EDGE OF THE CITY

DAN MAHONEY

St. Martin's Paperbacks

EDGE OF THE CITY

Copyright © 1995 by Dan Mahoney.
Excerpt from *Hyde* copyright © 1996 by Dan Mahoney.

All rights reserved. No part of this book may be used or reproduced in any manner whatsoever without written permission except in the case of brief quotations embodied in critical articles or reviews. For information address St. Martin's Press, 175 Fifth Avenue, New York, NY 10010.

Library of Congress Catalog Card Number: 95-15455

ISBN: 0-312-95788-2

Printed in the United States of America

St. Martin's Press hardcover edition/July 1995
St. Martin's Paperbacks edition/October 1996

St. Martin's Paperbacks are published by St. Martin's Press, 175 Fifth Avenue, New York, NY 10010.

10 9 8 7 6 5 4 3 2 1

OUTSTANDING PRAISE FOR THE NOVELS OF DAN MAHONEY

EDGE OF THE CITY

"Explosive . . . Mahoney is an excellent storyteller . . . a special talent."
—Tom Walker, author of *Fort Apache*, in *Wanted*

"Mahoney proves you can write an intelligent action thriller that makes sense . . . Mahoney scores because he has developed characters that are far more complex and interesting than the lineup usually found in thrillers."
—*Orlando Sentinel*

"A two-fisted thriller that throws several one-two punches."
—*Kirkus Reviews*

DETECTIVE FIRST GRADE

"A stunning piece of theater . . . Mahoney gives new meaning to the police procedural."
—*Los Angeles Times*

"The entertainment level soars."
—*The New York Times Book Review*

"Gripping and exciting all the way . . . Joseph Wambaugh, watch out!"
—*Publishers Weekly*

"Impeccably authentic . . . Astonishingly tight . . . The nuts-and-bolts of detection keeps the narrative energy pumping . . . A strong bet for police procedural fans."
—*Kirkus Reviews*

"Like Joseph Wambaugh, William J. Caunitz, and Robert Daley, Mahoney has turned his true-life adventures into a novel."
—*New York Daily News*

*St. Martin's Paperbacks titles
by Dan Mahoney*

DETECTIVE FIRST GRADE
EDGE OF THE CITY

Acknowledgments

When I first undertook this book project, I started with a basic story line without realizing the tremendous amount of research that would have to be done to get it right. Fortunately, I found help at every turn from wonderful people who unsparingly gave of their time and expertise. Accordingly, I would like to thank:

Ray Hegeman of the Staten Island Borough President's office for his invaluable help during my research of Staten Island ferries and bridges; Ken Cook, a retired TWA pilot who knows everything about the Boeing 727 and pointed me in the right direction; NYPD Detective Fred Rondina, who took out time from his Southwest vacation to help me with the research on Del Rio, Texas, and Ciudad Acuña, Mexico; Detective Fred Bleir of the Nassau County PD Bomb Squad for lending his expertise on bombs and detonators; Lieutenant Kevin Ward of the Port Authority PD for his help and guidance during my research of John F. Kennedy International Airport locations; Lieutenant Pat Picciarelli, NYPD (retired), a nationally recognized expert on polygraph and voice-analyzer testing; Lieutenant Vernon Geberth, NYPD (retired), *the* expert on murder and the author of *Practical Homicide Investigation*, which I used extensively in researching my autopsy reports; Captain Mike McCormick, NYPD (retired), who housed and entertained me while I did the Fort Myers Beach research; and, Staff Sergeant John D. Perkins, USMC, the toughest man alive (if he still is). Long ago and far away, he taught me more than I ever wanted to know about the M-60 machine gun and the 106-mm recoilless rifle.

Now comes that part where I would like to say that the characters represented in this book are fictitious and that any resemblance to persons living or dead is unintentional and coincidental. However, if I tried that one I'd be laughed out of town. The truth is, it's been my privilege to have worked with many of them during my time in the NYPD. Although I've taken some liberties with the particulars of their police careers and changed some of their names, the personalities remain. Knowing these fine folks has made this author business quite a bit easier; in writing the story, I simply set up the dilemmas for my characters, guessed how my real-life pals would handle those dreadful situations, and then told it that way. Conscience dictates that they receive some credit, so here they are:

My pal, NYPD Detective Bobby Gallagher (retired), was the most decorated detective in the history of the NYPD and also the hardest-working and most talented cop I ever saw. His personality and career form much of the basis for the Brian McKenna character. My pal, NYPD Captain Dick Savage, is the CO of that reservoir of talented and dedicated cops, the Street Crime Unit. His religion is NYPD, high-orthodox version. I used his personality and wit to complete McKenna. My pal, NYPD Inspector Walter Melnick, who could get his people to do almost anything and was the best police commander I've known. I used his personality as the basis of my Ray Brunette character. My pal and brother-in-law, Ray Brunette, a retired Department of Sanitation worker, who is also one of the brightest and funniest men imaginable. We had some laughs together when I made him the police commissioner, but there is still a lot of him in my Brunette. My pal, NYPD Sergeant Johnny Pao, a legitimate tough guy, sometimes cranky, and always cynical. In my story, I portrayed him as I know him—a real stand-up guy. My pal, NYPD Detective Sal Catalfumo (retired), also plays himself as I know him. He was a great detective who sometimes bent their rules to get the job done, always having fun in the process. My pal, NYPD Police Officer Dianne Halpern. Astute and unassuming, as well as being a good street cop, she can handle more paperwork faster and better than anyone I've known. I put some years on her and made her the basis of my Camilia Wright character. My pal, FBI Special Agent Bob Hurley (retired). He kept me laughing with his stories of following the Russians around in New York in the old days, so some of it is here. My pal, NYPD Detective Jerimiah O'Shaughnessy (retired). A fine detective and a real character in his own right, he is definitely *not* the basis of my Chief O'Shaughnessy. However, I always loved the name and wanted to use it somewhere before someone else did. My pal, Chipmunk, the world's greatest bartender, plays himself, as always. My pal, NYPD Lieutenant Gene Shields, a great detective commander. I felt I did the FBI no disservice when I put him in charge of their New York office. My pal, Steve Tavlin, president of the Holmes Detective Bureau, is a famous PI who keeps me laughing and employs me during my bouts with writer's block. Although he is unimpressed with titles, I still made him an inspector of police in this one and plan to promote him further in the future. A casual acquaintance, Suzy the bomb dog, is still alive and well and is always ready when needed. My pal, Mike Brennan, who, at one time or another, has been a reporter for every newspaper and TV station in town. He plays himself in the book, the guy who always asks the right question and won't be fooled by the answer. And my honey, NYPD Police Officer Yvette Camarena. Although she's never so much as dented a radio car, there's more of her in Angelita than I would care to say.

Finally, it should be known that, even with the help of all my pals, this book still would not have made it to the stores without three special people who must be mentioned: my dad, NYPD Patrolman Dan Mahoney (retired), who spent countless hours helping me by correcting my silly errors, just as he has tried to do in all things throughout my life. I relied on his judgment and have learned to always show my work to him for criticism before sending it on to the professionals. My editor and mentor, George Witte, who struggled to keep me somewhat literate, on track, and on time. I'm gratified that his fingerprints are on every page. And, my agent, Tim Hays, who was a source of inspiration and was tireless when working on my behalf. He is the guy who cut the deal that made my efforts worthwhile. These three deserve special thanks, and I gratefully and wholeheartedly give it.

—Dan Mahoney
New York City

Prologue

JULY 4, SAN JOSÉ, COSTA RICA—Felipe liked Juan Santamaría Airport. The Immigration agents were usually friendly, the Customs procedure was perfunctory, and security nonexistent. It was a terrorist's dream, and Felipe was a terrorist.

Nothing about his appearance suggested his lifelong occupation, which was one of the reasons he had achieved middle age in a field where an early end was frequently caused by a small mistake or a plan that failed to take into account all the variables. Failure meant quick death for the headstrong fanatics or a life in prison for the more practical.

Felipe had learned these rules through the unfortunate experiences of many others, and accepted them as a routine part of his work environment, or, as he called it, his profession. He was a careful planner and prided himself on analyzing every risk before deciding on a course of action. He was successful because he recognized and utilized the strengths and weaknesses of his own personnel, consistently overestimated the abilities of his opponents, and left nothing to chance. To those interested in promoting mayhem, a Felipe plan was a thing of beauty.

A casual inspection of Felipe as he waited in the Immigration line, passport in hand, showed nothing out of the ordinary. He exactly fit the role he had chosen for himself for this phase of the operation. He wore a pair of tan slacks, a white silk shirt opened at the neck, a navy blue sports coat, and a pair of well-shined brown Italian loafers, all bought in Buenos Aires the day before. His graying black hair was wavy, and combed straight back. He was what some women would call handsome without knowing exactly what appealed to them. His tanned face looked friendly enough, but something about

1

his expression suggested that his smile masked an attitude of condescending superiority.

Everything about him to the smallest detail conformed to produce the image he strived for. He appeared to be just another middle-management Argentine businessman, come to Costa Rica to arrange a deal to sell the friendly natives products they didn't want and couldn't use, but would probably buy anyway.

But to the more discerning eye, there were two things about the man that he could disguise but couldn't entirely hide. One thing was his height and build. Felipe was almost six feet tall, an unusual height in South America, so he stood with his knees slightly bent to appear an inch or two shorter and he slouched his shoulders and inflated his stomach to give the appearance that he was slightly overweight.

The other thing was his eyes. His expression looked bored, but, without moving his head, his eyes constantly darted from side to side, casually taking in everything and everyone in the large room. In a part of the world where at least a trace of Indian blood was commonplace, there was still something unusual about the way his eyes slanted. An astute anthropologist might surmise that there was a hint of the plains of central Asia in those eyes, generations removed.

Such an astute and discerning pair of eyes were watching Felipe, and they belonged to Lieutenant First Class Fernando Almeda of the Peruvian *Dirección Nacional Contra el Terrorismo*. Almeda was five persons behind Felipe on the Immigration line, listening to a rather staid, middle-aged, loquacious Argentine matron he had met on the plane. Wearing one of his cheap polyester suits, there was nothing remarkable about him to draw the attention of anyone. It was a look he cultivated as part of his job. He tried to concentrate on what the matron was saying, something about the volcanoes surrounding the city of San José, but he couldn't tear his gaze away from the back of Felipe's head.

After four years of searching for Felipe, a fruitless search that had taken Almeda to countless Third World capitals and through half of the most inhospitable jungles on the planet, he had begun to doubt the very existence of the man. Yet, by an unforeseen stroke of luck and with a little good police work on his part, there they were, in the same room, and Elena was with him. If his luck held, he could get both of them.

*　　*　　*

It was Elena who had led him to San José, to Felipe. Five hours earlier Almeda had been in Buenos Aires, in another airport in another country. He had just completed an assignment, giving a lecture on *Sendero Luminoso*, the scourge of Peru and Felipe's professional affiliation, to a class at the Argentine Army Staff Intelligence School. He knew his material and had offered a variation of the same lecture in most of the countries of the Western Hemisphere, so he considered these speaking commitments to be a welcome respite from the chase, something he did as part of his duties whenever the trail grew cold.

Then Almeda had seen Elena at the airport in Buenos Aires. He had been waiting at the Ladeco Airlines gate for his return flight to Lima. As usual, the flight was late in arriving and the passengers had been advised that their plane had experienced some administrative difficulties in leaving Lima Airport. When the plane finally arrived, Elena had been the first person off the flight.

Almeda had recognized her at once, in spite of her change in appearance. She had dyed her brown hair red and was expensively dressed in a dark blue business suit from some European designer, offset by a pair of bright red high-heeled shoes and purse that matched her new hair color. She looked exquisite, a far cry from the way she had looked in the jungle fatigues she had worn in the only picture they possessed of her. But she still had the limp, an unwelcome souvenir of a firefight with the Peruvian army in 1987. She disguised it with an exaggerated and provocative swaying of her hips as she walked, but Almeda had recognized it for what it was: a limp that resulted from a .223-caliber bullet ripping through her right thigh.

She had been in a hurry after she cleared her overnight bag through Argentine Customs, and Almeda had made a decision. He could have had her arrested right there, but he had wanted more. He wanted Felipe, so he had followed her to the Aero Argentina terminal. There she had caused Almeda to make a few more painful decisions. She had passed through the metal detectors on her way to the departure gates, but Almeda couldn't follow her, yet. He had still been armed, and he was only cleared with his weapon for the flight to Lima. Lacking time to make further arrangements, he had gone into a men's room and reluctantly dropped his prized S&W 9-mm Model 59 into a trash can. He then had passed through the checkpoint and found Elena just as she boarded Aero Argentina Flight 112 for Montreal, with stops in San José, Miami, and New York.

Almeda had rushed back to the ticket counter and bought a ticket for Montreal, since he had no idea where Elena would be getting off the plane. He had been the last person to board, so while his luggage was headed home to Lima, he was on his way to destinations unknown.

As he went to his seat in Coach, he had passed Elena, sitting alone in First Class and reading a magazine. She had taken no notice of him as he passed, but he had committed her seat number to memory. Then he had settled in to worry during the five-hour flight to Costa Rica, the first stop. He was acting independently and alone, following a known terrorist across South America, and none of his superiors knew where he was. Wanting to keep a low profile, he stayed in his seat.

Almeda had been less than gratified when Elena got off the plane in San José. Costa Rica had extradition treaties with very few countries, and Peru wasn't one of them.

Then the situation had escalated into something more dangerous. As he got up to follow Elena, he had seen Felipe standing among the passengers who had been seated three rows behind him in Coach. The shadow he had been chasing for years was getting off in one of the few places in the world where he couldn't arrest him, legally at least. Almeda knew that he had to find a phone as soon as possible.

Felipe was next in the Immigration line. He put down his travel bag, took a cigarette from his pack and put it in his mouth, and then searched his pockets for his lighter. Elena was ready, anticipating his needs as usual. She had a lighter in her hand and, without thinking, brought the flame to his cigarette. Felipe dragged deeply on his cigarette and the hint of a frown crossed his face before he smiled graciously and said, "Thank you, *señorita*."

Elena realized her mistake at once. They were not supposed to be together. She lowered the lighter, somewhat embarrassed, while Felipe took a few seconds to glance past her, casually examining his fellow travelers waiting on the Immigration line.

It was a typical collection of Argentine tourists and businessmen. Behind Elena was a family of four who apparently had come to enjoy the weather. The father carried the family's coats over his arm. It was July, winter in Argentina, but in the mountains of Costa Rica it was always late spring and the coats were no longer necessary. He was about thirty and held his young son in his arms while he stared at Elena with barely concealed interest.

Felipe was used to watching men watch Elena. After all, they were in Latin America, and a beautiful woman was always to be admired, much in the same way a fine painting or a breathtaking vista was to be admired.

The young man's wife obviously didn't agree with the convention. She held her daughter by the arm and concentrated all her energies into glaring a hole in the side of her husband's face. After a few seconds he felt the heat and, after giving his wife a sheepish sideways glance, decided that it was time to change his watch nonchalantly to local time. It wasn't done well.

Felipe took in the rest of the people waiting on line. Behind the Argentine family was an unremarkable couple, a middle-aged man in a polyester suit and a woman engaged in a one-way conversation. He assumed that they were married because the man nodded at everything the woman said but didn't seem to be listening at all.

Emilio was near the end of the line, looking as scruffy as ever, and maybe a little nervous. He was a five-foot-nine hulk of a man, with dull simian features, no neck, and shoulders that seemed freakishly wide. The overall effect was somewhat scary, but he was brave, resourceful, and totally dedicated to the cause. Felipe had put Emilio's bad looks to good use, placing him in charge of screening new *Sendero* recruits for past government connections. In other words, Emilio was his interrogator.

But looking at Emilio, Felipe saw that he had a problem. While the brute was perfectly at home in the jungles and mountains of Peru, he was definitely out of place in the International Arrivals Building of Juan Santamaría Airport wearing the first suit he had ever owned.

"Next!" the Immigration agent yelled.

Felipe turned around and put Emilio out of his mind for the moment. It was his turn and the young Immigration agent was sitting behind the counter, looking at him expectantly. Felipe picked up his travel bag and handed the agent his worn Argentine passport. He looked bored as the Immigration agent thumbed through it.

"Welcome to Costa Rica, *señor*. You have been here before?"

"No, sir," Felipe answered, putting a hint of an Italian accent into his Spanish, as many upper-class Argentines like to do. "This is my first time here."

"You travel quite a bit," the smiling Immigration agent observed as he continued looking through Felipe's passport, but Felipe was unconcerned. The passport was an expert forgery made the day before by a man who had since died.

"Today business means travel," Felipe observed dryly.

"Are you traveling alone?"

"Unfortunately, yes."

"How long will you be staying?"

"Two days."

"And where will you be staying, *señor*?"

"The Hotel Europa," Felipe answered, a hint of impatience in his voice.

The agent didn't seem to notice. He took his time going through the passport, looking for entry stamps from trouble spots like Peru and Nicaragua. There were none. "The Hotel Europa is very nice, *señor*," he said as he typed the information from Felipe's passport into the computer terminal in front of him, then pressed Enter. The screen changed and gave him the routine message: *No Restrictions, Cleared for Entry.* The agent stamped the passport and closed it. "Straight ahead to Customs. Enjoy your stay in Costa Rica, *señor*," he said, handing Felipe his passport. "Next!"

Felipe put the passport in his pocket, picked up his travel bag, and started toward Customs. From the corner of his eye he managed to catch a glimpse of Elena handing her Spanish passport to the Immigration agent. It appeared that the beautiful Spanish lady and the young Immigration agent were both looking forward to their official interview.

Felipe found his one suitcase circulating on the baggage carousel. He picked it up and waited briefly in the Customs line before he was waved through, his suitcase unopened and uninspected. There was a line of red Nissan taxis waiting outside, and he jumped into the third taxi in line. The taxi took off as Almeda watched.

While still waiting in line, Almeda heard Elena tell the Immigration agent that she would be staying at the Hotel Del

Rey. Her passport was stamped and she was passed through. He watched her pick up three suitcases from the baggage carousel and head for the Customs line.

Almeda was gratified to see that the Customs agent thought the pretty lady and her luggage deserved a special inspection. They talked and laughed while Almeda waited for the Argentine family to finish their Immigration inspection. Finally they were passed through and it was his turn.

Almeda handed the Immigration agent his Peruvian passport and it was received as if it were a pair of dirty socks. But then the Immigration agent remembered his manners and gave his official smile to the Peruvian. "Welcome to Costa Rica, *señor*. Have you been here before?"

"No, this is my first time."

"Business or pleasure?"

"Pleasure."

Almeda instantly saw from the perplexed look on the Immigration agent's face that he had given the wrong answer. The prefix on his passport number indicated that he was a Peruvian government official and the sharp young agent had caught it. "*Señor*, isn't this passport issued by your government for official travel?" he asked.

Almeda tried to recover. "Yes, it is," he answered confidently. "I'm with the Ministry of Agriculture. I was on my way to a conference in Montreal, but the conference isn't for another three days. As the plane was landing I saw how beautiful your country is and I decided to spend a day or two here."

The agent appeared dubious of Almeda's explanation. "May I see your airplane tickets?"

Almeda handed his ticket folder to the agent, and while he went through it Almeda saw the Customs agent close Elena's suitcases in the line in front of him. Panic was setting in, but Almeda forced himself to concentrate on his present predicament.

The Immigration agent handed him back his ticket folder and said, "This is very strange, *señor*. I see you have no baggage tags attached to your ticket folder."

"I didn't bring any. I had planned to shop in Montreal for some new clothes, but I guess that now I'll do my shopping here."

The Immigration agent appeared unconvinced at this explanation. While he typed Almeda's information into his computer, he asked sarcastically, "You would rather shop in San José than in Montreal?"

Elena was leaving the terminal with her bags. Almeda decided to go on the offensive. "Have you had any dealings with the French, *señor*?" he asked the Immigration agent, disgust dripping from his voice.

The agent immediately got the implication. "Only in my official capacity, fortunately."

"Then you should understand why I would prefer to spend my time in Costa Rica rather than with them in Montreal. I don't speak French and I find them to be less than understanding about my linguistic shortcomings."

"I see your point," the agent said as he finished typing the information from Almeda's passport into his computer. He hit Enter and received the routine clearance message. As he was stamping the passport, Almeda saw Elena get into a taxi outside the terminal. The taxi immediately drove off.

"Straight ahead to Customs, *señor*," the agent said as he handed Almeda back his passport. "Enjoy your shopping in Costa Rica."

Almeda was passed through Customs without a second glance. He went to a pay phone near the entrance to the terminal and, using his credit card, dialed Colonel Savraada's direct headquarters line in Lima. Savraada, the chief of Peru's antiterrorist force, picked up the phone on the first ring.

Ten minutes later Almeda hung up the phone with a better understanding of his situation. It was worse than he had imagined. There was no help available to him from the Peruvian embassy since the staff there consisted only of the ambassador, his secretary, and his driver. Almeda had hoped to be able to use a military attaché to help him, but there were none assigned to the embassy since there was no reason or plausible excuse to have any; Costa Rica didn't have an army for a military attaché to consult with.

But the colonel had made some arrangements. Reinforcements would be arriving in San José on the 10:00 P.M. American Airlines flight from Lima, and they would be carrying the diplomatic pouch. Savraada promised that it would contain everything they would need. Almeda was on his own until then.

Almeda had given him the seat numbers occupied by Felipe and Elena on the Aero Argentina flight and had suggested he use his influence to check with the airline and find out what names they were traveling under, since the names on their passports and on their plane tickets had to match.

Savraada had the information in minutes. Felipe was traveling as Enrique Velasquez on a forged Argentine passport. Elena was using the name of Janine Roldan, a Spanish national. Her passport was genuine, which meant that sometime during her life she had taken the trouble to set up a bona fide second identity for herself, or that her real name was Janine Roldan. Savraada had said he would have it checked out.

His instructions to Almeda had been brief and necessarily vague: Locate Felipe and Elena, find out why they were in Costa Rica, and take no action unless it looked like they were preparing to leave.

Almeda hoped the two terrorists planned to stay a while. He considered himself a detective, not a murderer, and didn't relish the prospect of drastic action.

Emilio, still waiting on the Immigration line, watched the dejected-looking man with no luggage hang up the phone and go to the currency exchange counter. Emilio's interest increased when he saw that the money Almeda took from his wallet to exchange for Costa Rican *colónes* was in *intis*, the currency of Peru.

As Emilio approached the Immigration counter, his Bolivian passport in hand, Almeda left the terminal for the bright sunshine outside and got into a taxi.

Once he arrived in town, Almeda called the Hotel Del Rey and asked for Janine Roldan and Enrique Velasquez. He was told that they weren't registered there, which came as no surprise to Almeda. He hadn't really expected Felipe and Elena to tell the Immigration agent where they would actually be staying. Next he bought a copy of the Costa Rican tourist guide and started calling every hotel listed.

He found that Elena was staying at the Hotel Aurola Holiday Inn as Janine Roldan. Felipe was not registered there or at any other hotel in San José under the name Enrique Velasquez.

He hired a taxi, which took him to the Holiday Inn. It was an imposing glass-and-marble seventeen-story behemoth, easily the tallest building in the city. The hotel faced a large plaza and there was a line of taxis pulled up in front, waiting for fares. Almeda had his driver park on the far side of the plaza so that the entrance to the hotel was visible to them. The driver was perplexed, but since the meter was running he kept his questions to himself.

Almeda settled back to wait and watch. Just before seven o'clock Elena, dressed in dark blue jeans and a red blouse, came out of the hotel. She was still wearing the red high heels and carried the red purse. She got into the first taxi in line and it took off from the curb with a screech of tires.

Time has passed the Gran Hotel by, and that is the historic establishment's saving grace, the quality that makes it unique. It is an Old World hotel still going strong in an awakening and rapidly modernizing part of the New World.

The hotel sits on a small plaza next to the National Theater and has all the amenities found in Old Madrid. Surrounding the entrance of the building is a café with tables and chairs that extend into the plaza. Inside the ornate front doors the lobby stretches to the front desk, with a restaurant occupying one side of the lobby and a casino the other. Both are open and busy all night long.

Sitting in the casino at a blackjack table, Emilio was passing time, losing money, and watching the front door of the hotel when Elena came in. Either she didn't see Emilio or she ignored him as she passed through the lobby and to the bank of elevators opposite the front desk. She pressed the elevator call button and waited.

Emilio shifted his attention from Elena to the front window of the hotel. He saw Almeda get out of a taxi and stand outside behind a palm tree to watch Elena through the front door.

Emilio went to the house phones hanging on the wall behind the blackjack table and dialed a room. When the phone was answered he said, "Elena's here and she brought a tail from Peru."

While Emilio was on the phone, he watched as the elevator doors opened and Elena got on. As soon as the doors closed, Almeda entered the hotel, went to the elevator bank, and watched the floor indicator light. Elena's elevator stopped on the third floor and stayed there. Almeda took a seat in the café and focused his attention on the elevators.

Emilio was still on the house phone while he watched Almeda. He listened for another minute, then hung up and walked out the side door of the hotel.

Fifteen minutes later the elevator doors opened and Elena came out, carrying a large manila envelope, but no purse. She headed straight out the front door, paying no attention to Almeda as she walked past him.

Almeda wasn't certain, but it looked to him like something new had been added to Elena's fine features. There was some swelling under her left eye.

Elena made a left as soon as she left the hotel and started across the crowded plaza at a quick pace. Almeda got up and followed her, staying 100 feet behind. She held the manila envelope to her chest as she walked, her other arm swinging free. She still had the wiggle and attracted quite a bit of attention, making her easy to follow.

At the end of the plaza she crossed the street, with Almeda still behind her. They were in the shopping district; the stores were all closed, and the streets were deserted. Halfway down the block, she turned into the large, open entrance of a new office building.

Almeda followed to the entrance of the building, stopped, and peered around the edge of the wall. It was a modern indoor shopping mall, with small shops occupying both sides of the corridor. They were all closed, but the corridor was well lit and the lights were on in every shop. He couldn't see Elena, but he could hear the rapid clicking of her high heels echoing off the walls, ahead and to the left. She was still in a hurry.

He took a good look around. He was the only one on the street. Following the sound of the high heels, he entered the mall, and came to an interior intersection. He stopped. He could still hear Elena walking. She had turned left at the intersection. He peered around the wall and caught sight of her. She was walking down a metal stairway leading to a lower level. He counted sixteen stairs as she disappeared from view, her heels ringing on the metal stairs. Then she took twelve more steps on concrete and the sound stopped.

Almeda tiptoed down the corridor and stopped at the top of the staircase. He peered down, but saw no sign of her. Then the sound of her footsteps on concrete resumed. She was again walking away from him, one level below. Trying to be silent, he descended the stairs and saw her. She wasn't bothering to disguise the limp, but something else was different. She turned at another intersection in the mall and he resumed following her.

Then it came to him. She had been swinging both arms freely as she walked. She had gotten rid of the manila envelope.

As the *click-click* of Elena's footsteps became more distant, he ran back to the staircase. There was a trash receptacle at the foot of the stairs. He quickly went through it, listening to Elena fade away. It contained nothing but trash.

He looked at the stores near the staircase, thinking. There was a travel agency, a shoe store, a gift shop, a photo shop, and a leather-goods shop. He focused on the photo shop and walked toward it, taking small steps. Twelve brought him to the front door, and he saw it.

Elena had pushed the envelope through the large mail slot set in the bottom of the glass door, and it was faceup on the floor inside the store. Written in large letters on the front of the envelope was *FROM FELIPE*.

He lay facedown on the ground in front of the door, opened the mail slot, and put his right arm through. He couldn't reach the envelope, but he was only inches away. With his arm still in the mail slot, he inched himself forward as far as he could go, until his shoulder was painfully pressed into the mail slot, his face against the glass. As his fingers tightened on a corner of the envelope, he heard footsteps behind him, close. Still holding the envelope, he tried pushing himself from the door with his left arm. He managed to slide just six inches back before his chest was forced into the concrete.

Almeda tried to turn his head to look at the man, but a foot on his neck forced his face into the ground. He was having a hard time breathing and his arm was hurting as it was pressed against the lip of the mailbox. He tried again to pull his arm from the mail slot, but it was impossible. He was caught good.

"*Sendero?*" Almeda asked, his lips brushing against the ground as he spoke.

"That's right," a harsh voice answered.

Almeda felt the man's weight shift on his back and neck as his passport was removed from his jacket pocket and his wallet from his back pants pocket. He heard the sound of pages turning.

"Where did you come from?" Almeda asked.

"Originally from Ayacucho, Lieutenant First Class Fernando Almeda. How about you?"

"Lima," Almeda answered, gasping for breath. "I mean, where did you come from just now?"

The man took his foot off Almeda's neck and placed it on the ground next to his face. The pressure on Almeda's chest eased slightly. Breathing was easier, but he still couldn't move. He took a few deep breaths.

The man was chuckling. "From under that staircase behind us, city boy, where I was waiting for you. I came to tell you a story, then you can tell me one. Okay?"

"I'm listening," Almeda answered, resting his forehead on the ground.

"I want to tell you a story about how the Indians used to catch monkeys in our country."

"I think I know that one," Almeda said, taking two breaths to say it.

"Maybe you used to know it, but you must have forgot. Otherwise, you wouldn't be in this fix." He sounded like he was enjoying himself. "Anyway, when the Indians wanted to catch a monkey, they cut a small hole in a coconut and put some berries in it that monkeys like. Soon a monkey would come along and put his hand in the hole and grab the berries in his fist. But, you see, the hole was too small to let the monkey's fist out, so the monkey just sat there with his fist in the coconut, holding the berries. He wouldn't let go of those berries, no matter what, even when the Indians came back. Of course, he would try to run, but he couldn't get far dragging the coconut. So the Indians would catch the monkey, and you know what they had to do to separate that monkey from that coconut?"

Almeda didn't answer. He hadn't been listening while the man was telling his story. Instead, he had been working on a cap on one of his rear molars with his tongue, loosening it and trying to get it off.

Almeda's silence seemed to enrage the man. He again stood on Almeda's back, this time with both feet, pulled his head by the hair with one hand, and put his other hand in front of his face. The thick hairy fingers held a long, ugly knife.

Almeda worked the cap free just as the man shifted his grip, letting go of Almeda's hair and clamping his hand over his mouth. Almeda watched in horror as the man slashed his trapped arm with the knife.

"I think you guessed it," the man laughed. "They had to cut that monkey's arm off."

Almeda was surprised that he didn't feel the cut. His arm was numb. But he saw the blood pumping out through his cut jacket and shirt. He couldn't breathe with the hand over his mouth, but he could smell the man's hand. It reeked of onions and sweat. He felt dizzy and struggled to stay conscious. He recognized the symptoms of shock and knew he wasn't going to last long. Then he heard the sound of high heels on the concrete of the upper level. Elena was returning.

"Now your story," the man commanded. He removed his hand from Almeda's mouth, pulled back his head by the hair, and put the blade of the knife under Almeda's throat. "Quickly, how did you know Elena would be here?"

Almeda rolled the cap around his mouth and the capsule fell out of the recess cut into the interior of the cap, but the capsule had rolled under his tongue. He tried to find it as his torturer applied a little pressure with the knife, cutting his neck. "We have an informant," Almeda answered. The knife cut deeper into his skin as he talked.

The pressure on his neck was relieved and once again Almeda could see the knife in front of his face. He felt the blood running down his neck.

"Who's the informant?"

"I don't know. But it's one of your big people."

"Elena? Is it Elena?"

"I don't know. Maybe." Talking had dislodged the capsule. He found it and pressed it against his upper teeth as he heard Elena descending the stairs.

"Maybe I believe you," the man said. "Now tell me another story. What are your instructions?"

With his tongue Almeda placed the capsule between his upper and lower molars as the man once again slashed his arm. This time Almeda felt the pain.

"Tell me, or I'll cut your arm off before you die."

"Emilio! Don't kill him yet," he heard Elena shout.

Emilio wasn't listening. "Tell me," he said as he slashed Almeda's trapped arm again. "What are your instructions?"

"I was told that Emilio's a filthy pig who doesn't wash his hands," Almeda rasped through clenched teeth, struggling against the pain. "I was to arrest you and get you a bath."

"Arrest me?" Emilio yelled, enraged, as he slashed Almeda's arm again and again.

Almeda was able to ignore him, fascinated by the sight of the blood pumping from his mangled arm. Then he bit into the capsule and swallowed.

*   *   *

Suite 306 was the biggest suite in the Gran Hotel and contained two bedrooms, three bathrooms, and a stateroom with a stocked bar. It was usually reserved for visiting heads of state and captains of industry, but Felipe had managed to reserve it for himself.

He poured two drinks at the bar and brought them to Emilio and Elena. Emilio sat in an overstuffed chair, with the manila envelope on his lap, looking totally relaxed and content. He took a small sip from his drink and put it down on the lamp table next to his chair.

On a sofa opposite Emilio, Elena perched erect, looking uncomfortable and pale except for the blue bruise under her eye. She accepted the drink gratefully and immediately took a long gulp, then held the glass tightly on her lap.

Felipe returned to the bar, turned around, and leaned back against it, facing them while he thought over the information he had just received. Emilio stared at him impassively, but Elena became more uncomfortable during the silence. She took another sip from her drink.

Felipe remained silent for a moment. Then he turned to the bar, poured himself a drink, and said, "Tell me again how this Lieutenant Almeda died."

Emilio and Elena looked at each other as Felipe sipped his drink. Finally Emilio turned to Felipe and said nervously, "He just died."

"One moment he was conscious and talking and the next minute he was dead?" Felipe asked, focusing on Elena.

Elena squirmed under his gaze while Felipe waited for his answer. "I think he swallowed a cyanide capsule," she finally volunteered.

"I thought so," Felipe said, turning back to Emilio.

"How? I had total control of him," Emilio protested. "He never had a chance to put anything in his mouth."

"I know that," Felipe said, patiently. "The poison was already there, a cyanide capsule located under a dental cap. All he had to do was loosen the cap with his tongue."

"How would I know that?" Emilio pleaded. "We've never had a Dinconte agent poison himself. They're all just capitalist lackeys and they don't have the balls."

Felipe stifled a smile at Emilio's rhetoric, surprised and gratified that after ten years this brute still believed the nonsense. "Well, this Dinconte agent did poison himself, and it wasn't a matter of balls," Felipe explained. "He knew he was headed for a painful death because he was questioned improperly. You left him no hope that he might live in exchange for the information he possessed. I told you to find out how he found us, and all you can tell me is something about an informant.''

The muscles in Emilio's neck tightened as he glared defiantly at Felipe, who coolly returned his stare. Finally Emilio lowered his eyes and said, ''I got everything I could from him.''

''You didn't get enough. All you did was tell me something I already knew. Obviously it's an informant, but who?''

Emilio turned his eyes to Elena, who glowered back at him. ''He said he didn't know who it was, but said that maybe it was Elena.''

Felipe regarded Elena dispassionately, while she stared into the empty glass on her lap, terrified. She kept looking into her glass as Felipe walked to her and she flinched when he removed the glass from her hands.

''Of course it isn't Elena,'' he said as he walked to the bar and poured Elena another drink. ''That was a classic piece of disinformation. I applaud Lieutenant First Class Almeda. Elena led them to us, but she is not the traitor. She was just careless in permitting herself to be followed in three countries without being aware of it. She has been punished for that, and it's over.''

He brought the drink to Elena and she took a long sip, then looked up at Felipe expectantly.

''It wasn't Elena because she knew she was coming here and Dinconte didn't,'' Felipe said. ''Otherwise, their agent would have brought luggage. Someone in Peru helped them locate Elena and told them she would lead them to me, but that someone, that traitor, thought I was still in Peru. So they followed her and she surprised them when she went to the airport and boarded the flight for Buenos Aires. Almeda had no choice but to follow her here, which is exactly what he did.''

''Then who is the traitor?'' Emilio asked.

''I'll find out sooner or later,'' Felipe answered. ''Unfortunately, this little matter is going to force us to advance our timetable. Colonel Savraada will be whispering to the police here once he finds out his man is dead, so I think it best we be out of the country by morning.''

''But the meeting with Alejandro isn't until noon,'' Elena said. ''Changing the time will make him suspicious.''

Felipe turned to Emilio. "I know I can count on you, Emilio," he said. "Alejandro trusts you and there's a fortune in this for him. Go talk to him. Tell him I'll be at his hotel at two A.M."

Emilio beamed at the compliment and searched his mind for a reply, but then the phone rang. Felipe nodded to Elena and she picked it up. "It's Cruzco," she said. "He's downstairs."

"Tell him to come up," said Felipe. Elena did and hung up the phone. Felipe put his arm on Emilio's shoulder. "Go now, but take the stairs down, Emilio. I think you make Cruzco nervous."

Emilio gave a small salute as he closed the door behind him.

Felipe waited with his hand on the doorknob, looking at Elena. "Sooner or later, I think Emilio is going to be a liability," he told her.

"It'll be my pleasure. Just tell me when," she said, then took her compact from behind the bar and applied some cover-up and blush to her cheeks. She checked herself in the compact mirror and asked, "How's this?"

"Perfect," he answered, regarding her impassively.

There was a knock at the door. Felipe opened it at once and embraced Cruzco, who then held him at arm's length and inspected Felipe. "Felipe, you still look like a playboy. It's good to see you."

"And you still look like Santa Claus must have looked when he was in his forties, old friend," which was an accurate description of Cruzco. He was big, overweight, with rosy cheeks, a wide smile, a gray beard, and a head topped by a thick mane of curly gray hair.

Cruzco looked over Felipe's shoulder and saw Elena standing at the bar, smiling at him. He walked to her and kissed her on the cheek. "You still look like a twenty-year-old beauty queen," he told her.

"I'm thirty, Cruzco, but I feel like I'm fifty."

Then Cruzco touched her cheek and Elena pulled away. "What is this, a battle scar?" he asked her tenderly.

Elena nodded, but said nothing.

"How are things going in Nicaragua?" Felipe asked, changing the subject.

"As well as can be expected, but you better put your plan in operation soon. The Sandinistas still have control of the army and most of the police, but we're losing power. I can't keep your men hidden forever.''

"We'll know tonight. It will be soon or not at all.''

The telephone rang again and again Elena answered it. "It's Burgos and Escudero,'' she said to Felipe. "They're downstairs.''

"You got the Cali and the Medellín cartels together in the same room?'' said Cruzco, astonished. "How did you do that?''

"They don't like it, but neither one can afford the price I'm asking. The only way for them to get it done is to pool their resources,'' Felipe answered. "Tell them to come up,'' he said to Elena.

Elena spoke into the phone, then hung up and looked to Felipe. "Get some rest,'' he told her.

She went to one of the bedroom doors, waved at Cruzco, then went in, closing the door behind her.

As soon as Elena left, Cruzco was all business. "What have you promised the Colombians?'' he asked.

"If they meet the price, every cop in New York and every federal agent on the East Coast will be otherwise occupied for five days at the end of this month. I'll let their imaginations work over the opportunities that will give them.''

"That's a lot, but we're asking a lot. Anything else?'' Cruzco asked.

"I'll explain to them that if we win in New York, then we'll win in Peru and they'll have a friendly government right next door to Colombia. I'll promise a sanctuary for their leaders whenever they have legal difficulties and a stable price for our coca leaves for the next three years.''

Cruzco thought that over for a moment, apparently not entirely convinced. "There's still three problems they're going to ask about before they come in on this,'' he said.

"I try to think of everything, but let's hear them,'' Felipe replied, smiling.

"Okay. The American government has a policy of not negotiating with terrorists or giving in to their demands.''

"We're going to modify that policy,'' Felipe answered with confidence. "They'll have no choice, but I'm going to give them an out that'll make it look like the federal government isn't involved. Next problem.''

"How about weapons?''

"I'm meeting with Alejandro de Leon right after the Colombians."

"That traitor is here, not a hundred miles from Nicaragua?" Cruzco asked, incredulously.

"Yes, and he's not to be harmed. He's got everything we need, and the beautiful part is that it's all in the United States."

"That's a hard pill to swallow, but if you say he's necessary, then he's safe," Cruzco stated. "Still, I'm curious. How did you get him to come here after my comrades tagged him last year?"

"Easy. He trusts Emilio."

"Emilio? Why would anyone trust Emilio?"

"They trained in Cuba together when Alejandro was still with the Sandinistas. It seems that de Leon got himself involved in an indiscretion with another man and was being blackmailed. Emilio disposed of the blackmailer and the lover for him and kept the whole thing to himself. That made him the only person Alejandro trusts."

There was a knock at the door, but Felipe ignored it and kept his attention on Cruzco. "You said there were three problems. The last has to be McKenna, right?"

"Yes. McKenna. He ruined the last *Sendero* operation in New York. Before you can win, you're going to have to kill him to restore some credibility to your movement. The Colombians know that, and I'm sure they know you've been looking for him. The old *Sendero* leadership has made it an issue you can't back down from."

"You know I've never agreed with the revenge vow of *Sendero*. It's sometimes counterproductive and it's one of the reasons most of the previous leaders are either dead or in jail. Still, I've devised a plan that'll bring Detective Brian McKenna into the open. We'll get him."

Cruzco smiled. "Then answer the door and let's change the world," he said.

Chapter 1

JULY 20, NEW YORK CITY—It started to drizzle just before three on Sunday morning, breaking the heat and producing a sparse vapor cloud that hung close to the ground as the raindrops hit the sidewalk. The city that never sleeps was at least taking a break. The streets outside the United Nations at East 45th Street and First Avenue were deserted, with no signs of life except for the uniformed cop assigned to the lighted police booth on the corner, outside the United States Mission to the UN. The post is covered twenty-four hours a day by a cop from the 17th Precinct, and his job is to protect the outside perimeter of the mission. The inside of the mission is guarded by a uniformed Federal Protective Service agent, who was visible from the street as he sat behind a desk in the lobby, reading.

A marked blue-and-white radio car turned onto First Avenue from East 44th Street and stopped next to the police booth. The uniformed cop left the booth, went to the driver's side of the car, and received the package of two coffees and two copies of the Sunday *Daily News*. After the radio car pulled off and made a left on East 47th Street, the cop went back to his booth and put one coffee and one newspaper on the counter. He brought the other coffee and newspaper to the federal agent inside the mission, who was waiting for him at the door. They chatted for a moment, then the cop went back to his booth and the agent returned to his desk after locking the front door.

Once inside his booth, the cop put the newspaper under the counter, stirred his coffee, and resumed studying his *Patrol Guide*, the New York City Police Department manual, which proscribed a procedure to be followed for each and every conceivable event. He would read a paragraph of a procedure, close his eyes and try to repeat what he had just read, then take a look around the street.

Tall and thin in an athletic way, he had a baby face accentuated by dimples that appeared at the corners of his mouth as he mumbled to himself the procedural banalities. He was handsome, with straight black hair and finely chiseled features, but looked too young to be a cop.

He was halfway into the manual and memorizing the nonsense contained in the three-page procedure titled "Processing Non-evidence Currency with or without Numismatic/Sentimental Value." It was an easy one for him because he had been studying that particular procedure for four years, which meant that three years before he even joined the police department he had been filling his young mind with police procedural trivia.

The young cop finished reading Steps 31 and 32 of the procedure, then looked up and was surprised to see a short, well-dressed man in his twenties coming toward him, slowly walking south on First Avenue under his open umbrella. He smiled as he approached the police booth, then stopped at the door. "Excuse me, Officer," he said politely in a soft, Spanish-accented voice, "but can you tell me what time the United Nations opens?"

The young cop did not like it. The man was looking at his name tag as he talked, not his face, but it was one of the usual questions.

"Yes, sir. The tours start at ten o'clock and cost seven dollars."

"Seven dollars? Is it worth it?" he asked, still smiling and talking to the cop's chest.

"I guess everyone should do it once."

"Thank you, Officer Brunette. I will." The man turned and continued his slow saunter down First Avenue. Brunette watched him until he turned at East 44th Street and disappeared from view, then returned to his coffee and *Patrol Guide*.

Angel DeSoto closed his umbrella and got into the backseat of the green four-door Chevy Caprice parked right off the corner of First Avenue, pushing two empty ladies' handbags onto the floor as he got in. Felipe sat in the front passenger seat and Emilio was behind the wheel. Turning in his seat to look at DeSoto, Felipe said, "Well? Let's have it."

"It's him," DeSoto reported. "He's six foot one, one hun-

dred seventy pounds, good shape, alert. He's wearing a bulletproof vest, but has only one gun. Looks like a six-shot
Ruger revolver. His radio is on the counter in the booth and
he's reading a book, but stops about every thirty seconds to
look around.''

The police scanner on the seat between Felipe and Emilio
crackled. ''Seventeen Charlie to Central, K.''

''Go ahead, Charlie,'' the female dispatcher said.

''We're leaving the station house with one prisoner for Central Booking.''

''Ten-four, Charlie. Time out five-oh-nine.''

Emilio wrote down the information on a clipboard.

''Give me the figures,'' Felipe commanded.

Reading from the clipboard, Emilio said, ''Right now we
got just two of their cars to worry about. Sector Adam and the
sergeant are in Bellevue Hospital with the lady who was
robbed, Charlie is on the way downtown with the prisoner,
David is in the station house eating, and Frank is on the East
River Drive handling the accident. That leaves just Boy and
Eddie. Four cops in two cars.''

''Perfect,'' Felipe said. ''Start it up and turn on the wipers.''

Emilio stuck a screwdriver into the hole on the steering
column and turned. The ignition caught and he turned on the
wipers and the defroster.

Felipe picked up a walkie-talkie from the seat and keyed
the mike. ''Everyone report.''

Felipe's men answered immediately. ''Post One at Second
and Forty-second. Light traffic and no police.''

''Post Two at Second and Forty-sixth. Light traffic and no
police.''

''Post Three at the subway and ready. No police.''

Felipe keyed his radio and said, ''It's on. Post Three, make
the call and get out.''

''*Sí, Comandante,*'' the radio crackled.

Felipe picked up a sawed-off Remington shotgun from the
floor and placed it across his lap. Emilio reached under the
seat and brought up two .45 Colt automatics. He put one on
the seat next to him and passed the other back to DeSoto. They
settled back to wait.

''Post Three, call made. I'm out,'' came over Felipe's radio.

Instantly the voice of the female dispatcher came over the
police scanner. ''In the Seventeenth Precinct we have a report
of a robbery one minute in the past, in the subway at Fifty-
first and Lexington, downtown side. Male caller reports to 911

that black male perp, five ten, dressed in black, robbed him at knifepoint and fled down the tracks, headed downtown. Complainant states he will follow perp on the tracks. What units to respond?''

"Seventeen Boy will respond to the Fifty-first Street station to help out John Wayne, if he needs us."

"Seventeen Eddie will respond to the Forty-second Street station. We'll head uptown on the tracks."

Sirens sounded in the distance as the dispatcher came back on the air. "Seventeen Boy and Seventeen Eddie. Be advised that Emergency Service is responding from the West Side with an ETA of three minutes, and Transit Police are notified."

The sound of distant sirens ceased.

"Seventeen Boy, ten-four. We're at the scene and going into the hole."

"Seventeen Eddie to Central. Same message. We'll chat again when we surface."

"That's it," Felipe said. "Their radios don't work in the subway." Felipe picked up his own radio and transmitted. "Post One and Post Two, put your people out."

Julio Montalvo left the rear seat of a stolen Dodge Caravan parked at Second Avenue and East 42nd Street. Small and slight, he looked about fifteen years old, although he was twenty-two. Without looking back, he walked briskly up Second Avenue.

At Second Avenue and East 46th Street Ingrid Troutmann left the rear seat of a stolen Honda and walked slowly toward East 45th Street. She was blond, in her thirties, and buxom, wearing heels, a short skirt, and a low-cut blouse that showed off her assets. She looked a little tipsy, but still smart enough to keep her shoulder bag clasped firmly to her side.

Julio was fast approaching her, still one short block down Second Avenue, when she made the left turn onto East 45th Street. She saw the police booth on the corner of First Avenue, one long block away and on the other side of East 45th Street. Her side of the street was a tow-away zone and clear of parked cars, but parking was permitted on the other side of the street and there wasn't an open spot.

She was a quarter of the way down the deserted block when Julio turned the corner of East 45th Street, crossed the street, and started running behind her, quickly closing the distance. Hearing the footsteps behind her, Ingrid also started to run, but Julio was too fast. She was halfway down the block when he overtook her and pushed her forward onto the sidewalk. He grabbed her bag and pulled on it, but she held on and kicked at him, screaming, ''Help! Police!''

The police heard her. Brunette looked up from his book and saw the lady on the ground fighting the small kid for her purse, half a block away. He keyed his portable radio and said, ''Seventeen UN Post to Central. Got a robbery in progress, Forty-fifth Street, First to Second,'' and hustled to grab his first arrest, anxious that no senior cop get there and steal his collar. As he ran on his side of the street, partially hidden by the row of parked cars, he heard the dispatcher transmit, ''UN Post reports a robbery in progress, Four-five, First to Second. Seventeen Units to respond?''

There was no response. Brunette smiled as he ran.

Across the street and down the block, the lady was putting up quite a fight and Brunette worried that she might not need him after all. Ingrid was on the ground kicking Julio in the legs, forcing him to jump around as he tried to pull her bag away. After seconds of dancing, and with Brunette still a quarter block away, Julio had had enough. He reached down, punched her in the face, and won. Ingrid fell back and released the bag.

Bag in hand, Julio glanced around and saw Brunette running toward him, still across the street, crouching behind the row of parked cars as he ran. Julio reacted as if he didn't see the cop, but looked past him to First Avenue and saw the green Chevy turn into the block and double-park at the corner, lights off.

Ingrid was still screaming and lights were coming on in many apartments on the block. Julio bent over and leisurely punched her in the face again. She screamed louder. Then he heard Brunette behind him shout, ''Police, don't move!''

Julio didn't.

''Put your hands in the air!''

Julio did, but he kept the pocketbook in his right hand when he raised them.

''Keep your hands in the air and turn around.''

Julio turned and faced Brunette, who was across the street, leaning over the hood of a parked car with his revolver trained on Julio's chest.

''Drop the pocketbook,'' the cop commanded.

Julio ignored him. Instead, with both hands raised high in the air and his right hand still holding the pocketbook, he turned and started walking down the sidewalk toward First Avenue.

"Hold it!" Brunette yelled. "Where do you think you're going?"

"Home," Julio said, still walking.

"You're letting him get away," Ingrid yelled from the sidewalk.

"Yeah, dummy, you're letting him get away," shouted a woman leaning out of a third-floor window.

Brunette ran across the street to cut Julio off, but Julio just turned and walked in the opposite direction, toward Second Avenue, with his hands still held high.

The green Chevy started from the corner.

"Stop and drop the pocketbook," Brunette ordered as he leveled his gun at Julio's back.

Julio still ignored him, so Brunette ran behind him and hit him in the head with his gun. Julio fell next to Ingrid just as the green Chevy pulled abreast of them.

Brunette turned to the car as Felipe fired his shotgun from the open passenger window, hitting the cop in the legs with nine .32-caliber pellets. The force of the impact swept Brunette's legs under him, but he fired twice before his chest hit the sidewalk.

Brunette's first bullet broke through the second-floor window of a studio apartment across the street, ricocheted off a brass ceiling fixture, and came to rest in the refrigerator door. His second shot caught Angel DeSoto as he was leaning out the rear window of the green Chevy, lining his sights on Brunette. The bullet entered DeSoto's right shoulder, ricocheted off his clavicle, took a trip through his right lung and liver, shattered his pelvis, and finally exited his body at his left buttock.

As DeSoto slumped out the window and dropped his gun to the street, Felipe pumped another round into his shotgun and fired. Six of the nine pellets hit the cop in the top of the head, exploding his skull and splattering Ingrid and Julio with blood and brains.

Julio got up from the wet sidewalk as Emilio jumped out of the car, but Ingrid was still on the ground, screaming. Emilio picked up the pocketbook and gave it to Julio, then leaned over Ingrid and pressed the barrel of his pistol against her forehead. She stopped screaming and her eyes went wide in surprise.

"Wait! What are you doing?" Julio yelled.

Emilio ignored the question and pulled the trigger, ending Ingrid's role in the charade. Then he turned and pointed his pistol at Julio's chest, but Julio didn't seem to notice. He was staring at Ingrid's body, trying to comprehend.

"Get in the car," Emilio ordered.

Julio looked at Emilio, then at the pistol pointed at his chest, and nodded.

Emilio put the pistol in his belt and slid back behind the wheel. Julio got into the rear seat behind him, threw the pocketbook on the floor, then leaned over and pulled DeSoto from the window onto the seat next to him.

Emilio drove to the corner of Second Avenue just as the light turned red. He stopped for the light and signaled for a left turn. Felipe put his shotgun on the floor and lit up a cigarette.

"How's Angel?" Emilio asked as he watched Julio in the rearview mirror.

Julio put his hand over DeSoto's heart. "Looks like he's dead."

"That's too bad," Felipe said. "He was always a good soldier, but I think he was always unlucky. His family's all dead, aren't they?"

"He has a sister left," said Julio. "I think she lives in Huancayo."

"If we survive this, we'll do something nice for her," Felipe promised.

"Good," said Emilio, surprising both Julio and Felipe. "I liked Angel."

"I liked Ingrid," Julio said, softly.

There was a moment of silence. Felipe turned in his seat and stared at Julio, but Julio avoided his gaze. "We all did," Felipe said. "But her death wasn't pointless, like Angel's."

The light changed to green. Emilio turned and drove down Second Avenue and caught the red light on East 44th Street as the drizzle turned to a downpour. "Seventeen UN Post, are you on the air?" came over the scanner. There was no response and the dispatcher transmitted, "Units in the Seventeenth and surrounding precincts, we are now getting multiple calls of an officer and a civilian shot on East Forty-fifth, First to Second. Units to respond?"

There were units to respond as every cop working in Midtown Manhattan dropped whatever he or she was doing and headed for East 45th Street.

Before long, every detective and every boss on duty in the borough of Manhattan would be standing in the rain on East 45th Street, and work would commence on the jigsaw puzzle. For them, it was the beginning of the game and they would have no idea of the big picture. But they had three important pieces to start.

There were the bodies of Ingrid Troutmann, occupation unknown, and Dennis Brunette, rookie police officer. Fortunately or not, Brunette's mortal and bloody remains on East 45th Street meant that there would be no shortage of manpower to work this double homicide. Young Brunette was now famous. Fame was something he had always wanted, but it came long before he ever intended.

Felipe had meant to leave only those two puzzle pieces for the NYPD to ponder, but the third piece had been left inadvertently. In the street, just ten feet from the two bodies on the sidewalk, lay Angel DeSoto's .45-caliber Colt semiautomatic pistol, Model US 1911A.

Chapter 2
Those who knew Brian McCoy in Fort Myers Beach, Florida, considered him to be one of the most content and well-adjusted of people. After all, he was just forty-five years old when, through hard work and a few lucky breaks in his insurance something-or-other business, he had been able to accomplish the one thing that most people only dream of doing: Brian McCoy had been able to retire to a life in the sun while he was still able to enjoy it. He had achieved the American middle-class version of nirvana.

And he had done it in style. He had everything going for him—all the comforts, all the toys, and a few of the other things that turn people green with envy and set idle tongues to wagging.

Take, for instance, his home. McCoy lived in a three-bedroom condominium in the nicest building in town, complete with, of all things, a regulation pool table. Everything was new, from the silverware to the paintings on the walls. McCoy had brought hardly a thing with him from his previous existence in some small town in New York state. Not a picture, not a trophy, not a scrapbook, not even a school ring, although everyone was sure he must have one somewhere, probably from some pricey eastern school. After all, he had money. That was for sure. He owned a new Lincoln, a new twenty-four-foot Baymaster that was docked in the canal right under his window, and at First Florida Federal he never had to wait in line. It was always, "So good to see you, Mr. McCoy. Please come right this way."

But he had brought one thing with him, the one thing that the gossips loved most. It was Mrs. McCoy, a twenty-something beauty who obviously doted on him. They conceded that McCoy was a fine-looking man in good shape, and getting in better shape all the time, what with running, swimming, water-skiing, and even karate lessons—but, give us a break! Twenty-something? And looking like she did? He had to be sitting on a pile of gold, said the general consensus of opinion.

Then he had given his more senior neighbors the ultimate affront. Apparently, McCoy had been exercising with young Mrs. McCoy. She was pregnant, and McCoy had already decorated both of his spare bedrooms, one in blue and, just in case, one in pink. He had dropped out of the Fort Myers Beach social circles to take his wife to this doctor or that health food store. He waited on her hand and foot and the only time he left her side was to socialize with *them*, which had everyone wondering.

Anyone who has been retired in Florida long enough knows who *they* are, that group of misfits who burden every retirement community in the state. They're easy to spot, always wearing last year's fashions, drinking too much while they tell their loud stories in coded language that no respectable outsider could possibly understand, and generally treating all the better people with an attitude of benign superiority, a sense of noblesse oblige.

They are like cockroaches. Where you see one, there are a hundred of them, just out of sight. No matter what northern city they retire from, they seem to find each other and cluster in social groups that exclude, by accident or design, every normal person, or anyone else for that matter who is not a retired cop.

Every normal person except for Brian McCoy, that is. When he went out at all, it was with some of them. He golfed with them, he fished with them, and although he was a teetotaler, he attended some of their frequently scheduled parties and always stayed late, laughing the night away while listening to their silly jokes and police stories.

Contrary to the expectations of Fort Myers Beach opinion makers, the cops seemed to appreciate his company and had even given him a nickname. They called him Buffy, which confused everyone until Joe McGuinness had explained it. Joe was a retired district attorney, a lawyer, and therefore someone to be believed. He said he used to know some of the cops (although they denied ever knowing him) and explained that, in the old days, a buff was anyone who always wanted to be a cop, but was either too short, too fat, failed physical agility tests, or possessed too much moral fiber to be accepted by any large and respectable police department. He added that the term was archaic, because anyone who would have been called a buff then is now called Officer.

Brian McCoy was aware of the controversy and curiosity that surrounded him in Fort Myers Beach, which was one of the reasons he chose to hang around with the retired cops. He knew they regarded his previous insurance-business story as just so much bullshit, and that was his own fault. In his conversations with them he had made a few slips. To them, it seemed that he knew a little too much about the law, which led some of them to believe that he was really a retired lawyer. But they didn't seem to mind. They thought he was a good enough guy, McCoy figured, and naturally ashamed of his past profession. They never bothered him with questions.

But that was only one of the reasons he sought their company. The other reasons he had only recently begun to articulate in his own mind, and they worried him. Like his pals, he found that the normal people didn't interest him. Of course, he could appreciate other people and talk with them about their accomplishments in life and their views on the state of the arts, the sciences, the economy, politics in general, and national problems in particular. He had prided himself on always laughing at the right time and nodding whenever appropriate.

But they bored him, those normal people, because they knew nothing about human nature, about the dark side of life. They believed in the rationality of things and were convinced, therefore, that events were subject to theoretical interpretations and logical predictions. But he knew better, knew that with the exceptions of droughts, earthquakes, hurricanes, and some fires, bad things were made to happen by people, many times just ordinary people. Experience had taught him that even the most rational of people had an irrational side, something that propelled them to do things without apparent motivation, and that sooner or later everyone let their irrational side loose, if only for an instant, and, if they were unlucky, drunk, or those outbursts occurred too often, then they got to meet the police. They didn't like the police because the police *knew*, had seen them at their worst in those moments, and probably talked about them and even laughed about them among themselves.

They were right about that. McCoy, Dominic Santini, Bobby Evans, and Mike McCormick were set to tee off on the sixteenth hole, which was a tough one for McCormick unless he fortified himself with a six-pack of Budweiser. Having already done so, he was transformed into a scratch golfer, an altered state that usually lasted five minutes. But before teeing off he had decided it was time to tell them the one about the gay guy, his pet gerbil, and the unusual predicament they had gotten themselves into together. According to McCormick, it had happened when he was a captain in Detroit, and naturally he starred in his version of the story as he, showing courage and dedication well above the line of duty, had found the tip of the animal's tail and saved both the guy and his gerbil from a horrible death, one possibly more horrible than the other. But McCormick had gone one better and thought to add the *Friends of Animals* posters that adorned the guy's bedroom.

Everyone had laughed at the story as they guided McCormick to the tee for what they knew would be his one good 250-yard blast, straight as an arrow.

McCoy had laughed along with the others, and just as hard, although he had heard each of them tell essentially the same story when they had been in similarly altered states. Except, of course, in each of their versions they had been the stars and it had happened in their cities. But a good story was a good story, he figured, and the names and places didn't matter.

As McCormick hit his ball, 260 yards this time and right in

the middle of the fairway, McCoy found himself feeling smug. Of course the gerbil story was true, he knew, but it hadn't happened in Detroit or Chicago or Cincinnati or any of those other small-town police departments. It had happened in New York, *the City*, the only place it possibly *could* happen. He knew it happened there because Detective Commander Vernon Geberth had told him the story ten years ago, and every detective in the City of New York knew that Vernon's stories were always true and that, if questioned, he had the pictures to prove it. Once again the out-of-towners had taken a New York story and made it their own.

McCoy chided himself as Santini teed off, telling himself that his attitude was just another symptom of his problem, a problem he didn't entirely understand. Here he was, retired in Florida with a great wife, plenty of bucks, and nothing to do all day but run, lift weights, water-ski, fish, play golf, and take lessons in this or that.

In short, he was miserable and bored to tears. All of this was great, but he wasn't ready for it yet. He wanted to be Detective First Grade Brian McKenna again, the gun-collar man, the most decorated cop in the city, a well-respected type of guy. He still longed for New York, with the crime, the filth, the degenerates, the rotten weather, and all those other things that made it the most exciting city on earth and the best place to be a cop.

Instead, he was in heaven and going nuts. He was worried about himself, so worried that he had even gone to one of those self-actualization courses. All it had taught him were things about goals and frustrations, things he knew already, deep down. His goal was simply to be himself and he was frustrated because it was impossible. Well, not impossible, he thought. Just unhealthy.

McKenna suffered from a potential health problem that was rarer than Lou Gehrig's disease, a problem that few people in the United States had ever heard of, and it was called *Sendero Luminoso*, the Shining Path of Peru. It was always fatal, and even killed the innocents around the victim when it struck. McKenna couldn't risk that, not with Angelita finally pregnant and happy.

He had caught the disease that forced this pleasant, comfortable, rotten life upon him the year before in New York, when he had thwarted a major kidnapping operation of *Sendero*'s and, in the process, eliminated a few of their prime-time players. He had embarrassed them, and they had a certain well-founded reputation as sore losers. They tried to enhance that reputation once, and he had barely survived. They would try again, if they could find him. Revenge was their guiding principle, and he was sure it was mentioned somewhere in every page of their manual of operations.

So he had had to leave. Fortunately for him, his best friend had been the chief of detectives and was now the police commissioner, so it was a pretty easy thing to arrange. Money hadn't been a problem because a first-grade detective's pension was the same as a lieutenant's and was the subject of an annual gripe-and-moan story by the New York newspapers. Besides, he had made a bit of a killing when he sold his apartment in Greenwich Village, so he could afford a few of the luxuries. Driver's license, passport, Social Security number? No problem either, when the chief of detectives of the City of New York decides to call you something else. Whatever he calls you is your new name. Even the banks had been no problem, even in Florida. Ray had friends everywhere, and those Brian McCoy checks and credit cards were backed by the full faith and credit of the former Brian McKenna.

Ray had thought of everything, including stashing him in Fort Myers Beach on the west coast of Florida. He had given McKenna a lesson in geography, explaining that cops from the eastern cities usually retire on the east coast of Florida, and cops from the Midwest retire on the west coast. He didn't want McKenna meeting anyone who could conceivably blow his cover.

He had been right about that, too. In a year of hanging out with a good bunch of degenerates he hadn't met a single retired New York cop, and here he was playing golf with three cops from cities in the Midwest, with none of them any the wiser.

Santini hit a long, beautiful shot into the woods, or the palms as they are called in Florida, and immediately headed for McCormick's Budweiser cooler for the obvious cure. He wasn't stupid, and the seventeenth was another long hole.

McKenna was next. He had teed up and was addressing his ball when he was interrupted.

"Goddamn, look at that one!" Evans exclaimed, but McKenna ignored him. He wasn't going to fall for that old trick, what with a possible sixty cents riding on the shot. He continued stroking his ball without looking up.

"That girl's not gonna make it," McCormick observed dryly. "We're gonna be fishing her out in another minute."

What the hell, McKenna thought. These yokels got Buffy again. He looked up and his heart went straight to his mouth.

Across the lake on the seventh hole someone was driving a golf cart at maximum speed, skirting sand traps, greens, and the edge of the water with two-wheel maneuvers and obviously no intention of slowing down. McKenna focused on the driver and watched the cart hit a bump on the fairway, approach the sky, and land neatly on four wheels, still rounding the lake. That convinced him. It had to be Angelita, because anyone else would have been killed on that one.

It wasn't that she was that good, it was just that she was that lucky. She didn't wreck vehicles, she just dented them. It was one of their secrets that their new nine-month-old car now had an extra four coats of paint applied at various body shops around town after they camouflaged her motoring adventures. McKenna used to figure that within another year or so he would have to sit on a telephone book to drive, in order to see over the new layers of paint on the hood.

But it wasn't that bad anymore. After her three consecutive months of driver training courses imposed by the wisdom of the Florida Department of Public Safety, she no longer had accidents, although McKenna was sure that she still caused them. She was still the worst driver he had ever seen.

McKenna wanted to wave and shout to her, but didn't dare distract her. She left the lake area, crossed the woods, and headed straight for them. He had a premonition of disaster and ran to meet her, leaving McCormick, Evans, and Santini standing at the tee. He knew that someone had died and thought about his mother, who hadn't been feeling well lately.

He got to the edge of the fifteenth green before she reached him and skidded to a stop. She looked terrible, frantic and red-eyed. She had been crying and was going to cry again. And then she did, putting her hands to her face and sobbing uncontrollably.

"Who?" McKenna asked.

She didn't hear him.

"Angelita, who was it?" he shouted.

"I'm sorry, Brian. It's Dennis," she sobbed without taking her hands from her face.

Dennis? McKenna thought. Not Dennis Sheeran? He's a health nut and he can't be fifty yet. Angelita liked him, but this Dennis she loved. Dennis who? he wondered.

"Dennis who?" he asked, feeling stupid.

She took her hands from her eyes and looked at him incredulously. "Dennis," she said. "Ray's son Dennis. They killed Dennis Brunette."

That Dennis? No wonder it hadn't occurred to him. After all, he was only twenty-two years old and in the Seventeenth Precinct, New York's Gold Coast, tucked away safe and sound with many of the other big bosses' kids.

His surprise was quickly replaced by a lump in his throat and he felt his eyes misting up. He loved Dennis, had watched him grow up, and was proud of him. But probably not as proud as Ray. Fifteen hundred miles away, he felt Ray's pain. Ray had five kids and loved them all, but, although he would never admit it, Dennis was the one. In every traditional police family, there is the one who carries on the tradition, and in the Brunette family it was Dennis. Everyone knew he was going places. Was.

"How?"

"The usual no-good reason. He was killed by some purse-snatchers in your filthy city."

McKenna reached for his handkerchief, blew his nose and wiped his eyes. Then he gave it to Angelita and climbed into the passenger seat. "You drive," he said, surprising them both. "How do I look?"

She managed to give him a little smile. "Just like big, tough, old Brian McKenna. A little older than him, maybe."

"C'mon. I have to go get my clubs."

Angelita slowly drove them to the sixteenth tee.

"Going?" Santini asked.

"Yeah, we have to," McKenna said. "Something came up."

"We heard. We're really sorry about it," McCormick said, stone-cold sober.

McKenna was confused. "Sorry about what?" he asked.

"I heard it on the news before we came out today, but we figured, why spoil your day? You were gonna find out anyway, and bad news can always wait. But we did take the liberty of booking Mr. and Mrs. McCoy on every flight into New York."

McKenna looked from one to the other, astounded. "You knew?" he asked no one in particular.

"Of course we knew," Evans answered in his Cincinnati drawl. "What do you think we are, a bunch of yokels?"

"Never," McKenna said with conviction, "but how come you never said anything to me about it?"

The three other cops shared a smile, which somehow made McKenna feel like the yokel. Then Evans said, "Well, big-city detective, I don't know if you ever noticed, but this place down here is kinda long on storytellers and a little short on audience. We figured it would be just plain stupid to take someone from the small group and transfer him to the big group. Besides, never know what kind of bullshit you might come up with if we put the spotlight on you, so why take a chance? we said to ourselves."

"You guys are a bunch of clowns," McKenna said admiringly. "You might even belong in New York."

"Yeah, Buffy. But don't forget, we're clowns with pensions. Make sure you get back soon to enjoy yours. Us good old boys hear that New York is a nasty place."

Just like a captain, McCormick always had the last word and there was nothing left to be said. Angelita drove while McKenna trembled, not altogether sure why.

Chapter 3

The taxi ride to the airport was a long one, with McKenna and Angelita not saying much to each other. Although Angelita had been born and raised in New York, she despised the city and hated the police department. She considered the department to be a cold and self-serving bureaucracy, and she felt she ought to know, having been a rookie cop when she had met McKenna before her problems with driving a police car in Manhattan had prompted her to quit.

That was all for the best, she thought. She was happy in Florida and never wanted to go back, but now they had no choice. It was only right that Brian attend the funeral of his best friend's son. Nevertheless, she was in a mood, which suited McKenna just fine. He felt like getting in a mood himself.

McKenna called Ray's house from the airport and got his daughter Ilene. Her father wasn't home, he was at the morgue. McKenna grimaced at the thought of seeing a son at that place. He had the number for Ray's mobile phone, but didn't want to disturb him at such a time, so he just asked Ilene to give her father the message that they were on their way to New York. Then he bought a copy of *The New York Times* at the airport and they headed for their plane.

Angelita still didn't feel like talking and neither did he, so he read the paper during the flight.

The headline read POLICE COMMISSIONER'S SON KILLED IN EAST SIDE SHOOT-OUT WITH ROBBERY RING. The story took three columns on the front page and was continued on page three in Section A, which was a break with tradition since crime stories and other metropolitan news were usually carried in the B section of the *Times*. On the front page was a picture of the crime scene on East 45th Street, with the two bodies covered by blankets and surrounded by detectives. Page three carried a picture of Dennis in uniform graduating at the top of his police academy class and a photo of the Brunette home in Bayside, Queens. As usual, the *Times* had a lot of information.

McKenna read how Dennis had been at his regular post at the United States Mission to the UN when he had observed a woman being beaten and robbed half a block away. Brunette intervened, and while he was struggling with the perpetrator, three accomplices drove up and one of them shot him with a shotgun. Wounded in the legs, Brunette returned fire and it was believed he hit one of the men seated in the car before being killed by a second shotgun blast. Then another accomplice, in a vicious act of revenge, executed the female victim with a single bullet to the brain before taking her purse and calmly driving away.

According to police, the victim was still unidentified and described as a well-dressed white female in her thirties. Police said that the car used in the robbery had been stolen in Coney Island the day before and had been identified in two previous purse-snatches during the evening, one in Queens Plaza and the other on the West Side of Manhattan. In both previous crimes the MO was the same. One robber followed the victim on foot, grabbed her purse, and was picked up by his accomplices in their stolen car. A police spokesman declined to comment further, but added that it was expected that the case would be solved and the perpetrators arrested.

The paper reported that Inspector Steven Tavlin of the Major Case Squad was assigned to supervise the investigation and a special confidential phone number had been set up for those willing to provide any information on the robbers. A reward of $100,000 was offered by the PBA, with an additional reward of $100,000 to be provided by Cop Shot, a New York philanthropic organization. The reward would be given to any person who could provide information leading to the arrest and conviction of the killers.

The Brunette family was described as devastated by the tragedy, but holding up under the pressure. The police commissioner declined to give an interview, but stated that he would not be personally involved in the case. He asked that all questions be referred to Inspector Tavlin, who, paradoxically, also declined to be interviewed.

The story ended with a short history of young Dennis Brunette, reporting that he had been a high school track and baseball star and had gone on to attend John Jay College of Criminal Justice, graduating as the class salutatorian with a degree in criminology before joining the police department. Several officers and supervisors in the Seventeenth Precinct described him as likable and competent, and as someone who would have had a bright future in the police department.

Throughout the article McKenna had noticed that the press attributed their information to "a high-ranking department source" or "a police official who spoke on condition of anonymity," and that worried him. It had been his experience that, when a newsworthy case was going well and arrests were expected soon, there was usually no shortage of chiefs who were willing to be propelled before the cameras to outline for their public the wonders their brilliantly supervised men had performed, ending the interview by giving the assembled press the correct spelling of his own name and none other. That wasn't happening here, which led McKenna to believe that the case wasn't going well.

Reading on, McKenna found that the *Times* featured an article summarizing Ray Brunette's police career on the front page of the B section. It stated that Brunette was a third-generation New York City police officer who had joined the department in 1964 after serving in the Marine Corps. He rose rapidly through the civil-service ranks after being treated for alcoholism in 1974, and was now a teetotaler. He spent most of his career in the detective division, obtaining a law degree from St. John's in the process, and rose to national prominence when, as chief of detectives last year, he supervised the rescue of a prominent Peruvian who was being held in New York by the Shining Path terrorist army.

The *Times* reported that as police commissioner Brunette was popular in the ranks and had recently been at odds with the mayor because of his advocacy of incentive pay for those members of the department with college degrees and those who spoke Spanish or Creole. The *Times* article speculated that the mayor was afraid to remove him because his popular police commissioner had been mentioned as a potential candidate for many statewide and city offices, including that of mayor.

McKenna learned nothing about Brunette that he hadn't already known, so he read the rest of the metropolitan section and found that not much else had changed in New York. There was a mounting budget deficit, a breaking scandal in the Department of Social Services with checks being issued to nonexistent clients, and the threat of a longshoremen's strike, which would close the harbor, the city's raison d'être.

Angelita snapped out of it as they were landing in New York. She had felt the baby move for the first time and she wanted to talk again about names, which was one of the things that drove McKenna crazy. They couldn't agree because she liked a couple of Spanish names he hated and, oddly enough, some Waspish names like Brad and Dane. He was only happy with the old Irish standbys that ran throughout his family. She didn't like those, he suspected, because she didn't like the people in his family that carried them. So once again they got nowhere.

McKenna was surprised to find Dennis Sheeran waiting for them when they picked up their luggage in La Guardia Airport. Sheeran was an old friend and the deputy inspector in charge of the NYPD end of the Joint Terrorist Task Force. A personable guy with a boyish grin, he was thought to be one of the department's rising stars.

"Glad to see you, Dennis, but what are you doing here?" McKenna asked.

"Ray told me to find you and get you to the Gramercy Park Hotel," Sheeran said as he shook McKenna's hand. "He's got a suite reserved for you. That okay with you, Mr. McCoy?"

"Just fine. You can give me the real deal on the case on the way in."

Angelita wasn't happy with that. "Can't we talk about something else?" she asked. "This whole thing is depressing enough as it is."

"Yes, we'll talk about something else, but after we talk about the case," McKenna answered, giving her his please-don't-break-my-balls look.

Angelita opened her mouth to say something, then thought better of it. They picked up McKenna's suitcase and Angelita's three bags and headed out.

Parked outside the terminal, Johnny Pao sat behind the wheel of an unmarked car. Pao was a big, handsome man, a former Marine, and one of the department's sharpshooters. He was half Chinese and half Irish and McKenna always used to kid him, telling him the only reason he was alive was because McKenna's father had run out of ammo when he was shooting at Johnny's father at the Chosen Reservoir in the Korean War.

They put the suitcases in the back, then Sheeran got in front while McKenna and Angelita took the backseat. "Yeah, Brian, my father's still fine," Pao said with a smile as they climbed in.

"That's good news, Johnny. Tell him my father sends his best."

"Yeah, right," Pao said as he pulled from the curb and headed for the Grand Central Parkway.

Pao's still the same grouch I remember, McKenna thought before asking Sheeran, "What's to know that I haven't read in the papers?"

"Tavlin's keeping quite a bit under wraps," Sheeran answered. "We got the getaway car this morning. The dopes ran it out of gas on the Jersey Turnpike near Newark Airport and left it there. Bad news is that they wiped it down and we got no prints from the car. Good news is that apparently Dennis killed one of them. No body, but we found a bullet in the backseat that had lung and liver tissue on it, and those are two organs you gotta have to stay alive. The medical examiner ran tests on the blood in the car and says the dead guy was probably an illegal alien from some Third World country in South America."

"They got that from his blood?" Angelita asked, suddenly interested.

"Yeah. No antibodies in the blood for rubella, mumps, or polio, so he had to be from the wilds of someplace poor. He would have been vaccinated if he entered the country legally, and the witnesses say he was Hispanic.''

"How about drugs?'' asked McKenna.

"None. He must've been a clean-living guy, a little unusual in his profession. No drugs or alcohol in his blood. But that's not all we got from the car. There were three pocketbooks in back, all empty, but the first two victims have identified them as theirs and the witnesses on Forty-fifth Street say the third one is the one they took from the lady before they killed her.''

"Got her identified yet?''

"Nope, it's gonna be a hard one. No jewelry and all her clothes were German. Fingerprints come back negative, no record. We asked all around the neighborhood and nobody knows her. She had some alcohol in her blood, so maybe she was lost. Some guys from the Missing Persons Squad are working on it and they sent her prints to Interpol.''

"How long before they get an answer?''

"A couple of days, if she was ever fingerprinted in one of their member countries.''

"How many witnesses you got?'' McKenna asked.

"Plenty. The victim made quite a racket and woke everybody up on Forty-fifth Street. The original purse-snatcher is a Hispanic, short and skinny, maybe fifteen or sixteen. The guy who shot the girl looked like Godzilla, Hispanic, maybe five nine, plenty well-built, real mean-looking, they say. Nobody could describe the guy with the shotgun because he never got out of the car. Funny part is, they said the guy Dennis shot was wearing a suit. Don't see that too often in a purse-snatcher.''

"What did the first two victims say about them?''

"That it was the same kid who took their purses, but they couldn't describe anybody else in the car. Said there were four of them, though, and these guys always drove away slow so they all got the plate number.''

"That was a little careless of them, don't you think?'' McKenna asked.

"Yeah,'' Sheeran said, "but they were real careful in their planning. In all three purse-snatches, right before they pulled them, they had somebody call in a phony run to 911, always a heavy job, and always at the opposite end of the precinct where they were gonna do the robbery. Same male caller, all three times. Had a bit of a Spanish accent. They did a voice-print match on the 911 tapes.''

"How about location of the calls?''

"They did their homework. They knew that when you call 911 now, the location of the caller comes up on the 911 operator's screen. So he was always at the location where he said he was, right near the bullshit job he was calling about."

"So they had to have radios. First they find the victim they wanna do, then they radio the guy to make the call," McKenna surmised. "Pretty sharp, but now we know there has to be four of them left."

"Yeah, they're pros," Pao said.

"Sounds like it," McKenna said, but it didn't make sense to him. What are the benefits of being professional purse-snatchers? he asked himself. How much could they make from ripping off some ladies' pocketbooks, split at least five ways? Not enough to justify all the trouble they went to, he concluded.

"Something on your mind?" Sheeran asked.

"A few things that don't add up, like driving so slow that everybody gets their plate. Then there's the deal with running out of gas on the Jersey Turnpike. Somebody must have seen them get out of the car and, once you let that into the papers, you're gonna be getting hundreds of calls from people looking to cash in on the reward, telling you they saw them there on the turnpike."

"Maybe they're sharper than we think," Sheeran mused. "Maybe they ran out of gas near the airport so we think they left town, but they're still here. They had to know that they're real hot after shooting a cop."

"Maybe," McKenna said, but he wasn't so sure.

"But there was one definite mistake they did make," Sheeran said. "They left something for us on Forty-fifth Street. When Dennis shot the guy, he dropped his gun. The witnesses said it bounced under their car and they never saw it when they took off. But that gives us an even bigger mystery."

"What did they do? File off the serial number?"

"They didn't bother. The gun was brand new, never been fired. There was still Cosmoline in the barrel. It's a forty-five-caliber Colt automatic, U.S. Model 1911A."

"Government issue?"

"Yep. We called the Colt company and they told us the gun was manufactured for the government in 1974. Then we called the General Services Administration and were told it was delivered to the Marine Corps. The Marine Corps said it was at the Marine Corps Ordnance Depot in Albany, Georgia, so we called them up and they checked their records. Said the gun was still there. So Tavlin said, 'Oh yeah? Then go get it.' "

"Then they found out they had a real problem," McKenna ventured.

"You got it. The whole case of guns was missing. The box was there, filled with scrap, but the guns were gone. So now they're doing a complete inventory."

"And?"

"It's not done yet, but a lot of their toys have disappeared. They don't know exactly what yet, but they've got a real scandal brewing and they're pretty upset about it. We won't get the complete inventory for a couple of days, when they finally figure out how bad they've been hit."

"What was the girl shot with?"

"Forty-five-caliber Colt," Sheeran answered.

McKenna thought long and hard as Pao drove onto the Triborough Bridge. Then he said, "I don't like it. If they have two of the stolen guns, they might have everything that's missing. That doesn't add up to purse-snatchers to me."

"What are you thinking?" Sheeran asked. "*Sendero*?"

McKenna noticed that just the mention of *Sendero* caused Angelita to shudder, but he still had to think it out. "Maybe," he speculated. "They sure wouldn't mind hurting Ray. But if they were gonna kill his kid, why would they go to all the trouble to make it look like an ordinary robbery instead of an assassination? If it were *Sendero*, they'd be bragging about it by now. There's still too much in this that doesn't make sense."

They were approaching Manhattan, and the panoramic lighted skyline of the city lay directly in front of them. Nobody seemed to notice except McKenna, and he couldn't take his eyes off it. God, that's beautiful, he thought. I'm home. But he dared not say it. He tried to take his mind off the thought and asked, "How's Ray holding up through all of this?"

Nobody answered.

"Well?" McKenna insisted. "Tell me."

"He's breaking up and blaming himself for all this," Sheeran said. "He says Dennis came on the Job just to please him and continue the tradition, but that the kid really wanted to be an architect, not a cop. His reasoning is that if Dennis didn't become a cop just to make him happy, he'd still be alive."

"That's nonsense," Angelita said, surprising everyone.

"Dennis always wanted to be nothing else but a New York City cop. If I know that, why doesn't Ray? He shouldn't be punishing himself like that."

"But he is," Sheeran said as Pao drove onto the East River Drive. "He doesn't care about anything anymore."

"How about the investigation? Tavlin isn't really running it, is he?" McKenna asked.

"Sure is, with no help from Ray. Ray says, 'What difference does it make if another four murdering lowlifes go to jail? They'll be quickly replaced in this city and nothing'll bring Dennis back.' "

"He might be right about that," Angelita said. "But it's still not his fault."

"It's even worse than that," Sheeran said, "which is one of the reasons I'm glad you're here."

"What could be worse?" McKenna asked.

"He's hitting the sauce again, heavy, and it shows."

That was the last thing McKenna wanted to hear.

Chapter 4

Surprisingly, it had been a great night and an even better morning. It was 11:00 A.M., they were in New York, and somehow, getting along famously. Angelita had snapped out of her dark mood and McKenna attributed the welcome change to location. There was just something special about the Gramercy Park Hotel, something romantic in an old-fashioned way.

From the outside there was nothing especially distinctive about the building. It looked nice, but all the buildings that surrounded Manhattan's only private park looked nice, from the brownstone private residences to the exclusive private clubs to the apartment buildings containing the mahogany-walled apartments with the very large rooms. Very old, very comfortable, and very nice, the Gramercy Park area was a little New York secret.

Inside the Gramercy Park Hotel, however, the character was European, certainly not posh, but still European with an accent on service; not friendly service, American-style, but rather deferential service, which seemed better. The staff somehow always knew what the guests wanted and needed before the guests did themselves, making it difficult to complete a request to them with a full sentence. Three or four words into a request the staff person simply nodded, said, "Of course, sir," and then it was done. More than a few well-heeled guests first stayed there on a whim and wound up living there, too spoiled to live anywhere else.

McKenna and Angelita had been led to their accommodations by an unsmiling bellboy who showed them around the suite, explaining everything. McKenna had been hungry, and the bellboy had known.

"Is the restaurant . . ."

"Of course, sir, it's open until ten. I understand the stuffed brook trout amandine is excellent tonight."

Stuffed brook trout amandine? My favorite, McKenna had thought. Great, maybe we'll eat before we start this unpacking chore.

"Good. We're a little hungry and tired, and—"

"Of course, sir, I'll have your luggage unpacked while you're eating. Will there be anything else?"

What else could there have been? It was then that Angelita had cracked her first smile since arriving in New York and, after all, there was something romantic about the place.

After awaking refreshed, they had showered together and Angelita applied some ointment to those new little scratches on his back, right before they had some more fun. Afterward, they had a good breakfast brought up to their room, dressed themselves appropriately in black, and by eleven-thirty the smiling was over for both of them. The ordeal had begun. McKenna bought a *Post* in the lobby and they went outside and hailed a taxi.

The first twenty miles of the trip to Queens were easy. It was a bright, sunny day and traffic was light. Angelita had been raised in Queens and she looked out the window, keeping her thoughts to herself while McKenna read.

The story was still page three and featured a quarter-page picture of Ray leaving the morgue after identifying the body of his son. He was unshaven, looking tired and quite a bit older than McKenna remembered. The story rehashed the crime with nothing new added except that the police had found the car on the Jersey Turnpike and the city had added $100,000 to the reward, boosting it to $300,000. The article ended with the information that police would like to talk to anyone who had seen anyone leave the car on the turnpike.

After half an hour their taxi exited the Cross Island Expressway at Northern Boulevard. It took their driver fifteen minutes to negotiate the next ten blocks, then traffic stopped altogether. McKenna paid the unhappy driver with a good tip, leaving him to find his own way back to the world, and led Angelita four blocks down Northern Boulevard to the funeral home. It was a large place, possibly the largest funeral home in Queens, but it was nowhere near adequate in size to receive the friends and acquaintances of Ray Brunette. Also there were hundreds of people who had never even met Ray or Dennis, but they came anyway to make a statement by their presence, hoping to show their appreciation for the family's sacrifice and loss. Most would be there for hours before they even got in. The line of people ran four abreast for three blocks from the front door of the funeral parlor.

Confounding the situation was the presence of the politicians, closely followed, naturally, by the cameras. Each of these frequently elected representatives of the people had awakened that morning feeling inspired by the opportunity as they hastily memorized excerpts from their best law-and-order campaign speeches, all of which had been written by somebody else. They were everywhere, their official cars scattered about, and they found to their chagrin upon comparing notes that many of their words of wisdom had been written by the same person. They didn't know who'd said what before they arrived, and they were terrified of being exposed by making the same speech that someone else had already made. They all wanted to leave, but didn't dare. It was tacitly decided among them that, for once, sympathetic silence was the best policy.

Still, they were beside themselves. Although a separate line had been established for the politicos, they were waiting in line like ordinary people with nothing to say as they concentrated on affixing their best sad faces while the cameras were rolling.

Inspector Edward Keller was officiating at the door, the right man for the job. An imposing giant, he was in full uniform and had a row of medals over his shield that ended at his ear.

He was talking to a state senator who was next in line when he saw McKenna and Angelita in front.

"Wait here, Senator," he said as he descended the steps, took McKenna's and Angelita's arms, and guided them past the politicians, through the crowded lobby, and left them at the door of the chapel.

Ray and his wife, Ann, were there, standing near the head of the closed casket. There was a picture of Dennis in uniform propped on top of the casket, with the Medal of Honor at the base of the picture. The room was full of seated chiefs and politicians, silently watching the people in line approach the casket, say a short prayer, and give their condolences to the parents on their way out. It was an assembly-line wake.

Ann saw McKenna and Angelita before Ray did, and she tugged at his elbow and whispered in his ear. He looked up, smiled when he saw them, and rushed over.

McKenna was shocked at the change in his friend. Ray and Ann had been down to visit them in June and he had looked the way he always looked: like an older, more distinguished version of his kids, with the trademark Brunette black hair and a smile that produced two dimples at the corners of his mouth and a twinkle in his eyes. He had always been in shape and appeared the perpetual forty-five, although he was fifty-five.

Now his eyes were red and as he smiled the dimples seemed like two scars. He looked sixty-five.

Brunette hugged Angelita first. "Don't say you're sorry," he whispered in her ear. "I know you are and I've heard it enough already." He kissed her on the cheek and then hugged McKenna. "And don't say I look like shit. I know I do and I've heard that enough already."

"Okay, I won't say it," McKenna said.

"Good. Now both of you go over and get the prayer thing over with and say hello to Ann. She's still glad to see you."

"You're not coming?" McKenna asked. "Ray, you know I don't handle these things too well and I won't know what to say to her."

"Don't worry, she understands. Turns out she's stronger than I ever thought she was, much stronger than me. I'll wait here, then we'll get outta here for a while. You understand, don't you?"

"No, but I'm not in your shoes, *amigo*, and I hope I never am," McKenna said. "We'll be right back."

McKenna and Angelita walked over, knelt in front of the

casket, and said their good-byes. Ann was waiting for them and gave them each a kiss. "Wipe your eyes, Brian," she whispered in his ear. "I'm glad you're here. I need you both to help us."

McKenna rubbed his eyes with his hands. "What do you want me to do?" he asked.

"Just help him get through this, any way you can," she said, looking directly into his eyes.

"Is it true he's been drinking again?" McKenna asked, not sure if he should.

"That's not what I'm worried about. After all, he drank like a fish for ten years before anyone even knew he had a problem. He'll get through the show today just fine. Just straighten out his mind a little, if you can."

"What about tomorrow?"

"Tomorrow's just family and close friends. You're going to have to do something before then to get him back for us."

"Any suggestions?"

"Of course. Don't you see it?" she asked. "Just get him interested in the case. You go with them, Angelita."

"What can I do?" Angelita asked. "Police work isn't really my thing anymore."

"Just keep them both strong and keep the common sense flowing. That's what we do, you know. Now get going. You're holding up the line."

Ann gave her first smile of the day to Angelita and sent them back to Ray, who was at the door talking to Sheeran. Sheeran nodded at McKenna and Angelita, then stood waiting like he had something to say.

"Get back to work, Dennis," Brunette said to Sheeran. "I'll talk to him about it."

"Yes, sir, but we need some weight here," Sheeran said, catching McKenna's eye as he left.

"What's that about?" McKenna asked.

"We'll talk about it upstairs," Brunette answered, motioning for them to follow. He led them to the manager's office and made himself at home behind the desk. "You two aren't gonna give me any problems, are you?" he asked as he opened up the bottom desk drawer.

"Have we ever?" McKenna answered.

"Good." Brunette took a bottle of Chivas Regal and two glasses from the drawer and put them on the desk. "Just this once, care to join me?"

McKenna stared at the bottle for a moment, then at Ray. "I can't, Ray. You know me. One is too much and ten is never enough. You'll be okay by yourself, but if we both get going this day will be worse than it is already."

"Then pull up some chairs, at least. You make me feel like I'm sitting in the electric chair."

McKenna and Angelita sat while Brunette poured a drink. He took a sip, then leaned back in his chair and closed his eyes. "I know everyone's been grabbing your ear, Brian, but I'm gonna be all right. It's just gonna take some time."

"I think it would help if you'd get yourself involved in this case."

Brunette sat up in his chair and shook his head. "Why should I? I've surrounded myself with competent people. It'll get done right. Besides, it wouldn't look good, especially if something went wrong and those dirtbags wound up getting killed instead of arrested. It would look like revenge, and we'd have the Justice Department breathing down our necks for a long time. If I were there when it happened, maybe we'd deserve it."

"Maybe," McKenna said without agreeing. "Now why don't you tell me what Sheeran was talking about?"

"He's going off on the gun thing. The Marine Corps had promised Tavlin a complete list of all the stuff they're missing, but we don't have it yet. Sheeran thinks they're dragging their feet, thinks maybe there's some kind of cover-up going on. He wants me to talk to the attorney general about it."

"Can you?"

"I think so. The president called me last night to offer his condolences and wanted to know if I needed anything. But I could call him back and have a chat."

"Maybe you should, especially if Tavlin doesn't get anything by tomorrow."

"Tomorrow? How's that?"

"Because if Tavlin doesn't get a call from one of the bad guys by tomorrow, then there's more to this thing than meets the eye."

"Sheeran told me you were making some *Sendero* noises, but it doesn't make sense to me. There's too many holes in it and you know it. They would have bragged about it by now, and it wouldn't have been this elaborate. But explain to me anyway what tomorrow's got to do with it?"

"Look at it this way. We're supposed to think Dennis was

killed by a gang of purse-snatchers. Vicious, sure, but still petty thieves, and at least four of them. Now there's a three-hundred-thousand-dollar reward and nobody's telling us nothing? That can't be. One of them should be talking to a lawyer by now and asking some advice.''

Brunette leaned across the desk. ''Which one?'' Then he answered his own question. ''The guy who made the phony call.''

''The likely candidate. He wasn't at the scene, so he doesn't go for the felony murder. If he says he didn't know they had guns, what would he get? Conspiracy to commit Robbery Second Degree, only a *D* felony? Makes a deal, and Lord knows what he'd get, if anything. But he would get three hundred thousand dollars and he'd be willing to do a little time for that.''

Brunette took another sip of his drink, deep in thought. Then he stood up and said, ''If nothing breaks by tomorrow, you may be right. It could be *Sendero* and, if it is, they must have something else up their sleeve.''

Then Angelita piped in. ''Ray, please pour me a drink,'' she said, surprising both Brunette and McKenna. Brunette had never seen her drink, and McKenna only saw her have one drink in the three years he knew her, which had made life easy for him.

Brunette stood up and poured her a stiff drink. She took a long gulp, made a face, and put down her glass. ''Ray, think about it. Do you know what all this means if it's them?'' she asked.

Ray had thought about it. ''Yeah, if it's them, then it didn't make any difference that Dennis was a cop,'' he snapped back, smiling sardonically. ''If it was part of their plan to kill him, they would have done it whether he was an architect, a street sweeper, or the president of Chase Manhattan.''

Brunette sat down again. McKenna and Angelita watched him intently as he followed his thought pattern to the logical conclusion. ''C'mon, Ray,'' Angelita said. ''Say it and get it over with.''

''Okay. Fortunately Dennis *was* a cop, and a pretty good one, I guess. He managed to get one of them before they finally killed him and because of that we've got the gun.''

McKenna was ready. ''If he wasn't good, we'd have nothing to go on, which could be real important if it is *Sendero*.''

''Exactly,'' Angelita said, following up in McKenna's

tracks. "Let's not waste the opportunity he gave us by sitting on our hands. Ray, you better make that call to whoever you gotta to get that inventory."

Angelita finished her drink while they watched her. Then she put down her glass and stared hard at Brunette. He still wasn't convinced, so she glanced at McKenna with a raised eyebrow.

"It's only common sense," McKenna said. "If it's them, we gotta know what weapons they might have and figure out what they're planning to do with them. After all, they're not smarter than us, are they?"

They were interrupted by a knock on the door. Keller came in and announced, "Commissioner, the mayor's downstairs. Mrs. Brunette says you have to come down and schmooze with him or he won't go away."

"Tell her I'll be right down," Brunette said. Keller left. Brunette picked up his glass and stared at it, thinking. Then he poured the rest of his drink back in the bottle, screwed on the cap, and put it back in the drawer. "No, they're not smarter than us," he said as he straightened his tie and went to the door. "And neither is His Honor, thank God."

Chapter 5 JULY 22, DEL RIO, TEXAS—It was just before dawn, and already Galindo, Manuel, and Pedro knew they were having a bad day. Ten minutes after crossing the border for the first time, dirty, wet, and hungry, they were spotted by a border patrol helicopter.

Following the plan, they split up and ran into the desert, but it was no use. The border patrol was suddenly everywhere, riding in Jeeps and on ATVs while searching the desert with their night-vision goggles. Twenty minutes after they had first seen the helicopter, Galindo, Manuel, and Pedro were reunited in the rear of a border patrol cage bus, along with ten other very recent immigrants.

They were brought to the border patrol station at Del Rio, Texas, and fed some salami-and-cheese sandwiches before being fingerprinted, photographed, and interviewed. Their cover stories held up and, two hours after their arrival in the United States, they were unceremoniously dumped back into Ciudad Acuña, Mexico, ready for another try.

They found a small cantina and talked strategy while they ate. Pedro and Manuel wanted to spend the day in Ciudad Acuña and try again that night, but Galindo was the group leader and he was worried. Their plane was leaving from San Antonio at seven the following morning and they had to be on it.

The issue was never put to a vote. They were already running behind schedule, so Galindo decided they would try again at once, but this time they would cross at the alternate spot. He telephoned their contact person on the other side and told him of their plans. The contact said he would pick them up at the designated place. Then Galindo called for a taxi and the three of them waited outside.

The taxi driver took one look at the disheveled condition of his passengers and asked, "Are you boys going to try again today?"

"Yes," Galindo answered. "Take us west on *La Avenida Cinco de Mayo* to the city limit, then drive another four kilometers."

"Whatever you say, but I know a better place," the taxi driver offered.

"We'll try our place," Galindo answered curtly.

The taxi driver followed Galindo's instructions and took the road out of town. It followed the Rio Grande, but three kilometers out of town the road veered southwest. Four kilometers from town they were a half-kilometer from the river. Galindo paid the driver, who told him, "The river is wide here. If you don't make it, give me a call this afternoon. We'll try my place."

"We'll make it," Galindo said and the three headed across the desert to the river.

The river was wide, but it was shallow. They waded across without a problem, scaled the fence on the United States side, crossed the border patrol road, and walked northeast through the hot desert. Although they saw helicopters and hid in the brambles as soon as they heard the rotors, they didn't see a single border patrol agent. After two miles they came to Route

90 and walked west, staying well off the road and out of sight.

Galindo's calculations had been almost perfect. After walking five minutes, they came to the meeting spot, a dry creek bed that Route 90 bridged. They sat down and waited.

They didn't have long to wait. At ten-thirty Ricardo Montoya pulled his blue van off the road at the east end of the bridge, got out, and opened the side door of the van. Montoya was a native Mexican-American, a local character in Del Rio, full-time thief and part-time smuggler of illegal aliens. He was a happy man that day, being well paid for this particular job.

Galindo, Manuel, and Pedro scurried up the creek bank and into the side door of the van. Montoya closed the door after them and got behind the wheel. The back of the van was filthy, with used batteries and other auto parts littering the floor. There were also three new suitcases.

"Welcome to *los Estados Unidos*," he said as he headed east on Route 90, toward San Antonio. "Just kick those things aside and make yourselves comfortable."

"You have the things we need?" Galindo asked.

"Everything. The suitcases are yours. You can sit on them, if you want. It's going to take us about four hours to get to the airport."

"What about the plane tickets and the money?"

"Got them right here," Montoya said, pointing to a briefcase on the passenger seat. "Three to New York and three hundred dollars. Got some ID for you, too, and there's a cooler back there with some cold beers, courtesy of the house."

Galindo was satisfied. The three sat down on their suitcases, ignoring the cooler. Montoya drove through Del Rio and was ten minutes past town when he slowed down.

"Shit!" Montoya said. "We're being pulled over. You boys might be going back to Mexico today, but I'll pick you up again tonight, same place. Just don't say anything."

Galindo heard a short siren burst and Montoya pulled onto the shoulder of the road and stopped, shutting off the van. Galindo positioned himself in the back so he could see behind the van through Montoya's side-view mirror. A white police car was behind them with the roof lights on. The policeman got out of his car with his pistol drawn and approached Montoya. "Whatcha doing, Ricardo?" he asked.

"Just runnin' some wetbacks, Deputy, trying to make a living."

"So I hear, but you've been falling a little behind on your

traffic tickets. They tell me you owe six hundred sixty dollars as of today.''

"I got the money, Deputy. Just let me deliver this crew and I'll get right to the courthouse and pay. I swear to God I will,'' Montoya pleaded.

It wasn't working for Montoya. "Gimme the keys,'' the deputy demanded.

Montoya pulled the keys from the ignition and gave them to the deputy, who put them in his pocket and said, "C'mon out and let's see what you got back there.''

The deputy opened Montoya's door and Montoya got out.

Galindo, Manuel, and Pedro watched through the windshield as the deputy followed Montoya to the right side of the van. Then Galindo shifted his position so that he could see the deputy and Montoya at the side door of the van through the side-view mirror. The deputy stood back with his gun raised as Montoya put his hand on the door handle. "Okay, open it up,'' the deputy ordered.

The door swung open and Montoya stepped back. The three saw the deputy with his gun pointed inside at them. The deputy looked them over without apparent interest, then checked around the inside of the van.

"Collecting a few batteries, aren't we now, Ricardo?''

"They're all mine,'' Montoya insisted.

"Got receipts for them?''

"I can get them.''

"You're gonna have to,'' he told Montoya. Then to Galindo, Manuel, and Pedro he said, "You boys just sit tight and we'll have you back home before you know it,'' before he slammed the door closed.

Galindo focused again on the passenger side-view mirror and heard the deputy say, "Sorry, Ricardo. I'm gonna have to take you in and impound your vehicle.''

"Please don't do this, Deputy Foster,'' Montoya pleaded.

"Got to, Ricardo. You're what we call a persistent violator. Now turn around, lean against your vehicle, and assume the position.''

Galindo watched the mirror in horror as Montoya leaned against the side door of the van and Deputy Foster frisked him, still keeping his pistol on Montoya.

"We're going to have to act,'' Galindo whispered to the others. "He's arresting him and taking the van.''

"So we'll go back to Mexico and try again tonight," Pedro quietly offered.

"No," Galindo whispered. "Plans have been made and the American is going to be waiting at the airport in New York to pick us up."

"This isn't our fault," Pedro protested, looking to Manuel for confirmation and support.

He got none. Pedro stared at Galindo, his face showing his confused reaction to the turn of events.

"We won't get to New York without money or plane tickets," Galindo whispered, urgently. "These cops won't let us keep that stuff. They'll ask too many questions, especially about the ID."

Neither Pedro nor Manuel made a move as Galindo watched the deputy holster his gun and take out his handcuffs.

"Felipe won't understand this," Galindo said.

That did it. Discipline was strict and uncompromising in their army, and Felipe was not known as an understanding man. Pedro and Manuel rose from their suitcases.

"What do you want us to do?" Manuel asked Galindo.

"He put away his gun. When I tell you, open the door quickly and we'll jump him."

Manuel put his hand on the side-door latch and Pedro stood behind him. The deputy had Montoya's arms behind his back and was handcuffing him as Montoya leaned forward with his head on the side door of the van.

"Now!" Galindo yelled.

Manuel quickly swung the door open and Montoya fell into the van. The deputy was still holding the cuffs and he was also pulled forward. Manuel, Pedro, and Galindo jumped over Montoya and swarmed over Deputy Foster. Manuel put him in a headlock while Galindo grabbed the deputy's gun, but he couldn't get it out of the holster.

"Put him down," Galindo yelled.

While Manuel held the deputy in the headlock, Pedro grabbed Foster's ankles from behind and pulled. Foster hit the ground with Manuel still holding on, but Foster was kicking and squirming while punching Manuel in the side. Galindo finally got the gun out. He put it to the back of Foster's head and fired one shot, killing him instantly.

Galindo rolled the body over, went through Foster's pockets, and removed the van keys. Then he emptied the deputy's bullet pouches and pocketed the twelve bullets.

Sitting up in the van with his legs hanging over the side and his hands cuffed behind him, Montoya was wide-eyed. "You boys shouldn't have done that," he said. "We're in a lot of trouble now."

"No, you're in trouble now, you ignorant asshole," Galindo answered. He raised the pistol and shot Montoya in the right eye.

Montoya fell back into the van and Galindo pushed his legs in. "Get him in, too," he said, pointing to Foster.

Manuel and Pedro picked up Foster by the arms and legs and swung the body into the van on top of Montoya. The three men looked around them. Traffic was light and flowing smoothly in both directions.

"You drive," Galindo ordered, giving the keys to Pedro. Galindo climbed into the passenger seat, Pedro got behind the wheel, and Manuel jumped into the rear of the van, closing the side door behind him.

"Get us out of here," Galindo said as he replaced the two spent shells in Foster's gun. "We have to get off this road and get rid of this van."

Pedro checked his side-view mirror, saw that the road was clear, and pulled onto the highway, leaving behind them the empty police car with the flashing red roof lights.

What he didn't see was the small flashing red light on the video camera mounted on the dash of Deputy Foster's car. He didn't know that in response to a rash of murders of officers during car stops Texas had joined the video craze and that Foster, following the new standard procedure, had turned on his camera before he made his last car stop.

Felix Rathbone liked living off the beaten track. Being a simple man, he eschewed things like cable TV, VCRs, microwave ovens, and strangers in general. He figured he already knew more people than he ever wanted to and wished people would leave him alone. People generally did.

Felix loved his simple farming life, which to him meant rising early, working hard, and living long. He was a man of few possessions, but those he had he cherished. They were his 1991 Mazda 626, his daughter Becky, his big hound, Deadly, and his wife, Sarah, in that order.

Those few people in Val Verde County who ever bothered to think about Felix considered him normal in all ways, except for the Mazda. Like them, Felix believed in buying American, and he could proudly state that he had never been in a Radio Shack in his life. But there was the Mazda, always parked directly outside his living room window.

Felix never tried to explain it to them because he didn't understand it himself. He just loved the car.

Sarah was in the kitchen mashing up some sweet potatoes for her sweet potato pie, the thing Felix liked best about her. He was in the living room listening to the farm report and petting Deadly when he heard the car pull off County Road 621. He took the normal precaution of getting his shotgun from the hall closet and putting the leash on Deadly. Then he stood at his front door with his dog and watched the blue van come slowly up his long driveway.

Sarah was watching from the kitchen window and yelled to him, "There's two of them in there. Be careful."

Felix was perturbed when the van parked next to his Mazda. The driver came out and was walking toward the front door when Felix came out onto his front porch, his shotgun cradled in his right arm and holding Deadly's leash with his left hand.

Deadly didn't like the man, or anyone else for that matter, and was straining at the leash. The man stopped in his tracks, twenty feet from the porch.

"I'm not hiring pickers till August," Felix said. "Come back then."

The man stood there with his hands at his sides, saying nothing.

"I said come back next month," Felix repeated as Deadly snarled. "Now get outta here."

The man just stood there.

Felix descended the porch steps with Deadly leading the way, growling and pulling.

Galindo was sitting in the van, the deputy's .357 Magnum ready, staring at Pedro's back. He could no longer see Felix and the dog, which meant they couldn't see him. He whistled and Pedro dropped instantly to the ground. Galindo stuck his gun out the window and fired one round through Felix's chest, but Felix remained standing and released the dog.

Deadly bounded over Pedro and ran straight toward the van. Galindo took aim and fired again. The bullet caught Deadly in the chest in midstride and he slid forward on the ground. He wasn't getting up.

Galindo switched his aim back to Felix's chest, but didn't

fire. He saw that Felix was dead but didn't know it yet. Felix dropped his shotgun, brought both hands to the hole in his chest, and fell forward, just as Galindo heard a door slam at the back of the house.

He jumped out of the van and yelled, "Take his gun and check the house!"

Pedro picked up the shotgun and Manuel slid open the side door of the van as Galindo ran to the back of the house. He saw Sarah fleeing through the cotton field in back. She was fifty and overweight, but running for her life and moving fast, about 100 yards from the house.

Galindo took off after her, pacing himself. Her endurance surprised him and it took him almost two minutes to catch her.

Pedro and Manuel were searching through the drawers in the kitchen when they heard the shot. There were so many keys, but none of them looked like car keys. Manuel went back to search the bedrooms and Pedro was searching through a chest of drawers in the living room when Galindo came in.

"Did you find them?" he asked.

"Not yet."

Galindo turned and walked out the front door to Felix's body. He stuck his hand in Felix's front pants pocket and removed a single key.

Becky Rathbone was driving home on County Road 621, still a mile from her house, when she saw her father's car coming toward her. She slowed down and beeped as the car with three men inside passed her. She hit the gas and drove home as fast as she dared.

Sheriff Jefferson Davis Parker was the high law in Val Verde County, and he figured he was in the perfect place to deal with the distressing information coming over his radio.

He had been in Barksdale that morning getting a mobile phone installed in his cruiser when his office called him with the news about Deputy Foster. Reserve Deputy Looney had come upon the empty cruiser on Route 90 and had played back the videotape. A statewide alarm had been put out for three male Hispanics in Ricardo Montoya's panel van.

The sheriff had been headed to his office in Brackettville to handle the emergency when the call came in from Becky Rathbone. Her father was dead, she couldn't find her mother, the blue van with Montoya's and Foster's bodies was in her front yard, and three men were headed north on County Road 621 in her father's Mazda. So the sheriff had settled in on County Road 418, 100 yards from where it crossed County Road 621 and 15 miles north of the Rathbone place. He figured these three fellas were heading north to Interstate Highway 10, which ran from San Antonio to El Paso, and also thought it likely they would stay on the back roads.

Parker loosened his Ithaca Model 12 pump-action shotgun and his Winchester Model 70 .30-06 rifle in their holders attached to the dashboard and was unwrapping one of his imported Mexican Te-Amo cigars when the Mazda crossed the intersection, still headed north on County Road 621. He slipped his cruiser into Drive.

Pedro was driving with Galindo in the front passenger seat and Manuel was sitting in the back behind Pedro. Pedro checked his rearview mirror and announced, "There's another police car behind us." Galindo and Manuel turned in their seats just in time to see Sheriff Parker put on his roof lights.

Then Galindo made the first in a series of mistakes. "Lose him," he ordered, and Pedro floored the gas pedal, letting all of the Mazda's 120 horses loose on County Road 621.

Behind them, Sheriff Parker chuckled as the Mazda shot forward. Knowing that County Road 621 went straight as an arrow for the next ten miles, he stayed behind the Mazda as he lit his cigar. Then he goosed the accelerator and activated the 300 horses that lived in the ram-charged Dodge 440-cubic-inch engine under the sheriff's hood.

Ten seconds later Pedro, Galindo, and Manuel were staring at the shotgun barrel the sheriff was holding out the passenger window as both cars proceeded north, side by side at 110 miles an hour.

"What should we do?" Pedro asked, panic-stricken.

Galindo made his second mistake. "He doesn't know anything about us, probably thinks we're just speeders. Keep going. They don't shoot people for speeding in the United States."

But Sheriff Parker did know something about them. Although he wasn't particularly fond of Deputy Foster because Foster had threatened to run in the next election for sheriff, Foster was still a lawman and entitled to a certain amount of respect, which these three gentlemen certainly hadn't given him. And although he didn't understand Felix's preference in vehicles, Sheriff Parker had still liked him since Felix was a lifelong resident of Val Verde County, a registered Democrat, and, incidentally, a second cousin to Lyndon Baines Johnson, twice removed. And perhaps most important, although these three men in the car next to him were theoretically in the United States of America, they were actually in Texas.

The shotgun blast tore into the side of the Mazda, peppering the driver's side with buckshot and causing multiple lacerations to Manuel's face and left side.

As the sheriff pumped another round into his shotgun, Galindo made his third mistake. "Ram him," he ordered Pedro.

It is doubtful that Galindo had ever seen the TV commercial that proclaimed Mazda to be the safest car in America, and if he had, he probably didn't know that this claim is based on driving a 2,000-pound test Mazda into a solid brick wall at five miles an hour, not into a 3,000-pound Dodge Police Cruiser Special while traveling at 110 miles an hour.

The Mazda careened off the side of the Dodge like a billiard ball off a rail. As it bounced out of the drainage ditch that ran along the side of County Road 621 and headed into the desert, it overcame gravity for a full four seconds before it reentered the atmosphere and headed back to earth in an unhealthy nose-first attitude. At the moment of impact, Galindo, Pedro, and Manuel exited their vehicle via the windshield. The Mazda teetered on its nose, threatening to crush the three recent occupants, then fell back, landing on all four wheels with Galindo, Pedro, and Manuel lying in front of the car.

Galindo was the first to wake up. Bleeding from the head with his face a mass of abrasions, at first he couldn't remember where he was or what had happened. He stared stupidly at his two unconscious companions lying on the ground next to him and then down at the gun still in his hand. It all came back to him as he saw the police cruiser on County Road 621 make a slow U-turn and head back toward them.

Galindo forced himself to his feet and staggered into the desert. He heard the cruiser stop on the road behind him and heard the door open and close. The next thing he heard was the sound of the .30-06 round pass over his head. And then Galindo made his final mistake.

Gun in hand, Galindo turned around and irrevocably enrolled himself in the patent-pending Sheriff Jefferson Davis Parker Weight Reduction Program, a program that operated on the theory that to lose a lot of weight quickly, first you have to gain a little. Galindo momentarily gained an ounce as the .30-06 round tore through his chest, broke two ribs, severed his aorta, and exited his back. But as his body lay faceup on the ground, Galindo lost four pounds when most of his blood was soaked up by the sand as it flowed from the new large hole in his back.

Sheriff Parker's mood darkened as he approached the two men lying in front of the heap of scrap. His cigar had gone out. With every molecule in his body screaming in pain, Pedro could still hear him say, "Goddamn Mexican cigar. You silly people just can't do anything right, can you?"

Chapter 6   JULY 23, NEW YORK CITY—McKenna

and Angelita had just left their suite when Inspector Tavlin and Johnny Pao stepped off the elevator. Tavlin was tall, thin, and balding, looking and dressing more like a successful accountant than a cop. He would never adorn an NYPD recruiting poster, as Pao had on two recruitment drives. Pao carried a large cardboard box.

"You two look like bad news," observed McKenna.

"Then we're good actors," Tavlin answered. "We should look like horrible news. Let's go back inside."

"We can't," Angelita protested. "We'll be late for the funeral."

"No you won't. Everyone except us is gonna be at least two hours early. It's been postponed until noon, at least. Maybe later."

"Then why are we standing out here?" McKenna asked, grabbing Angelita's arm and leading her back to their room. McKenna unlocked the door and everyone followed him into the stateroom. Pao put the box on a coffee table.

"Should we be sitting down for this?" Angelita asked.

"Might as well," said Tavlin. "We got the inventory from

the Marine Corps and it's gonna take a while." He took an envelope from his pocket and handed it to McKenna.

McKenna and Angelita sat on the sofa while Tavlin and Pao pulled up two armchairs facing them. McKenna opened the envelope, took out the four-page list, and read it to himself with Angelita looking over his shoulder. It took him ten minutes the first time, then he read it again while Angelita ordered a pot of coffee from room service.

Still reading, McKenna asked, "How much C-4 in a case?"

"Forty pounds," Tavlin answered.

"Two hundred and twenty cases, that's about four and a half tons of high explosive. Add in the remote radio relays, the 106-mm recoilless rifles, the Claymore mines, the M-60 machine guns, the M-79 grenade launchers, and enough small arms to supply a battalion. Then spice the pot with some tons of ammo, eight Stinger antiaircraft missiles, and what have we got?"

"Enough to fight a small war for a long time," Tavlin answered.

"And where do you think this war is gonna be fought?" McKenna asked grimly. "Here?"

"That's the only good news we've got. We think it's already been fought."

Already been fought? McKenna asked himself. Where? "Nicaragua?" he ventured.

"Yeah. How'd you know?"

"Educated guess. The only recent wars fought where American-made small arms played any part were in Nicaragua, Angola, and Lebanon. In Bosnia and Afghanistan they used Soviet weapons on each other, except for the Stingers in Afghanistan. I figured Nicaragua because it was the closest and there was a lot of politics involved. Now you tell me how you knew."

"When the war ended there the Sandinistas and the Contras agreed to turn in their weapons. Neither side did, of course, but they made a show of it. We checked with the new Nicaraguan government and found out that some of the weapons on that list were turned in by the Contras, mostly small arms."

"Any Stingers?"

"Nope. It's general knowledge that the Contras had them, which is one of the things that kept the Nicaraguan air force on the ground. Some C-4 was turned in, but we don't know how much, yet. We have to figure that a lot of it was used up by the Contras, so we'll never be sure."

"And the other stuff?"

"Still missing."

"Well, we know that some of this stuff is still loose or you wouldn't have the .45 Colt," Angelita said.

"We're going on the assumption that a lot of it is still loose," Tavlin said. "That's the reason for the delay in the funeral. The commissioner figured that with two thousand cops sitting in a church he wanted to take some extra precautions, so he—"

"Brought in the bomb dogs," McKenna said, interrupting Tavlin.

"All of them. They're doing the church, every house within a block, and the park across the street."

"Any ideas on how this happened?" McKenna asked.

Before Tavlin could answer, there was a knock at the door. McKenna got up and opened it for the room-service waiter. He was there with the tray of coffee, but McKenna was surprised to see Joe Sofia standing at the elevator. McKenna looked in the other direction and found Joe Mendez standing by the stairwell. Both men were old friends assigned to the Major Case Squad. McKenna exchanged waves with them both and followed the waiter into the room. He caught Tavlin's eye and gleaned from his expression that he should keep his questions to himself, for now. But he had bodyguards and knew Angelita wasn't going to be happy with this development.

McKenna sipped his coffee, then turned to Tavlin. "Well, Inspector? How did all this stuff come to be missing when it's supposed to be in a warehouse in Georgia?"

"We think it never was in the warehouse. Security is too tight there and they've had no reports of any break-ins."

"Who's 'we'?"

"Right now we is the attorney general and the FBI, but the list is gonna be growing soon to include a grand jury and some senators looking for some prime-time coverage."

"A Senate investigation?"

"Probably. It must've happened at the end of '84 when the Republicans were in, so it's kinda old news, but they'll still get some mileage out of it for the cameras. You see, in 1984 everything on the list was in the Marine Corps Ordnance Depot at Barstow, California. Then the marine general in charge there decided that the place was full and ordered that it all be moved to Georgia. It went by rail to Macon and by truck to Albany. . . . ''

"And the switch was made in transit?"

"It looks that way. Everything was inventoried at Barstow and put into sealed cargo containers, so they didn't check the containers when they got to Albany. It happened someplace between Macon and Albany. An outfit called Reliable Trucking was used to transport the stuff in Georgia. There's no listing for them now, so the FBI did some checking. They were in business for only four months, September to December of '84.''

"Who owned Reliable?"

"A guy named Frank Nesbitt. Turns out Nesbitt's a retired CIA guy. He's very popular now and everybody wants to talk to him, but he's made himself unavailable. He does have a lawyer now who says—''

"Yeah, I know what he says: 'This is outrageous, but my client will cooperate fully, et cetera, but he won't be the target of any witch-hunt.' ''

"Exactly what his lawyer said."

"What about the marine general? He had to be in on it."

"He's also retired now, but he's got a lawyer, too. He won't make a voluntary statement, so all this is gonna take time.''

"What's this general doing now?"

Tavlin shrugged. "Just being retired, as far as they can tell. Lives in San Diego, has a kid in the Marine Corps and another one in Annapolis. The FBI wanted to do a financial workup on him, but there's not much they can do without subpoenas.''

"Yeah, I know. They're good and pure and play by the rules," McKenna said, impatiently. "Did Ray do anything?"

Tavlin smiled. "Nothing official, but the general is clean, financially at least. He's got a mortgage, a car loan, and an ex–Mrs. General getting five hundred dollars a week. It looks like he's just scraping by comfortably on his pension. Ten thousand in the bank and he owes eleven thousand on credit cards. He didn't make any money on the deal, which means he was ordered to do it. But he must've known something was going on or he'd be talking to the FBI.''

"Weren't there any escorts when all this stuff was moved?"

"It was guarded by Department of Defense civilian guards from Barstow to Macon. They've been talked to and it looks like nothing happened while they had it. From Macon to Albany the Reliable trucks were supposed to be guarded by a company of MPs from the second MP Battalion from Camp Lejeune. The Department of Defense people said the MPs were there to meet the train, but the FBI checked the records of the second MP Battalion . . .''

''And they knew nothing about it?''

''There was no request made to deploy an MP company to guard the shipment.''

''So we know it was an inside job orchestrated by the CIA,'' McKenna said. ''That doesn't concern me too much. Everybody thought things like that were happening anyway. The thing that does concern me is the .45 Colt showing up in New York when it's supposed to be in Nicaragua.''

''Yeah, that's the mystery,'' Tavlin said.

''But it's probably not *Sendero*,'' Angelita said, smiling. ''The Contras were supposed to be anticommunist, right? And *Sendero* is a bunch of crazy commies. They shouldn't get along, so what's the big deal? What probably happened is that some unemployed Contra guy sold his gun to somebody.''

McKenna and Tavlin stared at each other, McKenna hoping that Tavlin would leave it at that and leave Angelita happy. He didn't.

''You might be right and I hope you are,'' Tavlin said somberly. ''But weapons are big business, so they don't always wind up where they're supposed to. I won't be satisfied until somebody bright talks to the Contra who handled the deal, but we won't even know who that is until somebody gets some of the players talking.''

''When will that be?'' Angelita asked.

''Months. Our system is slow, so they'll all be fighting subpoenas while they get their stories together.''

''But it still doesn't look like *Sendero*?'' Angelita asked, hopefully.

''No, but a lot of things still don't make sense, so the commissioner thought you should have these things.''

He turned to Pao, who stood up, opened the cardboard box, and took out two bulletproof vests and a Glock pistol in a holster. He offered one vest to McKenna and one to Angelita.

''That's your old pistol, Brian,'' Tavlin said.

''I don't have a permit.''

''Yes you do.'' Tavlin reached into his breast pocket, took out a pistol permit and a pen, and offered them to McKenna. ''All you have to do is sign it.''

Angelita was shocked. She stared at the vests. ''Ray thinks

they still want Brian?'' she asked.

"No, he's just being safe," Tavlin answered calmly. "As a matter of fact, he suggests you two stay home today."

"Not me," McKenna said, standing and taking the larger vest and his pistol from Pao and putting them on the coffee table in front of him. "I've been hiding long enough." He took the permit and pen from Tavlin, signed it, and gave the pen back to Tavlin. Then he took off his suit jacket and tie and unbuttoned his shirt. Angelita stood watching, her mouth open and her eyes wide.

"You don't mind Sofia and Mendez?" Tavlin asked.

"No, it's always good to see those two," McKenna said.

Angelita found her voice. "Brian, what the hell is going on?"

"Ray's got the two Joes outside. I guess he thinks we need company," he explained to her.

"I see," she said thoughtfully as she eyed the vest Pao offered her. "So you wanna play cops and robbers again?"

"I'm not playing," he said resentfully. "We're still leaving tomorrow. Let's just not take any chances. Put the vest on, Angelita."

Angelita eyed the vest thoughtfully. "I'll never fit that under this dress."

She's right, McKenna thought, looking at Angelita's sleek black dress. She was four months pregnant and showing it a little. It had been a team effort getting the back of her dress zipped. "Then you shouldn't go," he calmly said to her.

"If you're going, I'm going," she answered, just as calmly.

McKenna stared at her while Pao and Tavlin checked the shine on their shoes.

Finally McKenna said, "Look, Angelita, use your head. I have to go, but you've already made enough appearances. I really think you should stay here."

"If you're going, I'm going," she repeated.

"I'm going and you're not, and that's final," McKenna said, exasperated.

Sofia drove them to the church in Bayside, an affluent neighborhood where the white people lived. It was the last neighborhood before the Nassau County line, and to McKenna it seemed that the trip took forever. There was a total lack of conversation between McKenna and Angelita.

Three blocks before the church the formations of uniformed cops began, lining the street in groups of forty all the way to the church and for blocks beyond. They were from departments far and near, but most were from New York City. Sofia was passed through a checkpoint and drove to the front of the church.

It wasn't going to be the usual police funeral, McKenna saw. The Emerald Society Pipe Band was formed up in full regalia, and the print photographers and the TV news crews were set up across the street from the church, but something new had been added, something McKenna was sure would be the subject of much speculation in the press. At the entrance of the church were two Bomb Squad detectives holding their large dogs of indeterminate breed on long leashes. Inspector Keller was waiting, and he brought McKenna and Angelita inside.

Cops in uniform filled the church except for the first five aisles on the right side. The politicians sat there, the mayor and the governor among them. Keller brought McKenna and Angelita to the first aisle on the left side. The Brunette family was seated there, starting with little Kevin on the far end and ending with Ray on the aisle. Ray moved over so McKenna and Angelita could sit down.

"You shouldn't have come," Brunette said to McKenna.

"Sorry, but we're here anyway," McKenna answered.

Brunette smiled. "I know. I expected you anyway."

Then it began. The coffin was brought in and placed at the front of the altar. One of the police chaplains was officiating and he started the service. McKenna found his mind wandering. Like most of the people in the church, he had attended too many police funerals before, and after a while one seemed just like the other. Then Pao appeared in front of them, in the aisle between the altar and their pew. Leaning over the pew, Pao whispered, "Sorry to interrupt, Commissioner, but we just heard from Interpol. I thought you should know that the girl they killed was Ingrid Troutmann. Her brother was with the Baader-Meinhof Gang."

McKenna's heart skipped a beat. He knew the Baader-Meinhof Gang was a leftist radical terrorist group that frequently allied themselves with other like-minded organizations like the Japanese Red Army and the PLO. McKenna reasoned they would also probably sympathize with *Sendero Luminoso*.

Brunette got up, with McKenna and Pao following and everyone in the church watching, and went into the sacristy off the altar, closing the door behind them. He turned and faced Pao. "You did right. Now let me have it all."

"Interpol had her prints. She's a German citizen from Frankfurt. She was arrested in West Berlin in '81 after she punched a cop during a demonstration. No criminal record after that, but her brother was killed by the German police during a raid in '86. They were sticking up banks to finance their cause and the cops got on to them."

"What was she doing here?" Brunette asked.

"No idea. She arrived in the U.S. last week and Immigration told us she was here on vacation."

"What does she do?"

"Independent photojournalist, writes mostly for radical magazines in Europe. We checked with Immigration in Nicaragua and they told us she was never there, legally at least. Then we checked with Peru. She was there from March to June of this year, legally, doing an article on *Sendero Luminoso*."

"What was in the article?" McKenna asked.

"We're still checking, but as far as we can tell it was never published."

Brunette turned to McKenna. "What do you think?"

"I think they killed one of their own people to make Dennis's murder look like a purse-snatch. I'm still wondering why, but we might be standing in the reason right now. We got the mayor, the governor, and two thousand cops, including all the top brass, sitting in one place."

"You're right. This funeral is taking too long." Brunette turned and went back into the church. McKenna and Pao followed him, but stopped at the altar rail. Brunette went to the altar and whispered in the ear of the very surprised chaplain, who nodded, then Brunette rejoined McKenna and Pao at the rail. The three men took their seats as a murmur echoed through the church.

What followed was the fastest funeral within memory. Ten minutes after it began the casket was moved to the entrance of the church and the pews emptied in reverse order from the way they had filled, with the family and the politicians following the casket.

The church doors opened and caught everyone waiting outside by surprise. The limousine drivers had formed a group and were talking and smoking in front of the hearse and the press people were in another group across the street. The ranks of cops snapped to attention as the cameras started rolling and the limo drivers hurried to their cars. The pipe band drummers started a slow drumbeat while the bagpipe players blew into their instruments, filling them with air.

McKenna and Angelita watched from the steps as the pallbearer detail of uniformed cops picked up the casket and Brunette led his family, the mayor, and the governor to their waiting cars. Brunette was talking quietly and rapidly to the mayor as they walked, and it seemed, all of a sudden, that the mayor and the governor were ready to forgo an excellent prime-time photo opportunity.

The pallbearers carried the casket down the church steps toward the waiting hearse as the pipe band played. The driver opened the back door of the hearse as the pallbearers shifted the weight of the casket to load it in.

Then McKenna heard a dog whine to his left. He looked over and saw the leashed Bomb Squad dog running in circles around his handler, whining loudly. "Is that his signal?" McKenna yelled to the surprised detective.

The dog handler looked at McKenna and yelled, "Bomb!" at the top of his lungs.

My God! McKenna thought. The pricks put it in the hearse and the dog smelled it when the door opened.

Four thousand people froze, looking at the detective and the dog, but not for long. "Bomb!" the detective yelled again as he tried to untangle himself.

Pandemonium broke loose. The hearse driver was the first to run. Then most of the cops broke formation and started running down both ends of the block, but a few stayed, confused and awaiting orders. The official cars and the limousines backed down the block through the running cops as the pallbearers stood at the rear of the hearse with the casket, not knowing what to do with it.

"Run, Angelita!" McKenna ordered, but she held on to his arm. He shook her hand off. "For God's sake, listen to me. Run!"

She listened and ran down the stairs, leaving McKenna standing at the top of the steps.

"Close the doors and get down in the church," McKenna shouted. The Bomb Squad detective let go of the leash and ran into the church, pushing cops inside and closing the heavy doors after him. The dog ran straight to the hearse.

McKenna scanned the park. There's got to be of one of them

with the radio remote detonator, McKenna thought, and we caught him by surprise with the fast funeral. He wasn't in position and he wasn't ready, or we'd all be dead by now.

As the pallbearers finally got the casket into the hearse while managing to keep the dog out, McKenna thought he found what he was looking for. Through the woods at the far end of the park, at least fifty yards away, he saw a man climbing a tree.

God, I hope that's him, McKenna thought as he drew his pistol. He took aim and fired five times, with no apparent effect. He didn't have the range yet, but the man stopped climbing and looked toward the church. Then he started climbing again, reaching for the next branch.

That's him, McKenna thought. Anyone else would have climbed down when someone shoots at him. As McKenna raised his sights higher and took aim, he saw that he was the object of unwelcome interest from the cops who stayed on the street below. They had found their guns and they were all pointed at him.

"Get the guy in the tree!" McKenna yelled, but they kept their guns on McKenna as he saw the man pull himself onto a branch.

Keller appeared from nowhere and stood in front of McKenna. No one was ready to shoot a uniformed Inspector of Police, especially one who looked like Keller.

"Get the guy in the tree, you assholes," Keller roared, pointing into the park.

The effect was instantaneous. All but three of the cops, including the pallbearers, ran into the park toward the man in the tree. McKenna resumed firing over Keller's shoulder and the three cops still in the street joined in.

Over his sights and through the foliage, McKenna saw that the man was hit in the chest, but he held on with one hand to a branch over his head and reached into his pocket with his other hand.

"He's got the detonator!" McKenna hollered, still concentrating and firing.

McKenna fired the last round in his magazine as the hearse exploded. The three cops in the street were picked up by the blast and swept into the park while McKenna and Keller were blown into the wall of the church.

Young Dennis Brunette had made a final appearance, and he was everywhere.

Chapter 7

Slowly, McKenna regained consciousness to the sounds of sirens and men shouting all around him. He tried to open his eyes and move his body. He could do neither and started to panic.

He tried rolling his eyeballs in their sockets and they seemed to work, but he couldn't be sure. Next he wiggled his fingers and toes, and they also seemed to move. He figured that his eyes were glued shut and he was pinned to the ground by an enormous weight. But he was still alive, at least, and knew that help was on the way. The knowledge calmed him and he either fell asleep or slipped back into unconsciousness.

McKenna was aroused by a male voice, close and shouting, "This one's alive!" He felt the weight being pulled from his body and he tried to sit up. He couldn't. His head hurt and seemed to be stuck to the ground. But he could move his legs, although his left thigh hurt.

"Don't try to move," a voice told him.

"I can't, anyway," McKenna said. "I can't move my head and I can't open my eyes."

"Don't worry about that," the voice counseled. "It looks like your head is stuck to the ground by dried blood and there's scabs on your eyes."

"Whose blood? Mine?"

"We don't know yet. There's blood all around here. Does anything else hurt?"

"Everything."

"Okay. Just relax. We're gonna give you something for the pain. It'll calm you down."

McKenna felt his hair being cut in the back as a needle was slipped into his arm. He tried to concentrate, but couldn't. He relaxed and let the drug take over.

* * *

McKenna opened his eyes and looked around. He was in a hospital bed. Brunette, Pao, and Sofia were standing next to the bed, staring at him. Brunette and Pao looked as he had seen them last, but Sofia's suit was filthy and tattered and he sported a new shiner.

"What happened to you?" McKenna asked Sofia.

"Never mind him," Brunette said. "Are you ready to get up?"

"I don't know. Am I?"

"I think so, but Pao said you're a sissy and will probably spend a week in here, acting like a baby and soaking up the attention."

"Where's *here*?"

"North Shore Hospital. You're in the place where the rich and homely come to get their faces done over."

McKenna sat up in bed. His leg and his face still hurt. He touched the back of his head and felt a bandage partially covering a bald spot. Feeling under the sheet, he found another bandage on his left thigh. He wasn't so sure about getting up and asked, "How come my head and leg still hurt if I'm doing so good?"

"Toughen up," Pao admonished. "I've been beat up worse in a high school hockey game when I was fourteen years old. We won that one and I played again the next day."

"You've got a couple of stitches in the back of your head and a puncture wound in your leg," Brunette explained. "No big thing. You're laying here and preventing a paying customer from getting her boobies enhanced."

"How long have I been faking these injuries?"

"Six hours," Brunette answered.

"How bad was it?"

"Pretty bad. Lost four of our own, but the guy in the tree is history."

"Keller?"

"You didn't know?" Brunette asked. "He was lying on top of you when they found you. He's gone, but he saved your life. Cut to ribbons, but he was standing in front of you when it went off. Otherwise you'd be beyond pain like those other guys, instead of lying here crying."

Brunette's strategy worked. McKenna sat up and swung his feet over the bed. He felt dizzy at first, but it passed. The aches and pains didn't. "What happened to my leg?" he asked.

"You got stuck with a bone from Keller's leg. Nothing serious, just a few stitches."

"Tell me about the guy in the tree."

Brunette took a radio remote detonator from his pocket and gave it to McKenna. It was the size of a small TV remote control, with an On/Off toggle switch, an LED indicator light, and a large red button under a hinged protective cover.

"M129A radio remote detonator, serial number 46731," Brunette explained. "It's on the list. They found it on the ground next to his body. He was hit three times."

"I killed him?"

"No, but you helped. He was hit three times, two of your 9-millimeters and one .38 slug from one of the cops, but the range was too far. None of the wounds was fatal. You just pissed him off, so he pushed the button and then fell out of his tree. Broke his neck."

"Any ID on him?"

"What do you think?"

"That maybe we'll never find out who he was. How did they do it?"

"Expertly. They broke into the garage where the limos and the hearse were stored. There was no alarm, so they just picked the garage-door lock, opened the hearse with a Slim Jim, and put about twenty pounds of C-4 under the wooden bed in back that the casket's supposed to rest on."

"Twenty pounds?" McKenna asked. "I guess they wanted everyone."

"I don't think so. Just you and me. Everybody else would've been just icing on the cake, as far as they're concerned. They killed my kid just to get us together."

"I'm sorry about Dennis," McKenna said.

"About the body? Don't be. They could only kill him once, and they already did that. You know how I feel about the death industry. When I go, just wrap me in an old rug and put me out for Sanitation. It's just gonna be hard to find enough of him to bury, but I don't think he'd mind. Suzy the bomb dog is in the same shape as him, so we'll probably be burying parts of them together."

Can Ray really be that tough? McKenna thought. Probably not, was the conclusion he drew. They both shared the same feelings about the death industry and had talked many times about the socialized travesties that funerals had become. They agreed that anyone who had been in combat or on a homicide squad knew what happened to bodies as they decomposed, so they both had arrived at the same viewpoint, believing that the body was simply the place where the loved one lived and shouldn't be the subject of emotionalized rituals when the loved one died and left.

But McKenna thought what *Sendero* had done to Dennis's body was an extreme test of that belief, and Ray wasn't fooling McKenna. He knew that he was holding up because he had to. He was the man in charge, and if he fell to pieces, the show would not go on the way it should. Nobody's that tough, but Ray has to pretend he is, McKenna told himself. "How about Ann?" he asked.

"She doesn't feel the way I do," Brunette answered quietly. A silence descended over the room, but then Brunette chuckled and said, "But we screwed them a little. Before the funeral I made the area around the church a restricted area, no civilians allowed except residents of the block. So their man had to hang out on the other side of the park. He wanted to get you and me, but he couldn't see anything. He looked around and knew he had to be in the tree when the funeral ended, but he couldn't hang around up there, waiting, because one of the cops would see him. So he had to wait until the funeral was over, when everyone would be looking at the church, but we surprised him with the quick funeral. I think he started climbing when he heard the bagpipe music."

"But they still killed four cops," McKenna said.

"They'll pay for that, I promise," Brunette said firmly. "But it's not what they set out to do. It's a failure as far as they're concerned."

"They claim any bragging rights?"

"Between us and the press, we've had four groups nobody's ever heard of call up to take credit, but not them. Not *Sendero*, which is why I have to give you a medal in front of the cameras, for all America to see. That should piss them off."

"Ray, I'm not a cop. I'm a civilian. I don't get your medals anymore."

"Oh yeah?" Brunette said as he reached to the floor and came up with two small black boxes. He offered them to McKenna. "Pick one."

McKenna looked at the boxes and picked the one in Brunette's left hand. He opened it. Inside was a gold shield with an eagle on top, flying through a cloud of three stars. "What's this?" McKenna asked.

"Assistant commissioner of police."

"Assistant commissioner in charge of what?"

"Anything you want. Make up a title, but make it sound good. We have to live with it and we don't want those wise-guy detectives snickering. But you picked the wrong box, so you lose."

Brunette opened the other box. Inside was McKenna's old detective shield. "You could've got lucky and picked this one," he said. "Something with class and history. But the choice has been made. You're stuck with it."

"Does the mayor know about this?"

"He thinks it's a good idea. He already gave you a fancy line in the budget."

McKenna was confused. "Why?"

"Simple. I told him that you're the only man for the job, and with you as my assistant commissioner I'd probably be too busy to run against him come election time."

McKenna was awestruck. "You'd give up a chance to be mayor for me?"

Brunette leveled a stare at him. "It's not for you. Getting these douche bags is the most important thing in my life, and we've proved that we can do it together. If we don't, they'll try again and maybe kill some more cops in the process."

McKenna thought it over. What about Angelita? he asked himself. This won't make her happy. She'll say we can be safe in Florida or we can go someplace else, anyplace else. Can I do this?

McKenna felt uncomfortable with Brunette staring at him, waiting. Then Brunette broke the tension and smiled. "Think it over," he said, "and don't worry about me. I wouldn't want that mayor's job, anyway. It's just too hard being the mayor of this town."

Just as McKenna was feeling relieved, Mendez came in carrying a travel bag, a brown double-breasted suit, shirt, and shoes. McKenna recognized the suit as his own, a suit that he had left in the hotel. "Angelita gave you that?" he asked. "She hates that suit."

Mendez stopped short and looked at Brunette. McKenna saw that Pao and Sofia also were looking at Brunette and knew that something was wrong.

"Where's Angelita?" McKenna asked.

"Here," Brunette answered. "Upstairs in Obstetrics. There was a little problem. Hero Detective Sofia here was dragging her down the block while you were doing your act on the church steps. Then she decided that she wanted to go back, so she knocked Joe out and then the bomb went off.''

"How bad is she?''

"She was half a block away when it went off, so she got knocked around a bit. Some cuts, bumps, and bruises, nothing that's gonna last for too long.''

McKenna was relieved, but then noticed that Pao, Mendez, and Sofia were silent.

"I'm sorry. She lost the baby, Brian,'' Brunette said.

The news hit McKenna hard and everybody saw it as he stood up, grabbed his clothes from Mendez, and started dressing.

"I tried to hold her, Brian,'' Sofia said, looking a disheveled wreck. "She sucker-punched me, but I still tried to get her out of there.''

McKenna stopped to smile at Sofia. "I understand, Joe. It's not your fault. I understand because she got me once and then I looked like you do. She usually gets what she wants.''

Angelita's room was on the fourth floor. She was in bed and staring at the door as McKenna entered. She had an IV in her arm and her face showed a few bumps and bruises, but she still looked better than Sofia. She was the obvious winner.

"Where's my good-looking cowboy?'' she asked, smiling.

"Right in front of you, under the ugly-guy disguise,'' McKenna answered, looking and feeling battered.

"Complete with your ugly-guy suit. I told Joe to get the blue one.''

McKenna waited patiently while Angelita looked him up and down, then kissed her on the lips while she hugged him. Angelita started sobbing softly. He wasn't surprised.

"I know,'' McKenna said. "We'll do it again.''

She pushed him away and held him at arm's length. "I don't know if you understand, Brian. This innocent baby was a part of me, a part of us. I already had plans for our baby and even started talking to it.''

She let go of him and wiped her eyes with her sleeve, then sobbed again. "I felt its pain when it died. I can tell you the exact moment.''

"I think I understand,'' McKenna said, kissing her again and feeling helpless.

"Then you know what I want you to do," she whispered in his ear.

"Yeah, I know, baby. You want me to get you back to a normal life. I will, I promise. As soon as we can get you out of here, we'll be on the first plane back."

"Brian, you don't know me at all," she whispered, looking at him like he was one of the slow kids.

McKenna was confused. "What do you want me to do?"

She stared him straight in the eye with a look he had never seen before. "I want you to get them all. Kill them, if you can get away with it, but get them all. They're heartless savages and I don't want them on the same planet with our children. When you're done, come back to me. I'll be waiting."

McKenna was speechless. What have they done to my Angelita? he asked himself. I don't know this girl. "Where are you gonna be until then?" he asked her.

"Right here, for the next three or four days, they tell me. Don't worry about me, because you're going to be busy. Call but don't visit. Ray's assigned the two Joes to take care of me."

Things were moving too quickly for McKenna's tastes. "He already knows about this? I just finished telling him I'd think about it."

"Of course he knows. I'm the one who told him you had to be a big shot on this case so none of the department drones could get in your way."

"Ray already got rid of the drones," McKenna told her confidently.

She smiled at him patiently. "It's a civil service, Brian. That's where they live. You get rid of the ones he missed if they get in your way. Now go to work. Ray needs a lot of help to keep his sanity."

McKenna searched for reasons to stay there with her, but under these new circumstances he couldn't think of any. He knew that Angelita was pretty tough, but she would still need some consoling from him, eventually; she was telling him that she could wait. He kissed her again and went to the door. As he opened it, Angelita asked, "Brian, you know they shaved the back of your head, don't you?

"Some men don't look bad when they go bald, but you're not one of them. Get a hat."

McKenna was relieved to see a bit of the twinkle back in her eyes.

Chapter 8

Avoiding the swarm of reporters at the hospital, Brunette and McKenna slipped out through the basement entrance close to where Brunette's car was parked. Ray drove as they headed for the news conference at police headquarters.

Incredibly, Brunette seemed to be in a good mood, smiling and humming to some oldies on the radio, but McKenna was visibly nervous. He just couldn't seem to get comfortable, and fidgeted in his seat. As they crossed the city line, Brunette turned down the radio and asked, "What's bothering you? The job?"

McKenna thought he was being cool and the question caught him unaware. "Am I that obvious?"

"To those who know you."

"I was never a boss before, and you just made me a big boss," McKenna said, looking out the window. "I hope I can handle it."

"You never took a sergeants' test, right?"

"Nope."

"Why not?"

"I never wanted to be a boss because I liked being a detective too much. Still do, I guess."

"It's what you do best, but you'll still be a better boss than most. You see, the bosses are supposed to be smarter than the cops and detectives, but it's just pretend, because sometimes they're not, and frequently they're not as sharp, which is more important. These civil-service tests are mostly memorizing *Patrol Guide* trivia, which doesn't mean a boss is smart, it just means he spent a lot of time in the book."

McKenna turned to Brunette. "I dunno. Some of them are smart."

77

"A fortunate aberration of the system. Are you as smart as Sheeran and Tavlin?"

"Maybe," McKenna said, but he wasn't so sure.

"As smart as O'Shaughnessy?"

"I hope so," McKenna said, sitting up straight. "Everyone knows O'Shaughnessy's a jerk."

"Yet he's a chief, a living, breathing, walking testament to the failure of the civil-service system, and he's not the only one. He's not smart, he's not sharp, and worst of all, he's a prick."

"So why do you keep him around?"

"You're gonna find out that you need a guy like him around just to keep the men on their toes. Otherwise you've got to do it yourself, and who wants to do that? Try and get a sharp prick, if you can."

"Like Hardcass?"

"Perfect, although I suspect he just pretends to be a prick. But that's okay, as long as the men believe his act. I'll have him assigned to you."

"What is it I do, exactly?"

"Technically, you're a political appointee just helping me out. Unofficially, you'll be running the Joint Terrorist Task Force and the Major Case Squad while I'm doing everything else I'm supposed to do."

"But those are Sheeran's and Tavlin's outfits."

"I said unofficially. They're both smart enough and sharp enough to know that you're smarter and sharper than they are, and they'd probably admit it if you asked them. They'll be a big help to you."

McKenna still wasn't convinced. "Who's gonna go for this besides you?"

"Why, everybody, of course. The bosses will like it because you'll cut their heads off if they don't, the press will like it because you're a hero and heroes sell papers, and the public will love it because it's like a rags-to-riches story. Even the politicians will like it, because if anything goes wrong they can blame me, and I think they'd like to do that."

McKenna was still skeptical. "It's as simple as that to be an assistant police commissioner?"

"In this case it is because there's no middle ground. It's cut and dried. We're either gonna win or we're gonna lose, because I don't think *Sendero*'s going away. At least I hope they're not."

No, they're not going away, McKenna thought. We'll get

another crack at them or they'll take one at us. This thing was too involved to be a simple hit, even a tremendous hit. And there's a high probability they have a lot of explosives and firepower here, which means they're planning something big. One failure won't stop them; it never has in the past. They're not going away.

The two men spent the next ten minutes in silence, but just before the Midtown Tunnel McKenna had to know. "Ray, you're not really this tough, are you?"

Brunette gave the question some thought. "I feel like breaking down and crying, and I probably will when this thing is over. But not until then. I have to stay rational and professional about all this."

"We both have to," McKenna added.

The mayor and Gene Shields were waiting in Brunette's office and sipping on a scotch apiece when Brunette and McKenna arrived.

The mayor looked tired and was having another bad day. But they were all bad, and he was fond of saying his last good day was election day, two years before. He looked older than his fifty-six years because the job had aged him. Under his administration the city had fragmented into vocal special interest groups, so he spent his day meeting and bartering with this group pushing their policy or that group with an ax to grind. He hadn't yet learned that when you try to please everybody, you wind up pleasing nobody.

Gene Shields was another story entirely. He was the director of the New York office of the FBI and had been for some time. He was good at his job and loved it enough to have turned down many higher federal positions just to keep it. Fifty and looking forty, personable, well dressed, trim and fit, he traveled in the society circles and loved the theater, the restaurants, the museums, and all the other things New York had to offer. Originally from Baltimore, he was that rare breed of person who came to visit and found he could live nowhere else. New York wasn't for everyone, but it was for him. Having worked with Shields before, McKenna considered him a stand-up guy.

Brunette introduced McKenna to the mayor, and the mayor seemed genuinely pleased to meet him. "Thanks for being there today and doing what you did," he said as he shook McKenna's hand. "It was bad enough with you, but it would have been horrible without you.''

Before McKenna could thank him for the compliment, the mayor turned to Brunette. ''Stroke of genius, Ray. The press is gonna love him. You know, young, good-looking hero. It's gonna take the pressure off us.''

Turning back to McKenna, he asked, ''You don't mind that, do you?'' but before McKenna could give his answer, if he had one, the mayor sat behind Ray's desk. ''Okay, let's get our stories straight. What are we gonna tell them?'' he asked, looking from Shields to Brunette.

Shields and Brunette exchanged glances and Shields nodded to Brunette to take the floor.

''You're gonna tell them that the brave people of this city will never tolerate this type of uncivilized terrorist attack, unspeakable atrocity, et cetera, and that you've charged me with finding those responsible and bringing them to justice. Then you go straight to me. I'll tell them we believe it's the Shining Path and that they killed my son in order to get me and McKenna and all the brave dignitaries who risked their lives to attend my son's funeral, defying the implied terrorist threat in order to show their support for everything good and decent in our society.''

''I like it,'' the mayor said, nodding and smiling. ''It's got a nice ring.''

''Then I'll say that you and I, after serious consultation, have appointed police hero McKenna, a *Sendero* expert, to—''

''I know about them,'' McKenna interrupted, ''but I'm not an expert.''

''Not important,'' the mayor said. ''You will be by tomorrow. Go ahead, Ray.''

''Next I'll give a brief history of Brian and turn the floor over to him.''

''And what do I tell them?'' McKenna asked.

''Look grim and open the floor for questions,'' Brunette instructed. ''Tell them whatever you can that won't compromise the investigation, which just means leaving out the part about the weapons.''

''We don't know much more than that,'' McKenna protested.

''Then just give them background, but smile at them when they ask you a question. They aren't too tough on heroes. Tell them you'll keep them informed. Then turn the floor over to Gene. He'll tell them that we will have the complete cooper-

ation of the entire United States government with all the resources necessary. They won't be too hard on him either, since
every reporter in town owes him a round of drinks.''

"Just the local guys," Shields said. "We're gonna have
CNN and the national networks here tonight.''

"You'll manage, I'm sure," Brunette said, smiling. "Any
other questions?''

"I have just one," the mayor said seriously, staring at Mc-
Kenna. "What are you gonna tell them about your plans for
the future, because they're sure gonna ask.''

"I'm gonna tell them I'm leaving as soon as the case is
over. I won't answer any of their other personal questions.''

The mayor showed his appreciation of McKenna's response
with a wide smile. "The white knight syndrome," he said.
"Save the city and ride off into the sunset. They'll like that,
too, and so will I. You'll do. Raise your right hand for the
oath of office.''

McKenna looked at Brunette, who smiled and nodded. He
raised his right hand.

"Do you swear that you will help get me reelected by getting these criminals, that you'll follow the Constitution within
reason while doing so, that if you succeed you will never run
against me for anything, and that you'll keep the press off my
back in all matters big and small?''

"I will, to the best of my ability.''

"Good. Welcome to politics, Assistant Commissioner of
Police McKenna. Enjoy your day in the sunshine because it
rains a lot around here.''

The mayor went to the door and held it open. "Gentlemen,
let's go climb into the ring and take our punches.''

Chapter 9
McKenna got a wake-up call at 5:00 A.M. and he rolled out of bed, determined to adhere to his running and exercising program, but he changed his mind as soon as he stood up. Everything hurt and he felt stiffer than he had when he went to bed. He hobbled to the shower and winced under water as hot as he could stand it for twenty minutes. It seemed to work, a little, but he knew it was going to be a tough day, physically at least.

He ordered the papers and three breakfasts: one for himself, one for the detective guarding his door, and one for the detective watching the lobby. He dressed in his blue suit while he waited.

Ten minutes later he answered the knock at the door. The waiter was there with the breakfast cart. Also there was Cisco Sanchez, another friend from the Major Case Squad, with *El Diario* tucked under his arm. He gave McKenna a small salute with a smile.

"*¿Cómo te vas, Cisco?*" McKenna asked.

"*Regular*, Commissioner. *Buenos días.*"

Commissioner? McKenna still hadn't gotten used to the sound of it. "*Tu sabes que me llamo Brian, Cisco. Ven a dentro y comamos juntos.*"

"Sorry, Brian, but I'd rather eat out here on my toes. I've been reading about your pals from Peru and I'm convinced they're serious. But congratulations and thanks for the chow. I love to see something good happen to one of us peons."

"Thanks, but it's only for a while."

"Too bad," Cisco said.

McKenna took a breakfast serving and gave it to Cisco, then the waiter rolled the tray inside and McKenna followed him in.

After breakfast, McKenna read the papers over coffee. The bombing was headlines in all three papers, with the story continuing on pages three, four, and five in the tabloids. It was described as the worst terrorist attack in the United States since the Oklahoma City bombing.

The press conference was reported in detail, complete with pictures, and at first McKenna was surprised that they could spread the little he said over so many pages. But as he read on he realized that he had said quite a lot, most of which consisted of background on the Shining Path. The *Post* even reported that he had conducted his part of the press conference in a confident and relaxed manner.

McKenna smiled at that. Fooled them, he thought.

The *Times* ran a complete transcript of the press conference and also a four-page background article on *Sendero Luminoso* and the efforts made by the Peruvian government to combat the insurrection. Although he had previously read everything he could find on *Sendero* and their war, he still learned a few things from the *Times* article.

It was a no-quarter civil war that had been going on since 1982, with both sides frequently cited for atrocities by Amnesty International. Most of the *Sendero* soldiers and supporters were Andean Indians who had suffered through a history of government oppression. *Sendero* controlled 25 percent of the country, mostly mountainous and rural areas, but their area of control was shrinking because of some recent successful government operations against them. Most of these successes were attributed to a new elite unit of the national police, the *Dirección Nacional Contra el Terrorismo*, nicknamed Dinconte and headed by a Colonel Savraada. He had a reputation for scrupulous honesty and demanded the same from the people he recruited for his unit, the result being that *Sendero* no longer had advance knowledge of government operations and intentions.

Among the successes attributed to Dinconte was an operation orchestrated by Savraada that resulted in the capture of Abimael Guzman, one of the founders of *Sendero* and their *jefe supremo*. Savraada was demoted after the operation, reportedly because Guzman was captured instead of killed, but he was restored to his position by President Fujimori. *Sendero* was also losing a portion of its financial base since, at the urging of Colonel Savraada, the government began spraying the coca crop in areas under *Sendero*'s control. This effort was financed by the United States, and the troops and pilots used were trained by Special Forces troops based in Peru. The result was that *Sendero*, which previously had been totally apolitical regarding events outside Peru, had recently begun vilifying the United States in their literature and propaganda.

McKenna made a mental note after he finished the article. He thought that Colonel Savraada was certainly a person he'd like to talk to, if possible.

After washing up, McKenna took his new Glock and a cleaning kit from the closet, cleaned his new gun, and loaded three magazines with thirteen rounds each. As he loaded a round into the chamber and a magazine into the butt, he marveled that he was still alive while his original Glock had been damaged beyond repair as a result of the explosion that had blown him into the church wall and his pistol against the church door.

As he donned his jacket and hat, he checked himself in the mirror. His new look left something to be desired, but he put on a brave face anyway and opened the door.

Cisco folded up the paper he was reading and handed it to McKenna. "You should read this," he said. "It's got a lot on *Sendero* in it."

"I already read about them in the *Times*," McKenna answered.

"So did I, but *El Diario* has more. It sounds like they have somebody on the inside."

"Thanks, I will," McKenna said, taking the paper and putting it under his arm. They took the elevator down together and Eddie Morgan, another old friend, met them in the lobby. "Good morning, Commissioner," Morgan said.

"Have a heart, Eddie," McKenna said. This commissioner stuff was getting him down already.

"Sorry, Brian, but you did it to yourself," Morgan admonished.

"I know. Stupid, huh?"

Not wanting to give Morgan the opportunity to vent his opinion, McKenna went outside and they followed. Parked in front was a new Mercury limo with four antennas mounted on the trunk. The car made an obvious public statement: riding inside in appropriate luxury is a politician of some importance on his way to spend your tax dollars somewhere, somehow.

McKenna didn't like it, but Johnny Pao didn't seem to mind. He was sitting behind the wheel with the air conditioner on full blast and looking rather content.

McKenna turned to Cisco and Morgan. "You guys aren't coming?"

"Nope," Cisco answered. "We're assigned to guard your room to make sure nobody puts any surprises in there while you're gone."

Jeez! McKenna thought. Aside from the fancy salary and the obvious perks, the public is sure spending a lot of money in police salaries on this particular commissioner. I hope I can give them their money's worth.

McKenna reached into his pocket and gave Cisco his room key. "Do me a favor and guard it from the inside. The Mets are playing the Dodgers today."

McKenna opened the passenger door, but Cisco and Morgan waited while Pao got his digs in.

"Sir, the commissioners usually sit in the back," Pao said with a straight face.

"Oh yeah? And where does your partner usually sit?"

"In the front, of course. Hop in, partner."

Ten minutes later Pao had the city's newest dignitary at police headquarters, One Police Plaza, commonly known as the Puzzle Palace and rumored to be harboring 5,000 cops and bosses who had taken refuge behind their desks as noncombatants in the war on crime while they dreamed up new orders and procedures to be memorized and followed, thus ensuring that the cops remaining in the trenches could linger on in misery, always unhappily aware of the building's existence.

McKenna got the shudders every time he saw the building, and nothing had changed. He made another mental note: Make sure I don't become one of them, no matter how comfortable they make me, because whatever the occupants of this building have, it must be highly contagious. How else could there be so many of them, men and women who came on the Job to be cops and are transformed by the disease into high-paid secretaries?

McKenna attempted to bring his attitude under control, admitting to himself that some police work was done in the building. The Communications Division was there, handling the millions of 911 calls and dispatching the cops to handle them. The Identification Section was there, classifying the fingerprints of the thousands of persons arrested daily. Many specialized citywide detective squads like the Missing Persons Squad and the Major Case Squad also had offices in the building.

McKenna felt a little better about the place as Pao drove down and parked in a spot marked v.i.p.

"Good luck," Pao said as McKenna got out of the car.

"Thanks. Where are you gonna be?"

"Wherever you want me." Pao wrote a telephone number on a slip of paper and handed it to McKenna. "That's the phone number for the car."

McKenna walked to the small elevator door near the entrance to the garage. Standing next to the elevator was an old cop whose only mission was to ensure that only the commissioner, the deputy and assistant commissioners, and the chiefs gained entry to the small private elevator that went directly to the fourteenth floor.

"Good morning, Commissioner," the cop said, pushing the elevator call button.

"Good morning," McKenna answered, wondering why he had never liked this cop before. He didn't seem like such a bad guy.

The elevator doors opened. Fifteen seconds later McKenna stepped off into the inner sanctum. He looked on the directory to locate his office number, but his mind went blank. There were quite a few assistant commissioners listed by full title, but for some reason he couldn't remember the title he and Brunette had invented. But he knew it when he saw it. The Assistant Commissioner for Special Projects' office was in Room 1414. He made a right off the elevator and found Chief Jerimiah O'Shaughnessy leaving room 1414 carrying a large cardboard box.

O'Shaughnessy looked a little flushed when he saw McKenna. "Good morning, Brian," he said, somewhat embarrassed, then added, "I really don't know what to call you now. Is Brian okay?"

McKenna remembered back to some of the many hard times O'Shaughnessy had given him over the years and thought, Your Excellency would be better, you slimeball. But instead he answered, "Brian's fine. Jerry, isn't it?"

"Right. All my friends call me Jerry."

You don't have any friends, McKenna thought, and everybody else calls you Dog Dick. I'll probably be the only person in the world to call you Jerry, with the possible exception of Mrs. Dog Dick if such an unlucky person exists.

"Whatcha doing in there?" McKenna asked, pointing to the door of his new office.

O'Shaughnessy's face turned even redder, and McKenna couldn't tell if it was from anger or embarrassment. "This was my office," O'Shaughnessy said. "The commissioner called me last night and told me you needed it. He told me to get in here early today and clear my things out."

McKenna tried suppressing his smile, but he wasn't sure if he was pulling it off as O'Shaughnessy looked at him. A few tense seconds passed before he knew he had when O'Shaughnessy said, "I'm sorry, I'm just finishing up now. I didn't expect you in so early."

"What exactly was it you used to do in that office?"

"I'm a deputy chief in the Inspections Division," O'Shaughnessy answered proudly. "My area of responsibility is uniform inspections and appearance. You've been away, so I don't know if you've noticed that now the cops—"

McKenna cut him off. "I have noticed and figured that somebody competent was in charge of that. These cops are spic-'n'-span and shine so much that now you need to wear sunglasses just to talk to them. Good job, Jerry," McKenna said as he tried to calculate how much misery the nitpicking O'Shaughnessy caused the uniformed cops on patrol. McKenna was sure he couldn't begin to imagine.

But O'Shaughnessy preened. "Thank you, Brian. Do you think you could mention that to the commissioner?"

"First thing, next time I see him. He'll be happy to hear it." Actually, Ray had spent most of his time in the Detective Bureau and personally wouldn't care if the cops rode around in bathing suits, McKenna thought. But Ray was right about one thing. It helps to have a prick like O'Shaughnessy around.

As O'Shaughnessy carried his belongings to the elevator McKenna opened the door of his new office. He was surprised at the size, with a well-furnished reception area fronting his office. His door was open and he could see that it was grand, with a large desk, a PC, a library of books, a conference table, and a sofa.

Behind the receptionist's desk was a prim-and-proper gray-haired woman who reminded McKenna of Mrs. Rodriguez, his first-grade teacher forty years ago at St. Columba's Grammar School. He figured that Mrs. Rodriguez must now look like this woman, if she were still alive.

The woman sprang up as soon as he entered the room. "Good morning, Commissioner. I've been assigned as your secretary and I didn't wind up on the fourteenth floor by accident. If you need anything, just tell me and it'll get done. Don't make any lists, just tell me. My hours are whatever hours you work, and I'm available anytime. I'm always early and I don't get sick. My name is Camilia Wright, but you may call me Camilia.''

She offered her hand and McKenna, momentarily speechless, shook it. Then he found his voice. "Thank you, Camilia. It's a pleasure to meet you. You can call me Brian.''

She was shocked. "Brian? I could never do that, Commissioner.''

"You'll have to. I'm new to this commissioner business and Brian is the only name I answer to, except for a few others that a lady like yourself wouldn't know.''

It took her a moment, but finally she appeared to accept it. "All right, Brian, what do you want me to do?''

"Get me all the files on the Dennis Brunette shooting and on the church bombing.''

"Inspector Tavlin brought them over this morning. They're on your desk.''

"Good," McKenna said, trying to convey: Of course. Where else would they be?

"By the way," she added. "I put some direct lines on your phone. If you want to reach the commissioner, dial 'star' one. Inspector Tavlin is 'star' two, Inspector Sheeran is 'star' three, and Mr. Shields is 'star' four. Your calls will forward to their mobile phones if they don't pick up by the fifth ring. If you need me, press 'star' six. If I'm not here, the call will forward to wherever I am, day or night. Your mobile phone is in your top desk drawer.''

Of course. My mobile phone? Where else would it be? McKenna thought. "What time is the commissioner coming in today?''

"He isn't, and nobody's supposed to know where he is.''

McKenna waited for a moment while Wright watched him. "Well?''

"He's at St. Charles Cemetery burying what's left of his son. He wanted it to be very private.''

"I see. Thank you.''

McKenna went into his office and closed the door behind him. He spent five minutes sitting at his desk as he once again tried to imagine Brunette's grief and pain while he stared at the two large stacks of reports on his desk. But all he felt was anger, his own and Brunette's, and it was entirely directed at

Sendero Luminoso. This was doing him no good, so he got up and inspected his office.

An American flag and a New York City flag hanging on six-foot flagpoles stood on either side of his desk. A large coffee machine brewing two pots of coffee, decaf and regular, was set up on top of a small refrigerator. The refrigerator contained milk, cream, sugar, and a bottle of Gorilla anisette. Above the coffee machine hung a rack of coffee cups, one of which had COMMISSIONER MCKENNA inscribed on the front. The bookcase contained two shelves of books of police rules and procedures that McKenna had never read and hoped he never would, a complete set of *McKinney's Law Review*, and a set of the *Encyclopedia Americana*. On one wall hung a six-foot-square detailed map of the city and on another wall hung a set of individual portraits of all the chiefs and commissioners. His own wasn't there yet, but he was sure it would be as soon as Camilia Wright could get her hands on a camera.

So McKenna wasn't surprised at the knock on his door. Wright breezed in, camera in hand, and positioned him in front of the New York City flag. She wouldn't let him wear his hat, so her stock climbed in his estimation.

As soon as she left, McKenna sat down and started on the files. Everything done by each detective assigned to the case was listed on a separate "Complaint Follow-up" form, called a DD-5. He went through the Dennis Brunette shooting first.

There were diagrams and photos of the crime scene on East 45th Street and pictures of the bodies of Dennis and Ingrid Troutmann. It wasn't pretty, and McKenna could see the reason for the closed-casket wake for Dennis.

For all the work that had been done on the case, he didn't learn much that he didn't already know. Seven hundred and sixteen residents of the block had been interviewed and eleven of those were classified as witnesses. None had seen the initial confrontation between Troutmann and the purse-snatcher, but eight of them had seen Dennis confront the purse-snatcher, and all eleven had been witnesses to the two murders.

He made himself a cup of coffee and read on. The Federal Protective Service agent at the U.S. Mission to the UN stated in his interview that he had seen Dennis talking ten minutes before the murders to a man who matched the description of the person Dennis had shot in the assassin's car. That also made sense to McKenna.

Ingrid Troutmann was another story. Every hotel clerk in

the city had been shown her touched-up picture, but no one recognized her. Where she had been staying before she was killed was still a mystery.

The reward offer had produced some results. Fourteen people had been interviewed who said they saw one man leave the assassin's car on the New Jersey Turnpike and get into a van that had been behind the car. All described it as a dark van, and although none could give a make, a description of the driver of the getaway car emerged and it matched the description of the man who had killed Ingrid Troutmann on East 45th Street.

The file on the church bombing enlightened McKenna a bit. The crime-scene pictures showed the condition of the hearse after the bomb went off, and it wasn't as bad as he had imagined. The chassis and the front of the hearse were intact, but from the front seat to the rear of the hearse there was nothing but scrap. In other photos he found pieces of the hearse, the casket, Dennis, and what he presumed was Suzy the bomb dog. They were spread over a one-block area. The church was still structurally sound, although all the stained-glass windows in the front had been blown out.

He found no sign of himself in any of the photos and presumed he had been removed to the hospital before they were taken. But there were photos of Inspector Keller and the three dead cops. Two of the cops were mangled and one of them had lost both legs. Incredibly, the third dead cop looked like he was just taking a nap. Keller was unrecognizable in the crime-scene picture of his body.

McKenna went to the Keller autopsy report. He had been killed instantly when a piece of the hearse rear door and another piece of shrapnel from the cover of the casket hit his chest area. Altogether, he suffered twelve fatal wounds, including one inflicted by the jawbone of Dennis Brunette, which lodged in his left lung.

McKenna had to stop for a moment when he realized that he was reading what should have been his own autopsy report if Keller had not taken the initiative of standing in front of him, fully aware that a bomb was set to go off in the hearse in front of them. He had worked with Keller before and had always considered him one of the toughest men alive. In the end, Keller had proved him right, and McKenna resolved that the Keller family would always know who Brian McKenna was and the debt he owed them.

McKenna remembered reading that Keller left a wife and three children, ages fourteen to twenty-two. He took a credit card from his wallet and dialed "star" six. He heard the phone ring once outside and Wright was instantly at his door. McKenna gave her his credit card.

"Find out where Inspector Keller is being laid out and send the biggest wreath we can buy, inscribed *With Gratitude*," he told her. "Okay?"

"Yes, sir," and she was gone, closing the door behind her.

McKenna went on, his mounting depression somewhat relieved, but not for long. Forty-three pounds of human remains presumed to be Dennis Brunette had been found and cataloged.

McKenna thought he'd had enough, but there was more, and it was finally something he didn't mind reading. The crime-scene photos showed how potentially dangerous urban tree climbing could really be. Even from the photo, McKenna could see that the bomber's neck was broken. He was lying on the ground with his head at a thirty-degree angle to the rest of his body, eyes open and staring at the gates of hell. The three bullet wounds were clearly visible and McKenna went to his autopsy report.

The report stated that the subject was a male Hispanic in his thirties who had suffered three recent bullet wounds, none of which were fatal. Cause of death was suffocation induced when his neck was broken, causing his fourth vertebra to puncture his windpipe. The subject also showed evidence of an old bullet wound, which had been inflicted approximately four years before. A bullet, probably a high-velocity military round, had pierced his right calf, broken his tibia, and exited the front of his leg. He had been fingerprinted and remained unidentified, with no military or criminal record in the United States.

McKenna leaned back in his chair and sought a conclusion from the volumes of reports he had just read, and the answer disturbed him. After spending thousands of man-hours and using all the available resources of the largest police department in the country, they had nothing. Even the $300,000 reward hadn't shaken much loose. Arrests were not imminent, and he wasn't sure if arrests were even likely. They needed a break of some kind.

He remembered the *El Diario* Cisco had given him. He spread the paper on his desk, took his small Spanish dictionary from his pocket, and started reading.

Cisco was right. *El Diario* did have someone on the inside of *Sendero*. Aside from the information contained in the New York papers, there was a four-page article by a man named Maximo de la Vega, who was listed as a contributing editor. De la Vega had been in Peru in May and June and spent six weeks living in the field with a number of *Sendero* units. He described the abject living conditions in the countryside, the *Sendero* goals and philosophy, and had even participated as an observer in a number of *Sendero* operations against government troops and installations.

In one operation *Sendero* initiated a diversionary attack on a small government outpost and then ambushed the landing zone when government reinforcements arrived by helicopter. Two government helicopters were destroyed and sixteen government soldiers were killed. One *Sendero* soldier was killed and one was severely wounded. The wounded man was killed by the *Sendero* leader to keep him from falling into government hands.

In a second operation de la Vega traveled by bus with four *Sendero* soldiers to Lima. They were met there by a *Sendero* agent who supplied them with explosives and that night they blew up two electric pylon towers. They spent the next three days living with sympathizers in a Lima shantytown and then returned to the *Sendero* stronghold in Ayacucho by car.

The reporter described the third operation as a disaster for *Sendero*. Government troops had surrounded a village east of the city of Huancayo in a *Sendero*-controlled area, and had taken all the male adults to Lima for questioning. The *Sendero* leader, following their standard practice, sent forty men to the village to also take hostages to ensure that the recent government prisoners would remain loyal to *Sendero* during questioning. As they approached the village, the *Sendero* force was ambushed by national police agents who had lined the trail with Claymore mines. After detonating the mines by remote control, the national police raked them with small-arms fire. Twenty-nine *Sendero* soldiers failed to return, and de la Vega was also wounded in his chest and arm by shrapnel. He was evacuated to a *Sendero* hospital in the city of Pucallpa, where he spent nine days recovering from his wounds. He eventually left Peru by flying from Pucallpa to Bolivia in a private plane operated by Colombians.

As McKenna finished the article, Wright knocked, came in,

and gave him his credit card back. "Flowers on the way to the funeral home. Five hundred dollars even," she said.

"That's good news, I guess. Now call the Peruvian mission to the United Nations and see if you can get me an appointment with their ambassador."

Wright left and McKenna read the article again to get a handle on the reporter, this time using his Spanish dictionary to ensure that he was getting the correct meaning of some unfamiliar Spanish words. It took him half an hour.

Considering that the writer had been living with *Sendero*, he found the article to be fairly objective, criticizing both the government and *Sendero* in a tongue-in-cheek fashion. McKenna concluded that the article was slightly slanted in *Sendero*'s favor, but considered it to be quite a piece of professional journalism on the part of Maximo de la Vega. But it was the timing of his visit to Peru that interested McKenna most. He had been with *Sendero* in May and June while Ingrid Troutmann, another journalist, had been there from March to June.

Had their paths crossed? McKenna wondered. He took the touched-up photo of Troutmann from the pile of reports and stared at it. Her eyes were closed, there was no sign of the bullet hole in her forehead, and her mouth was slightly open, like she was just about to say something.

Not a bad-looking girl, McKenna thought. I bet you'd have something to say to me now, knowing what your pals had in store for you.

As McKenna put the photo in his pocket, Wright came in again. "I called the Peruvian mission and they told me that their ambassador had been called back to Lima last night for consultation. I asked them to forward your request and he's on the line now. Should I put him through?"

"Yes, please. What's his name?"

"*Señor* Cudero, but they referred to him at the embassy as Mr. Ambassador."

"Thank you."

Wright left and the phone rang once before McKenna picked it up. "Hello, Mr. Ambassador?"

"Yes, Commissioner. I heard you wanted to speak with me. But before we begin, on behalf of my government I want to offer you our sincerest condolences and apologies for the misfortunes you have suffered at the hands of some of my misguided countrymen."

The connection was fuzzy with a bit of an echo, but McKenna could make it out.

"Thank you, Mr. Ambassador. I appreciate your concerns and I need a little help from you, if you can give it."

"Of course. This must be my day to help American policemen. Let me guess. You would like to talk to Colonel Savraada, is that correct?"

"That's right," McKenna answered, a little surprised. "How did you know?"

"Because I had the same request from Mr. Shields of your FBI an hour ago." McKenna felt a little knot in his stomach as the ambassador continued. "As I told Mr. Shields, I have been instructed by my government to offer you any and all assistance we can provide. But I'm a little embarrassed to say that we can't seem to locate Colonel Savraada at the moment."

"Is that unusual?"

"Uncommon but not unusual, if you can understand our situation here. You see, for security reasons, very few people know where Colonel Savraada is at a given time or what he is doing. He reports directly to the president. However, I have already forwarded Mr. Shields's request to Mr. Fujimori and I will do the same with yours. I am sure you will hear from Colonel Savraada as soon as he becomes available, but I can't tell you exactly when that will be."

"I see. Might I ask when you will be returning to New York, Mr. Ambassador?"

"Certainly. Within the next couple of days. Commissioner, while I have you on the line, I'd like to make an informal request that your department provide our UN embassy and our consulate in New York with some extra security for the next couple of days, at least."

Good idea, McKenna thought. "Of course. I'll see that it's done."

"Thank you. Can you think of anything else I can help you with right now?"

"Not at the moment," McKenna answered.

"Good. I look forward to meeting you as soon as I get back. If you need anything else before then, you can contact me through our embassy."

"Thank you, Mr. Ambassador."

"Good luck, Commissioner," the ambassador said and then hung up.

McKenna replaced the phone and stared at it. I have to be sharper and quicker, he thought. I'm playing in the major leagues now and the FBI beat me to first base. But it's a long way to home plate and I don't care if we get there together, as long as we get there. Good thing is, if a sharpie like Gene Shields is thinking about Colonel Savraada, then I must be on the right track, but just a little slow. I have to talk to my federal pal real soon.

As if thinking of something could make it happen, the phone rang. It was Gene Shields, and he wanted to meet McKenna for lunch at Forlini's. He had some developments in the case he wanted to run by McKenna.

"I'll be there," McKenna said. "What time?"

"One o'clock okay with you?"

"Fine. See ya."

McKenna hung up the phone and happened to glance at the clock on the wall. He was shocked to see that it was twenty to one. He had been in his office since 7:00 A.M., but felt like he had been there for only an hour or two. He called Wright and told her to get in touch with the chief responsible for security at the embassies and tell him to provide extra security, both visible and covert, to the Peruvian embassy and consulate. As an afterthought, he said he wanted a report detailing what extra measures would be taken, figuring he might as well let the chiefs know there was a new boy in town.

Wright assured him that, naturally, it would be done.

He took his mobile phone from his desk drawer and considered calling Pao, but Forlini's was on Baxter Street in Little Italy, just four short blocks away. He put the phone in his pocket.

It's a nice day and why bother Johnny? McKenna thought. I'll walk, he decided as he put on his hat and left his office.

Chapter 10 It was hot and uncomfortable, in the nineties with high humidity, when McKenna left police headquarters. Still, McKenna thought he would enjoy his stroll through Chinatown. He was wrong. He had become a police celebrity, too famous to walk anywhere around headquarters in a hurry.

The area was loaded with cops returning from their lunch breaks taken in the many fine restaurants of Chinatown or Little Italy. The two small neighborhoods were adjacent to one another with Canal Street the official dividing line, but in places the border was indistinct, with Italian and Chinese restaurants operating side by side. Eating was the primary industry in both neighborhoods, with ten or more restaurants on each block.

Most of the cops returning to their assignments worked in headquarters, but quite a few of the detectives were downtown for court appearances in Criminal Court or Supreme Court, both located within a few blocks of headquarters. Whatever they were doing there, it seemed they all knew McKenna, and although he was sure he had worked with many of them in some capacity at one time or another during his twenty-three-year career, he only recognized some of their faces and couldn't remember most of their names. It took him ten minutes to walk the first two blocks, stopping to receive the cops' congratulations while being placed in the embarrassing situation of talking with people who seemed to know everything about him and whose names he couldn't remember. It was like a two-block receiving line, with McKenna managing to disengage himself from one conversation only to turn to the next cop or detective waiting to say hello. By the time he reached the corner at Elizabeth and Bayard Streets, he was fresh out of glib conversation. He put his head down and walked quickly, looking neither right nor left and avoiding eye contact with anyone. He brushed past people who had stopped to greet him, pretending not to see them. In short, he behaved like a typical New Yorker, like a victim passing through a gaggle of muggers, quickly walking the gauntlet and hoping to make it to his destination unmolested.

He turned right at Baxter Street and continued his routine, passing Forlini's before he realized it. He looked up and sheepishly took stock of his surroundings. A few people had stopped to stare at him, and they waved when he looked in their direction. He waved back, turned around, and walked back to the restaurant.

Given their choice, most cops on their lunch breaks eat in the Chinese restaurants because of their cheap prices, healthy servings, and varied menus. But for some reason, when a cop makes detective or boss, he seems to lose his taste for Chinese food and winds up eating in the Italian restaurants, where the food is still great but certainly more expensive. It isn't the food or the prices that prompts this change in culinary preference, though. It's the ambience. Wearing his suit and tie and feeling good about his small successes in life, the detective just feels better in the Italian restaurants, and finds himself happily surrounded by others of similar station and attitude. Usually, whatever extra money the new detective gains by his promotion isn't wasted on the wife and kiddies precisely because of this change in diet, but that can't be helped. It's expected of detectives and goes with the territory. Those who continue to eat in the Chinese restaurants are regarded by their contemporaries as lacking in stature and unsuited for the position.

This phenomenon affected everyone. Although he liked the food, McKenna hadn't eaten in a Chinese restaurant near headquarters in twenty years. But he had eaten many times in Forlini's, and the owner, Victor, greeted him like a son and guided him through the restaurant crowded with well-wishing detectives to the table in the rear where Gene Shields was sitting, sipping on a martini. Victor summoned a waiter and returned to his post at the door.

As soon as the waiter left, McKenna got right down to business. "Making any progress on the Georgia connection?"

"Alejandro de Leon is his name. He was a Contra spokesman in the U.S. in the eighties."

"Anybody talk to him yet?" McKenna asked.

"Like to try, but we haven't found him yet. Our Atlanta office is handling it. They say he owns a trucking and shipping business operating out of Macon, Georgia. None of his employees have heard from him since Monday and he didn't tell any of them he was leaving. Some of them think he might be dead."

"What do you think?"

"He might be, but I think he cut out. There was quite a commotion down there last year. He was ambushed leaving his house by some folks with automatic weapons. Alejandro was hurt bad and his two bodyguards were killed."

"Who did it?"

"Nobody was ever caught, but Alejandro says it was the Sandinistas. Nothing was ever found to link anybody from Nicaragua to it and the case is still open."

"Why the Sandinistas?"

"He thinks they're mad at him. He comes from a big-shot shipping family in Nicaragua. When the revolution started they were smart enough to see that Somoza wasn't going to last, so they supported the Sandinistas. After the Sandinistas won, the family did pretty good for themselves in Nicaragua, got all the government shipping contracts. Then the Contra thing started and young Alejandro joined the Sandinista Army and turned out to be a natural military man. They eventually made him a colonel and his unit kicked the stuffings out of the Contras every time they tried something. He had a bright future with the Sandinistas, but he figured out one thing."

"That the Sandinistas were going to lose?"

"Yep. His family was the first to see the handwriting on the wall. Being in shipping, the U.S. trade embargo devastated their business, and they came to the conclusion that there was only room for one Cuba in their part of the world. They knew the Sandinistas weren't going to last, not with the Reagan Administration so pissed off at them, and they figured that Reagan was gonna be around for a while."

"So Alejandro switched sides," McKenna said.

"Yeah. He didn't mind the Sandinista politics, but he was used to being rich and his prospects for continued luxury didn't look good. His switch was a big boost for the Contras and maybe the Sandinistas never forgave him. We know now he was a front man in the Contras' weapons-acquisition schemes."

"What happened to his family?"

"Living in luxury in Miami."

"Now you gonna tell me how you know all this?" Mc-Kenna asked.

"It's a long story."

"Okay, save it for later. Let's stick with trying to find Alejandro. Did he get more bodyguards after the attack?"

"He got everything. Made his house into a fortress. More bodyguards, dogs, lights, alarms, and a big wall all around. He was worried and hardly ever left the place. Didn't even go to work. Ran his business with a phone, a fax, and a computer, but it wasn't working for him. According to his employees, the business was going downhill."

"Anybody at the house?"

"Just the maid. She came in on Monday morning and found the place empty and the dogs starving. She called one of the bodyguards at home and he told her that Alejandro had given them both a month off, with pay."

"He ever do that before?"

"Yeah, a couple of times, but never for a month. They took him to the airport on the fourth of this month and he was gone for two days, but he didn't tell them where he was going."

"Did you find out?"

"The Atlanta office checked with Customs and Immigration. He came back to the U.S. through Miami on the fifth on a flight from Costa Rica."

Costa Rica? How does that figure in? McKenna asked himself. "Does he have any business there?"

"His employees say they've never shipped anything to Costa Rica."

"How about his house?"

"The Atlanta guys had no warrant, but the local police went through it for them using the missing-person thing. It was real nice, but nothing unusual. The maid thinks some of his clothes and three of his suitcases are gone."

"Is there anything to connect Alejandro to *Sendero*?"

"Nothing we can find."

"Did you do a financial work-up on him?"

Shields shrugged his shoulders, looking disappointed. "We'd like to, but we won't be able to get subpoenas with what we've got. It's not enough."

McKenna didn't know what to say. Here we've got five dead cops and Lord knows what else and the FBI is worrying about subpoenas. What can I say to that? he wondered silently. Doesn't our very efficient FBI understand that any information on just about anybody can be bought by the right person with enough money? Shields must know somebody who can get into Alejandro's finances without a subpoena to find out whom he's been dealing with, so what's the problem?

Their food came and McKenna dug right in, but Shields ignored his food and just stared at McKenna, smiling.

Then it came to McKenna. Of course he knows somebody to do it. He knows me.

"I'll handle it," McKenna said in between mouthfuls.

Shields smiled as he picked up his knife and fork. "I'll go half with you, whatever it costs."

"It's gonna be expensive."

"That's all right. It's better this way, just between us. I could run a scam and have some of my agents do it, but that might blow up in our faces. Then there'd be a scandal and some good people and me would lose it all. I'd do it if I had to, but why take a chance?"

"I understand," McKenna said. "I've got the guy for the job. He's a retired detective who runs a PI business that specializes in skip-tracing. He knows all the ins and outs and all the tricks. He'll do it for me."

"Bob Hurley?"

"How did you know that?" McKenna asked, surprised.

"Because I hear he's the best and he wouldn't do it for me. I called him and hinted around, but he made like he couldn't hear me. He's got a low trust level."

No wonder, McKenna thought. The feds have been spending a lot of time lately busting private investigators who step over the line. They even set up a few sting operations to get them, pretending they were clients with big money who needed financial information and records not ordinarily available. McKenna knew that since then the whole PI industry had been on its toes and had become very cautious about whom they dealt with.

Shields took a folded piece of paper from his pocket and McKenna opened it. Written on it was de Leon's name, address, Social Security number, and date of birth.

"Will he need more than that?" Shields asked.

"He never has before."

The two men ate their meal in silence, but McKenna's estimation of Shields had gone up once again. Stand-up guy, and smart too, he thought. After all, it's only money.

They finished eating and the waiter brought them two coffees. A few tables away McKenna noticed a woman eating alone, her back to them, head cast down, and he suddenly felt a pang for Angelita. They sipped in silence for a few moments before McKenna asked, "Ready to give me the rest of the story?"

"About how we found out it was Alejandro?"

"Yeah, and why you can't get enough legally for the subpoenas we need."

"Since the bombing, this case has gone national and there's a lot of pressure to solve it quickly before something else blows up. I talked to the director and he convinced the attorney general that Nesbitt, the CIA guy, and the marine general are just pawns in this game. We're not interested in prosecuting some people who thought they were doing their jobs, right?"

"It's been done before to keep the cameras rolling, but what we need to know right now is, How much stuff is really missing and what's *Sendero* doing with some of it in New York?"

"Exactly what I told the director. So the Justice Department cut the bullshit to get the ball rolling. They offered them a deal."

"Immunity?"

"Better than that," Shields said. "Immunity if they told what they know plus protection from prosecution for whatever else comes up from this deal."

"And?"

"A guy named James Montgomery arranged the whole thing. He used to be with the CIA, then he got a political appointment for a job with the National Security Agency. Later on, he was a fringe character in the Iran-Contra investigation, but he never got grabbed for anything. Denied under oath having anything to do with illegal government-arms transfers to the Contras. The general's and Nesbitt's statements put him up for perjury, for starters."

"But that's still long and involved and I don't care about it," McKenna said.

"Yeah, I know. He's retired now, living in the Bahamas. The Democrats are in and all this happened when the Republicans were running the show, so the attorney general wanted two things from Montgomery."

"Find out who got the stuff and who gave him his orders," McKenna offered.

"Yeah, but he wouldn't go for it. The Justice people visited him in the Bahamas and offered him immunity from prosecution for what they wanted. Unfortunately for them, it turns out he's a loyal tough guy with terminal cancer. Makes G. Gordon Liddy look like a blabbermouth. He told them to get lost, said he'd hang out in the Bahamas, fight extradition, and maybe even win. If not, he said he'd die in jail. He's not gonna give up his bosses.''

"They're not used to guys like that,'' McKenna said, "and I think maybe I'd like him myself, except for one thing. He screwed it up and put us in this mess.''

"The Justice people don't think like you, or maybe even me, but he put them in a bind. They don't like him at all, but there's a lot of pressure on them.''

"I hope they said, 'Just tell us who the Contra contact was and we'll forget everything else.' ''

"He got it in writing. Everything was delivered to a warehouse in Macon, Georgia, owned by Alejandro de Leon.''

"So what's the problem getting subpoenas?''

"Many. First of all, Montgomery wouldn't make a written statement, wouldn't let the interview be taped, wouldn't sign anything, and said he'd deny saying a word if anybody ever asked him about it again. The only reason Montgomery told them anything at all was because the Justice people told him how some of the stuff was being used in New York.''

"So he has a conscience?''

"Not at first. Said he hated New York and never met a New Yorker he liked. Said he'd like to blow it up himself, but the thing that worked with him was that he doesn't like anybody killing cops, even New York cops.''

"I see,'' McKenna said. "No statement, no subpoena.''

"We could waste some time and write one, but we can't find Alejandro to serve it. Besides, I'm sure he has a lawyer on retainer who'd fight it, and no judge would sign it without some evidence on our part that Alejandro's involved in something illegal. The Justice Department has nothing to show a judge except hearsay, so it would be a big waste of time.''

"And time might be something we don't have a lot of. Did anybody look at the warehouse in Macon?''

"That's another problem. Montgomery didn't remember exactly where it was, except that it was near the railroad tracks in Macon. Alejandro's employees don't know anything about a warehouse near the tracks, and there's hundreds of warehouses there. I could have the Atlanta office run it down, one by one, but I think Hurley will get it done quicker.''

"I hope so, but if you can't get a subpoena, you sure won't

be able to get a search warrant.''

"I know," Shields said as he finished his coffee. "I'll go down and handle it myself."

McKenna sipped his coffee, realizing that the director of the New York office of the FBI had just told him that he was going to travel across seven states to do something that might amount to a burglary in the eyes of an overzealous prosecutor. Shields was rapidly becoming one of McKenna's heroes.

McKenna's thoughts were interrupted by the phone ringing in his pocket. It was Camilia Wright and she was frantic. "A Detective Pao came up and I think he may be insane. I don't know what to do."

"Why? What did he do?"

"He said some dreadful things about you."

"Where is he now?"

"He's in your office. I told him he couldn't go in there, but I can't repeat what he said to me then."

"What did he say about me?" McKenna asked.

"For one thing, he said you're the dumbest bastard he's ever worked with."

"That's a lie."

Wright didn't get it. "No, it's not," she answered indignantly. "That's exactly what he said, I swear."

"I know it's what he said," McKenna explained, patiently, "but he's worked with dumber people than me. See if you can calm him down, and then ask him to pick me up at Forlini's."

Wright was beside herself. "Calm him down after the things he said?" she asked, her voice rising. "He's just a detective."

"So am I, Camilia. Please just do it," McKenna said, then hung up. I'm in for it, he thought, and Johnny's right. I'm just gonna have to take it like a man.

Shields was looking at him with eyebrows raised. "A little personnel problem?" he asked.

"Kind of. I did something stupid and I think my partner's gonna kick the shit outta me in a couple of minutes."

"Too bad," Shields said, not looking sympathetic. "You ever hear of a Colonel Robert Savraada?"

McKenna was relieved to hear the question. He didn't think that Shields was going to hold out on him, but was ashamed to admit the thought was scurrying around someplace in the back of his mind.

"The head of Dinconte," McKenna answered. "I heard you were trying to get in touch with him."

Shields looked surprised, which made McKenna feel good. Got to keep him on his toes, he thought. But Shields recovered quickly. "It makes no difference which one of us talks to him, but I'm sure he can help and I think he'd rather talk to you."

It was McKenna's turn to be surprised. "Why?"

"Because you're not with the federal government. Not many people know it, but Savraada grew up here and his family's still here. His father owns a drugstore in Queens. If *Sendero* knew that, your department would be guarding them all the time or his family would be history."

"Do you mean to tell me that the head of Dinconte is working for us?"

"Not at all. He's been approached by the State Department and the CIA, but it seems Savraada is not a man of divided loyalties. When he was here, he was an American, but when he went back he became a Peruvian and nothing else."

McKenna couldn't imagine leaving New York, Queens even, to go live in the Third World and take a job where his life had to be in danger. "Why'd he go back?"

"Because he's a strange guy. Real smart, but strange. He was in pharmacology school here during the Vietnam War. One day right before he graduated he just quit and enlisted in the army. They trained him as a medic and offered him a commission, but he said he'd rather stay an enlisted man and then he volunteered for Vietnam. They put him in some community action programs, you know, treating the civilians and the refugees over there, but then he got into some trouble."

"He found out the war was bullshit?"

Shields was surprised again. "Yeah, that's what he thought. How'd you know?"

"Because you said he was smart. I spent two years of my life over there and I didn't find out the whole thing was bullshit until I was back a couple of years. Means he's smarter and faster than me."

"I won't get into the politics," Shields said, "but let's just say that Savraada had some ideas that the army thought were pretty strange at the time. He developed an antiwar attitude, but then he surprised them and extended his tour for another six months. He had this clinic and he treated anyone who walked in, no questions asked. Turned out that some of his patients were wounded Viet Cong soldiers and he didn't say anything to anybody. He felt that everybody was just soldiers, theirs and ours, all involved in something stupid."

"Maybe he saw the big picture when the rest of us were standing too close to know what we were looking at," McKenna said thoughtfully. "What did the army do with him?"

"Nothing. The antiwar thing was raging here then and they didn't want to create another martyr. So they just sent him home and gave him an honorable discharge. He finished school and went to work in his father's drugstore. Got married in eighty and divorced in eighty-three. Then he went back to Peru and joined their army."

"What? Over a divorce? Why not the Foreign Legion?"

"We don't know. Something happened and his family doesn't talk about it. They stay entirely out of the politics. But we do know that they're originally from Huancayo, and *Sendero* started operating around there in nineteen-eighty-one, right before he left."

"Are they American citizens now?"

"Sure, and so was he. But he sent back his passport and renounced his citizenship."

"How did he get to be the head of Dinconte?"

"Just smart and hardworking, I guess. His U.S. Army psychological tests indicated that he had the kind of mind that's especially suited for intelligence work. I could get someone to tell you about it, but in essence he's got an unusual way of looking at things and adapts well to changing situations. The Peruvians were smart enough to see it, too, and he just worked his way up. They made him a captain in their national police and now he's in charge of Dinconte, which is their intelligence arm."

"They must know he lived in America?" McKenna asked.

"Of course, but they were sharp enough to keep it a secret and give him a new name. His real name is Bernard Velasquez. That's why I think he'd prefer to talk to you. He can't appear to be a running-dog lackey of the American imperialist government and a paid informant for the warmongering CIA, which is exactly what *Sendero* would say if they knew. It would destroy him."

"I see. I just hope we hear from him."

The check came and McKenna picked it up, but Shields wouldn't hear of it. "You get the next one and I'll really make a pig out of myself," he said.

"Good, but I need one more thing. You ever hear of a journalist named Maximo de la Vega?"

"No. Why?"

McKenna loved that answer and felt better about himself than he had in a long time. "He wrote an article in today's *El Diario*. Pick it up and have somebody translate it for you. It's interesting reading and I want to go see the man."

"I will. Anything else you want me to do?"

"Get me everything you can on him, and I need it soon. I wanna go see him as soon as I hear from you."

"It should be easy. There can't be too many de la Vegas. Soon as I get it, I'll give you a call."

The waiter returned and Shields paid the bill. McKenna left the tip, and the two men got up and headed for the door.

Pao was standing next to the Mercury parked outside, looking big, mean, and unhappy. Shields took one look at him and said to McKenna, "Good luck," as he hurried up Baxter Street, leaving McKenna to his fate.

Chapter 11 McKenna climbed into the passenger seat under Pao's glare and sat by himself for a few moments before Pao got behind the wheel.

"I'm sorry, Johnny. It was stupid," McKenna said as Pao started the car without looking at him. He pulled out of the spot and made a left on Bayard Street while McKenna waited for the explosion. It was slow in building. Pao stopped at a light at the corner of Elizabeth Street and turned to McKenna, the tension rising. But Pao was all smiles, it seemed.

"Do you know how I look if I'm sitting in the garage listening to the Bee Gees while you get shot doing your community affairs act?" he asked.

McKenna put on his very best altar boy look. "I'm sorry, Johnny. It won't happen again."

It wasn't working. Pao's blood pressure was too high for him to hear McKenna. "How come half the people I know tell me you're prancing around the neighborhood doing autographs and I don't even know where you are?" Pao was still smiling, but his voice was getting louder.

What a grouch, thought McKenna. Unfortunately, he's a very large, tough grouch. Time to be diplomatic. "I just thought you'd appreciate the break," McKenna offered, weakly.

"Do I look like I'm breaking my ass?" Pao was calm again, but his question dripped sarcasm.

McKenna didn't know what to say. No, was the only thing he could think, so he said it and braced himself.

"No, I'm not," Pao yelled. "If you get shot, Ray expects to go to two funerals, yours and mine. You got it?"

The light had changed, but the Mercury limo had become the neighborhood center of attention. People in third-floor apartments were leaning out their windows, looking for the source of the high-decibel agitation. Traffic was backing up behind the Mercury and horns were blaring, but Pao ignored them all as he glared at McKenna, waiting for an answer.

"I'm sorry, Johnny. If I get beat, maimed, murdered, or blown up, I promise you'll be standing right next to me for all the fun."

The cloud passed and it was like it never happened. "Good," Pao said, calmly. "Where we going?"

"Twentieth and Fifth."

"Does Hurley know we're coming?" Pao asked as he made the left.

"I'll call him now," McKenna said, reaching for the phone. Apparently Hurley did know they were coming. "I was wondering when you were gonna give me a call to come up," he said.

"I have to," McKenna protested. "You won't talk to Gene Shields."

"Nice guy, but I never trust the feds. They're subject to politics and they can turn on you after any election."

"What about me? Maybe you haven't heard, but I'm a politician now."

"Yeah, Brian, but I don't have to worry about dealing with you because I've got enough on you," Hurley said. "If I ever go away, I could tap out a message to you by banging my cup on the bars, and it won't be long distance. See ya soon."

Hurley hung up, having given McKenna something to think about. In the world of push and shove, Hurley had always been there for him. Whenever McKenna needed anything to make a case, some little piece of information that could snowball into jail time for some bad guy who nobody else could get, Hurley had it, most of the time without McKenna asking for it. He would just call and say, "You'll never guess what I just heard about so-and-so. Seems he came into some money and changed his bank to . . ."

In the detective business, you just had to know which way to point yourself and where to plant your shovel, especially when looking for motive or evidence of the fruits of a crime. Of course, you still had to make a case, pretending that you were just lucky, but one of the funny things about life is that lucky people always seem to be lucky. After a while, it's expected of them. McKenna had been thought of as an unusually lucky detective, but there were lots of them.

Suffice it to say that with the current difficulty of obtaining eavesdropping warrants and subpoenas for financial records, if you were a criminal and the IRS wasn't chasing you, then you had nothing to worry about from the feds or your local police. That is, unless one of them was a friend of Bob Hurley. In that case, you'd better pack a toothbrush, a jar of Vaseline, and a small bag, and make sure to tell everyone you know it'll be a while. Good-bye.

Incredibly, Pao found an open meter in front of Hurley's building. McKenna offered him a fistful of change, but Pao declined with the comment, "This is the first time I've found a legal parking spot in Manhattan in twenty years. Don't spoil it for me."

Change in hand, Pao approached his meter, but first he checked the three signs, which hung one over the other, that were attached to the pole over his particular meter, describing for all to see and none to understand the times and conditions of the legality of the parking spot. McKenna smiled as he watched Pao, knowing that the second-grade detective was confused beyond all hope by those masters of double-talk who wrote the parking signs for the New York City Department of Traffic. With apparent total confidence, Pao put his quarters in the meter as McKenna got out of the car.

"Are you sure we're good?" McKenna asked.

"I'm sure."

McKenna wasn't. "Why don't we play it safe and put the police pass in the windshield?" he asked.

"Why should we? Read the signs," Pao said as he crossed the street.

Knowing his own limitations, McKenna was too smart for that. He followed Pao into the corner building and they took the elevator to the ninth floor, the last stop. Then they had to take another smaller elevator to arrive at the eleventh-floor penthouse office of the Holmes Detective Bureau.

Tracy, Hurley's pretty young black receptionist, was dressed as always in something provocatively demure. She looked up from the *Cosmo* perched atop her PC as McKenna and Pao entered. "Mr. McKenna. Mr. Pao," she said, smiling. "Good afternoon. How good to see you."

Bob Hurley was no dope, McKenna thought. Once a prospective customer wandered into his office to check some prices on investigative services, the first thing he saw was Tracy. Then he was a client and just had to see what was behind Door Number One. He was always disappointed. After Tracy, it was all downhill and not too glamorous.

Tracy led McKenna and Pao through the door to a large room filled with retired detectives sitting in front of computer monitors or talking on their phones. Screens were flashing and printers were making a racket. Although the room was air-conditioned, the heat of the electronics was eating up the comfort, prompting McKenna to loosen his tie.

Tracy pointed to Door Number Two. "Mr. Hurley's expecting you," she said as she turned and resumed her post in the reception area.

McKenna and Pao walked through the room, apparently unnoticed by anyone. Not a word of greeting was exchanged, although both men knew many of Hurley's employees. "Less to see, less to deny" was the rule of the office. McKenna and Pao? Never heard of them.

They walked into Hurley's office without knocking and were hit with a blast of cold air. Hurley was sitting in his well-appointed office playing cards with Sal Catalfumo, his vice president in charge of gin rummy. Sal was another retired detective and an old friend of both McKenna's and Pao's.

Hurley and Catalfumo could have been brothers; same mother but different fathers. They were the Irish and Italian versions of the same man: both were thin and fit, slightly balding with Fu Manchu mustaches, and both wore their silk shirts with a debonair manner that indicated that their bodies hadn't been touched by plebeian cotton in years.

"Close the door," Hurley said as he threw a card. "You're letting out the air-conditioning."

"What about those guys out there?" Pao protested.

"What guys?" Hurley answered, innocently.

"The guys in the steam box making your money for you."

Hurley bowed his head. "Your Honor," he said, "I had no idea there was anyone in my office doing anything illegal. They must have sneaked in to use my computers while I was at church making novenas for the continued success of the Democratic Party."

"Yeah, he's been set up," Catalfumo said as he picked up a card. "I can swear to that. There was nobody out there when I came in."

It took Pao a moment. "Okay, I got it. Why don't you do something with all that empty space?"

"Maybe we will someday, when business picks up," Hurley said. "You guys in a hurry?"

"Kind of," McKenna answered.

"That's too bad for you, Sal. Gin!" said Hurley, laying down his cards in front of Catalfumo with a flourish. "I was gonna keep playing with you, but these men are in a hurry."

Catalfumo didn't seem to mind as he displayed his own cards. "I've got gin, too, wise guy. I thought you were gonna quit on me so I'd have to go back to paying my own mortgage."

"See what I'm up against here?" Hurley asked McKenna and Pao, looking for sympathy. He got none and looked hurt. "Okay, I guess it's down to business. What do you need?"

McKenna gave Hurley the slip of paper with de Leon's information. "Everything you can give me on him."

"Everything?" Hurley asked. "With a name, a Social Security number, and a date of birth, given enough time and money, I'll tell you who his grandfather was dating before he met his grandmother. Are you sure you need everything?"

"We've got the money but we don't have the time. What I really need to know is how much money he's got, where it's coming from, and where he is. I also need to know if he owns or leases a warehouse that's near some railroad tracks in Macon, Georgia."

"This have anything to do with the bombing?"

"Yeah. We think he may have supplied the C-4."

Hurley gave the paper to Catalfumo and said, "Then you got it at my cost. I don't make money off dead cops," Hurley said, then waited a moment before asking, "Isn't there something else you need?"

What am I missing? McKenna asked himself. What else does Hurley think I should be asking for? And why is he looking at me like I just got left back in kindergarten?

Catalfumo couldn't take it anymore. "You ever read *El Diario*, Assistant Commissioner McKenna?" he asked.

"Oh, yeah. I forgot to mention it," McKenna said, trying to recover but failing miserably. "I need anything recent you can get on a Maximo de la Vega."

Assistant Commissioner McKenna had to suffer.

"Maximo de la Vega? Maximo de la Vega? Now where have I heard that name before?" Hurley asked himself, searching the ceiling while jogging his memory.

Fortunately, Hurley had an assistant in place. "Don't you remember, O Wise One?" Catalfumo asked. "This morning you asked me to get everything I could on him. You said that the new snot-nosed assistant commissioner would be smart enough to figure out that Maximo should be put under our microscope."

"I did?" Hurley asked, surprised at his forgetfulness. "That wouldn't be the same Maximo de la Vega who was born in Lima, Peru, on March 21st, 1949, and who came to the United States on August 18th, 1969. You know, the guy who makes $17,000 a year as a contributing editor for *El Diario*, but whose real job is running a newspaper called *El Peruano* out of 95-21 National Boulevard in Corona, Queens, circulation about three thousand a week."

"I can't be certain, Your Worship," Catalfumo said. "I'll have to ask the assistant commissioner to make sure we've got the right Maximo de la Vega. Lord knows there's so many of them. Commissioner," Catalfumo said, turning to McKenna. "Would the Maximo de la Vega you're thinking of be the same one who has a $119,000 mortgage on his house located at 95-41 Denman Street in Corona, yet interestingly enough, put $97,000 in a money-market fund last month, June 30th to be exact?"

"No, wrong Maximo de la Vega," McKenna said, backing out the door, but backing into Pao instead. He turned and saw that Pao was staring at Catalfumo and Hurley like Adam must have stared at Eve on her first appearance. Like poor Adam, Pao obviously couldn't appreciate what they were up against.

Seeing that Pao was going to be no help and certainly wasn't going to move, McKenna turned back to Hurley and Catalfumo to receive a few more needles under his fingernails.

"That's too bad," Hurley said, "because our Maximo de la Vega might be quite an interesting character. Although he's the husband of Carmen de la Vega of the same address, and the father of little Miguel and Tonia, on July 11th he asked that an additional Banco Popular MasterCard charged to his account be issued to a Janine Roldan and he instructed the bank to make sure they send the bills to his office, not his home. Then, on July 16th Janine showed up at the bank to have her PIN number validated, knocked their lecherous eyes out, and showed her Spanish passport for identification. Get this. She's five-foot-five, one hundred and fifteen pounds, with gorgeous red hair. It set us to wondering what Mrs. de la Vega looks like."

McKenna saw an opportunity to exhibit his Man of the World expertise. "If you two would get some sunlight every once in a while, you'd know that gentlemen with good-looking wives usually stray with good-looking girlfriends, if they do at all."

It didn't take with either Catalfumo or Hurley. "What do you think half this business is?" Hurley asked, then answered his own question. "I'll tell you, it's finding out whose wife is boffing whose husband. We get to see them all."

"Yeah," Catalfumo chimed in. "I can't believe they write books about this PI business. Usually it's about as exciting as watching paint dry. The only time we have any fun is when we get to give the client his bill."

Catalfumo had said the B-word, which got McKenna thinking. "Can you give me any idea how much this Alejandro business is gonna cost?" he asked.

"Depending on how deeply he covered his tracks, no more than ten grand, my cost," Hurley said, somehow still managing to look like Santa Claus.

God! They are good at this bill business, McKenna thought. But that's only five grand, my end, and Shields looks like he can afford it.

But McKenna was still worried. Could have a problem here, he thought. What about the Maximo de la Vega thing? Shields never said anything about paying for that.

"And how much for Maximo?" McKenna asked, bracing himself.

Hurley dispensed with the question with a wave of his hand.

"You weren't smart enough to ask about it, so we'll be stupid enough not to charge you. It's a free-o." Hurley took a folder off his desk and gave it to McKenna. "Here's his information in case you forgot anything I told you. Get rid of it as soon as you can."

"Thanks," McKenna said. "I owe you."

"You always do and maybe one day I'll collect. Until then, don't worry about it. Any more questions?"

"Yeah, I got a question," Pao said, finding his voice. "How do you guys do it?"

Pao instantly regretted his inquiry. McKenna, Hurley, and Catalfumo looked at him as if he were a schoolchild caught trying to peek up his teacher's dress, not knowing that what was up there was none of his business, yet.

"Weren't you guys in a hurry?" Hurley asked without emotion.

"Yeah, thanks a lot," McKenna said. "We gotta go." As McKenna and Pao walked past the zombies in the outer office, Hurley yelled to them, "You guys better stick to civil service. It's tough on the outside."

"Yeah, the competition is pretty sharp," Catalfumo had to add.

McKenna and Pao said nothing until they got into their car. It had started to drizzle lightly and the weather didn't lighten their mood.

Pao started the car and pulled out of the spot. "Where to?" he asked. "Corona?"

"Yeah, let's go."

As Pao turned on East 14th Street, he said softly, "That was pretty ugly up there, wasn't it?"

McKenna didn't need to be reminded. "Yes, it was," he said, hoping to end the conversation.

No good. "They treated us like we were a couple of dopes, didn't they?" Pao commented. "Especially you," he had to add.

Yeah, they did, McKenna thought. But I hope they know that I'm not as dopey as you. *How do you guys do it?* Good question, Johnny. Notice how they couldn't wait to show you all their tricks, you big dummy?

In the interests of domestic tranquillity and exercising a commendable team spirit, seasoned with a healthy instinct for self-preservation, McKenna kept his hopes to himself.

Pao was smiling away until the rain started coming down

harder. Then he turned on the windshield wipers and made McKenna's day. Those friendly public servants from the Department of Traffic had criticized Pao's understanding of their trio of signs by rewarding him with a parking ticket, which, in their usual straightforward fashion, they had hidden under the windshield wiper. Knowing that the American public finds a gaudy display of windshield wipers to be offensive, those fine Mercury people had hidden the wipers in the windshield-wiper well, which was another reason that the Parking Violations Bureau got to charge their hefty overdue fines on their summonses issued to the owners of the finer automobiles.

For the first time, McKenna knew how Gene Kelly felt, and he started humming the tune as the parking ticket went back and forth in front of Pao's face.

I love this, McKenna thought as he watched Pao pretend that the four-by-eight-inch parking ticket impeding his vision wasn't really there.

Pao tried turning off the wipers and found that he couldn't see the ticket, or anything else. He turned the wipers back on.

"Aaaghh!" he said, quite distinctly, as he rolled down his window and put out his hand, trying to grab the ticket and finally catching it on his fourth try. He brought his drenched arm and his prize into the car and closed the window, then looked at McKenna defiantly.

Chapter 12
It took them a half hour to drive to Corona, an area McKenna considered to be one of the more vibrant parts of the city. At one time Corona was just another Italian neighborhood in Queens, but in the seventies the neighborhood started changing to reflect the large influx of immigrants from South and Central America. Spanish was the lingua franca on Roosevelt Avenue, the commercial main drag of Corona, and the street was crowded with travel agencies and restaurants that specialized in the various cuisines of all

the countries south of the border.

Pao stopped in front of a candy store and McKenna went in and bought a copy of *El Peruano* and two containers of strong Latin coffee. They sat in the car drinking their coffee while McKenna read the paper. It was a learning experience.

El Peruano was a thin weekly newspaper of twenty pages and concerned itself with events in Corona as well as the news from Peru. McKenna's issue had been published four days before, so it contained nothing about the bombing, but he was surprised at what it did contain. McKenna's understanding was that *Sendero* had a policy of refusing all contact with the press as they fought their war, declining all requests for interviews and relying instead on creating a mystique of the unknown to further their cause. As McKenna read, he realized that the policy had changed. *Sendero* had gone public.

In reporting the news from Peru, *El Peruano* treated *Sendero* like the opposition party, and reports on government programs and operations were balanced by criticism and comment from *Sendero* spokespersons. There was no news on any military operations by either the government or *Sendero*.

By page five McKenna was out of the news and into the pictorial coverage of weddings and social events, the type of coverage peculiar to Spanish-language newspapers. McKenna concluded by reading an editorial that gleefully speculated that the war in Peru was coming to an end, without mentioning which side was the winner.

As McKenna folded up the newspaper, Pao asked, "You learn anything?"

"One pretty important thing. Our Maximo de la Vega seems to hear fairly regularly from *Sendero*."

"Does he like them?"

"I don't know, but he writes what *Sendero* has to say about whatever the government in Peru is doing. I find that interesting and I think we'd like to meet whoever it is who's talking to him."

Pao parked outside the storefront *El Peruano* office on National Boulevard and McKenna went in. Behind a counter just inside the store was a young man with ink on his hands who smiled when he saw McKenna. "Glad to meet you, Mr. McKenna. Mr. de la Vega is expecting you," he said, surprising McKenna, and then led him past the printing presses to a cluttered office in the rear of the store. The clerk knocked, opened the door, and went back to the front of the store.

Maximo de la Vega was a tall, dapper man with a twinkle in his eyes and a face dominated by his large nose. McKenna knew de la Vega was in his forties, but he looked to be thirty-five at the most. Still, as de la Vega rose from his desk to greet him, McKenna's first thought was, This guy's got something I don't see if he has the girlfriend Hurley described.

"Glad to meet you, Mr. McKenna," de la Vega said as he shook McKenna's hand and pointed at a chair opposite his desk. Both men took their seats.

"How did you know I was coming?" McKenna asked.

"If you didn't, I would have been surprised. I thought that someone would bring my article to your attention, and that you'd naturally have some questions."

"Which you don't mind answering?"

"Not at all. That bombing was a filthy business."

"So you don't sympathize with the Shining Path?"

"That's a difficult question. Something has to be done in Peru, and because of *Sendero* some things have changed, but I don't think *Sendero*'s the answer. Let's just say that I agree with some of their goals without agreeing with their methods."

"How did you manage to get to *Sendero* to do the article in Peru? My understanding was that *Sendero* shunned publicity of any kind."

"All that changed after Guzman was captured. Whoever's in charge now has decided to seek favorable publicity, which made my job easy. But I didn't get in touch with them, they contacted me, and it wasn't to do the article you read. I just put that together after the bombing, figuring that the time was right for it. Before that, I couldn't sell a *Sendero* article to any of the other newspapers here. Nobody wanted to hear about them."

"So what did they want you to do in Peru?"

"They wanted a documentary on *Sendero Luminoso*, shot on location there. They used me as a scriptwriter."

"How did it turn out?"

"They were very happy with it, and so were many of the other people involved in the production, but I wasn't. It started as a legitimate documentary, but turned into a rather clever propaganda film."

"Since you were writing the script, didn't you have anything to say about it?" McKenna asked.

"Not really. I wasn't there as a journalist, I was there to do the job they paid me to do. I protested at first, but I went along with their program."

"Because the pay was that good?"

"Yes."

"Do you mind if I ask how much it was?" McKenna asked, thinking about de la Vega's recent money-market deposit.

"Yes," de la Vega answered defensively. "Next question, please."

"Can you describe the film for me?"

"I promised them that I wouldn't. That was part of the deal."

"Okay, then can you tell me what you didn't like about it?"

De la Vega thought over McKenna's question before deciding to answer. "Let me just give you an example. They made a big thing out of atrocities committed by government troops. While I'm sure these things have happened, I didn't like the way *Sendero* set it up. While I was in Peru there was a battle in a little village called Roncayo. A company of government soldiers occupied the town and then started a house-by-house search, questioning everybody and looking for weapons and Senderistas. They found more than they were looking for."

"They were ambushed?"

"Yes. Somehow, *Sendero* knew the troops were coming. There was a little shoe factory in the middle of town that *Sendero* figured the army would use as their command post, and they were right. They had set it up with explosives and blew it up. Then they attacked the town and wiped out the rest of the soldiers who stayed to fight. Only about a dozen of them got away."

"So what's the problem?" McKenna asked. "Sounds to me like the perfect situation for some good press."

"The problem is that the army was using the shoe factory as the place they did their interrogations of the townspeople, and *Sendero* had to know they'd do that. They blew them up, too."

"How many?"

"Hard to tell. They brought us there about an hour after the attack, and there were pieces of them everywhere. It had to be at least ten, but that wasn't the worst part. They had me rewrite the whole event into something that never happened. They had lots of bodies lying around, and the final version will show that the government attacked a defenseless village and were in the process of torturing some innocent townspeople when *Sendero* came to the rescue. They mutilated some of the soldiers' bodies and dressed them as villagers, and the film crew took footage of the torture victims. The way it was done, it was pretty convincing.''

''I'd sure like to see that film,'' McKenna said.

''I wouldn't show it to you, even if I could. That was part of the deal.''

''Don't you have a copy?''

''Nobody does. They were very strict about control, which was one of the things that annoyed everyone. We weren't allowed to see the completed product we all worked very hard to make.''

''Who else was involved in making the film?''

''I can't tell you. I will say that, to lend credibility to their project, *Sendero* used professional production people from all over the world, and when the film is released they will naturally be listed in the credits. None of us is famous and it should give a lot of careers a boost.''

''When will that be? You must all be looking forward to it.''

''I am, and I'm sure the rest are, too, but *Sendero* never gave us any idea.''

''Okay, can you tell me where they're from, at least?''

De la Vega took some time before answering, ''I see no harm in that. Besides myself, there was another scriptwriter from Los Angeles, there were some still-photo people from Germany, some film people from Argentina, and some makeup people and a special-effects crew from France. Oh, and the narrator was from Spain. I wrote some of her dialogue and coached her through it.''

Her? Janine Roldan? McKenna wondered. He decided not to push it. ''How many foreigners altogether?'' he asked.

''Sixteen of us involved in the actual production. It was a good crew.''

''So you got along with everyone?''

''Pretty much so. There was some grumbling among some of us when we saw the direction the project was taking, but we were all well paid and stayed to the end. The working conditions were miserable and there was an element of danger, so we had to cooperate to put the project together as quickly as possible. Most of them just wanted to finish and get out.''

"Most of them?" McKenna asked. "Does that mean that some wanted to stay?"

"A couple of us. As you know, I went on some of their operations while the film people were scouting locations and setting up interviews with villagers. I had nothing to do with that part of the project, and I knew there was other news there. It was a great opportunity and I might still be there if I wasn't wounded."

"Who else wanted to stay?"

"Somebody who turned out to be a good friend of mine. She's a photojournalist and got very involved in their cause, politically, I mean, which surprised most of us. We were all at ground zero and could see what *Sendero* was up to, but she took it all seriously. Some people in *Sendero* really liked her."

"Was it Ingrid Troutmann?" McKenna asked.

His question drew a blank look from de la Vega. "Ingrid Troutmann? The girl who was killed in Manhattan? No, she's German, but that wasn't her."

It had to be, McKenna thought. There's not that much room for this many coincidences. A German photojournalist whose brother was a terrorist and who was in Peru at the same time as de la Vega? McKenna took Troutmann's picture from his pocket and showed it to de la Vega. The journalist's eyes went wide.

"That's Marlene. Where did you get this picture and what's wrong with her? She looks terrible."

"What's wrong with her is that she's dead. She's the girl that *Sendero* killed on East 45th Street."

The news hit de la Vega hard, and he looked like he was going to cry. But he didn't. McKenna watched de la Vega's face as rage replaced grief. "We were very close," de la Vega said softly, without moving his lips.

"Do you mean close close, in the biblical sense?"

McKenna realized that he had hit on something as he watched de la Vega's reaction to his question. He thought de la Vega was going to deny it, but instead he lowered his eyes and said, "Yes, we were that close. I'm very sorry that this happened to her."

"It didn't just happen to her. She was murdered."

De la Vega was beginning to understand, but he had to ask anyway. "Why did they do it? And why did she tell us her name was Marlene Kohlmann?"

"Don't you see it?" McKenna asked. "They did it because

they needed another body on East 45th Street and hers was available. And she didn't tell you her real name because she was one of them. She was their spy in your camp.''

"Then I guess she brought it on herself," de la Vega said, apparently resigned.

McKenna didn't want a resigned de la Vega. He wanted to keep him fired up. "Nobody brings that much on themselves," he said. "She was murdered by her friends, her comrades-in-arms."

It worked. "They're cold, calculating savages," de la Vega said through gritted teeth. "I suspected that, so I shouldn't be surprised."

"Is any of your crew still with them?"

"No, thank God. But we keep in touch. I'll tell them about this, although there's nothing we can do about it."

"Are any of them in New York?"

The question caught de la Vega by surprise, and he didn't think before he answered, "Why yes, as a matter of fact, the narrator is here now. Why do you ask?"

"Because New York is my area of responsibility and I think you might all be in danger. *Sendero* might want to get rid of any dissenting voices before they release the film."

McKenna's theory gave de la Vega something to think about, but he reached a different conclusion. "If so, then why didn't they just kill us in Peru when we finished?" he asked. "It would have been easy for them there."

"You see how cleverly they think. Were you in the country legally?"

"No, I went in through Colombia. But some of us were legally there."

"Then that's your answer. They can't afford to have a bunch of journalists and filmmakers, even relatively unknown ones, just disappear while they're with them. It takes all credibility away from their project, and it sounds to me like they worked very hard and spent a lot of money just to get credibility."

De la Vega thought that over. "I see what you mean," he said. "You may be right. What should I do?"

"You can start by helping me out."

"How?"

"I read your last edition and it sounds to me like you've been in contact with someone from *Sendero*."

"That's not entirely true. They're in contact with me. I get a call every Monday and the person gives me the *Sendero* position on what's happening in Peru."

"And you run it?"

"Sometimes I do and sometimes I don't, but my contact doesn't complain about it. I think they want the coverage and they try to be pretty honest with me. But sometimes their position is patently absurd or I find other information to refute their claims. Then I just don't print it."

"Where do you get your other information from?"

Now de la Vega did look embarrassed. "I should tell you that, being a great newspaperman, I have sources all over Peru. But you've seen the size of my operation here. What I really do is call the Peruvian embassy here and they put me into their information section. I talk to them a lot and they're really quite helpful."

"I can understand that," McKenna said. "They need good press here as much as *Sendero* does."

"You're right. I think *Sendero* now attaches as much importance to their political operations as they do to the military phase of the war. Their whole emphasis has changed and I think that now their leadership is looking for some kind of a political victory."

"Do you know who the leadership is?"

"No, but I can surmise who at least one of them is."

"How?"

"Just because of the way he's treated. He was around sometimes and everybody snapped to whenever he said something."

"So? Being a big shot doesn't put you in the leadership circle. Every army has generals who have nothing to do with making policy."

"I know that, but does every army threaten journalists with death just for taking a picture of their generals?"

"Did that happen to you?"

"Not in so many words. But once when he was in our camp, I had a camera around my neck and one of the *Sendero* leaders told me they had a policy. Take a shot of Felipe, get shot by *Sendero*. He was laughing when he said it, but I believed him."

"But you did get some other pictures?" McKenna asked, his hopes rising.

"Everyone did, but I'm the only one who got them out of the country. They let us take as many pictures as we wanted, but the others told me that *Sendero* took all their film right before they left the country. We all realize now that they let us take the pictures just to keep us happy.''

"Then what made you different?"

"I didn't leave like the rest of them. I was wounded before the project was over, and they sent all my stuff to the hospital in Pucallpa. I didn't mean to be sneaky, but I had hidden some film in my computer battery pack. If they searched it, they missed the film.''

"Can I see it?" McKenna asked hopefully.

"I've already decided that. If I wasn't going to let you see it, I wouldn't have told you about it. I assume you'd be able to get a search warrant based on what I've inadvertently told you.''

"I see," McKenna said. "If you were to give it to me voluntarily, it would look to *Sendero* like you were in collusion with the enemy. If they had anything bad in mind for you, that would certainly accelerate their plans.''

"Am I that crafty?" de la Vega asked, then laughed at his question. "I guess I am. If you think these pictures would be of some value, please make the raid well publicized." As an afterthought, he said, "It wouldn't hurt my circulation any, either.''

Yes, you are that crafty, McKenna thought. "If I were to get a search warrant, where do you think would be a good place to look?"

"If I were you," de la Vega said, smiling, "I think I would start on the bottom drawer of this desk. But before you do that, I would look under the rug exactly where I'm sitting. You might find a spare desk key there.''

"Wouldn't it look better for you if you had some pictures of your broken desk to publicly complain about?"

De la Vega liked it. "You're right. You seem to be thinking a little faster than me today, Mr. McKenna.''

"I'm getting better," McKenna said. "So far, I haven't been having a great day."

"Then you're due for some improvement. When you find the pictures, the one on the top will be of Felipe.''

"You risked your life to take a picture of him?" McKenna asked, surprised.

"Don't be shocked and don't let the size of my operation here fool you. I'm still a journalist under it all, even though I took a lot of money to help make a film that can best be characterized as straight propaganda. Maybe it'll make up for that breach in ethics. It just seemed to me that it might be an important picture.''

"How did you do it?"

"From a distance. You'll see."

"Thank you," McKenna said, getting up. "We'll be meeting again soon. Would you mind if I supplied some protection to you for a while?"

"If it wasn't too obvious or intrusive," de la Vega answered, smiling. "Sometimes I'm busy." He smiled like McKenna should understand, and he did.

McKenna could imagine the tall journalist with the big nose being busy with Janine Roldan. He thought that Maximo was turning out to be quite the hummingbird, flitting from flower to flower. McKenna decided to give him some room. "I understand. You call the shots," he said with the same smile. "How about your friend who's here?"

"Her? I don't think that would be necessary. *Sendero* couldn't possibly know where she is."

If I can find out, and I will, McKenna thought, so can *Sendero*. But I can't push this man too far.

"Suit yourself," McKenna said, offering his hand, but de la Vega was lost in thought. He came to a conclusion and saw McKenna's hand for the first time. He shook it and said, "There's something else you should know, something that none of us could figure out while we were shooting the film. When we started, we naturally thought it would be for domestic consumption, but it's not and it's certainly too gory to be shown on TV anywhere. We couldn't settle on their purpose, but I'm reaching some conclusions now, and it's pretty scary."

"Conclusions? Such as?" McKenna asked, waiting.

"You tell me. The entire film is shot in English."

Chapter 13

For once, McKenna experienced some of the perks of his new position and felt good about it. He was in and out of Queens Supreme Court in under an hour with the search warrant de la Vega wanted, plus three eavesdropping warrants he didn't want and wouldn't know about. Two of them covered de la Vega's office phone and home phone and also covered the installation of two PENS registers to record the phone numbers incoming calls were made from. The third one permitted the installation of a locating transmitter on de la Vega's car.

To obtain the warrants, all McKenna had to do was articulate the importance of finding de la Vega's *Sendero* contact and interviewing Janine Roldan. Ordinarily, obtaining such warrants would be a tedious all-day affair for any detective, with some assistant district attorney troubleshooting and second-guessing the need and legality of the detective's warrant application before the judge got his shot at the same job.

But that wasn't the way it was for the newly famous assistant commissioner. As soon as he showed up in the District Attorney's Office, he was brought directly to the DA himself. All other business stopped. A staff of typists was rounded up to punch out the applications and the warrants, and a short time later McKenna found himself in the chambers of the senior judge, who was only too happy to help. He didn't have a single question for McKenna concerning his need for the four warrants, and even wished him good luck on the way out, with the request that McKenna give his regards to the mayor.

McKenna and Pao got back to headquarters at five o'clock, just as the rest of the building was emptying out. But Wright wasn't going anywhere, and she was a wealth of information.

"Inspector Tavlin and Inspector Sheeran are waiting in your office."

"Fine, thank you."

"Three literary agents and four authors called. They say you're the hottest property in town and they all want to do your story."

"Fine, thank you."

"The mayor's office called. There's a six o'clock news conference at city hall. He's going to announce that the city's going to offer an additional one-million-dollar reward on the church bombing. He wants you there, prepared to say something appropriate."

"Fine, thank you."

"Your wife called. I gave her your mobile number, but she said she wouldn't bother you."

"Fine, thank you."

"The sheriff of Val Verde County, Texas, called. He sounded pretty impressive and said he had some information on your case. He wants you to call him back. Here's his number," she said, handing him a message slip.

"Fine, thank you. When are you going home, Camilia?"

"Right after you."

McKenna took the message slip and went into his office. Both Tavlin and Sheeran looked like they could use a good night's sleep, but they weren't going to get it.

McKenna described for them his activities of the day and gave them the warrants. They would use detectives from both offices to handle it, as the job would require some manpower around the clock. Aside from the installation of the electronics, they would need men to monitor the two wiretaps, a team to provide some obvious protection for de la Vega, and two teams to do a surveillance on de la Vega by following the signal of the locating transmitter. They would go into action as soon as de la Vega requested the discontinuance of his protection.

Tavlin would personally handle the search of the *El Peruano* offices, and McKenna asked him to make a show of it and even throw de la Vega around a little bit, if it seemed that was what he wanted. McKenna wished them both luck and they went to work.

McKenna had to rush to arrive at city hall just in time for the news conference. The media was there in force as the mayor described how the hearts of the good citizens of the City of New York went out to the families of the murdered cops. For that reason, he was offering an unprecedented reward on their behalf, bringing the total to $1.3 million. His Honor received a round of applause before bringing McKenna to the lectern to handle questions.

The first question was, "Would you mind removing your hat for the cameras, Commissioner?"

"Sorry, can't do it. I'd get into too much trouble at home. Next question."

"How do you feel, Commissioner? Can you do the job after the injuries you suffered in the bombing?"

McKenna received the impression that the Fourth Estate wanted to make sure he was in fighting form before they tore him up. "A little sore, with just some bumps and bruises," McKenna said. "I'll survive."

Then the questioning shifted to the investigation, specifically the lack of apparent progress in the endeavor. McKenna assured them, time after time, that everything was proceeding smoothly, although arrests were not imminent.

The press didn't go for it. They came for a story and they wanted specifics. McKenna wouldn't give them any. It made them crazy and they wouldn't leave it alone. The same questions came in different forms, until McKenna got visibly annoyed with them. Then they remembered the rule about picking on heroes where everyone could see them do it and they calmed down. But McKenna knew that the next press conference would be a no-holds-barred affair. He felt five years older by the time he returned to his office at six-thirty.

Wright was still there, but she had another visitor. A small, slight man was sitting at attention in the receptionist's office with a briefcase on his lap, patiently waiting for the assistant commissioner. He was the kind of man who was easily ignored, and at first McKenna did ignore him.

"Call the chief of detectives and tell him we're gonna need more men to man the phones," McKenna told Wright. "That extra million for the reward is going to have every screwball in the city calling and the press cornered me on it. Every call has to be taken seriously."

"I'll handle it," she said, then pointed to the visitor. "This is Mr. Savraada. He insisted on seeing you and is under the impression that you would want to see him."

Wright was surprised by McKenna's facial reaction to the news, but she misinterpreted it. "I told him he should have called first for an appointment," she said.

"You've got it wrong, Camilia. I should have to call Mr.

Savraada for an appointment, and I've been trying to do just that."

McKenna turned to Savraada and held out his hand, which surprised the colonel. He stood up, shook McKenna's hand, and asked, "You know who I am?"

"Of course, Colonel. Didn't you get my message?"

"No. To whom did you address it?"

"To your embassy here in New York."

"I'm sorry. I've been out of touch for a few days. Travel is very difficult for me and it took me some time to get here. I didn't want our adversaries to know I was coming, and they have people everywhere. I couldn't take a chance on flying out of Lima, so I had to drive to Ecuador and take a flight from there."

Now McKenna was surprised. "You were coming even before I asked your embassy if I could talk with you?"

"Of course. I started here as soon as I heard about your bombing incident. I knew that could be the work of only one man and I think you need my help."

Chapter 14 Savraada sat in one of the comfortable chairs across from McKenna's desk and arranged his briefcase on his lap while McKenna made two cups of coffee. He gave Savraada one and sat down at his desk, sipping his coffee and waiting for Savraada to begin.

The colonel took his time. He took a sip of his coffee, obviously enjoying it, and said, "It's been a while since I had a cup of American coffee. Our stuff might be better, but it gives me the runs."

"Does a while mean since 1983?" McKenna asked, innocently.

Savraada smiled. "So you know about me? I'm embarrassed to be the subject of discussion, but I must admit that I'm a little impressed."

"Don't be impressed with me. Gene Shields gave me the information. He's also trying to get in touch with you."

"I see," Savraada said. "For reasons of my own, I prefer to deal with you and you can pass on my information to whomever you think appropriate."

"I understand. Thank you."

Savraada smiled and said, "You might tell Mr. Shields that he can update his file on me. Actually, I've been back a few times since 1983, but I don't think your government is aware of it. They're so nosy and they make me a little nervous."

"You're not alone. They are nosy, but I trust Gene Shields and right now we need him."

"Of course." Savraada took out a cigarette and lit it, pulling an ashtray on the desk toward him. The little man had an air of authority about him, making McKenna feel like he was sitting in Savraada's office. Without knowing why, McKenna said, "I hear you're winning your war. Congratulations."

Savraada took the time to stare at McKenna. "Nobody wins a long civil war, Mr. McKenna. You just end it, any way you can."

"Any way you can? Does that include surrender?"

Savraada thought over the option. "If that is the only way possible to end it, then yes, surrender. Of course, compromise is preferable, but I've come to the conclusion that the type of government we suffer or enjoy isn't worth the total destruction of our society, which is what is happening now."

"An answer like that surprises me, coming from a man in your position."

"Don't be surprised. It's just common sense. We spend forty percent of our national budget on defense, and there is no threat of invasion from anyone. No country can afford to waste that much for too many years, and we are a poor country with enormous social needs. We have tremendous economic potential, but none of it will be realized as long as this war drags on. It must be ended and the wounds healed before Peru becomes a basket case."

McKenna was amazed at Savraada's ideas. He made the absurd seem practical and necessary. "Does anyone else in Peru think like you?" he asked.

"Unfortunately, I am alone in my position. Too many people on both sides are in entrenched positions for anything positive to happen anytime soon, especially from my side. The war has slowed down and the government appears to be winning. But because of your bombing, I anticipate a rapid rise in hostilities.''

The idea that a bombing in New York could have a tangible effect on the civil war seemed preposterous to McKenna. "You're gonna have to explain that to me. We tend to look at it as an act of retribution, not something connected to any grandiose battle strategy.''

"If I am right, and I hope I'm not, you will come to realize that the bombing was just the first act reflecting a change in strategy by *Sendero* and the opening of a whole new campaign that will deeply affect you.''

McKenna finished his coffee and sat back in his chair. "Okay, Colonel, you certainly have my interest. Why don't you convince me?''

"Good. If you will just hear me out, I'll answer any questions you may have as best I can when I am through.''

It was like turning on the radio. Savraada began.

"Three weeks ago in Argentina one of my agents stumbled upon Elena Castellena. She's with *Sendero* and is a known associate of one of their most able leaders, a man we know only as Felipe. Elena boarded a plane and my agent followed her. Felipe was on the flight and they both got off in San José, Costa Rica. My agent reported back and I found that both Elena and Felipe were traveling under false names. Felipe was using a forged passport and Elena was using the passport of a Spanish TV producer who is currently missing in Peru. I instructed the agent to maintain his surveillance while I arranged for some reinforcements for him. That was the last we heard of him. His body was discovered that night in San José by the police. Two more of my agents arrived that night and found out about the murder. After some difficulty they were able to get some assistance from the local police.''

"Why should they have any difficulty with the police?''

"Because the people of Costa Rica traditionally have a very narrow field of vision when it comes to world affairs. I'm convinced that many of them believe the civilized world ends at their border, and those who don't couldn't care less about the rest of the world anyway. The police reflect the national attitude and usually aren't very helpful. Fortunately for us, it was a newsworthy murder.''

"What was so newsworthy about it?'' McKenna asked.

"My agent was being tortured before he killed himself by swallowing a cyanide capsule. Made a big splash in the Costa

Rican papers and put some pressure on the police.''

''You give your agents cyanide capsules?''

''Of course. Death is preferable to a vigorous *Sendero* session. I have one myself under a cap in my mouth.''

''That's something to think about,'' McKenna said, obviously impressed. ''I'm sorry. Please continue.''

''Anyway, the Costa Rican police found a taxi driver who had delivered my agent to the Gran Hotel in Costa Rica while he was following Elena. With our assistance, they found that Felipe and another man had been staying at the Gran Hotel, and that he had some visitors the night of the murder. We have helped the police to identify all of the parties involved but one.''

Savraada opened his briefcase and took out a stack of photographs.

''This is the man who was staying with Felipe at the hotel,'' he said, handing McKenna the top photo. ''His name is Emilio Aponte. From the descriptions I read in your newspapers, I believe he was instrumental in the killing of your commissioner's son.''

McKenna looked at the photo of Emilio and felt himself go from anger to hate. It was a prison photo of a face that was easy to hate.

''He escaped from prison five years ago. This is a photo of Warren Burgos,'' Savraada said, handing McKenna another picture. ''He is a lawyer for the Medellín drug cartel.''

McKenna studied the photo and came to the conclusion that Burgos looked like many lawyers he knew.

''This is the chief negotiator for the Cali drug cartel,'' Savraada said, handing McKenna another picture. ''His name is Jose Escudero.''

It was a front- and side-view prison picture. Escudero seemed cunning and dangerous. McKenna looked up and Savraada continued.

''We were able to identify them because of some unusual air traffic into the airport in San José. They arrived in San José together in a private plane from Colombia at seven-thirty on the night of the murders. They flew back at one A.M., returned to San José at five in the morning, and flew back to Colombia for good at seven that morning.''

Savraada gave McKenna a moment, and the conclusions that McKenna was forced to draw from the information were staggering. Savraada's face had a look of total self-assurance, a look that said to McKenna, I told you this would change your thinking, as he continued. He handed McKenna another photo.

"That is a photo of Elena, taken three years ago, but don't be guided by it. She is reported to be quite beautiful and quite deadly. When my agent saw her in Buenos Aires, she had dyed her hair red to match the description of the missing Spanish TV producer, Janine Roldan."

"Janine Roldan?" McKenna asked as his heart jumped in his chest, but he tried to keep a straight face. So *Sendero* had both Elena and Ingrid spying on the journalists, McKenna thought. Old Maximo is in deeper than he knows, and we're closer than I thought.

McKenna looked at the picture. It was obviously a surveillance photo taken from some distance and showed her in camouflage fatigues, complete with hat. Her hair was dark and he looked closely at her face. Yes, she could be beautiful, he decided.

"Elena matches Roldan fairly closely," Savraada said, eyeing McKenna. "She is five foot five and weighs one hundred and fifteen pounds. She has a limp as a result of an old wound, but she is clever in disguising it." Then he handed McKenna a sketch. "That is Felipe. There are no known photos of him and the sketch is made from a composite of many descriptions. I'm told by those who have seen him that it is very accurate."

McKenna glanced at the sketch. This guy could fit in anywhere, he thought. He even looks like a few cops I know. But he didn't spend much time looking, knowing that their intelligence picture was about to improve. He was holding a few cards Savraada couldn't possibly know about.

Savraada continued. "Felipe and Emilio checked out of the Gran Hotel at six-thirty that morning and haven't been seen since. There was another man present at their meetings in the hotel, but we haven't been able to identify him, yet. I'm told that he's described as a younger version of Santa Claus."

Santa Claus? McKenna thought. What's he doing mixed up with this crew? Isn't there anything left to believe in anymore?

But Savraada wasn't through. "Let me give you some additional information to think about. During the past three months, *Sendero* offensive military operations in Peru have virtually ceased and they are rapidly losing territory, but they don't seem to mind. They fall back every time government troops confront them. I also have reports from my informants in *Sendero* that many of their most reliable and trusted soldiers have vanished and there are rumors of a major operation in the near future. To complicate matters, six members of their Revolutionary Council have been killed this month, some in some very unsavory fashions. It's either a power struggle or a purge. We no longer have any idea who is in charge of *Sendero* in Peru, but we suspect that Felipe is running the show overall.''

''From here?''

Savraada smiled. ''Doesn't that lead you to any conclusions?'' he asked.

''Just that you may be right,'' McKenna admitted, not liking the conclusions he was drawing. ''Maybe the *Sendero* operational strategy has changed and the new battleground in your war might be right here. I'll know more in a few minutes.''

McKenna picked up his phone and dialed Wright. She answered immediately. ''Can you get me the chief of OCCB on the line?'' he asked.

Sure she could. No more than five minutes, she promised. McKenna looked at his watch and hung up.

''What is OCCB?'' Savraada asked.

''Organized Crime Control Bureau. Consists of our Narcotics Division and our Public Morals Division.''

''I see,'' Savraada said, with total self-assurance. ''He will confirm our thinking.''

Savraada was getting a little too smug for McKenna's taste, so he decided to take him down a notch or two. ''You ever heard of a gent named Alejandro de Leon?''

''The old Contra spokesperson who is reputed to have just sold two Stinger missiles to the Afghans so they could sell them back to the CIA? What about him?''

God, this guy's infuriating. What doesn't he know? McKenna thought, but he still said with a touch of pride, ''Well, he was also in Costa Rica on July 4th and he supplied the stuff *Sendero* is using in New York. It looks like he made a deal with Felipe and split.''

''Interesting,'' Savraada said, dryly.

Interesting? McKenna thought. Well, try this one out. ''Have you ever heard of a man named Maximo de la Vega?''

''The journalist who publishes *El Peruano*? Actually I know him, although he's not aware of who I am now.''

McKenna sighed. ''How?'' he asked meekly.

''He always used to come into my father's drugstore in Corona for the latest in aphrodisiacs. You see, Maximo's always had a reputation as a bit of a Romeo who wouldn't last long, yet he's still around and still living on the edge. He has this incredibly ugly but insanely jealous wife who's always just a half-step behind him, and if she ever gets ahead of him, he's done for.''

''What do you know about *El Peruano*?'' McKenna asked. Everything, I'm sure, he thought.

''Everything, I think,'' Savraada answered without a trace of emotion. ''I make sure our embassy here supplies Maximo with all the information he needs. He doesn't know it, but I helped arrange his entrance into Peru from Colombia. I saw him briefly in Peru over the sights of my rifle near a little village called Esperanza. I believe he wrote about our meeting in an uninformed manner in his article for *El Diario*. I had set up an ambush for *Sendero* and Maximo happened to be with them, which dampened the success of our operation. When I saw he was wounded, I had my men cease fire so he could escape.''

McKenna was astounded. ''Why?''

''A few more dead *Sendero* soldiers is not going to make any difference in the war. What is important is that we had a psychological victory in Esperanza, and I knew Maximo would write about it. Psychological victories are more decisive than military victories and the side with the most psychological victories wins, not the side which kills more of the enemy's soldiers. But in hindsight, I must admit it was a mistake not to capture him.''

A mistake? You? McKenna thought. He was gratified at the admission, but he had to figure out for himself what the mistake was to feel really good about it. Then it came to him. ''I guess at the time you didn't know about *Sendero*'s film,'' McKenna said, hearing the smugness in his own voice.

''I see you've been talking to Maximo. You're right. We didn't find out about the film until later. When I saw Maximo, I believed that he was in the country doing a straight reporting job.''

''How did you find out about the film?''

''From Ingrid Troutmann. I believe you must know her role in this by now?''

McKenna was glad he could nod that he did. He didn't answer the question, but his face said to Savraada: Of course we know who Ingrid Troutmann was. What do you think we are, stupid or something?

It must have worked. "I'm sorry," Savraada said. "Of course you know about Troutmann. Anyway, she had a penchant for paramours, including Maximo, I believe, and one time she slept and talked with a *Sendero* soldier who used to talk to a person who talks to me from time to time. I would love to see that film, and I'm sure it must disturb you that it's in English."

It did disturb McKenna, but the ringing phone disturbed him more. He looked at his watch again. Four minutes. He found himself running up a real dislike for very efficient people like Camilia Wright and Robert Savraada. He picked up the phone and almost bit off his tongue after he said, "Detective McKenna. Can I help you?"

"Commissioner McKenna?" the voice asked, unsure.

"Yeah, I'm sorry. You know how it is. Rank is coming a little fast around here lately and you get promoted before you know it."

McKenna could imagine the chief at the other end pulling his hair out, if he had any. The chiefs didn't have the reputation as a particularly gracious bunch when it came to other people's promotions. Actually, sometimes it made them physically sick to go to the promotion ceremonies of their supposed friends when they themselves hadn't received an extra star on their collar in the previous week or two.

"This is Chief McNamara of OCCB. You wanted to talk to me, Commissioner?"

McKenna noticed that when the chief said "commissioner," he sounded a little hoarse. It made McKenna smile and gave him a pleasant little tingle in his ear.

"Yes, Chief. Can you tell me anything about the amount of drugs coming into the city from Colombia since July 4th?"

"Funny you should ask," the chief said. "It looks like there's been nothing coming in since then. The price is skyrocketing, the streets are drying up, and neither the Coast Guard nor the DEA has made even a modest seizure this month. Then just today I got a report from the DEA. They have an informant in Colombia who's an aircraft mechanic for the Cali cartel. He says they're running out of places to put the stuff down there, but nothing's moving. All their planes are fully serviced, cleaned, and tuned up, but they're just sitting on the end of the runway."

"Anybody have any information on when they're gonna start shipping again?" McKenna asked.

"Not as far as I know, but it has to be soon."

"Thanks, Chief. You've been a big help," McKenna said before he hung up. Unlike the chief, he didn't think it was funny. He thought it was scary. He looked back to Savraada and saw that the little man was staring intently at him.

"I'm sorry. Where were we?" McKenna asked Savraada.

"From the look of you and the sound of that conversation, we were sitting in the wheelhouse on the *Titanic*."

"We are. For Felipe to bring the Cali and Medellín drug cartels together, he had to promise them something big. No drugs are coming in right now, so I think that in exchange for financing he's gonna do something here that will immobilize or distract law enforcement all over this country so they'll be able to bring their stuff in without risk. He convinced the Colombians. They paid and they're waiting."

"Then we have a lot to think about. I'm really sorry about all this," Savraada said.

McKenna thought he detected something in Savraada's voice, but he wasn't sure what it was. It could have been sorrow, it could have been fear, but it just as easily could have been smug superiority prompted by Savraada's thinking: I told you that you had problems, stupid. McKenna figured it was time to give Savraada a left hook to see if he could really take a punch.

"How much would you give for a picture of Felipe right now, Colonel?"

"I've already given up the lives of three good agents trying to get one, and I still don't have it. But that's not too important right now because he's your problem. It seems to me you need his picture more than I ever did."

Not only could he take a left hook, he could counterpunch, and he was pretty accurate, McKenna thought. He reeled from the blow while Savraada looked at him straight-faced. Finally, Savraada had to say, "Well, you have something you want to tell me, Mr. McKenna?"

"Yes, and I would consider it an honor if you would call me Brian."

The impassive mask dropped and Savraada laughed, then reached over and gave McKenna a little shot in the arm. "Okay, tell me, Brian."

McKenna did and Savraada listened intently as he learned about the search warrants on Maximo, and McKenna's belief that Maximo would lead them to Elena, and hopefully the rest of the crew.

When McKenna finished his account, Savraada said, "I'm glad to see you haven't been sleeping on the job up here, Brian."

Coming from Savraada, McKenna decided it was the greatest compliment he had ever received.

Chapter 15

By the time Tavlin returned from Corona, McKenna and Savraada had cemented a working relationship based on mutual respect and trust. McKenna made the introductions and then asked Tavlin, "How'd the search go?"

"Perfect," he said, handing McKenna a stack of photographs.

The one on top was Felipe. It was very grainy and had obviously been taken from a distance with a telephoto lens. While Felipe's features were clear, the jungle background was fuzzy. Felipe was standing, wearing a camouflage uniform without insignia, and obviously talking to someone else who wasn't captured in the photo.

McKenna gave the photo to Savraada, who sat down and stared at it as McKenna examined the other photos. Ingrid Troutmann was there, posing in the middle of two *Sendero* soldiers, her arms relaxed on their shoulders. Elena was there as a redhead, looking gorgeous and oblivious to the camera as she studied a sheet of paper. There were photos of the film crew working on their equipment while drinking beer, and there was a group photo of a *Sendero* platoon, mugging it up and looking vicious with their weapons pointed at the camera. Most of the soldiers were very young.

There were also photos of a burned village with four dead government soldiers lying in the street and three photos that portrayed only scenic mountain vistas and looked like postcards.

McKenna handed them to Savraada, who went through them without comment.

"You get everything else done?" McKenna asked Tavlin.

"All the electronics are being installed right now. It shouldn't take too much longer."

"How'd Maximo behave?"

"What a character! He put on quite a show when we served the search warrant. Kicking and screaming with the whole neighborhood watching. That didn't bother us too much, but his wife was there and she's scary. We couldn't wait to get out of there."

"Face like a pan of worms?" McKenna asked.

"Exactly. And mean, too. I think if she ever catches Maximo in the wrong place, she'll torture him to death and enjoy it."

"Where's Maximo now?" McKenna asked.

"Home, tucked in bed with her, God bless him."

McKenna explained the new developments to Tavlin and the inspector had some suggestions. "We've got pictures of the people we're looking for, so we should get them out."

"But I don't want them going to the newspapers," McKenna said. "I don't want Felipe to see his picture in the papers and then take off."

"If they went to this much trouble already, they're not gonna be scared off by their picture in the paper," Tavlin reasoned. "We should have the pictures ready to go, just in case. And we should have some firepower ready in case Maximo leads the surveillance teams to them."

"All good ideas," McKenna said. "Anybody hungry? I haven't eaten since breakfast."

Neither had Tavlin or Savraada. Rosie O'Grady's was decided upon for a late steak dinner and McKenna's stomach was grumbling as they stopped at Wright's desk on the way out. "Camilia, we're going to dinner, but I have a few missions for you while we're gone, okay?" McKenna asked.

"Sure."

"I want three Emergency Service trucks with heavy weapons standing by in every borough with nothing to do but wait until we need them."

"Okay, I'll get it done, but it's going to be tough. The longshoremen went on strike at eight o'clock and the chief of patrol just ordered overtime for five hundred men a tour."

What is this? McKenna thought. A conspiracy? Then he

handed the photos of Felipe, Emilio, and Elena to her and said, "I need five hundred copies of each picture tonight."

"Yes, sir. What size?"

What size? All she can say is, "What size"? McKenna thought. Not "Are you out of your mind? Fifteen hundred copies? Tonight? Don't you know it's nine o'clock at night, you dummy"?

Instead, Wright sat patiently waiting, with McKenna secure in the knowledge that she was going to be making many people absolutely miserable who thought they had a good job in police headquarters.

"Make them five-by-sevens."

No reaction but "Yes, sir."

"Thank you, Camilia. We'll be back soon."

"Did you call the sheriff back yet?" she asked.

The sheriff? McKenna thought. I forgot all about it. "I'll call Andy at Mayberry when we get back," he told her and turned to join Savraada and Tavlin, both of whom were shuffling impatiently at the door.

"He said it was important, and I believed him," Wright said.

"I'm sure it can wait an hour."

"I think you should call him now," Wright said defiantly.

McKenna looked to Tavlin and Savraada and the two men shrugged. They followed McKenna back into his office and he found the sheriff's message slip on his desk. He dialed the number and the phone was answered on the fourth ring.

"You got the sheriff himself. Go on." The voice was deep with a heavy drawl.

"This is Commissioner McKenna in New York, Sheriff. I got a message that you wanted to talk to me."

"You got the wrong message, Commissioner. It should read that you want to talk to me. You're lucky, too. I was just set to head home, and then y'all would have to solve your own case."

McKenna took the phone from his ear and stared at it, then he smiled. Apparently superefficient Camilia Wright wasn't properly screening his calls. A bedbug had slipped through her mattress cover. He decided to continue the conversation to gather more evidence against her.

"I'm sorry, Sheriff. I didn't get your name."

"Sheriff Jefferson Davis Parker, son."

Jefferson Davis Parker? Perfect. Strike Two, Camilia. "And

what was it I wanted to talk to you about, Sheriff Parker?''

"Well, it's like this. We had three immigrant fellas slip the border yesterday morning and git themselves into a ruckus. I had to—''

"Excuse me, Sheriff. A ruckus? What might that be?'' Here comes your final pitch, Camilia, and the thought made McKenna smile. Get ready for the old ruckus pitch, baby.

"You figure it out. In this particular ruckus they killed a common low-life thievin' rascal and one of my deputies. Then they stole a car and killed a good, honest, God-fearing farm couple in the process. Shot them all dead. You gittin' any understanding out of all this?''

McKenna closed his eyes and swore he heard the crack of the bat followed by, *Ladies and gentlemen, that ball is going, going, going. . . .* But he was getting understanding. "Yes, Sheriff. I'm sorry. Please continue.''

"As I was sayin', I had to end one of them but the other two—''

"End one? You mean you killed him?''

"What language y'all speak up there, Commissioner? Of course I kilt him. But the other two desperadoes are currently reposin' as my guests. 'Course, they're not feelin' too good, but they can still talk. I come to find that they're jabbering away to each other in some Indian language. I figured they was Indians from Guatemala trying to pass themselves off as legitimate wetbacks, but I had some interest in their conversings, especially since they had three airplane tickets to New York on them when they ran afoul of me. You gettin' all this, son?''

Ladies and gentlemen, this is incredible. Our batter, Camilia Wright, playing for the headquarters home team, has just fired a shot off the head of that newcomer snot-nose pitcher, the visiting assistant commissioner. Bounced right off his head, I tell you. "I'm getting it, Sheriff. I'm getting it all. I have some other people here with me. Do you mind if I put you on the speakerphone?''

"Suit yourself.'' McKenna pressed the button and the three were treated to some local home-grown wisdom, which included a how-to-do-it course on police work.

"As I was sayin', they was jabbering away, understood only by themselves. So I slip a tape recorder under one of the beds and they fill it up for me, unbeknownst. Meanwhile, I read how you folks are having a few problems up there with some

Peruvians, so I have one of my boys run the tape over to the
university in San Antone. They got themselves a Professor
Witte over there who's the world's specialist in Indian languages. You know what we come to find out?''

McKenna had to close his eyes again as Tavlin and Savraada crowded around the speakerphone. ''That they're from
Peru?'' McKenna asked.

''Now you're hittin' on all eight, Commissioner. That's
right. Them boys is speakin' Quechua, which I'm told is peculiar to Peru.''

McKenna couldn't get it to stop. *Ladies and gentlemen, I
know you're not gonna believe this, but we just got a flash
over the wires. That ball sailed right out of the park and kept
going and landed right smack plumb dab in the middle of—*
''Where are you located, Sheriff?''

''Right now, I'm in Brackettville, Texas.''

Folks, it landed in downtown Brackettville, Texas. ''And
what is Brackettville near, Sheriff?''

''Why, it's just a holler away from Del Rio, Texas.''

''Please help me out on this, Sheriff. What is Del Rio
near?''

''Del Rio's not near anyplace. It just sets by itself.''

''Does Del Rio have an airport?''

''What do you think?''

''No?''

''Quit funnin', Commissioner. Of course we got an airport.''

''Sheriff, what time is it in Del Rio?''

''You mean now?''

No, later, McKenna thought. ''Yes, please. Now.''

''About eight o'clock.''

''Sheriff, we'll be there before midnight. Could you possibly have somebody waiting at the airport for us?''

''Don't see no need for that. Kyle Farnsworth lives right
near the airport and he wakes up every time a plane comes in.
He'll call me when you get close.''

''Whatever you say, Sheriff.''

''I think y'all gonna find that's the way it always is in Val
Verde County, Commissioner. It's whatever I say. See y'all
soon.''

The sheriff hung up and McKenna didn't waste any time
hanging out. He had learned the best way, maybe the only
way, to get impossible things done quickly and efficiently.

''Camilia!''

Chapter 16

Camilia made all the travel arrangements while McKenna called Angelita. She had been sleeping when he called, but was glad to hear from him and said she was feeling better.

"I have to go to Texas for a day or two," he told her.

"Just hurry up and finish this and let's go home," was all she replied.

She hadn't asked him how the case was going or what he was doing to solve it. She just expected he would finish it and they'd go home. Her confidence in him gave McKenna confidence.

"We'll be home before you know it, baby. Just get some sleep and take it easy."

He closed with love and kisses.

McKenna decided that Texas was going to be just himself and Savraada, with Tavlin left to mind the store. A police helicopter was waiting for them when Pao dropped them off at the East 34th Street Heliport. Half an hour later they were on a chartered Gulfstream jet, headed out of Teterboro Airport for San Antonio, Texas.

By the time they reached San Antonio, McKenna owed Savraada eighty-three dollars in gin rummy debts. He paid up and swore off the game forever, again. Camilia had chartered a Bell Ranger helicopter for the trip from San Antonio to Del Rio. They came up on it fast after a ride over dark countryside, and the place surprised McKenna.

Del Rio was a city. It wasn't big, it wasn't fancy, but it was still a city. McKenna figured that if a place had an airport, then it had to be a city.

Del Rio International Airport was a small private airport with two small runways, but McKenna had seen smaller that still called themselves *international* airports. But then he guessed that anyplace a plane could land near Del Rio was an international airport since Mexico was right across the river.

The pilot radioed the tower and was directed to Sheriff Parker's location. They saw the sheriff standing next to his car and holding on to his Stetson as the helicopter descended onto the landing pad. Unfortunately, the pilot took off again as soon as McKenna and Savraada were out, and McKenna found himself chasing his own hat around the landing pad while the sheriff watched him impassively. The hat blew Parker's way and he stopped it with his foot, picked it up, and held it out for McKenna.

"First time you ever been in a helicopter, son?" he asked.

"First time with a hat on. I'm Brian McKenna," McKenna said as he took his hat from the sheriff and put it on. "And this is Colonel Savraada. He's a policeman from Peru."

"Glad to meet you gentlemen," Parker said, holding out his hand. "Jefferson Davis Parker, but just call me Jeff. Everybody does around here."

Sheriff Parker could have won first prize in any *Looks Like the Sheriff* contest. About fifty years old and six foot four, he had to be fifty pounds overweight, but most of the extra poundage was stored in his hands and feet. He was carrying a small roll of fat around the middle, but his hands were the biggest McKenna had ever seen and he thought a herd of steers must have given their hides to make the sheriff's boots. With his Stetson low on his head, his crisp tan uniform with the gold star pinned on his chest, and the wide gunbelt around his waist that supported the .357 Magnum Colt with a six-inch barrel, there was no doubt in McKenna's mind that here stood the primary police official in this part of the country.

McKenna shook Parker's hand and braced himself for the squeeze, but it never came. Parker left his bones intact. The sheriff was a little harder on Savraada's small hand, but it was unintentional. Savraada grimaced, but took it without complaint.

"What you gentlemen want to do first?" Parker asked. "See the prisoners, maybe?"

"What else is there to do?" McKenna asked.

"You could come over to my place and Mrs. Parker will roast you up some ribs like you never tasted before. That's what I'd do, if I were you. Those boys will keep."

It sounded good to McKenna and he didn't want to be rude, but Savraada was all business. He had traveled thousands of miles on a mission and wasn't going to let his appetite slow him down. "I'm sorry, Jeff. But we're really in a hurry. Maybe later," Savraada said.

"You're making a mistake, but suit yourself. Git in."

Parker climbed behind the wheel, McKenna got in the passenger seat, and Savraada got in the back. McKenna was surprised to see that the front seat of Parker's car looked like a high-tech police equipment display. He had everything: shotgun, rifle, radar, video camera, Breathalyzer machine, phone, two radios, computer screen, keyboard, and printer. There wasn't any police gadget that McKenna had ever read about that wasn't right there in front of him.

"The citizens around here treat you pretty good, equipment-wise," McKenna observed.

"Why shouldn't they? I just tell them what I need to do the job and they give it to me. They know you gotta have the tools 'cause sometimes out here there's not another lawman for twenty miles. You on your own."

He's right, McKenna thought. One of the good things about working in New York City was that you were never really alone. In Manhattan, just yell 10-13 into your radio and you usually had ten cops to help out in under a minute. But still, McKenna couldn't imagine Parker ever needing help. Once you'd seen what he looked like, he could arrest you over the telephone and just tell you where to report to do your time.

Parker drove at a good clip and before long they were out of Del Rio, traveling along a straight, dark highway while Parker explained the circumstances surrounding the capture of his prisoners.

"Are you still recording their conversations?" Savraada asked.

"Not much. They don't seem to be talking much anymore. They wised up when they saw my deputy take the recorder out to put in a new tape. He thought they were sleepin', but they weren't."

"That's too bad," McKenna said. "But it doesn't make too much difference. It helped us, but I don't think you could use anything they say on tape against them in court."

Parker was surprised. "Why not?"

"Because they're in custody. You could record conversations between them and any visitors, but I think you'd need

an eavesdropping warrant to legally record conversations between them.''

The sheriff didn't seem impressed with McKenna's legal
expertise. ''So?''

''You mean you got a warrant?''

''Of course I did.''

''Wasn't that a lot of trouble on such short notice?''

''No trouble at all. If you're gonna do something, you might
as well do it right.''

There were some secrets to be had here, McKenna thought.
Getting a judge to sign a warrant that broke new legal ground
was almost impossible, since they all worried about looking
bad if the warrant should be controverted by a higher court.
Stretching it, conversations between two persons in custody
and arrested for the same crime might be considered privileged
communication. They could say that they planned to represent
themselves and were discussing their defense.

''I don't think I'd be able to get a judge to sign a warrant
like that in New York,'' McKenna said. ''How'd you do it?''

''Let me explain how it works around here, Commissioner.
Everybody's elected, including the judges. Now, I've been the
sheriff of Val Verde County for seventeen years and was reelected last November with eighty-nine percent of the vote.
Don't know who's in that other eleven percent 'cause everyone
I've ever talked to said they voted for me, some of them twice.
So, if I were to inform the citizens that one of their duly
elected judges was deviatin' in his duties and impeding the
flow of justice in Val Verde County, then come next election
time he'd be chasing ambulances and doing house closings,
and it wouldn't be around here.''

It can't be that easy, McKenna thought. ''It's that easy?''
he asked.

''Yep. I just write up the warrant and show 'em where to
sign. Don't take but a minute, so I get me warrants for everything.''

''Have the prisoners told you anything?'' Savraada asked.

''Not even their names, but one of them might talk yet. He's
real nervous, but the other one's a real hard-ass. I told them
we got them on video killin' my deputy and Texas is gonna
fry them unless they make a deal.''

''What kind of deal?'' asked McKenna.

''Now that's up to you, isn't it?'' Parker said. ''I don't need a thing from them, so you're the one who's gotta provide them with some incentive.''

What exactly can I offer them? McKenna wondered. I have no authority in Texas and nobody gave me a blank check. By myself, I couldn't help them beat a parking ticket down here.

Savraada must have read his mind. ''One of them will talk,'' he said confidently as the sheriff slowed down and turned into a low and modern prison compound, the Val Verde County Detention Center. If they had passed through Brackettville, McKenna hadn't noticed.

Parker pulled into a spot reserved for the sheriff, next to another police car. McKenna could see a lighted sign in the lobby of the building that pointed to the sheriff's office.

''They're in your office?'' McKenna asked.

''Sure. Got me a fine jail in there. Where'd you think they'd be?''

''From the injuries you described, I figured they'd be in a hospital.''

''Naw, wouldn't waste the taxpayers' money on that, what with guarding them and all. Anyway, they just got themselves some broken bones, nothing life-threatening. I have the doctor come over to visit them from time to time, but the pain in the ass is one of my deputies got to spoon-feed them.''

''Why's that?''

''You'll see,'' the sheriff said as they exited the car.

From what he had seen of the area, McKenna had expected a modest operation, but he was wrong. Any good-sized city would be proud to have Sheriff Parker's police station. They followed him into an enclosed reception area and a deputy behind a bulletproof glass window buzzed them into the main office. Inside, the duty officer sat behind a large desk with a police radio base set, a logbook, eight video monitors, and a computer in front of him. He was a sergeant and he saluted the sheriff as he walked in.

''Morning, Otis,'' Parker said. ''How they doin'?''

The sergeant checked the video monitors. ''One of them's sleepin' but it looks like the other one's wide awake.''

Parker went around the desk to sign into the logbook as McKenna looked around. There was a small glassed-in office behind the sergeant where a rather elderly civilian worker was typing at her PC while she was talking on the phone. Off the main office there were a series of closed doors leading to other rooms. They were marked LOCKER ROOM, COFFEE ROOM, AR-

MORY, PROPERTY ROOM, INTERROGATION ROOM, DETECTIVES, and SHERIFF JEFFERSON DAVIS PARKER. A heavy metal door at the far end of the main room was marked CELLS. The entire area was modern, spotlessly clean, and well lit by fluorescent lights.

Parker opened one of the desk drawers and took out a set of large brass cell keys. Then he took his pistol from his holster and handed it to the sergeant.

"Sorry, boys. Don't allow no guns in the cell area," he said to McKenna and Savraada.

Savraada was unarmed. McKenna took out his Glock and handed it to the sheriff, who looked contemptuously at the latest in police hardware before he handed it to the deputy. Then Savraada and McKenna followed Parker to the outside cell door and waited while he unlocked it.

There were six large barred cells along one wall, with a separate video camera mounted high on the passageway wall, each camera peering into the cell opposite. Each cell was clean and contained a sink and a commode, but there was one thing that couldn't be disguised by all the scrubbing, cleaning, and disinfectant that kept the place up to Parker's standards. To McKenna, it smelled like jail. He couldn't put his finger on it, but all jails shared a common smell, like being inside a giant sneaker. Some were worse than others, and this one wasn't bad, but it was still jail.

The first two cells were occupied by two men apiece, sleeping on beds complete with sheets and blankets. The next three cells were empty. The last contained the Peruvians.

Both men were in bed, and it looked like they had no choice. The man on the far wall was sleeping, but he moaned in his sleep. His left leg and left arm were in casts and his whole head and face were wrapped in bandages.

The other man was in a bed at the opposite end of the cell. He wore a turbanlike bandage on the top of his head, but his entire upper body was in an immobile cast that made him look as if he were frozen on a cross with both arms extended straight out from his sides. He was propped up on pillows and wide awake. He ignored two of the three visitors standing outside his cell. His gaze was fixed on Savraada, who returned his stare.

"*Buenos noches, soldado,*" Savraada said, and the man nodded, never taking his eyes off the colonel.

"Sheriff, I think I'd like to listen to those tapes now, if you don't mind,'' Savraada said, still staring at the prisoner.

"I'm told there's not much on them. Just chitchat. We got three tapes covering three hours, with maybe just an hour of conversings between them. They don't talk much.''

"We'll see.''

Savraada abruptly turned and walked to the cell-block entrance, followed by McKenna and the sheriff. Parker locked the cell-block door after them and they followed him into his large and comfortable, well-appointed office.

"I take it you and that prisoner know each other,'' McKenna said to Savraada.

"We've met. Pedro Cabrera is his name. He's a veteran *Sendero* soldier from Ayacucho. I interrogated him after he was wounded and captured about five years ago. I offered him everything I could, including his freedom, but he would give up nothing. Finally, he was sentenced to life in prison, but he was freed in an exchange of prisoners last year. *Sendero* gave us back one of our army majors for him, so I know they value him.''

"So we've got problems,'' McKenna said.

"More than you know. He's an expert on explosives.''

McKenna and Parker entertained each other for an hour, telling police war stories in the sheriff's office while Savraada listened to the tapes in the interrogation room. It wasn't long before McKenna had concluded that, while they might be in Mayberry, Sheriff Parker was no Andy and there wasn't a Barney in sight. Sometimes big things happen in small places, and he was thankful it was Parker who was there for the three Peruvians.

McKenna was glad when Savraada returned. He had run out of his own stories long before the sheriff did, but naturally that didn't stop him. He just told other cops' stories and substituted himself into the starring role. He suspected Parker was doing the same, because if he wasn't, then Tombstone wasn't the toughest town in the West. It was Brackettville.

"Learn anything?'' Parker asked Savraada.

"They were talking in a roundabout way, but I got some of it. My Quechua isn't as good as it should be.''

"Is it good news or bad?'' McKenna asked.

"Depends. Sheriff, which one of them is the one you think might talk?''

"The one who was sleepin'. He got hit in the face with some buckshot and he's in pain. Better than that, he seems to be scared."

"Well, then there's some hope. Pedro is not worried about being in your jail. He thinks that Felipe will free them. He's just worried that Felipe might be angry with them because they were supposed to be in New York today. But the man who's sleeping isn't sure. He thinks they should offer some information to make a deal with your government."

"Who the hell they think this Felipe is that he can break them out of my jail?" Parker wanted to know.

"He's not gonna break them out, Jeff," McKenna said. "Felipe must be planning something so big that the government will release them in exchange for something."

"Doesn't that dope know the U.S. government doesn't bargain with terrorists?" Parker asked.

"He knows that," McKenna said. "It's my guess that whatever he's planning is big enough to change that. This country's never been put to the test."

Parker scoffed at that. "I can't imagine the U.S. government—"

He was interrupted by the sound of the sergeant outside shouting. "Sheriff! Come quick! Sheriff!"

The three men ran outside to the sergeant's desk.

"He's killing him!" the sergeant shouted, pointing to a monitor. They all looked to see Pedro in black and white with his mouth on the throat of his fellow prisoner while the other man struggled to release himself, pounding Pedro's cast with his own as he lay in bed with Pedro on top of him like a cross lying on his body.

"Goddamn it," Parker exclaimed. He had left the cell keys on his desk and ran back to get them.

By the time they got to the cell, Pedro was back in bed, again sitting propped up on his pillows, but with blood dripping from his mouth onto his body cast. He spit out a piece of his partner's neck and smiled at Savraada as the sheriff opened the cell door.

The other man was dead and his body twitched as blood flowed from his ripped neck onto the sheets. There were pieces of muscle, tissue, and skin on the floor next to the bed, and a trail of blood led to Pedro's bed. As they gazed into the eyes of the dead man, behind them Pedro said, "*Ahora mismo, yo soy el unico que pueda hablar con tigo, Colonel.*"

"What did he say?" Parker asked.

McKenna and Savraada turned and stared at Pedro in re-vulsion and amazement.

"He said that now he's the only one who can talk to me, Sheriff." Savraada answered. "Please bring him to someplace where myself and Pedro can talk, alone and uninterrupted."

Parker didn't like that. "I don't stand for beatin' no pris-oners," he protested.

"Neither do I," Savraada said calmly as he returned Pedro's glare. "And unfortunately he knows it."

Chapter 17 "Jeff, these boys are sure boosting the mortality rate around here. This keeps up, I'm gonna need your help to get me a raise."

That was all the taciturn county coroner had to say for the record before the body was removed to the county morgue. After he left, Parker had Pedro's bed brought to the interro-gation room, with Pedro still lying in it. As requested, Sa-vraada and Pedro were left alone in the room.

McKenna and Parker were on their third cup of coffee apiece when Savraada returned to the sheriff's office. "I need a major Spanish-language newspaper."

"Yesterday's or today's?" Parker asked.

"It makes no difference, as long as the bombing and the reward are mentioned."

"Yesterday's would be better," McKenna said. "Today's won't be out yet, but I'm sure we don't need him to know the reward is up to one million three."

"As I said, it makes no difference," Savraada said. "I never lie when I'm trying to get information or make a deal. I'll tell him the truth. I just want the paper as confirmation."

Unusual questioning technique, McKenna thought. Not lie to him? What kind of police work is that?

"I got a deputy reads the Spanish paper from San Antone,"

Parker said. "I'll send him home to git it."

"How are you doing with him?" McKenna asked Savraada.

"Good, I think."

"I don't get it," Parker said. "If he wanted to talk and make a deal, then why did he kill his buddy and give himself another murder count?"

"I've seen it before," Savraada answered. "When he saw me, he knew that *Sendero* must have done something big here and you knew that he and his partner were Senderistas. He also figured there would be a sizable reward for information, a much larger reward than we could possibly offer in Peru, and he knew his partner was ready to talk. The rest is easy to figure out."

Easy? McKenna thought. Let me see how easy it is. A reward divided by one is always much better than a reward divided by two, if Pedro were to get a shot at it. If his pal were around, maybe he wouldn't. He knew his partner was going to talk anyway, so we were going to get some information and someone's situation was going to improve, and it wouldn't be his. They were already just about convicted of murder in Texas, which meant that life had taken a real bad turn. He also knew that part of any deal his partner made would have to include testifying against him in the state trial, which meant the death penalty. So one more murder wouldn't make any difference if he was the only one with the information we need. We'd have to deal with him if he was the only one left. Easy.

Dawn was breaking when Savraada came back for the second time. He looked haggard, but confident.

"Where do we stand?" McKenna asked.

"It depends on how much clout you've got."

"I've got none, but maybe I can get some. Let's have it."

"He'll plead guilty to one murder or six, it makes no difference to him. And he'll do it today, as long as he doesn't have to do more than five years in jail."

"That's easy," Parker said. "I can guarantee that one myself. Texas will execute him long before then."

"I'll call Gene Shields," McKenna said. "I imagine the attorney general will have to work it out with the Texas governor. It's just politics and trading favors, but whatever sentence he gets, the governor can commute it to five years."

"Only if he doesn't plan to run for reelection," Parker interjected.

"Why's that?" McKenna asked. "If the information's good enough and we do the right thing with it, he might wind up looking like a political hero."

Parker was skeptical. "Saving Yankees some trouble in New York doesn't exactly make for heroes in Texas."

"Okay. We'll work on it," McKenna said, trying to sound optimistic. "What else?"

"He wants three hundred thousand of the reward," Savraada said.

"I should be able to pull that off, depending on what he can give us. What else?"

"The last is the hardest part, and I have to do it. He wants his wife and two children here before he'll talk. He knows that *Sendero* will kill them if he does and they're still in Peru."

"We still need the feds for that," McKenna said. "I'm sure he doesn't want them here as illegal aliens."

"No, but I'm assuming you can take care of that. Naturally, Pedro and his family have to be given legal status here. The hard part is that his family lives in Ayacucho."

McKenna knew what that meant, but Parker didn't get it. "So?" the sheriff asked. "What's so hard about that?"

"Ayacucho is the heart of *Sendero* territory and I'm sure they're being watched," Savraada explained. "I'm going to lose some men getting them out of there, and still I might not be successful. It would have to be a major military operation."

"Are you sure his information will be worth that?" McKenna asked.

"You be the judge of that. The only thing he told me was that an entire *Sendero* company was formed to train for their operation here. He said he didn't know the final objectives, but the type of training they received will give us some clues. Add to that the fact that he knows the people involved, and we should have a good starting point if we plan to stop them."

"How many people in a *Sendero* company?" McKenna asked.

"Eighty, more or less."

Eighty? McKenna thought. That's a lot of bad guys to deal with. Of course, they're down five that we know of. The bomber, the one Dennis shot, and the three here. And we have to figure that they all didn't get to New York as planned if these two didn't. Let's be optimistic and say fifty. Fifty? Still a lot to handle.

Savraada interrupted McKenna's thinking. "I have a way that this should be presented to the federal authorities that should get them right behind you," he said. "What do you call it when a military unit from one country travels three thousand miles to accomplish an objective in another country?"

"An invasion?" McKenna asked, not liking the way it sounded as he said it.

"Exactly. Tell them that. A Peruvian military unit has invaded the United States of America."

"You're right," Parker said. "It's a lot like Pancho Villa. He was a rebel too, but we still treated it like an invasion from Mexico and sent troops down there."

"I'm sure my government will see the analogy," Savraada said. "And yours will, too."

"Looks like we're gonna be waking up some politicians," McKenna said, smiling, as he reached for the phone on Parker's desk.

In the next couple of hours it got bigger faster than McKenna had ever imagined was possible. The President became directly involved, and by 9:00 A.M. both the mayor of the City of New York and the Peruvian ambassador to the United States were not exactly enjoying themselves in the Oval Office while they awaited the arrival of the governor of Texas.

By 10:00 A.M. McKenna was not exactly enjoying himself either. Mrs. Parker had come by the office, bearing a load of Texas chili and a rack of ribs. She looked like she could have been the sheriff's twin sister, which might make her the ugliest woman in Texas. But Savraada and the sheriff didn't seem to notice. The food was great.

The chili was the hottest McKenna had ever tasted, but still very good. The ribs had been expertly barbecued and needed nothing else, in his opinion. But Mrs. Parker had brought her own very special hot sauce. Savraada and the sheriff couldn't get enough of it and sloshed every rib around in the bowl.

"You'll really have to write down the recipe for this sauce for me," Savraada told Mrs. Parker, who absolutely preened.

"Sorry, that's not possible," the sheriff told him. "Mrs. Parker's special barbecue sauce is a Texas state secret and it's not covered by the NAFTA agreement.''

Then the sheriff noticed that McKenna thought his ribs were good enough without Mrs. Parker's sauce and he pushed the bowl over to him.

"You really should try it," Parker recommended. "It'll wake you up a bit."

Why not? McKenna thought. Angelita is a great Mexican cook and I can take anything she can dish out. How bad can it be?

McKenna rolled his next rib around in the sauce and took a bite. He instantly became aware that he wasn't the toughest guy in the room. Even Mrs. Parker was tougher than he was, but he already knew that.

The mayor called the sheriff's office at ten-thirty, but McKenna was indisposed in the men's room and it was ten-forty before he could get to the phone. In the interim, the governor had talked to Parker and the ambassador had spoken with Savraada.

"Commissioner, where have you been?" the mayor wanted to know.

"Sorry, Your Honor. I seem to have developed a little gastrointestinal problem."

"Well, you better get over it in a hurry," the mayor admonished. "You are instructed to do whatever you think is necessary to end our problem in New York."

The blank check? No such thing from a politician, McKenna knew. I make one big mistake and they'll run for cover and deny they ever knew me.

"Can I get that in writing?" McKenna asked, hopefully.

"Don't be ridiculous. We'd also like you to keep this on a local level as much as possible and limit the involvement of the federal authorities. Do you understand?"

Sure I understand, McKenna thought. I'm to be the only sacrifice if it goes wrong, but you'll all be around to receive the accolades if it goes right. But I guess that's the way it's gotta be. "Yes, sir. I understand completely."

"Good. Get back here as soon as you can. The colonel will be going to Peru for a day or two. When he returns here, we hope to complete arrangements to transfer custody of the prisoner to you in New York."

"Yes, sir."

The mayor hung up and the phone rang again. McKenna picked it up.

"You sure are a hard guy to track down."

"Sal?" McKenna asked. "How did you find me here?"

"Your secretary gave me the number. Try and guess where I am?"

A tough one, McKenna thought. When Sal Catalfumo was still on the Job, all the chiefs spent a lot of time guessing where Sal really was while he was doing his version of police work, and they never got it right.

Then McKenna got some help. Through the phone he heard a long, low, distant wail. After a moment, he recognized the sound. It was a train horn.

"That's an easy one. You're standing on some railroad tracks in Macon, Georgia, looking at Alejandro's warehouse. Where else could you be?"

"Damn, Brian! I'm glad you were never a boss while I was still on the Job."

"It was just a lucky guess. How's it look there?"

"I guess you wanna know what's inside?"

"Yeah, but I still can't get a warrant."

"I'm assuming you're gonna do it anyway," Sal said.

Nothing's ever easy, McKenna thought. Shields told me he'd handle this part, but he'd be risking everything: his job, his reputation, and his pension. On the other hand, I'm in sort of a temporary political job, don't have much to lose in the way of a sanctimonious reputation, and I'm already retired from the NYPD, which means I'd keep getting my pension in jail if everything went real wrong. Looks like I'm about to advance my criminal career. "Yeah, I'm gonna do it anyway," he said.

"Then I'll give you a hand, but we're gonna need some more help. The place is alarmed and there's an armed guard."

"I'll call Gaspar and ask him to help."

"Perfect choice, and he'll be glad to do it," Sal said confidently.

Sal's right, McKenna thought. I could never order Gaspar to help commit a burglary, but just like Sal he'll take the risk and do it because it has to be done.

McKenna ended his musings on the motivations of his accomplices. "Find out anything else on Alejandro?"

"Lots. Alejandro has spent the month liquidating. His employees don't know it, but he's already sold his shipping business and his house is for sale, cheap. Looks like the only thing not for sale is this warehouse.''

"How about his finances?"

"He must be doing okay because he had the funds from the sale of his business transferred to an offshore account in the Bahamas, and that takes at least ten million. They're not in our computer network, but the good news is that we've got a contact there.''

McKenna felt it coming. "What's the bad news?"

"We'll have to spread some cash around if you want to find out how much he's got. If we do, the ten-grand figure we gave you is no longer good.''

Take it like a man, McKenna told himself. "I see. Is there anything else?"

"Maybe good news, maybe bad. You tell me. Last Saturday Alejandro made a mistake. He used his American Express card to call his folks in Miami.''

Saturday? McKenna thought. That's right after he left Macon, so he's probably still alive. "I guess you don't know what he told them?"

"What do you want, miracles? The important thing is where he called from, right?"

"Right. From where?"

"From thirty-five thousand feet over where you're sitting right now. He used his American Express card to call from the plane, American Airlines Flight 107 from New York to Lima, Peru.''

Good news or bad? McKenna wondered. He didn't know. "Can you meet me at the Macon airport in five hours?" he asked Catalfumo.

"See you then.''

McKenna hung up and told Parker and Savraada the information he had just received. "What do you think, good or bad?" he asked Savraada.

"Both," Savraada answered after giving the matter some thought. "If he's still in Peru, I'll get my hands on him. But we have to consider why he went there. He must know that after *Sendero* pulls whatever they're planning, the United States would be too hot for him.''

"He might have thought that before this," McKenna said. "Don't forget, he's been having some security problems. But why Peru? If he made a lot off this deal, he could always find someplace more pleasant.''

"But not as safe. He must think that *Sendero* is going to win. He must think that, before long, *Sendero Luminoso* will *be* the government in Peru."

That gave them something to think about.

Chapter 18 JULY 25, MACON, GEORGIA—At four

o'clock Catalfumo was standing on the tarmac next to a rented van as McKenna's chartered Gulfstream jet taxied in. Ten minutes later they were both sitting in a restaurant in the main terminal, waiting for Pedro Gaspar's flight to arrive from New York. During dinner, neither man mentioned a thing about the impending burglary. That happened over coffee when McKenna asked, "How's it look?"

"Easy, if it weren't for the guard. The alarm is a Remex connected to four flashing red lights and klaxons mounted on the outside of the warehouse. Since they have a guard inside, they won't be using motion detectors. Just the doors and windows will be protected."

"How about the phones?"

"Just one line into the building. The Remex alarm has a power-interruption feature, which means a signal is sent through the phone lines every five seconds that checks the building power and the phone line. So if the power goes out or the phone lines are cut, a signal is sent to the alarm response company, and I imagine also to the police."

"I assume Gaspar's bringing all the equipment we'll need to handle that," McKenna said. "Can you tell me how you found this place?"

Catalfumo smiled. "So you want to look up the magician's sleeve?"

"Just this once, and only because people are going to ask me. I can't look stupid, you know."

"Okay, Brian, just this once. It wasn't that hard, so the bill won't kill you. We found out the only company that Alejandro owned was his shipping company, and this warehouse isn't theirs. Then we started looking at his father's businesses. Found out he's listed as the president of a company called Pemco, a business that does no business. They write only five checks a month, month after month: the alarm company, the guard company, the power company, the phone company, and the real estate management company. Talked to the real estate company and found out Pemco's had the warehouse since 1985.''

"So Alejandro's got his father fronting for him?''

"That's what I figured. Just to be sure, I decided to come down here and take a look.''

"You could have just given me the location,'' McKenna said. "I think you came down here because you were bored and figured that maybe I'd need some help on this one.''

"Well, I *was* bored. Maybe I was hoping you'd need some help.''

This is one solid guy, McKenna thought as he watched his friend pretend there was nothing to it. "Thanks, Sal. I do need some help.''

Pedro Gaspar was assigned to TARU, the detective bureau's Technical Assistance Response Unit. He was a thin, dark man with an easy smile and had a lot of luggage for a one-day stay. McKenna and Catalfumo treated him like royalty, carrying his four heavy suitcases into the van.

The drive to the warehouse took twenty minutes, and Catalfumo parked across the street from it. The fenced-in building stood among a row of other small warehouses that backed onto the railroad tracks. There was a loading dock in the back next to a fenced-in railroad siding, another on the side for trucks, and a small parking lot in front.

Two things about the building attracted Gaspar's attention. One was the power and telephone lines running to a corner of the building from the same utility pole in the street, and the other was the roll-down-type steel loading-bay doors.

"How long you expect to be in there?'' Gaspar asked.

"Half hour, tops,'' McKenna answered. "I'm hoping there's something left in there.''

"There has to be,'' Catalfumo said. "Otherwise, he'd have discontinued the guard service and probably have gotten rid of this place.''

As they were talking, they saw a marked car from the guard company stop at the front gate. A uniformed supervisor got out of the car, opened the lock on the gate, and drove up to the front entrance. He knocked on the door and waited.

"That's good," McKenna said. "I don't think the guard inside has a radio or the boss would've just radioed him to open the door."

"I'll be able to make sure of that," Gaspar said. "And in case he does have one, I'm gonna jam his frequency when you go in."

A uniformed guard opened the door for the supervisor. He was in his fifties and had a pistol on his belt. The supervisor went in and was out again in ten minutes.

"We seen enough?" McKenna asked.

"It's all I need," Gaspar said. "What time you want to do it?"

"About four in the morning. Let's get a hotel and get some sleep."

Gaspar woke McKenna at three o'clock. "It's a good time to go," he said. "The supervisor just checked the guy working the late tour at the warehouse, so he shouldn't be getting any more company except us."

"How long were you there?"

"Since one. There's been no radio transmissions from inside. How about we do the equipment check in our room in ten minutes?"

Gaspar and Catalfumo had the equipment spread on the bed by the time McKenna walked into their room. There was a dart rifle with a scope mounted, a dart pistol, bolt cutters, two pairs of night-vision goggles, latex gloves, a police scanner, three portable radios with headsets, an electrician's toolbox, a tent, and a black box housing an electronic device that McKenna didn't recognize.

"I'm ready to learn," McKenna said.

Gaspar was ready to teach. He held up the black box. There were four wires running from the box that terminated in alligator clips. "This is the only piece of magic we need," he said. "I just have to climb the pole and splice it into the power line and the phone line. Then we simply cut the power and the phone to the building. The alarm will be out, but this little box will be lying to the alarm-response company every five seconds, telling them the building still has power, the phone is okay, and everything's secure.''

McKenna picked up the dart rifle. "I guess when the power goes off inside, the guard should come out to see what's wrong.''

"Hopefully. The rifle has an effective range of fifty yards and the tranquilizer dart will knock him out in about five seconds.''

"Five seconds?" Catalfumo asked. "He might be able to get a few shots off.''

"Yeah, but his aim will be terrible," Gaspar answered. "If the guard comes out, the rest is easy and you'll just go in the front door. If not, I've got an acetylene torch in the van. You'll have to cut in the loading dock door and go in and get him with the dart pistols.''

"We're gonna be vulnerable when we're cutting the door," McKenna said. "He's gonna see the sparks from the inside.''

"I know, but once you're in you've got the advantage," Gaspar explained. "You've got the night-vision goggles and he'll just have his flashlight.''

"You know, a lot could go wrong with this plan," Catalfumo said. "The police could stumble on us or this guard may be a Wyatt Earp. But unfortunately I don't have a better one.''

"Then let's get it over with," McKenna said.

McKenna checked the three out of the hotel while Catalfumo and Gaspar loaded the van. Catalfumo drove them to the warehouse and parked next to the utility pole. The parking lot was well lit and there was a light on inside the warehouse, near the front. Gaspar put on a tool belt and hung his black box from it. Then he attached pole-climbing spikes to his legs, put on his radio headset, and climbed the pole. McKenna got the dart rifle ready and served as the lookout as he lined up the front door of the warehouse. Catalfumo monitored the police scanner from inside the van, with the motor running.

Five minutes later the lights went out and Gaspar clambered down the pole. "He should be out in a minute or so," he said.

McKenna kept the crosshairs on the front door for five minutes. Nothing. Catalfumo opened the side door of the van and took out the torch kit, a pair of fireproof gloves, and a portable tent. "Looks like it's gonna be Plan B," he said.

"Okay," McKenna said to Gaspar. "Once we're in, take off. I'll call you when we're ready to leave, but keep your ear to that scanner.''

McKenna put the dart pistol in his belt, and both he and Catalfumo put on their radio headsets and latex gloves. They carried the torch, the tent, the bolt cutters, and their night-vision goggles to the side loading dock after McKenna cut the lock on the front gate.

Catalfumo snapped the tent in place next to the steel roll-up door. McKenna got in, put on the fireproof gloves, and lit the torch. As quickly as he could, he cut a two-foot-by-four-foot hole in the door, nerves tensed as he waited for the shots from inside. As he finished, he caught the cut steel rectangle and gently lowered it to the ground before turning off the torch.

The van took off. "Good luck, guys," sounded in Mc-Kenna's headset.

McKenna pushed the tent to the side and collapsed it. He and Catalfumo put on their night-vision goggles and the world turned light green. McKenna took out his dart pistol and peered around the edge of his new door into the warehouse. The building was empty except for one large cargo container. There was no guard in sight and no place for him to hide in the main part of the warehouse.

With Catalfumo following, he entered the warehouse and headed for the offices at the front of the building. McKenna put his ear to the office door and heard the sound of heavy rhythmic breathing. The guard was sleeping through their visit.

McKenna slowly opened the office door. The guard was sprawled on a couch, his head propped up on a telephone book. He had a large flashlight at his side and a windup alarm clock next to his head.

McKenna shot him in the side, and the guard snapped up, looking around in the dark room. He felt the dart in his side and put his hand on it before he fell back onto the couch. He twitched a little, eyes open, before his rhythmic breathing resumed.

McKenna closed the guard's eyes and pulled the dart from his side. Catalfumo followed him into the warehouse and snapped the lock on the large metal cargo container. They opened the doors and went in.

The front part of the container was empty, but the rear held thirty wooden boxes of M-16 rifles, six to a box. Perched on top of the rifle boxes were two long wooden boxes marked with an FSN stock number that McKenna recognized from Tavlin's list. "Two Stinger missiles," he said. "This must be

Alejandro's retirement policy, just in case anything goes wrong.''

"What do you want to do with them?" Catalfumo asked.

"We're gonna open them up and leave them here."

They carried the two boxes to the warehouse floor and popped the covers on the boxes. The Stingers were inside, looking long, deadly, and ugly.

McKenna looked around the warehouse, then focused on the floor on one side of the cargo container. The floor was cleaner on that side and he could see the outline marked in the dust and grime where another two containers had been. "There were three of these containers here not too long ago," he observed.

"Now you just have to find out what was in them."

"We will. Alejandro's gonna tell us. Wanna do something nice for the guard before we go?"

Catalfumo understood at once. "Yeah, let's do it."

They went back to the office and carried the guard to the loading-dock door, gently placed him on the ground, face-down, then took his gun out of his holster and put it in his hand.

They stepped back and admired their handiwork. "Do you think he'll rise to the starring role we're giving him?" Catalfumo asked.

"I think so. It sure sounds better than 'I was taking a nap and I don't know what happened.' "

McKenna pushed the transmit button on his radio. "C'mon back for us," he said.

"Two minutes," Gaspar answered.

As they were carrying their equipment out, Gaspar pulled up. He climbed the utility pole and yanked off the black box as McKenna and Catalfumo loaded the van.

Ten minutes later they were halfway to the airport when the police call reporting a burglary in the warehouse sounded over their scanner.

Chapter 19
JULY 26, NEW YORK CITY—Pao picked them up at the East 34th Street Heliport at 8:00 A.M. He dropped Catalfumo at his office, then McKenna and Gaspar at the hotel. Cisco stood in the lobby and Morgan was up in the room watching CNN.

The burglary in Macon was already news. Thieves had broken into a warehouse and were in the process of stealing a large cache of weapons, including two Stinger antiaircraft missiles that had recently been reported stolen from the Marine Corps Ordnance Depot in Albany, Georgia, when they were discovered by an alert guard. A struggle ensued, and the guard was knocked out by the thieves before the alarm sounded and the thieves escaped. The FBI was endeavoring to locate the owners of the warehouse for questioning.

McKenna showered, shaved, changed into a fresh suit and, by nine o'clock, he and Gaspar were on their way to police headquarters. Pao brought Gaspar to his car in the garage and McKenna took the elevator to the fourteenth floor, reporting directly to Brunette's office. Gene Shields was also there, on the phone.

Brunette looked fresh, but Shields needed some sleep.

"I hear you've been busy," Brunette said.

"Yeah, traveling first class and putting on the frequent-flyer miles."

"How's our situation look?"

"It all depends on what happens in Peru."

"Then we'll know tonight. Your colonel found Alejandro de Leon living in luxury in a suite at the Lima Hilton. As soon as we get him indicted here, he's gonna grab him."

"When will that be?"

Shields hung up the phone. "Soon," he said. "The guards

at the warehouse got to see a picture of Alejandro and have identified him as the man who ran the warehouse. They had only seen him twice before and the last time was July 16th. He showed up with a driver in a tractor trailer and they loaded two cargo containers into it."

"Any way to identify the truck?"

"No. The guard who was there that day wasn't the sharpest knife in the drawer. All he can remember is that it was a blue tractor."

"You gonna get his father indicted, too?" McKenna asked.

"Might as well," Shields said. "It'll give us some leverage on Alejandro. I have the guards testifying in the federal grand jury right now, so Savraada will have his warrants and an extradition request sometime this morning."

"Do we know anything about what's going on in Ayacucho?" McKenna asked.

"At two A.M. Savraada's going in with an army battalion and two companies of his national police," Brunette said. "Security is a problem for him and only the army commanders know about it now. They hope to be out with Pedro's family by dawn tomorrow, if everything goes as planned."

"Did he give any indication how he feels about it?"

"Better, now," Brunette said. "A naval task force including the *Tarawa* will be off the coast of Peru by eight tonight. The marines are busy painting a squadron of helicopters with new colors for transfer to the Peruvian army. They're gassed up, loaded with ammo, and ready to go."

An unusual way to give military aid, McKenna thought. Congress is not gonna like that if there's a screwup. "Does their army have the pilots?" he asked.

"Plenty of pilots, not enough helicopters. They'll be on-board by six for some orientation and training. Meanwhile, I'm having some manpower problems of my own."

"The longshoremen's strike?"

"Yeah, they're getting a little crazy, as usual. Everyone's on overtime and everyone wants the days off to go to the funerals. I've got two funerals today and two tomorrow, so I put O'Shaughnessy in charge of the manpower requirements. He doesn't mind denying the day-off requests and I think by tomorrow I might have to supply him with a bodyguard. If this strike goes another week, I'm gonna be over our budget for the year by November first."

"Did I get all my manpower requests?"

"Everything you wanted."

"When's Keller's funeral?" McKenna asked.

"Eleven tomorrow morning, but don't think about going. Both myself and the mayor are going to all of them and the security arrangements are a nightmare. Don't add to the problems."

I'm gonna miss Keller's funeral after he saved my life? McKenna thought. I don't think so, Ray.

But instead he asked, "How is the Maximo thing going?"

"Nothing going on with Elena, but Maximo's *Sendero* contact called him yesterday from a phone booth in Brighton Beach," Brunette said. "The conversation only lasted four minutes and by the time we got somebody there, he was gone."

"Brighton Beach? That's all Russians now. What would he be doing there?"

"Lord only knows, but Brighton Beach has got a little bit of everything. It just looks all Russian because they own so much real estate there and they put a sign in Russian on everything they own."

"What did the contact talk about?"

"Just the bombing. He said it wasn't *Sendero* because if it were, we'd all be dead."

McKenna felt a tingle of self-satisfaction. "So we did embarrass them. What did Maximo say to that?"

"He called them on it and got a little cranky. He's really mad about Ingrid Troutmann. The contact wound up hanging up on him, but the next time he calls from that area, if he does, we'll be ready. We rented an apartment overlooking the phone booth and I've got Hardcass living there with a team."

Living with Lieutenant Hardcass? McKenna imagined. That's like living with your drill instructor. "They must be a pretty unhappy team."

Brunette laughed. "They don't have time to think about it. I hear Hardcass already has them shining and cleaning. He says if they stay there a week, he's gonna have them paint the place."

"They won't be there a week," McKenna said. "I don't think *Sendero*'s gonna give us that much time."

"Ray, we gotta get out of here," Shields said, checking his watch. "First funeral is ten-thirty."

Brunette looked at his watch and headed for his door. "Go hide someplace and keep thinking," he told McKenna on the way out. "I'll be back tonight sometime."

Think about what? McKenna wondered. Nothing came to

mind, so he walked down the hall to his own office.

Camilia was there, surrounded by flowers. McKenna had sent them from Del Rio and Macon, but she looked unhappy.

"What's happening?" he asked her and braced himself.

"Thanks for the flowers, but I've got nothing to do."

"Me neither," McKenna said as he walked into his office. She's got nothing to do and it's bothering her, McKenna thought. I've got nothing to do and it feels great.

He made himself a cup of coffee and reread the case folders for a few hours, looking for ideas. He found none, and didn't feel good about it. Needing a boost, he called Angelita. She was up and sounding chipper. For the first time, he explained the problems with the case to her. She listened intently and asked a few questions. In the end she agreed with him. *Sendero* was up to something big and he would have to think of a way to head them off.

"By the way, was that you in Georgia this morning?" she asked as he was getting ready to hang up.

How could she know about that while she's sitting in a hospital in New York? McKenna wondered. "What makes you ask?"

"Joe Sofia's wife called this morning. She got a call from Gaspar's wife. Seems he got a call from you yesterday and he ran out of the house. He didn't get home until this morning and she found a boarding pass in his pocket. He's taking the Fifth, but then she saw the news."

"I'm taking the Fifth, too. We'll talk about it when we get home."

"Have any idea when that'll be?"

"Soon, I hope."

"Me too."

God, there are no secrets in this job, McKenna thought after he hung up. He was trying to decide where to go for a late breakfast when Tavlin called and snapped the boredom. "Elena just called Maximo on his office phone," Tavlin said. "He came out of his office with a beach bag and told the protection team that he wouldn't need them for the rest of the day. He's on his way to meet her at the Petrograd Restaurant, Brighton 4th Street and the boardwalk."

Brighton Beach again? McKenna thought. What can that have to do with anything? "Where did she call from?" he asked.

"No signature on the PENS register. It had to be a mobile phone."

"Where is Maximo now?"

"Driving on Roosevelt Avenue approaching the Grand Central Parkway. It's gonna take him about forty-five minutes to get there. We got three teams behind him, but staying back. They tell me they're getting a good signal from Maximo's car."

"What kind of car's he got?" McKenna asked.

"Easy to follow. It's a new red Toyota minivan."

What else is there to do but get there? McKenna thought. Only one thing came to mind. "Have Hardcass check out the restaurant and set his team up there," he told Tavlin. He regretted it immediately.

"I already did that," Tavlin stated matter-of-factly. But to McKenna it sounded like: "Listen kid, this is what I've been doing for a living while you were hiding out in Florida trying to take some strokes off your game."

"Of course. I'm sorry, Inspector. That slipped out and I should have known better. Anything else I should know?"

"No offense taken, Brian," Tavlin said, sounding sincere. "I have two Emergency Service trucks going to Ocean Parkway and the boardwalk and one to Brighton 8th and the boardwalk. They'll be out of sight, but close enough if we need them. There'll also be a helicopter up one mile offshore in ten minutes. Did I miss anything?"

Do you ever? McKenna thought. "I can be there in half an hour," he said before hanging up. Next he called Pao in the garage and told him to get another car and a radio.

"What's wrong with the one we've got?" Pao asked.

"Too conspicuous. Our high-flying days are over," McKenna said. "Be down in two minutes."

Pao wasn't happy. "Two minutes? You want another car in two minutes?"

"I have faith in you, Johnny. Do your best."

Pao was parked at the elevator door when McKenna got out. He was seated behind the wheel of a four-door battered Plymouth that looked like it should have been retired from service sometime in the last decade. McKenna climbed in and Pao took off up the garage ramp.

"Where to?" Pao asked.

"Brighton Beach, as quick as you can get us there in one piece."

"Music to my ears," Pao said as he placed the red light on the roof and turned on the siren. "Hold on."

McKenna did. As the G-forces mounted up, he found himself searching for his seat belt, figuring that he needed it more than any astronaut ever did. He felt better once it was on. "Is this the best car you could get?" he asked, only because he felt the need to say something to show Pao how relaxed he was.

"Best deal I could make in two minutes," Pao said as he headed onto the Brooklyn Bridge, against the light, against the sign and, it seemed to McKenna, against their mutual self-preservation instincts. But Pao made it. For once in New York, all vehicular obstacles heeded the siren and pulled to the side and out of the way as Pao took the middle lane to Brooklyn, making good time.

Then McKenna did relax. "What happened to our old new car?" he asked.

"I traded it to two guys I know from the Two-Eight Squad, on your orders. They said they were sure glad they had to come to headquarters today."

Oh no, McKenna thought. How am I going to explain why a new city limousine is now assigned to two detectives from Harlem? And why does Johnny look so happy? "Did they at least throw in a radio?" McKenna asked.

Pao reached under the seat and pulled out two portable radios. "Are you kidding?" he asked. "One of them was willing to throw in his firstborn to get that car. Besides, they don't need radios. Your car had a phone."

That's right, McKenna thought. Maybe I can talk them out of this. He took out his mobile phone and dialed his old new car, but knew it was no use when he got a busy signal. He suspected two Harlem detectives were calling their wives and friends to inform them of their phone number in their new fashionable location.

Chapter 20

Brighton Beach is New York City's Little Russia and has been since Russian immigration to the United States started in the late seventies. It is a small neighborhood by Brooklyn standards, tucked into the stretch of beachfront between Coney Island and Manhattan Beach. Primarily residential in character, two-family homes and six-story apartment buildings line the narrow streets running from Ocean Parkway to Brighton 15th Street along the Atlantic Ocean. Cutting the middle of the neighborhood is Brighton Beach Avenue, a commercial strip of small Russian grocery stores, restaurants, and clothing stores operating in the shadow of the New York City Transit Authority elevated train line running above the avenue.

It is that train line that keeps the Russians complaining and on their toes. The D train runs along these tracks, coming from the Bronx via Manhattan and bringing the majority of the visitors who crowd the neighborhood in the summer. Most are unwelcome, but they don't seem to notice. The Russian immigrant residents of Brighton Beach are not a notably tolerant bunch, especially when it comes to Puerto Ricans and blacks from Manhattan and the Bronx. But over the course of time the Russians have been forced to the realization that there is nothing they can do about it. They have been blessed with the beach and cursed with the D train, and they take their summer visitor problem in stride by pretending that it doesn't exist. In the summer, they simply close their stores, lock their doors, and ignore the hordes of brightly dressed brown and black people, most of whom are carrying children, coolers stocked with malt liquor, and large radios tuned full-volume to rap music or salsa. The D train brings them in the heat of the early afternoon and takes them home when the sun goes down and the neighborhood is returned to the Russians.

*   *   *

The trip took McKenna and Pao half an hour, and they listened to a steady chatter coming over the radio from Tavlin's men as Pao drove. The surveillance teams were still behind Maximo and fifteen minutes away from Brighton Beach when Pao took the Ocean Parkway exit off the Shore Parkway and drove south, toward the beach.

McKenna hadn't been in that part of Brooklyn in years and he took in the neighborhood as Pao stopped for a red light at Brighton Beach Avenue and Ocean Parkway, two blocks from the Atlantic Ocean. White shoppers crowded Brighton Beach Avenue, and the storefront glass of the avenue's shops were covered with hand-lettered signs advertising sales and prices in Cyrillic.

As they waited for the light, a subway train pulled into the Ocean Parkway station above them. McKenna and Pao heard the music from above as soon as the train doors opened.

"Watch this," Pao said, pulling the car to the curb, and McKenna did. It looked like a reverse-order fire drill. Before the train had left the station and the first passenger descended the stairs, the Russians had cleared the street. They all found a hole in a hurry, most of them in the stores before the doors were locked behind them. There was no one left to greet the hundred or so black and Puerto Rican visitors the D train had brought. There was no one for them to talk to, nothing for them to buy, and not much for them to see on deserted Brighton Beach Avenue.

It must have been as the poorer and darker visitors expected. They quickly left the deserted avenue and walked down the side streets leading to the beach. When the music faded, the Russians returned to the streets.

"Never saw anything like that," McKenna remarked, thinking that the Russians seemed to be used to invaders and, over the centuries, probably gave the same routine to the Germans, the Cossacks, the Tatars, the Mongols, and the Huns. His musings were interrupted by a radio message from one of Tavlin's teams. "Maximo's getting off the Shore Parkway at Coney Island Avenue."

"That gives us ten minutes," McKenna said to Pao. "Let's find a place to wait for him."

"I got the place. He's gotta dump his car and the only place he can do that is the municipal parking lot, Brighton 2nd and the boardwalk,'' Pao remarked as he pulled away from the curb. He drove the two blocks to the beach and parked between the two Emergency Service trucks standing by at Ocean Parkway and the boardwalk, four blocks from the Petrograd Restaurant. Before leaving the car, McKenna checked with Tavlin by radio. There was a team staked out in the Petrograd and still no sign of Elena.

Pao and McKenna took off their ties and suit jackets and put their guns and radios in the jacket pockets. They left the car with their jackets over their arms and started strolling up the boardwalk, toward Brighton 2nd Street.

There were some people on the crowded boardwalk in street clothes, but most were in bathing suits. The beach wasn't crowded yet, but McKenna expected that it would be jammed within a few hours. It was already hot and sunny, and the afternoon promised to be a scorcher.

Leaving Pao standing outside, McKenna stepped into a novelty shop tucked into the row of stores and snack bars on the boardwalk facing the beach. He emerged a minute later wearing sunglasses and a beach hat and carrying a shopping bag. "How do I look?" he asked Pao.

"Like an asshole, but less conspicuous."

What a charmer, McKenna thought as he handed Pao the shopping bag. "Make that two assholes," he said over his shoulder as he resumed walking toward Brighton 2nd Street.

Pao took a pair of sunglasses and another beach hat out of the shopping bag. He donned the sunglasses, but discarded the hat and shopping bag in a trash can as he followed McKenna to Brighton 2nd.

From the elevated boardwalk they had a good view of the municipal parking lot and the street. The parking lot was filling up fast, and traffic was backed up for blocks on Brighton 2nd Street with cars dropping off bathers at the boardwalk or waiting to get into the lot.

As McKenna and Pao waited, they saw another D train pass on the elevated tracks two blocks away. Two minutes later the first of the passengers broke into view, coming toward them along Brighton 2nd Street.

McKenna raised his jacket, reached into the pocket, and pressed his radio transmit button. "This is McKenna. Where is Maximo now?" he whispered into the radio.

"Chase Unit Two, Commissioner. We're two blocks behind

him. He just turned onto Brighton 2nd from Brighton Beach Avenue.''

McKenna shaded his eyes with his hand and saw the top of Maximo's red Toyota van two blocks away in the line of cars approaching the beach. He pressed his transmit button again. ''Any sign of Elena yet?''

''Nothing yet, Commissioner,'' another voice answered. ''We'll key the radio three times when she comes into the restaurant.''

McKenna monitored the slow progress of Maximo's van and saw that the subway passengers were making much quicker progress than the motorists. As the first of them crossed Brightwater Avenue, one block away, his attention was drawn to two men standing on the corner. Both were Hispanic, in their twenties, and dressed for the beach, wearing shorts, pullover shirts, and sunglasses. There was a large cooler on the sidewalk between them and both were looking toward Brighton Beach Avenue.

One of the duo could have blended in with any of the people passing them on the sidewalk, but the other was a well-built menacing-looking figure, and McKenna noticed that the passing people seemed to go out of their way not to look at him. But McKenna couldn't take his eyes off the man. As he watched, the object of his attention took a mobile phone from his pocket and brought it to his ear. He said nothing into the phone, just listened. Then he put the phone back in his pocket and said something to his partner.

''I think those two are gonna whack Maximo,'' McKenna said softly to Pao. ''The big, ugly one matches the driver on the Brunette hit.''

''I see them, but don't turn around,'' Pao replied without moving his lips as he propped his elbows on the boardwalk railing. ''Elena's gonna pass behind us in a second.''

Taking a cue from Pao, McKenna also casually leaned on the railing, listening intently and watching as the two men picked up the cooler between them and placed it on the hood of the third parked car from the corner. Maximo's van was still half a block away from them.

Perfect spot Emilio chose, McKenna thought. Maximo will be helpless in his van between two stopped cars. Then McKenna heard the approaching click of Elena's high heels on the wooden boardwalk behind them and the two men remained motionless as she passed behind them.

What's she doing here? McKenna wondered. If I'm right, she must know that it isn't in the plan for Maximo to make it to the restaurant. What did she do, come to watch?

The sound of her footsteps stopped abruptly and McKenna ventured a sideways glance. Elena was thirty feet away from them, dressed in a red sarong and red high heels, with a towel wrapped around her wet red hair as she also leaned over the boardwalk railing. Obviously, she *had* come to watch the end of her fling with Maximo and was staring at the two men on the corner a block away from them. Then she glanced toward McKenna and Pao and recognition quickly crossed her face. She reacted in an instant, turning away from them as she stepped out of her high heels and ran across the boardwalk to the beach.

"Stay with her, Johnny," McKenna yelled as he pulled his radio from his jacket pocket. But Pao didn't move as McKenna raised his radio.

"McKenna to chase units. Close in on Maximo in a hurry. Two male Hispanics are set to whack him at the corner of Brightwater and Brighton 2nd."

Pao was still in front of him, watching and waiting. As McKenna pulled his gun from his jacket pocket, he looked toward the beach and saw Elena shed her sarong and towel as she ran toward the water in a skimpy two-piece bathing suit, the center of attention for every man on the beach.

"I said get her," McKenna yelled, exasperated, as he gave Pao a shove. Pao reluctantly turned and started after Elena at a brisk trot.

This is getting worse every second, McKenna thought as he hopped the boardwalk railing and hurried through the approaching crowd of bathers toward the two men on the corner, his jacket slung over his arm concealing his gun and radio as he walked. But I'm gonna reach them before Maximo does. I'll pull this off and have two *Sendero* prisoners as long as they keep their eyes on the van and don't turn around. Just another half a block.

Maximo's van was five cars from the corner when Emilio took the lid off the cooler and both men reached inside.

McKenna started to run through the crowd and three things happened at once. Behind him on the beach he heard Elena screaming in the distance, "Help, police!" over and over. From his left and right came the sirens of the Emergency Service trucks approaching from both directions on Brightwater

Avenue. And in front of him, in the street on the other side of Maximo's van, he saw two of Tavlin's men, Richie White and Patrick Early. Early and White were both removing their pistols from the holsters on their belts as they ran across the street in a crouch.

Emilio and Juan Sanchez saw and heard everything McKenna did, but they still didn't see McKenna. They responded in a military fashion by removing two stiff rolled towels from the cooler and addressing the nearest threat they saw, the two approaching detectives. They each pulled a cut-down M-16 rifle from their towels and fired on full automatic, unleashing twenty rounds of high-velocity .223-caliber rounds in three seconds and total pandemonium on Brighton 2nd Street, but they had made a mistake.

Both had fired at Early and neither missed. He went down in front of Maximo's van, hit many times in the torso and legs. As his lifeless body slumped to the sidewalk, Maximo and the occupants of every other car on Brighton 2nd Street ducked under their dashboards while people fled in all directions from the scene, many of them screaming. But not Richie White. Early's death had given him a one-second reprieve on life and he used it, jumping behind Maximo's van and returning fire with his pistol.

White missed, but he induced a degree of caution in the Senderistas. They split up. Emilio moved to the other side of the street, firing into the front of Maximo's van as he ran and took cover between two parked cars, the barrel of his weapon pointed at Maximo's van at the spot he had last seen White.

Then Juan Sanchez fired his M-16 at the ground in front of Maximo's van, hoping to catch White's legs with a ricochet or force him into the open.

White screamed, hit by a bullet in his left foot, but he didn't go down. Instead he responded, extending only his pistol around the rear corner of the van and firing five rounds in Juan's direction.

The bullets came closer to hitting McKenna than they did to hitting Juan. McKenna dropped to the sidewalk as White's rounds whizzed over his head, but he kept his eyes fixed on Juan's back, still twenty feet away.

Juan stood up and fired a five-round burst at the place where White had shown his hand and his bullets tore into the right rear quarter panel, spreading metal, glass, and plastic along Brighton 2nd Street.

Patrick Early, was all McKenna could think as he got up and closed the distance between himself and Juan. Wife's name is Christina. Pretty, a little heavy-set, but funny and personable once she got a few drinks in her. Three kids or four? He couldn't remember as he reached Juan and pressed the barrel of his pistol against the back of Juan's head and placed his left arm around Juan's neck.

Juan froze and McKenna thought any conversation between them would be superfluous under the circumstances, but Juan did have one thing to say. "Emilio!" he yelled as he struggled to turn and face McKenna.

From the corner of his eye, McKenna saw Emilio crouched between the two parked cars across the street. The barrel of Emilio's gun was swinging from Maximo's car to McKenna and Juan.

McKenna squeezed his trigger and sent one round of 9-mm parabellum high-velocity copper-jacketed lead into the back of Juan's head. Then he pulled Juan up, placing the body between himself and Emilio.

McKenna had wasted a round on Juan. Emilio had found his aiming point and fired a long burst. The bullets went through Juan's body and slammed into McKenna, hitting him in the chest. He was wearing a bulletproof vest and the rounds didn't penetrate, but the force slammed McKenna back and he went down hard on his back, still holding on to Juan's neck with his left arm. As he hit the sidewalk, his right hand hit the pavement and, without realizing it, he lost the grip on his gun.

McKenna, lying on the sidewalk under Juan's body, raised his right hand to fire at Emilio and was surprised to see that he was no longer holding his pistol. Over his empty right hand, he focused on Emilio, who was staring back at him as he pulled his magazine from his weapon.

Thank God! McKenna thought. He's out of ammo.

McKenna's gratitude to the Almighty was short-lived. Emilio turned his magazine over, inserted it into the weapon, and slid the bolt home. McKenna realized that Emilio had taped two magazines together and had just inserted a fresh thirty rounds into his M-16.

Looking to his right for his pistol, McKenna saw it, lying three feet away on the sidewalk. No time for that, he thought. But I do have access to an M-16.

Juan was still holding his weapon in his dead hands. McKenna reached around Juan's body and placed both hands on the weapon and managed to swing the barrel in Emilio's direction. But Juan's hand still covered the trigger and McKenna couldn't find it as he saw Emilio smile and stand up. Emilio calmly started across the street toward McKenna, smiling all the time, his weapon pointed at the two men on the ground.

As McKenna contemplated the fragility of his existence while staring at the approaching terrorist, he heard a fusillade of gunfire from the direction of Brighton Beach Avenue. More of Tavlin's men, he thought. He heard the rounds slam into cars on Brighton 2nd Street, and it seemed to McKenna that some of the bullets came close to hitting Emilio, but the big man didn't seem to notice. He just kept coming, smiling. He was in the middle of the street, standing over the body of Pat Early, when he put the stock of his M-16 to his shoulder and lined up on McKenna's head.

All McKenna could see was the quarter-inch black opening at the end of the barrel and all he could think was, Will I see the muzzle flash before the bullet that kills me slams into my head?

The sound of ineffective gunfire continued from the direction of Brighton Beach Avenue as McKenna lifted his eyes to stare into Emilio's. He was consoled by the thought that Emilio only had one or two seconds more to live than he did.

Then McKenna heard the sound of a single distant shot from his left, from the direction of the boardwalk. It seemed to him that Emilio had also heard it, and had started to turn his head when the bullet entered his right ear on its way to his left ear. As Emilio slowly slumped to the ground, on top of Early, three more rounds caught him in his left side.

Richie White, McKenna thought as pulled himself from under Juan's body. But where did the first round come from? He stood up, then bent down again and retrieved his pistol. When he looked up again, White was standing over Emilio, blood flowing from a hole in his shoe, but his pistol pointed at the dead gunman as he cursed him. Then, as McKenna watched, he pulled Emilio's body off Early and started the obviously useless procedure of giving Pat Early mouth-to-mouth resuscitation.

McKenna realized his mind was shifting from *Act* to *Record* as he listened to White's labored breaths escape from the holes in Early's lifeless and shattered chest and neck. No bulletproof vest, McKenna observed, but knew that a vest wouldn't have made the slightest bit of difference in this case. Early just had too many holes in him.

McKenna looked up again and was surprised to see that he was standing in the middle of a police crowd. Tavlin was there, along with a bunch of his detectives pinning their shields onto their coat lapels. Four Emergency Service cops were also there, wearing heavy-gauge ceramic bulletproof vests and casually carrying Mini-14 automatic rifles. Sirens were sounding in the distance, coming closer from all directions.

McKenna felt faint and realized he was hyperventilating, but no one was paying any attention to him. Everyone's focus was on Richie White as he tried to breathe life into Early's mouth. All that McKenna could think was, No head damage. Open casket.

Then McKenna became aware that Tavlin was tugging on his sleeve, and he focused on the inspector.

"Where did it come from?" Tavlin asked, pointing to Emilio's body.

McKenna shifted his gaze to Emilio's lifeless body, eyes open and staring at the sky. He had forgotten about that. Where had the bullet come from that hit Emilio in the ear and saved my life? McKenna wondered. From the left, from the boardwalk.

McKenna looked in that direction and saw Johnny Pao, half a block away, casually strolling toward them with his jacket on and his hands in his pockets. From the boardwalk? Pao from the boardwalk? McKenna asked himself. A head shot from a block and a half away? "I don't know. I'd better ask Pao," he said to Tavlin as he continued watching Pao.

Pao stopped on the corner of Brighton 2nd and Brightwater Avenue to let two ambulances pass in front of him. They squealed to a stop at the scene of the carnage, but McKenna paid them no mind. He started toward Pao, still woozy and out of breath. He felt like he was sleepwalking and realized that he must have lost at least five seconds from his life, because there was Pao, standing in front of him, sporting a blackened left eye.

"You look like shit," Pao said.

McKenna looked down at himself and was surprised to see that he was still holding his pistol. He holstered it and was forced to agree. He did look like shit. His white shirt and his pants were covered with Juan's blood, and his shirt had five bullet holes in it that he could see. He ripped the shirt open and checked his chest. None of the blood was his. He looked again at Pao, who was staring at him and showing not the slightest bit of concern.

"Did you do it?" McKenna asked.

"Sure."

"You shot him in the ear from a block and a half away?"

"Had to. I knew we only had time for one shot and I didn't know if he was wearing a vest. His ear looked like the best target, under the circumstances."

McKenna took a moment to digest this piece of ballistic information. Then he remembered something else. I'm mad at this guy, he thought. He's supposed to be with Elena, not wasting valuable department time saving my life. "Where is she?" he asked, sternly.

"I don't know," Pao answered, totally unconcerned. "Last time I saw her, she was taking a swim and she looked pretty strong. England, maybe?"

"You mean you let her get away?"

Pao just smiled at him.

This isn't working, McKenna thought. Got to remember I'm the big boss and this big, mean, very bad detective just disobeyed my direct orders to stay with Elena. But what happened to his eye? McKenna asked himself, almost as an afterthought. "So you just let her get away?" That sounded good, McKenna thought. Tough and sarcastic, just like a real boss.

No effect on Pao, however. The big detective simply put his arm around McKenna's shoulders and said, "She had some help, you know."

"Who?"

"Every male Puerto Rican on the beach with an ounce of testosterone."

"Is that what happened to you? They beat you up?"

"Tried to. She was running to the water screaming, 'Help! Police!' Now I know that none of them were the police, but they all helped. But I understand. Put yourself in their places."

McKenna tried and found it wasn't hard. A half-naked, very good-looking young woman being chased along a beach loaded with young, virile male Puerto Ricans with machismo, muscle, and hormones spilling out of every pore. They hear her screaming and then they see that she is being annoyed and antagonized by someone who looked and acted like Johnny Pao. It wasn't a pretty picture.

"Are we in trouble?" McKenna asked.

"A little," Pao answered as he guided McKenna back toward the growing crowd in the middle of the block. "What I suggest, Commissioner, is that you take some very patient and understanding detectives from CCRB or Community Affairs or one of them other hideouts and send them to the beach with a packet of civilian complaint forms and a few typewriters to interview those unfortunate victims of some recent police brutality. You might also send a few ambulances down there when you get a chance, just to show your concern."

McKenna was hit by a thought and stopped short. He looked around and saw that hundreds of people were coming from the beach to join the spectator pool, and knew that the potential for further disaster was high. Riots had started before in New York under circumstances less drastic than the one he found himself in. "You didn't shoot any of them, did you?" he asked, not really sure of the answer.

For the first time, Pao looked hurt. "Now wouldn't that be unprofessional?" he asked.

"I don't know anymore. After all, you still let her get away. I didn't expect that."

Pao took his arm off McKenna's shoulder and looked him square in the eye. "It's time you knew something," he said sternly. "For one thing, according to Police Commissioner Ray Brunette, my primary mission is to keep you alive. Everything else you might want me to do is secondary."

I should have known, McKenna thought. Brunette, of course. It was no coincidence that Ray assigned Pao as my driver. But Pao had left himself open when he said, "For one thing . . ." "What's another thing?" McKenna asked.

Pao replaced his arm around McKenna's shoulder and they continued walking. Then Pao whispered in McKenna's ear, "Just between us, another thing is that I can't swim."

Chapter 21

What a mess this turned out to be, McKenna thought. From his vantage point in the cab of the big Emergency Service truck he had a good view of Brighton 2nd Street, but he felt like closing his eyes tightly and wishing it would go away. He knew that he was hiding out while he left Tavlin to try and straighten things out as much as possible. Only to himself, he justified his avoidance of duty with three reasons.

First, he knew he was no good to anyone just then. He just wasn't thinking fast enough and hoped it wasn't a permanent state. He realized he was suffering from poststress syndrome, trauma, or whatever name the doctors give to the things that happen to the mind when too much violence occurs too fast.

Second, McKenna knew Tavlin had the experience to do a better job than he could in handling this aftermath. Like many cooks, McKenna loved brewing up a pot of trouble, but hated cleaning the pots. Tavlin, on the other hand, was great at cleaning up and handled it the way he handled every other task: objectively and efficiently. Tavlin knew all the things that would have to be done in order to best answer all the questions that would be asked.

Third, McKenna knew he needed some time to sort things out under the new circumstances that had evolved on Brighton 2nd Street. He forced himself to take in the street scene to get a better sense of the new realities in the investigation.

Barriers had been set up at each end of the street to keep the large and still growing crowd from the crime scene and a line of cops from the local precinct was manning the barricades. McKenna figured the beaches must now be empty. Everyone was there, standing and pushing on the other side of the barriers.

The three bodies were still on the street, waiting to be photographed by the Crime Scene Unit. Early's wife had to be notified, and McKenna figured that was his job. He knew her, and she deserved to be told how her husband died by someone who was there and knew the reasons it happened.

Sitting on the hood of a parked car, Maximo was talking rapidly and excitedly while Richie White took notes. The top of White's left shoe was cut off and his big toe was bandaged. Juan's bullet's ricochet had just skinned the top of White's toe, taking off some skin and the toenail, but White refused to go sick. His partner was dead and White wasn't stopping.

McKenna figured Maximo would be of no further use to the investigation. Their one link with *Sendero* was burned but it couldn't be helped. A live Maximo was the one bright spot. If it wasn't for the police, he would be dead.

Detectives were writing down the license plate numbers of the cars parked on the street and noting the locations of bullet holes in the cars with yellow crayon circles. From where he sat, it looked to McKenna like every car on the block was adorned with at least one yellow circle, and he knew the city would be paying for the damage.

Johnny Pao was leaning against the side of an ambulance, enjoying a cigarette, looking as calm and collected as the most perfectly innocent bystander. But McKenna knew there was something wrong with that picture, and it gave him a little tickle. Pao didn't smoke.

In the middle of the block, like the Rock of Gibraltar, stood Tavlin. A steady flow of cops and detectives were arriving and were all directed to him. He found something for everyone to do, and had a five-second conversation with each new arrival, after which they hurried away to perform their assigned tasks.

As McKenna watched, Sheeran arrived with four detectives. He talked with Tavlin and, during their conversation, Tavlin pointed to McKenna. Then Tavlin took his phone from his pocket. Someone had called him and something important was happening. Tavlin listened for thirty seconds, then made three short phone calls before he folded his phone.

Sheeran rounded up ten detectives, and Tavlin took less than a minute to give them a series of instructions while they wrote and nodded. When he finished with them, they left on the run. Tavlin and Sheeran then headed for McKenna's truck, engaged in animated conversation while they walked.

McKenna got out and waited for them on the street. Tavlin and Sheeran were both smiling by the time they got to him.

"Heard from Hardcass," Tavlin said. "He's with one of them on the D train."

Hardcass? I forgot all about him, McKenna thought, which is a very hard thing to do, once you know him. "How?"

"He was standing on the corner of Brighton Beach Avenue and Brighton 2nd before all this went down and he saw a young Spanish lad call someone on a mobile phone as soon as Maximo's van came into sight. At the sound of the first shot, this young lad walked to the Ocean Parkway station while everyone else was running in a panic. Being a naturally suspicious kind of guy, Hardcass decided to follow him, saw him drop a little package in a trash can on the station platform, and managed to retrieve it. A Colt .45 in a paper bag."

So the hit team for Maximo had three people in it, McKenna thought. One lookout and two killers. That was the phone call Emilio got on the corner. The lookout told them to get ready, then tried to get lost once the shooting started. He must've gotten very nervous when he saw all Tavlin's men run past him, and decided to get rid of his gun just to play it safe. But Hardcass still had him. "Where are they?"

"Last we heard, at the Neck Road station. He got on the city-bound D train and Hardcass hung out in the next car. Got off two stops later at the Neck Road station and, last we heard, the subject's waiting on the platform for the next train to take him back this way. Hardcass says the guy's real nervous and looking all around. He's gonna let him go after he gets on the train and I've got men at every station to follow him when he gets off."

"How many stations before the end of the line?"

"Two in Brighton Beach and two in Coney Island."

"Why did it take so long for Hardcass to get to you?"

"He doesn't have a radio. He had to wait till the guy got off at Neck Road before he could call me." Then Tavlin smiled. "But tell me, what's your definition of so long?"

"I don't know, but it's been a while since the shooting started."

"How long?"

Tavlin and Sheeran seemed to be sharing a joke as Sheeran checked his watch, giving McKenna the feeling that they expected him to say something stupid. He did.

"Maybe an hour?"

Tavlin looked like the cat that swallowed the mouse, but Sheeran just shook his head. Tavlin turned to Sheeran and asked, "What time is it, Dennis?"

"Ten-forty-nine."

Tavlin turned back to McKenna. "Brian, the first shot was fired at ten-thirty-two, seventeen minutes ago, and the last shot was fired less than ten seconds later."

Ten seconds of shooting seventeen minutes ago? How is that possible? McKenna asked himself. It seemed the firefight lasted for an hour and I'm sitting here wondering why the sun hasn't gone down yet. Am I okay?

No, I'm not, was the conclusion McKenna was forced to draw.

Tavlin and Sheeran watched the mounting confusion spread over McKenna's face until Sheeran broke what was becoming an embarrassing silence. "Mind if I put this in perspective, Brian?"

"Do I mind? No."

"Okay. How long have you been back from Florida?"

McKenna had to stop and think because it seemed to him that the days were running into the nights, and he had a tough time telling when one day ended and another began. "Is it five days?"

"More or less. Six, actually. In that time you've been to the wake of a kid you've known for most of his life, been blown up, had your wife lose a baby, witnessed a murder in Texas, did a burglary in Georgia, and now killed a man here. Twice this week you've had your life saved by the bodies of dead men. Add to that the fact that there's a bunch of well-armed maniacs out there who have your death and destruction as one of their primary goals, throw in a little political pressure to solve maybe the biggest case this department has ever seen, and I'm forced to conclude that what we have here is a stressful situation, one that anybody would have a tough time handling."

Sheeran stopped to take a breath while McKenna waited for more, but there was no more to be said.

Thank God, McKenna thought. I didn't realize it was that bad until Sheeran said it. What he didn't say was that it was gonna get worse, and I'm in no shape for it right now. "What should I do?"

It was Tavlin's turn. "Because of funerals, right now you are probably the senior official working in the police department. There's a lot to be done here, but you need a rest."

"How long do you think?"

"Maybe an hour, maybe a day, maybe a week. You'll know when you're ready again. Remember, we're in a war here, and everybody gets rotated out of the front lines every once in a while."

They were interrupted by Sergeant Goldblatt, one of Tavlin's detective supervisors. McKenna stepped back, expecting that Goldblatt had something to say to Tavlin, but instead it was to McKenna that he reported.

"Excuse me, Commissioner, but I thought you should know. The subject came out of the Brighton 8th Street D train station. My men have got him in a diner at Coney Island Avenue and Brighton Beach Avenue, sitting in a booth with two other male Hispanics."

That's good news, right? McKenna asked himself. But maybe it's bad news. Suppose they split up after they leave the diner? Then we'd need a lot of men and vehicles standing by to do a proper leapfrog surveillance. We need them soon, and Goldblatt's standing there expecting me to tell him what to do. "Looks like we're gonna need a lot of men and equipment," McKenna said, feeling stupid as soon as he stated the obvious.

Now Goldblatt was staring at him the same way Tavlin and Sheeran were. Tavlin saved him.

"The Communications Division truck and the manpower you ordered is on the way, Commissioner. You still want me to coordinate the assignments when they get here?"

"Yeah, do that," McKenna answered, then turned to Goldblatt. "Scrape up all the men and equipment possible until the cavalry gets here, Sergeant, and do the best you can to see where those three are going. If you think they wise up and the operation is burnt, then take them."

"Yes, sir," Goldblatt said. He saluted and left at a trot.

"Nice recovery," Sheeran said.

"Yeah, thanks. Now why don't you two tell me all the other things I was smart enough to do."

"Not too much, yet," Tavlin said. "You've got the Street Crime Unit coming to handle the surveillance and the Bomb Squad is on the way with their dogs and bomb disposal trucks. They're all reporting to the Kingsborough Community College campus, about a mile from here, and you've authorized overtime for everyone."

McKenna was impressed at his own intelligence. "How did I get all that done so quickly?"

"Just three phone calls while you were sitting here."

McKenna remembered watching Tavlin make the short phone calls and had to admit that everything he did seemed exactly right and showed a lot of foresight. In short, Tavlin made him look like a police organizational genius.

"I won't forget you two for this," McKenna said.

"Nothing to remember," said Sheeran. "We all sink or swim together."

"Now tell me what I should be doing next."

"You can keep the press off our backs. They listen to our radios and there must be a bevy of reporters on their way here."

"I'll try. What else?"

"You've just killed a man, so you have to be interviewed by the DA. He might not be happy with the way it went down. Shooting that guy in the back of the head might not fit into his perfect justifiable-homicide scenario," Sheeran said.

"But does it fit into ours?"

"Like a glove," Tavlin said.

"That's all I'm worried about. Just have the union lawyer tell them I'm injured and I can't make a statement yet."

"There's a problem there," Sheeran said. "You're a politician now, and politicians don't have a union."

"Then I'll get my own lawyer. What else?"

"Take a rest," Tavlin said. "You need some medical attention, a bath, and a new suit."

Sheeran summed it up: "Yeah, Brian. You look like shit."

Pao drove back to Manhattan like a normal person, fooling everyone else on the road. McKenna was on the phone for most of the trip, implementing Tavlin's suggestions much in the same manner as Moses implemented God's.

First he called the Deputy Commissioner for Public Information's office and left a message. His call was returned within five minutes. Since the man technically outranked him, McKenna took a political tack in explaining the need for a press blackout, and offered a few suggestions on how it should be presented to the press. McKenna thought he was impressing the deputy commissioner and scoring some points because he answered, "I see. That's a good suggestion," to every idea McKenna offered. But he wasn't saying much else and McKenna ran out of suggestions. There was a lull in the conversation until the deputy commissioner said, "Well, which is it?"

McKenna was confused. "Isn't that your decision to make?"

"What makes you think that?"

"Because you outrank me."

"Are you joking? Let me tell you something about politics, kid. Right now you're Brunette's fair-haired boy and the public's darling. As for me, I got my job because somebody owed a favor to another guy who owed a favor to me, but I still never know who's gonna be sitting at my desk tomorrow. So what's it gonna be?"

"Okay, go with the one that promises full and honest disclosure after it's over, with the implied threat that, if they don't play ball, and somebody gets killed by *Sendero* because the press spilled our operation, then the department will put their First Amendment rights under some pressure and publicly blame any errant reporter and his publication. Think you can tell them that in a nice way?"

"It'll be tough, but I'll manage."

"Thanks."

"Okay, kid, but remember one thing. You've got the spotlight for today, but tomorrow it might be my sacred duty to assassinate you in the press if you step on your dick."

"Thanks for the tip," McKenna said, but realized he was talking to himself. The deputy commissioner had hung up. McKenna took it in stride and called the Health Services Division and made arrangements for his medical needs. A department surgeon would visit him at his hotel at two o'clock.

Last came the call to Brooks Brothers. His adventures had run him out of suits in New York, and he needed a complete wardrobe. He talked to the very competent manager and old friend, Mr. Schmidt. After exchanging some pleasantries, McKenna placed his order. Schmidt assured him that his sizes were on record with the store and everything he needed would be delivered to the Gramercy Park Hotel by four o'clock.

Then Tavlin called. The M-16s used in the shoot-out and the Colt .45 dropped by the surveillance subject were all part of the stolen Georgia shipment. The three *Sendero* soldiers were still in the Seabright Restaurant.

But that changed while Pao and McKenna were stuck in traffic on the Brooklyn Bridge. The three Senderistas left the diner and McKenna monitored the surveillance on the police radio. They were cautious and did some slips and pirouettes around Brighton Beach, but Sheeran and Tavlin were prepared, since their manpower and vehicles had arrived in time. With all their turns and moves, it took fifteen minutes to traverse a total distance of six blocks, and by the time McKenna and Pao were on the East River Drive, the subjects had entered 1143 Brighton Beach 15th Street, a private house off the corner of Brighton Beach Avenue. One of them had used a key to unlock the door.

Sheeran called just as Pao pulled up in front of the Gramercy Park Hotel. "You were listening to the radio?" he asked.

"Yeah. Tell me about the house they crawled into."

"It's a detached one-story house that was probably built as a beach bungalow fifty years ago. But it's been renovated and a garage has been added in the back. It looks nice and neat."

"Any idea what they're doing there?"

"Not yet. We're working on finding who the owner is, but that's not the reason I called. I saved you some grief and sent Richie White to notify Pat Early's family."

That's a relief, McKenna thought. White knows them better than I do. But there's one more thing, and I know I've remembered it and forgotten it ten times in the last half hour. What was it?

Then it came to him. "How about Emilio's phone?"

"Emilio?"

I didn't tell them? McKenna thought. That's right. I'm the boss, so nobody asked me anything about the shooting. Nice. If I were still a working detective, I'd be under virtual arrest until I was debriefed. "Sorry, I should have told you. That was the big one's name. Savraada showed me his picture and figured he was the one who shot Ingrid when they ambushed Ray's kid."

McKenna's apology was accepted without comment. "Elena used the credit card Maximo got her to buy his phone and two others," Tavlin said. "Bought all three at the Wiz Electronics Store two days ago and she used the card to have them all hooked up with NYNEX. We've got the three phone numbers and frequencies, and we're working to get a court order directing NYNEX to give us the billing records."

"It would be nice to know who they've been calling," McKenna added.

"It would be wonderful, and we'll get it. Until then, we're set up to monitor their conversations, if they're stupid enough to use those phones again. Get some rest. I'll get in touch with you if anything real important develops."

Chapter 22

The phone was ringing and McKenna closed his eyes tighter, waiting for someone to answer it and stop the noise. Nobody did. He was conscious by the fourth ring, knew who and where he was by the seventh ring, and found the phone on the nightstand in the darkened room on the ninth ring. It was Brunette. "Morning, buddy. I was just about to call the troops and have them break down your door," he said.

"It's morning?"

"No, actually it's six at night, but it's a new day for you. How do you feel?"

How do I feel? McKenna took a few seconds before he gave the stock answer. He felt the back of his head and checked the police surgeon's work. The stitches were out, the bandage was off, and there was no blood. Next he felt his ribs. He was taped up and it hurt a bit to breathe deeply, but he thought he could manage. "I feel fine."

"Good enough to come back to work?"

"Meaning you've got something for me to do?"

"Meaning we're gonna take their Brighton Beach house sometime after midnight. Figured you wouldn't wanna miss it."

"I don't, and midnight gives me a lot of time. I'll be there by seven-thirty. Where should I meet you?"

"Pao will show you. He'll be there soon."

"Pao? I sent him home for the night."

"Really? I got here at four and he was here when I arrived. Tavlin's been keeping him busy."

"Are we doing good?"

"We'll know after midnight, but we might do better before that. Elena wants to talk to you."

"Elena? How?"

"She called your office and finally got through to Camilia. Said she wants her red dress back."

"Her red dress? Do we have it?"

"Nobody knew what she was talking about until I mentioned it to Pao. And no, we don't have her dress. Somebody swiped it off the beach while he was off chasing her. The shoes, too."

She wants her dress back? What kind of nuts are we dealing with here? McKenna asked himself. "Did she leave a number?"

"She says you have her number."

Of course we do, McKenna thought. One of the other two cellular-phone numbers must be hers, and she figured we'd get that information after we got Emilio's phone. Which means we're wasting time and money monitoring those frequencies. She knows we're listening and they probably won't use the phones to talk to each other.

"They're playing with us, Ray. Is NYNEX cooperating yet?"

"In every way they can. We've got the billing records and, except for Elena's call to you at headquarters, they only used the phones to call the other mobile phones. All the calls were in Brighton Beach cells. We can get a cell location one minute after the next time they use them."

"A cell location? That doesn't help much, does it?"

"Better than nothing. We can narrow their location down to ten square blocks in Manhattan, maybe twenty anyplace else in the city."

"Where was Elena when she called me?"

"On the East Side, someplace between East 42nd Street and East 53rd. I have people showing her picture at all the hotels in that area, but there's more than a hundred and we've got nothing so far."

"So we can talk to them anytime we want," McKenna said.

"That's one of the reasons I want you to get here. You can make your call to your new girl, and then we'll talk."

"Fine. Anything else?"

"Yeah, thanks for getting those two." Brunette hung up, leaving McKenna feeling uncomfortable. He thought Brunette's expression of gratitude strange and out of character.

But he had more on his mind and lay in the darkness while contemplating this turn in events.

Why would Elena want to talk to me? he asked himself. Why not Ray, the mayor, or even the President? Any one of them would take her call at this point. So why me? Is she ready to turn and take a shot at the reward, or did I look stupid to her in person? Maybe she figures she can get some information out of me because the others would be too smart for her.

I hope she's wrong, but I've got a lot of thinking to do before I call her, McKenna thought as he reached over and turned on the nightstand light.

Showered, shaved, and dressed in his new clothes, McKenna was ready and anxious to leave a half hour later. But he had two more calls to make. He had retained Harry McCrystal, Esquire, to handle any potential problems the DA might have with his conduct that afternoon. He called Harry at home to get an indication on his legal health.

"You're always doing fine when you've got me for a lawyer," Harry said. "I called Mulvey this afternoon and he insisted on an immediate statement from you about some illegal alien who died somehow on Brighton 2nd Street."

McKenna knew Bruce Mulvey, the Brooklyn district attorney, and thought that Mulvey would be a problem for him. Mulvey had a history of prosecuting cops, and although he lost most of the time, he always considered the publicity a plus. "So what did you tell him?"

"That you would love to make a voluntary statement and get this behind you, but that you also wanted me present if there were going to be any questions. He said there would be, so I told him that, due to my pressing schedule of house closings and divorces, I wouldn't be able to squeeze his session in until April of next year. Mulvey said April would be fine."

"What does that mean?" McKenna asked.

"It means that Mulvey's no dope. Prosecuting heroes is bad politics, but if you fall from grace and lose your popularity, then he's got a prime chance to jump on you and make some headlines."

I keep hearing this same thing, McKenna thought. If I'm not a hero, I'm in trouble. Isn't there any middle ground? He thanked Harry and hung up, then called Angelita.

"How's my hero feeling?" she asked.

"Pretty good, considering."

"It's on the news. Two more, right?"

"Yeah, two more."

"Congratulations. I knew you were too good for them."

Another one out of character, McKenna thought, worried at the change in Angelita. What have they done to my usually sweet little girl?

"Brian?"

"Yeah, honey. I'm still here."

"Be careful and don't get cocky. How much longer?"

Good question, McKenna thought. How much longer? "Not long, I hope. We're doing pretty good."

"A week?"

"Yeah, maybe a week." I hope not another week like the last one, he thought. "I have to get back to work."

"Good luck and stay in touch."

"I will. 'Bye, baby."

After hanging up, McKenna sat down and watched CNN while he waited for Pao to arrive, and he caught the top of the show. The Brighton Beach shoot-out was featured in the national news coverage, but for once CNN seemed to be reporting in the dark. His name was mentioned, which led the newscaster to speculate about the involvement of *Sendero*, but there was nothing about the surveillance on Maximo de la Vega. However, CNN did call the news piece a continuing story, leading McKenna to conclude that they knew more than they were telling their audience.

So far, so good, McKenna thought. If we managed to keep CNN in line, every other news organization must be in step.

The following CNN national news piece was also set in New York and reported on the growing level of violence on the New York docks as the striking longshoremen battled for a better contract. The report documented vandalism against trucks and machinery and illustrated the rising level of rhetoric and violence directed by the longshoremen on the picket lines against the replacement workers brought in by the shipping companies. Three assaults were captured on camera, showing the replacement workers being beaten and the subsequent arrests as uniformed cops jumped into the fray to maintain a semblance of order on the picket line.

It looked to McKenna like a losing battle for all concerned. The longshoremen were losing clout and jobs because of the mechanization of the docks made possible by the container ships used by the shippers. The shipping companies were losing business as cargo was routinely routed to other East Coast cities with lower freight handling and manpower costs. The replacement workers were enduring beatings and threats in order to work a week or two and make a decent wage for the duration of the strike. Even the police department was a losing party, in the middle and paying high overtime costs to the cops, who were perceived by all sides to be biased against them.

McKenna shook his head, shut off the TV, and went to the mirror next to the door. He had combed his hair in back to cover his cut, and he craned his neck as he looked at his reflection, trying to see if the cut was showing. He couldn't tell, but decided his hat days were over anyway. Then Pao called to say he was downstairs.

Eddie Morgan was outside, leaning against the elevator door as he read the *Post*. He stood up straight as McKenna entered the hallway and closed the door behind him.

"Hiya, Brian," Morgan said. "Off to do battle again?"

"Looks like it, Eddie. Is Cisco downstairs?"

"Yep, but he'll be up as soon as you leave."

"Don't you guys ever go home?"

"At these rates? Are you kidding? We're working twenty-four hours a day, sixteen of them on overtime, and it's not too tough."

Good news for Cisco and Morgan, McKenna realized, but bad for the police department. The Job hated paying overtime, but the combination of the longshoremen's strike, the funerals, and the Brighton Beach surveillance had stretched the largest metropolitan police department in the world to the limit. And there was no end in sight for the next couple of days. Those cops and detectives not on overtime would soon be working at time and a half.

Cisco was outside talking to Pao, who was still wearing sunglasses in a vain attempt to hide his shiner.

"Mind telling me why you're still working here?" McKenna asked as Pao pulled from the curb.

"Easy. I went home and my wife started breaking my balls. Today's our anniversary and I was supposed to take her out, but she gave me a routine. Seems she didn't like my new look and she didn't wanna be seen in public with me."

"All that over a black eye?" McKenna asked, trying to sound consoling, but agreeing in his heart with the Mrs. Pao position. Pao looked like a "Wrestlemania" commercial, and Patty Pao was a classy act.

"Yeah. Hard to believe, isn't it?" said Pao. "So I found myself with time on my hands and went down to the Six-One Precinct to see if I could save us some trouble on a few civilian complaints. Did pretty good, too."

Wouldn't that be nice? McKenna thought. Nobody's asked about it yet, but I'm still gonna have to explain this car away. So I could do without his civilian complaints thrown in when I'm standing on the carpet. Civilian complaints he earned while under my direct supervision would just be the poison on the arrows I'm gonna have to take. They wouldn't do Pao too much good either, but he didn't seem to mind.

"Just how good did you do?" McKenna asked.

Pao looked annoyed by the question, but answered anyway. "When I got to the station house, there were two guys there I had run into on the beach. They had been to the hospital and were complaining about being assaulted. I guess they were real mad at me and got a little excited when I walked in. I think the desk officer was gonna have me arrested until I mentioned your name."

"My name? Good thinking, Johnny," McKenna said. I really need that, he thought. Some icing on the cake for Mulvey when he decides to cook me.

"Yeah, it worked like magic," Pao continued. "He let me talk to them in private, and I told them Elena was wanted for throwing lye on her boyfriend's sensitive parts after she caught him with another woman. That got them thinking. They agreed they were wrong for interfering and that she belonged in jail, no matter how good she looked."

"And that was it?"

"Sure. We shook hands, apologized to each other, and went out for a few drinks. Now we're all pals. Case closed, no civilian complaints."

"Then what did you do?"

"Went back to Brighton 2nd and everybody was gone, except for some reporters. They told me that Tavlin was at Kingsborough Community College, so I went over there and he stuck me with Maximo."

"And how is Maximo?"

"When I got there, real worried and very mad at you. He's terrified his wife is gonna find out he was on his way to meet another woman when everything went down, and he thought you set him up.''

I guess I did set him up, McKenna thought. And from what I hear about Mrs. de la Vega, Maximo's got something to worry about.

"But you fixed that?" McKenna asked, not sure he wanted to hear the answer.

"Sure. He's in the clear with his wife and he's your new best friend. I called his wife and told her that Maximo was working undercover for you on this investigation, following your orders. Said he was a real hero, and she agreed. She can't wait to get her fat, hairy arms around her wonderful man again.''

"So he's cooperating?"

"Fully. He gave Tavlin the names and addresses of all the foreigners involved in making the film in Peru, and Brunette's gotten through to a few of them. Told them what *Sendero* tried to do to Maximo when he strayed from the party line, and speculated that their lives were in danger. He suggested that they lie low for a while, and have no contact with anyone from *Sendero.*''

"Did Maximo give Brunette anything on the film?"

"He described it frame by frame."

"And?"

"You'll have to ask him," Pao replied.

A corner of Kingsborough Community College had been converted into a police camp, but looked more like a truck stop along an interstate highway with all the tractor trailers parked in a row. The Bomb Squad disposal truck, Communications Division truck, the Mobile Headquarters truck, the Special Operations Division disaster control truck, and the Emergency Medical Service mobile operating room were there, along with three Emergency Service heavy weapons trucks. But there were no press vehicles, which surprised and pleased McKenna. Pao dropped him off in front of the headquarters truck.

Brunette, Shields, Tavlin, and Hardcass were hunched over a map table set up near the front of the truck when McKenna entered by the rear door. No one else was there, and they didn't see him come in.

"I want to make sure we get some prisoners out of this," Brunette was saying. "If not, this operation will be a failure, and I don't know if we'll get another opportunity quite as good as this one.''

The truck was silent as everyone thought over the implications of Brunette's statement while they stared at the map. It was Hardcass who broke the silence.

''We can't miss. If the plan works, we lose none, and they might lose a couple. But there's sure to be plenty of prisoners left over. It's so easy that it's boring.''

Just like Hardcass, McKenna thought. Short, concise, and to the point.

Like everyone else in the police department, McKenna respected Lieutenant Hardcass. He had more than thirty years in the detective division, was experienced, clear thinking, and competent, but he was also a hard taskmaster and tough as nails. Still, McKenna found it difficult to like him, which really didn't matter at all, since McKenna and the rest of the department were always glad that Hardcass was on their side when things got tough.

Hardcass's comment brought the planning session to an end, and Brunette, Tavlin, and Shields breathed a sigh of relief. Obviously, if Hardcass liked the plan, then it must be a good one. Then Brunette looked up and saw McKenna standing by the door. ''You look better than the last time I saw you,'' Brunette said. ''How do you feel?''

''Ready for work.''

''Good, because you're gonna be in charge of this thing.''

''Me? Then what are you gonna be doing?''

''Sitting in my office, waiting for reports from the field.''

Why would Ray abdicate responsibility and leave it to me? McKenna wondered as he turned to Shields. ''And you?'' McKenna asked.

''Same thing, different office.''

The responses left McKenna deep in thought as he approached the map table. Tacked to the table was a large map of Brighton Beach and blueprints of 1143 Brighton 15th Street. ''Why me?'' McKenna asked as he studied the map, looking for hints of the plan.

''Simple,'' Brunette answered. ''Politics. The mayor has backed me into a corner. He wants to waste some time talking these folks out, but I see no reason for that. Time is too valuable, and we want to keep *Sendero* off balance. So I told him that you're in charge, and you want to go in and get them.''

It was becoming clearer to McKenna. ''And if something

goes wrong?'' he asked, fearing the answer.

''Then the mayor was right and I fire you, but that's just a ploy and it still really leaves us in charge to finish the job with these people. We're not gonna be able to keep the press at bay for too much longer, and His Honor has to worry about the newspaper performance polls. Our function is to get the job done while making him look good. If there are any setbacks, we know that some political sacrifices have to be made, starting with you.''

It was the answer McKenna expected. ''That makes you the next sacrifice,'' he said to Brunette.

''If we screw this one up, and the next one goes bad, then I'm up for the slaughter,'' Brunette said frankly.

''After that, I'm up,'' Shields said. ''The mayor will request that the investigation be turned over to the FBI, and we'll officially take over. But it will still be the three of us calling the shots, although two of us will be technically unemployed. We just had to build in some political escape hatches for His Honor to make sure this is done right.''

''The mayor knows all this?'' McKenna asked.

''He's no dope,'' Brunette answered, ''and he knows this *Sendero* thing is politically dangerous and fraught with variables. We don't have to put it into words for him.''

''I see,'' McKenna said. ''We know how many of them we'll be dealing with?''

''Eleven, we think,'' Brunette answered. ''At six-thirty this evening the surveillance teams saw a Domino's Pizza van make a big delivery to the house, and they questioned the delivery man when he came out. Five sandwiches, three pizzas, and eleven cans of soda.''

''He ever make a delivery there before?''

''Yeah. He's been making big deliveries to the house for about a week. Difference is, it used to be thirteen cans of soda.''

''That makes sense,'' McKenna said. ''We brought them down two. But what are they doing in Brighton Beach? You get anything on the owner of the house?''

Tavlin took a notepad out of his pocket and turned the pages as he talked. ''According to city tax records, 1143 Brighton 15th Street has been owned since 1983 by a man named Sergei Ivankovich. We saw that they had an ADT Alarm Company sticker on the front window, so I sent somebody to their office to talk to them. They installed the alarm in 1986 and their monthly bill goes to the Brighton Realty Management Corporation, so we talked to them. In 1986 Brighton Realty was hired to rent the place by a lawyer named Mr. Jacob Stern. Apparently he was the only one who ever met Ivankovich, and he hired the realty company to run the building."

"What does Stern say?"

"Nothing. He died in 1991."

"Interesting. So nobody we can talk to has ever seen this Sergei Ivankovich. Are we even sure he exists?"

Tavlin turned a page in his notepad. "He exists, but he's a bit of a mystery man. Checked with Immigration and Naturalization, and they have nothing on him. He applied for and received a Social Security number in 1979. Social Security records indicate that he presented a birth certificate from Coney Island Hospital saying he was born there on September 21st, 1947. Checked with the hospital and the New York City Bureau of Records. The birth certificate was a forgery. Shields got to the IRS and convinced them to divulge what they had on him, which turned out to be nothing."

The IRS cooperation surprised McKenna. Their records were never available to local law enforcement agencies and, by law, could only be made available to federal agencies charged with specifically investigating tax fraud. That wasn't the focus of this investigation, so some rules were being bent and laws were being broken. "What does the realty management company say about the present tenants?" he asked.

"Not much," Tavlin answered. "The last tenants left in April and the realty company received a letter from Ivankovich instructing them to leave the house vacant. On July 17th, a big ugly guy came into their office and showed them another letter from Ivankovich which authorized him to use the house."

"Emilio?" McKenna asked.

"Yeah, the manager identified the body. Anyway, the letter was in Russian, just like all of Ivankovich's previous correspondence with them, and Emilio had the keys. So they took the letter at face value."

"Then we can assume that Emilio at least met Ivankovich, but I don't see the connection," McKenna said. "How does the realty company get paid?"

"Commission basis. Emilio paid them two months' rent in cash, but all the previous tenants paid the realty company by check. After their commission, maintenance, and real estate taxes, they send what's left to Ivankovich's account with the

Third Federal Savings and Loan in Miami. Got to the bank and they say the money's just been sitting there for years.''

"Anything else on him?"

"Nothing. No credit cards under that Social Security number, no phone listing nationwide, and no driver's license issued by any state in that name with that date of birth.''

So what do we really know about this mystery man? McKenna asked himself. He can write in Russian, but was probably born in the United States, or at least speaks perfect English since the clerk at Social Security never questioned his birth certificate. The building he owns is in Brighton Beach, a very expensive real estate area, so he has money. And he went to the trouble fifteen years ago of setting up a false identity for himself. But for what purpose? It didn't have anything to do with *Sendero*, since their movement didn't get started in Peru until 1982, three years after he applied for the Social Security card. So what's the connection and where are the rest of the *Sendero* soldiers staying? McKenna asked himself.

"Does Ivankovich own any other real estate in New York City?" McKenna asked.

"No."

"Has there ever been a passport issued in the name of Sergei Ivankovich?" McKenna asked.

"No," Brunette answered. "Give up?"

"For now."

"So do we. It just doesn't make sense yet. We're hoping his new tenants will be able to shed some light on Mr. Ivankovich for us, once we introduce ourselves later on tonight.''

Brunette, followed by Shields, walked to the back door of the truck. Then Brunette turned to McKenna. "Coming?" he asked.

"Where?"

"To the communications truck to call your new girlfriend. I have some people there to help you out.''

Chapter 23
McKenna knew Lieutenant Pat Picciarelli as the department's polygraph expert and had worked with him many times in the past. Like everyone else, he respected Picciarelli's expertise and the way he used the mystique of the polygraph machine on the witnesses and suspects brought to him by detectives working a dead-end case. And like everyone else, McKenna detested Picciarelli's full head of black hair. Picciarelli didn't have a gray hair on his head, and had never lost a strand. If anything, McKenna thought with a twinge of jealousy, Picciarelli had even more hair than ever before.

Still, Picciarelli was the Interrogator of Last Resort when detectives were unable to crack a suspect's or witness's story and suspected they were being fed a line. The liars were brought to Picciarelli's office in the Police Academy, where he used the polygraph machine merely as a prop for the interrogation session. With the subject he was personable and caring, while at the same time he instilled in his prey a belief that the machine was infallible and that the truth would come out.

Smarter subjects refused to be tested after they got a measure of Picciarelli. Dumber ones gave him confessions before they were even hooked up to the polygraph machine. But it made no difference. The polygraph machine was only an investigative tool, and no results gained from it could be used in court. However, after his interrogation routine, and whether the subject cooperated or not, Picciarelli would always have a close approximation of the truth for the assigned detective.

But Picciarelli seemed to have a new trick up his sleeve, and McKenna was unfamiliar with it.

"Simple," Picciarelli explained as he ran his hand through

his hair before pointing to his new toy. "It's a voice stress analyzer. Anything we get from it won't be accepted by the courts, but at least I'll be able to give you some indication when she's lying."

"What do I have to do?" McKenna asked.

"Write yourself a little script of things you'd like to ask her, and include a question you think she'll lie about. That will give me a base line for the machine so I'll be able to differentiate between truth and fiction."

"I don't think she's gonna be giving away any secrets," McKenna said.

"Makes no difference," Brunette said. "If you know something she tells you is a lie, we'll be in a better position to guess the truth."

"Besides," Shields added, "she's got something on her mind and this call might give us an opportunity to locate her, if you can keep her on the line long enough."

"Ready?" Brunette asked, handing McKenna the phone. McKenna took it and stared at the two phone numbers written at the top of the piece of paper in front of him. One of them would ring Elena's cellular phone, but the other would ring *Sendero*'s second cellular phone, the one in their apartment on Brighton 15th Street.

Which number should I try? McKenna asked himself. How about "first things first"?

He dialed the top number on the list and waited. It was picked up after the second ring and a female voice asked, "Brian?"

She sounded so nice, so familiar, surprising McKenna so that it took him a second to answer. "Yeah, it's me. McKenna."

"You certainly took your time returning my call," she said sweetly, chiding him. "Be a dear and call me back in five minutes."

The line went dead, exactly as they had expected. Elena knew they were going to get her approximate location from the signal of her cellular phone, and she would be moving when he called back. Brunette, Shields, and McKenna stared at the back of the Communications Division technician's head while they waited for NYNEX to relay the news to them. Picciarelli sat stroking his mustache, appearing totally unconcerned.

The wait was less than a minute. The technician took off his headset and swiveled in his chair to face them. "Same East Side cell she was in when she called Headquarters. She's somewhere near the middle of the cell, but she didn't give them enough time to get a better location."

"Put the East Side map up," Brunette ordered.

"It's already up, Commissioner," Picciarelli said. He got up and switched on a backlight for a map-display case that hung on a wall of the communications truck. "Mr. Shields's teams are marked on the map."

McKenna walked over and studied the map. The FBI radio-direction locating vans were marked at the corners of the NY-NEX cell, East 42nd Street and Fifth Avenue, East 42nd Street and Third Avenue, East 53rd Street and Third Avenue, and East 53rd Street and Fifth Avenue.

"As you can see, she's where we hoped she'd be," Brunette said. "If she hits the streets, I've got an extra fifty uniformed men assigned to stop traffic if Shields's men can get close to her."

Still a long shot. Someplace in those densely populated fifty square blocks Elena is waiting for my call, McKenna thought. And we're supposed to locate her in the next five or ten minutes by following her phone signal? We're grabbing at straws, but I guess all the bases have to be covered.

McKenna looked from the map and saw that Brunette had put on a pair of headphones. Brunette nodded and McKenna dialed the number again. It was picked up immediately.

"Hi, Brian. Do you have my dress?" Elena asked.

McKenna could hear the sounds of traffic in the background over her slight Spanish accent. He waited a second before he answered, thinking the question ridiculous. "No, I'm sorry. Somebody swiped it while my pal was chasing you. They got your shoes, too."

Elena sighed. "That's too bad. It was a Paris original, you know. I really loved that dress."

"It looked great with your red hair. Good taste in a bad woman," McKenna said.

Elena took it as a compliment. "Thank you."

Try to shake her up, McKenna thought. "We almost got you today. We could be talking in person."

"I know. That was a very tough man you sent after me. He was so good I almost stopped to watch him fighting with those men on the beach. Is he Chinese?"

"Chinese and Irish."

"Good combination," she said with admiration in her voice. "Anything else on your mind?"

"Lots. You got time to talk?"

"You should know by now. I guess I've got a while before your people get too close."

So much for shaking her up, McKenna thought. Brunette handed him a note. *Going south, probably on Lex Ave., about 20 mph. Taxi?*

McKenna looked at the script, specifically at the question he figured she would lie about. "Okay, first question. Is red your natural color?"

"Of course not, but I like it. Do you?"

And so much for Picciarelli's base line, McKenna thought. What kind of woman doesn't lie about her hair color? "Very much," was all he could think to say.

"Too bad. I'm probably going to have to change it after our adventure today."

McKenna decided to try another tack. "I'm sorry about your friends today."

"Don't be," she stated with schoolgirl innocence. "One was a pig and I hardly knew the other. You were just doing your job, and they certainly would have killed you."

"Emilio was the pig?"

There was no surprise in her voice that McKenna knew the name. "Yes, a degenerate sadistic pig. He won't be missed."

"Speaking of sadistic, you didn't have to come today. It seems to me you wanted to watch Maximo die."

"Then I admit it," she said frankly. "I wasn't happy with the decision to kill him, but I wanted to see how he died. You have to acknowledge that he is a little impressed with himself, in an annoying sort of way."

"I don't know him as well as you do. I never went to bed with him."

Elena laughed. "Of course not, but you aren't missing much."

Brunette handed McKenna another note. *Out of initial NY-NEX cell, south on Lex. Taxi?*

McKenna wasn't ready to ask the taxi question that might end the conversation. Instead he asked, "Why did you really call me? Surely it wasn't just the dress?"

"I liked the dress, but I also wanted to ask you something else. No, tell you something."

"I'm listening."

"You wanted to go to your friend's funeral tomorrow, right? The one who saved your life."

"Yes, I want to go. Keller was a good man."

"But you won't go, because you feel we may try something there."

"I might still go."

"Then do it. It's safe for you to go. We have no plans for you there."

"Thank you. Should I believe you?"

"Of course."

For some reason, McKenna did believe her. Brunette passed him another note. *Eastbound in the 30s. Closing in.*

"But your people will still try to kill me?"

"Probably, but not tomorrow."

"Will you be there to see how I die?"

The line was silent. For a few seconds, McKenna thought she had hung up. Then she answered. "I hope not. I think I like you. Call me back in five minutes, if you want." The line went dead.

"Damn," Brunette said, disgusted. "They were only a couple of blocks away from her."

"Close as we're gonna get, I think," said Shields. "She knows she's being tracked."

"What did you think of her?" Brunette asked, tapping Picciarelli on the shoulder.

"She's real smooth. I need a few more minutes to examine the voiceprint tape, but off the top of my head I don't think she told a single lie. However, she might be a complete psychotic, which I don't discount. That would make the voiceprint results useless."

"Why?" McKenna asked.

"Psychotics frequently believe their own lies as soon as they form them, so their voices show no measurable stress when they tell them."

"So she really called about the dress?" McKenna asked.

"Hard to believe, but that's it."

And to tell me I could go to the funeral, McKenna thought. Very nice of her, but why? Because she likes me? That couldn't really be it, could it? "What do you think?" he asked Brunette.

"We got nothing useful from her. I think you have to show our hand a little and see if you can shake her up. If that works, give her an offer to come in."

"What kind of offer?"

"Immunity, our guarantee that she won't be extradited to Peru, and one million cash. That should move her."

McKenna was stunned at the offer. "Would we give her all that?"

"Yes," Brunette answered unequivocally. "To get the rest of them and end all this, it would be a cheap price."

"Shaking that girl up isn't going to be easy," Picciarelli said.

"I've got a few things to tell her that might shake her up," McKenna said. "Besides, I think I'm beginning to understand her."

"Really? Care to share this wisdom?" Brunette asked.

McKenna wasn't ready to, and was saved from answering by the communications technician. "They got a confirmed fix on her last location. East 32nd Street and Third Avenue. Nothing there now."

She might as well have been there last year, McKenna thought as he picked up the phone.

"It's not five minutes yet," Shields said.

"Who's in charge, us or her?" McKenna asked as he dialed the phone. It went unanswered until the recorded message from the NYNEX operator came on. "She shut her phone off," McKenna told his bemused colleagues. They whiled away the next few minutes staring at the clock on the wall.

"Five minutes," the technician said and McKenna redialed. Elena was there and spoke first. "Was that your men in the furniture truck on Third Avenue?"

"Hold on. I'll check." McKenna held his hand over the mouthpiece. "One of your teams using a furniture truck?" he asked Shields, who nodded. "Yeah, that was one of ours," McKenna told Elena.

"Very good. You were close."

"Thanks. Is Felipe with you?" That should shake her up a bit, McKenna thought.

It didn't. "No, he's not. I guess you've been talking to Colonel Savraada."

"Yeah, nice man. Very well informed."

"He's an honest man, I'll say that for him," Elena said. "A rarity in the government."

"Does Felipe know you're talking to me?"

"Yes, but does Angelita know you're talking to me?"

Elena's mention of Angelita's name sent a chill up Mc-

Kenna's spine, and he took a moment before answering. "No, she doesn't. But I'll tell her."

"Why?"

"What difference does it make? We're strictly business, aren't we?"

"I guess so. Too bad for both of us."

"I don't know. You're beautiful, and I'm sure you're exciting, but I don't think you're my kind of girl."

"Maybe you'll change your mind after you meet me again."

"You're planning on meeting me again?"

"Soon."

"You might be right," McKenna said. "Maybe I'll visit you in jail. We're gonna get you, whether you believe it or not."

"Do you think you're close?" she asked innocently.

She's mocking us, McKenna thought. He was about to reply when he stopped himself. Wait a minute. I'm supposed to be getting information from her, not the other way around.

Brunette handed McKenna another note. *Northbound on Mad Ave. in the 40s. Closing in. Get her excited and keep her talking.*

"Do you want me at the funeral tomorrow because you're planning something big someplace else?"

"I'm surprised at you, Brian. You're flattering yourself."

For the first time, Picciarelli came to life. He stood up and waved to McKenna. "She's showing stress," he whispered.

"Please answer the question, Elena."

"I'm hanging up."

"Wait. Talk to me for another minute, for your own good. If you surrender and cooperate, I'm authorized to offer you one million dollars, immunity from prosecution, and a guarantee that you won't be extradited."

Elena was laughing.

"You don't believe me?" McKenna asked.

It took her another few mirthful seconds before she answered. "I'm sorry, Brian. I believe you, but how's this? I'm authorized to lift your death sentence and give you two million dollars to join us. Think about it, okay?"

"I can't."

"Then you understand how I feel. I have to go now. Traffic is slowing down and there's a good chance your men are responsible. But I'm going to do something nice for you tomorrow just to see how sharp you are.''

Over the phone McKenna could hear horns blaring. ''Elena. My offer's good right now. Are you in a taxi?''

''No.'' The line went dead.

''She's in a taxi,'' Picciarelli yelled. The technician repeated the information to the FBI teams on the East Side while everyone settled down to wait.

''Turn the radio up so we can hear it,'' Brunette ordered. The technician flipped a switch on his console and took off his headphones.

''Team Two to Base. We found the taxi she was in. Driver says his fare was an old lady talking on a cellular phone. She paid and left the cab two minutes ago when he got stuck in traffic at Madison and 43rd. Gray hair, blue dress, walks with a limp, carrying a Macy's shopping bag. He didn't see which way she went.''

Two minutes is too long, McKenna thought. She's gone, this time.

The radio remained silent for the next five minutes, but the next transmission proved McKenna right. ''Team Four to Base. We've got the shopping bag. She dumped it under a car at East 43rd and Vanderbilt. Contains a gray wig and a new pair of ladies' red shoes, size seven. Hot dog vendor on the street states a good-looking redhead in a blue dress passed him and walked into Grand Central Station five minutes ago. No limp, but she really swung her undercarriage.''

McKenna tried her number again, but that was the last they heard of Elena that night.

Elena generally didn't like traitors, but the American she particularly despised. For what she considered to be a pittance, he was prepared not only to betray his country, but to help murder his countrymen. She wasn't looking forward to meeting him again and sincerely hoped Felipe's plan succeeded so the American's ingredients wouldn't have to be used. She believed in revenge, but to kill thousands because a plan failed seemed to her to be overstating a point. Felipe did not know that she disagreed with his perspective on this question.

Elena almost hoped the American wouldn't be there, but he was, sitting on the bench on Central Park South and feeding the pigeons a few bread crumbs from a jar. There was a pretty brown-and-white pigeon among the group of feeding birds and it seemed to Elena that the American liked that one best. With his foot he kept the other pigeons away from the bread crumbs, permitting his favorite to feed. A closed Thermos sat next to him on the bench.

Elena paid the taxi driver, got out of the cab, and walked over. The pigeons scattered as she approached and sat next to the American. Without looking at her, he asked, "Do you like pigeons?"

"No."

"Good. Do you know what to do with the formula?"

"Yes."

Without saying another word, the American screwed the top on his jar of bread crumbs, got up, and started walking toward Fifth Avenue. Elena waited a minute before picking up the Thermos and examining it thoughtfully. Something made her look up: a brown-and-white pigeon fell off a window ledge on the other side of the street. It hit the sidewalk, fluttered its wings a few times, and stopped moving.

Elena crossed the street, stepping past the dead bird with the practiced indifference of a native New Yorker. She got into one of the taxis waiting in line in front of the Plaza Hotel.

Chapter 24 JULY 27, BRIGHTON BEACH, NEW YORK—Just after midnight McKenna arrived on the corner of Brighton 15th Street and Brighton Beach Avenue, looking for his surveillance teams. Seeing no sign of them on the deserted street, he raised his radio and transmitted, "McKenna to Surveillance Team One. How's it look?"

"Pretty good, Commissioner. Looks like most of them went to bed. Only light on is in the living room, near the front of the house."

"From where you are, can you see inside?"

"No, sir. The blinds are closed tight."

"Any sign of a lookout?"

"No, sir."

McKenna took another long look down the block, but still couldn't see where his surveillance teams were hiding. "Can you see me?" he asked.

"Yes, sir. Glad you lost the hat."

So am I, McKenna thought. He raised his radio again. "McKenna to Headquarters Truck. Let's get started."

"On the way," Tavlin answered.

McKenna saw a long line of police vehicles approaching Brighton Beach Avenue. The avenue was blocked off as soon as the convoy stopped near McKenna's corner. Leading the procession were three Emergency Service trucks, followed by two paddy wagons, the headquarters truck, the Bomb Squad bomb-disposal truck, the communications truck, and two civil-defense chemical decontamination trucks. Bringing up the rear were five ambulances.

The rear doors of the two paddy wagons swung open and the seventeen members of the assault team assembled on the sidewalk, looking like an invading force from another world with their heavy vests and helmets, the air tanks on their backs, and the goggles on their eyes. McKenna could distinguish Hardcass only by his size as he formed them into line, then led them around the corner. Four men with gas grenade guns fell in behind Hardcass, followed by eight men carrying two heavy battering rams between them and four men with shotguns held in the ready position.

Hardcass stopped his team line one house short of 1143 Brighton 15th Street, unslung his shotgun, and looked to McKenna for the signal.

In the living room of the house sat three men watching TV. Only their leader, Jesus Arroyo, was armed, but he was having a difficult time. It had been a tough day for Squad One of the Second Platoon, Fifth Sword of Marxism Company. They had received no further instructions from Felipe after the failure on Brighton 2nd Street, so the men were nervous and uncertain of their next course of action.

Things had happened that night that would have been unthinkable if Emilio were still there. Arroyo had told his troops that their part of the operation would proceed as scheduled, and three of them had openly disagreed with his decision.

In Peru, Arroyo would have had them and their families

shot and the discussion would have been over. But they were in New York. Each man had been trained in a specific part of the assigned mission and he needed them all to ensure success. Fearing mutiny, Arroyo had collected the weapons and locked them in the attic, leaving himself with the only pistol. He sensed that his men resented his action, but nobody voiced their opinion after he pointed out to them that they had been relieved of the tedious and boring task of cleaning and recleaning their weapons, a chore they had performed twice a day since arriving in New York. Then Arroyo had ordered pizza and gave another training session after they ate.

Only Arroyo knew that other units would commence hostilities against the Americans in the morning, but that his squad wasn't scheduled to go into action for another three days. Only he knew that there was plenty of time for Felipe to issue further instructions or changes in the plan. But he wasn't permitted to soothe the nerves of his young combat veterans by giving them that information.

As he had expected, the training session proved to be unnecessary. They had been over it a thousand times in Honduras and in New York, and each man knew exactly what he had to do when the time came. Every contingency was covered by Felipe's plan, and Arroyo's training session simply bored them. One man had actually fallen asleep while Arroyo was talking. Unthinkable!

Without Emilio, discipline was crumbling, but Arroyo wasn't too worried. He was sure that whatever Felipe was planning for the first part of the operation would be on the news, and discipline and esprit de corps would be restored. They had experienced a setback, but Arroyo was confident that Felipe had taken setbacks into account when he formed the plan for the operation.

Bored with the Mexican western they had watched a few times since arriving in New York, Arroyo aimed the remote at the TV and changed the channel to CNN.

"Hey, I was watching that," Julio Montalvo protested from the sofa.

Unthinkable! thought Arroyo. He got up, walked over to Montalvo, and punched him in the face. Montalvo offered no resistance, but glared up at him. Arroyo had raised his fist to strike again when the lights and the TV went off.

Arroyo yelled a warning to his men, but his shout was covered by the sound of the back and front doors splintering. He dropped to the floor in the darkness as he heard the windows breaking, but the floor was the worst place for him to be. A gas grenade exploded next to his head, burning his face as he sucked in the choking fumes. He got his pistol out of his holster, and through his tears searched the darkness for a target. He heard movement in front of him and raised his pistol to fire, then heard the explosion from a shotgun, close. He felt a jolt of pain in his hand, but still concentrated on squeezing the trigger. He was confused when nothing happened.

It came to him as he felt a fist crash into his face. He no longer had a functioning right hand.

Instinctively, McKenna started running toward the house when he heard the shotgun blast, but he caught himself and stopped. He watched as the three Emergency Service trucks pulled in front of the house. The backup team poured out of the trucks and deployed around the building, each man carrying a Mini-14 automatic rifle.

They weren't needed. McKenna waited and heard shouting inside the house, but no further gunfire. Then Hardcass appeared at the shattered front door and waved to him. It was over, and none too soon. The tear gas was seeping out of the house and affecting the backup men outside. They looked happy to get back in their trucks and leave, making room for the chemical decontamination trucks.

McKenna radioed the headquarters truck and ordered the power restored. The streetlights went on instantly. Then he walked toward 1143, but stopped two houses away when he got a whiff of tear gas. He decided that he could see all he needed to see from there.

A minute later ten choking and handcuffed prisoners were brought out and dragged into the decontamination truck by the Emergency Service cops. Next McKenna heard Hardcass call for an ambulance over the radio. When the ambulance pulled in front, Hardcass and an Emergency Service cop carried another prisoner out between them. The man was wearing a shoulder holster, his right hand was badly mangled, his face was burned, and he was choking.

They placed the prisoner on the ground and Hardcass kept him still by planting his foot on his chest while the Emergency Service cop ran to the decontamination truck. He returned a moment later with a fire extinguisher and Hardcass sprayed the prisoner with water until he stopped choking. Then they lifted him into the ambulance, the Emergency Service cop got in behind the prisoner, and the ambulance took off.

Hardcass took off his Scott Pack and gave it to another one of the Emergency Service cops, along with a string of orders. Then he walked over to McKenna, impervious to the effects of the tear gas.

McKenna could smell the gas on Hardcass's clothes, but was determined not to be a sissy. However, his eyes started to tear and he did back six feet away from Hardcass.

Hardcass didn't seem to notice. "Complete success," he reported. "I had to blast that one guy, but he'll live. Funny thing is, he was the only one armed, but all he had was a .45 Colt in a shoulder holster."

"Find any other weapons in there?"

"In the attic, but not all the stuff we're looking for. Just enough to arm a military squad, with a couple of machine guns thrown in. This place is just a housing outpost, not their main base."

"Any explosives?"

"Didn't see any."

"Any injuries to your men?"

"Nothing they'd complain to me about."

McKenna understood perfectly. They might have some cuts and bruises, but unless they were shot or missing some limbs, they'd keep it to themselves rather than engage Hardcass's questionable sympathies.

"We ready to start the cleanup?" McKenna asked.

"Might as well. I'm gonna go back in and take another look around."

Two houses on either side of 1143 were evacuated, and the Russian residents didn't seem to mind or even notice the tear gas. McKenna theorized that they probably had built up an immunity to the stuff in the old country. They expressed no curiosity about the fate of their recent neighbors as the decontamination truck left to take the prisoners to the interrogators waiting at police headquarters.

Large exhaust fans were brought into the house and placed at the doors and windows to clear the tear gas. It took longer than McKenna expected, and he and Sheeran were waiting impatiently when an Emergency Service cop approached them.

"There's a blue van in the garage," he reported.

"Is it stolen?" McKenna asked.

"Yes, sir. Stolen in Coney Island on July 19th."

Figures, McKenna thought. Stolen on the same day and in the same neighborhood as the car they shot Ray's kid from. Looks like we found the van that was spotted on the Jersey Turnpike.

McKenna and Sheeran followed the cop to the garage and watched as the detectives from the Crime Scene Unit dusted the outside door handles and lifted a few fingerprints from them. Then they opened the rear door of the van and the smell of rotting flesh hit them hard. The source was a body tightly wrapped in two large plastic garbage bags, which didn't surprise McKenna. The Crime Scene detectives pulled the wrapped body from the van and placed it on the garage floor.

"Should we open it, Commissioner?" one of them asked.

"Go ahead," McKenna said, wishing he could find an excuse to say no and avoid the next unpleasant task.

They cut the bag open and the smell got worse. Inside was the body of a short man dressed in a suit. The right side of his jacket and pants were stained with dried, matted blood.

"Looks like we found the one Ray's kid shot before he died," McKenna said. "The clothing description matches."

"I wonder why they didn't get rid of the body," Sheeran said.

McKenna wondered the same thing until he thought he found the answer. "They figured they didn't have to, because whatever they're planning is going to happen soon."

Sheeran thought that over. "You're probably right. It would have to be soon, before the smell got out of the garage and annoyed the neighbors."

Without exchanging another word, McKenna and Sheeran decided that, whatever the house smelled like, it had to be better than the garage. They left to search the house through their tears, but were pleased to find that the exhaust fans had done a good job of clearing the gas. They saw that very little damage had been done during the assault, and everything had been left in place after the prisoners were removed. The interior of the house was neat, clean, and furnished.

The search of the two bedrooms yielded nothing but sleeping bags and ten battered old suitcases of different colors and brands. Each contained two fresh sets of clothes, four sets of underwear, and toiletries. They found no pictures or papers of identification.

The kitchen, the bathroom, and the dining room were spotless, but there was nothing there to interest McKenna and Sheeran. They saved the living room for last as that was the place where the gas had been strongest. There were three suitcases arranged along one wall, and they started with them. The search of the suitcases was unproductive, but McKenna knew that one he searched belonged to Emilio; the clothes in it were too big to fit any of the other prisoners. Again, there were no pictures or papers of identification.

It wasn't until they searched the dresser in the living room that they found anything that shed any light on *Sendero*'s plans, and what they found gave them a lot to think about. In one of the dresser drawers was a map of Kennedy Airport, schematic drawings of the Northwest Airlines terminal, and a model of a Boeing 727.

"Looks like they were planning to hijack a plane," Sheeran observed.

"Looks like it," McKenna answered. "Let's go see what they've got in the attic."

Stacked in the center of the attic they found the weapons Hardcass had described. There were ten loaded .45 Colt pistols with spare magazines, six M-16 rifles, a wooden box containing more loaded magazines for the rifles, two M-60 machine guns loaded with 400-round assault packs, and a box containing twelve M-29 fragmentation grenades.

"They'd have no trouble taking a plane with all this stuff," Sheeran said. "Looks like we did good."

"Not good enough," McKenna said, unsmiling, as he opened the breech of one of the machine guns and removed the belt of ammo. "They still have all the explosives and most of their weapons, along with a lot of manpower. What we have here is just the tip of the iceberg, and we're still in big trouble."

"Maybe our prisoners will shed some light on whatever they're planning," Sheeran volunteered.

"I hope so," McKenna said as he took his phone from his pocket. He called Brunette at headquarters and told him what they had found.

"Leave Tavlin and Sheeran there to clean up and get over here," Brunette ordered.

"Anything else?"

"Yeah. Don't have the body sent to the morgue yet. Bring it here."

"The body? Why?" McKenna asked.

"Because I wanna have a look at it."

"Are you sure? He really stinks."

"Good."

Something else out of character, McKenna thought. He hung up and relayed Brunette's orders to Sheeran.

"I'm not surprised," Sheeran said. "This afternoon he had the two bodies from Brighton 2nd Street brought to the college campus, and he spent a long time just staring at them. He did the same thing with the guy you shot at the funeral."

That was news to McKenna. Very unusual conduct, he thought, bothered by the evidence that his friend might be cracking up.

Brunette wasn't delighted with the results of the operation. "We're going to have to beef up security at the airports and get some information from those prisoners," he said after looking at the diagrams of the Northwest Airlines terminal and the model of the Boeing 727.

"You've got nothing from them yet?" McKenna asked.

"Nothing. I've got them all separated on the thirteenth floor, and they haven't talked to each other since we got them. We've offered them lawyers, but they still won't say a word. Won't even give us their names. What bothers me is that they all still look confident."

"We're gonna have to offer them a deal, just like we did in Texas. One of them has to talk."

"It's got to be soon. The mayor's under a lot of pressure and we have to give him some kind of a plan. Otherwise, he's gonna come clean with the press, and our pictures of Felipe and Elena will be on the front page of every paper in the country with the HAVE YOU SEEN THIS PERSON? caption underneath."

McKenna didn't get it. "Is that bad?" he asked.

"Maybe not, except bringing the public into it forces us to admit we can't catch these people on our own," Brunette said, looking dismayed at the prospect.

"You're forgetting we still have an ace in the hole," McKenna offered, hoping to cheer up Brunette a bit.

"What's that?"

"Colonel Savraada."

Chapter 25

JULY 27, AYACUCHO, PERU—Until the 1970s, the descendants of the conquistadors who ruled Peru regarded Ayacucho as the small and unimportant district capital of one of the more backward and rural departments of the country. The area was dismissed as commercially unproductive since there were no sizable mineral deposits and the soil and climate were not suitable for the type of large-scale farming established elsewhere in the country.

Even the natives were not worth exploiting. The city was peopled by a particularly surly and rustic bunch of Indians who spoke Quechua, the ancient language of the Incas, a linguistic ability that entitled them to a permanent place at the bottom of Peruvian society. The majority were poor and illiterate sustenance farmers or small traders who eked out a living in their barter society, barely making enough to stay alive and reluctantly pay their rents to the absentee landowners in Lima. As a result, Ayacucho was treated to official benign neglect.

Its location on the remote eastern slopes of the Andes, far from the western coastal cities, made Ayacucho easy to ignore. The first road to connect the city to the rest of the country was not built until 1924, there was no river running through Ayacucho to facilitate commerce, and the nearest railroad station was 100 miles away.

But Ayacucho did have a history, and this was what caused it to be brought into the national spotlight. First established in 1537 as a military outpost by the Spaniards in their war of subjugation against the Incas, the city figured prominently in all wars fought during subsequent Peruvian history. It was at Ayacucho in 1824 that the last battle of the War of Independence was fought, when forces under the command of the great liberator, Simón Bolívar, defeated the royalist army and ended three centuries of Spanish domination of South America. The next defense of the nation occurred in 1847, when a military unit from Ayacucho stopped the Chilean invasion of Peru in the War of the Pacific and earned the natives of the region their reputation as fierce and uncompromising warriors.

But time passed, and Ayacucho was forgotten by the ruling class in Lima until it was discovered by foreign tourists. The reason they wanted to see Ayacucho was indirectly the fault and fortune of the government. Ayacucho had been so neglected that it was the best place in Peru for them to see authentic examples of Spanish colonial architecture. No new government buildings had been erected for centuries and the ones built by the conquistadors still served their original purposes, unencumbered by modern plumbing and lighting.

But while the tourists were snapping their pictures and spending their money, they couldn't help but notice that the colorful and interesting natives were totally excluded from Peruvian society and living in dismal poverty. They inquired about this and learned that their hosts were disenfranchised because of their language, since literacy in Spanish was a requirement for voting. Although many of the natives professed a desire to learn the language, there were few schools and the university had been closed by the government. Most went no further than the first grade, which was taught in Spanish.

Not long after the arrival of the tourists, international aid began pouring into the region and the government was pressured to reopen the University de San Cristobal de Huamanga in Ayacucho. Hired as head of the Philosophy Department was Professor Carlos Abimael Guzman, a kindly, highly educated man who was, incidentally, a dedicated communist. His lecture manner and his ideas electrified his students so that he was idolized by them, and he was a master of organization.

Guzman had a plan and a vision of the role he was to play. He had prepared himself well by learning English, German, French, and even Quechua. Before his appointment to the university, Guzman had traveled to China and became a great admirer of Mao and the agricultural and social reforms he had instituted. He decided that Mao's revolutionary ideas would work in Peru, if accompanied by a few twists from the mind of Guzman to fit the locale.

He saturated his students with dialectic materialism, but explained to them that their ancestors, practicing the Inca communal method of farming, were actually the first communists, predating Karl Marx by 400 years. He also pointed out to them that Ayacucho was located at the exact geographic center of the Inca Empire, which had to mean something. Blending mysticism, history, ancient traditions, and communist theory into a creed for his students, he motivated them to go forth and recapture their rightful place in the world. His teachings replaced Catholicism as their religion and they came to view the church, with its repression of their ancient beliefs, as just another controlling influence of the conquistadors.

Ordinarily, Guzman and his disciples would have been a minor Indian problem, the kind of thing that the descendants of the conquistadors had gained experience in dealing with over the centuries. But a few things were happening around Peru that altered the environment Guzman was operating in and furthered his efforts.

First was agrarian reform. In Lima, a leftist government had taken power in a coup and the large *hacienda* estates were being broken up with the stated intent of turning the land over to the families who actually farmed it. Of course, Peru being Peru, it didn't work that way. One way or the other, the estates remained in the same hands, but the owners now looked on their low-paid tenant farmers as a potential source of trouble. They decided to mechanize their farms to dispense with the problem, the result being that millions of newly unemployed, unskilled, uneducated, and landless Indians had no place to go, so they wound up looking for work in the cities. The population of Lima doubled, then tripled as shantytown slums sprang up in the desert surrounding the city. The new residents lived in abject misery, and the government made little effort to improve their lot.

Into this environment came the new graduates of San Cristobal University, armed with their degrees and an enhanced sense of self-esteem, ready to make their place in the white man's world.

They were neither needed nor wanted. The labor market was saturated, and any prospective employers they found asked themselves the same question: Who needs another snotty Indian around, especially one with a degree who thinks he's just as good as I am, maybe even better? The result was that most found themselves back in Ayacucho within a short period of time, and many took employment in the university. There Guzman had been promoted to head of personnel, and he was busy hiring teachers who agreed with his philosophy and purging those who didn't.

The returning natives also found that something else was

happening in Ayacucho. The people of the Western world had discovered the little trick that the descendants of the Incas had always known about and used to alleviate the sickness and fatigue that comes with living at high altitudes and being employed at hard and mindless labor. The little bush that grows like a weed on the eastern slopes of the Andes between 5,000 and 7,000 feet was used as the source of the fashionable new drug of choice: cocaine. Ayacucho was at 8,000 feet, and overnight the town was filled with Colombians buying the coca crop and somewhat mystifying the natives. The coca leaf had always been used as a form of currency among the people of the high Andes, but the surprising appetite of the foreigners for their simple home remedy made things a lot easier for them. Green cash was much easier to carry around than a basket full of leaves.

They had discovered the American dollar and were surprised how the mere possession of this foreign currency changed their social status. There is a saying in Peru that money whitens, and suddenly there were white people from Lima everywhere, treating the the townspeople with deference while selling them everything under the sun. The town, which ten years before had boasted a dozen cars and two buses, began experiencing traffic jams. Televisions, radios, and VCRs gave them their first glimpse of the outside world, and they saw the things they had been missing.

Naturally, the arrival of cash in town was followed by police and politicians from Lima. The people of Ayacucho had been discovered to the extent that they were worth exploiting. They were told that the sale of the coca leaf was illegal, which meant in effect that only the politicians could sell it. There were some protests and minor acts of violence directed at the government and the police, and these expressions of discontent were quickly followed by more police.

Guzman was gathering strength and biding his time through all of this when international and domestic pressure forced the government to schedule an election. Quechua had been added as the second official language of Peru, so for the first time the Indians were going to be permitted the vote. The elections were scheduled for May 18, 1980.

The prospect of elections threw Guzman into a panic. He had spent his life preparing for the armed confrontation between the righteous peasantry and the oppressive forces of racist international capitalism, but the government was set to remove one of the major grievances. He suspected the election results would be manipulated in any event, leaving the oligarchy in power, and he convinced his followers that the vote was a duplicitous trick. He set out to disrupt the electoral process.

On May 17 six armed masked men burned the ballot boxes in the Ayacucho town hall, and the armed struggle was launched. Shortly thereafter, the police and other government representatives were ejected from town. Guzman went underground and directed the movement under the nom de guerre of Chairman Gonzalo. He wrote copiously and his works, called *Gonzalo Thought*, were studied, memorized, and recited by his followers—who called themselves *Sendero Luminoso*, the Shining Path—as religious tracts that served to propel them to unleash a bloodbath.

Within a year both the government and *Sendero* were identified by Amnesty International as culprits in numerous atrocities against the civilian population. Thirteen years later *Sendero* dominated 40 percent of the country, and 30,000 people had died.

Most of the residents of Ayacucho slept, but *Sendero* was wide awake and on guard in the person of Sinsi Althapaca. Cradling his M-16 in his arms as he sat on the roof of the Hotel Samay on Callao Street, Sinsi was a deeply troubled young man, unsure of himself and unsure of the direction the revolution was taking. The yellow fever that still made him cough and shiver had brought him close to death two weeks before in the Amazon jungle, and had also given him a new perspective on life. In his delirium he had seen God, only briefly, but Sinsi knew who He was and saw that the Almighty was angry with him.

Before his sickness, Sinsi had not doubted the existence of God. Rather, as a result of his *Sendero* training, he had been absolutely convinced that He did not exist. He had been taught since adolescence that the concept of God was simply an instrument of oppression used by the oligarchy to keep the proletariat productive, docile, and in line. Sinsi had accepted without reservation all the teachings of Chairman Gonzalo, and with *Gonzalo Thought* always in his mind, had aspired to be a hero of the revolution and servant of the proletariat. He had been considered a good soldier by his comrades and had thought some of the unpleasant things he was called upon to do were necessary for the new order, and therefore justifiable, but his fever had produced the realization that he was a murderer many times over.

Without knowing why, Sinsi found himself staring at the bell tower of the San Francisco de Paula Church, one block away. Then it came to him. He felt an overwhelming need to confess, which would be a difficult thing to do in Ayacucho. In a city of thirty-three churches, there were only two priests left. But he knew that Padre Ramon had braved the threats and beatings over the years, and was still there, at San Francisco de Paul, the church Sinsi had attended as a boy before the madness began. Padre Ramon would hear his confession and save him from the fire. He had so much to tell, so much to be forgiven for, so many spirits to exorcise and put to rest.

It wasn't the soldiers he had killed in combat or during ambush that weighed on his soul. Nor was it the informers and traitors he had been called upon to dispatch. It was war, and he reasoned that those killings were an acceptable part of warfare, not murder. What bothered him were three particular souls and a host of others without faces who had recently been making recurring appearances in his nightmares, people he had blindly murdered under orders from his superiors.

It was in the village of Cayera that it had happened. Since the village had failed to make the suggested contribution to the cause, Sinsi's squad went there under orders to investigate and take appropriate action. When they arrived, Sinsi saw that Cayera was poor, even by Andean standards. All the homes were made of dried mud, with earth floors, and had no electricity or running water. The villagers were hungry and dressed in rags. Still, they were rounded up in the small plaza to witness the trial of the village headman.

The trial was perfunctory, but the headman put up a spirited defense. He explained that the soldiers had come and, after beating them and accusing them of being *Sendero* sympathizers, stolen their crops and livestock and removed half the families in the village to a *ronda,* one of the government's fortified hamlets.

"Did you fight the soldiers?" the squad leader asked.

"We had no weapons to fight them with," the headman replied.

"Were any of the villagers killed by the soldiers?"

"Beaten, but not killed."

"Have any of the families escaped from the *ronda* and returned?"

None had. "Why should they? Look around," the headman pleaded. "You see we have nothing."

From his own mouth the headman had assured his fate. He was responsible for the conduct of his people. Submitting to the government without a fight and allowing families to be placed under government influence in a *ronda* was sufficient justification for the death sentence for the headman.

But first there had to be an official verdict, so the squad leader explained the situation to his men in terms of *Gonzalo Thought*: "For the revolution to succeed, it is necessary to kill one to terrorize a thousand." The verdict was unanimous and the squad leader pronounced the sentence. The headman, his wife, and his son would die by the knife.

Sinsi disagreed with the sentence. The headman and his wife he could understand, but their three-year-old son? He was answered by the squad leader with more *Gonzalo Thought*: "We are in a struggle that will take generations, so leave no enemies for your sons to fight. Act without malice, but without mercy."

As a result of his disagreement, Sinsi was designated to carry out the sentence before the assembled villagers. Sinsi had no choice and was accustomed to obeying the most ruthless of orders. The headman and his wife were seized by the squad and the sentence was pronounced. Sinsi had expected screaming and pleading, but the headman surprised him and accepted his fate stoically. The only emotion he displayed was a tear that dripped from his eye as Sinsi lifted the unprotesting child off the ground and plunged his knife into the heart.

The child died without uttering a sound and Sinsi placed the body on the ground and attended to the woman. She was in uncomprehending and silent shock as she stared at the body of her son. Sinsi slashed her throat and believed she died without ever feeling the blade.

But Sinsi felt something. For the first time, he felt self-conscious and ashamed in front of the villagers, who were watching him with an emotion he couldn't name. It wasn't hate and it wasn't anger. It wasn't even fear. If anything, he thought it might be resignation. He approached the headman, who wore the same expression as the rest of the villagers. The difference was, the headman had something to say. "Why do you do this?'' he asked. ''We are poor farm folk, just like you.''

The headman's attitude and question confused Sinsi, but only for a moment. ''Because you are guilty!'' he screamed as he plunged his knife into the man's chest.

The headman didn't appear to notice the knife in his chest. ''No, you are guilty, and we will be with you always,'' he said calmly as he stared into Sinsi's eyes.

Sinsi pulled his knife from the headman's chest and stabbed him again. Again, the headman didn't seem to notice. He just stared at Sinsi as the life left his eyes. Sinsi pulled his knife out and wiped it on the man's shirt before he sheathed it and his companions released the body.

While the squad leader appointed a new headman and gave instructions for the disposal of the bodies, Sinsi stared at his victim's back, almost expecting him to get up again.

As the squad was marching from the village, the squad leader fell in next to Sinsi. ''Comrade, that was badly done,'' he admonished. ''You let them die looking like heroes.''

''I did something wrong?'' Sinsi asked, confused.

''Yes, Comrade. You should have thought of something to make them scream and give the villagers something they would remember.''

''That man would never scream,'' Sinsi answered.

''Maybe you're right,'' the squad leader conceded, with the hint of a smile on his lips. ''It is usually the guilty who scream their innocence.''

The squad leader's analysis confused Sinsi. ''Then they were innocent?'' he asked.

The squad leader stared at him, but didn't answer. Then he smiled and shook his head, apparently at Sinsi's ignorance.

Sinsi's mind worked furiously as they marched. He reached a conclusion and knew that he shouldn't ask the question, but he did. ''Comrade Squad Leader, if they were innocent, then why did we kill them?''

The squad leader was waiting for the question. ''I thought so,'' he said with disgust as he stopped the column and turned to Sinsi. ''Comrade, you have been lax. You must read more of Chairman Gonzalo's works for better understanding. The answers are there.''

Sinsi did study harder, but understanding still eluded him. Recent events had served to confuse him further. He had so many questions to think about.

For instance, why the long march into the jungle, where he had contracted the yellow fever, and why were they formed into a battalion there in the first place? And why did they kill and bury all the Amazon Indians they saw during the march? They were not part of the struggle and Sinsi was sure that the primitive Indians they killed didn't even know about the war. They were more innocents, and their faceless souls haunted his dreams.

Another question bothered Sinsi. Why had so many senior comrades disappeared without a trace? He had even dared to ask his squad leader about them. Were they killed or captured? Worse yet, were they deserters or traitors? The way his squad leader answered led Sinsi to believe that he didn't know the real answer himself. "The senior comrades are operating under secret orders," the squad leader told him. "Do not concern yourself with it."

The answer confused Sinsi even more, and did nothing to explain his present assignment. He knew Senior Comrade Pedro as one of the most experienced, promising, and dedicated of Senderistas. It was he who had recruited Sinsi into the movement, and Pedro was one of the missing comrades. Sinsi couldn't understand why he was assigned to watch Pedro's family if the senior comrade were performing a secret mission and wasn't suspected of being a traitor. Compounding Sinsi's confusion were the explicit orders he had received: no one in Senior Comrade Pedro's family was permitted to leave Ayacucho, but they should not know that they were being watched.

Remembering his duty, Sinsi peered over the roof parapet at Pedro's door, across the street and two floors below. All was dark and quiet as it should be and he figured that Teotica and the children were asleep. The lights had gone out in the house hours before. The streets were deserted, but he could hear the snores of some of his comrades from the hotel below him.

The roof door opened and Comrade Tupac came up, armed with a pistol in a holster on his belt and carrying two hot cups of Quechua tea laced with coca leaf. "May all be enlightened by *Gonzalo Thought*," he said as he handed Sinsi one of the cups.

Sinsi gave one of the stock replies to the *Sendero* greeting as he put down his rifle and took the cup. "May the revolution keep progressing in our great-grandchildren's lifetime."

Tupac placed his cup on the parapet and looked across the

street. "Anything happening?" he asked.

"Nothing," Sinsi answered, savoring the tea's pleasant and numbing effect on his tongue. He found it strange that Tupac, one of the younger comrades, had never once questioned their assignment, displaying a total lack of feeling or curiosity as he followed orders to the letter. Until recently, Sinsi would have described Tupac as a promising and dedicated Senderista. Now he regarded him as just another fanatic, which he had come to surmise was the same thing.

Without warning, a wind came up and blew Tupac's cup off the parapet. Sinsi was instantly on his feet, his rifle raised and his ears cocked as he searched the sky. The moon had gone behind some clouds but he heard something, a low-pitched buzzing noise.

"Helicopter?" Tupac asked.

"Impossible," Sinsi answered as he continued searching the sky. Whatever it was, there were more of them. The buzzing noise was coming from all directions. Sinsi realized that it was helicopters, but didn't understand how it could be. The army bases were all watched, and they would have heard if army helicopters had taken off for Ayacucho. Sendero had spies everywhere in the army, and they had enjoyed two days' notice before the last army surprise visit.

A machine gun was fired from the roof of the university, four blocks away, and Sinsi saw sparks as some of the bullets hit metal in the sky. The response was instantaneous, and tracers from many points in the sky converged on the university rooftop. There were no more shots fired from the university, but other comrades opened up from other rooftops at the unseen attackers. There were more sparks in the sky as Sendero bullets found targets, but all the rooftop fire was answered. Then a burst of fire from above hit two feet from where Tupac and Sinsi were standing, although Sinsi had not fired. As both men flung themselves to the ground and hugged the side of the parapet, the only possible explanation came to Sinsi.

"It's the gringos," he said.

Tupac didn't understand. "The gringos? How?" he whispered frantically.

The firing had stopped, but Sinsi didn't bother to answer the young comrade. He had heard that the gringos used amazing new helicopters at their DEA base at Santa Lucía that were armor-plated, made very little noise, and were equipped with

devices that enabled their gunners to see in the dark. He saw
that bullets bounced off the machines overhead and the men
in the sky could see them, even though he and Tupac hadn't
revealed their position by gunfire as the other foolish comrades
had. The gringos were the only answer he could come up with.
But he couldn't understand how there could be so many of
them, where they came from, and what they were doing in
Ayacucho.

The moon broke through the clouds and Sinsi could see that
the sky was full of helicopters of two types he had never seen
before. There was more ineffective gunfire from the rooftops,
which was quickly answered from the sky. Sinsi and Tupac
huddled close to the parapet and watched from shadows.

Then Sinsi and Tupac did hear the loud, distinctive sound
of helicopter rotors. They peeked over the parapet and saw
that one of the helicopters had landed in the Plaza de Armas,
two blocks away. Sinsi understood that somehow those clever
gringos had found a way to direct the noise of their machines
upward so that they could not be heard from below. He was
still marveling at the scientific achievement as a squad of
troops disembarked from the machine and headed toward them
in a skirmish line while helicopters overhead covered their
advance.

"Let's get off this roof," Tupac said.

It seemed like an excellent idea to Sinsi, so the two men
started crawling to the roof door. As soon as they left the
shadow of the parapet, a helicopter overhead opened fire on
them. They got up and ran, pursued by a trail of bullets. But
they made it to the door unharmed and ran to a room on the
second floor that overlooked the street. Sinsi was surprised to
find that it was his own room. He shared it with another two
comrades, but they had fled to a safer refuge. However, that
option was closed for Sinsi and Tupac. The troops were too
close. They cautiously peered from the window as the troops
took up positions around Pedro's house. One of them, directly
below, raised a loudspeaker.

"Teotica Cabrera. We are Dinconte agents. We will not
harm you. Please come out."

Sinsi was astounded. It wasn't the gringos. The man was
speaking in Quechua.

The Dinconte agent raised his loudspeaker again when a
shot was fired from Pedro's window. As the agent clutched

his chest, he dropped the loudspeaker to the ground, then fell on top of it.

While admiring the bravery inherent in Teotica's desperate action, Sinsi waited for the fusillade of return fire from the Dinconte troops. But it never came. Instead, another agent calmly placed his rifle on the ground next to his fallen comrade, rolled him onto his back, and placed his ear to the man's heart. Then he picked up the loudspeaker and raised it to his lips. "Teotica Cabrera. This is Colonel Savraada. I must speak with you. I am unarmed, so please don't shoot me."

Sinsi heard Tupac gasp next to him as he stifled his own gasp.

"Colonel Savraada!" Tupac whispered urgently. "We must shoot him. Then we will be heroes."

Sinsi ignored his comrade's death wish for the both of them as Savraada again lifted his loudspeaker.

"Teotica! I have a message that your husband wants me to give to you. We won't hurt you, I promise."

Savraada put the loudspeaker on the ground, walked to Pedro's door, knocked a few times, then waited casually with his hands in his pockets, like he was waiting for a bus. The door was slowly opened and Savraada entered, closing the door behind him.

Sinsi could comprehend none of this, but knew that Tupac was right. He knew that he must shoot Colonel Savraada when he came out, or his comrades would learn of his cowardice and painfully execute him. But he realized that either way, he would be dead. As he prepared to join his murdered victims, he stepped back from the window, aimed his rifle at Pedro's door, and waited.

The door opened and Teotica came out first, holding a sleeping child in her arms. Colonel Savraada followed, carrying Pedro's four-year-old son.

"Shoot now," Tupac whispered in his ear.

Sinsi looked at Teotica over his sights, remembering the times she had watched him as a child while his mother went to trade in the market.

"What are you waiting for?" Tupac asked as he unholstered his pistol. "We have our orders. Shoot."

Sinsi shifted his aim to the colonel, but he couldn't be sure of hitting him without hitting the child.

"Shoot," Tupac whispered over his shoulder as he raised his pistol to the window.

Sinsi made his decision. He shifted his aim and fired a burst into his comrade.

On the street, the rifles of twelve Dinconte agents swung toward Sinsi's window, but they saw no target. As they waited, a rifle was thrown from the window and landed on the street. "Don't shoot. I'm unarmed," Sinsi yelled from inside.

"Show yourself," one of the agents commanded loudly.

Sinsi appeared at the window with his hands raised in the air. "I wish to surrender, Colonel," he yelled down. "I've had enough."

Chapter 26

Before he finally went to bed, Keller's funeral was foremost in McKenna's mind. He wanted to go and pay his respects to the man who had died saving his life but realized that he shouldn't. The voice analyzer had told the story, if purportedly scientific instruments could be believed. After analyzing the voiceprint of the conversation with Elena, Picciarelli was sure that *Sendero* wanted McKenna at the funeral and out of the way because they were planning some other event to take place at the same time as the service.

McKenna had dismissed the scientific arguments and decided to go to Keller's funeral anyway. He saw no harm, as he felt powerless to prevent by his absence from his office whatever mischief *Sendero* was planning for the City of New York. But mainly he felt that he owed Inspector Edward Keller and his family a show of gratitude expressed through his appearance at the funeral, whatever the consequences.

Awakened in his hotel room at eight o'clock by Eddie Morgan, McKenna was still groggy after a strenuous night of press conferences, decisions, and politics. "The commissioner wants you to call him after you read the papers," Morgan said as he dropped the newspapers on the bed and left.

McKenna read the papers over breakfast, and they did nothing to improve the way he felt. The *Post*'s red banner headline of TERRORISTS SET TO ASSAULT CITY, with POLICE INSTITUTE DRASTIC ACTION AT AIRPORTS underneath in smaller letters, summed up the results of the press conference. The bottom half of the front page featured Colonel Savraada's photo of Elena and Maximo's photo of Felipe.

The press conference had been a chaotic affair and the gloves were off. The reporters had to have their story, and at the insistence of the mayor, they got it. McKenna answered to the best of his ability whatever questions they asked about *Sendero*'s activities in New York, although he managed to leave Maximo out of it.

The police plan to protect the airports was a matter of particular interest to the press. After taking a look at the prisoners, Brunette, Shields, and McKenna saw that they were all Indians from the Peruvian highlands and recognizable as a type. So the plan called for roadblocks on the airport approach roads to Kennedy, La Guardia, and Newark Airports. The officers manning the roadblocks were instructed to stop every vehicle entering the airport, and if any of the occupants were suspicious looking—that meant Spanish or American Indian in appearance—they were to search the car or truck for weapons before allowing it to proceed.

However, it soon became apparent that the simple plan was going to be a logistic nightmare. They weren't dealing with the usual type of hijacking scenario, where one or two people slip a gun aboard a plane and take it over. Rather, it was apparent from the captured maps and the plane model that *Sendero* was going to take their plane by force, using at least eleven men armed with military weapons. Knowing that there were still sixty or so Senderistas in New York City who were still unaccounted for, the police manning the roadblocks had to be backed up by heavily armed Emergency Service units. Manpower reserves were stretched to the breaking point, but McKenna and Brunette speculated in private that the overtime being paid might be a waste of money. They wanted to have public buildings, bridges, and tunnels guarded also, just in case Felipe changed his target, but they didn't have the manpower left to do it.

McKenna finished thumbing through the papers and turned on the TV. Traffic was the local news story. It was backed up ten miles from the airports and, according to the announcer, was the worst ever experienced by the city.

McKenna turned off the TV, then called Brunette. He was

pleased to hear his friend sounding upbeat.

"Good news, I think," Brunette said. "Your colonel's on his way back. He's got Pedro's wife and kids."

"When's he getting in?"

"About two o'clock. His government chartered him a plane, so he's stopping off in Texas first to pick up Pedro. I sent Richie White down to meet him and present the official extradition request. Then they're all flying into La Guardia."

"How about Alejandro de Leon? Did he get him?"

"He said it's complicated and Alejandro's not coming yet. But Savraada spoke to him and he's bringing the list of weapons Alejandro sold to *Sendero*. That's all he would tell me on the phone, except he said he did better than he expected in Ayacucho."

"Hopefully he's doing better than we are. Any other developments?"

"We've been getting a lot of phone calls. I've got ten detectives answering the phones and another two hundred following up the leads. Since the papers came out it seems half the people in the city think they've seen Felipe or Elena and the other half think *Sendero* is holed up in the building next to them."

From Brunette's tone of voice, McKenna deduced that Brunette thought the whole thing was a waste of time. McKenna wasn't so sure. Felipe and the rest of his *Sendero* troops had to be somewhere in the city or close to it, and somebody had to have seen them. It was just going to take some time to sort it out. "Maybe something will come of it," he offered.

"Maybe," Brunette answered. "We might find out where at least some of them are, but I think it'll be too late. See you at the church."

Brunette hung up, leaving McKenna to sort out his thoughts. It didn't take long, and he wasn't happy with the conclusion he reached. He feared that Brunette was right. They would find *Sendero*, but it would be too late. He was ready to leave when the phone rang. It was Joe Sofia at the hospital. "We've got problems here," Sofia said, causing McKenna's heart to skip a beat.

"Tell me."

"We got a basket of fruit from Elena. It's for Angelita."

They know where she is, McKenna thought, his anxiety increasing. "Was it checked?"

"Yeah, nothing but fruit, but that's not your problem. There's a note."

Sofia was whispering, leading McKenna to the conclusion that Angelita was in the room and listening. "What did it say?" he asked Sofia.

But Sofia was no longer on the line. He had given the phone to Angelita, and she wasn't afraid. She was angry. "What the hell is going on with you and that girl?" she demanded.

"What do mean? What could be going on? She's the enemy," McKenna answered, trying to sound indignant.

"Oh, yeah? How's this sound to you? 'To Our Poor Skinny Angelita—Eat some fruit and put some meat on those bones if you want to keep that man. He deserves better.' She signed it, 'Your Friend Elena.' She doesn't sound like one of your enemies to me."

Uh-oh, McKenna thought. Elena said she was going to do something nice for me. This is nice? What to say now? "Heavy girls always are jealous of thin girls," he blurted out, almost reflexively, but got nothing but silence for his efforts. "I mean, they're jealous of just-right girls," he added, thinking that sounded much better.

It wasn't working. "So you're telling me she's fat?" Angelita asked, sarcastically.

The picture of Elena in her bikini running away on the beach jumped into McKenna's mind. "No, not fat. Just a little chunky," he lied.

"I bet."

Think quick, McKenna told himself. Why's Elena doing this? Why is she telling me she knows where Angelita is? Is it a warning?

He didn't know what to make of it, but he knew he had to do something. "I have to get you out of there," he said.

"Don't worry about that. I'm checking myself out. Something tells me I should be with you."

"What do the doctors say?"

"They want me to stay a while, but I feel fine."

"That doesn't work. Can you please calm down and listen to reason for me?"

It took a while, but she could and she did, finally agreeing to a transfer to Bethesda Medical Center, the place the presidents go and the most secure hospital he could imagine. Then he called Gene Shields who said he'd arrange it. Angelita would be on her way to Maryland by helicopter in half an hour. Next McKenna called Angelita back and gave her and Sofia the plan. She had changed her mind again, but he finally prevailed.

Chapter 27
The Williamsburg Bridge is one of the three bridges that connect Brooklyn to Lower Manhattan. Built in 1903, it had since become a constant source of embarrassment to whatever mayor occupied the office and a constant drain on the city's capital-works budget. The trouble began with a 1975 *New York Times* study that concluded that the bridge was so poorly maintained that it was in danger of falling into the East River. The city rounded up its own engineers and sent them to inspect the bridge, and the mayor was horrified to learn that the *Times* study had understated the case. It seemed the only thing holding up the bridge was the paint clinging to the rust.

At the time, the city was in the midst of one of its frequent budget crises. The municipality's creditors were closing in and cash was desperately short, so an impact study was done to forecast the consequences of closing the bridge rather than repairing it.

The study concluded that closing the Williamsburg Bridge would be madness. The bridge carried four narrow lanes of traffic in each direction, two on the inner roadway and two on the outer roadway. The commerce of Lower Manhattan was dependent on the 300,000 cars and trucks a day that used it. Compounding the problem would be the impact on mass transit if the bridge were closed. Tracks from the Transit Authority BMT line ran down the center lanes of the bridge, and more than a quarter million commuters a day traveled that subway line to commute to their jobs in Manhattan from their homes in Brooklyn and Queens.

Worst of all, closing the bridge would virtually ensure a

Republican mayor in the next election. At the time that prospect was unthinkable, so the city scraped up the money, partly
by laying off massive numbers of city workers. The bridge
was repaired, but future studies would indicate that the repairs
were of a stopgap nature. Sooner or later, the Williamsburg
Bridge would have to be replaced.

Felipe agreed wholeheartedly with that assessment. He had
changed his appearance dramatically by shaving his head,
growing a beard, and hiding his eyes behind sunglasses, but
underneath his new look he was still the same fun-loving guy.
At exactly eleven o'clock he drove the tractor trailer onto the
Williamsburg Bridge exit of the Brooklyn-Queens Expressway, following his two men in the stolen Oldsmobile station
wagon in front of him. The Oldsmobile took the outer roadway
and Felipe followed, chuckling to himself as he passed under
the sign that read COMMERCIAL TRAFFIC PROHIBITED ON OUTER
ROADWAY. Traffic was heavy, but moving.

In the middle of the span, at the point where the steel suspension cables holding up the bridge almost touch the roadway, the Oldsmobile stopped. So did Felipe as he turned the
truck and blocked the two lanes of traffic on the outer roadway. A hundred motorists behind him immediately displayed
their displeasure at the new traffic jam by leaning on their
horns, but they weren't bothering Felipe. He calmly got out
of the truck and was joined on the bridge roadway by his two
men, both of whom were carrying M-16s. One of them fired
a burst over the roofs of the stopped cars, and the honking
stopped as people ducked under their dashboards. Felipe's
other companion walked around the truck, firing into the tires.
He stopped to reload once, and when every tire was flattened
he fired the remaining bullets from his second magazine into
the engine of the truck.

Felipe inspected the truck and, satisfied that it wouldn't be
easily moved, removed a can of spray paint from his pocket
and wrote *BOMB* in big letters on the side of it. The three
men then got into the Oldsmobile and headed for Manhattan,
while the people they had left in traffic behind them got out
of their cars and ran for their lives back to Brooklyn.

Felipe was in a good mood as he sat in the backseat. When
the Oldsmobile left the bridge and headed west on Delancey
Street, he took a cellular phone from his pocket and dialed
911.

"Police Operator Two-Six-Nine. Where's your emergency?'' the female operator said dispassionately.

"Wrong, Miss Two-Six-Nine. It's *your* emergency. This is Felipe. Do you know who I am?"

"Yes, sir."

"Then listen carefully. In the name of the oppressed peoples of the world, I have just closed the Williamsburg Bridge. There is a truck loaded with a ton of explosives in the middle of the bridge. If I set it off, your bridge will drop into the East River. Do you understand?"

"Yes, sir. Go on, please."

"Good. We will have the truck under observation at all times. If anyone approaches it, the explosives will be detonated. From this moment on, no one is permitted on the bridge. Do you have that?"

"Yes, sir. I understand."

"Good girl. Now, I believe that Assistant Commissioner McKenna is attending a funeral in Brooklyn. Would you kindly give me his mobile phone number?"

"I don't have that number, sir."

Felipe smiled, thoroughly enjoying himself as the Oldsmobile turned south onto Broadway. "Of course you don't. Please get it. I'll hold."

McKenna and Brunette were sitting together in the second row of Our Lady of Perpetual Help Church in Bay Ridge, Brooklyn, as the monsignor concluded the sermon. They were surrounded by politicians, dignitaries, and chiefs, all of whom were bored to tears. It was the fifth funeral most of them had attended that week, and the monsignor was playing to an audience that had seen the show too many times.

But McKenna was glad he had come. Keller's family still managed to be charming, in spite of their grief. He had met them for the first time at the funeral home, just before the casket was loaded into the hearse. "I'm glad you came, Brian," Mrs. Keller had told him. "Edward always spoke well of you, although he said you could use some discipline."

"I'm glad I came, too," McKenna had replied. "And he was right, as always. I wish I could tell him that." He immediately felt awkward at his statement, but Mrs. Keller was a strong woman. She just smiled and touched his hand. "So do I," she had said. "It's going to take us a long time to get used to the fact that we can't talk to him anymore. At least not directly.'' She had been gracious enough to leave him as his eyes filled with tears.

The turnout of about 2,000 cops was less than both McKenna and Brunette had expected, but they attributed it to the fact that most of those who ordinarily would attend were working overtime somewhere else. As he sat there, McKenna again felt anger at *Sendero* building up in him. Another one I owe them, he thought. Because of them, we can't even properly bury the dead.

Then McKenna's and Brunette's phones started ringing at the same time, and McKenna felt that everyone in the church was staring at them. He considered turning off his phone, but Brunette answered his so McKenna did the same.

''Hello, this is McKenna,'' he whispered into his phone as he noticed that Brunette was just listening to his own phone and not saying a word.

''This is Felipe, Commissioner. I figured it was time we talked.''

''We should, but you really caught me at a bad time, Felipe,'' McKenna said calmly through his barely suppressed rage. ''Would you mind calling back in half an hour or so?''

''Oh, I'm sorry. I understand,'' Felipe said, sounding like he meant it. ''I was going to call you later anyway, but I wanted you to be the first to know that we just took over the Williamsburg Bridge.''

''Good for you. Talk to you later,'' McKenna said, then hung up and put the phone back in his pocket. He waited for Brunette to finish his call.

''Just do it,'' Brunette said before hanging up.

''Was it Felipe or Elena?'' Brunette whispered to McKenna.

''Felipe. Is it true?''

''Yep. They're set to blow up the Williamsburg Bridge.''

Brunette stood up, got out of the pew, and walked around to the front pew where the mayor was sitting. The monsignor stopped the ceremony and everyone in the church watched while the mayor and Brunette had a short conversation. Then the mayor got up and headed for the door and Brunette went to the altar and whispered to the monsignor.

It looked to McKenna like it was going to be another short funeral.

Chapter 28

They parked the Oldsmobile at a fire hydrant at Bowling Green and Broadway. Felipe's men broke down their M-16s and placed them in a gym bag, then the three of them left the car and quickly walked one block to the Staten Island Ferry Terminal. As they entered and climbed the stairs to the large waiting room, Felipe saw the NEXT BOAT sign change from 05 MINUTES to 04 MINUTES. They were right on time.

Felipe took a casual look around the waiting room and was satisfied to see more than 400 people waiting for the eleven-thirty boat. About half were obviously tourists, families with cameras and children out to enjoy the greatest bargain New York City has to offer. For fifty cents round-trip, they would get a good view of the Statue of Liberty and Ellis Island, both from a distance of a mile, and for the rest of the twenty-five-minute trip they would usually stand at the rail, the children throwing popcorn to the flock of seagulls that followed the boat while their parents enjoyed the sights and sounds of one of the world's busiest harbors, watching the sailboats, the tugboats pushing barges loaded with sand, gravel, or more commonly, mounds of garbage, all navigating between ships from all over the world entering or leaving port.

Among the tourists were the usual collection of day visitors to Manhattan returning to their homes in Staten Island, salesmen returning from a visit to the home office, and domestic workers on their way home after a night and a morning of scrubbing other people's apartments, washing other people's dishes, pots, and laundry, or watching other people's children. There were also bus drivers and transit workers who had toiled through the night shift and the morning overtime rush, city-dwellers on their way to the Staten Island Zoo, folks crossing to visit friends and relatives in Staten Island, and others who were only there for the ride, taking the ferry just to get out of the house.

To the tourists, the trip usually seemed like ten minutes and they thought it went too quickly. To the others used to traveling the boat, the crossing seemed to take an hour and they were always happy to finally reach Staten Island. But all the routine passengers would be particularly glad to reach shore after the next crossing of the *Samuel I. Newhouse*, if they ever did, because interspersed among them and scattered around the terminal were twenty-five *Sendero* soldiers, each one innocuous looking in a city of immigrants, apparently alone and talking to nobody.

A loud buzzer went off, and the large steel doors leading to Slip One were opened. Everyone in the waiting room converged on the doors. The eleven-thirty boat was right on time.

Police Officer Gus Hoffmann was a nut who loved his job, but it hadn't always been that way. He was always a nut, but he used to hate his job. People who knew Gus found him annoyingly strange and they longed to tell him of his mental deficiency, but unfortunately for them, Gus happened to be a big, tough, ugly nut, so they always thought it better to keep their opinion to themselves.

Being single and having no close friends, Gus never found out what people thought of him. A lifelong resident of Staten Island, he had joined the department twenty-two years before after a four-year stretch in the navy, and then spent fifteen years really working for a living, on patrol in the 79th Precinct in Bedford-Stuyvesant, traveling two hours each way to get to the station house by bus, ferry, and subway.

The trip didn't have to take Gus that long. Neighbors of his who worked in the 79th Precinct made the commute in forty-five minutes tops, driving over the Verrazano-Narrows Bridge to Brooklyn. They didn't understand Gus and, taking pity on him, many times offered to drive him back and forth to work with them, but Gus would have none of that. They couldn't know that Gus hated the Verrazano-Narrows Bridge and had never been on it in his life. If he had his way, he never would.

Gus grew up in rural Staten Island, then an isolated and almost forgotten borough of the city. Home to farms, woods, and isolated towns that looked like Norman Rockwell settings where everybody knew everybody else and most people liked each other, Staten Island was an anomaly in the largest and most densely populated city in the country. Gus cherished his childhood memories of the place as it used to be, until 1964. Then the Verrazano-Narrows Bridge was opened and everything changed, drastically, and not just in Staten Island.

Spanning the bottleneck entrance to the harbor, the bridge connected the Brooklyn neighborhood of Fort Hamilton to the Staten Island town of Fort Wadsworth, two neighborhoods that were separated by a mile of water and a disparity of cultures. On opening day, the second, fourth, and ninth commercial vehicles to cross the bridge were moving vans, loaded with the possessions of Brooklyn residents seeking a change of lifestyle. They were the first, but they weren't the last, as whole Brooklyn neighborhoods of white people pulled up and moved to the newly convenient Promised Land, then just a twenty-five-cent toll away, quickly selling their old homes to some of the city's darker residents before they left. The result was that Staten Island got very crowded very quickly, with acres of tract homes growing out of the farmland, while Brooklyn was set on its way to a new reputation as the culturally diverse borough. Neither place was ever the same once the bridge went up.

Most of the original Staten Island residents took the change in stride, making fistfuls of money by selling their land to real estate developers, while at the same time griping about the newcomers and bemoaning their presence.

But not Gus. He accepted none of it, and the changes he couldn't ignore, he avoided. He never went to the new shopping centers, nor did he socialize with any of the new people, and traveled the old back streets whenever possible, preferring the scenic route to the new highways. And of course, he loved the ferry, the only symbol of *his* Staten Island that endured. He didn't even mind when the fare jumped in one day from a nickel to a quarter, knowing that the bridge fare had steadily increased over the years to three dollars, a sort of tax that the bridge users paid twice a day. Like a true nut, Gus thought everyone else was crazy and considered himself to be a fine judge of character.

So for fifteen years Gus traveled to his ghetto precinct, hating the Job, but doing his part like most of the cops there. He viewed his task simply, as he viewed most other things: sort the predators from the victims, and then take proper police action. Over the years he got good at it, which involved making many arrests, dealing with a few disciplinary complaints, taking a few punches, and ducking an occasional bullet. Besides being considered a nut, with the passage of time Gus also gained a reputation as a pretty good and very tough street cop.

Then one day a drug dealer/gunslinger/robber Gus had arrested offered Gus $10,000 for his freedom and Gus subsequently awarded him with the additional charge of bribery. Gus was commended by his superiors and sent to the Integrity Review Board, a tribunal that had the power to reward him with promotion or transfer to a precinct of his choice, and everyone in the 79th Precinct thought he would return as Detective Gus Hoffmann, or that he would at least be transferred to Staten Island to save four hours a day commuting time.

But they had forgotten that Gus was a nut. He didn't want the pay raise and prestige associated with the detective promotion, and he didn't want to work on patrol in Staten Island among the newcomers. Actually, in his mind, he wanted more. He wanted to work the Staten Island Ferry detail, which was not an assignment coveted by many officers with his experience and seniority.

So Gus got his way, riding the ferry all day long and getting paid for something he would have done for free. He learned everything he could about the boats and soon came to be regarded by the deckhands and even the captains as an expert. His disposition improved and he made friends with some of the steady passengers, selecting for this honor those who always enjoyed the ride and disdaining all others who wasted time by reading newspapers, working on computers, playing cards, or doing crossword puzzles when they should have been on deck enjoying the sea breeze or looking out the windows at all the wonders to be seen in the harbor. To those passengers Gus had chosen as friends, he was known colloquially as *the Admiral*, the diminutive form of Grand Admiral of the New York City Navy, Transport Division.

Like most famous admirals, Gus ran a tight ship. Since major crime was not a problem on the ferries, Gus devoted himself to the little things like loud radios, littering, graffiti, and drunkenness. None of these violations were tolerated or overlooked by Gus, as persistent violators soon learned. Although Gus would have preferred to have them walk the plank, he was constrained somewhat by those crazy people who ran the police department, so he simply arrested them and removed them from his fleet. It wasn't long before the word got out to those inclined toward social deviance, the result being that any boat Gus was on became problem free, making Gus's job easier. So easy, in fact, that Gus figured he had gone about as far as a man could go in life. Although he was eligible to retire, he never once even considered leaving.

Gus was the last person to board the eleven-thirty boat, and he almost didn't make it. He had arrested a man on the eight-o'clock boat who had foolishly persisted in placing his feet on the seats, so after the trip to Beekman Downtown Hospital where the prisoner was treated for injuries resulting from his lack of social graces, Gus was tied up with the arrest paperwork at the First Precinct station house for nearly two hours. But Gus had hurried through because he knew that the eleven-thirty boat was the *Samuel I. Newhouse*, the pride of his fleet. He was happy to arrive at South Ferry just in time, but his joy wouldn't last.

As was his custom upon boarding, Gus stood on the rear lower deck, chatting with the deckhand who was untying the boat under Gus's unwelcome supervision. But his police radio proved to be an annoyance to Gus, with the dispatcher going on and on, directing units to some terrorist disturbance at the Williamsburg Bridge. Gus listened with half an ear, heard something about South American Indians, then decided that the constant chatter was interfering with his duties. He figured that it had nothing to do with the more important work of policing the ferry, and therefore was none of his business, so he turned his radio off before making the first inspection of his boat.

Two minutes later, with the skyline of Manhattan receding at the speed of fifteen knots, Gus realized that he might have a problem. He had traveled on the eleven-thirty boat a thousand times, and knew what the complexion and makeup of the passengers should be. But this time his boat was loaded with a profusion of short, young, swarthy types. He recognized that South American Indians were a recent phenomenon in New York, most of them being illegal immigrants employed by the Korean owners of fruit and vegetable stands throughout the city, and he was used to seeing a few of them on each trip. But there were more of them onboard than he had ever seen before at one time, and although they didn't appear to be hostile, they were spread throughout the boat. Gus correctly figured that the presence of so many of them onboard defied the laws of probability.

As he continued his tour, Gus noted that there were Indians standing or sitting near what he considered to be every strategic location. They were at the hatches, at the stairwells, dispersed among the passengers, on the outer forward and aft decks, and at the engine-room doors. Without being obvious, he visually inspected some of them for weapons and saw none. But he did notice that they must be an athletic bunch. Many of them had gym bags placed at their feet.

As he walked around the boat, Gus kept it casual, frequently stopping to chat briefly or exchange a greeting with some of his regular passengers. He didn't appear to notice any of the Indians, and they avoided eye contact with him. But with his street cop's sense, he knew that he was an object of their intense interest.

His survey of the upper deck confirmed his suspicions. There were two of them seated next to each of the two locked steel doors of the forward and aft ladderways that led to the bridge decks.

Gus figured he could make no overt move to alert them to his suspicions, so he descended to the salon deck and bought four hot dogs and a can of Pepsi from the restaurant concession. He felt the tension on deck subside as he took his bag of provisions down the stairs to the main deck.

As he approached the steel door leading down to the starboard side of the engine room, he saw that one of them was leaning against it. Gus casually took out his pass key and said, "Sorry, buddy. You can't lean on that door. Safety violation."

The young man didn't seem to understand English, so Gus pointed to the row of seats and said, "Sit down. You can't stand here."

The man was confused, but he followed the direction of Gus's finger, then understanding came to him. He smiled at Gus, nodded, then took a seat. Gus opened the door and descended the ladderway to the cavernous, noisy engine room. At the bottom of the ladderway there was a steel watertight hatch. He placed his bag of food on the ground, swung the hatch closed, and spun the locking wheel that made it watertight. When he turned around again, he saw the chief engineer, standing and watching him with a quizzical expression on his face.

"Don't move. Wait for me here," Gus ordered.

"What's going on?" the chief engineer asked, naturally suspicious since Gus was a nut.

"We'll know in a minute," Gus said before he crossed the beam of the ship and went up the port ladderway to the main deck. He opened the door and, as he expected, there was another Indian leaning against the bulkhead next to the engine-room door. The short young man was surprised to see Gus, and Gus had another surprise for him. Like a moray eel darting out of its hole to grab a fish, Gus gave him a short chop to the Adam's apple, then reached around the man's neck and dragged him through the door. Before the door closed, Gus took a quick look around the main deck. Some astonished passengers had seen his actions, but none of the other Indians were close.

Gus's prisoner offered some resistance on the way down the ladderway, but it was futile. Gus was too big and strong. The chief engineer just stood and stared with his mouth open as Gus entered the engine room with his prisoner. Gus held the struggling man from behind with one arm while he searched him with his free hand.

Gus found what he was looking for. Something cold and hard was taped to the man's stomach, so Gus choked the life from his victim, dropped the body to the floor, swung the ladderway watertight steel hatch closed, and spun the locking wheel tight.

The chief engineer was joined by another two crewmen, but none said a word as they stood staring at the body. Gus ignored them. He reached down, pulled up the man's shirt, and ripped off the .45 Colt automatic taped to the Indian's stomach. Then Gus figured it was time to turn his radio back on.

Felipe was sitting in the cabin on the top deck when his phone rang. He wasn't expecting any messages, so he knew it wasn't good news. It was Elena. "There's police transmissions coming from your boat," she said. "They know. The captain was just ordered to return to Manhattan."

As soon as Elena said it, the boat shuddered as the aft engines were cut and the forward engines engaged, causing the boat to slow.

But Felipe wasn't worried. "It's too late for them," he said. "We're ready to go."

"You better hurry," Elena warned. "The police are preparing quite a reception for you on the Manhattan side."

Felipe hung up and dialed Alfredo Stesso, the commander of his troops on the ferryboat *Andrew J. Barberi*, which was still four miles away and approaching the *Samuel I. Newhouse* from the Staten Island side. Stesso answered instantly.

"Are your men in position?" Felipe asked.

"Yes, *Comandante*."

"Good. Take the boat as soon as I hang up."

"But, *Comandante*, I can see your boat. You're still miles away."

"A problem has developed. Follow my orders." Felipe replaced the phone in his pocket and took out a whistle. He stood up as his twelve men on the upper deck watched him. He joined his two men at the locked steel door leading to the bridge deck and blew the whistle, startling the rest of the passengers. Then they heard a series of whistles sound from other parts of the boat. As the passengers stared at Felipe, his men went into action. Some drew .45 Colt pistols from under their shirts while others reached down into the gym bags at their feet and assembled their M-16s.

"Nobody move!" Felipe yelled to the hundred passengers on the upper deck. He had their attention. "I am Comandante Felipe and you are all prisoners of the Shining Path Army. If you obey our orders instantly, you will greatly improve your chances for survival."

None of the passengers protested as they glanced around the cabin at the young men who covered them with weapons held menacingly. The passengers just watched from the corners of their eyes as people who had been on the outside deck were herded by other Senderistas into the cabin and roughly pushed into seats. One of the deckhands was pushed forward by two of Felipe's soldiers. He was a middle-aged Hispanic-looking man, clean and dapper, wearing his uniform as if he were the captain. He stared at Felipe sullenly.

"The pass key, please," Felipe said to him.

"*Tu madre, pandejo*," the deckhand spit out in reply.

"Foolish," Felipe said, seeming to take the insult in stride for a moment while the passengers watched, holding their breath. Then he reached under his shirt, took out his pistol, and shot the deckhand through the heart. Before the body had even hit the deck, Felipe's men were going through the deckhand's pockets. One of them produced a key ring and handed it to Felipe.

Seeing that the boat was reversing direction and satisfied that he was no longer needed on the upper deck, Felipe unlocked the steel door and climbed the ladderway to the bridge deck, followed by two of his men armed with M-16s. From the window of the bridge cabin, the captain and the first mate saw the armed terrorists as soon as they came on deck. They locked the doors and ducked under the bridge console.

"Take the glass out," Felipe ordered and one of his men opened fire on the forward bridge windows, shattering them. Then Felipe leaned into the window opening and placed his pistol against the head of the captain, who was cowering under the control console. "I'm ready to accept the surrender of your boat, Captain," he said.

"We surrender," the captain said immediately.

"Good. Both of you get up and unlock the doors."

Felipe took his pistol off the captain's head and they quickly got up, unlocked the doors, and stepped back. But Felipe didn't enter. Keeping his pistol pointed at the two men, he ordered, "Reverse course. All Ahead Full."

The captain returned to the control console, grabbed the engine control handle, and swung it from *Reverse* to *Forward*. Nothing happened, so he tried it again. Still nothing happened. The boat continued heading for Manhattan.

The captain turned to Felipe, fear etched into his face. "The engine room isn't responding to the control commands," he said.

"Don't you run the engines from here?" Felipe asked impatiently.

"Yes, sir, but I think they've disconnected my controls."

"Who?"

"The crewmen in the engine room."

"Why would they do that?" Felipe asked, perplexed.

"I don't know. I really don't know."

"Then I suggest you talk to them, Captain. Tell them your life depends on *Full Speed Ahead*."

The captain pressed the ENGINE ROOM button on his intercom console. "Engine Room, this is the captain. Restore control to the bridge."

There was no answer.

The captain waited a moment, then tried again. "Engine

Room, please restore control to the bridge at once. Our lives depend on it.''

Still there was no answer. Felipe pointed his pistol at the first mate and shot him through the head. The captain watched, horrified, as the first mate fell to the floor.

''Think you can be more convincing now?'' Felipe asked calmly.

''Yes, sir.'' The captain put his mouth to the intercom mike and shrieked, ''Engine Room, they've just killed the first mate and I'm next. Please restore power to the bridge. Now, please.''

There were a few seconds' silence before the intercom crackled. ''Sorry, Captain, but this boat's going back to Manhattan.''

''Who is this?'' the captain demanded.

''Gus.''

The captain slumped over his console, exasperated and afraid.

''Who's Gus?'' Felipe screamed.

''He's the policeman who rides this boat,'' the captain answered without looking up. ''He's a nut.''

''Damn,'' Felipe said. ''How many men do you have in the engine room?''

''There should be four of them down there.''

''They would know how to reconnect the controls?''

''Sure,'' the captain answered, hopefully. ''All of them should.''

Felipe threw one of his men the pass key and said in Quechua, ''Get that policeman out of the engine room, but make sure that at least one of the crewmen lives.''

''*Sí, Comandante.*'' The Senderista turned and ran down the stairs, leaving Felipe to ponder this unexpected development. Then a thought came to him. ''He can't see from the engine room, can he?'' he asked the captain.

''No.''

''Then tell him we're going to crash into the dock.''

The captain stood up and screamed again into the intercom. ''Gus, you must return control to the bridge. We're gonna crash into the dock.''

''Yes, sir, we are gonna crash, but not yet and probably not into the dock, unless I get real lucky,'' Gus answered. ''We will hit somewhere in Manhattan, but I figure that shouldn't be for another five minutes. I suggest you folks up there look for something to hold on to."

Felipe looked toward Manhattan and figured that Gus was just about right. In about five minutes they would be arriving someplace on the Battery at fifteen knots. "Do you have control of the helm?" he asked the captain.

The captain swung the wheel, but the boat stayed on course for the Battery. "No, sir, he's disconnected the rudder controls."

"Shit!" Felipe yelled, followed by a long string of curses in all the languages he knew. He had almost exhausted his supply by the time the Senderista soldier returned and reported.

"*Comandante*, we can't get into the engine room. There are steel doors at the bottom of the stairs to the engine room, and they are locked from the inside."

"So? Blow it."

"Lazarus is rigging explosives to one of the doors and he is awaiting your command."

Felipe looked to Manhattan and figured he had three minutes left. In the distance, he saw many blue uniforms and the red lights of many police cars and ambulances waiting for them in Battery Park. Then he was momentarily distracted by the noise of a police helicopter far overhead. He looked up and decided that the machine posed no immediate threat, so he pointed to one of his men. "You stay here and watch the captain," he ordered before bounding down the ladderway, followed by the other soldier.

On the way down to the engine room, Felipe was gratified to see that all of the passengers had been brought to the upper deck and had been made to lie on the floor with their hands behind their necks. Many of the children were crying, but Felipe expected that.

Six of his soldiers were waiting for Felipe at the engine-room door. He ran past them, down the ladderway, and joined Lazarus at the watertight door. There were four C-4 charges placed at the hinges and locks of the door, with wires running to the detonator in Lazarus's hand from the blasting caps embedded in the explosives.

Felipe inspected the door and wasn't satisfied. "This door is too strong," he said. "Use more explosive."

Lazarus took a knife and cut four more chunks of C-4 from his two-pound pack and pressed one into each charge already on the door.

"Good enough. Let's go," Felipe ordered. They ran up the ladderway to the main deck. "Take cover," Felipe ordered, and he ran to the middle of the boat and into the men's room, followed by his six soldiers and Lazarus, who was playing out the detonator wire behind him.

Felipe pointed to one of his soldiers. "Paco, after the door blows, take your men down and get the policeman. But remember, we need one of the crewmen alive."

"*Sí, Comandante*. Trust me. We are ready."

As Lazarus placed his hand on the detonator switch, the engines stopped. Felipe looked toward shore and saw that Gus was on his approach run and planned to drift into shore. Felipe figured he still had two minutes, maybe more since the boat was no longer under power. He held his hands over his ears and gave the order. "Do it now!"

Lazarus twisted the detonator switch. The sound of the blast was muffled somewhat by the closed steel door leading to the engine-room ladderway, but still loud enough to cause Felipe's ears to ring. He ran to the door, opened it, and peered down the ladderway. Through the smoke, he saw success. The watertight door was blown off its hinges. Felipe stepped aside to let Paco and his men down.

Paco was the first one into the engine room and the first one to die, taking two bullets in the chest. Then the soldier behind him fired a burst at the unseen marksman in the engine room before he too was hit and went down. But the *Sendero* soldiers never wavered. They jumped over their fallen comrades into the engine room, searching for a target.

Felipe heard another short burst of fire before one of his men yelled up, "Clear, *Comandante*."

Felipe ran down the ladderway and was unprepared for the sight that greeted him. Two crewmen stood there with their hands held high, being covered by his four remaining soldiers, but bodies were everywhere. There was Paco and his man, the soldier Gus had strangled, and a crewman, shot dead.

There were two things that surprised Felipe. One was the chief engineer, uninjured but standing with one hand handcuffed to an overhead pipe. The other was that there was no sign of the policeman.

"Who shot that man?" Felipe asked, pointing to the crewman lying on the floor.

One of his men raised his hand. "I did, *Comandante*. Sorry."

"I'm sure it was unavoidable," Felipe answered. "Where is the policeman?"

"He is not here, *Comandante*," his men answered in unison.

Felipe faced the two crewmen with their hands in the air. One was in his twenties and the other was in his fifties, and they looked like they could be father and son. He was annoyed to see that the younger one was staring at him defiantly. "Where is the policeman?" he asked them.

They didn't answer, so Felipe shot the younger one in the left foot. The crewman screamed in surprise and pain as Felipe shifted his aim to the older crewman, but he didn't have to repeat his question.

"Don't shoot him," the chief engineer yelled, pointing with his free hand to an open manhole on the deck of the engine room between two of the engines. The manhole cover was lying next to it. "He went into the bilge. I saw him go in."

"Who disconnected the bridge controls?" Felipe asked.

"He did. I tried to stop him, but he's a nut," the chief engineer said. "Look what he did to me. This is all his fault."

Felipe turned back to the older crewman. "Did you help the policeman?"

"I would have, but he never asked."

"I understand," Felipe said. "But you two have another problem. You have thirty seconds to have these engines started and we must be at All Ahead Full."

"You got it, Chief," the older crewman said, resigned. "Looks like you're the boss for now." He went to a console in the engine room and started the engines. Felipe was instantly hit in the back by a stream of hot oil squirting from a bullet hole in one of the engines, but he merely stepped aside, unconcerned, knowing that the boat had four engines.

The crewman switched the transmission into *Forward*. The boat shuddered and was still heading for shore, but Felipe knew it wouldn't be long before the engines overcame the momentum of the drift and the boat resumed its course into the harbor. He just didn't know if it would be before the boat hit the Manhattan shore at the Battery.

"Now," Felipe continued, "we are a little pressed for time. You two gentlemen have two minutes to restore engine control and helm control to the bridge."

"Might take a little longer than that," the older crewman said.

"Then your boss has just two minutes to live," Felipe answered without emotion, before turning and saying to his men in Quechua, "Give them three minutes. If any of you think it necessary, kill the engineer."

"*Sí, Comandante.* What about the policeman?" one of them asked.

"He'll keep. Replace the manhole cover, then stay down here to guard these three and make sure the policeman doesn't surface," Felipe ordered before he turned and climbed up the ladderway. He saw through the rear doors that they were about 100 yards from shore, and slowly getting closer, despite the forward pull of the engines. Police onshore had rifles trained on the decks above. He ran up two flights of stairs to the upper deck.

"Stand these people up!" Felipe yelled, realizing that only his soldiers were visible to the police.

With threats and a few blows, all the hostages were quickly made to stand. "Now get some of them on the rear deck," Felipe ordered, and twenty passengers were herded to the rear deck. Felipe and some of his men followed them out and covered them from the rear. As the boat stopped fifty yards from shore, he could see the faces of some of the cops over their rifle sights as they crouched behind their cars and the sea wall, but none of them fired.

"I have one of their police generals in my sights," a soldier with a rifle to his shoulder reported to Felipe. "Should I shoot?"

"Not yet, Comrade. We don't want to make them too angry to think."

As the boat lurched forward, a warm feeling of relief came over Felipe. His schedule was disrupted, but he was in control. "Wave good-bye to the nice policemen," he yelled to the hostages, and they did.

Chapter 29

In the police helicopter 2,000 feet above the harbor, Brunette glumly watched the *Samuel I. Newhouse* pull away from Manhattan, but McKenna was relieved. "Just as well, Ray," he volunteered. "It would have been a bloodbath."

"Not as bad as it's gonna be. It doesn't look like they have their heavy weapons yet."

Ray might be right, McKenna thought. They couldn't have brought their recoilless rifles or missiles onboard, yet. Those weapons were just too big, and Gus Hoffmann would have seen them. So they must be planning on getting a delivery, and it has to be from another boat.

Brunette raised the radio mike to his lips. "Brunette to Detective Hoffmann. You still with us, Gus?"

"At your service, Commissioner."

"How you doing down there?"

"Okay, I guess, except I can't see a thing, and I'm up to my chest in filthy water," Gus answered as calmly as if he were commenting on the weather. "But they seem to have forgotten about me," he added.

"They didn't forget, Gus. You caused them a lot of trouble and it doesn't look too good for you."

"Not too much you can do about that now, Commissioner. Just try to keep my boat afloat."

"We'll try, Gus," Brunette said. "Don't transmit unless you have to. Remember, you have to save your batteries, and we want to be able to get in touch with you if we need you for something."

"Okay, Commissioner. Just one more thing. Now that I'm a detective, does that mean I can't work the boats anymore?"

Brunette turned back to McKenna and shook his head. They

were both sharing the same thought: Where do we get these guys from? Then Brunette raised the mike again. "Gus, if you get out of this, you can work wherever you want for as long as you like. I promise."

Brunette replaced the mike on the dash and retreated into his own thoughts.

From the backseat of the helicopter, McKenna surveyed the scene below him. The sky was clear and visibility was good, so with his binoculars he had a good view from the Bronx to Staten Island and beyond.

In the middle of the harbor, still three miles from the approaching *Samuel I. Newhouse*, lay the *Andrew J. Barberi*, dead in the water and answering no communications from shore. There were three small pleasure boats circling it, and McKenna figured they belonged to people curious about the stopped ferryboat. They seemed to be treating it as a gala event, and other pleasure boats were approaching the *Andrew J. Barberi* from all directions.

A disaster waiting to happen, but why isn't *Sendero* waving them off or shooting them up? McKenna wondered. "We have to get those boats out of there," he said.

"Harbor will get rid of them," Ray said, looking out the window from the front seat, next to the pilot. Then he pointed down. "Looks like the first Harbor Unit will be there in a couple of minutes."

McKenna raised his binoculars and saw the blue flashing light on top of the Harbor Unit launch as it rounded the far tip of Governors Island, heading for the *Andrew J. Barberi*. Then he saw another two Harbor Unit launches in the East River cross under the empty Williamsburg Bridge, racing south toward the harbor.

McKenna also could see that traffic was stopped dead on the East River Drive in Manhattan and the Brooklyn-Queens Expressway because of the Williamsburg Bridge closing, and it was bad on every other highway he could see, which was the reason they happened to be in the helicopter when *Sendero* took over the *Samuel I. Newhouse*. Brunette had figured it would be bad and, after Keller's very short funeral had ended, he had had the helicopter pick them up so they could check the situation on the Williamsburg Bridge.

But by the time they had arrived over the Williamsburg Bridge, the First Division dispatcher had heard from Ferry Post One. Brunette had instructed Police Officer Hoffmann to surrender to *Sendero*, but Hoffmann protested that that was impossible since he had already killed one of them.

Once again, McKenna had been disturbed by Brunette's strange smile on hearing the news of the death of another *Sendero* soldier, and he was even more astonished when Brunette promoted Hoffmann to detective from 2,000 feet, which had to be a first. "Do whatever you think you have to, Detective Hoffmann. You're in charge on that boat," Brunette had told him over the radio. "And keep us informed, if you can."

Gus's first transmission from the bilge had told them that he had taken his instructions quite seriously. For a few minutes, he had been in charge, and it cost *Sendero* another two men to regain control.

Brunette then had the four precincts in the First Division switched to another radio band, leaving Hoffmann as the only one on the frequency.

"How much fuel we got?" Brunette asked the young-looking pilot.

"Enough to stay up about another twenty minutes, Commissioner."

"Good," Brunette said as he picked up the radio handset. "Switch it to the Harbor Unit frequency for me."

The pilot did.

"Brunette to the Harbor Unit rounding Governors Island."

"Harbor Unit Six standing by, Commissioner."

"Harbor Unit Six, you are to clear the pleasure craft from the *Andrew J. Barberi*, if possible. Be aware that the boat is probably under *Sendero* control, with hostages onboard, so you are to retire if you see or even sense the possibility of confrontation with the *Sendero* soldiers aboard."

"Harbor Unit Six. Understood, Commissioner."

"Brunette to the Harbor Units proceeding down the East River."

"Harbor Unit Two standing by, Commissioner."

"Harbor Unit Three standing by, Commissioner."

"Harbor Units Two and Three, it is possible that the *Andrew J. Barberi* and the *Samuel I. Newhouse* will be reinforced by additional *Sendero* personnel with heavy weapons. You are to assist Harbor Unit Six in maintaining a blockade of the ferries."

"Harbor Unit Three, Commissioner. Be advised that we are armed with three thirty-eight revolvers and two shotguns on each launch."

Tough decision coming up, McKenna thought as he watched his friend agonize over the coming prospects. Glad it's not my call.

But Brunette didn't waver. "Sorry, Harbor Units. You're all we've got right now. Ram any approaching craft if you have to, but don't let them through."

"Harbor Unit Two, ten-four."

"Harbor Unit Three, ten-four. We predict an ETA of five minutes."

It looked to McKenna like the first Harbor Unit was going to get to the *Andrew J. Barberi* about the same time as the *Samuel I. Newhouse* would. He also noticed that there was another police helicopter and a news helicopter over the harbor. Then a large pleasure boat caught his attention as it sped into the harbor from the Brooklyn shore. He examined it through his binoculars and thought it was a big Chris-Craft, about sixty feet long, and traveling at about thirty-five knots, which was faster than any of the police launches. *Harbor Launch Six* was closer to the *Andrew J. Barberi*, but the pleasure boat was going to overtake it. Then he scanned the hull of the cruiser and knew.

"It's them," he said. "The registration numbers are painted over."

Brunette looked down and saw it. "Get lower," he instructed the pilot as he raised his radio.

"Brunette to *Harbor Launch Six*."

"*Harbor Launch Six*, Commissioner. We see him."

McKenna felt a knot in his stomach as he watched *Harbor Launch Six* make a short turn in the water and head for the approaching pleasure craft. There were two cops on the deck of the launch with shotguns, but he saw nobody on the large cabin cruiser. Still, he had a premonition of disaster and felt totally helpless. He saw that the other two Harbor Unit launches were at least a mile away. Then the waiting was over.

The front windows of the main cabin of the cruiser were blown out as a machine gun opened up from the bridge, raking the Harbor Unit launch with sustained fire. The cops raised their shotguns and fired, but the range was too great for them. McKenna saw first one, then the other cop on deck get hit and go down, but the launch continued on a collision course with the cabin cruiser.

"Put us on top of them scumbags," Brunette yelled to the pilot, who put the helicopter into a steep dive. By the time

they were twenty feet over the cabin cruiser, the Harbor Unit
launch was smoking from the sustained machine-gun fire, but
it was still on course for the cabin cruiser. The wind was up
at sea level and the pilot was having a tough time keeping his
machine over the speeding cruiser.

Both McKenna and Brunette took out their pistols and
opened their cabin doors as the pilot did his best to keep pace
with the cruiser. McKenna got off the first shot into the roof
of the covered cruiser, and it turned hard to port. The pilot
turned the helicopter to stay on top, but he wasn't as fast as
the captain of the cruiser, which was swerving back and forth
in short, sharp turns. Still, by the time McKenna and Brunette
had to reload, there were twenty holes in the roof of the cabin
cruiser, but the course alterations had spoiled it for *Harbor
Launch Six.* The cruiser was too fast and too agile, and the
big boat swept by the launch as it was trying to turn into the
cruiser to ram it.

By the time McKenna and Brunette had completed the difficult job of reloading their pistols in the violently swerving
helicopter, the Harbor Unit launch had made a wide turn and
was pursuing the cruiser, but it would never catch it. They
were too close to the *Andrew J. Barberi,* and the *Samuel I.
Newhouse* was tying up next to it.

As McKenna and Brunette opened the cabin doors to resume
firing at the speeding cabin cruiser below them, the Senderistas
aboard the ferries decided to get into the fray. They had come
into rifle range, and streams of tracer bullets were fired at the
helicopter from many spots on the ferries, and despite the
range, some bullets hit it, although it was a difficult target with
just the narrow front profile visible to the Senderistas. The
right pane of the windshield shattered and a few bullets
whizzed through the cabin, but Brunette and McKenna weren't
deterred. They managed to fire four more rounds into the roof
of the cabin cruiser before another round from the ferries shattered the left pane of the helicopter windshield and clipped the
pilot's left arm.

That was enough for him. He pulled the helicopter up and
turned for the Brooklyn shore. Brunette was on him in an
instant. "Turn back around and ram that cruiser, while we still
got time," he ordered.

Great, McKenna thought. Now we're kamikazes, but it's
typical Ray. He would never ask his men to do something that
he wouldn't do himself. He was relieved when the pilot said

nothing, but the helicopter kept gaining altitude.

Brunette tried a different tack on the pilot.

"Officer, if we don't ram that boat, they'll deliver their weapons and a lot more people may die."

The pilot finally found his voice as they heard a round hit the rear of the machine. "Nobody I know," he said.

McKenna, knowing what was coming, reached around Brunette's seat and held him down. As Brunette struggled to get at the pilot, another bullet hit the rear of the helicopter. Then there was an explosion in the engine behind them that caused the machine to shudder. They heard the rotors slowing as the pilot checked his gauges. "Hold on. We're going down," he said as he pulled out a knob on the dashboard that inflated the pontoons on the machine's runners.

The young pilot was good. He fought the stick and kept the helicopter level as it hit the water hard. He had a seat belt on, but both McKenna and Brunette were thrown from their seats on impact. Brunette hit his head hard on the dash, and McKenna's head and shoulder smashed into the back of the front seat. After shaking his head to clear it, McKenna checked Brunette. His friend was alive, but unconscious.

The pilot opened his door, climbed onto the runner, and as the waves lapped over his feet, he pulled the cord that inflated his life vest.

"What are you doing?" McKenna asked. "You're wounded. Get back in here."

"Don't worry about me," the pilot answered. "I'm resigning, effective immediately. I don't think I have much of a future in this job anymore."

"Don't be crazy. He'll forget all about it."

But the pilot didn't think Brunette would forget. "Sorry," he said. "Please tell the commissioner when he wakes up that he wanted me to make our wives into rich widows today, but that I don't like mine that much."

"Tell him yourself," McKenna sneered, not knowing if he was mad or glad at the pilot's decision not to ram the cruiser. Then the pilot further surprised McKenna when he jumped into the water and started swimming toward Brooklyn.

"Where are you going?" McKenna yelled to him.

Without missing a stroke, the pilot yelled back, "To the Fire Department. I'm three names away on their list."

Before McKenna could think of anything else to say to the pilot, he heard a distant explosion behind him. He climbed out onto the runner and saw *Harbor Launch Six* burning furiously, about 100 yards from the ferries and half a mile from his helicopter. He had forgotten about the launch, but the Senderistas didn't have that luxury. He saw that the cabin cruiser was tied up next to the *Andrew J. Barberi* and surmised that the launch had persisted in its suicide run for the cruiser. But he knew that small-arms fire wouldn't account for the violent explosion that destroyed the launch.

As the launch sank, bringing the charred and shattered bodies of three brave men to the bottom of the bay, McKenna saw that *Sendero* had accomplished what the NYPD could not. The small pleasure craft that had surrounded the *Andrew J. Barberi* were fleeing from it in all directions, using all the speed they could muster.

Another police helicopter landed next to his as McKenna scanned the ferries with his binoculars and saw two men passing a long tube from the small rear deck of the cruiser to another two men on the *Andrew J. Barberi*. It was the thing he feared, the weapon that explained how they were able to sink Harbor Unit Six, blowing it up from a distance of 100 yards. They were loading onto the ferry the recoilless rifles they had obtained from Alejandro, but McKenna didn't have time to think about it.

Over the racket produced by the helicopter next to his, he heard the sound of boat engines to his right. *Harbor Launch Two* and *Harbor Launch Three* had arrived and, still following orders, they were racing for the cabin cruiser. Horrified, he looked back to the *Andrew J. Barberi*. The Senderistas had also seen the launches and were mounting a recoilless rifle on a tripod on the lower deck of the ferry.

"Stop them!" McKenna yelled to the helicopter pilot, but the pilot, although looking straight at him, couldn't hear him and the launches continued on course.

"Stop them!" McKenna yelled again and again while pointing at the rapidly receding launches.

Finally the pilot understood and McKenna saw him raise his radio mike to his lips. He prayed as he watched the launches, and didn't stop until he saw them make a sharp turn and head back toward him. Then he thanked God and promised a lifetime of novenas and clean living, just in case He was listening.

Brunette came to and mumbled a few noises before he started to make sense as one of the launches pulled up between the two helicopters. He had a gash topping off a large lump on his forehead, and it looked to McKenna like his nose was broken, but Brunette didn't even bother to wipe the blood from his face. He just turned in his seat and watched the cruiser being unloaded for a couple of minutes while he sat in the rocking helicopter. "Harbor Unit Six?" he finally asked.

"Gone. No survivors. Got them with a recoilless rifle."

"Damn, they were good men." Brunette finally did wipe his face and eyes before he asked, "Where's the pilot?"

McKenna pointed to the swimming figure in the distance. "He thinks you're mad at him."

McKenna was relieved to see Brunette smile his famous old smile. He pointed to the pilot and yelled to the launch, "Go get that man and take him to Bellevue Hospital, no matter what he says. And tell him I love him."

"What should we tell him?" a cop on the launch yelled.

"Tell him I love him. Now go!" Brunette yelled back.

The first launch took off and the second launch took its place between the two helicopters, but Brunette wasn't ready to go. He had thinking to do and wouldn't be distracted. His phone rang ten times before he turned it off without answering. Two minutes later a cop stuck his head out of the cabin and yelled, "Commissioner, the duty chief says the mayor is trying to reach you."

That wouldn't do it, either. "Have him tell the mayor that I'll call him later," he yelled back.

Brunette and McKenna silently watched the activities on the ferries, keeping count as five more recoilless rifles and forty-six boxes of various sizes and shapes were unloaded onto the *Andrew J. Barberi*. McKenna took a break for a minute or two to watch the kicking and screaming pilot being dragged onto the launch, but Brunette didn't. Fifteen minutes later, when the Senderistas finished their unloading and jumped onto the ferry, Brunette asked, "Can you guess what's in them?"

"You know, the usual," McKenna answered. "Stinger missiles, a ton of ammo, lots of explosives, and enough food for a week or so."

"And what are they going to do next?"

"I think they're going to take those ferries to the entrance to the harbor, near the Verrazano-Narrows Bridge. That would give them control of the harbor from both ends. If ships try to get in by coming down the East River from Long Island Sound, they blow up the Williamsburg Bridge and block the river."

"If that's so, you're forgetting about the back door."

"The Kill van Kull?" McKenna asked.

"Yep. It's narrow, but it's deep. Ships can get in that way. Matter of fact, most of the ones heading for Port Newark do it."

McKenna smiled. "No, I'm not forgetting, and I bet Felipe isn't either. He's shown us he's a pretty good planner, and if closing the harbor is part of his plan, then he's thought of that."

"So what do we do?" Brunette asked.

"If it isn't too late already, close the three bridges that go from Staten Island to New Jersey before he gets to them."

Brunette smiled again. "That's sure gonna make a lot of people mad at us, especially if we're wrong."

"So what? I think they're mad at us already."

Then Brunette called the mayor back. The mayor had a hundred things on his mind, but all Brunette wanted to talk about was closing the bridges. The mayor tried to explain that he didn't have the authority to close them as the bridges were run by the Port Authority, which was under the joint control of the governors of New York and New Jersey. Brunette told him to get the authority, but that he was going to close the bridges until he did.

Brunette hung up, called the duty chief, and told him to have NYPD cars block the three bridges until the Port Authority police officially closed them. Then he got back to McKenna. "Looks like it's gonna be the worst rush hour in history," he said. "Almost makes me glad we're gonna be working all night."

"Makes me sorry I'm not in Florida."

Brunette looked skeptical. "Listen, pal, this isn't Angelita you're talking to. I think that's bullshit. I have a feeling there's no place you'd rather be than right here in the middle of all this."

McKenna hadn't thought about it, but he was afraid that Brunette might be right. "Maybe, but let's keep that to ourselves."

"Okay, suit yourself. Now, let's get back to business. What do they do next?"

"Make some outrageous demands and threaten to kill some hostages."

"And then what do we do?"

"Negotiate."

Brunette didn't like that. "Negotiate? With them?"

"Until we think of something else, I don't see any other way. But it won't be us doing the negotiating. It's gonna be out of our hands because they'll wanna talk to some real big shots, not us."

"Can't you think of a single thing that we should be doing now?"

"No. Can you?"

"Unfortunately, me neither. They're holding all the cards right now."

Then the ferries started moving slowly, side by side toward the harbor entrance, leaving the cabin cruiser behind them. Both ferries came to a stop after a quarter mile.

"Now what?" Brunette said.

In response, McKenna's phone rang. He knew who it would be before he answered it. "What now, Felipe?"

"Did you get wet?" Felipe asked.

Damn it! McKenna said to himself. If he knew it was me in the helicopter, they must be monitoring our radios. "Just my feet, thank you. What do you want?"

"I want to commend you and Commissioner Brunette on that little demonstration. Your men surprised us with their dedication and we offer our condolences."

"Too bad it was all for nothing."

"But it was close. You and Commissioner Brunette managed to hit two of my men in our delivery boat."

McKenna felt good about that, but wondered why Felipe would give him that information. "Are they dead?" he asked.

"You must realize that wounded and dead are the same thing in our situation. We have made no provision for the wounded, and we can't allow them to fall into your hands."

"I see. So you want to show me how dedicated your men are. Kill your own wounded. That'll make good reading in the papers."

"Yes, this will be the biggest media event since your Gulf War and good press never hurts. But I want you to remember one thing."

There was something about Felipe's condescending tone of voice that really irritated McKenna. He tried to bring his anger under control, and partially succeeded. "Yeah, what's that?" he asked, shortly.

"Just this. We're the ones who are supposed to be the mindless fanatics, not you and your civil-service policemen. You're not prepared for us, so keep the heroics to a minimum and we'll both prevent unnecessary losses to both sides.''

''We'll try to keep that in mind. Is it time for you to give us your demands yet?''

''Not yet. I just wanted you to see this. Watch.''

McKenna thought he knew what was coming, and didn't want to give Felipe the pleasure of surprising him. ''What are you gonna do?'' he asked. ''Blow up your cabin cruiser with a recoilless rifle round?''

''Commissioner McKenna, you're taking a lot of the fun out of this business.''

As McKenna and Brunette watched, the spotter round, a fifty-caliber tracer, was fired from the stern of the *Samuel I. Newhouse*. It hit the cabin cruiser at midship just above the water line. It was followed a second later by the 106-mm round that hit the cruiser in the same place, destroying it in a ball of flame and smoke. What was left of it sank immediately.

''Pretty good,'' McKenna had to say. ''You hit the fuel tanks.''

Felipe couldn't keep the pride out of his voice. ''You know, it was a new weapon for us. I could only give my men five days' training with it.''

''Congratulations, Felipe. What next?''

''Haven't you figured it out yet?''

McKenna could tell that Felipe was really enjoying himself. ''Sure. You're closing the harbor.''

''Exactly. We'll wait here while you have the Verrazano-Narrows Bridge closed and cleared of traffic. If there is a single car or person on that bridge when we get there, we are going to cause some very expensive damage to it. Do you understand?''

''Yeah. Just give me a minute.'' McKenna turned to Brunette and said, ''Close the Verrazano now. No cars or people on it.''

Brunette nodded and dialed his phone as McKenna returned to Felipe. ''It's being done,'' he said.

''Good. Here are the rest of the rules. As soon as we get there, the harbor is closed. If any vessel passes under the Williamsburg Bridge, we will drop the bridge into the water and kill one hundred prisoners. If any vessel comes within one mile of our position, we will destroy it and kill one hundred prisoners. If any aircraft, including commercial aircraft, passes over the harbor, we will destroy it and kill one hundred prisoners. Any questions?''

"That's sure gonna piss off the airlines. I presume you have Stingers?''

"Would you like a demonstration? Do you see that news helicopter that has been annoying us for some time?''

A knot formed in McKenna's stomach. The news helicopter was a mile from the ferries, hovering at about 2,000 feet. "That won't be necessary, Felipe," McKenna said, embarrassed that he was pleading. "Please, I believe you.''

"Good. I never realized that you had such affection for the press. I myself thought they were rather antagonistic with you at your last press conference.''

"That was your fault, not theirs. Are you going to give us a list of the people you're holding?''

"Of course, as soon as we find out who they all are.''

"What about our man?''

"Detective Hoffmann?''

"Yeah, Detective Hoffmann. What are you gonna do with him?''

"I was very impressed with him. Let me think about it. But for now, I prefer he stay where he is. I think he's the type to cause trouble with the other passengers.''

"You're not gonna kill him?''

"Only if we have to. I promise you, if he has to die, it will be right before I do.''

"Thank you," McKenna said, meaning it.

"You're welcome. Here's another favor. Since you have so much to do in both of our interests, you and Commissioner Brunette can leave in your helicopter, just this one time.''

"Thanks, but maybe we'll take the boat.''

"You don't trust me?'' Once again, Felipe sounded hurt.

"Aren't you the guys who have been trying to kill me for almost a year?'' McKenna asked.

"Yes, and we will. But not today. Think of it as a sporting gesture. Could you excuse me for a minute?''

"Sure.''

McKenna took a look at Brunette while he waited. It was obvious that Brunette was in a barely controlled rage, as McKenna expected he would be, since no one had ever accused his friend of being a good loser. McKenna searched for a way to explain to him that some terrorist who had killed his son was going to permit him, the police commissioner, to travel in his police helicopter in his city, and still make it sound good.

Felipe came back on the line before McKenna had formed an answer. "I have just learned that you have closed the three bridges between Staten Island and New Jersey. Good thinking, but that wasn't necessary. You are inconveniencing a lot of people for nothing."

"Just a precaution. We try to plan ahead from time to time."

"I see. Do you know the old railroad bridge that's just north of the Goethals Bridge?"

The knot returned to McKenna's stomach. "I know it."

"Then you won't want to miss our next event, so I suggest you use your helicopter. You have five minutes to get there."

The line went dead as the ferries resumed course for the Verrazano-Narrows Bridge.

Chapter 30

Most people who lived in Staten Island had seen the B&O Railroad Bridge a thousand times without really noticing it. Those who did knew nothing about it. It was just an old, nameless feature in the landscape, a neglected monument to Staten Island's industrial past.

Until the sixties, the Staten Island docks on the east shore of the island were a rail terminus for industrial cargo shipped up and down the East Coast and overseas and were used by many large American companies like US Gypsum and Bethlehem Steel, along with smaller factories located in Staten Island and New Jersey that produced finished wood products for export. Within a period of ten years a number of things happened that made the docks and the rail lines feeding them unprofitable.

First was the collapse of the American steel industry. In the 1960s the United States went from being the largest exporter of steel in the world to a net importer of cheaper foreign steel, much of it produced in Japan and transported to the booming

West Coast, far from the Staten Island docks.

Then came the container ships, which amounted to a revolution in the way cargo was transported. But container ships required specialized loading and unloading equipment, and the Staten Island docks didn't have it. The new facility at Port Newark in New Jersey did, however, and those docks weren't ruled by the longshoremen, who in a bid for survival had engaged in a series of crippling strikes in New York City. So the new container ships went to Port Newark, bypassing the harbor completely by traveling up the Kill van Kull, a narrow dredged waterway between the west shore of Staten Island and New Jersey. Along the way they passed under the Outerbridge Crossing, the Goethals Bridge, and the B&O Railroad Bridge.

Of course, the Staten Island docks could have been modernized, saving the railroads that served them in the process, but the opening of the Verrazano-Narrows Bridge in 1964 precluded that expensive possibility. Within ten years the population of Staten Island nearly doubled, and land was more profitably used for residential purposes. The small factories gave way to tracts of middle-class houses and the docks themselves became the sites of high-rise luxury condominiums with spectacular views of the harbor and the Manhattan skyline. The Staten Island docks and the railroads that served them were finished.

But the management of the Baltimore and Ohio Railroad foresaw none of these events when they commissioned the building of their bridge over the Kill van Kull in the 1950s. At the time, the railroad business between Staten Island and the industrial northeast was booming and they had been transporting their freight cars between their lines in New Jersey and Staten Island by ferry across the Kill van Kull, which was a time-consuming and expensive process. So they contracted for an efficient, relatively inexpensive, and common bridge design, a railroad lift bridge with a useful design life of seventy-five years. In 1958 construction of the B&O Railroad Bridge was begun.

The bridge consisted of a pair of 200-foot towers on each side of the Kill van Kull, separated by 500 feet. The tracks ran 37 feet above the Kill van Kull. To enable shipping to pass under the bridge, an elevator mechanism in the towers used 12 heavy steel cables to raise and lower the bridge section between them to 137 feet above the water, providing enough clearance for all but the largest of ships.

The B&O Railroad Bridge opened to great fanfare in 1959. Twelve years later the lift section of the bridge was raised for the last time and left in that position. The railroads had closed their operations on Staten Island.

Senior Comrade Electrico Amarutsi was in fear of his life, and fear was not an emotion frequently felt by him. In his youth he had worked as a guide for American mountain climbers and gained a reputation as a sure-footed and fearless climber, skilled in navigating the steepest gorges and mountain faces in the high Andes. Then the war came, tourism dropped, and he found himself in the movement with a new job that required his skills. He was charged with destroying the electric pylon towers that spanned the mountain passes, and he excelled at his job. By the time he had blown up his one-hundredth tower, he was known throughout the central Andes as Electrico, and he relished the honor as his fame spread.

He remembered how he had scoffed at the ease of the mission he had been assigned in New York. It had been a simple matter for him to climb the bridge towers during the night and wrap the C-4 detonation cord around the steel cables holding up the track bed, especially since the bridge wasn't guarded by soldiers as were many of the electric pylon towers in Peru. But even if it had been guarded, he knew he would have succeeded. The bridge hadn't been lighted and it was his experience that soldiers never look up. Still, he had allowed himself three hours for a job that only took two.

After he had completed his task and was picked up by the American, he rejoined his squad at the motel in Elizabeth, on the New Jersey side of the Kill van Kull. They congratulated him on his success, but there was no celebration since everyone had to be combat ready for the morning's action. Although the American had driven the rest of them to the ferry terminal in Staten Island many times during the past week for practice runs on the ferry, and although every man knew exactly what he had to do for his part of the mission, they had all been tense when he returned. All except for him, as the major part of his work was done. He had tried to sleep, but they kept him up all night with their nervous chatter, right through till morning, when the American came in his van to pick them up.

The taxi had come an hour later, right on schedule, to take him to the gas station near the railroad bridge. Then they had hit the traffic, still a mile from the gas station, and had progressed only two blocks in the last ten minutes.

In a panic, Electrico checked his watch for the tenth time. Twenty-five minutes after twelve. He had only five minutes to get to the gas station and blow the bridge.

"Can you find out what the problem is?" he asked the Cuban taxi driver.

The driver radioed his base and Electrico heard the answer. The New York City Police had closed the Goethals Bridge and traffic was backed off the New Jersey Turnpike into the streets of Elizabeth.

Knowing that a traffic jam would not be sufficient excuse to deter Felipe's wrath, Electrico paid the driver and started to run for the gas station. He figured he had a mile to go. Running as fast as he could, he covered half the distance and could see the B&O Bridge when the blue-and-white New York City Police helicopter swept in and hovered over it. As he ran, he reached into his pocket, turned on his M129A radio remote detonator, and pressed the "Fire" button.

Nothing happened. The M129A had a range of 1,000 yards, and he was still too far away from his explosives. He kept running toward the bridge and saw the helicopter hover close to the top of the tower on the New Jersey side. The helicopter's rear door opened and a man hung out, looking at the tower through binoculars. Electrico was sure the man could see the white det cord wrapped around the black steel cables. He pressed the "Fire" button again.

Still too far. He kept running and saw the helicopter hover over the tower and drop a rope ladder. The man with the binoculars started climbing down. Electrico tried again. He had finally gotten close enough.

The radio remote receivers attached to each cable picked up Electrico's signal and sent nine volts of high-amperage electricity to the blasting cap embedded in each strand of C-4 det cord. The resulting explosion severed each steel cable and caused the helicopter and the man hanging on the rope ladder to gain rapidly fifty feet of altitude while the raised-track roadway suspended between the towers almost as rapidly lost 137 feet of altitude.

At thirty-three minutes after twelve as the middle section of the bridge descended into the Kill van Kull Channel, the path to Port Newark and the back door to New York Harbor were slammed closed.

Chapter 31

The police helicopter returned to Manhattan by flying north over New Jersey, then crossing the Hudson River and Manhattan at Midtown. It landed briefly at the 34th Street Heliport, where Brunette got off and jumped into a waiting police car for the short trip to Bellevue Hospital, then took off again, rose to 2,000 feet, and followed Third Avenue and the Bowery south, passing over miles of stopped traffic.

McKenna struggled to put his thoughts in order as the helicopter headed south. He was more shaken than he cared to admit to himself, and he couldn't ignore the twitch he had developed in his right thigh muscle. He tried changing position a few times in the cramped backseat of the helicopter, but the tic always returned. His leg persisted in giving his brain false information, telling it that he was running somewhere, fast. But he knew he was going nowhere and hoped it would take a while to get there.

The helicopter reached police headquarters, descended to 1,000 feet, and hovered. McKenna looked down quickly, then concentrated on staring at the back of the pilot's neck, trying to will his stomach to cease jumping and hoping that he wasn't going to throw up.

He had discovered with his brief glance downward that he had developed a fear of heights in the last half hour, a phobia he never had suffered before. He tried rationalizing and attributed his fear to his narrow escape at the B&O Bridge, but still it surprised him. Over Brunette's objections, he had left the helicopter and gone down the rope ladder without a second thought, knowing he was in a position to disrupt at least a part of *Sendero*'s plans if only he could remove the blasting caps from the explosives wrapped around the bridge cables. His pride had demanded the attempt, even though he had thought it would be futile and figured he would be killed in the process. It was one of those perfect moments in life when he was totally without fear and ready to meet his fate, which made his visceral reaction to the explosion difficult for him to explain to himself.

When the blast forced the helicopter upward, he thought he was lost, and was actually surprised to see that he was still holding on to the rope ladder. He had looked down, then yelled up, begging the pilot to land. He had thought his hands were frozen to the ladder, and he couldn't will them to pull his body up the ladder. It was Brunette who had finally gotten him up.

First Brunette had tried coaxing and pleading, but McKenna still couldn't move his hands. Then he had gone into pure Brunette, cursing down at him, spitting at him, and talking bad about McKenna's mother. That got McKenna's hands working, and he climbed up the ladder like a gymnast, eager to get into the helicopter so he could bash his insolent friend.

Of course, he couldn't do it. By the time he had climbed back in, Brunette was back in the front seat and talking on the phone. McKenna had sat behind him and thought of strangling him from behind. Then Brunette had put his hand over the mouthpiece, turned, and said with a smile, "Welcome back. Now, isn't it nicer in here than out there?"

Looking at Brunette's broken nose and battered face, McKenna had been forced to return the smile as his anger vanished. "It's a little too hot in here," was all he had been able to say.

Brunette had continued his phone conversation with Gene Shields. Shields would arrange that the Coast Guard station three cutters at the New York Harbor approaches to turn away incoming ships. They would also act to close all the marinas within 100 miles of New York City to prevent pleasure boats from undertaking sight-seeing excursions to the harbor.

Then Brunette had surprised McKenna when he fell asleep as soon as he finished his call, leading McKenna to believe that his friend was suffering from a concussion and needed medical attention. It had been difficult, but he was finally able to persuade Brunette to get a quick checkup at Bellevue.

"Ready to meet the press, Commissioner?" the pilot asked, pointing down.

McKenna forced himself to look. Twenty cops had the small

plaza cordoned off and they worked to keep a crowd of hundreds away from the landing zone. McKenna saw a mobile press van with its large roof antenna raised and knew they were transmitting live. From his vantage point he could see three more press vans coming from city hall.

"I don't wanna do this," was all McKenna could think to say.

"Which is it, Commissioner? Do you want me to land or not?" the pilot asked.

"Got no choice. Put her down."

As the pilot lowered the machine, a group of reporters and a camera crew ran from the parked van and rushed the police line. The reporters were pushed back, and McKenna saw what appeared to be a heated exchange between a uniformed sergeant and a reporter. The sergeant won, and order was briefly restored when he ripped the press pass from the reporter's jacket.

As the helicopter touched down, McKenna took a deep breath and opened the cabin door. Even over the noise of the rotors, he could hear the shouted questions begin, questions he wished he had the knowledge to answer. He stepped out and walked to the line of cops holding back the reporters, still feeling wobbly and sure they could see it.

If they did, they kept it to themselves. He stopped and a dozen microphones were thrust in front of his face.

"Sorry, but I'm not feeling too good right now," McKenna said, looking straight into the cameras. "I'm sure there will be a press conference soon and I promise to answer all the questions I can."

There wasn't another question. They still held the microphones in front of his face while the cameras continued to roll, but they didn't ask another question.

"Excuse me, please," McKenna said as he aligned himself on the headquarters garage door and started walking. The crowd of reporters parted and he passed through. They remained standing on the sidewalk as he crossed the street, walked down the ramp, and entered the garage.

Not a bad bunch of guys after all, he thought as he got into the elevator. Camilia was waiting at his office door with a cup of coffee for him. It was exactly what he needed, of course. He took a long sip, then asked, "What now, Camilia?"

"Your wife wants you to call when you get a chance."

"That's it?" Wouldn't that be wonderful, he thought.

"Of course not, but you can imagine the rest. The mayor

and the rest of your public are waiting for you in the commissioner's office, but I think that you should wash up first. There's a fresh suit in your bathroom.''

He had learned to do whatever Camilia suggested. One look in the bathroom mirror told him she was right again. His face and hands were filthy, his suit was a wreck, not a strand of his hair was in place, and he was pale white without a hint of color. But a new suit, shirt, and tie were hanging on a hook behind the door. He marveled at Camilia's foresight in having his clothes brought from the hotel. While he was fighting for his life over the harbor, she was busy ensuring he would look good for the mayor, just in case he survived, which was exactly the kind of thing that made her Camilia.

McKenna took ten minutes to wash up, change, and rearrange himself as best he could, but it wasn't good enough for Camilia. When he came out of his bathroom, she gave him the once-over. ''You look like a corpse,'' she said, then pinched his cheeks with both hands long enough to bring tears to his eyes, so that he looked better, but felt worse. She gave him a pat on the back and sent him to work.

Chapter 32 The mayor and all the chiefs and deputy commissioners were in animated conversation when McKenna entered Brunette's conference room, but silence prevailed as he walked to the only empty chair at the table, trying to look casual. It was difficult. All eyes were on him, which made McKenna wonder if he had left his fly open. A quick glance downward told him that it was something else. He took his seat and they all sat there, just staring at him. Then McKenna realized that he was the star and that they had been waiting for him to begin.

''I presume you know everybody, Brian,'' the mayor said.

McKenna didn't. He knew Jackie Townsend, the chief of detectives, had met Frank Gibbons, the first deputy commissioner, and had spoken briefly to Reginald Rivers, the deputy commissioner for public information. The chief chaplain had officiated at Keller's funeral that morning, and McKenna recognized the rest of the chiefs only because their pictures were hanging in his office. The mayor introduced a man McKenna didn't recognize as John Rinaldi, the deputy mayor for transportation.

Everyone stood up and shook McKenna's hand over the table and took the time to repeat their names for him. As he sat down, it gave McKenna a little chuckle to think that a short time before he would have been saluting and standing at attention before these personages. But for the moment, it looked like he was in charge.

He was. "First let's get a few things out of the way," the mayor said as he stood up. "I spoke to the chief surgeon at Bellevue, and he tells me that Commissioner Brunette is suffering from a broken nose and a concussion that he describes as potentially serious, but not critical, whatever that means. He recommends he be hospitalized, maybe for a week or so. However, Ray called me fifteen minutes ago and said he would be back long before that. In his absence, the first deputy commissioner will run the department, as provided for by the city charter."

Frank Gibbons looked less than happy at that prospect. He was a tough old guy who had risen through the ranks and hung around long enough to be rewarded with the largely ceremonial position of first deputy commissioner. His main mission in the department was to approve disciplinary penalties, run interference for Brunette, and make sure that all the chiefs' sons and daughters went to the nice places they wanted to go in the department. Now, at possibly the most critical moment in the history of the New York City Police Department, he was being handed the ball when his offensive line was down and in disarray and the defense was coming in to crush the life out of him.

"However," the mayor continued, "Commissioner Brunette recommends that Assistant Commissioner McKenna, being the one most familiar with the problem confronting us, should be charged with the specific responsibility of getting us out of this mess. I told him I agree. Are there any objections?"

McKenna was sure there were a gazillion objections colliding with each other in the assembled chiefs' heads, but none were heard as the mayor looked around the room.

"I'm glad we're all in agreement," the mayor said with a straight face. "Now let me give you the big picture on all this, and I'm going to talk straight so there'll be no misunderstandings. For the moment, I have ordered that Kennedy Airport and La Guardia be closed to incoming flights, since most of the approach runs to those airports take the planes over the harbor. That means that the city and the tourist business are going to lose millions that will never be made up. Right now there are thousands of people sitting in airports with paid tickets for New York in their hands, along with hotel reservations, car rentals, and Lord knows what else, and they're never gonna get here to spend their money.

"Next, Staten Island is effectively cut off from the rest of the city. The Verrazano-Narrows Bridge is closed and we can't use the two ferryboats we have left. The only way people are going to be able to get home tonight is to drive through New Jersey in the biggest traffic jam any of them have ever seen, cursing me and you the whole time. Worse yet, the governor has unilaterally suspended the tolls on the bridges and tunnels so traffic will move a little easier, which means we lose millions while he looks like a hero and I look like shit."

The mayor paused a moment to let that sink in. The animosity between him and the governor was common knowledge, but it ran deeper than that. Actually, the mayor hated the governor, considered him the cause of most of the city's problems, and was diametrically opposed to him on almost every issue ranging from the death penalty to welfare reform. One of His Honor's favorite questions was, If this governor is so popular, how come I can never find anyone who admits voting for the douche bag? To those who knew the mayor, the answer was obvious, since whenever he said "douche bag," he was thinking about the governor, and no one would admit to him that they had voted for the man he detested. Speculation was that if the mayor were locked in a room with the governor's mother, even she would deny voting for him.

The mayor could see that his point was not lost on the chiefs, so he continued. "Then we have the hostages. There's somewhere between five hundred and a thousand of them, and they have to be foremost in our minds, especially since I carried Staten Island in the last election and I'll need them more than ever in the next election."

Of course, they all knew the mayor was right. He was living in Gracie Mansion only because the white voting blocks that dominated politics in Staten Island and Queens had put him there, and he always played to his fans.

"Now for the price tag," the mayor continued. "Aside from the overtime your department is racking up on all this, those two ferries are the best and newest ones we have. Cost the city thirty-two million in nineteen eighty-one and would probably cost twice that today. As for the Williamsburg Bridge, the 1975 *Times* study estimated that it would cost eighty million dollars to replace it. We don't even have a figure, so we'll use theirs and say it's a hundred and fifty million in today's dollars. But all that's just a drop in the bucket compared to what American business is losing. Since eleven o'clock this morning, when all this began, the stock market has lost almost two hundred points. That means billions, and it's affecting everything, which means that *Sendero*'s actions here have shaken investor confidence in the ability of the American system to handle people like them. Interestingly enough, the only stock rising through all this is a company called Equitable Shipyards, which just happens to be the company that built those two ferries. So it looks like the market is anticipating another big order for them, which means they think we're gonna lose those boats."

There was a knock at the door. Madeline, Brunette's secretary, opened it and waited to be recognized.

"Well?" the mayor shouted to her.

"I just thought you should know, Your Honor, that a cop has been shot in the Bronx. He got in a shoot-out with a drug dealer. The bad guy's dead, but then the cop was shot by the guy's girlfriend."

"What happened to her?"

"Cop's partner shot her. She's still alive, but there have been some local disturbances."

"Local disturbances? What's that mean?" the mayor asked.

"It means they're rioting and looting," Gibbons answered.

"Then why don't we say they're rioting and looting and forget this 'local disturbances' bullshit!" the mayor roared.

"Yes, sir," Madeline said, unperturbed. "They're rioting and looting on University Avenue in the Four-Four Precinct."

"Thank you," the mayor said, somewhat placated. "How's the cop?"

"Serious but stable. He's in Montefiore Hospital." She left and closed the door behind her.

The mayor sat down while he thought over this new development. Then he turned to the first deputy commissioner. "Frank, you can't fool around up there because your department doesn't have the manpower right now. The governor already offered to activate the National Guard, and I turned him down. I'm sure not gonna ask him now, so I'm gonna say this only one time and I'm not gonna deny later that I said it."

McKenna found himself leaning forward in his chair to catch every word, then noticed he wasn't the only one. Everyone in the room knew that the mayor hadn't carried the Bronx in the last election, and never would.

The mayor spoke clearly and slowly. "I want you to scrape up all the manpower you can get and go up there. Be firm, be fair, but most important, be fast. Whatever's going on up there, I want it over tonight, and I don't care how many arrests you have to make. Understand me?"

It was exactly what Gibbons wanted to hear. "Yes, sir."

"Good. It shouldn't be as hard as it could be, since most of the press will be tied up at the harbor. If you do it right, I should be reading about your activities someplace between the sports and the funnies tomorrow."

"Will you be going to the hospital?" Gibbons asked.

"No. If I did, it would draw the press. So for the first time I can remember, the mayor of the City of New York is not going to the hospital to visit a cop who has been seriously shot. Instead, I'm going to lock myself in my office and wait to hear the excellent plan the rest of you gentlemen are going to cook up. Then, I'm going to announce a five o'clock press conference, at which time I will tell the world that the situation in the harbor will be handled by our expert police department under the supervision of our highly paid chiefs. In the meantime, I expect that I'll be getting a call from the President offering me his unqualified support, and I'll try to off this whole thing on him, if he's stupid enough to let me."

But none of that was Gibbons's concern. "I should be on my way?" he asked.

"Exactly," the mayor answered.

Gibbons got up and left, looking glad to be going.

Then the mayor stood up and McKenna couldn't help thinking that sometimes, in periods of crisis, otherwise mundane politicians are transformed into the great leaders the nation needs. The mayor headed for the door and everyone stood. But then he decided he wasn't done.

"I just want to leave you all with a few heartfelt thoughts, and then I'll be a nice guy again. McKenna?''

"Yes, sir."

"I seem to have created a political monster when I appointed you. I understand that the press helicopter got some great footage of you and Brunette during your harbor adventure, so right now you're politically untouchable. But I've been a politician a long time, and I know all the filthy ways to play. Understand?''

"Yes, sir," McKenna answered, not really understanding.

The mayor shifted his stare from McKenna and took in every man around the room in turn. "As for the rest of you, I suggest you cooperate with McKenna and come up with something good, because if you screw it up and cause me to lose my job, I'll go gracefully, taking my deputy mayors and my deputy commissioners with me to the unemployment office. But before I do, I'll make sure every one of you chiefs is a captain again, meaning no more stupendous salaries, no more city cars, no more cellular phones, no more pretty secretaries, and I promise that you'll be working in some forgotten, filthy, crime-infested precinct that I wouldn't even feel safe flying over."

Then the mayor smiled. "I know it's unfair and you all worked hard to get where you are, but I just wanted to let you gentlemen know how I feel. Good luck."

It was then that McKenna realized that great political leaders are, first and foremost, great politicians. He turned back to the table, but the chiefs weren't ready yet. Each of them was still staring at the door, mesmerized while contemplating his own uncertain future.

"Exactly where are the ferries now?" McKenna asked softly, but they responded as if he had yelled the question into each of their ears. All heads snapped to McKenna, with total attention focused on the new supreme leader.

"They're at anchor, fifty yards this side of the Verrazano-Narrows Bridge, tied bow-to-stern," the chief of patrol answered.

"There's nobody on the Verrazano Bridge?"

"Nobody."

McKenna focused on the deputy mayor for transportation. "Mr. Rinaldi, tell us about those ferries."

McKenna had jumped into Rinaldi's backyard, and he was happy to answer. "The *Samuel I. Newhouse* and the *Andrew J. Barberi* are identical. Each is licensed to carry six thousand passengers, which is far more than any other ship in the world. They're three hundred and ten feet long, powered by four diesel engines generating seven thousand horsepower in either direction, have a maximum speed of seventeen knots, and are operated by a crew of twelve, counting the captain.''

Three hundred and ten feet long, McKenna figured. Tied end-to-end, that's six hundred and twenty feet. ''What's the span between the bridge towers on the Verrazano-Narrows?''

''Two thousand feet.''

''Could ocean vessels still navigate around those boats and get into the harbor?''

''It would depend on the time of day and the tides. There's a heavy current running through the Narrows, but a good pilot could get a large vessel through if the tide were right.''

''How deep is the water under the bridge?''

''Runs from forty-three to ninety-eight feet.''

''And how high are those boats?''

''Forty-five feet above the water line, thirteen feet below. I see what you're getting at, Commissioner. You want to know if they could close the Narrows passage into the harbor if they sank those boats there, right?''

''I'm sure it's gonna be one of their threats when they finally give us their demands,'' McKenna said.

''If you're right, the answer is yes, they could keep the harbor closed, presuming they have accurate charts and know exactly where to sink them. A skilled pilot would still be able to bring a ship in, but the question is academic because he wouldn't be permitted to. The maritime insurance companies would place New York Harbor off limits if there were two underwater obstacles the size of our ferryboats at the bottom of the Narrows.''

''If they were to sink them, could they be removed?''

''Anything's possible, but I'm sure it would be very expensive and would take some time.''

''How far could they take those boats, if they wanted to?''

''They both were fully fueled at four this morning, so I'd say Boston, Massachusetts, if they went north or Norfolk, Virginia, if they went south.''

''They're seaworthy?'' McKenna asked.

Rinaldi beamed. ''Of course. They were built in New Orleans and came to New York under their own power.''

''Okay, let's get on to the Williamsburg Bridge. If that tractor trailer were loaded with explosives and they set it off, what would happen?''

"I asked the chief city engineer the same question before I came here,'' Rinaldi said, "and he told me that it depends on how much explosive they have in the truck. But assuming they have enough to snap that suspension cable with the explosion, then the roadway and tracks between the Williamsburg Bridge's two towers are going into the East River, just like *Sendero* says they are.''

"And I presume that would close the East River to shipping?'' McKenna asked.

"Definitely. The channel under the bridge is thirty-five feet deep. If that bridge goes down, the center span would be sticking out of the water in most places.''

"How long would it take to remove?''

"At least a year, I presume. It will probably take that long to clear what's left of the B&O Bridge out of the Kill van Kull and get that open again.''

"What would be the economic impact if all those things happen?''

"Offhand, I'd say New York City would be done for. Without the harbor, we'd be an economic basket case. Massive layoffs in the transportation, fishing, and shipping industries; high unemployment; loss of tax base; and you can imagine the rest. Besides that, we'd lose the subway line running on the Williamsburg Bridge, and the bridge would have to be replaced, not to mention that the traffic would be intolerable. There would be massive capital flight, companies would move out, and the city would be broke in a week. I assume that federal disaster relief funds would blunt some of the more immediate effects, but in the long term it would be over for us.''

"And if we get out of this with the Williamsburg Bridge intact and the Narrows clear?''

"It's still bad. They already caused us a major problem when they blew the B&O Bridge. Most of the city's solid garbage is transported across the harbor by barge and then up the Kill van Kull to the Fresh Kills landfill on Staten Island. It's the largest dump in the world, and *Sendero* just made it much more expensive and time consuming to get the garbage there. Until we get the B&O Bridge out of the Kill van Kull, the barges are going to have to go out the Narrows and up the Kill van Kull from the ocean side. That's going to add six hours to the round-trip and we won't be able to move the garbage barges into the ocean if the weather's bad.''

"But the city would still survive?''

"Yes. Confidence would be shaken, but, in my opinion, we'd survive.''

"Thank you, Mr. Rinaldi. I have just one more question for you. Would they be able to get those ferryboats to Jamaica Bay and beach them at Kennedy Airport?''

"I don't know. The ferries need thirteen feet of water to operate. I'd have to get the charts for Jamaica Bay and see how deep it is. I have them in my office.''

"Then please do that.''

"Now?'' Rinaldi asked.

"Yes, now, Mr. Rinaldi. I think Felipe already has that information, so we're entitled to it also. We know he was planning to hijack a plane at JFK, and logic leads me to conclude that's where he was planning to bring the ferries before we captured his men in Brighton Beach. I think he would have beached the ferries, then taken his men and as many hostages as he needed to fill up a Boeing 727 before heading off for parts unknown.''

"But he can't do that now," Rinaldi protested. "The mayor closed JFK.''

"Yes, Felipe can. I'm sure we pissed him off when we captured his hijack team, but he went ahead with his plan and hijacked the ferries anyway, so he must have something else in mind in the way of an escape plan. The airport's closed, but they still have planes at JFK, don't they?''

"Yes, of course," Rinaldi answered. "There must be hundreds of them stuck there now.''

"Then one possibility is that his men will storm a parked plane there. Then Felipe will still beach his ferries and start shooting hostages until we open the airport and let him take off. Another possibility is that he has men in place to hijack a plane someplace else in the world and bring it here, or to any airport close to the water that's within the range of his ferryboats, and I'm sure that's a lot of airports. He could take them to La Guardia if he wanted to. In any event, we need to know exactly where it is possible for him to beach those ferries, and JFK is number one on my list.''

Rinaldi stood up. "I'll be back in twenty minutes. I'll bring the charts for Flushing Bay around La Guardia also, just in case you want to look at them.''

"Good. You can also find out how many airports on the East Coast we're talking about and order the charts for them."

"Of course," Rinaldi said as he got up and left.

McKenna turned his attention to the chiefs and said, "I know we all heard the mayor's fine speech, and I have some bad news for you. We're not going to have a plan for him soon, unless one of you is much smarter than I am. Right now, Felipe is in charge of this city, not the mayor, and there's nothing we can do about it. Forgetting about the Williamsburg Bridge for the moment, we don't have the capability to take those ferries back. Maybe the military could, and I'm sure we'll be hearing from them soon. In any event, if they tried, I'm sure there would be tremendous loss of life on both sides, hundreds of dead hostages, and the ferries would probably wind up at the bottom of the Narrows."

McKenna saw that his assessment wasn't going over well with the chiefs, and he sympathized with their position. At the moment, they were politically vulnerable and subject to the mayor's whims, while he was not. McKenna wished he had something to boost their confidence, but he didn't. What he had to tell them was going to make it worse.

"We will make every attempt to keep His Honor happy, but this thing is not going to go away easily," he said. "What we have to remember, and I hope that you're all in agreement with me, is that we work for New York City, not the federal government."

"I think we all agree on that," Townsend said. "But why is that important?"

"It's important because whatever happens in the harbor is going to affect the city, but Felipe didn't take those ferries to get anything from us. When he finally makes his demands, they're going to be things that only the federal government can do, not us. So the feds are going to want to take charge of this thing, and the mayor wants them to, but we're not going to let them."

"Why not?" the chief of detectives asked. "That would get the mayor off our back."

"Because the feds don't live here. We do. I think Felipe's demands will be so outrageous that they will contemplate military action, but we're not going to let them. Those are our citizens on those boats right now, and it's our city that goes down the tubes if they fail."

"When do you think he's going to make his demands?" Townsend asked.

"When he's good and ready. He's organized quite a show, and for a number of reasons he's going to take his time. He'll want to wait until tomorrow, at least. By then the entire world press will be in place here and focused on the harbor. Another thing is that we can presume this whole thing is being financed by the Colombian drug people, so we have to figure the drug people have a stake in this."

McKenna turned to Chief McNamara and asked, "Anything new on large drug shipments into this country since the last time we talked?"

"Nothing new," the chief of the Organized Crime Control Bureau answered. "The last I heard, they had all their planes full and sitting on their runways in Colombia."

"That's gonna change now," McKenna said. "The Coast Guard has three cutters heading here, and I'm assuming at least a couple of them were assigned to drug interdiction duties. I'm also assuming that in the next couple of days, this city is going to see the largest buildup of federal law enforcement forces ever assembled, and a lot of those forces are going to be people who would ordinarily be assigned to something to do with narcotics."

"Sounds like a good assumption," McNamara said.

"And what are your people doing now?" McKenna asked.

"As soon as this broke, I suspended all narcotics investigations and put them in uniform."

"Who told you to do that?" McKenna asked.

"Nobody," McNamara answered defensively. "I figured you could use an extra two thousand experienced bodies, and narcotics investigations seemed a pretty low priority to me under the present circumstances."

"I'd say you did exactly right," McKenna said. "Because that's exactly what I would have suggested you do. Drugs is the least of our problems right now, but it's going to be a big problem for the feds. I'm sure part of what Felipe promised the Colombians was that they'd be able to move their stuff into this country quite easily once he started his show, and those planes are going to be taking off soon."

"So what should I do?" McNamara asked.

"Get your men up to the Bronx to help out Commissioner Gibbons and get things quieted down up there. We don't need the festivities to spread to other parts of the city."

"I'll do that."

"Good. Do it now," McKenna instructed.

"Now?" McNamara protested. "What about the rest of this conference?"

"Oh, I'm sorry," McKenna said. "Are you the one with the plan to solve all this?"

"No," McNamara answered, his face reddening.

"Then give me a call later and I'll tell you how much the mayor hates the rest of us after I tell him Felipe's in charge of this city, not him. Think of it this way: if you're not here for the whole meeting, you might be the only one he still likes."

"I see," McNamara said as he got up and left, still not a very happy chief.

Next McKenna focused on the police chaplain, whose presence at the meeting seemed unusual. "What exactly are you doing here, Monsignor?"

The chaplain seemed to expect the question. "To tell you the truth, I don't exactly know. I came here to discuss a problem with Commissioner Brunette, but the mayor was here and he told me to sit down and pray for all the people on those ferries."

"And have you?"

"Fervently."

"Could you tell me the problem?"

"Of course. The families of the Harbor men who were killed today are on their way here and I don't know exactly what to tell them. You see, we've never had any cops killed before where we didn't at least have their bodies. In this case, we have nothing, and I don't know when we'll be able to recover the remains and make proper arrangements. I just don't know what to tell them."

"Me neither, except that they were heroes. Do you have their names?"

"Sergeant Michael Sweeney, thirty-one years on the Job, nineteen years in Harbor. Police Officer Wayne Crandall, twenty-six years on the Job, eleven years in Harbor. And Police Officer Bob Crandall, twenty-four years on the Job, nine years in Harbor."

"Brothers?" McKenna asked, hoping it wasn't so.

"Yes."

Oh no, McKenna thought. This was going to be a tough one, especially since all of them could have retired years ago.

But the Harbor Unit, commonly known throughout the Job as the Poor Man's Yacht Club, had a lot of gray-haired cops assigned. Nobody retired from Harbor until they were ready to collect Social Security. "When will their families get here?" McKenna asked.

"Soon. I sent helicopters to pick them up. Otherwise, they'd never get here, with the traffic."

"Good. When they do get here, have them wait in my office. But make sure you're there with them, because I don't think I'm going to be too good at this."

"Don't worry. I'll be there," the chaplain said as he got up and left.

McKenna turned to Jackie Townsend, the chief of detectives. "Can you give us anything we don't already know?"

"A little bit, but not much that helps us now. We've received over one thousand calls since Felipe and Elena's picture appeared in the papers this morning. I've got a hundred men answering the phones and six hundred men following up the leads. We found out where Felipe and Elena were staying, but it was too late."

"A hotel in Midtown?" McKenna ventured.

"The Summit Hotel, East 51st Street and Lexington Avenue. The bell captain called us at nine-thirty this morning, after he saw the pictures in the papers. He was off, but he said he thought Felipe was one of their guests in a nice suite, Room 1407. But he wasn't sure because his guest was bald and had a beard. We called the hotel and found out that the guy in 1407 had checked out at four this morning, so we had the Photo Unit do a workup on Felipe's picture. Made him bald, gave him a beard, and brought it to the bell captain's house. That was him, he was sure of it. But he never saw Elena."

An unwanted thought popped into McKenna's head and wouldn't leave: If we would have run Felipe and Elena's picture in the newspapers a day earlier, maybe we could have prevented all this. But Ray didn't want that because he didn't want to scare them away. Is the desire for revenge ripping Ray's judgment apart? McKenna wondered. He got rid of the thought without reaching a conclusion. "Search the room?" he asked the chief of detectives.

"Got to it at eleven this morning, and it hadn't been made up yet. There were two beds and both of them had been slept in. Found a red hair on one of the pillows, but nothing else. Then we went to the night doorman's house and he remembered, since not many people check out at four A.M. Identified both Felipe and Elena. Said they got into a tan van with their luggage. Had four pieces.''

That would be her, McKenna thought. Elena doesn't strike me as the kind of girl who travels light. But 4:00 A.M.? Sounds a little early for her. Felipe must have had a lot of organizing to do, and maybe he wanted to get an early start. Or maybe the truck with the explosives was stored a couple of hours away from the city.

McKenna felt he was missing something, that there was a question he should have asked that slipped his mind. Then it came to him. ''How did Felipe pay for his room?''

''Cash.''

''Any room charges? Phone calls?''

Townsend wasn't missing anything. ''Nothing.''

Exactly as McKenna expected. ''We manage to get anything from our prisoners yet?''

''Not a thing. They're just not talking, and that's it. We're gonna have to arraign them before long, and that puts them into the legal process and out of our hands.''

McKenna wouldn't accept it. ''There's eleven of them, all young men under a lot of pressure in a strange country,'' he pointed out. ''There must be a way to crack one of them, even a little.''

''Maybe not,'' the chief said. ''I'm sure one of Felipe's demands will be for their release, and maybe they know that, or at least expect it.''

''They don't know what's going on in the harbor, do they?''

The chief treated it as an offensive question. ''Of course not,'' he retorted with a trace of indignation. ''They haven't spoken to anyone but their interrogators, not even to each other.''

McKenna decided to try a different approach with the chief. ''Okay, they're not gonna crack. But if you had to stake your life on getting something from one of them, and you could use any dubious method you wanted, is there one you'd choose?''

Townsend must have already asked himself the same question, because he had an answer ready. ''There is one, and at first both myself and Picciarelli thought we had a shot with him. He's the one who was ID'd as the phony purse-snatcher when they killed Brunette's kid, so he has the most to lose.''

McKenna sat up straight. ''Wait a minute. I didn't know any of them had been ID'd in that. When did it happen?''

If the chief was surprised, he was a master of self-control. "Last night. He fit the description, so we rounded up some witnesses and put him in some lineups. He was picked out by eight of them. Of course, I told the commissioner right away, so I figured you knew."

Now why wouldn't Ray mention that to me? McKenna had to ask himself. He didn't like the answers his mind bounced back. "What did the commissioner say?" he asked.

The chief was noncommittal. "Not too much. Said to keep working on him, and maybe he'd try himself if all else failed."

"Anything else about this guy I should know?"

"One thing, but I don't know what it means. He's sporting a fresh shiner. We didn't do it, so I talked to Hardcass. He swears that his men didn't touch him. Hardcass was there in the living room when they took him and he says the guy was choking and offered no resistance."

"So maybe he's a *Sendero* problem child and one of them figured he needed a little discipline." McKenna figured it was time to change the subject before his frustration became too apparent. "Any other worthwhile leads come in from the public?"

"Most of them seem good when you first hear them. We're finding so many illegal immigrants from Central and South America that I'm beginning to wonder who's left down there. There's lots more leads to work on and they're still coming in, but nothing solid yet. I don't know if it's that important to find out where they used to be, since they're all on the ferries now."

"Not all of them," McKenna said. "Maybe we can narrow the search to what is important. Felipe told us that both bridges are under observation, so . . ."

"I get it," the chief of detectives said. "We should concentrate on the tips that come from places where they can see the bridges."

"At least do them first," McKenna said. "Maybe they have two places rented overlooking the bridges, probably apartments they rented this month. And maybe whoever is in the apartment close to the Williamsburg Bridge has the detonator that will blow up that truck, so it has to be handled carefully."

The chief of detectives knew when to leave, which McKenna figured was one of the reasons he got to be the chief of detectives. "I'll get right on it," he said on his way out.

Kenny Kleber, the chief of patrol, was next, and he knew

it was his turn. Before being asked, Kleber gave his report. "Right now, we have eight hundred people a tour on overtime. I have three thousand men a day assigned to the longshoremen's strike, twelve hundred men a day assigned to the airports, two hundred men right now at the bridges, a hundred men assigned to the marinas around the city to keep them closed, and whatever men the precincts can spare are assigned to traffic duty. I don't know yet what kind of manpower Frank Gibbons will be using up in the Bronx, but I think by tomorrow things will be better."

Better? McKenna thought. That's good news. I figured we would be in deeper shit by tomorrow.

Kleber smiled when he saw the perplexed look cross McKenna's face. "It's simple," he explained. "We won't need that many people on the docks because it doesn't look like there will be any ships loading or unloading to piss off the longshoremen, and after the traffic mess clears up sometime tonight, late I would guess, I don't think too many people will be coming back to work tomorrow once they get home. It's my bet that many businesses will stay closed until this is over. So we'll have manpower to spare."

"Now if only we had a plan to use them," McKenna said.

"A more immediate concern is that right now we are experiencing a 911 overload amounting to a breakdown. The emergency operators are getting a couple of thousand extra calls an hour from people who think their husbands, fathers, mothers, or sons are on those ferries. Some of them are pretty hysterical. Unfortunately, there's nothing we can tell them, but it takes time to do even that."

"Nothing to be done about that until we get a list from Felipe," McKenna said, turning to the chief of personnel.

The chief of personnel was also ready. He put on his glasses, took a pad from his pocket, placed it on the table, and consulted it as he reported. "Right now, the department has never been stronger. We have just under thirty-one thousand sworn personnel. We have two hundred and eight on terminal leave prior to retirement, twenty-nine long-term sick due to injuries, one hundred and eighty-five on regular sick, two hundred and nine on maternity leave, and about thirty-one hundred on vacation."

Something about the way the chief of personnel so precisely crunched his numbers irritated McKenna, but he couldn't put his finger on it. The man is doing the job he was paid to do, so what's the problem? McKenna asked himself. He decided it was just that the chief didn't look like a cop and didn't act like a cop. He was more like a high-paid accountant.

"There's one thing I don't understand," the chief said at the end of his recitation.

"What's that?" McKenna asked, really curious to know what the one thing the chief didn't understand could possibly be.

"We should be losing strength, but in the last week our manpower figures have gone up considerably. People are canceling their vacations, thirty-three men have put off their retirement, and only seven people went sick today, when the average number is two hundred and eleven. Then this morning a female police officer who had a baby four days ago came back to work, even though she's entitled to six weeks' sick leave, with pay. The numbers just don't make sense to me."

Not to the chief of personnel, but they did to McKenna. He remembered the Big Blackout of July 13, 1977. He and his partner had been on vacation, fishing on a lake upstate, when they heard the news on the radio. The lights had gone out in New York City, and there was looting, burning, rioting, and other forms of related merriment going on. So they rowed to shore, jumped in their car, and three hours later they were in Manhattan Central Booking with their first arrests of the many more to be made during the course of the following three days. He saw every good cop he knew at one time or another in Central Booking during the blackout. At the time, he figured that cops would bitch and moan more than any other city workers, but they'd always come in and sweat when things went wrong in their city. Add in the fact that *Sendero* had been killing a lot of cops, and you had a bunch of pretty angry people in blue playsuits spoiling for a chance to get even. Of course nobody was staying home. "Chief, what were you doing in 1977?" McKenna had to ask.

"Nineteen seventy-seven?" The chief needed some time to think. "Let me see. That was the year the department sent me to Harvard for my master's degree in Urban Studies."

It figures, McKenna thought as Mr. Rinaldi returned, carrying an armload of charts. "I think I have everything you need," he said as he spread the chart for Jamaica Bay on the table and pointed. "As you can see, they could take those ferries from the Narrows and follow the Ambrose Channel past Coney Island. The water gets a little shallow there, but at high tide they'd have no problem. Then they're into the Rockaway Inlet Channel, all deep water until they get here.'' Rinaldi pointed to a spot in Jamaica Bay, a half mile from Kennedy Airport. ''If they force us to open the two drawbridges over the channel, and I'm assuming they can, at high tide they could get in here, probably put the ferries right on the beach if they came in at full steam.''

McKenna marked the chart at the place Rinaldi indicated. He saw that the spot was off a runway at Kennedy Airport. ''What runway number is this?'' he asked.

''Runway Four Right.''

''How about La Guardia?''

''They could do it, but it wouldn't be as good for them. Flushing Bay is more shallow and the runways at La Guardia are built on high landfills. They'd have to wade ashore for thirty yards, even at high tide, and then they'd have to climb the landfill wall.''

McKenna came to the conclusion that Mr. Rinaldi was a pretty good thinker. ''How about the other airports within their range?'' he asked.

''Unfortunately, there's thirteen of them adjacent to the water and capable of handling jet aircraft the size of a Boeing 727. I found all the charts and I'll leave them with you to figure out.''

''Thank you, Mr. Rinaldi. You've been a big help, but I have one more question. It might sound like a stupid one to you, but I have to know just in case anyone dopier than me asks it. Then I'll certainly need to know the answer.''

''Yes?'' Rinaldi said, waiting patiently, but McKenna noticed that the chiefs had developed a special interest in the boy wonder's next question.

''Who were Andrew J. Barberi and Samuel I. Newhouse?''

McKenna expected the chiefs to laugh, but was glad to see that they also didn't know who Barberi and Newhouse were. But, of course, Mr. Rinaldi did. ''They were two very popular figures on Staten Island. Andrew J. Barberi was a teacher and coach at Curtis High School on Staten Island for more than twenty-five years and Samuel I. Newhouse was a prominent Staten Island businessman. He founded the *Staten Island Advance*, the local newspaper over there.''

McKenna was flabbergasted. A coach and a publisher? he asked himself. The biggest and best ferries in the world named after a coach and a publisher? ''I'm sure they were both swell

guys,'' he said, ''but correct me if I'm wrong. I seem to remember that they used to name the ferryboats after war heroes,
especially since the people on Staten Island were always a
pretty patriotic bunch and they always seemed to have more
than their share of honored dead.''

''I guess they don't do that anymore,'' Rinaldi answered
simply.

It figured.

Chapter 33
Gene Shields was sitting on McKenna's
desk, having a cup of coffee and browsing through the *Patrol
Guide* when McKenna returned, carrying the harbor charts under his arm.

''This is pretty straightforward and well written,'' Shields
observed. ''Nothing like the ambiguous gobbledygook regu-
lations they give us to live by.''

''Oh yeah? I could never make any sense out of it,'' Mc-
Kenna answered as he slumped into the chair behind his desk.
''What happens next? Politically, I mean.''

''You have any kind of a plan?''

''You mean to kick Felipe and his boys off our ferryboats?
No. The mayor wants one, but I don't have one. We just have
to wait and see what *Sendero* wants. It'll be more than we can
give, so the mayor's hoping you'll be in charge of this soon.''

''But you're not?'' Shields asked.

''Depends on your plan. But I'm not gonna sit still for any
kind of Waco plan that entails a substantial risk of sending our
citizens to the bottom of the harbor. You and I both know
Felipe and his people are serious. In their entire history, *Sendero* has never made an idle threat.''

''Don't worry about that too much because I don't think it's
gonna come to that. Unless I miss my guess, nobody in Washington is looking to take over what's basically a no win situation. I think your department's going to be left in charge,

unless it drags on so long that public pressure gives the President no other choice but to intervene. That is, if you don't screw it up along the way and force his hand."

"How will he avoid it? We have more than five hundred people kidnapped in the harbor. Isn't kidnapping one of the federal statutes you use to push local police departments around?"

The FBI boss took a long moment before answering. Then he responded to the slap with a smile. "My, Brian, we are being especially candid today, aren't we?"

But McKenna could sense the anger rising in Shields, although Shields gave no outward sign. He knew he was out of line with his Waco and kidnapping remarks. "Sorry, Gene," he said. "I'm not having a great day."

"All's forgiven, buddy. Just try and remember I'm not from the Omaha field office. I know we're not too popular around the rest of the country, but I'm a New Yorker now and I'm not sending our town down the tubes."

"I will. I know you've never crossed us before, but this is bigger than anything that's ever happened in this country and I'm afraid your boss might sacrifice us in the name of principle."

"You're wrong. Principle is the excuse Washington is gonna use to stay out of this. In theory, the United States has a policy of not negotiating with terrorists. Now, everyone knows that's bullshit. When they took the hostages in Iran, we couldn't wait to talk to them. But still, that's the principle they like to think they have. And they'll swear by it after the President calls the National Security Agency and orders his contingency plans for hijacked ferries and bombs on bridges, and they tell him they don't have one."

"So what's it all mean?"

"It means that the President won't want the black eye he has to get on this one, so he'll talk to the mayor, promise him all sorts of federal disaster aid and anything else he can think of if things go real bad, and tell him to run with the ball."

"What about *Sendero*'s demands?"

"The president will do everything he can to help out, but he'll want the mayor to front for him so it doesn't look like it's the federal government that's collapsing to *Sendero*. That's important since he'll still want to maintain good relations with the Peruvian government, if possible."

Shields had given McKenna much to think about and he

wanted some time to digest it, but he wasn't getting any time. Camilia appeared and announced, "The monsignor is here. He has a lot of people with him."

McKenna took a deep breath. "Give me a minute, please, then send them in."

"You got it," Camilia said as she closed the door.

"Is that the families of the Harbor cops?" Shields asked.

"I'm afraid so."

"Then I'm out of here," he said as he stood up. "I'm no good at this stuff. I'll call you if I hear anything." Shields left and, as he opened the door, McKenna got his first glimpse of his somber visitors. Camilia ushered them in and made a quick exit, closing the door behind her.

As soon as McKenna saw Virginia Crandall, he knew it wasn't going to be as bad as he expected. She was a tall, stout woman in her sixties, dry-eyed, obviously a tower of strength and in charge of the delegation of women and children.

The monsignor made the introductions. Virginia was the mother of the two Harbor Unit brothers, and she had an arm around the shoulder of each of her daughters-in-law, both younger women in their forties. At first glance it looked like they were holding her up, but the opposite was true. They had been crying, their makeup was smeared, and they were relying on Virginia's strength to get them through the day.

Jennifer Sweeney, the dead sergeant's wife, was a prim and proper small woman, also in her sixties. She appeared resigned to her loss, but McKenna got the impression that she wasn't really there. She was accompanied by her teenage grandchildren, Lois and Roger.

Everyone was casually dressed, as McKenna expected. They were wearing the same clothes they wore that afternoon in their suburban homes when they had been notified that their lives had been suddenly, violently, and irrevocably changed.

Virginia set the pace. "We're not going to take up a lot of your time, Mr. McKenna. I can imagine how busy you must be right now."

"You can have all my time you want," McKenna said. "I just wish we were meeting under different circumstances."

"We all do. I understand you were there when my boys died?"

"Yes. I was in a helicopter above them."

"Tell us about it."

McKenna looked at the other family members and wondered

if it was the time and place to get into that. Just thinking about it could make him cry, and all of them sitting and sobbing in his office wouldn't improve the situation. But Virginia looked adamant, so he knew he had no choice. "After *Sendero* took the ferries, your men were ordered to intercept the boat that was delivering weapons and supplies to the terrorists. They—"

"Who gave the order?" Virginia interrupted.

"Commissioner Brunette did, but if he hadn't, I would have." McKenna paused, expecting some recrimination, but there was none. She had just wanted to know, so he continued. "They drove their launch straight at the terrorists' boat, and the terrorists opened fire on them with a machine gun. I think that two of your men were killed then. But I'm sorry, I don't know which two it was."

"I think that would be my sons," Virginia said. "They were always complaining that Sergeant Sweeney never let them take the wheel when anything good was going on. They were all friends, but he was definitely the boss on their boat."

McKenna looked to Jennifer Sweeney for a reaction, but she had none. She was staring right through him, focused on something outside, on the other side of his office window. But her two grandchildren were looking at him expectantly, obviously waiting for him to tell them how their grandfather died. "Should I go on, Mrs. Sweeney?" he asked.

He had surprised her with the question. "You might as well," she said. "I guess I'm going to see it all a thousand times. A news helicopter got it all on film, didn't they?"

"I haven't seen it yet, but I believe they did."

"Then please go on."

It wasn't what McKenna wanted to hear, but he continued. "After your husband's boat missed ramming the terrorists the first time, he turned around and tried again. When he was almost to them, they fired at his boat with a recoilless rifle and blew it up. I presume he was killed instantly. The police launch burned and sank in a few seconds."

"What's a recoilless rifle?" Virginia asked.

"It's like a cannon."

"He didn't have to try a second time, did he?" Mrs. Sweeney asked, her eyes still not focused on McKenna.

"No, nobody ordered him to do that. He decided on his own it was the thing to do."

"Did he have a chance of succeeding?"

"Yes, a small chance. But he probably would have been killed anyway if he was able to ram their boat."

"It's exactly what I would have expected Mike to do," Mrs. Sweeney said, apparently resigned. "He was the thickest man I ever met, and he always finished whatever he started." She started to cry again and was consoled by her grandchildren.

McKenna felt very uncomfortable, but Virginia Crandall hadn't come to watch other women cry. "So they were all heroes, but they died for nothing," she stated.

McKenna searched his mind for another way to say it, but there was none. "Yes, they were heroes and they died for nothing. But if they had succeeded—and they came close to doing it—then those terrorists wouldn't be in as strong a position as they are now."

"Are you going to get them?" Virginia asked.

Here comes the hard part, McKenna thought. "Mrs. Crandall, we'll recover your sons' bodies as soon as we can. The problem is that—"

"I don't mean the bodies," Virginia Crandall said. "I mean those terrorists. Are you going to get them?"

"I don't know. I hope so, but they may win. They have this city by the throat."

"But you'll still try to get them, even if they get away from you here?" she asked again.

"If it takes me the rest of my life," McKenna stated, surprising himself with the quick answer that came from the back of his mind.

"That's why I came, and that's all I wanted to hear. Thank you for telling us the truth, Mr. McKenna. I hope to see you at the funerals, whenever that will be." She turned to the door, taking her two daughters-in-law with her. Mrs. Sweeney didn't seem to notice that Virginia Crandall had decided the meeting was over. She remained standing, looking out McKenna's window at nothing in particular.

Mrs. Crandall escorted her sons' wives to Camilia's reception area and came back for Jennifer Sweeney. "Mrs. Sweeney," she said in an admonishing tone of voice. "Come on. We can't be taking up any more of Mr. McKenna's time. He has a lot of people depending on him."

Mrs. Sweeney, guided by her grandchildren and the chaplain, followed Mrs. Crandall out, leaving McKenna thinking of something his own mother once said. It's a terrible man who lies to widows and children, she had told him when he was growing up. He had never thought of himself as a terrible man, and he had told them he would get *Sendero* if it took him the rest of his life. For the first time, he knew he would, or die trying.

Chapter 34

Colonel Savraada arrived at McKenna's office at two-thirty, carrying a large suitcase and, although he wore a fresh suit, looking beat.

"Glad you're here, Colonel," McKenna said as he rose from his desk and shook Savraada's hand. "I guess you've heard what's going on here."

"Yes, I heard," Savraada said, taking a seat across from McKenna. "Well, we expected something spectacular from Felipe, didn't we?"

"Not quite this spectacular. He's put us in a real bind. You learn anything from Alejandro and Pedro to help us out?"

"I've learned a lot, but nothing that will remove Felipe from your ferryboats. I spoke to Pedro on the flight from Texas and he gave me some information, but he would prefer to talk to you directly since you are the one paying for his information."

"That's fine," McKenna said. "Where is he now?"

"Waiting downstairs with your Detective White. I thought it best we speak privately before you interview him. The information he did give me needs to be discussed."

"He's cooperative?"

"Very. I've seen it before with the Senderistas. It is very difficult to get them to turn, but when they do, they frequently give everything they know."

"Can you be sure he's telling you the truth?"

"I found no reason to disbelieve him. As soon as he saw his wife and children, he was ready to talk."

"Where is his family now?"

"Living in the sheriff's jail until you're done with Pedro in

New York. I don't think his wife is quite ready yet to join law-abiding Texas society.''

"Why not? She give you some trouble?" McKenna asked.

"She killed one of my men in Ayacucho. She's a dedicated Senderista and needs a little time to get used to the fact that the war's behind her and she'll be staying in America with a new life and quite a bit of money. Until she adjusts, I thought Brackettville would be a safer place with her staying in the sheriff's jail.''

"His children are in jail too?" McKenna asked.

"Yes. Mrs. Parker offered to look after them, but Pedro's wife wouldn't hear of it. The sheriff has made it as comfortable as he could for them, and Mrs. Parker is going to bring them in meals.''

Not her special chili sauce, I hope, McKenna thought, or the kids will be more dedicated Senderistas than their folks. But McKenna kept that thought to himself. Instead he asked, "What did you find out?"

"Quite a bit. I'll start with Alejandro de Leon.''

"I heard you didn't arrest him.''

"Of course I did, at his suite in the Lima Hilton. But I had a problem. He had committed no crime in Peru. I could have charged him with some vague conspiracy against the government, but he had two million dollars in currency in his possession, and I was sure he could get his hands on more. With the current dubious state of justice in my country, we both knew that a man with that kind of money to be spread around in his defense could be convicted of nothing. So I threatened to extradite him.''

"To the United States?" McKenna asked. "We've built up a pretty good case against him after his warehouse was burglarized in Georgia, but I don't know if a warrant has been issued for his arrest yet.''

"No matter. If we were to extradite him here, his release would undoubtedly become another of Felipe's demands. He hadn't taken your ferries yet, but I knew he had something spectacular in mind. So I told Alejandro I was going to extradite him to Nicaragua, and that I had a plane standing by to take him there.''

"Nicaragua? I don't get it," McKenna said, although he knew Alejandro had some powerful enemies there.

"Yes, Nicaragua," Savraada stated. "When the Sandinistas were in power there they filed some charges against him and issued an arrest warrant, a copy of which I had in my possession. Now ordinarily, a warrant of that type would not merit serious consideration by most governments, but mine thought it was entirely legal, under the circumstances. Keep in mind that, although there is a duly elected neutral government in power in Nicaragua right now, the Sandinistas still control the police and the army under their power-sharing arrangement. Anyway, I told Alejandro that the plane would be taking him to Villegas in Nicaragua, which is an area under the military control of one General Hildago, who just happened to be the Sandinista official who signed the warrant.''

"And I guess they would kill him?''

"Let's just say that Alejandro's continued survival would be a matter of conjecture once the plane landed. He has few friends there, and when it becomes known that he held out on the Contras and sold *Sendero* the weapons they were supposed to have gotten, he would have nothing but enemies.''

"So he told you what he had sold Felipe?'' McKenna said.

Savraada took an envelope from his pocket and gave it to McKenna. "I'm sorry to tell you that they are quite well armed, but I guess you expected that.''

McKenna opened the envelope, extracted the list of weapons, and immediately saw that Savraada was right. There were four Stinger missiles, 72 cases of C-4, blasting caps, M129A radio remote detonator kits, six 106-mm recoilless rifles, 100 Claymore mines, ten M79 grenade launchers, ten M-60 machine guns, 60 M-16 rifles, and what looked like a ton of ammo for all the weapons.

He did some quick calculations in his head and figured that *Sendero* had a ton and a half of C-4, the thing that disturbed him most. That had to be more than enough to blow the Williamsburg Bridge, he figured.

"How much did they give Alejandro for this stuff?'' McKenna asked.

"He didn't say. I'm sure any figure he gave me would have been a lie, so I didn't bother to ask.''

"Where is he now?''

"At his hotel in Lima, under guard.''

"What are your plans for him, if I may ask?''

"We arrived at an understanding. In return for the list and certain other considerations, Alejandro will be free to go when this is over. He is a wealthy man and will have no trouble finding a country of refuge, as long as your government doesn't press the issue. I felt time was of the essence, so I might have overstepped my boundaries in assuming the posture your government will take. However, no matter what, I will endeavor to hold up my end of the bargain.''

"I see," McKenna said. So Alejandro goes free because he had the good sense to collapse, he thought. And it falls on me to convince the U.S. government that he should not be prosecuted in a case I sort of initiated against him, which is going to be a very hard thing to do if all this goes bad in New York. Savraada knows that, so he must have something else up his sleeve. "What are the other considerations in your deal with him?" McKenna asked.

Savraada pointed to the suitcase at his feet. "There is two million dollars in cash inside. Alejandro offered it to me as a form of penance, after a little persuasion. My government thought you might have some use for cold, hard cash in your predicament here, so I have been instructed to place it at your disposal.''

"Two million dollars at my disposal? Are you kidding?" McKenna asked, incredulous.

"No," Savraada answered, smooth and unshaken.

"What am I supposed to do with that? I'm sure that *Sendero* is going to ask for a lot more than that when they make their demands.''

"For starters, it has been my experience that when you offer a prisoner you are interviewing a sum of money in exchange for information, whatever figure you mention possesses only an esoteric value in his mind. However, when you place the money on the table when you talk to him and give him enough time to let his mind wander over the possibilities, results are more easily forthcoming.''

"So we bribe these guys for information, even though some of those we've got have been involved in killing our cops?"

"Of course.''

McKenna saw the logic, but didn't know how he could ever present it to Brunette, given his present state of mind and the fact that the prime candidate for Savraada's largesse was one of those involved in killing his son.

But Savraada made it clear that it had to be done. "Didn't you do just that in Texas?" he asked, without emotion. "And the one you bribed helped kill one of Sheriff Parker's deputies. Pedro's here with us now and going to be a rich man, but the sheriff isn't complaining, though I'm sure he'd still like to strangle Pedro. You better look at the big picture, Brian.''

''You're right, of course,'' McKenna said contritely and feeling foolish. ''Under the circumstances, principles have to be bent and feelings disregarded. But I'm sure it's not going to take two million to get them to talk.''

''Probably not,'' Savraada stated. ''As I said, the money is placed at your disposal to do with as you see fit. Might I suggest that whatever money you don't require for this case be used as a small form of compensation for *Sendero*'s victims in this country?''

A gesture that would, incidentally, cause the stock of the Peruvian government to rise in the public opinion polls, McKenna speculated. ''The way things are going around here, that two million might be spread pretty thin, Colonel,'' he said.

Savraada shrugged his shoulders.

''I'll have to clear this with the mayor,'' McKenna said.

''Of course, but I'm sure that any politician would see the inherent wisdom in the proposal.''

''I'm sure you're right. Let's get back to Pedro.''

''All right,'' Savraada said as he settled back in his chair. ''He's got an interesting story that shows how long and how carefully Felipe has been planning your present predicament. Pedro's twenty-six years old, been with *Sendero* nine years, is experienced with explosives, and was considered a loyal and dedicated Senderista, something they call a senior comrade. Last May Pedro and twenty other senior comrades in the Aya-cucho area were given one hour's notice, then transported to Trujillo on our northern coast.''

''Is travel that easy for them in Peru?'' McKenna asked.

''No, it's difficult for them, with army checkpoints and roadblocks. It still took them a week to reach Trujillo. Then they were put on fishing boats and worked as fishermen for almost a month until they were put ashore in a small Nicara-guan coastal village, Piedra Blanca.''

''Didn't it make anybody suspicious when a boat from Peru traveled one thousand miles to land some people in Nicara-gua?''

''Not at all. Peru is a maritime nation and it may surprise you to know that we have the second largest fishing fleet in the world. Our fleet fishes the Humboldt Current, primarily for tuna and anchovies, and they frequently put in to Central American ports to sell their catch. Transporting eighty men in a fleet numbering hundreds of boats with thousands of workers is not as hard as it may seem, especially if large amounts of money change hands, as I suspect it did.''

"So there were eighty of them?''

"Originally, eighty of them made it to Nicaragua. Later three were killed and another four were injured in a training exercise and had to be left behind. Pedro said that seventy-three men completed the month's training.''

"A month? They trained in Nicaragua for a month, right under the noses of the government? Are they in on this?''

"No, they trained in Honduras, and I think it unlikely the Nicaraguan government was involved, although there is evidence of some Sandinista involvement. They were met in Piedra Blanca by a Sandinista official and transported in an army truck across Nicaragua to an old Contra camp in Honduras on the Nicaraguan border.''

"How did they manage that? Honduras lets foreign military units train on their soil?''

"Probably not the Honduran government. More likely a local military commander was paid, which was how the Contras obtained the bases when they used them.''

"But aren't the Hondurans supposed to be anticommunist and not exactly in love with the Sandinistas?''

"Enough money has a way of numbing political sensitivities in that part of the world. Anyway, whoever was paid might have thought it was more Contras training there.''

"Did he tell you how they got from Nicaragua to Texas?''

"I asked, but he said he'd rather talk to you about that. He told me about the training they received only because he feels I'm going to have to deal with the men in his company in the future. Apparently, he still believes *Sendero* will accomplish their mission.''

"Does he know what's going on here?''

"No, he's been kept in the dark.''

"Okay, let's talk about their training,'' McKenna said. "Who trained them? The Sandinistas?''

"Just the military training. They also received intensive political training, indoctrination really. They were told they were selected as the saviors of the nation, and the struggle they had always been led to believe would take generations would be accomplished by them in a few months, after one daring operation.''

"Were any of them given the details?'' McKenna asked.

"No, except that they were going to the United States. Silence was the rule and they weren't allowed to speculate about it amongst themselves. The political training was conducted by a man named Alfredo Stesso, whom we know as a very powerful speaker who used to teach political science at the university in Ayacucho. They were told that many of them would die, but that the families of those killed would be rewarded with a just share of the *mistis'* wealth.''

''*Mistis*?''

''Slang for the white upper class in Peru. Those who survived would be made company commanders in the new Peruvian army after the struggle was won and they would be honored as heroes with a place in the history books. They were given a tremendous amount of anti-American propaganda, with your country portrayed as the root of most of Peru's problems. The most important part of their political training, as far as you should be concerned, is that Stesso prepared them psychologically to kill large numbers of American hostages.''

Yeah, that's important, McKenna thought. Felipe's threatened to kill hostages, and I guess it's important to know he won't have any problems getting his men to comply. ''How did Stesso do it?'' he asked.

''He told them that, with the exception of Nazi Germany, the United States has killed more civilians in warfare than any other nation in history. They were shown film clips of the German and Japanese cities bombed by the Americans in World War II, along with the civilian casualty figures, which numbered in the hundreds of thousands. They were told that two million civilians were killed by the United States in the Vietnam War, and then they were shown clips of that bunker that was bombed in the Gulf War. Five hundred and thirty civilians were killed in that, and Stesso told them that five hundred was possibly the number of American civilians who would be killed by them during their operation. He portrayed it as a small price to pay for victory, given the fact they are enemy civilians.''

''In your opinion, would they do it? Would they line up a hundred hostages at a time and shoot them in cold blood?''

''If Felipe told them to, absolutely. Keep in mind that none of them are choirboys. They are all dedicated *Sendero* veterans, and I don't doubt that each of them has participated in many assassinations.''

McKenna didn't want to dwell on it any longer. He knew that hearing that five hundred people were killed and seeing five hundred bodies were two different things, and he would be the one seeing the bodies and explaining his actions to the families, if it happened. "Tell me about their military training."

"The Sandinistas trained them to use the Stingers, the 106-mm recoilless rifle, and the Claymore mines, which were all new weapons to the *Sendero* people. A few select people were also given training in the use of C-4 explosives and radio remote detonators, which was something else new for them to learn."

"C-4 is new to them?" McKenna said. "What have they been using to blow your country up for the past ten years?"

"Simple dynamite, stolen or extorted from the mining companies. Most of their weapons are captured or stolen from our army, so they were already proficient with the small arms. Except for one squad, their training centered on squad tactics, securing a number of hostages in a large room, and defending it from attack."

The ferry, McKenna thought. Three large rooms, one on top of the other. "What did the other squad train in, hijacking a plane?"

"Pedro didn't know, but it's safe to assume that was the squad you captured. In addition, they were all parachute trained, and Felipe put a lot of emphasis on it. They made six practice jumps in Honduras."

"Parachute jumps?" McKenna asked, astonished at this revelation.

"Yes. If you think about it, you should come to the conclusion that this is the piece of information you're paying Pedro for, and it might be worth the price if we can use it."

McKenna did think about it. He knew that most armies trained airborne troops just to build up esprit de corps within their elite units, with no intention at all of ever dropping them from the sky. Helicopters had made the airborne soldier obsolete, since the high casualty rate sustained by these troops was no longer justifiable in the minds of the military planners. Was Felipe simply building esprit de corps in his troops, or was he going to use their new abilities? McKenna wondered. "Was Felipe there for their training?" he asked.

"Only at the end. He insisted on a practice combat jump into the jungle for the whole company, which is a very dangerous thing to do carrying a full load of weapons and a sixty-pound pack. They lost people on the jump when they hit the trees. Three killed and four injured with broken limbs. But Felipe thought it was worth it. He was very happy with the way they organized themselves into a combat unit once they hit the ground, and congratulated them on their training.''

"So he jumped himself?''

"Yes.''

A few things became apparent to McKenna. He had wondered where Felipe was going to land the jetliner after he hijacked it and escaped from the United States. What country would permit the hottest terrorist, the most wanted criminal in the world, to land on their soil with all his men and a load of hostages, thereby provoking the rage of the United States? No country, not Lebanon, not Cuba, not even Libya. And certainly not Peru, since Felipe would be arriving with the avowed purpose of overthrowing their government. "So that's it,'' he said to Savraada. "They're going to jump back into Peru with their loot, probably someplace in the Amazon jungle.''

"Only if they have to,'' Savraada said confidently, giving McKenna a look that told him Savraada knew something he didn't. "They would much rather land the plane and avoid the risk a jump into the jungle would entail, and I think I know where they're planning to do that.''

"Where?''

Savraada reached down and opened his suitcase, giving McKenna a brief glimpse of what two million in cash looked like before he took out a map and zipped the suitcase closed. He unfolded the large map of Peru and pointed to a spot on the Amazon River near the eastern edge of the country. "Here is where he wants to land,'' he said. "Iquitos.''

McKenna studied the map. It showed roads and cities, with the Andes along the coast in brown and the Amazon jungle in green. Iquitos was in the middle of nowhere, surrounded by green, with no roads connecting it with the rest of the country. "Why Iquitos and how?'' he asked.

"The why first,'' Savraada answered. "Although the Amazon Basin covers sixty percent of Peru, it contains only five percent of our population, mainly indigenous Indians, some of whom are still living in the Stone Age. The area was never seriously contested by *Sendero*, simply because there's nothing there.''

"Except Iquitos.''

"Yes, except Iquitos, and that's a recent phenomenon. The government has recently invested a sizable portion of our national budget in the Amazon Basin and developed the lumber and fishing industries that are now thriving there. Then oil and gold were discovered nearby, and Iquitos has jumped to three hundred thousand people. There are very few Indians from the high Andes living there, and those are the people who constitute *Sendero*'s political base, so the city is lightly defended by the government. Besides the local police, there's only a company of national police, a small army detachment, and a naval squadron that patrols the rivers there. But suddenly it became clear to me that Iquitos has something that Felipe will need very much if he succeeds in hijacking a plane and getting out of New York.''

''An international airport?'' McKenna ventured.

''Yes, an international airport capable of handling a Boeing 727.''

''Why have you built an international airport in the middle of the jungle? Tourists?''

''Yes. Quite recently, exotic destinations became the rage for the well-heeled traveler, and you'll have to search the world to find someplace more exotic and backward than Iquitos. But it has what they want, in the middle of the Amazon jungle and on the river. With the present new environmental consciousness pervading the minds of the well-to-do, Iquitos has become the destination for them. They want to see the jungle, the Indians, and the wildlife before they all disappear, and they're willing to pay nicely for the opportunity. Since they're coming to spend money, my government thought it expedient to build an airport there for them, especially since it's the one place in the country not feeling the effects of the war.''

''Until now, you think.''

''Yes, until now. I believe that *Sendero* is planning to take the airport for long enough to allow Felipe to land there with his men, which brings us to how I think Felipe plans to do it. How is he planning to secretly get enough men to take the airport through three hundred miles of jungle from his nearest base?''

''What's his nearest base?'' McKenna asked as he studied the map.

''*Sendero* has virtual control of Pucallpa, here,'' Savraada said, pointing to the map. McKenna saw that the only thing breaking the long expanse of green between Pucallpa and Iquitos was the Rio Ucayali that ran through both cities. ''And the navy has total control of the river," Savraada added.

McKenna stated the obvious. "Through the jungle seems the only way for them to get there," he said.

"Yes, through the jungle, and preposterous as I would have thought, that is exactly what they are doing. A battalion of *Sendero* soldiers is advancing through the jungle toward Iquitos as we speak."

McKenna had seen his share of jungle warfare, and the idea didn't seem that preposterous to him. Moving a battalion through expanses of jungle in total secrecy had been done before. He knew from personal experience, because he had seen it done and felt the movement's startling effects when the North Vietnamese army's 324B Division dispatched a battalion to attack the Ninth Marines outpost at Cam Lo during the Tet Offensive in 1968. The NVA had achieved total surprise when they emerged from the jungle, and McKenna and his comrades who lived through the attack all felt that their lives began anew that day, the day they barely beat off the massive attack and survived when so many others died.

But 300 miles undetected? McKenna thought. That's a feat if they can do it. The NVA only had to travel fifty miles from Laos to Cam Lo. "How do you know they're doing this?" he asked Savraada.

"Because when I went to Ayacucho to get Pedro's family, I had the extraordinary luck to meet a young man named Sinsi Althapaca. He was a Senderista assigned to watch Pedro's family. Fortunately for me, he was a friend of Pedro and Teotica Cabrera, or I would be dead right now. Just before I met Sinsi, he killed his comrade who was preparing to shoot me, Teotica, and Pedro's children."

"And then he told you about the *Sendero* battalion advancing on Iquitos?"

"Not in so many words."

"And you believed him?"

"Yes."

"Why?" McKenna asked.

"Because he'd had enough of the war. I believed him because it was the only thing that made sense."

"If it's such a secret movement, so secret that you had no intelligence on it, how would a *Sendero* soldier in Ayacucho know about it?"

"Because he was with them. He was evacuated two weeks ago after he contracted yellow fever in the jungle."

"How was he evacuated?"

"By seaplane. That's the way they're being resupplied during their march. Airdrops from seaplanes."

"Doesn't that make anybody suspicious?"

"There's nobody there but tourists in seaplanes and indigenous Indians. Another couple of seaplanes flying around didn't make anyone suspicious, and to keep their march secret they're killing and burying all the Indians they come across."

"Little cold-blooded, isn't it?"

"That's *Sendero*, and that's one of the reasons we know about it. After years of killing, the deaths of those Indian families found Sinsi's conscience and disillusioned him with *Sendero*."

"How many have they killed?"

"He doesn't know for sure. They've split up and are traveling in company formations, but he says his company has killed six families, twenty-seven Indians. Men, women, and children, all killed. It was too much for him."

"How many companies in a *Sendero* battalion?"

"Five, but we didn't know that before. This is the first time *Sendero* has organized in battalion strength. Before this, they always operated in small units and avoided direct confrontation with government forces, except for hit-and-run attacks and small-scale ambushes. It's a drastic change in tactics for them, something our generals always hoped for, the same as your generals did in Vietnam. They would see it as their chance to use their superior military technology and troop strength to annihilate a large enemy force in a pitched battle."

"What do you mean, 'would see it'? What are they going to do about it?"

"They don't know about it yet. I haven't told them."

McKenna was astounded. "Why not?" he asked.

Savraada didn't answer at once. He smiled and said, "Think about it."

McKenna did. He figured the generals would immediately marshal the biggest force they could muster and insert them someplace between Iquitos and *Sendero*'s position. Once the army engaged them, it would be a short battle. The bulk of the *Sendero* force would be wiped out by airpower and the generals would have their victory. "Five companies means four hundred *Sendero* soldiers, right?" McKenna asked.

"Less than that. Malaria and yellow fever have been hitting them hard."

"Still, wiping out this *Sendero* battalion would be their biggest victory of their war, especially since *Sendero* has only how many soldiers? Six thousand?"

"I believe the figure is closer to five thousand," Savraada stated. "But the opportunity would be irresistible to our generals, especially if you take into account that they would be eliminating *Sendero*'s most experienced soldiers. It might even win the war for them."

But where does that leave us in New York? McKenna wondered. Felipe was bound to hear of the battle, and he would make other plans. Assuming he manages to hijack a plane, and he must be confident of that or he wouldn't have gone this far, where does he go? He'll still need an airplane and hostages. McKenna thought about it some more and thought he saw what Savraada was driving at. "What is the range of a Boeing 727?" he asked.

Savraada smiled. "Twenty-five hundred miles."

"How many air miles from New York to Iquitos?"

Savraada had the number on the tip of his tongue, leading McKenna to believe he was on the right track. "Three thousand thirty-six air miles."

"I'm assuming that he chose the Boeing 727 because it is possible to parachute from it. Otherwise he would have selected a plane with longer range to hijack, right?"

"Theoretically, it is impossible to parachute from any commercial jet plane, but it wasn't always. The airline companies built some safeguards into their designs after D. B. Cooper hijacked a plane and parachuted out over Idaho. These safeguards and modifications prevent the airplane doors from being opened while it is in flight, but I'm sure Felipe has thought his way around that. I've made some inquiries and found it can be done on the Boeing 727."

"How? Blow the doors?"

"Easier than that. The rear ramp door of the 727 is secured by something called a slipstream lock while it is in flight. It is attached to the fuselage at the rear door and as soon as the plane surpasses forty miles per hour, the pressure of the passing air activates a spring that causes the lock to swing closed and block the door. When the plane stops it pops open again and the ramp door can be lowered."

"So once they have the plane, they just cut the lock off with a torch while it's on the ground, right?"

"Exactly. Except for its limited range, the Boeing 727 is

the perfect plane for him because of the rear ramp door. He wouldn't have to worry about getting sucked into the engines or getting hit with the tail wing. The Boeing can also slow to one hundred and ten miles an hour without stalling, which would make jumping easier. We have to consider that he'll have to stop someplace to refuel.''

So it's Iquitos or jump, McKenna thought. He took another look at the map. There was no city within 500 miles that wasn't green, and he had never heard of any of them. He figured the chance of any of them having an international airport where a 727 could land to be zero.

Savraada was smiling. "I see you've got it," he said.

"I think so. *Sendero* couldn't hold the airport for long against the government reinforcements that are sure to follow. So they plan to take it while Felipe's plane is in the air and they'll just hold it long enough for him to land. Then they'll split up and fade into the jungle.''

"I believe that's his plan, with one added possibility. Felipe could also commandeer some of the smaller planes at Iquitos Airport and take them to one of the many airstrips used by the Colombian drug smugglers in the areas controlled by *Sendero*.''

And then he'd be out of our hands, McKenna thought. "Without advance knowledge, how long would it take the government to get sufficient forces to Iquitos to retake the airport?''

"Without use of the airport to land troops, days.''

McKenna was surprised at Savraada's estimate. "Days? Wouldn't your military send in troops immediately? Why days?''

"Because there are no roads to Iquitos, so they would have to send their troops in by helicopter. Unfortunately, our helicopters have limited range and troop-carrying ability, and the nearest base where the army has sufficient helicopters to mount any kind of offensive is at Tingo María, four hundred miles from Iquitos. It would take them time to position fuel along the way so the helicopters carrying the reinforcements could land and refuel.''

Days for them to get troops to someplace in their own country? Ridiculous, McKenna thought. "There's no other way for them?'' McKenna asked.

Savraada smiled. "There is, but our generals wouldn't consider it. They could use the Sinsi Battalion.''

"Wasn't Sinsi the name of your informant?"

"Yes. It means 'warrior' in Quechua. It's quite a common name among the Senderistas."

"Is the Sinsi Battalion an airborne unit?"

"Yes. It's supposed to be our best, in spite of a terrible human-rights record."

"And why wouldn't they want to use it?"

"Because the battalion is currently involved in drug-suppressing efforts in the Huallaga Valley, where most of the coca crop in Peru is grown. It's often thought that the battalion really acts as a sort of tax collector for the military, since the Colombians seem to be moving their crop out with no more than token interference from them. You must understand that narco-dollars fuel our economy. It might be our largest industry."

"So they won't use the Sinsi Battalion."

"No, especially if there was a chance the battalion would lose the battle. The damage to army prestige would be irreversible."

"Wouldn't Fujimori order them to, if Iquitos were under attack?"

"You have to understand that things do not run in Peru the same way they do here. In theory, our military is under civilian control. In practice, our senior military men have found a way to salute and nod at whatever civilian orders they receive, and then do exactly whatever it is the generals want."

"Let's see if I understand all this," McKenna said. "Felipe must figure it will take days for the government to get troops to Iquitos by helicopter, and he'll probably make the runways unusable before they leave the airport, so helicopters will be the generals' only option."

"Yes, unless the Sinsi Battalion is used."

"Which means he'll have days to escape into the jungle, or wherever else he's planning on going."

"Exactly."

"Now let's look at the situation here. Unless we can figure a way to get him off our boats, we want Felipe out of this country as soon as possible, which means acceding to his demands so he doesn't kill too many of our people or blow up any more of our things. Right?"

"Yes, but keep in mind that our military doesn't mind too much that he's here and not in Peru causing them aggravation, although I'm sure that he's going to drive our government crazy with his demands. Although the generals would like him dead, they aren't too concerned with his activities in New York. However, they would do anything to keep him from returning to Peru.''

''Including, if they knew he was on his way to Iquitos, shooting down an airliner full of hostages?''

''Possibly. Accidents happen, and they seem to happen with alarming frequency to Senderistas who fall into the military's grasp. While we might think of it as an airplane full of hostages, our generals might see it as a plane full of Senderistas and a few foreigners.''

''We'll get back to that. As for the Senderista battalion in the jungle, if the military ever found out about it they would destroy it and prevent it from reaching Iquitos, right?''

''Correct.''

''But we want Felipe to leave his hostages and parachute into the jungle, and then have a military force in place to destroy him.''

''Yes, I think that would be the optimal result as far as you are concerned in your present predicament.''

''And that would involve permitting the Senderista battalion to reach the Iquitos Airport, take it, and keep it until Felipe's plane was close, and then having sufficient government forces in place to prevent his landing.''

''Yes. Keep in mind that there are bound to be casualties among the government troops in Iquitos, although it has been my experience that most of them will flee in the face of a determined attack.''

''Then it would help if the government commander there was privy to our plans.''

''Yes.''

''And your generals have to be notified that the *Sendero* battalion is close to Iquitos. This notification has to be late enough so they will not have enough time to plan an attack to destroy them, but soon enough to give them enough time to get forces in place to retake the airport from *Sendero* before Felipe's plane lands there. Add in that they have to be ready and willing to deploy their Sinsi Battalion to engage and destroy Felipe's company after they parachute from their plane.''

''Yes. An enormous amount of pressure must be brought to bear on our generals. It's a gamble, and if all this works out, they will be considered masterminds and national heroes. But remember this: They are not considered a gambling breed and are already very content with their present condition.''

"It sounds like we're going to be talking to a lot of people in high places if we're going to sell this one.''

"The highest place. We should be talking to God and begging his understanding and forgiveness if this plan of ours is put in place,'' Savraada said solemnly.

"God?'' McKenna said, perplexed. "Begging God for forgiveness? What for?''

"I might as well tell you now, because you'll think of it later. As the *Sendero* battalion progresses toward Iquitos, they are killing Indians as they go. We could prevent that killing of innocents simply by telling the generals where they are. But for our own reasons, we won't.''

Would I have thought of that? McKenna asked himself. How much innocent blood am I going to have on my hands? "Do you have any idea how close they are to Iquitos?'' McKenna asked.

"I've given it some thought and I have an idea, although it's only a guess. Although Sinsi didn't know where they were going, he told me they were making ten miles a day during the forced march. Even though many of the men were sick, the pace never slowed. So every soldier knew they were on some kind of timetable. They left Pucallpa on July 2nd, twenty-five days ago. So they should be about fifty miles from Iquitos.''

"Five days!'' McKenna said, stunned. "That means Felipe plans to drag this thing out that long, no matter how quickly we cave in to his demands.''

"Of course he does,'' Savraada said, like it should be obvious to everyone. "He'll want to give the Colombians as much time as he can to move their stuff in.''

"Felipe certainly has his way of giving us a lot to think about, doesn't he?'' McKenna asked.

"Consider yourself lucky, my friend. He's been doing it to me for years, and I'm getting a little tired of it.''

I can imagine he has, McKenna thought. "Mind if I ask you a personal question, Colonel?''

"Ask.''

"What would you do if you captured Felipe in Peru after all this?''

"Alive?''

"Yes, alive.''

"You might not understand.''

''Try me,'' McKenna said.

Savraada took some time to think, then stared at the floor while answering. ''You must understand that in my country I am allowed much more latitude than the police here, and in the case of Felipe's capture, I would be expected to stretch that latitude to the limit. But I believe that, in order to win this struggle, we must be the good guys, and that savagery and lawlessness are not defeated by savagery and lawlessness. *Sendero* will be defeated by the rule of law, justly applied.'' He looked up and saw that McKenna was staring intently at him. Savraada smiled and added, ''I must confess that mine is a minority opinion in our government circles.''

''So you would arrest him and bring him to trial?'' McKenna asked.

''Yes, although my superiors would rather I dealt with him otherwise.''

''I think I knew that already, but I had to ask.''

''I'm not sure you would agree with me at this point, so I won't ask if you do,'' Savraada said with a rueful smile.

Suddenly, McKenna felt such compassion for the brilliant, fine, troubled man in front of him that he felt like hugging him. But he didn't. Instead he asked, ''Are we ready to go down and talk to Pedro?''

''Of course. Isn't that how I spend my time? Talking to killers, every day?''

Savraada followed McKenna to the door, but McKenna stopped short with his hand on the doorknob. ''Wait a minute,'' he said. ''I hate to say this, but I just got a thought.''

But Savraada was ahead of him. ''You mean your bridge?'' he asked.

''Yes,'' McKenna said, even more impressed with Savraada. ''How did you know?''

''I've been studying Felipe a lot longer than you have. Of course he's planning to leave his truck of explosives on your bridge until he's safe and sound.''

''And if things go wrong for him in Peru, he'll leave someone here to detonate it, right?''

''I'm sure that's his plan. He always had a vindictive side, and I'm certain nothing would anger him more than dying at his moment of victory.''

''So what do we do about that?''

''You have two options,'' Savraada said seriously. ''The

hardest one would be talking Felipe into removing the explosives before he leaves.''

Fat chance, McKenna thought. "I think I'll take the easy option," he said.

"I would too, if I were in your place. You simply have to do some police work, find out who has the detonator and where this person is, and prevent him from pushing his detonator button after Felipe leaves," Savraada said with a smile.

McKenna had to laugh. "That's the easy option?"

Savraada seemed puzzled by McKenna's reaction. Then he had to laugh himself. "It's a very old bridge anyway, isn't it?" he asked, laughing so hard that he started to cry.

The two men laughed some more as they pondered the imminent possibility that Williamsburg and Lower Manhattan were about to lose their close relationship.

Chapter 35 Richie White left the room as soon as McKenna and Savraada entered, leaving the two men alone with Pedro. Sitting with his arms spread out in his body cast, Pedro looked the picture of discomfort as he sipped soup from a straw. He didn't acknowledge McKenna or Savraada until he sucked everything he could from the cup.

"You ready to talk to me?" McKenna asked Pedro.

"Sure. Let's get this over with and get me back to Texas. The food there's much better than the stuff you serve here."

McKenna pulled up a chair opposite Pedro while Savraada remained standing at the door. "Let's start with how you got from Nicaragua to Texas," he said.

"After our training was over, each squad was loaded into the back of a big truck going north."

"Who drove the trucks?"

"I don't know. They was just regular truck drivers, I think. I saw our driver before they loaded us in the back, but we didn't talk to him."

"What do you mean, loaded you in?"

"When our truck came to the base, the trailer was filled with mangos. We had to unload all the mangos and we built a wood shelter on the floor of the trailer. Then we crawled into the shelter and they loaded the mangos on top. It was terrible. We couldn't move much, it was dark, and we had to pee in bottles."

"The mango truck took you to the Texas border?"

"No, it took us to the city of Tuxtla Gutiérrez in southern Mexico."

"Didn't the truck stop at the Guatemalan or Mexican border for Customs inspection?"

"The truck stopped many times, but I don't know what for. We couldn't see or hear anything outside. Once we heard somebody banging on the outside of the truck, but nobody bothered us."

"How long were you in the trucks?"

Pedro grimaced at the remembrance. "A long time. Two days and a night."

A long time to be lying under some tons of mangos, McKenna thought. Without wanting to, he found himself admiring the dedication of his adversaries. "Did you have any weapons?" he asked.

"No."

"Any identification?"

"No."

"Any money?"

"No, nothing. Galindo had some money, but the rest of us had nothing but one change of clothes in a plastic bag."

"Who's Galindo?" McKenna asked.

"Our squad leader. He's the one the sheriff shot."

"What did you do in Tuxtla Gutiérrez?" McKenna asked.

"Galindo split us up into four groups and gave out some Mexican pesos. He had a bus schedule with him, and he assigned each group to a different bus going north. It was then he told us our squad had been assigned to cross the American border at Del Rio, but that was okay. We had three days off to wander around the city. We had learned about it, but it was better to see it."

"Was that where you were supposed to be from if you got captured by the border patrol?"

"Yes. In the training camp we learned the history and geography of the city, along with the names of the mayor, the churches, and the schools.''

''Was Tuxtla Gutiérrez chosen because most of the people there are Indians like you?''

''We don't call ourselves Indians,'' Pedro said, coldly. ''We are *campesinos*, country people. In Peru, the Indians are the savages who live in the jungle.''

''Sorry, but you know what I mean,'' McKenna said without sounding sorry.

''Yes, they look like us, but their faces are rounder. It seems to me they laugh a lot.''

''Where did you stay in Tuxtla Gutiérrez?''

''In different places every night. All small, cheap hotels full of people from Guatemala going north.''

''Where did you go after you left Tuxtla Gutiérrez?''

''Galindo, Manuel, and me took the bus to Monterrey. We were the last ones in the squad to leave, I think. At Monterrey we changed buses and took the one to Ciudad Acuña, but it broke down and we were stuck for a day in a filthy little place called Dos Palos. It was bad because Galindo was getting nervous. He told us we had to be in Del Rio by the twenty-fifth. That's when he first told us we were going to New York.''

''Nobody knew but Galindo?''

''The others in the squad knew because Galindo always went to the bus station in Tuxtla Gutiérrez to see them off and give them instructions. But Manuel and me didn't know until Galindo told us in Dos Palos.''

''What happened next?''

''The next day another bus came and we took it to Ciudad Acuña. We got in at dawn. Me and Manuel wanted to stay there for the day, but Galindo said we were late and had to cross. So he called the smuggler in Texas.''

''Would that be Ricardo Montoya?'' McKenna asked.

''Who?''

''The man you killed after you killed the deputy.''

''Oh, I'm sorry. I didn't know his name,'' Pedro said, displaying no emotion. ''Yes, he called Montoya and arranged the place to meet on the other side. Then Galindo gave us our final instructions, in case we got split up, and we joined up with—''

''Wait a minute,'' McKenna said. ''What were the final instructions?''

''That, even if all of us didn't make it across, we were to

go to New York. The smuggler would have airplane tickets and money for us and would take us to the airport. When we got to New York, we were to wait outside the Southwest Airlines terminal at Kennedy Airport with our hands in our pockets. An American would pick us up there.''

"An American?" McKenna asked, surprised. "What's his name?"

"I don't know."

"Well, what was he supposed to look like? How would you know him?"

"He would be driving a van and the numbers on his license plate would add up to either eleven or seventeen."

McKenna sat back and digested this information. An American? he thought. Of course. Felipe wouldn't risk his men being driven around by other illegal aliens without licenses or knowledge of the city. There would be too much risk of running into the cops, and Felipe was too careful and had done too much planning for that. He would have to have some local help and I should have thought of that sooner, McKenna told himself. This American could answer a lot of questions for us, if we could find him. "Can't you tell me anything else about this American?" he asked.

"I don't know anything else."

"Too bad. Go on with your story. What happened when you crossed?"

"We joined with many other people crossing just before dawn. I think we were all captured right after."

"By the border patrol?"

"Yes. They took us to their building, gave us some sandwiches, asked us some questions, and then took us all back to the border and kicked us off the bus."

"What did they ask you?"

"Nothing much. You know, names, ages, where we were from. We told them we were from Tuxtla Guitérrez, and I guess they believed us."

"But you had no identification, right?"

"We told them we had been robbed by smugglers."

"And what happened next?"

"Galindo called the smuggler and we crossed again, by ourselves this time. He met us, he had our plane tickets and money, and we were on our way to the airport in San Antonio when the police stopped us. I think you know the rest."

"Most of it," McKenna said. "Mind telling us why you

killed your pal? What's his name, Manuel?''

''You would have done the same thing in my position,''
Pedro said, brushing off the question. ''When do I go back to
Texas and when do I get paid?'' he asked.

''Soon,'' McKenna answered, getting up. He went to the
door and Savraada followed him out into the hallway while
White went back inside to guard Pedro.

''You want to find that American, don't you?'' Savraada
asked.

''I'm hoping we can.''

''How do you plan to do it?''

''Like you suggested. Money.''

''For one of your other prisoners?''

''Yes. Maybe when they arrived here they were picked up
from the airport by the same American. And maybe one of
them remembers the license plate number. I have to know. If
I can get the mayor to clear it, I'm going to use the cash you
gave me to find out. Put it on the table right in front of them.''

''Do you have a particular prisoner in mind?''

''Yes.''

McKenna took out his phone and dialed the mayor's number. He was surprised when the mayor himself answered.

''McKenna here, Your Honor.''

''When are you getting here?'' the mayor asked.

''I'm sorry. Not for a while.''

''What's keeping you? I'm locked in my office, hiding from
the press. We have to give them something, soon.''

''We have nothing to give them.''

''What? You and all those chiefs couldn't come up with
some kind of a plan?''

''The plan is to give in to Felipe's demands. There's nothing
else for us to do.''

Complete silence greeted McKenna's assessment.

''Has he made any demands yet?'' McKenna asked, wondering if the mayor was still on the line.

''Nothing,'' the mayor said and sighed. ''We've been ra-
dioing both boats, but he hasn't answered.'' The mayor
paused, then asked, ''Can't you give me anything?''

''Just a hope. The important thing is getting him off these
boats, saving the hostages, and getting the truck off the Williamsburg Bridge. The only way I can see to do that is give
in to his demands when he makes them. We stand a chance
of getting him when he returns to Peru.''

"How do you know he's going back to Peru?"

"I'll explain that later. In the meantime, the government of Peru has donated two million to our efforts."

"Two million? How?"

"In cash. Colonel Savraada brought it with him. I need your permission to use some of that money to try and turn one of the prisoners. I also need you to get in touch with the DA to make sure that any deal I make sticks."

McKenna had expected some objections, or at least some questions, but got none. "Do what you think best," the mayor said. "I'll take care of the DA. Get here as soon as you can."

Julio Montalvo sat, handcuffed to his chair, facing Pat Picciarelli across the table in the center of the small room. Picciarelli hadn't spoken in some time and Montalvo hadn't spoken at all. Montalvo shifted his gaze to the door when McKenna and Savraada walked in. McKenna was carrying a briefcase and he placed it on the table.

Montalvo's face showed no expression, but he kept his eyes fixed on Savraada as the two newcomers took seats opposite him at the table. McKenna opened the briefcase and removed twenty stacks of wrapped one-hundred-dollar bills, then arranged the bills in five stacks on the table in front of Montalvo. But Montalvo didn't seem to notice. He kept his eyes locked on Savraada.

"You know who I am, *soldado*?" Savraada asked.

"*Sí*, Colonel," Montalvo said, shocking Picciarelli.

"This man is Brian McKenna," Savraada said, pointing to McKenna.

"I know who he is," Montalvo said.

"Good," Savraada said. "Listen to what he has to say about your future."

Montalvo shifted his impassive gaze to McKenna.

McKenna sized up Montalvo before saying anything. He took in the black eye and thought the young terrorist looked like a kid, much too young to be involved in the kind of trouble he was in. At the same time, Montalvo seemed to be taking McKenna's measure, but whatever he thought wasn't revealed on his face.

"Are you ready to listen?" McKenna asked.

Montalvo's face remained noncommittal.

"The reason I'm talking to you is that you're in more trou-

ble than your friends and have more to lose than them," Mc-
Kenna said. "You have been implicated in the murder of a
police officer, and you will be found guilty. That means you
will be sentenced to life without parole, and I assure you that
you will spend your life in the most miserable jail in this
state."

Montalvo maintained the impassive mask on his face, causing McKenna to wonder if he was talking to himself.

"Let me tell you what we know so far," McKenna said.
"We know that at the beginning of this month a company of
Sendero soldiers set out from Honduras after training there a
month. We have captured quite a few and some of them are
talking."

McKenna paused and was gratified to see a flicker of interest
cross Montalvo's features. Then, as quickly as it appeared, it
was gone. He just continued staring through McKenna.

"We also know that your squad was planning to hijack a
Northwest Airlines Boeing 727 at Kennedy Airport. We assume that another squad was also trained in hijacking planes,
and we think Felipe still plans to hijack one. What that means
is that you and your squad are no longer essential to Felipe's
plan. I want you to think about that for a moment."

If Montalvo was thinking about it, nothing showed on his
face. Still, McKenna waited a minute before continuing. "We
also know that Felipe has promised that all *Sendero* soldiers
captured on this mission will be released and will return with
him to Peru."

A smile briefly crossed Montalvo's face and he sat up
straight in his seat.

That's it, McKenna thought. They won't talk because they
believe that Felipe will free them. But they don't know his
plan and they don't know what's happening in the harbor, so
I have to use that to my advantage. "We will never release
you," McKenna said. "The others, maybe, but not you. You
helped murder our police commissioner's son. You murdered
the son of my best friend, a kid I watched grow up. You we
will never give up."

Montalvo still looked uninterested, so McKenna tried a different tack. He decided to lie. "So far we have killed six of
your soldiers and captured another thirty-nine," he said. "You
know better than me, so I want you to ask yourself a question.
Does Felipe have enough men left to complete whatever he's

planning? Because if he doesn't, you're going to rot in jail for the rest of your life.''

McKenna saw another emotion cross Montalvo's face. Was it fear? he asked himself. He couldn't be sure.

"Now I'm going to give you the alternative," McKenna said. "There is one hundred thousand dollars on the table in front of you. It could be yours to start a new life. I could guarantee that you would receive a jail sentence of no more than five years, and if you help enough, I could reduce that to zero. I could also guarantee that you would be permitted to stay in the United States with a new identity, which means that no one in *Sendero* could ever find you. I'm offering you a new life, a rich life, in the United States."

McKenna saw Montalvo look down at the stacks of money in front of him. For a moment McKenna thought he had him, but then Montalvo looked up and resumed staring through McKenna, his face a noncommittal mask.

"You only have to tell me one thing," McKenna said. "I want the license plate number of the American who picked you up at the airport when you arrived here."

Montalvo didn't say a word or move a muscle. Maybe he wasn't picked up by the American, McKenna thought. But he should still talk. He should tell us something, even if it's a lie. "I need to know now," McKenna said.

Montalvo said nothing. McKenna returned his stare and wondered what the young man could be thinking to turn down such a deal. He gave Montalvo another minute, then got up.

But Savraada had something to add. "*Soldado*," he said, "you know me and you know my reputation. I consider myself an honorable man and would do nothing to harm my reputation. I personally guarantee the provisions of this agreement. I urge you to accept it, for your own sake. You are so young and should have so much to live for."

Still Montalvo said nothing. McKenna got up, went to the door, and held it open for Savraada. Savraada shook his head, then got up.

"JTV 962," Montalvo said. He shifted his gaze from McKenna to the stacks of money.

Nine-six-two, McKenna thought. Adds up to seventeen, so he's probably telling the truth. I've got to keep him talking, open him up. "What kind of car?" he asked.

"Brown Dodge van."

"What did he look like?"

"Blond hair, beard, short, maybe forty years old."

"What's his name?"

"I don't know."

McKenna sat down in front of Montalvo and took out his pad and pen. Montalvo was still staring at the money and ready to talk.

Chapter 36
Microphones were set up on the steps of City Hall in front of the hundreds of reporters standing behind the police barricades, and the front of the building was illuminated by scores of television camera lights. But no one was standing in front of the mikes. The steps of City Hall were conspicuously empty.

McKenna arrived just before five o'clock and needed a squad of cops to help him get through the reporters. Inside, he found there was a veteran cop posted outside the mayor's door. He told McKenna he was expected, and that his orders were to admit no one but him. McKenna knocked and went in.

The mayor was sitting behind his desk watching the news on TV. "You might as well see this," he said. "It looks like you and Brunette are gonna be the stars of your own shows."

Brunette was being interviewed in front of the 44th Precinct station house in the Bronx. His nose was bandaged, another bandage covered the gash on his forehead, and his eyes were blackened. But there he was, standing in front of the microphones and fielding questions.

McKenna was surprised to see it. "What's he doing up there?" he asked.

"Lord knows," the mayor answered. "Checked himself out of the hospital and went up."

Brunette announced that the outbreak of rioting and looting following a justifiable police shooting had been ended by a massive deployment of police manpower. More than 300 had been arrested and he thanked local community leaders for their help in quelling the disturbance. He added that he thought it rather unpatriotic for criminal elements to have taken advantage of the national emergency taking place in the harbor by rioting and looting. The camera cut from Brunette to scenes recorded earlier that showed people of all ages looting stores and police making arrests. Then it was back to Brunette.

As the mayor had predicted, the reporters were treating the problem in the Bronx as a mildly interesting sideshow. What they really wanted to know was how the police department intended to deal with Felipe and *Sendero* in the harbor. Brunette had nothing to say on that, except that options were being examined and the mayor would be conducting a news conference at City Hall shortly.

"Thanks a lot, Ray," the mayor said as a commercial came on. Then he turned to McKenna. "You got any good news for me?" he asked.

"Some news, but nothing you'd consider good."

"Then you might as well see this first," the mayor said as he clicked on his VCR with a remote control.

It was the footage shot from the news helicopter in the harbor that afternoon. McKenna watched as *Sendero*'s cabin cruiser opened fire on *Harbor Launch Six* and he saw the Crandall brothers killed for the second time that day, followed by himself and Brunette leaning out of the police helicopter while firing at the roof of the cabin cruiser and ending with their helicopter crash. The news crew had also captured Sergeant Sweeney's last rush for the cruiser and he saw how it ended. A *Sendero* crew set up a recoilless rifle on a tripod on the small rear deck of the cruiser. Sighting through the eyepiece on the top of the weapon, they fired the spotter round into the hull of the approaching harbor launch. A second later they fired the 106-mm round and the police launch exploded, burned, and went down.

For the next fifteen minutes the video clip showed *Sendero* unloading their boxes from the cruiser onto the *Samuel I. Newhouse* and setting up their recoilless rifles on the front and rear decks of the ferry. When the video ended, the mayor shut it off with his remote control.

"Can I have a copy of that video, Your Honor?" McKenna asked.

"What for? To save it for your grandchildren?"

"No, sir. I'd like to show it to somebody in the military who would know what's in those boxes they unloaded. Probably somebody in ordnance who could recognize the crates by their size and shape."

"You can have that one," the mayor said, pointing to his VCR. "I don't ever want to see that film again. The press is gonna torture me over that one."

"Why's that?"

"Politics, my boy. They have to have someone to blame. Ordinarily I'd shift the blame to the police department, but this time I can't even do that. You guys look like heroes and they're gonna make me look like shit, unless I can get the feds to assume responsibility."

"Have you heard from the President?"

"Yeah, twice. He even gave me his private number, but he's not going to be much help. He's ordered the Delta Force to Fort Dix from their bases at Fort Bragg and Camp Pendleton, but he insists the final decision to use force to retake the ferries rests with the civil authorities."

"Meaning you?" McKenna asked.

"Who else? You don't think I could get the douche bag to leave his palace in Albany and take over, do you?"

"No, but it's just as well. I think you have to resist all temptations to use force to retake the ferries. It won't work, and Felipe is prepared to kill five hundred hostages. He might even be planning on it."

The number hit the mayor hard. "Five hundred?" he said to himself, over and over. "What do we do?"

"Aside from satisfying Felipe's demands, we have to try and prevent the plane hijacking so we'll have some room for negotiations. Maybe he'll tone down his demands in return for his escape airplane."

"And then what?" the mayor asked.

"Then we have to trust the Peruvian government to get him." McKenna outlined his and Savraada's theory on Felipe's intentions, and the difficulties to be expected from the Peruvian government and their military before they could get Felipe and his men on the ground in the Amazon.

"I don't like it and the President will never go for it," the mayor said. "Leaving our work to a foreign government to screw up won't be good enough."

"I think as time goes on, it will become apparent that there's no other choice," McKenna said, trying not to sound overbearing. "Remember, their government has a vested interest in destroying Felipe before he destroys them, and I'm sure that some of his demands are going to entail some things they will be very reluctant to do. In any event, some high-level consultations with the Peruvians are going to be necessary.''

"That's just another reason the feds should be taking this over," the mayor said, talking more to himself than to McKenna.

"But they won't," McKenna said. Then he told the mayor what he thought were Felipe's intentions regarding the Williamsburg Bridge.

"So if you don't find the person with the detonator, we lose the bridge," the mayor said.

"I'm afraid so, Your Honor."

"And how are you doing?"

"I'll know more by tomorrow. One of the prisoners we got in Brighton Beach is telling all he knows, and we have some leads on finding that person. I have Inspector Tavlin working on it now."

"What else did your prisoner tell you?"

"That Felipe plans to be broadcast live on national television."

"That figures," the mayor snorted. "He could do that anytime he wants. The press would jump at the opportunity to board the ferries and interview him." For the first time that day the mayor smiled. "I almost wish he'd invite them tonight and get those reporters off my lawn," he said.

"Ready to face the music, Your Honor?"

"No, but we might as well get to our very short news conference," the mayor said as he stood up. "We have nothing to tell them, and they're not gonna like that."

Neither man looked overjoyed at the prospect.

Chapter 37

McKenna was surprised how well he slept. He woke up feeling refreshed in his hotel room at seven o'clock, not having been disturbed once during the night. He had left instructions that he was to be awakened if anything new developed, and apparently nothing had. He figured that Felipe was still sitting on his boats and biding his time.

After showering and dressing, he ordered up some breakfast and watched CNN while he ate. The only story being covered was the drama in the harbor. They had a camera with a powerful telephoto lens on the roof of the World Trade Center, focused on the Verrazano-Narrows Bridge and the two ferries underneath. The bridge was empty and nothing else was moving in the harbor. CNN had analysts, experts, and commentators reporting and speculating on every aspect of the story.

One aspect proved the chief of patrol right. Many businesses remained closed, people were staying home, and traffic was light. *Sendero* had closed the City of New York, and street scenes shown by CNN made McKenna think it looked like Sunday morning.

CNN also ran segments of the previous evening's news conference at City Hall, and watching it caused McKenna to smile. Although the mayor had opened the conference with a brief statement, he then had turned the microphone over to McKenna, who told them there was nothing new on the story that hadn't already been seen on the news and that they would formulate a plan after they heard what Felipe wanted.

Naturally, that was not good enough for the reporters. But they refused to beat up McKenna, who was standing at the microphones with his guard down. Instead, they shouted questions at the mayor, who made sure he was nowhere near a mike. In response to their questions, the mayor moved his lips

and made some expansive gestures while pointing to Mc-
Kenna, but McKenna was sure he wasn't making a sound. It
looked plausible on film, but wouldn't play too well on the
radio. The end result was that McKenna promised a daily brief-
ing session.

McKenna was in for a lift when he left for work. "Chipmunk's
waiting for you in the coffee shop," Morgan announced when
McKenna stepped into the hall.

"Chipmunk? Did he say what he wants?"

"Just that he's waiting for you and it's important."

"Then it must be," McKenna said as he got on the elevator.
But on the way down he couldn't imagine what it could be.
He knew Chipmunk as the world's greatest bartender and a
good friend. Chip worked at Churchill's, a bar and restaurant
on the East Side that was frequented by many detectives and
FBI agents. He knew them all, and there was nothing going
on in either agency that Chip didn't know about, although he
never crossed secrets or took a side in the frequent and petty
interagency disputes. For that reason he was one of the most
popular men in town, and his advice was valued.

He found Chipmunk sitting in a corner booth, having breakfast and a few laughs with Cisco and Pao. They shoved over
to make room for McKenna, and he sat down.

"Heard you've been busy," Chipmunk said after rising and
giving McKenna a kiss on the forehead, the standard Chipmunk greeting.

"Yeah, Chip. Sorry I didn't get up to see you."

"That's all right. How's Angelita doing?"

"She's just a barrel of laughs. Be out of the hospital in a
few days."

"I know. I heard from Joe Sofia and he says she's driving
them crazy. She's not sleeping and tuned to the news twenty-
four hours a day."

It didn't surprise McKenna that Chipmunk knew what his
wife was doing and he didn't, but he knew that whatever Chipmunk said was true. He was just glad for the insight. "Thanks,
Chip," he said. "I didn't know that. I talk to her every day
and she sounds fine on the phone."

"I know. It's an act. She's a strong girl, but she's worried
sick." Chipmunk finished his cup of coffee and poured himself
another. "Ever hear of Joe Gleason?" he asked.

McKenna rolled the name around his mind. It sounded familiar, but he couldn't quite place it. "Maybe, but I can't picture him offhand."

"Joe's a good friend of mine in a little bit of trouble. He had nineteen years with the Bureau. Used to work in New York in counterintelligence in the early eighties. Anyway, Joe likes to drink, maybe a little too much, and he likes the ladies. You know how the Bureau frowns on the two pastimes."

McKenna did. In the Hoover days agents who enjoyed those diversions soon found themselves with other like-minded agents assigned to field offices in places like Missoula, Montana, and Nome, Alaska. It wasn't quite that bad anymore, but it still wasn't good. "So where did they put him?" he asked.

"He'd go gladly wherever they sent him, but he's sinned too often. He's suspended and he's gonna be fired, meaning no pension after nineteen years. He's living in Florida, awaiting his fate. But yesterday he flew up to Philadelphia, rented a car, and drove to New York. He wants to talk to you."

"Why?" McKenna asked.

"He wants you to use your influence with Gene Shields or whoever to help him keep his pension."

McKenna was mystified by Chipmunk's suggestion. He couldn't stick his nose where it didn't belong, and it certainly didn't belong in an FBI personnel management decision. But turning down Chipmunk was another story. "I don't know if I could, Chip. Why me?"

"Because he saw Felipe's picture in the paper yesterday and came right up, since it seems that nobody that matters in the FBI is taking his calls right now. So he wisely decided he doesn't want to talk to them after all. He wants to talk to you."

"Why?"

"Because he knows Felipe, but not under that name. Says he's not even from Peru."

A big shot in *Sendero Luminoso* not from Peru? McKenna had his doubts about that one. "Then where's he from?" he asked. "Cuba?"

Chipmunk took another sip of coffee, put down his cup, and smiled. "Nope. Get ready for this one, buddy," Chipmunk said. "He's a Russian."

"A Russian? How can that be?"

"I don't know. But if Joe Gleason says it, then you can take it to the bank. And he says that man on the ferryboat holding this city hostage in the name of the Shining Path of Peru is a goddamn Russian spy."

*　　*　　*

First, McKenna called Gene Shields and reached him in his office. Shields said he knew Gleason and was familiar with his problems, but hadn't seen him in years. He described Gleason as a nice guy, a good agent, an expert on Soviet spies operating in the United States, and a hopeless alcoholic and womanizer. Each divorce and affair had been followed by a stay at the Bureau's alcohol rehabilitation center. But finally his bosses had enough. Gleason had just been to the trough too many times and had exhausted their patience.

"Can I promise him he'll get his pension if his information's good?" McKenna asked.

Shields didn't need a second to think about it. "Brian, if it's good, you could promise him my job and he'd probably get it."

McKenna didn't like that. "Feeling some heat?" he asked.

"Yeah, it's pretty hot here."

A half hour later McKenna was knocking on Gleason's door at the Tudor Hotel on East 42nd Street. It took Gleason some time to get to the door, but when he finally opened it he was dressed in his Sunday best, looking pleased to see McKenna, but a little nervous.

"C'mon in, Commissioner," Gleason said, offering his hand. "I was hoping it was you."

As McKenna shook Gleason's hand, he took the measure of his new best friend. He was a stout man in his fifties with a full head of black hair and a friendly smile, who looked like an IBM executive except for the two things that marred his appearance. One was his nose. It was wide, red, with one small vein bulging near the tip. The other was that he had cut himself shaving, McKenna guessed sometime within the last two minutes. In short, Gleason resembled a moderately successful rummy on an interrupted bender, but a nice guy to have a drink with. McKenna knew the look well, having frequently practiced it himself in his distant past.

McKenna followed him in and saw that Gleason had rented himself a nice large room with two beds, a sofa, an upholstered chair in each corner of the room near the window, and a large dresser that ran half the length of one wall.

The first thing that caught McKenna's eye was that the bed had been slept on, not in. The second was the half-empty bottle of Jack Daniel's on the dresser. But Gleason had taken the trouble to unpack. An empty open suitcase lay on top of the dresser, next to the bottle, which brought McKenna to the conclusion that Gleason planned to be in town for a while.

"Offer you a drink?" Gleason asked.

"Not me. I'm in the program," McKenna answered as he sat in one of the chairs.

"Too bad," Gleason said. "Mind if I do?"

"Suit yourself."

Gleason poured himself a neat drink into a plastic cup. McKenna noticed that Gleason's hands shook a little as he took a long sip while McKenna waited, hoping that Gleason's first, or maybe second, blast of the morning would relax him a bit.

It did. McKenna could see the alcohol work its way through Gleason's body until it reached his fingertips. The shaking stopped and the nervousness was gone, replaced by a look of confidence on Gleason's face.

"I guess you can see I'm in trouble," Gleason said with a smile.

"I can see it and I heard about it," McKenna answered. "But you don't look like you're beyond recovery to me. I was in the same shape myself, more than once."

"I heard. That's one of the reasons I came to you. Are they gonna take me back?"

"That wasn't the deal I got for you," McKenna said. "You've got your pension if you have the information Chipmunk said you do, but I don't think they want you back."

"Who'd you talk to? Gene Shields?"

"Yeah. He said you were good when you were good and bad when you were bad, but bad too many times."

McKenna expected an argument, but got none. "Probably just as well," Gleason said. "I'd just screw up again. The pension's good enough, especially since I'd give you the information anyway."

"Why? Patriotic duty?"

"Yeah, let's call it my patriotic duty," Gleason said through a wry smile. Then he took another sip and added, "But mostly it's because I just don't like that prick sitting in the bay getting over on us again."

"Again?"

"Yeah, again. He got over big time on me."

McKenna sat back to listen as Gleason talked, pacing in small circles. "In 1981 I was assigned to counterintelligence working out of the New York office, doing not much of anything but following Soviet diplomats around, mostly their small people working at the UN. One time I'm outside their residence assigned to follow their second cultural attaché when he comes out and starts walking, looking all around.''

"Why him? Did you have something on him?"

"Not that I know of. It was just one of the things we did to keep them on their toes. They did the same thing with our people in Moscow. So I'm following him and he does a couple of moves that make me think he's hot. You know, doubling back, going into office buildings and taking the elevator up, coming out and jumping into a cab for a few blocks. All their standard stuff.''

"Did he know you were on him?"

"No. As soon as he went into his act, I got on the radio and called for some help. Our office used to be right down the block from the Soviet mission, so I got a good response in a hurry. Had maybe ten agents on him, and he never saw the same face twice. After an hour or so of his precautionary measures, he loosened up and we got him going into a bar on the East Side, and it just happened to be one of the places where I was well known.''

"Which bar?"

Gleason stopped pacing. "Jameson's. Ever been there?"

"Has it been around a while?"

"Ages."

"Then I guess I've been there, but not in a while," McKenna said.

Gleason resumed his pacing. "Well anyway, after a few minutes I follow him in and it's perfect. He's sitting at the end of the bar chatting with a couple of the regulars and the bartender gives me a big greeting, so our boy doesn't get suspicious. He orders another drink and I have a few while I'm hanging out. Then he went downstairs to the men's room. He's up after a minute and I go down to check it out.''

"What are you looking for? A drop?"

"Yeah, I figured he didn't go to all that trouble making sure he wasn't being followed just to sit down and have a drink. I look around real quick and I don't find anything. As I'm coming out, your boy comes in.''

"Felipe."

"Yeah. He had been sitting in the back having dinner with a girl. I can't hang around in the john, so I run upstairs just in time to see the Russian leave. I'm behind him, along with everyone else, and he goes straight back to their residence. Then I knew.''

''What? That you missed it?''

''Had to be. So I went back to Jameson's and talked to Keith, the bartender. He says the Russian comes in from time to time, has a couple, then leaves. Friendly guy, good tipper, only a small accent. I asked him about Felipe and he didn't remember him, but the waitress did. She said he stops in for dinner every once in a while, always with a different girl. Likes the leg of lamb. Said he had no accent she noticed, so she thought he was American.''

''But I've spoken to Felipe,'' McKenna said. ''He's got a Spanish accent. Not bad, but it's there.''

''It's bullshit. He's putting it on for you. He speaks English like you and me.''

McKenna was surprised, but it made sense when he thought about it. If Felipe wanted to keep us and everybody else thinking he was from Peru, then he knew we'd expect to hear a Spanish accent. This wasn't the time to be showcasing his linguistic talents, McKenna thought, a little annoyed to find his respect for Felipe growing.

Gleason had stopped his pacing and was smiling at McKenna, enjoying himself and adding to McKenna's annoyance. ''Go on,'' McKenna said.

Gleason wiped the smile off his face and resumed pacing. ''So I gave Keith my beeper number and asked him to get in touch with me the next time the Russian or Felipe came in. He did, about a month later. I was on my day off in another joint in Midtown, enjoying myself when Keith called. The Russian was there, but Felipe wasn't. I was in a little trouble with the bosses at the time and knew I was in no shape to be talking to them, so I figured I'd handle it myself.''

''Wasn't that breaking the rules?'' McKenna asked.

''Yeah, but my boss was a guy named Weatherby and I was on his shit list, so I couldn't call him. Besides, he'd take the credit himself and send me back to the rehab.''

''You were right about one thing. That's Weatherby's style.''

''You know him?'' Gleason asked.

''Obsequious little prick?''

''Yeah, you know him. Anyway, when I got to Jameson's I saw no sign of the Russian, but Felipe was having dinner with a girl in the back. Keith points down, so I know the

Russian's in the men's room. He comes up in a minute and I go down. This time I find it, in the toilet-paper roll. The Russian had taken the roll of toilet paper off the holder in the commode booth, put the message inside, and hung the toilet paper back up. So I think I got the clever bastards and everything's gonna be okay for me with the bosses. I'm sitting pretty."

Gleason poured himself another drink, smiling more to himself than at McKenna as he remembered the moment. McKenna waited as he finished his drink, but then Gleason poured himself another.

"How about telling me what the message was before you have that one," McKenna said.

"That's the problem. I don't know," Gleason said. He drank his drink in one gulp, screwed the cap onto the bottle, and sat on the bed, staring at McKenna.

"You screwed it up?" McKenna asked.

"Yep. It was in code, so I put it in my pocket and figured that somebody else could figure it out later. But your Felipe had other plans. I didn't see him until I was leaving the men's room, and then only for a second."

"He got the jump on you?"

"Big time. Gave me a shot right in the kisser. Did this," Gleason said as he loosened his upper dental bridge with his fingers and offered it for McKenna's inspection.

The move caught McKenna by surprise and he didn't know what to say as he stared at the wide gap in Gleason's smile. He settled on, "Nice bridgework."

"Thanks," Gleason said. He put his bridge back in and added, "Looks good, but these things never fit right. Gives me blisters on my tongue. But it could have been worse."

"Because he didn't kill you?"

"No, never happens. That would be against the rules. We don't kill their people and they don't kill ours. No, it would have been worse if I would have lost my lowers. He loosened them up, too, but the dentist managed to save them. Fortunately, he was pretty good."

What am I supposed to ask next? McKenna wondered. Who's your dentist? or maybe, How's that Bureau dental plan, anyway? No, he decided, because Gleason would tell me and he's got a quarter of a bottle left to drink while he does. McKenna hoped he was giving a hint when he looked at his watch, then asked, "What happened next? You woke up in the men's room?"

Gleason took the hint. "Yes, sir. Handcuffed to the sink with my own cuffs, and *sans* Russian message and my handcuff key. But he was nice enough to leave my gun and ID. Keith found me. Said the Russian left right away, and he came down after Felipe left with his girl, casual as can be. But I was in trouble, puking and feeling like shit, and Keith couldn't get me loose. He had to run upstairs and borrow a handcuff key from an off-duty cop."

"And you were in trouble again?"

"Not right away. Keith agreed to keep quiet about the whole thing because I was in no shape to be interviewed by Weatherby. But I had to take a week off to get my teeth fixed and Weatherby figured something was up and sent me back to the rehab anyway."

"That still doesn't make Felipe a Russian," McKenna said. "He could have been an American working for them."

"That's what I figured at the time, but I ran into him again."

"Not at Jameson's?"

Gleason was looking at his bottle again as he answered. "No, not Jameson's. They knew they were blown there. The Russian was called back home and everybody on our side was wondering what was up, since he had only been here for a couple of months. Everybody but me, that is, but I kept it to myself."

McKenna waited, getting exasperated as Gleason shared the joke with himself. "Where did you see him again?" he asked, trying to maintain a patient tone.

Gleason got the point. He composed himself, placed his hands on his lap, and stared straight at McKenna. "About six months later. In Brooklyn."

"Brighton Beach?"

"Yeah, Brighton Beach. Myself and a few other agents were tailing one of the Soviet members of their trade mission. He was running around Brighton Beach collecting information from some of his moles. It was kind of a boring day since this guy was a real dope, had no training. We could have followed him in an ambulance, so I left him with my partners and took a break. I stopped in to—"

"Wait a minute," McKenna said. "Do you mean you left your partners while they're watching some spies?"

"Don't get excited. They didn't mind," Gleason said. "Besides, they weren't really chasing spies, just ordinary people the Soviets infiltrated into this country with all the other Russian immigrants who were coming over. They all had technical backgrounds and were supposed to give the Soviet contact everything they learned in their new jobs here. You know, work for the big companies and get the trade secrets, new industrial processes. Just technical stuff.''

''And wasn't that important?''

''Not very. Most of them agreed to work for the Soviets just to get out. Once they got here, they liked what they saw and just refused to cooperate or give the Soviets anything. Some of them even came to us and we had some fun feeding the Soviets some secrets that would cost them a bundle, but wouldn't work too well.''

''But some of them must have worked for them,'' McKenna objected.

''Yeah, a few. But we knew who they were and we never let them get into a position to cause any damage.''

''Why weren't they just deported?''

''Wasn't done. At that time immigration from the Soviet Union was one of those politically correct things. Pointing out that the Soviets were sending over some spies here along with legitimate immigrants wasn't worth the hassle. People would question the policy and the Soviets would probably retaliate by slowing immigration, even though they were getting some other benefits from it.''

''Such as?''

''They got rid of a lot of their crooks. The gulags were no longer politically feasible for them, so the Soviets doctored their papers and sent them here. Must've given them quite a laugh when we started getting some major problems from their freedom-loving Russian mafia.''

''All right, so you just left your partners and stopped in for a drink.''

Gleason didn't answer, just glared at McKenna, which got McKenna thinking. What am I doing playing the high and mighty? he thought. This guy's got the information and I gotta get it. ''Sorry,'' he said. ''Go on with your story, please.''

But Gleason continued glaring at McKenna for another minute. Then he smiled. ''All right, but just remember this,'' he said. ''If I didn't stop in for a drink on that particular day, I wouldn't know what I'm about to tell you.''

And you remember that if you didn't know it, you'd be out

your pension, McKenna thought, trying to smile through his mounting aggravation. He succeeded and said, "Okay, I'll remember."

Gleason was riding a high. "Good," he said. "Anyway, I stopped into this Russian place, the Club Sevastopol. The place is crowded with some heavy Russian types, but it's dark and nobody's paying much attention to me. I order a vodka and I'm enjoying my drink when he walks in with another guy."

"Who? Felipe?"

"Yeah, but that wasn't his name then. He's coming from the outside and it took a moment for his eyes to adjust, so I see him before he sees me. I hunch down on my stool and they walk right past me into the back. They got a little dining room back there, sort of private. So once again I got a problem."

"I see," McKenna said, trying to sympathize with Gleason's predicament. "You can't call for backup because you're in a place you're not supposed to be in doing what you're doing. You got to do him on your own, by yourself again."

"Pretty concise evaluation, and that's what I did. They have dinner and I get close enough for a second to hear them talking. Can't hear what they're saying, but I know it's Russian. Caught a couple of words."

"You speak Russian?" McKenna asked, a little surprised.

"Is that a shock?" Gleason asked, enjoying McKenna's reaction. "Russian language major at the University of Pennsylvania, four years, then a graduate degree in Russian literature. It's easy once you get by the Cyrillic alphabet, the three genders, and the six noun cases. But what makes it really easy is it's a pretty good language to drink in. Go ahead, ask me anything in Russian."

Gleason was beginning to slur his words and was having a good time, but McKenna was out of patience. "Mr. Gleason, finish this story now," he said in the most authoritative tone he could manage.

Gleason took it like a punch on the chin. He shook his head to clear it and stared at McKenna with his mouth open. When McKenna saw that Gleason's bridge was coming loose, he felt a pang of guilt and said softly, "Try to remember that if what you're telling me is true, it might be the most important thing you've ever done in your life. It'll make up for a lot of sins."

"Okay, there's not much more to tell, really," Gleason said, measuring his words. "I followed them to a house on Brighton

7th Street. Your Felipe was cagey, looking around a bit, but he didn't see me. They were walking on Brighton Beach Avenue and I followed them by running along the tracks overhead. They never looked up. I was still on the tracks when they walked into the driveway, and then I couldn't see them. A minute later a car comes out of the driveway and takes off, heading away from me. I saw there was only one guy in it and that it had diplomat plates, but I was too far away to get the number. I waited maybe a half hour and I don't see the other guy. So I go down to get the address. As I'm walking past on the other side of the street from the house, your Felipe comes walking out of the driveway. There was a garage in back and the door was open. He takes a short look at me, but I didn't think he recognized me. He just made a left and walked back to Brighton Beach Avenue, casual as can be. That was it.''

"You didn't follow him?"

"I couldn't just turn around and walk back the way I came, so when I got to the corner I ran around the block back to Brighton Beach Avenue to see if I could pick him up, but I never saw him again.''

"That's it?" McKenna asked. "No follow-up investigation?"

"Nothing official, but I did a lot on my own. I went back that night in my own car and the garage door was still open. He never went back to that house.''

"Then he recognized you, didn't he?"

"He must have. I only saw him for a second in Jameson's, but he had all the time he needed to take in my face when he was handcuffing me and going through my pockets. Seeing me in front of his house spooked him and he never went back.''

"How do you know it was his house?"

"I checked. I drove by every time I got a chance for the next week, and the garage door was still open. I checked the Municipal Real Estate and found the house was bought by an Ilya Garonovich in 1980. There was no mortgage, so I guess he paid cash. Then I talked to the neighbors, said I was working a missing persons case on him. Nobody really knew him, but they had seen him from time to time. Said he lived alone and wasn't home much. All the descriptions they gave me of their neighbor fit.''

"What happened to the house?"

"It was vandalized and burglarized a few times, then the city took it over for taxes."

"You do any of those burglaries?"

Gleason smiled at the thought and McKenna wasn't sure if he was going to answer, but he did. "I might have looked around. There was nothing there."

"Did you check with DMV or do a credit check?" McKenna asked.

"That's not allowed without a case," Gleason answered, defensively.

"I know, but did you?" Gleason still didn't answer and McKenna knew why. It's okay to admit a break-in when there's no complainant to make a beef, he thought, but making unauthorized credit checks and DMV inquiries leaves a paper trail. "Statute of limitations is up by now," McKenna said. "And just between us, I would have checked the DMV, the credit bureaus, and even the underwear drawer of any guy who knocked my teeth out."

"He had no credit cards in that name, but he had a driver's license," Gleason said, almost under his breath. "Got the license with a forged birth certificate in 1979. It's expired now. No moving violations."

"Thanks. Now what about the car with the DPL plates?"

"When I was working another case, I got a chance to go through the State Department photo file of all the diplomats. The other guy was listed as a chauffeur attached to the East German mission to the UN. By the time I found out he had already been recalled. There were no active cases on him."

"His name?"

"Werner Bachmann. You gonna look him up?"

"I'm gonna try. It's a new ball game in Germany now, and I'd like to know how he's doing. But I need one more name from you to make this perfect."

"What name?"

"The name of the Soviet cultural attaché you followed into Jameson's."

McKenna watched Gleason straining to remember, going back through the years. But he couldn't do it. "Sorry, I just can't bring it back. It was a long time ago and we followed so many of those jokers."

"But there's a record of it?"

"Sure. Check with Mr. Shields. Tell him to find out who I

was watching a couple of weeks before they put me in the rehab in '81.''

''I will, but I've got another deal for you. I'm going downstairs to pay for your room for another couple of days and I'm going to send you up some breakfast from room service. After you eat I want you to take a nap.''

''Sounds good to me, but why?''

''Don't take this the wrong way, but there's somebody coming to see you at noon, and you have to be sober and well rested. His name is Lieutenant Picciarelli and he's gonna give you a polygraph test on what you've told me.''

It looked to McKenna like Gleason was going to take it the wrong way. He stood up, looking angry, with his veins bulging out of his neck. McKenna stood up also, fearing that Gleason was going to hit him.

But he didn't. Gleason sat back down on the bed, closed his eyes, took a few deep breaths and said, ''I understand. Nobody would believe this stuff came from a drunk with my record.''

''I do believe you, but put yourself in my place,'' McKenna said. ''I'm going to be shaking some pretty big trees with the information you gave me, and if you weren't polygraphed I'd have a much tougher time getting taken seriously. It's got to be done.''

''I'll be ready. Send him up,'' Gleason said in a whisper, still not moving.

McKenna put his hand on Gleason's shoulder and it seemed to him that Gleason was melting under his touch. ''For what it's worth, Joe Gleason, I think you were a pretty good agent with some real tough problems,'' McKenna said. ''It's never too late to get a new start, and you're gonna be eligible for the law-enforcement hall of fame if I can do my job right.''

Gleason remained seated, but drew himself up straight. ''Thanks, but I'll settle for my pension,'' he said, and McKenna wasn't sure if he said it with stubbornness or pride.

''You'll get it, but what are you gonna do? Use it to drink yourself to death?''

''Yep.''

Stubbornness.

Chapter 38 At nine-thirty Pao was headed downtown to headquarters from the Tudor Hotel, weaving in and out of the light traffic, when McKenna's phone rang. McKenna knew who it was before he answered. Since Felipe had taken the ferries, his phone number was reserved for only Brunette and *Sendero*. He had just spoken to Brunette to apprise him of the Gleason interview, so he knew it was the call he had been expecting and dreading. "Pull over, Johnny," McKenna said as the phone kept ringing.

As soon as Pao stopped, McKenna answered it.

"Good morning, Assistant Commissioner McKenna. Did I wake you?" Felipe said, sounding chipper.

"No, I've been up for hours."

"Been keeping busy?"

"No. There's not much to do around here since you took over the show," McKenna said. "How about yourself?"

"Just taking care of some odds and ends. Wanted our place to look just right when the press gets here."

"And when will that be?"

"I want to extend an invitation to them through you. We're prepared to receive a delegation of reporters at eleven-thirty this morning."

"That's just two hours from now," McKenna protested.

"I don't think you'll have much of a problem getting reporters to come, will you?"

"No, but suppose we don't let them go to your press conference?"

"Don't be ridiculous. I am able to communicate with the press directly, if I wish, and I will announce to them that at eleven-thirty-five I will shoot one of the passengers and throw the body in the bay, and that I will shoot another one every

334

five minutes pending their arrival. By noon, once the press started on you, there would be a new mayor, a new police commissioner, and six unnecessary new navigation hazards floating in the bay.''

Scratch that option, McKenna thought. ''Just kidding, Felipe,'' he said. ''Don't get cranky on me, okay?''

''Fine. No reason to spoil both our days this early in the morning. Are you ready for the arrangements?''

McKenna took his pad from his pocket, poised to write. ''Go ahead.''

''We are expecting two open boats, no more than thirty feet long, and carrying no more than twenty reporters, including their film crews. They are to approach the *Samuel I. Newhouse* from the commuter ferry pier at 69th Street in Brooklyn, traveling no faster than five knots. Naturally, if there is any deviation from these instructions the boats will be sunk.''

''Any preference on reporters?''

''Of course. I expect to meet representatives of CNN, *The New York Times*, and *Noticias Telemundo*. You may allot the rest of the spaces as you see fit.''

''Do you guarantee their safety?''

''Yes, as long as they follow instructions and don't interfere. Of course, they must all be accredited members of the press, with identification.''

That scratches what was probably a bad idea anyway, McKenna thought. Slipping people aboard masquerading as reporters would never get by Felipe. ''Are you going to give them a list of the people you're holding?'' McKenna asked.

''Not for their knowledge. That's for you. I will give them a list of our guests in a sealed envelope, along with instructions on the things that must be done to end our visit here. They are to deliver this envelope to you, unopened. At this point, I see no reason to involve the press in what are bound to be some sensitive communications between your side and mine.''

''We'll be under a lot of pressure to release your demands anyway,'' McKenna said.

''What you do is up to you. I'm just trying to make it as easy as possible for you by insulating you from public pressure.''

''Why are you sending it to me?'' McKenna asked. ''I'm not in charge. Why not the governor, the mayor, or even the President?''

''That's just the point, Commissioner. I'm placing you in charge. We will deal only with you.''

"But you haven't told me why," McKenna said.

"It's simple. I have found you to be a sensible man, and you don't have the same agenda in this affair as an elected official, which means your job doesn't depend on concluding this affair to the satisfaction of your superiors. Since some painful decisions have to be made and since we have, quite inadvertently, made you into something of a public hero, I think that your voice will prevail in this matter."

"That's not too flattering. In other words, you think I'm the one most likely and most able to cave into your demands."

"Yes, only because you'll realize that's all you can do. I know you must harbor some personal animosity toward me, but you'll still do what's best and sway others in that direction."

"I guess we'll have to see about that. How's Detective Hoffmann doing?"

"Fine, as far as I know. We monitored a conversation between him and Commissioner Brunette a half an hour ago. He seems to be in good spirits, although I can't imagine why. He's dirty, wet, and he must be hungry and very tired by now. In the predicament he's placed himself in, he can't sleep without drowning."

"Are you ready to let him out if he surrenders?"

"Maybe after the news conference."

"I hope you're not planning anything dramatic at this conference?"

"Like shooting some passengers to show how serious we are?" Felipe asked.

"Yes. There's no reason to do that. We already know you're serious."

"Quite frankly, I am planning on shooting five of them for viewer gratification just to make sure we have a good Nielsen rating for our next news appearance. We really plan to be the top show in our time slot."

"Felipe, please don't do that," McKenna pleaded.

"Be sensible, Commissioner. It's only five and we have so many mouths to feed here. A lot of people are going to die before this is over. Maybe even you and me."

"There's no reason for any more to die, Felipe. We can work this thing out between us, without the gory stage shows. Please, I'm begging you."

"I'm surprised you don't see the big picture yet, Commissioner. These silly sensibilities have no place in the situation we're in right now."

McKenna's mind was racing. He had suspected that Felipe was going to start shooting hostages for dramatic effect, and nothing he could say or do would deter him. But five? He took a gamble, just hoping to save at least one life for the present. "Please, Felipe," he pleaded. "Not five."

Felipe took his time in answering. "Okay, as a personal favor to you I'll make it three. Now stop your sniveling and get busy. I'm sure you have a lot to do if our visitors are to arrive on time. You have one hour and fifty-five minutes."

The line went dead. McKenna turned to Pao, who was totally unconcerned and busy rubbing his tie, trying to remove a stain McKenna was sure had been there a year. He got Pao's attention when he put on his seat belt. "Where to?" Pao asked.

"The 69th Street Pier in Bay Ridge, *tout de suite*. We have to dig up some lifeboats and motors."

Five seconds later McKenna was in fear of his life as Pao followed his orders. He called Brunette and gave him Felipe's instructions, trying not to pay attention to the blur of vehicles they were passing at somewhere near Mach Two as he talked.

"You on your way to the pier now?" Brunette asked.

"As fast as we can."

"Take your time and get there in one piece. I figured Felipe would pull a stunt like this. Everything and everyone you need will be there by eleven o'clock."

That was good news to McKenna. "Bring us down to Warp One, Mr. Sulu," he said to Pao, who complied, although he didn't look happy about it.

"How are you arranging that?" McKenna asked Brunette.

"Sheeran and I just figured it out in our spare time. We knew Felipe would want to talk to the press, and we figured he would give us short notice and that he'd insist on open boats. The Bay Ridge pier seemed the natural place for them to leave for his position. So Sheeran scouted it out last night. There are two lifeboats from the old Brooklyn ferry there. He's having them pitched and tarred and the Harbor Unit is bringing the motors by truck."

McKenna was awed by Brunette's and Sheeran's foresight. "I'm impressed, Ray. I wouldn't have thought of all that."

"It's not your job. You just worry about getting these guys and we'll handle the logistic details."

"How about the press?"

"No problem. They're all here. You can't spit outside without hitting a reporter. Once we let them know what's going on, they'll all be running for the pier. I'm sending Reginald Rivers over to handle the press assignments. Once we load up the *Times*, CNN, and *Noticias Telemundo*, he'll decide who else gets to go. He's been dealing with the press a long time and knows them all."

"What do you want me to do there?" McKenna asked.

"Just keep thinking. I'm sending the communications truck over so you'll be comfortable."

"You got anything more for me to think about?"

"A few things. Tavlin's got a surveillance going at the house of that American your new pal Julio said was working for Felipe, but our people haven't seen him or the van yet."

"Are you sure we got the right guy?"

"Has to be. What's the odds of Julio making up a license number that adds to seventeen, and then it just happens to fit a tan Dodge van? Then Tavlin pulled his DMV record and got a look at his picture. Just the guy Julio described."

"What's his name?"

"Seymor Cranston."

Seymor? McKenna thought. His parents must have hated him to give him a name like that. Being short with a name like Seymor can add up to a miserable life. Could make him bitter enough to engage in some antisocial behavior, maybe even treason. "Where's he live?" McKenna asked.

"Way out in Suffolk County. Port Jefferson. He's got a three-bedroom house in one of those luxury condo developments, but we got lucky on that. There's only one road in and out of the development. We'll know as soon as he gets home and whenever he leaves. Already got a wire on his phone and we're gonna put his house under permanent video tonight to see who's visiting him. Shouldn't be hard because there's woods all around."

"Where's he work?"

"This is where old Seymor gets interesting. We ran his credit history and found out he worked for Brookhaven Labs, out near his house. Good job, eighty grand a year. They do a lot of government work, so Shields called up the personnel manager and told him Brookhaven Labs would be a parking lot if he breathed a word of the inquiry. Anyway, Seymor was a research biochemist, graduate of Stanford University, worked for them since '79. Top Secret clearance. Then last November he up and quits. Surprised everyone. No fights, everyone liked him, no policy disagreements, and he was due for a promotion and a large raise. But he quits to drive a truck for Allied Maintenance, making twenty-one thousand a year.''

''What did they say about that at Brookhaven Labs?'' McKenna asked.

''Nothing. They didn't know where he went. We got it from the W-2 on his tax return.''

''You seem to be getting a lot of information very fast,'' McKenna observed. ''We doing this legal?''

''Very. It's all simple now. We've got National Security Agency authorization for everything we want in this case. Credit checks, wiretaps, tax returns, everything. It's easy for the feds once you prove the involvement of a hostile foreign power, terrorist groups, or espionage. Then it's minimum probable cause necessary, no parading informants before a judge. Just your basic NSA warrant. Good for gathering information, but whatever you get can't be used against the defendant in court in a criminal prosecution, except for espionage cases.''

Very nice tool to have, McKenna thought. No wonder the feds make it look so easy sometimes. ''What's Allied Maintenance say about him?''

''We haven't contacted them yet. We don't know what his position is there and we don't want to risk tipping him off.''

''But you know he's driving a truck?''

''Assume. He went to the trouble of getting his driver's license upgraded last November, right after he quit Brookhaven Labs. Now he's legal on the big rigs.''

''It doesn't figure to me yet,'' McKenna observed. ''Doesn't Allied Maintenance do the major jobs like the cleaning and the maintenance at the stadiums, the hospitals, the universities, and the bigger office buildings? Why would Seymor quit a good-paying job to do that?''

''You're missing the big one, buddy,'' Brunette said, and McKenna could almost feel him smiling through the phone. What am I missing? he thought.

It came to him in a flash. ''They do the airports,'' he said, surprised at himself for yelling the answer like he was a contestant on a game show. ''They do everything at the goddamn airports!''

''You got it. Opens up some interesting possibilities, doesn't it?''

''Yeah. Means he's been on Felipe's payroll since November, and probably longer. Add the fact that Felipe has spent years setting up safe houses, and we have to conclude he's been planning this for some time. That's why he's beating us every step of the way.''

''We're only in the middle innings,'' Brunette said. ''It's the endgame that counts. We've got to unravel the web he's been weaving for years, but we're getting there and we haven't given him a clue yet. That's why we have to be real careful with Seymor.''

''I agree. What about Seymor's finances?''

''We're going through his life history with a fine-tooth comb, and later on you and I will decide what to do about him.''

''Okay. I'll put him out of my mind for now. What do you want me to do with the reporters after Felipe's done with them?''

''Debrief them thoroughly, and don't put up with any of that First Amendment crap. Any one of them that doesn't co-operate gets locked up as a material witness.''

''Got it. But I have one other question, and give me a straight answer, okay?''

''Shoot.''

It was the question McKenna couldn't get off his mind, a simple one. He had been worried about his friend's state of mind in general, especially his bizarre desire to view the body of every *Sendero* casualty. But one thing had brought it to a head. Why had Ray not told him that Julio Montalvo had been identified in the lineups as being implicitly involved in his son's murder? he wondered. McKenna had expected some adverse comment from Brunette regarding the lucrative deal he had offered Montalvo, just about guaranteeing his freedom.

In the back of his mind, and as hard as it was for McKenna to believe, he feared that Brunette intended to murder Montalvo while he was in custody. Therefore, he wasn't concerned about any deal Julio was offered by McKenna. So he took his time in asking the question. ''How you feeling, Ray? I know it's personal, but I'm worried and I've got to know. Tell me the truth.''

''You mean physically, emotionally, or psychologically?''

''All of them.''

It was Brunette's turn to take his time, and for a few moments McKenna was afraid he wasn't going to answer. But he did. ''Just for you, buddy,'' Brunette said in a slow, measured tone. ''Physically, I feel lousy. I've got a broken nose that makes it hard for me to breathe and a concussion that makes me want to sleep most of the time. Emotionally, I'm a wreck, but the Job keeps me going. I had to get out of the hospital and get back to it, no matter what, or I'd be crying and making a fool out of myself. So here I am, performing credibly, I think."

"How about psychologically?"

"You notice something?"

"I'm not the only one."

McKenna braced himself for a tirade of denial, but he didn't get it from his friend. "Psychologically, I'm bent," Brunette said. "But the important thing is that I know it. I have some crazy thoughts running around my head. I'm suffering from a fixation. Really suffering, I mean. Fortunately, I also have you. You understand me better than anyone on this job. We understand each other."

"You're not thinking of cutting me out of your thought process, are you?"

"No. I was, but I won't do it again. I know I still have a wife, a family, and a reputation to think about, and I'll get through this. I just feel emasculated by that scumbag in the harbor, but I'm counting on you."

"You can, amigo. I promise you, but it's gotta be done right."

"Then I'll promise you something. I won't make another move unless you're standing next to me. Maybe we'll be stupid together. Is that a deal?"

"Deal."

Chapter 39   From the bridge of the *Samuel I. New-house*, Felipe monitored the approaching reporters' progress through the sunlit bay, satisfied that his instructions were being followed to the letter and a little surprised that they were precisely on time. The tide was going out, rushing through the Narrows and causing his ferries to strain against their anchors. He thought the docking procedure was going to be difficult,

but was pleasantly surprised to observe there were some yachtsmen among the reporters. Each open boat in turn was thrown a line by one of his men on the aft deck of the *Samuel I. Newhouse*, pulled in, and its cargo of reporters and their equipment taken aboard without incident.

Felipe went down to meet the press. The twenty reporters and cameramen were assembled in a group on the rear deck, guarded by a ring of six of his men carrying M-16 rifles pointed at the new arrivals. All of the *Sendero* soldiers wore black ski masks except for Alfredo Stesso, a handsome, muscular man in his forties, with a full head of long, dirty blond hair and a boyish grin, who looked like he belonged with the reporters, not *Sendero*.

The reporters paid no attention to Felipe as he stood in the stairwell inside the main cabin. The group was focused on the seven bodies placed in a line on the deck in front of them.

Felipe opened the cabin door and stood in the doorway, still unnoticed. "They were killed when we took these boats," Felipe said loudly, and the reporters swiveled to face him. "You will be taking these bodies with you when you leave. I am Felipe. I know you have many questions and I will answer some of them later. But we have a number of things to do before that. First, you will each be searched and present your credentials to that man." Felipe pointed to Stesso, who held up his hand, then slung his rifle over his shoulder and removed a pad and pen from his pocket. "His name is Alfredo. When he is satisfied with your identity, you will be given a tour of this boat and the defensive arrangements we have made will be explained. You may take as many pictures and shoot as much film as you like. However, you are not to speak to any of my men or to any of the passengers. You are merely to obey any directions my men give you. All questions are to be directed to myself at the appropriate time. Any one of you who deviates from these directions will be shot."

One of the reporters raised his hand, seeking permission to speak, and a scowl crossed Felipe's face.

"This is not the appropriate time," Felipe said.

The hand was quickly lowered.

"Place your cameras and equipment on the ground and line up in single file in front of Alfredo," Felipe ordered. "The reporters first, followed by the cameramen and technicians."

Felipe smiled, satisfied, as they silently followed his instructions, lining up in front of Stesso like schoolchildren. The process took thirty minutes, but there was no objection from the malleable reporters, not even a grumble of protest as they regarded the line of bodies with morbid fascination as they waited their turn to be interviewed. Felipe recognized some million-dollar smiles on the faces of some of his better-known guests and was gratified that the media had sent those they considered their best, just as he had expected.

After the last technician was registered, Stesso returned his identification and nodded at Felipe.

"Thank you for your patience, ladies and gentlemen," Felipe said. He walked over to a 106-mm recoilless rifle mounted on a tripod on the rear deck. There were two wooden boxes of shells stacked next to the rifle. "I believe you all have seen the effectiveness of this weapon on television last night. According to the manufacturer, it has an effective range of one mile. We have eight shells next to each of our six recoilless rifles, and each shell delivers approximately two pounds of explosive to the target."

Felipe pointed toward the Brooklyn shore. "As you might imagine," he said, "we are in a position to devalue quite a bit of Brooklyn real estate." Then he pointed to a tanker riding at anchor outside the harbor. "According to our range finder, that tanker is nine hundred and eighty yards from us. If provoked, we can ensure that no one will be swimming on any of the city's beaches for the rest of the summer." Felipe smiled to his audience. "Naturally we insist that tanker remain exactly where it is for the remainder of our visit."

Felipe was the center of the reporters' attention as he went to the cabin door and opened it. "We will now travel as a group around the main deck," he said. "I ask you to notice that eighteen Claymore mines have been attached to the outside of the ferry at thirty-foot intervals, four feet above the waterline. These mines are U.S. military issue and have been effectively used by government forces against our troops in Peru. For your information, the Claymore is a directional mine, electrically detonated, and when activated it explodes forward, producing an effective semicircular killing radius of twenty-five meters. Please follow me, and be careful not to trip over any of the wires."

Followed by the reporters and cameramen, Felipe went inside to the center of the cabin. Eighteen pairs of wires ran along the deck from the windows around the cabin and terminated at a console set up in the middle of the large cabin.

As the cameras rolled, Felipe opened a window on the port side of the boat and pointed outside to a Claymore mine attached by ropes to the bottom of the window frame. The green mine was rectangular and slightly convex in shape. Felipe stood back from the window. "You may photograph and film this particular mine, if you like."

One by one the reporters went to the window, climbed over the seat, and looked at the mine outside. They were followed by the still photographers and cameramen, who took photos and footage of the device. Felipe waited patiently until they were finished, then said, "As you will see later, there are another fifteen Claymores set up on the bridge, directed upward to discourage anyone dropping in on us from the air. We'll now go up to the upper deck."

Felipe climbed the stairs, followed by the reporters at a respectable distance. Two more *Sendero* soldiers wearing ski masks waited at the top of the stairwell on the salon deck, covering the reporters with their M-16s. Felipe turned the stairs and continued up, followed by the reporters and Senderistas. On their way up, the reporters saw that the large salon cabin was vacant.

More *Sendero* soldiers waited at the top of the stairwell on the salon deck. Felipe stood aside to let the reporters pass. They were directed to a yellow line painted on the deck, twenty feet from the stairwell. Approximately 400 passengers were seated in the middle of the cabin, watching the reporters with undisguised interest, but none of them moved or said a word. Each passenger wore a large plastic card around his or her neck that had written on it the passenger's name, age, employer or business, and nationality.

The passengers were well guarded. Two M-60 machine guns were set up astride the yellow line, each pointing down the aisles leading to the area occupied by the passengers. Each gun was manned by two Senderistas. Three more *Sendero* soldiers stood astride the line, covering the passengers with M-16 rifles. All of the soldiers on the upper deck wore bandoleers of grenades around their shoulders. The reporters could see an additional five *Sendero* guards standing on the far side of the boat with their M-16s pointed at the passengers.

"You may photograph the passengers from here for five minutes," Felipe said.

The cameramen took full advantage of the five-minute session, taking still photos of the unsmiling faces of the passengers while the video cameras panned the unmoving crowd. Then Felipe looked at his watch and said, "That's enough." The cameramen immediately stopped their activity and looked to him.

"Next we will now take a quick tour of the bridge and then we will attend to some unpleasantness on the main deck," Felipe said. For the first time, the reporters noticed that the steel door leading to the bridge stairwell had been removed.

There were four masked Senderistas on the bridge, each one carrying an M-60 machine gun with a 400-round assault pack attached. Two additional canvas assault packs were at the feet of each man.

The tour was brief. Felipe walked along the bridge deck, pointing at the Claymore mines tied to the bridge railing and facing upward. The wires from the mines ran along the bridge deck to the forward wheelhouse. In the wheelhouse stood the uniformed captain, guarded by another Senderista. The captain regarded the reporters dispassionately as Felipe stopped the group at the rear of the wheelhouse and pointed to a Stinger missile lying on top of three wooden boxes.

Felipe picked up the missile and said, "I believe you gentlemen know the capabilities of this weapon, maybe even better than we do. My men have been trained in the use of the missile, but I admit we haven't actually fired one. They were terribly expensive and we lacked suitable targets during our training for this mission."

He put the missile down, then laughed, more to himself than for the benefit of the reporters. "The range is classified, but perhaps your government will give us an opportunity to investigate the weapon's capabilities," he said.

Felipe led the group along the bridge and stopped at the forward stairwell leading down. He turned around and pointed to the top of the wheelhouse. "I would like to point out that our radar is functioning and we can monitor all traffic moving toward us, day or night. Both the boats we control have the same defensive arrangements," he said.

Felipe descended the stairs to the main deck. The reporters followed him down and saw that some changes had been made. The bodies were no longer on the rear deck outside, but in the main cabin stood three blindfolded men, guarded by three Senderistas. The prisoners' arms were tied behind their backs and pieces of tape had been placed over their mouths.

One of the blindfolded prisoners was a white man wearing

a disheveled pin-striped suit. His name tag read *Alvin Baker, age 52, Mobil Oil, American.* The second man was also white, wearing jeans, sneakers, and a cut-off YANKEES sweatshirt. His name tag identified him as *Colin McAllister, age 24, U.S. Marine Corps, American.* The last was a black man wearing baggy jeans, black sneakers, a red CHICAGO BULLS T-shirt, and a blue baseball cap. His name tag stated that he was *Tyrone Greer, age 20, Thief, American.*

The reporters were directed by the Senderistas guarding them to stand along the bulkhead and they quickly complied, keeping their attention and their cameras on Felipe. "The bodies you saw before have been removed to your boats, but there will be more. You would all be wiser to keep your cameras focused on these three men," Felipe said as he walked and stood in front of Alvin Baker. Felipe pointed to Baker and stated, "This man is an executive with the Mobil Oil Corporation, an American company that has been exploiting the people of Peru for forty years. They accomplish this exploitation mainly by paying corrupt politicians to avoid paying taxes."

Next Felipe pointed to Colin McAllister. "This man is a sergeant in the American Marine Corps, an imperialistic and brutal organization that for the last two hundred years has been suppressing the rights of poor people living in the Third World."

Tyrone Greer was the last to receive Felipe's attention. "This man is a thief," Felipe said. "When we took control of this boat he had in his possession the wallet of another one of the passengers. He has admitted that he is a heroin addict and a pickpocket and has told us that he steals one or two purses or wallets a day."

Felipe turned and walked to the bulkhead opposite the reporters. As he faced the newsmen he appeared annoyed that the cameramen still had their cameras on him, not the prisoners, so he pointed to his captives. The cameramen took his hint and switched their focus back to the prisoners. So did Felipe. "*¿Estás listo, Pablo?*" he asked one of the Senderistas guarding the captives.

"*Sí, Comandante,*" Pablo answered. He stood behind the prisoners, gave his M-16 to another Senderista, and took a .45 Colt pistol from his belt. As the reporters watched and the cameras rolled, he put the pistol to the back of Alvin Baker's head. Pablo looked to Felipe and Felipe nodded.

It was over in less than two seconds. Pablo fired a shot into

Alvin Baker's head, put his pistol to the back of Colin McAllister's head and fired, then shot Greer in the head before Baker's body had hit the deck. The three victims fell to the ground like a row of dominos and the cameras remained fixed on their bodies, lying facedown and close together. The blood from their head wounds flowed along the deck to form a single pool.

Felipe was satisfied with the reaction of the press. The younger newsmen stood horrified, staring at the bodies, while the old hands glared at him with hatred and disgust on their faces. Then Pablo pulled off his ski mask and the newsmen, sensing an event, turned their cameras on him. Many of the reporters were surprised to see that this cold-blooded killer looked like a child with the face of an innocent angel.

Still holding his pistol in his hand, Pablo stepped between the bodies in front of him and faced the press.

Felipe shifted his position so he was in the camera frame, behind Pablo, and said, "This man has something to say to you that might explain in a small way what you have just witnessed. Unfortunately, he has been too busy fighting all his life, so he has not had the time to learn English. I would like the reporter from *Noticias Telemundo* to come up and translate for him. Who would that be?"

A young reporter raised his hand.

"What is your name, sir?" Felipe asked.

"Miguel Rivas."

"Good, Señor Rivas. Please stand next to Pablo and do as I ask."

Rivas left the group of reporters and stood on Pablo's right side.

"Listen carefully and make sure you get it all," Felipe ordered.

Pablo started speaking slowly in Spanish, taking the time to survey his audience and looking each reporter in the eye in turn. After a minute he stopped speaking and cast a sidelong glance at Rivas.

"He said his name is Pablo Santiago," Rivas said loudly to the other members of the press. "He is twenty-one years old and is from the small village of Callera in the Department of Ayacucho. On the morning of May 2nd, 1982, a truck carrying government soldiers was ambushed near his village by *Sendero Luminoso*. An army captain, a sergeant, and eight privates from the Sinsi Battalion were killed. Pablo said he was just a boy at the time, but he knew the people of his village had nothing to do with the ambush. They were very poor and just wanted to be left alone to work their farms. They knew nothing about the ambush until a company of government soldiers came to his village that afternoon. They arrested every villager they could find, men, women, and children, and brought them to the church.''

Rivas turned to Pablo, who continued his narrative in slow Spanish. As he spoke, tears formed in the young killer's eyes. He spoke for another minute, then turned again to Rivas, who was obviously moved by Pablo's story.

"Pablo said that he and his mother had been working in their field next to the church when the soldiers came, and they hid there as the soldiers arrested the rest of the villagers, including his father and his two young sisters. He said he was related to everyone in the village in one way or another and he saw the soldiers bring his cousins, his grandparents, and his aunts and his uncles into the church. While they were hiding, they heard many people screaming inside the church. It went on for hours, but Pablo and his mother were afraid to move. Then they heard a lot of gunfire and more screaming. After a minute the screaming stopped and they heard laughter. Then the soldiers took the bodies out of the church and put them in the back of an army truck.''

Rivas turned back to Pablo, who spoke for another minute, weeping openly. When he stopped talking, Rivas continued translating the narrative. "He said he saw the bodies of everyone he knew in his life, all his friends and relatives. They had all been shot many times, thirty-nine people. They were all dead. Men, women, and children. The soldiers got into their trucks and drove away, taking the bodies with them. Pablo said that was when he became a Senderista, although he was very young and it was many years before he got a chance to kill any soldiers.''

Pablo made another short statement, this time speaking rapidly in Spanish. Then, as the press looked on, horrified, he raised his pistol to his head. He took a moment to stare at his audience, then smiled and pulled the trigger.

The single shot reverberated throughout the main cabin as the side of Pablo's head exploded, covering Rivas with blood. The young reporter watched in shock as Pablo's body fell to the deck. Not a word was said as the cameras continued rolling.

Felipe surveyed the press corps, satisfied at the effect Pablo's suicide had on them. They stood staring at his body, uncomprehending and transfixed. He waited until one of them, then another, raised their eyes to stare at him. "Tell them what he said," Felipe ordered.

But Rivas said nothing. He kept his eyes on the body on the deck next to where he stood, unconsciously wiping Pablo's blood from his face and neck with his hand. Then he stared at his bloody hand.

"Señor Rivas, tell them what he said," Felipe ordered loudly.

Rivas heard him this time and made an effort to compose himself before translating Pablo's final statement. "He said that he regretted killing those three people, but that they had to die. He said that *Sendero Luminoso* was the only hope for the people of Peru and that he would show us that Senderistas are not afraid to die. He said he was doing this to show us they are prepared to fight this battle in New York to the death."

"Thank you, Señor Rivas," Felipe said. "Please rejoin your comrades and I will give you the epilogue to the history of Pablo's village."

Rivas followed Felipe's directions, and the other reporters shuffled aside to make room for him in front.

"Now I will tell you what the government of Peru did after the atrocity endured by Pablo and his family became generally known," Felipe said. "I'm sure the incident must ring a bell with some of you who have been around a while, and you will hopefully guide your younger colleagues to the appropriate source materials that verify that what I am about to tell you is true to the smallest detail."

Felipe saw that he was right. It did ring a bell. Mike Brennan, the senior Fox News correspondent, nodded at him, almost imperceptibly. Felipe caught it, but gave no acknowledgment. "After the massacre at Callera, Pablo's mother took him to live in a shantytown outside of Lima and they became street vendors. In June of 1982 she went to the Ministry of Justice and told the officials there her story. They took a statement, but nothing was done. On March 3rd, 1983, she risked imprisonment by going to the Amnesty International office in Lima. She had no proof, but they believed her. They were able to substantiate that the Sinsi Battalion had been operating in the area of Callera in May of 1982, so they went to the Ministry of Justice for assistance, which we find laughable.''

Felipe's comment provoked a chuckle from a few of his soldiers. Felipe paused a moment before continuing. ''Amnesty was surprised to find that the Ministry of Justice had actually done something of an investigation on Pablo's mother's complaint. They found that a platoon from the Sinsi Battalion had been ambushed by our forces on May 2nd, 1982. According to army records, the platoon chased the *Sendero* force to Callera, where a battle took place. The records state the village was deserted, but six Senderistas were killed. Members of the battalion had substantiated the story. The case was closed by the Ministry of Justice, but Amnesty persisted in their investigation. However, there were no results for a long time. Then they got lucky. Or I should say, we got lucky.''

Felipe paused again. ''Should I go on, or is this revolutionary rhetoric boring you?'' he asked. No one dared answer. ''Mr. Brennan?'' Felipe asked.

''Go on,'' Brennan answered.

''Thank you,'' Felipe said. ''In 1985 our forces captured a sergeant from the Sinsi Battalion. He was questioned closely and we learned that he had been in Callera on May 2nd, 1982. He signed a statement indicating what had happened and who was involved. On September 9th, 1985, he was released to Amnesty International, unharmed. He took them to the place the bodies were buried. Amnesty thought to bring some members of the press along, including a correspondent from the Associated Press. I believe that correspondent was you, wasn't it, Mr. Brennan?''

''Yes, it was me.''

''Then I am exceptionally lucky today and a little tired of talking. Would you mind telling your colleagues what was found?''

''Thirty-nine decomposed bodies. Men, women, and children, all wearing civilian clothes,'' Brennan stated. ''Autopsies determined they had all been shot or beaten to death. Jacinta Santiago, Pablo's mother, identified the clothing of her husband and two daughters. I interviewed her and I actually met Pablo in 1985, during the interview. I submitted the story and it was run in most of the papers in this country.''

''Did you submit any follow-up stories?'' Felipe asked.

''Yes, as the case progressed.''

''Were those stories published?''

"Sometimes."

"Were any of the soldiers involved ever arrested?"

"Not while I was there."

"Did this surprise you?" Felipe asked.

Brennan was obviously uncomfortable, but forthright. "At the time, I was near the end of my tour with Associated Press in Peru," he said. "No, it didn't surprise me."

"Why not?" Felipe asked.

"Because there wasn't much interest in this country about what was going on in Peru. No pressure was brought to bear on your government to resolve the matter."

"What was the end result of the investigation?"

"It was alleged that the commander of the Sinsi Battalion had personal knowledge of the massacre and impeded the investigation. He was relieved of command and transferred."

"Do you remember his name?"

"I believe it was General Ramon Hidalgo."

Felipe smiled. "Correct, Mr. Brennan. Now, tell us. Do you know who is in command of the Sinsi Battalion right now?"

"No."

"It is General Ramon Hidalgo." Felipe paused for effect, and was a little disappointed to see that the newsmen were not in a state of shocked indignation. He surmised it would take more than the story of a little massacre to get the experienced reporters going. He planned to give it to them. "I will now take your questions, but please identify yourself when you ask them," Felipe said.

The reporters all looked at each other, taken unaware, before Rivas found his voice. "Miguel Rivas, *Noticias Telemundo*. How many hostages are you holding?" he asked.

"More than we'd like. We're now down to seven hundred and fourteen."

"Joe Monaghan, *New York Post*. Does that mean you're going to shoot some more of them?"

"Probably, but not necessarily. That depends on Commissioner McKenna, your government, and the illegal government of Peru. However, as a gesture of good faith, I propose to release one hundred hostages today at four o'clock in return for certain supplies. If Commissioner McKenna agrees, he will send the same two boats you ladies and gentlemen arrived in. Each boat will be operated by one police officer and must contain fifty gallons of number-two diesel oil in five-gallon containers, five hundred TV dinners, and four new microwave ovens. You might tell Commissioner McKenna that we have equipment to test the quality of the diesel oil, and that we have brought enough provisions to feed ourselves during our stay in his city. The TV dinners are for our guests, so he needn't bother putting something tricky in them. Each boat will make five trips back and forth, and we will release ten hostages for each boat loaded with the provisions I have described.''

"Alice Racuglia, *Washington Post.* Why are you choosing to deal with Commissioner McKenna? Hasn't your organization sentenced him to death?"

"Yes, we have sentenced him to death, but that was not done personally by me and mistakes have been made in the past. We are dealing with him and only him because I have chosen to do so. Next question."

"Tom Blackman, CNN. What is your position within *Sendero Luminoso*?"

"Obviously, I am in a position of leadership. If I am still alive when *Sendero Luminoso* finally replaces the illegal government of Peru, I expect that I would be consulted on certain affairs of state, although I seek no position in the new government."

"Roger Gainsford, NBC Nightly News. What do you expect to get out of all this? What are your demands?"

"I cannot tell you that right now, Mr. Gainsford. But since you asked the question, if I give you a sealed envelope containing our demands and a list of the passengers we are holding, would you give it to Commissioner McKenna, unopened?"

"Yes, but why not make your demands public?"

"I have my reasons, but you might hear more from me later on that. Next question."

"Steve Paquette, CBS News. Have you given any thought about how you will leave New York if your demands are met, and if you succeed in returning to Peru, do you anticipate that the United States will act militarily against your forces?"

"Yes, we have thought about it, and no, we don't believe the United States will react militarily against us. Your experience in Vietnam has taught you that a nation cannot wage war against another distant nation without overwhelming public support for a just cause. To ensure that your government is not permitted to engage in such unwise and unjust action, we have prepared three copies of a videotape that must be shown to the nation tonight at seven P.M. on the three networks.

This film was professionally produced and will correctly explain our position to the American public. Mr. Paquette, I will give these videotapes to you when you leave.''

"Suppose our employers decide not to run these videotapes?" Paquette asked.

"They will, because if I am not watching it on TV at seven tonight, we will shoot one hundred passengers. But aside from that, the film will delight their capitalistic hearts. It has been edited down to forty minutes, which leaves them plenty of time for the commercials in a one-hour time slot. They will figure a way to make quite a bit of money on the presentation, as I believe most Americans close to a TV will be watching it. One more question.''

"Mike Brennan, Fox News. Why did you kill those three innocent people?" Brennan asked, pointing to the bodies of Baker, McAllister, and Greer.

The expression on Brennan's face told Felipe that no answer he gave would satisfy the veteran reporter, but Felipe was prepared for the question and was surprised it had not been asked sooner. He knew he didn't have to convince all of them, or even most of them. He just had to win a little sympathy or understanding from some of the reporters, and he was sure he could do that.

"Those men were guilty of the crimes we charged them with, but I will say that in an ideal situation they would not have been shot, but rather incarcerated.''

Felipe gauged the reporter's reaction to his statement and saw he was going to have to do better. "We are not in an ideal situation. Possibly the death of those three will convince your government we are serious and will prevent a foolish military assault on these boats. If so, those three died so the rest of the passengers could live.''

Felipe saw he had found the chord to play. "There is something else I have noticed throughout my lifetime that you ladies and gentlemen of the press are going to illustrate for me once again, and that is this,'' he said. "Every year thousands of people are executed by Third World governments which enjoy the support of your government. These executions receive scant attention in the world press, if they are reported at all. Yet, the execution of those three Americans in New York will be front page in every newspaper in the world. Ask yourself why. Is it because those three were better than the simple people of my country, people our military executes routinely without notice or complaint from the American press? If we have done something to change that policy even a little, then those three deaths might be worthwhile. Think about this. If our government wasn't so callously executing our citizens, then we wouldn't be here executing yours.''

Felipe saw he had at least a few of the reporters thinking, so he was satisfied with his performance. ''This interview is over.'' Felipe signaled one of his men, and the Senderista ran to the console in the middle of the cabin and removed a cardboard box from underneath it. He ran back to Felipe and handed him the box.

''Mr. Gainsford and Mr. Paquette, would you come here please?'' Felipe asked.

The NBC Nightly News correspondent and the CBS News reporter left the group of newspeople and approached Felipe. Felipe took a large manila envelope from the box and handed it to Gainsford. ''As we agreed, Mr. Gainsford, here is the information you are to give to Commissioner McKenna.''

Gainsford accepted the envelope without comment, placed it under his arm, and returned to the group of reporters.

Felipe gave the box to Paquette. ''These are the videotapes to be run by the networks tonight, Mr. Paquette.''

''Thank you,'' Paquette said as he accepted the box. ''I'll try to see that they do.'' Paquette returned to his colleagues.

''Thank you, ladies and gentlemen,'' Felipe said. ''Please select some volunteers to carry these bodies, then follow the directions of my men and return to your boats.''

As Felipe expected, the reporters directed their cameramen and technicians to pick up the corpses, then they all headed for their boats, shepherded by the *Sendero* soldiers. Brennan was at the rear of the group and Felipe caught his eye. ''Mr. Brennan, could I have a word with you?'' he asked.

Brennan didn't look happy at the invitation, but shuffled over to Felipe. ''Quite a show you put on,'' he said.

''Thank you, Mr. Brennan. I value your professional opinion.''

''See if you value this,'' Brennan said. ''You're not fooling me. I've been around a long time and I've seen your type before.''

''I'm not trying to fool you, Mr. Brennan,'' Felipe said without anger.

''Who then? Them?'' Brennan asked, pointing over his shoulder at the departing reporters.

Felipe laughed. "Maybe," he said. "But just remember that from time to time good things have been accomplished by bad people. Maybe that is what's happening here."

Against his will, Brennan had to smile. "Bullshit," he said, looking Felipe straight in the eye.

Chapter 40

It took McKenna and Sheeran two hours to debrief the protesting reporters. It was a difficult thing to do since the newspeople were stars in their field and therefore people not used to being pushed around, especially when there were limos waiting to bring them to their offices so they could file their stories. During the process some were cajoled, some were threatened, and some cooperated gladly, but by the time the newspeople were released to their public McKenna and Sheeran were certain they knew to the smallest detail everything they had seen on the *Samuel I. Newhouse.*

It was four o'clock before McKenna arrived at police headquarters. Brunette, the mayor, and a man McKenna didn't know were waiting for him in Brunette's office, all seated around Brunette's desk. McKenna thought it looked like a card game where everyone was losing.

"Find out anything new?" Brunette asked.

"Except for who the passengers are, little we don't already know. I *can* tell you that Felipe and his boys are still smart, still crazy, still armed to the teeth, and there's still a lot of them."

McKenna reached across Brunette's desk to hand him the envelope. "Here's what Felipe wants," he said. He was surprised when the stranger, a distinguished-looking man in his fifties wearing a pin-striped suit, rose from his chair and extended his hand across Brunette's desk. "May I see that?" he asked.

"Who are you?" McKenna asked, a little offended by the brusque action.

"I'm sorry," Brunette said, without taking the offered envelope. "I should have made the introductions. This is Ashton Heresford, the national security adviser to the President."

Good time to set the tone, McKenna thought. "Pleased to meet you, Mr. Heresford. And sure you can see this, if Commissioner Brunette wants to show it to you."

Heresford's hand was instantly withdrawn as his mouth opened and closed a few times, but not a sound came out. Brunette smiled as he took the envelope, opened it, and removed a thick pack of papers. He began reading as Heresford remained standing in front of his desk.

"Take a seat, Mr. Heresford, unless you're prepared to publicly take over this situation and really be in charge in front of all the cameras," the mayor said.

Heresford looked at the mayor, astonished, but the mayor just smiled at him. "C'mon, sit down," he repeated. "You're blocking the air-conditioning and I'm sweating my balls off."

Heresford did as he was told, but he managed to restore that dignified look to his face before he sat down.

Brunette took a few minutes to read through Felipe's demands. When he was finished, he rearranged the papers in a neat pile and handed them to the mayor, who thumbed through the pages, squinting, before reaching into his pocket for his glasses. "Goddamn, how many pages is this thing?" he asked as he put on the glasses.

"Twenty-four, but it's not that hard to get through," Brunette answered. "Most of it consists of lists of names of people he wants released from jail in Peru or people he says the government in Peru captured or arrested, then executed. He wants 321 people released and 2,288 others accounted for. That's why it's so thick. Names, with the dates of arrest or disappearance."

The mayor started reading the document line by line, becoming more frustrated as he did so. "I'm having a hard time just getting out of the first paragraph. What is this guy, a terrorist or a lawyer?" the mayor complained. "Listen to this," he said as he read from the top page. " 'In view of the military, moral, and political advantage currently exercised by our military forces in New York, the Communist Party of Peru following the Shining Path of Jose Martinguez, hereinafter referred to as *Sendero Luminoso*, DEMANDS that the following fair and just concessions be made by the present illegal government of Peru, hereinafter referred to as the Government of Peru, acting alone or in conjunction with any governments interested in resolving the military impasse in New York Harbor.' ''

"Sort of reads like a mortgage, doesn't it?" McKenna observed. "Like he's holding the mortgage on this city."

"You read it?" the mayor asked, looking up at McKenna.

"Down to the smallest detail," McKenna answered. "It was even thicker when I got it because it included the list of hostages."

"What did you do with that?" Brunette asked.

"Dropped it off with the chief of detectives on my way up here. The Missing Persons Squad is going nuts with the inquiries from the families, so he was glad to get it."

"Good," Brunette said. "I'll give it to the press, too."

"I'll make a little bet with anyone who cares to take it," the mayor said. "I'll bet by tomorrow morning we're going to be hearing from a new pressure group calling themselves the Families of the Hostages or something like that."

Nobody cared to take the mayor's bet.

"I don't blame them for any pressure they put on us," McKenna said. "When you see the news tonight, you'll see those families have a lot to worry about."

"I guess the pressure goes with the job," the mayor said. "What else does he want?"

"He's made seven demands. A lot of what we expected, but little the City of New York can provide," McKenna said. "There are a few surprises in there, but some of his demands sound fairly reasonable, things he'd be able to sell to the American public."

"Give me one of his surprises, for instance," the mayor said.

"Okay, how's this? He demands that the capitalist money-grubbing shippers settle their dispute with his fellow members of the exploited working proletariat, the International Longshoremen's Association."

"That's just great," the mayor said as he slumped in his chair. "Bill Kearns gets to maul the shippers and the whole thing will play well in a labor town like this."

"Who is this Bill Kearns?" Heresford asked.

The mayor looked at Heresford like he was a total illiterate before he answered. "Bill Kearns is the president of the ILA whenever he's not in jail."

"In that case I see your problem," Heresford conceded.

"Unfortunately, he also wants two hundred and fifty million dollars, but he doesn't mention the United States government once. According to that," McKenna said, pointing to the packet of papers on the mayor's lap, "he wants it all from the government of Peru as reparation for war crimes, but he invites interested third-party nations to help in the resolution of the crisis."

"Isn't that us?" the mayor asked sarcastically. "He certainly managed to get our interest, didn't he?"

Heresford found his voice for the first time. "Naturally, the President will not expect the City of New York to pay that amount of money to a foreign terrorist group."

"You mean you think Peru is going to pay it so we can ship them back some rich terrorists to deal with?" the mayor asked. "I sort of doubt that."

Heresford was unfazed by the mayor's sarcasm. "Once we examine the military options—"

McKenna cut him off. "There are none," he said. "After anyone with a brain sees the defensive arrangements *Sendero* has made on those ferries, and then hears the things they plan to do if they are attacked, they'll come to the same conclusion."

"In any event, the military option has to be examined," Heresford said calmly. "General Sneadman is standing by at Fort Hamilton. He's the commanding officer of the Delta Force, and I propose to bring him the statements of the reporters and the films they made during their visit to the ferries—"

"We'll give you *copies* of the films," the mayor said, interrupting Heresford. "Just in case the army tries to do something stupid, I want to retain some evidence here that justifies my stand. I want you to know that I am against using force to retake those ferries."

"For your information, Mr. Mayor, General Sneadman is a marine general." Heresford paused to smile at Brunette and McKenna, and was happy to see them return his smile, in spite of themselves. "I expect that General Sneadman will reach the same conclusion. Then we will get on to the next phase, which is: How do we get *Sendero* out of town and still save some face for the United States government? Felipe has made it easier for us by addressing most of his demands to the government of Peru. So the next steps must be diplomatic. Extraordinary pressure must be brought to bear on the Peruvian government to meet whatever demands the American public will see as reasonable.''

"After you see Felipe's little documentary tonight, you'll realize that's going to be quite a few members of the American public,'' Brunette said. "From what we've learned, it's a propaganda showpiece.''

"I guess there's no question that the networks will run it?'' the mayor asked.

"None. I met with a few of their executives on the pier after the reporters got back, and they were already taking calls from sponsors,'' McKenna said. "If they didn't want to run it, I'd insist that they did. We'd look like the bad guys if Felipe started shooting hostages because he couldn't see his film on TV.''

"I see,'' Heresford observed. "Felipe has done well for himself. He has managed to commit murder, mayhem, and violence in your city, and also managed to make himself look like a legitimate revolutionary hero at the same time. He has both our government and the government of Peru in the box, so to speak.''

"We already know that,'' the mayor observed dryly. "Can you get the Peruvians to give in to his demands?''

"It will be expensive for us, but I think we can. After all, world public opinion will be against them by eight o'clock tonight.''

"What about the two hundred and fifty million dollars?'' the mayor asked. "Do the Peruvians have that kind of cash lying around?''

"Of course not,'' Heresford answered. "If it has to be paid, the money will come from us, naturally in the name of the Peruvian government. I anticipate that we'll advance the Peruvian government some type of credit.''

The mayor wasn't altogether happy with Heresford's appraisal. "Remember, when you say 'we,' you mean the U.S. government, right?'' he asked.

"Yes, the President has asked me to tell you that in appreciation of the support you have shown for his understandable reluctance to directly involve the federal government in this affair, he will try to push emergency legislation through Congress to cover all your costs.''

Heresford's answer appeared to satisfy the mayor and he looked like a new man for a moment. Then he remembered he was a politician in a position of some strength. He wanted more. "What about the B&O Railroad Bridge? Who's gonna pay to get that out of the Kill van Kull?"

"The federal government," Heresford answered smoothly, suddenly making himself a popular man.

Brunette decided to jump onto the merry-go-round while there was still a supply of brass rings. "How about the police overtime this whole thing is costing us?"

"The federal government," Heresford said.

The mayor had another idea. "How about—"

But Heresford cut him off by raising his hand. "Mr. Mayor, the President has authorized me to communicate to you that he will try to pay for everything within reason in connection with this fiasco. However, he did warn me to keep my hand on my wallet when I talked to you, or the federal government would wind up paying your entire budget."

The mayor took it as a compliment. "All right, as long as the President understands this is going to be an expensive proposition," he said, satisfied. Then he turned back to Mc-Kenna. "I'm sure we'll all study his demands later in detail, but can you briefly tell us what else Felipe wants?"

"It's pretty vague, which seems to me that he's leaving himself room for negotiation," McKenna said. "He mentions something about setting up a war-crimes tribunal and both sides allowing Amnesty International and the International Red Cross free access to territory controlled by each side."

"Christ, the American public is going to love that," Heresford said, shaking his head. "It just sounds so . . . What's the word I'm looking for?"

"So fair?" McKenna suggested.

"Yes, so fair," Heresford said, not liking the sound of it.

"It's bullshit, that's what it is," the mayor said. "Just smoke and mirrors. What he really wants is the two hundred and fifty million and that's it. If he manages to get some good press out of this, so much the better for him."

"No, Your Honor, he wants them both," Brunette said. "Without at least some favorable public opinion, the money's no good to him. He figures if he gets both and does manage to get back to Peru, public opinion will prevent our government from sending General Sneadman and his boys down to Peru to kick the shit out of him and get our money back."

"I don't know if that's even an option," Heresford said. "Intervening militarily in a faraway civil war where both sides seem repugnant to the American people would be a chancy maneuver, unless we managed to attain total victory very quickly.''

"What happens after we get him off our boats is none of my business,'' the mayor said. "What else does he want?''

"The return of the people we captured in Brighton Beach,'' McKenna said.

"We expected that,'' Brunette said. "I guess he doesn't know one of them has been talking to us, so we're gonna have to stall him on that one.''

"Does he mention any time frame before he does anything drastic?'' Heresford asked.

"No, but we sort of expected that, too,'' McKenna said. "We know he intends to take his time out there, and the food he ordered today proves that. He has to give the Colombians enough time and latitude to move their stuff into this country while we're otherwise occupied.''

"What do you think about the diesel fuel, Commissioner McKenna?'' Heresford asked. "Do you think it's possible he doesn't intend to take those ferries to JFK after all?''

"It's a clever red herring to keep us guessing. Everything we know still points to JFK.''

"I agree,'' Brunette said, closing that point of inquiry. "Has the administration any thoughts on what to do about the drug shipments that are sure to be coming here, Mr. Heresford?''

"Yes. Some pretty drastic courses of action are being rolled before the President for his consideration, and I'll let you know when a decision has been made.''

"That's it?'' the mayor said. "No hints?''

"No. No hints,'' Heresford answered, considering the matter closed as he turned back to McKenna. "Let's get back to the demands. You said there were seven and I believe you've only mentioned six.''

"I don't understand the last one completely myself,'' McKenna answered. Then he turned to the mayor. "Do you mind if I read it, Your Honor?''

"Go ahead,'' the mayor said, handing McKenna the pack of pages.

McKenna leafed through the pages until he found what he was looking for. "Here it is,'' he said as he began to read. " 'We reserve the right to request the presence of three persons to be named at a later time, with the understanding that such persons will voluntarily remain with the *Sendero Luminoso* forces currently in position in New York Harbor to ensure the safety of these forces after the present military position is evacuated. We will guarantee the safety and security of such persons as long as the *Sendero Luminoso* forces currently in position in New York Harbor are not attacked by the military forces of any nation.' "

"So he expects us to surrender another three hostages to him," Brunette said.

"Not surrender," McKenna answered. "He said they will *voluntarily* remain with them until he gets away."

"Anybody have any ideas on who he's going to ask for?" Heresford asked no one in particular.

"It would have to be three public figures, and pretty big ones at that," Brunette answered. "No one else would voluntarily put themselves in that kind of situation." Brunette shook his head. "Old Felipe sure seems to have covered all the bases," he said with a kind of admiration.

"Yeah, he's beating the stuffing out of us in our own ballpark," McKenna said. "But we might have a few surprises in store for him when we play in his backyard."

"Yes, Commissioner Brunette has explained the theory you and Colonel Savraada have on his plans," Heresford stated. "I have already informed the President and the National Security Council of the possibility that he can be taken when he gets to Peru, and some plans are being made. But Felipe's last demand might end whatever plans they're coming up with, depending on the importance of the three additional hostages he takes with him."

"All their plans are going to be so much hot air unless they can manage to get the Peruvian military straightened out and onboard," McKenna said.

"I believe they already know that and are taking it into consideration," Heresford said dryly. "Let's get back to where we are right now. Is it true that Felipe has appointed you as the negotiator for our side?"

"He calls me an intermediary. It's right at the end of his list of demands. Kind of makes me blush," McKenna said, handing the pack of papers to Heresford.

Heresford thumbed through the papers.

"It's the last paragraph before the list of names," McKenna said.

Heresford thought he found it. "Long live Chairman Gonzalo?" he asked, smiling snidely.

"Okay, the next-to-last paragraph," McKenna said.

Heresford read, obviously not liking what he was reading. "Let us all hear it," the mayor said.

Heresford didn't like that either, but he read the paragraph loudly. " 'Being familiar with, and recognizing the courage and integrity of, Assistant Commissioner Brian McKenna of the New York City Police Department, we designate him as the only intermediary acceptable to *Sendero Luminoso* in the ensuing and necessary negotiations to resolve this matter.' "

He handed the pack of papers back to McKenna and said, "No offense intended, Commissioner, but that is the first matter that will have to be resolved with Felipe. It's very clever of him, totally in keeping with his plan to keep the U.S. government out of the negotiations, and it insulates us from any embarrassment sure to ensue, but you must realize that you are not equipped to handle the negotiations."

"I don't know," Brunette said. "It makes sense to me, and I'd think you should be happy with his choice. Like you said, it keeps your boss out of it."

"It does," Heresford said. "But these negotiations will necessarily be delicate, and should be handled by a person skilled in diplomacy so we don't wind up giving up more than we have to."

"I presume you mean a person like yourself," the mayor said.

"Not necessarily me, but someone like me," Heresford answered defensively. "We must remember that, appearances aside, whoever it is will be negotiating on behalf of the United States government and the government of Peru."

"Wish whatever you like, Mr. Heresford," McKenna said. "But as far as I can see, it's me. Of course I'm going to take all the advice I can get from yourself or people like you, but it's still me."

"We'll have to see about that," Heresford said. He wanted to say more, but they were interrupted by McKenna's phone ringing in his pocket. He answered it while everyone in the room watched him intently. "Yeah, Felipe. What is it?" he asked.

"Sorry to bother you, Commissioner McKenna," Felipe said, sounding contrite. "I'm sure you're very busy."

"I can spare the time. What do you want?"

"Well, I can see your men on shore are busy loading your boats with the items we requested, and I must admit I forgot something. I try to think of everything, but sometimes it's so difficult. We've run into a little emergency here, so I'd like to amend the deal I offered your reporters.''

"I'm sorry to hear that, Felipe. What do you need?"

"I'm informed we've just run out of toilet paper. When your men have delivered the supplies I requested, could you possibly load up one of the boats with some toilet paper and paper towels?''

"Sure," McKenna said. "That is something of an emergency. How about I throw in some sanitary napkins and Pampers, too?"

"Good thinking," Felipe said. "Naturally, I will send the boat back with an additional ten passengers to compensate you for your trouble and expense.''

"You've got a deal. Anything else on your mind?"

"Yes, as a matter of fact I was wondering if you'd be free at four o'clock tomorrow to discuss some of our mutual problems. I thought that should give you enough time to contact other interested parties so that we would have at least an idea of where we're going.''

"Four o'clock would be fine," McKenna said. "My place or yours?"

"Actually I'd prefer we meet at Elaine's. Tomorrow baked Idaho brook trout is her special. Have you ever tried it?"

"Yeah, it's pretty good," McKenna said.

"Yes, but under the circumstances, I think I would feel rather unsafe walking the streets of New York, so why don't we meet here, on the *Samuel I. Newhouse*?"

"Fine. What's the travel arrangements?"

"Naturally, for the sake of appearances, I don't expect you to travel by lifeboat like a common reporter. If you give me your word that your people won't be trying anything underhanded while we're talking, you can get here by either police launch or helicopter, but please tell me which it will be.''

"You've got my word. I think I'll come by boat. You've sort of killed my love of flying. Do you mind if I bring my secretary?"

"Not at all. I'll see you at four."

"One more thing, Felipe," McKenna said. "I'm running into a bit of a problem with your selection of me as the person you want to talk to. Right now I have with me Mr. Ashton Heresford. He's the—''

"I know who he is," Felipe said curtly.

"Would you talk to him for a moment and see if you can work something out?"

"Of course not," Felipe said. The line went dead.

McKenna put the phone back in his pocket and turned to Heresford, who was eyeing him suspiciously. "He says he's very sorry, but he doesn't want to talk to you," McKenna said.

Chapter 41 McKenna left Brunette's office feeling very much in charge, but not sure he was happy with that development.

"Any calls?" was the first thing McKenna asked Camilia as he walked into his office.

"A few. Mr. Shields and Lieutenant Picciarelli both called. They wanted to talk to you, but they also wanted to talk to each other, so I put them in touch. Apparently they're cooking up something together in Mr. Shields's office right now, but they asked me to tell you they'll be right over to see you."

So the Russian connection is working out, McKenna thought, not sure yet exactly what it meant.

Camilia leafed through the message sheets on her desk, throwing all of them away but one, which didn't bother McKenna in the slightest. He had come to realize that, if it was important, she would tell him. If not, she wouldn't, and she was possibly the best judge of exactly what was important. "Chief McNamara would like you to call him at your convenience," she said before she threw that message sheet in the trash can. "He said he heard that they're warming up their planes in Colombia."

To be expected, McKenna thought. Nothing I can do about that. He filed the message in the back of his mind, having something else to discuss with Camilia. "Do you take shorthand, Camilia?" he asked.

Camilia looked at him hard without answering, making him

feel foolish for asking such a question of the most competent secretary in the world.

"I'm sorry," McKenna continued, "but I need you tomorrow and I may have placed you in some danger. I'll be going out to the ferries to talk to Felipe and I'd like you to be there. I know I have no right to ask you to volunteer, but I'd like you there to take down every word said and to give me your impressions."

"Please get to the point, Commissioner," Camilia said.

I thought I just did, McKenna thought. What else could she be thinking? More pay? A promotion? "I'm sorry, Miss Wright," he said. "I don't understand. What else would you like to know?"

She looked at him like he was a dunce. "I don't know what you must be thinking," she said. "The point is, will I be on TV if I go with you?"

"I guess so," McKenna said. "Probably on every station in the country."

"Well, I have to know things like that," she said as she emptied her top drawer of a cosmetic pack, a brush, and hair spray and shoved them in her pocketbook. She surprised McKenna when she said, "I have to go right now. I'll be back in a few hours, okay?"

She was at the door before McKenna got a chance to ask, "Where are you going?"

She paused at the door to look at him for a second, giving McKenna the impression that she was checking to see if his dunce cap was where it belonged, squarely in place on the top of his head. "To Macy's, of course," she said. "I haven't bought a new dress in ages, and I can't be seen on national TV wearing just any old rag. Hold down the fort, will you?"

She was gone before McKenna could say another word, which made him feel fortunate. No reason to further expose my stupidity, he thought. Macy's, of course. Why couldn't I figure that out?

McKenna went into his office and poured himself a cup of his always hot, always fresh coffee and sat down at his desk. He was still enjoying his coffee when Shields and Picciarelli came in.

"I hope this is good news," McKenna said. "I've had enough bad news for one day."

"You tell me," Shields said. "Is it good news that Felipe definitely is, or at least was, a Russian spy?"

"I don't know. Is it?" McKenna asked.

"It opens up some possibilities with widespread international implications, but we have to find a way to use the information to our advantage," Shields said.

"Then pour yourselves a cup of coffee and enlighten me," McKenna said. "But try to be patient. Camilia just informed me in her own little way that I'm not thinking too good today."

Picciarelli savored a sip, then said, "I polygraphed Joe Gleason and everything he told you is the truth, as far as he knows it. He does believe that Felipe is a Russian agent and he did hear him speaking Russian. As instructed, I gave that information to Mr. Shields for further investigation. Then I went to Jameson's to check out what I could on Gleason's story."

"Don't tell me the same bartender is still there after more than ten years," McKenna said.

"I won't. Keith is one of the owners now, doing a pretty good business there. Sharp guy with a good memory for faces. He remembered the whole Gleason incident, remembered getting him out of his handcuffs in his men's room. Then I showed him a picture of Felipe. He said he hadn't thought of it before, but he was pretty sure that was the guy who had followed Gleason into the men's room."

"What about the Russian Gleason was following?"

"Keith says he never came in again after Gleason got bonked. So I brought Keith to see Mr. Shields," Picciarelli said, then turned to Shields.

"I checked our records and found that the guy Gleason was assigned to follow was named Leonid Kantorovich. Listed as the second cultural attaché to the Soviet Mission to the UN, one of their usual KGB positions. Showed Keith his picture. 'That was the guy,' Keith said. I did some checking and found that Leonid Kantorovich is now the military attaché at the Russian embassy in Berlin, which leads me to believe that he's still KGB, or whatever they're calling themselves in these enlightened times."

"What about the East German? The one Gleason saw Felipe meeting with in Brighton Beach?" McKenna asked.

"Checked on him too," Shields said. "Werner Bachmann. Called a friend in the German intelligence service and it turns out they're also very interested in Bachmann, especially since they went through the records of STASI, the old East German intelligence service. Turns out Bachmann is a Volga River German, those people who lived in Russia before World War II. His father served in the Soviet army, fighting the Germans, and then Werner shows up in Berlin in 1962 and, somehow, the East Germans put him in STASI. But the records the Germans have now indicate that Bachmann was KGB, all the way."

"So where is he?"

"Only the Russians know. Remember when the last East German president fled to the Soviet Union?"

"Erich Honeker? Sure."

"Well, Bachmann was with him. Maybe arranged the whole thing. The Germans say they've built up a pretty good espionage case against Bachmann and have requested his extradition, but the Russians tell them they never heard of the guy."

"So they're protecting their man. Good for them," McKenna said.

"Think about it," Shields said. "It's good for us, too."

McKenna did think about it. Why is it good for us that Bachmann, if he's still alive, is probably in Russia? Well, first of all, if we were to accuse the Russians of complicity in this affair, the fact that he's living in Russia would tend to confirm that, once we laid out what we know to them. But why would the Russians be pulling a stunt like this in the first place, especially when they're trying to get loans and credits from us right now? Certainly doesn't seem like a good business practice. So why? McKenna thought a few moments more without coming up with the answer, much to Shields's obvious delight.

"I told you I'm slow today," McKenna said. "Give me a hint."

"Sure," Shields said, smugly. "More than ten years."

"More than ten years? That's the hint?"

"Yep."

More than ten years? McKenna thought. Well, Felipe hasn't been seen around here in more than ten years, and he must have been in Peru most of that time. The Soviets were exporting revolution all over the world then, and the *Sendero* thing must have pissed them off when they made Mao their hero. So they sent Felipe there to straighten out *Sendero*'s thought processes when they felt he was burned in the U.S. by Gleason. Pretty good thinking on their part. Felipe's risen fast in *Sendero*, and the prisoners we have never mentioned thinking he wasn't Peruvian like he wants everyone to believe.

But a lot of changes have taken place in Russia since he went to Peru. Maybe his bosses forgot about him or, worse yet, this whole thing could be the work of one of those big-shot KGB hard-liners it seems are always popping up over there, looking to embarrass the new Russian government and get that old Cold War going again. But what does all that have to do with Bachmann?

Then it came to him. "I guess you got a look at some birth certificates, didn't you?"

Shields smiled. "Yep. I got copies of both the forged birth certificates he gave DMV and Social Security to set up his new identities. Gave them to our Documents Section. Know what they said?"

"Excellent KGB forgeries," McKenna answered.

"It's a sure thing. They've seen the type before."

"And we can assume that if he went to the trouble to buy two houses that we know of under two different names, then, for whatever reason, there might be more houses and more identities."

"Exactly what I thought," Shields said.

"And we're looking for some more of his real estate over-looking the Williamsburg Bridge and the Verrazano-Narrows Bridge."

"Which he might have bought for the KGB back in the eighties, or maybe he bought some on his own. Rather recently, I'm thinking," Shields said.

"But it makes no difference when," McKenna said. "For whatever reason, the KGB had him buying houses here, probably for use as safe houses, and they supplied him with the ID to make the purchases legal. Someone in the KGB must know the names on whatever other birth certificates they gave him. If we knew what other names Felipe's been using, we could track down what real estate he owns here."

"So it is good that Werner Bachmann is in Russia, isn't it?" Shields suggested, smiling.

"It's great," McKenna said, surprising himself with how excited he was over Bachmann's choice of nation of domicile. "Once we lay our cards on the table, the Russians are gonna go into a panic. If they have any doubts we're telling the truth about Felipe, they're gonna drag in Werner Bachmann and Leonid Kantorovich. Matter of fact, we should insist on it. Either one of them could lay out the KGB people they were working for in those days and explain exactly what Felipe was supposed to be doing here."

"All this is good, but we have to make sure the Russians tell us," Picciarelli said.

"They will," McKenna said as he picked up his phone and started dialing.

"Who are you calling?" Shields asked.

It was McKenna's turn to be the bright guy. "Do I have to do all the thinking around here?" he asked. "I'm calling the mayor, of course. He's got the President's home phone number."

Chapter 42 JULY 30, PORT JEFFERSON, NEW YORK—Just after dawn, Seymor Cranston was the object of very intensive scrutiny as he left his housing development and turned left, heading for the Long Island Expressway. Five miles later he pulled into a 7-Eleven located near the expressway entrance. Without looking around, he left his van and went in, apparently another unconcerned commuter fortifying himself for the long trip to the city.

Tavlin walked in behind him, only to satisfy his curiosity. He couldn't understand why Cranston had betrayed his country. All indications were that Cranston was a bright man, a man with a family and an excellent education, a man who had given up a good job with a secure financial future to somehow advance Felipe's plans.

It made no sense to Tavlin. He knew it was money, of course, but just money didn't explain Cranston's treachery to Tavlin's satisfaction. So Tavlin wanted to hear Cranston speak and see how he acted with other people.

The short stop surprised Tavlin. He had expected an introverted loner seeking revenge on the world for some perceived suffering and abuse that had been heaped on him all his life. Instead he got Cranston, apparently a courteous and smiling

soul who chatted with everyone in the store, was friendly with
the salesclerk, and even touted Tavlin on the taste and aroma
of the nondairy creamers sold by the store with the coffee.
After they prepared their coffees together, Tavlin paid and left
while Cranston continued chatting with the salesclerk, both spy
and immigrant employee complaining about the disruption that
jerk in the harbor's activities had caused in the Mets' home-
game schedule.

Cranston finally came out, got in his van, and led his caravan westbound, toward the city.

It didn't take long for any empathy Tavlin might have felt
for Cranston to evaporate. The man was infuriating, driving in
the center lane at exactly the legal speed limit, fifty-five miles
an hour in the light traffic with everyone else passing him like
he was standing still—everyone except for the cops in the
three unmarked cars trailing a half mile behind him. They were
using the locating transmitter that had been installed in Cranston's rear bumper the night before to keep track of him. Without seeing his van again during the trip, they followed the
beeps to the employee parking lot of the Allied Maintenance
building at Kennedy Airport. They arrived in time to see Cranston lock his van and enter the building.

McKenna was also up early. By 7:00 A.M. he had already
showered, dressed, and read the newspapers. He smiled at an
editorial in the *Times* that just about lauded Felipe as a grand
humanitarian for freeing the 110 women and children from
peril, paying scant attention to the fact that it had been Felipe,
after all, who had placed them in danger in the first place.

The *Times* editorial piece also had some good things to say
about Felipe's documentary which had been run on all the
networks the night before. The editorial called for an international investigation into the government atrocities it portrayed, something McKenna knew would play right into
Felipe's hands if his demands were made public.

Over breakfast, McKenna reviewed Sheeran's report on the
interrogation of the 110 hostages that had been released by
Felipe the day before. All of them were women or children.

The freed hostages were able to tell almost nothing Mc-
Kenna hadn't already known or suspected. They were a mix
of people from both the *Samuel I. Newhouse* and the *Andrew
J. Barberi* and said they had been kept under constant guard

on the ferries, huddled in the middle of the salon deck of both boats. After the ferries had been taken by *Sendero*, they had heard the shooting when the police launch was sunk, but none of them had witnessed the unloading of weapons and supplies from the cabin cruiser to the ferries since they had all been ordered to lie on the floor and couldn't see out the windows.

What McKenna did learn from the interviews was that there were approximately twenty-five Senderistas on each boat and, more important, that they had increased their communications ability when they confiscated cellular phones belonging to the passengers.

Working from the list of hostages, Sheeran had found by calling their families that fourteen passengers on the boats had mobile phones. He got the phone numbers and those phone frequencies were being monitored, but no calls had been made or received on those phones since the ferries were taken.

After reading Sheeran's report twice, McKenna reread the report that had been prepared for him by General Sneadman. The film footage taken by the newspaper helicopter had been thoroughly analyzed and every box and crate that *Sendero* had unloaded from their cabin cruiser was identified by a military logistics specialist as containing either rations, Claymore mines, M-16s, hand grenades, small-arms ammunition, 106-mm recoilless rifle rounds, or Stinger missiles.

Sneadman's report was comprehensive, but there was one thing missing from the *Sendero* inventory, the thing that McKenna knew Felipe needed for his backup escape plan.

McKenna was mulling over the possibilities and trying to put himself in Felipe's head when Tavlin called. "You might find this interesting," the inspector reported. "We've got Cranston at Kennedy Airport."

"Where in the airport?"

"He's operating a tractor at the edge of Runway Four."

McKenna couldn't help smiling and felt like laughing outright. "Where are you?" he asked.

"In the control tower."

"I'll be right there."

"There's more about this that might interest you," Tavlin said.

"I'm sure there is, but I've got to see this. Tell me the rest when I get there."

"Suit yourself," Tavlin said. "I'll have a Port Authority police car meet you at the second checkpoint."

"Half an hour," McKenna answered before he hung up and left, walking as quickly as he could without running.

Both McKenna and Pao were impressed by the measures Brunette had instituted at Kennedy Airport. It wasn't just closed, it was locked tight and made into a fortress. Concrete barriers had been placed across two lanes of the Van Wyck Expressway at the airport entrance and the third lane was blocked by a large Emergency Service truck. McKenna could see that there was another similar roadblock a couple of hundred yards farther up the expressway. The first checkpoint was manned by a couple of Port Authority cops, strongly complemented by fifteen Emergency Service cops carrying Mini-14 automatic rifles.

There were three cars and a delivery van in front of them in line. "Want me to swing around to the front of the line?" Pao asked.

"No, let's wait. I wanna see how they do this."

So they waited in line and watched. One car at a time, the Port Authority cops checked the identification of the occupants before searching the rear seat and trunk of the car. Then the Emergency Service truck pulled forward and the cleared car was permitted to drive to the second checkpoint while the Emergency Service truck backed up, again blocking the roadway. The procedure was repeated for each car waiting and took only a couple of minutes. The delivery van was another matter, and it took the Port Authority cops three minutes to search it. While McKenna and Pao were waiting they were spotted by the Emergency Service cops. Their lieutenant came over and saluted McKenna. "Why don't you just pass through, Commissioner?" he suggested. "You don't have to wait here."

"Wouldn't miss this show," McKenna answered, self-consciously returning the salute. "How many people we got in the airport?"

"Ten sergeants and ninety cops a tour, plus another hundred from the Port Authority police. Got the other airport entrances blocked just like this one and the rest of the men are spread around the airport fence."

"Heavy weapons?"

"Lots. Do you think he's still gonna try to take a plane here?"

McKenna really didn't think so and sounded like a real boss

when he answered, "Maybe." Feeling bad about the lie, he wanted to change the subject. "How many people came in here so far today?" he asked.

"Maybe five hundred. All airport employees or people making deliveries. But nobody's doing much of anything in there and I hear they're enjoying themselves."

The delivery van in front of them was cleared and passed through. "Thanks for the information," McKenna said as Pao pulled through the checkpoint behind the delivery van. At the second checkpoint McKenna saw that the process was being repeated again, but there was also a Port Authority police car parked on the other side of the concrete barriers. The driver got out of the car and waved to them.

"Are we gonna wait again?" Pao asked.

"Not this time."

McKenna was amazed at how much could be surveyed from the control tower. They could see virtually everywhere in the airport.

There were fifteen air-traffic controller stations in the room, but only two were occupied, by men looking at mostly nothing on their radar screens. Tavlin was standing at the window facing the runways, looking through binoculars. A Port Authority lieutenant was standing next to him, wearing a uniform with the sharpest creases McKenna had ever seen and looking too young to even be a cop, no less a lieutenant.

Tavlin hadn't seen McKenna enter the room, but the Port Authority lieutenant did and he nudged Tavlin's shoulder. To McKenna, it appeared that the inspector had put on ten years in the last week, looking haggard and tired with dark circles under his eyes.

Tavlin introduced Lieutenant Kevin Ward of the Port Authority police and added that Ward seemed to know more of what was going on in the airport than anybody else.

"Wanna take a look at our boy?" Tavlin asked, offering McKenna the binoculars.

"That's what I'm here for," McKenna said, looking out the window.

"That's him, on the tractor mowing the grass at the edge of the last runway," Tavlin said.

McKenna could see him. Cranston was the only one in that direction who seemed to be doing much of anything. He raised the binoculars to his eyes and took a closer look. Cranston was riding his tractor on the far side of the runway and McKenna could see that he had already done quite a bit of work that day. A thirty-yard strip of grass parallel to the runway had already been cut, and it looked like he had another thirty yards to do. Beyond that, the grass ended and the bulrushes took over the landscape. They were thick and high and stretched another fifty yards beyond the runway, ending at Jamaica Bay.

McKenna focused on Cranston and could see nothing special about the man. "What more do you know about him?" he asked Tavlin.

"More than his mother does. Comes from a broken home. Only child. Married, wife and two kids, a daughter and a son, ages seven and five. His mortgage is paid up and he's got a great credit rating, always pays his bills on time. Has fourteen thousand in the bank and another forty thousand or so tied up in his pension plan at Brookhaven Labs. He left it there, so I think he's planning on going back after this is over. Takes the family to Europe every summer to his little cottage in San Sebastián in Spain, also paid for. Speaks Spanish and French. Hobbies are sailing and flying model airplanes."

"So you did a credit check on him, checked with the courts, and ran the whole family's passports."

"Yep. On the surface he looks like a pretty ordinary guy for a genius," Tavlin said. "He's got a lot of toys, but he always made a good salary."

McKenna was impressed by what Tavlin had accomplished in a day, but realized that it just involved looking at documents and credit receipts. However, Tavlin seemed too smug and McKenna was sure he had more. "What do you know that his mother doesn't?" McKenna asked, waiting for the punch line.

Obviously, it was the question Tavlin wanted to hear. "She doesn't know that she's a very wealthy woman, and she probably never will," Tavlin answered. "She had a minor stroke in 1981 and has been in a nursing home near Seymor's house ever since. She gave him power of attorney and he set up a money market account for her in Spain. From 1981 to 1984 he built her up quite a nest egg every summer. All cash deposits, all under ten thousand dollars, all perfectly legal. He does her taxes and he makes sure to declare the interest."

"How much?"

"Stands at close to a quarter million right now."

"Very clever," McKenna said, impressed at the precautions

Cranston had taken. "From '81 to '84 he's selling secrets to
Felipe, and he doesn't want to show the cash. So he gets it
when his mother dies."

"That's the way it looks."

"Uncover any recent financial transactions?"

"Nope. Either Felipe's blackmailing him or he promised
him a bundle when this is over."

"Blackmail, I'd say," McKenna ventured. "Otherwise he
would have taken his money out of the Brookhaven Labs pension fund. What I don't understand is how he could start a
new job and manage to be working at the exact spot we think
Felipe's gonna bring the ferries to. He must have some pretty
big connections at Allied Maintenance."

"He can go anywhere he wants in the airport, and it's not
because of who he knows. It's because of who he is. You see,
last October Seymor took the test and became a licensed exterminator."

Exterminator? McKenna thought while Tavlin watched him,
enjoying himself. What's that got to do with anything? Of
course, being a biochemist, he'd have no trouble with the test.
But why? Why is he an exterminator working for Allied Maintenance with the run of the airport? "Bugs on the runway?"
he asked, weakly.

"Nope. Birds. Seagulls, to be exact."

Seagulls? Of course, McKenna thought. Always a problem
for any airport on the water. They breed in the bulrushes and
cause damage to planes taking off and landing. Heard stories
of them getting sucked into the engines and cracking cockpit
glass when planes hit them in the air. Think they even caused
a few accidents. "Okay, seagulls," McKenna said, feeling like
he was finally stating the obvious. "Tell me more."

Tavlin turned to Ward. "Tell him, Kevin."

It was the right question for the right man. "Last year there
were one hundred and thirty-nine documented instances of
damage caused to aircraft resulting from a midair collision
with birds in flight in the proximity of the airport. Most of
these birds were identified as seagulls," Ward said. "The task
of discouraging the birds from nesting in the airport used to
fall on the Port Authority police. We used to shoot birds and
destroy the nests and eggs. As you might imagine, we received
some rather unfavorable publicity for our efforts, including a
few lawsuits from the Sierra Club and the Audubon Society.

Then Allied Maintenance told us they might have someone with a better way."

"Cranston?"

"Seymor Cranston, licensed exterminator and biochemist. He said he had developed a seagull repellent on his own and wanted to test it out. The Allied management was a little skeptical, but they came to us to see if we wanted to try it. We did."

"And the results?" McKenna asked.

"Inconclusive at first, but he seems to be getting some promising results lately, and this is the nesting season. So far this year we've had only thirty-three planes damaged, and the year is more than half over. The next month will tell."

"But nobody's been shooting birds or crushing eggs, right?" McKenna asked.

"That's the good part. He's doing it without publicity, which is exactly what the Port Authority wants. Better yet, whenever he's not busy spraying he mows the grass around the runways. He's a real good deal for Allied."

"What hours does he work?"

"I think the deal he has is forty hours a week, any way he wants to break it up," Ward said. "Most of the time, I see him in the daytime, but I have seen him working nights a few times. Says it's easier to check the gulls at night because they don't like to fly in the dark."

"You know him?" McKenna asked.

"Spoke to him a few times. Always thought he was a nice guy."

"I got close to him today and that's the impression I got," Tavlin added. "Guess you can never tell about people."

"Can you figure out why he'd need a license to drive big commercial vehicles?" McKenna asked Ward.

"Sure. He needs it to transport his chemicals. He uses Allied's big hazardous materials truck."

"And where does he keep his stuff?"

"See that steel shed over there?" Ward asked, pointing.

"Yeah, I see it," McKenna said, raising the binoculars to his eyes.

It was a good-sized shed, a little smaller than a one-car garage, set at the spot where the bulrushes began on the far side of Runway Four Right. McKenna smiled when he saw the international hazardous materials symbol painted on the side of the shed. That would discourage any visitors, he thought. "You got a key for it?"

"No. Want me to check with Allied?"

"I don't think so." McKenna answered, turning to Tavlin. "You got somebody who can get in there without damaging the locks?"

"Sure. Gaspar should be able to do it."

Good choice, McKenna thought. One of Gaspar's duties in TARU was to install the electronic surveillance devices and wiretaps for the detective bureau, which frequently entailed getting around some locks. Gaspar always succeeded. "Can you have him here tonight?" McKenna asked.

"You want him, he'll be here. What do you expect to find in there?"

"About seventy-five parachutes, I hope."

"Parachutes?" Tavlin and Ward asked at the same time.

It was McKenna's turn to be the smart guy. "Think about it," he suggested while he thought it over himself, hoping he was right.

It has to be, McKenna thought. Felipe doesn't have the parachutes with him now, and we know he went to a lot of trouble training his men to jump. That's why he let that news helicopter photograph his men unloading their supplies on the ferry. He wanted us to know about his firepower, but not the parachutes. That's something he wants to be a surprise in case his men fail to take the Iquitos Airport on time, since most military planners will acknowledge there's nothing much worse than jumping from a plane when that's what your enemies on the ground expect you to do.

McKenna watched Tavlin's methodical mind at work as he thought over the theory. Then the inspector smiled. "They're in there, or they will be soon," he said as if it were an absolute fact. "It's the only thing that makes sense. It's Seymor who's gonna provide them and probably mark the landing site for him so he'll know just where to bring the boats in. You can figure Felipe will be coming at night so we don't see him loading his chutes."

"All of this opens up some possibilities for us, doesn't it?" McKenna asked innocently.

The question showed McKenna something about human nature. He saw that even a nice man like Tavlin was capable of a perfectly evil smile. "Sure does," the perfect inspector answered.

Chapter 43

After leaving the airport, it was a morning and afternoon of meetings for McKenna. First he went to Brunette's office to report and found him there with General Sneadman, the commander of the Delta Force.

McKenna was impressed with Sneadman. Although the general was casually dressed in civilian clothes, everything about him suggested who he was. He had that something, but he couldn't claim credit for all of it. God had given him a helping hand. Tall, muscular, and ramrod straight, he looked every inch the leader of men. But that was just the start. His intelligence and personality did the rest. He seemed to be a shy man until he had something to say, but when he spoke it was obvious that he was used to being in charge.

From the outset, Sneadman made it clear that one thing he didn't want to be in charge of was any mission to retake the ferries, which was right in line with McKenna's and Brunette's thinking. The general stated that he was merely there to present the military option, but suggested it be used only as a last resort. He had studied past *Sendero* actions and was convinced that Felipe would do everything he said he would in the event of attack. Taking into account the dedication of Felipe's men, the number and type of weapons they had at their disposal, and the fact that there were still 604 hostages onboard the two boats, he predicted a disaster in the event that force was used.

Then Sneadman surprised both McKenna and Brunette when he went on to say that he was still willing to undertake the operation if ordered to do so, as long as his objections were noted on the record. Without specifically describing his plan, he stated that he expected a casualty rate of 50 percent among his attacking force, a large number of dead hostages, and he still thought the ferries might wind up at the bottom of the harbor anyway.

After listening to Sneadman's numbers, McKenna and Brunette felt no desire to listen to his plan, which was just fine with the general. As he said, he was merely there to present the military option and he wanted to make sure they understood the exact risks involved before they considered using it.

After Sneadman left, McKenna briefed Brunette on Cranston's activities at the airport. Brunette found the implications to be fascinating, but suggested waiting until Tavlin found out if the parachutes were really there before deciding on a course of action. Then he gave McKenna his dance card for the day, all of which was designed to prepare him for his meeting with Felipe at four that afternoon.

First up at 10:00 A.M. was Bill Kearns, the president of the International Longshoremen's Association. From eleven to one was Cristobal Cervantes, the Peruvian ambassador to the United States. Both of these meetings were to take place in McKenna's office. Then there was to be a change of venue. One-thirty to three was lunch at city hall with Ashton Heresford, the mayor, and Brunette.

The scheduling made sense to McKenna. First try talking to Kearns to have him remove himself and his union as a point of contention in the negotiations with *Sendero*. Next he would hear what the Peruvians were willing to do to comply with *Sendero*'s demands. The wrap-up belonged to Heresford, the national security adviser to the President. It fell on him to make up the difference between what the Peruvians were willing to give and what Felipe wanted before he would leave the harbor.

"Heresford's gonna tell you anyway, but I think you should know that Felipe might be very cranky at your meeting today," Brunette said.

"Wonderful. Why's that?"

"Because between two and four this morning aircraft from the USS *Abraham Lincoln* shot down twelve planes off the coast of Colombia."

The news made McKenna smile. "So we've stepped up our drug interdiction efforts?"

"Considerably. We had an AWAC up to spot them and the pilots all had the registration numbers from the DEA informant. Not one of the drug-runners got through."

"I didn't see anything in the papers about it."

"And you won't. Smugglers don't file flight plans, so officially it never happened."

"Yeah, Felipe's gonna be cranky all right. I'll bet his financiers will want his blood over this once he gets out of here."

McKenna could see it was going to be another long and arduous day for the new assistant commissioner of police, but also realized that Brunette was right about one thing: It sure beat hitting golf balls all day in Florida.

Chapter 44   The weather had taken one of those quick July turns so common in New York, changing from miserable, hot, and sunny to miserable, warm, and wet. There had been no sign of rain when McKenna and Camilia Wright boarded the police launch at Wall Street, but it started to drizzle just as the sergeant operating the launch put the boat in neutral and let the tide carry it to the rear deck of the ferry. Wright instantly produced two collapsible umbrellas from her bulky briefcase and offered one to McKenna.

McKenna accepted the umbrella without comment and opened it without bothering to ask himself what Camilia was doing with two umbrellas on what had promised to be a sunny day. He had come to expect that Camilia would always be perfectly prepared for any eventuality.

There were eight Senderistas waiting for them on the rear deck of the ferry. Two were manning a recoilless rifle, two stood ready at an M-60 machine gun aimed at the launch, and the other four were just generally looking menacing with their M-16s pointed at the cop on the bow of the Harbor launch. As it drifted closer, one of the Senderistas slung his rifle over his shoulder and threw a line to the cop on the bow. The cop caught it and pulled the launch in until the bow touched the rear of the ferry. Then the Senderista threw another line down to McKenna on the rear deck of the launch, surprising him. McKenna dropped his umbrella and barely caught the line.

As McKenna pulled the stern of the launch in, Felipe appeared on the rear deck of the ferry. He was perfectly dressed for the occasion as a yachtsman receiving some visitors to his vessel, wearing white pants, a white shirt, and a navy blue blazer. As McKenna secured the stern line, Felipe said something to his men and they lowered their weapons. Then he bent down at the edge of the deck and offered his hand, asking, "May I help you aboard?"

McKenna just looked at him, inclined to refuse all help. But not Camilia. The rear deck of the ferry was still a foot higher than the rail of the police launch and she was not one to quibble over proprieties. "Yes, thank you," she said and handed Felipe her umbrella. Felipe gave it to one of his men, and he stood on the deck next to Felipe, holding the umbrella over Camilia on the launch below. Then Camilia passed her briefcase up to Felipe, stood on the rail of the launch, took Felipe's hand, and he lifted her onboard. Next Felipe offered his hand to McKenna as Camilia picked up her briefcase and adjusted her dress.

"No, thanks, I can make it by myself," McKenna said, aware that newsmen on the Brooklyn shore must be photographing the whole scene with telephoto lenses.

"Of course," Felipe said, smiling as he withdrew his hand and stood back.

McKenna stood on the rail of the launch, placed his hands on the deck of the ferry, and vaulted onboard. Then he took a handkerchief from his pocket and wiped the deck grime off his hands as Felipe watched, still smiling. He waited until McKenna had put his handkerchief away before he extended his hand again. "A pleasure to finally meet you, Commissioner McKenna," he said.

"Likewise, I guess," McKenna said as he shook Felipe's hand. "But why don't you just call me McKenna and forget the commissioner crap?"

"Fine. A pleasure to finally meet you, McKenna."

Felipe then turned to Camilia and offered his hand. Camilia took it.

"This is my secretary, Camilia Wright," McKenna said.

"Delighted to meet you, Miss Wright," Felipe said, the picture of continental hospitality. "I hope you don't think it presumptuous of me to say that is a lovely dress you're wearing."

McKenna wouldn't have thought it possible, but Camilia actually blushed. Like Felipe, she was suitably dressed for a nautical occasion, wearing a prim navy blue business suit with brass buttons, and a white scarf. Damn, McKenna thought. It *is* a lovely dress. Why hadn't I bothered to tell her that?

"No, I don't mind," Camilia said, taking the time to shoot McKenna a reproachful look. "So nice of you to say so."

"Why don't we make ourselves comfortable inside?" Felipe asked as he led the way inside to the main cabin.

"What about the launch?" McKenna asked.

Felipe turned around and looked at the three cops on the Harbor launch. All three had pistols in holsters on their belts, but Felipe seemed unconcerned. "You can give them whatever instructions you like," he said. "They can wait for you here, or cast off and await your signal to return."

McKenna knew that Felipe's well-armed men could counter any move the cops might make and he appreciated the small gesture of respect for him, but he wanted to avoid any possible confrontations. He signaled to the cops to cast off and they began untying the lines as he and Camilia followed Felipe into the main cabin of the ferry.

There was only one other Senderista in the large cabin, which McKenna took as another sign of respect, especially since neither he nor Camilia had been searched. In any event, he had left his own pistol onboard the launch, but could see that Felipe was also unarmed. There were no bulges under his jacket indicating possession of any kind of weapon. As they followed Felipe, McKenna took note of the control table set up in the center of the cabin, manned by the lone Senderista.

Taking care not to step on any of the wires, McKenna also saw the door leading to the engine room that had been damaged by explosives when *Sendero* took control of the ferry away from Gus.

Felipe stopped just past the middle of the cabin. A card table had been set up between two benches that faced each other. There was a portable radio on the table, a coffeepot, milk, sugar, and three cups. "I hope these arrangements will be all right," he said as he turned and faced McKenna and Camilia. "Coffee, anyone?"

"Fine by me," McKenna said. "Black, please."

"Milk and sugar for me, please," Wright said.

Felipe poured the coffee and gave them their cups, then poured himself a cup of black coffee and slid onto one of the benches. McKenna and Camilia took his cue and sat on the bench facing him.

Felipe finished his own cup, then placed it on the table in front of him and stared at McKenna. "Before we go on, I feel that this would be a good time to get the ground rules out of the way," he said. "I presume you are not wearing any type of recording device."

"No, I'm not."

Felipe looked to Wright.

"Me neither."

"Good. Miss Wright, you may take any notes you wish, but I would like us to have the ability to go off the record from time to time whenever the commissioner or myself feels the need to do so."

Wright looked to McKenna for an answer.

"What do you mean by 'off the record'?" McKenna asked.

"It's very simple. I anticipate that you and I will be negotiating in good faith since we both have the same objective in mind. We both want me to leave your city without causing too much damage here. During the course of any sensitive negotiations such as these, we might feel compelled to reveal things that we wouldn't want to be public knowledge. I realize that you have people you must report to, and so do I, and everything discussed here will be revealed to them. But if I say something is off the record, what I mean is that I don't want it repeated in the press or reported to the government of Peru. It is just between you and me. Is that agreeable?"

"A very hard thing to do since you have placed me in the position of negotiating for the government of Peru. I'm not a professional diplomat and I'm not familiar with the amenities used in situations like this."

Felipe smiled. "Then, to illustrate, I'll go off the record for the first time and state the obvious," he said. "I am sure you realize that is a sham. You are actually negotiating for the United States government. I expect that the strongest and richest country in the world will exercise pressure on the present government of Peru to acquiesce to our demands, but for obvious political reasons the government of Peru would prefer to maintain the pretense that they are working to end this situation purely for humanitarian reasons. Things will work out better for all concerned if we maintain that pretense."

So that's how these things are done, McKenna thought. I guess he's right and, diplomatically, it makes sense instead of wasting time trying to tiptoe around the obvious. "All right," he said. "I agree. Anytime either of us feels it necessary to go off the record to keep these negotiations moving, we will do so, as long as we're both in agreement."

"Good. Just one other rule. I realize that it is your job to try to undermine my situation by either killing or capturing me and my men, no matter what we agree to here.''

Pretty much the point, but it doesn't state the overall picture, McKenna thought. ''That's not exactly the case,'' he said. ''If we agree to something, I will do everything in my power to ensure that our agreement is carried out. That is also the position of my government.''

Felipe laughed at McKenna's comment.

''Did I say something funny?'' McKenna asked, piqued at Felipe's attitude.

''I'm sorry,'' Felipe said, still smiling. ''I have total faith in you, but very little in your government. Off the record, while I have placed you in a position of speaking for them, I really don't expect them to make more than a pretense of complying with anything we agree to.''

''Then they're fooling me,'' McKenna said.

''Yes, they are.'' Felipe was no longer smiling. He said it as a matter of fact. ''In any event, the second rule should be this: I will not ask you about any of your plans to kill or capture me and my men, and you will not ask me anything regarding our future plans. All right?''

It sure is, McKenna thought. Hopefully, he doesn't suspect that we already know almost as much as he does about his future plans, and I sure don't want him asking me what we've been up to. It's a rule almost custom-made for me. ''Agreed, with one stipulation,'' McKenna said.

''Which is?''

''The matter of an airplane. You are aware we have captured your people who were supposed to hijack one for you?''

''Yes, of course,'' Felipe said, appearing unconcerned. ''Congratulations.''

''We believe that you have other people who will still attempt to hijack a plane somewhere and bring it here or to another city within the range of these ferries. We regard that as an unnecessary escalation that would place more innocent people in danger and result in additional casualties.''

McKenna stopped to gauge Felipe's reaction, but the *Sendero* leader's face was an impassive mask. ''Do you intend to suggest to me that your government will provide an airplane for our use when we leave?''

''Exactly.''

''I will consider that option and let you know,'' Felipe said, sitting back on his bench. Apparently, he considered the matter closed.

"Good," McKenna said. Bullshit, he thought, but it was worth a try. This guy is very careful and doesn't trust the U.S. government at all. I think he would rather select a plane at random than take one from us that might have a few surprises installed onboard. He's still going to hijack a plane, if for nothing more than the dramatic impact, but I'm sure he expected me to make the offer.

Wright opened her briefcase and removed two copies of the list of Felipe's demands that he had given to the reporters the day before. She put one on the table in front of McKenna, put the other in front of Felipe, then took out a notepad and pencil and waited.

"Any particular place you would like to start?" Felipe asked without touching his copy.

Camilia recorded Felipe's words in shorthand, then looked at McKenna, bored, as he picked up his copy.

"How about with the one demanding that the longshoremen's strike be settled before you leave?" McKenna asked.

"Yes?" Felipe asked, somewhat surprised at McKenna's choice of a starting point for the negotiations.

"This afternoon I met with Bill Kearns, the president of their union," McKenna said. "The meeting was supposed to last an hour, but took only five minutes. He is aware of your demand and gave me a letter to be given to you." McKenna turned to Wright and she took a sealed envelope from her briefcase and offered it to Felipe.

Felipe didn't take it. "What does it say?" he asked.

McKenna smiled. "It's very short and rather pointed. Basically it says that he doesn't want any godless commie foreigners interfering in any strike by the loyal and patriotic members of his union. He says thanks anyway, but he or any of his men would kill you themselves if given the chance. He also asked me to relay a personal message to you, but it's rather impolite. Care to hear it?"

Felipe smiled. "No, that won't be necessary. The demand was just a thought and possibly ill-advised."

It was a nice piece of politics, McKenna thought, realizing Felipe had been planning this operation for a long time, long before the longshoremen's strike, and he had made the demand just to generate good press in the event he felt it necessary to publicize his total list of demands.

"Which one would you like to discuss next?" Felipe asked.

"Let's do the three hundred and twenty-one prisoners you want the government of Peru to release. But before we do, I have to tell you that enormous pressure has been put on your government and they won't budge. Seems the people you want released are the heart and soul of *Sendero*, and it wasn't easy capturing them over the years. Your government says if they let them all go, then they've—"

"Lost the war?" Felipe said, smiling smugly.

What's he smiling about? McKenna wondered. I just told him he's demanded something that's not gonna happen, which might mean these negotiations and my diplomatic career are over. "That's what they say," McKenna said, trying to sound reasonable. "Take Carlos Abimael Guzman, for instance. He was your number-one man, the guy who started the whole *Sendero* thing and did most of the planning. Maybe if you left him out of your demands, we could stay on track."

"No. I want them all back, but I'm not going to be unreasonable," Felipe said, still smiling. "I have an alternative solution the government should be able to live with, once you explain it to them. They may even like it. You see, our people are a lot of trouble for the government. *Sendero* prisoners run the prisons and it costs a lot to keep them in jail. I will guarantee that, once they are released, they will no longer participate in the war effort."

"Your government will never believe that," McKenna stated.

"Yes they will. I've negotiated with them before, things like prisoner exchanges. They know I've always meticulously observed my end of any bargain we've made. Tell them I would be satisfied if our people were released and transported to a neutral country."

A nice proposal, but there's still a problem, McKenna thought. "What country would want them?" he asked.

Felipe had thought of that and had the answer. "I guess your government will have to use the power of persuasion, but you'll come up with one. If you do, we will pay to maintain our people."

I might be able to sell that, McKenna thought, then thought of another problem. "What's to stop them from returning to Peru?" he asked.

"My word. But if that's not enough, it would be agreeable with me if they were kept in camps under the supervision of the UN," Felipe said, still smiling.

Then McKenna understood the reason for Felipe's smile. That's exactly what he wants, McKenna thought. He doesn't want senior members of *Sendero* free in Peru. This way, he gets the glory of releasing them and still keeps them out of his way. It pretty much leaves him in charge of *Sendero*, or at least in a position to make decisions. For the first time since he boarded the ferry, McKenna had to smile.

"I see you get it," Felipe observed.

"Yeah, I get it, and the way you present it I don't see how your government can refuse."

"Good. Let's get on to the next point."

"All right. Let's talk about the war-crimes tribunal."

"All right. We demand that an international war-crimes tribunal be established with subpoena power to command the presence of anyone in Peru to investigate allegations of war crimes. I guarantee that every member of our forces will respond to these subpoenas and I also guarantee safe conduct through areas controlled by us for any tribunal member investigating war crimes. Naturally, we expect the government of Peru to make the same pledge."

What a wonderful propaganda point, McKenna thought, and very easy to sell. But there's a big problem with this one. "From what I hear, this tribunal is going to be very busy, and not only investigating the actions of the government. Your people haven't always behaved in a civilized fashion, and you're bound to have problems with your actions here," McKenna said, stating the obvious.

"I don't intend that this tribunal go raking up old news. It will be empowered to investigate only those allegations of war crimes occurring thirty days from the conclusion of the agreement between us and the government."

"And all the previous crimes committed by all you folks down there?"

"Amnesty for members of both sides. It would be a new start and would tend to civilize our struggle."

Again, very clever, and something public pressure would force the Peruvian government to agree to, McKenna thought. Felipe comes out of this looking like a hero righting past wrongs and he gets carte blanche to do whatever he thinks necessary to get out of here. "I stand a good chance of selling that," McKenna said. "It might even get a few of their generals out of some hot water."

"It will also be an incentive for them to give a truthful accounting of what happened to most of our people they've captured. Has the Peruvian government done any work yet on the list?"

"Some. You gave us a list of two thousand two hundred and eighty-eight people you allege the government has taken into custody. I'm told it will take a lot of time to account for all those people."

"I understand that."

He understands, but time is something I don't have a lot of, McKenna thought. We want him out of here. "I'd like to go off the record for a moment," he said.

Felipe's smile returned. "I'm sure you would. Go ahead."

Camilia stopped writing and put down her pencil. The look on her face gave both men the impression that she was no longer listening to them and wouldn't remember a word of their off-the-record conversation.

"You and I both know what happened to most of those people," McKenna stated. "They've been executed. The Peruvian government is never going to admit to that."

"Don't you think their families deserve to know what happened to them?"

"Sure, but the government's not gonna buy it. It would be an international disaster for them, making them a pariah among nations. Besides, as they see it, they were just responding to atrocities committed by your side."

"Every one of which they publicized every way they could," Felipe said sternly. "We haven't been angels and have done some unpleasant things, admittedly. There's no use denying it because all the world knows about it. But the government has managed to pull their crimes in the dark, so we look like mindless killers and they look like the good guys preserving civilization in our country."

"Some of what you say is true, and that's why they won't go for it. Between us, it would antagonize the generals so much that civilian rule would be jeopardized."

"Do you have a suggestion?"

"How about this: demand that Amnesty International get full access to the records of the Ministry of Prisons and the Ministry of Defense. Their investigation would take time and they could release their findings in dribs and drabs."

"Has Fujimori agreed to this?"

"In essence, yes."

It was Felipe's turn to sit back and think. Then his smile returned. "I think I might be doing him a favor."

"You mean helping him to get rid of some generals he's not crazy about."

"Yes. Under the terms of our agreement, we wouldn't demand their prosecutions, and he might not either. But it would give him a lot of leverage when he suggests their retirement to them." Then he turned to Camilia. "We're back on the record again."

Camilia snapped out of her state of self-induced stupor and picked up her pencil, ready to write.

"We demand that Amnesty International be given full access to the records of the Ministry of Defense and the Ministry of Prisons in order that they may ascertain the fate of the persons listed in Appendix B of this agreement," Felipe stated for the record. "We realize this cannot be accomplished quickly, so if President Fujimori agrees to this demand, we are satisfied that he will honorably comply."

"Then I think we've got that point covered," McKenna said, satisfied with himself.

"That brings us to my eleven men you're holding."

"One of them is in the hospital and should stay there," McKenna said.

"Are his injuries life-threatening?"

"No. His hand was injured and it's been operated on. He's going to need physical therapy."

"I want them all back."

Now how are we going to do that? McKenna wondered. I made a deal with Julio, and if we don't return him Felipe will know that he talked. I have to play this right or Felipe will figure out that we know more than he thinks we do right now. It's time to plant a seed and shake him up a bit without giving up the game. "Suppose some of them don't want to come back?" McKenna asked.

Felipe didn't like that. He frowned and scratched his chin before saying, "You can keep any of them who cooperates with you. I won't take anyone back against his will."

That settled it. McKenna suspected that Felipe had some questions about his captured men, but he had formulated the ground rules himself, so he had to respect them. "Agreed."

"Good. Then the rest is just money," Felipe stated in an almost offhand manner.

He said it like it's simple, but the money is a real problem,

McKenna thought. "Two hundred and fifty million is just too much," he said, hoping he sounded convincing. "You must realize it's more than your government can possibly pay."

Felipe looked surprised by McKenna's tone of voice. Then his face hardened. "They can get it," he stated simply.

"From where? Us? I thought you put me in the position of negotiating for the government of Peru, and I'm telling you they can't get it," McKenna said with finality, waiting for Felipe to show his hand.

Felipe stared hard at McKenna for a few seconds, then smiled. "Off the record?"

"Go ahead."

Camilia put down her pencil again before Felipe continued. "We'll cut the bullshit for a moment. I expect your government to loan it to them."

"That won't work. Everyone in this country would know that the administration caved in to you. It's too much money, and Congress would have to approve it."

"Nonsense. It's just the cost of one of your Stealth bombers and one-tenth the cost of one of your aircraft carriers."

"It's too much," McKenna repeated.

"Then consider it an emergency loan to the government of Peru. Do you know how much money your country gives away every year in foreign aid?"

"I didn't before you came here, but I do now. Between seven and eight billion."

"Correct. There are five countries that get more than I'm asking you to loan to the government of Peru. Egypt and Israel each get eight times that figure, and they're not quite in the position of strength we are."

"And how would the government of Peru pay us back with you and your people wrecking the economy down there?"

Felipe settled back on his bench and smiled. "The present government wouldn't," he said. "But we would."

It was a possibility that McKenna and Heresford hadn't even considered at lunch that afternoon, one that definitely put a new slant on the monetary part of the negotiations. "You mean, if you won?" McKenna asked.

"Yes. If we win, we would honor all international monetary commitments, starting with this one. Of course, that's just between us, but you can consider it a promise."

God, this guy's good and he's got brass balls, McKenna thought. We give him the money to get out of here, money that incidentally will help him overthrow the government of Peru, and now he's telling me it's just a loan and he's gonna pay us back after he wins. After all this, he'll have some members of the American public in his corner, along with some congressmen and lots of bankers. But I still don't think I can sell it, especially since we know he got here on drug dealers' money. Which brings me to the point I'll use. "How are you going to pay us back if you win? Increase the coca crop?"

"No. Regulate it for a while, but never increase it, and that also is a promise."

Very candid, McKenna thought, and then Felipe surprised him even further with his honesty. "Off the record, you know that I've recently fallen out of favor with certain parties in Colombia, don't you?"

McKenna had to smile at Felipe's frank admission, then answered, "Off the record, do you mean that the drug cartels who financed your operation up to now aren't very happy with their investment?"

"Yes," Felipe said, giving no indication he was surprised that McKenna knew of his financial backers.

"By 'recently,' I guess you mean since last night?" McKenna asked with a straight face.

Felipe glared at McKenna for a moment, then found something funny in his remark. "Yes. I've heard their aircraft are experiencing some navigational difficulties, which I attribute to your efforts," Felipe said, laughing. Then he got serious again. "There's twelve of them unaccounted for, none of which is my fault. I just provided them with an opportunity, as I agreed to do, but they are not used to such losses and I suspect they will try to vent their anger on me at the first available opportunity."

"So?"

"So their failure presents us with a unique opportunity that should soothe some minds in Washington. Do you know where the world's coca crop comes from?"

"Sixty percent from Peru and forty percent from Bolivia."

"More or less. Some is grown in Colombia and Ecuador, but Peru provides the bulk. If we win, we will endeavor to wean our economy off the narco-dollar. Three years after the date we assume power, the export of Peruvian coca leaves will be cut to zero."

"How will you do that?" McKenna asked, skeptically.

"Persuasion and crop substitution, if possible. If not, force and terror. I can't go on the record with that, but it's a promise between you and me. To sweeten the pot, we will ensure that the Colombians don't fly over Peru with coca leaves from Bolivia,'' Felipe stated before he thought to add, ''Three years after we assume power, that is.''

God, this guy *is* good, McKenna thought once more. We must spend at least ten billion a year in drug enforcement, and he's just told me that if we give him the money, he's gonna cut our problems in half. What's better, once he's in, our government will be inclined to give him the three years he needs to fulfill his promise. What's worse, I believe him. But who else would? ''How could we be sure you'd do what you say?'' McKenna asked.

''You have a DEA base operating in our territory right now. For that, the government of Peru is holding you up for thirty-one million dollars a year. We would allow you to have ten such bases and might even welcome the help. You see, we intend to get respectable.''

''When would we get those bases?''

Felipe was conducting a sale, but he wasn't giving away the store. ''A while after we win, if we do.''

''I'd like to go back on the record,'' McKenna said.

Camilia made a show of picking up her pencil.

''I will try to persuade my government to loan the government of Peru one hundred and fifty million dollars if you will modify your demand to that amount and also agree never to publicize the source of the money.''

McKenna expected some haggling over the figure, but got none. ''Agreed,'' Felipe said so quickly that McKenna regretted not saying one hundred million.

''I believe that covers all points to be negotiated by us, doesn't it?'' Felipe asked.

''You're forgetting one thing.''

''You mean the small matter of the three additional distinguished guests who will accompany us when we leave?''

''Yes.''

''That's not open to negotiation.''

''I presume I'll be one of these volunteers,'' McKenna said.

''If you would be so kind,'' Felipe answered graciously.

''I accept your invitation,'' McKenna said, just as graciously. ''Who are the others?''

''We extend invitations to Mr. Ashton Heresford, since he's in town and apparently wants to get involved. We also extend an invitation to the Peruvian ambassádor to the United States."

McKenna had expected the ambassador to be one. Cristobal Cervantes was well known and respected in the international diplomatic community and was related by blood or politics to many of the traditional rulers of Peru. The generals there would think twice before shooting down a plane he was a passenger on. But Heresford was a surprise, and a pleasant one to McKenna. He looked forward to giving the news to the distinguished national security adviser to the President. "Would you like me to extend your invitation to them?" he asked, trying hard not to smile, but failing.

"If you would," Felipe said, puzzled by McKenna's reaction. Then he got it. "Off the record, Heresford is a pompous pain in the ass, isn't he?" he asked.

"Off the record, he sure is."

"Then you're happy with the choice?"

"Ecstatic. But now I have a request."

"Detective Hoffmann?"

"Yes."

"As a gesture of good faith, if you can persuade him to leave, that's fine with me."

But then the *Sendero* leader gave McKenna something else to worry about. "I have enjoyed our little chat and I hate to end it on a down note," he said. "I believe that you personally will attempt to implement the points we've discussed, but I feel your government will need some stimulus. Therefore, I've made a contingency plan that might seem vindictive to you."

"You mean that after you leave, you will still keep that truck on the Williamsburg Bridge for a while?"

"That goes without saying. What I mean is that we are in possession of a rather virulent biological reagent. If we do not safely arrive at our final destination, one of my people will release this biological reagent in New York. As a result, thousands will die."

Damn that Seymor Cranston, McKenna thought. He was a biological researcher; it had to come from him. What would it be, something released in the water supply? McKenna concentrated on putting a concerned look on his face, not wanting Felipe to suspect that he could have Cranston arrested any time he wanted.

Then a thought came to him that did concern him: Elena. He knew she wasn't onboard since none of the released passengers reported seeing her. Taking a chance, he asked, "Who are you leaving behind? Elena?''

Felipe wasn't perfect after all, and the question had caught him unawares. A surprised look crossed his face, and he knew it was evident to McKenna. ''Possibly,'' he said noncommittally, but McKenna had his answer.

''Let's conclude our negotiations,'' Felipe said impassively. ''At four o'clock tomorrow afternoon I will expect you here with seventy-five million dollars in military duffel bags, along with a currency counting machine. This money will be from federal reserve banks from all over the United States. They will be old bills and not sequentially numbered. If you are not here at that time, I will shoot one hundred passengers.''

McKenna had expected something like that. ''What denominations?'' he asked.

''Fifty million in hundreds, ten million in fifties, ten million in twenties, and five million in tens. If you do bring it, you may return with two hundred of the passengers.''

''I'll be here with the money, but I don't know if I'll be able to get your government to agree to all this in one day.''

''I will respect your efforts. We'll talk about it tomorrow, as long as you can pay the fare,'' Felipe said, standing up. ''Now, let's see if you can talk your stubborn detective out of the bilge.''

Chapter 45
McKenna noted the damage to the engine room as he followed Felipe down and McKenna concluded that the *Samuel I. Newhouse* wasn't going to be making any long voyages in the immediate future. There was oil everywhere and he counted four bullet holes in the engines as they passed through the room to the end, where two armed Senderistas were waiting.

In contrast to the relaxed reception McKenna had received, Felipe and his men were not taking any chances with Hoffmann. There was a large ammo box on top of the bilge manhole cover, and the Senderistas had their M-16s pointed at it.

"I'm going to contact him before we move that box and open the manhole," McKenna told Felipe.

"Good," Felipe said. "Tell him to throw his weapons up before he comes out. He had two pistols."

McKenna nodded as Camilia took a portable radio from her briefcase and gave it to him. "Can you read me, Gus?" he said into the radio. "This is McKenna."

Hoffmann answered immediately. "I read you, Commissioner. Good to hear your voice."

"I'm in the engine room, right on top of you. You ready to go home yet?"

"If that's what you want. You been dealing with those rascals up there?"

"Have to, Gus. They're holding all the cards. Here's what I want you to do. Get away from the manhole cover and knock on the overhead so they know where you are."

Hoffmann was nowhere near the manhole cover. They heard his knock on the deck behind them.

McKenna looked to Felipe, who nodded at him. Felipe said something in Quechua and one of his men slung his rifle and rolled the ammo box off the manhole cover.

"Okay, Gus. Stay where you are. They're ready to open the cover."

The Senderista put his hands in the recessed handle of the cover, lifted it up, and rolled it to the side while the other Senderista covered the hole with his M-16.

The stench from the bilge was foul, a mixture of grease, oil, and standing water. "Gus, walk to the edge of the hole and stop," McKenna said into his radio.

Gus didn't answer, but they heard the sound of him approaching as he sloshed through the water. The sound stopped at the edge of the manhole.

"Gus, you're gonna have to throw your guns up!" McKenna yelled into the bilge.

"If you say so, Commissioner. Just give me a minute to get my eyes used to the light."

"Take your time, Gus."

Gus did. The tension built as everyone waited at the hole. Both Senderistas had their rifles pointed into the manhole. The first word spoken was from Gus. "Here's the first one," he yelled as he threw a .45 Colt up.

The gun sailed up and, reflexively, McKenna caught it with

his right hand. From the corner of his eye he caught the movement as the Senderistas swung their rifles to him. McKenna raised both hands in the air as Gus threw his service revolver up. McKenna had to duck or catch it, so he caught the revolver in his left hand, before raising it again. He shifted the guns in his hands so that he was holding them by the barrels.

"Please put your hands down, Commissioner," he heard Felipe say behind him.

McKenna did and turned to face a very amused Felipe. "I guess you want these," McKenna said, offering the pistols to Felipe butt-first.

Felipe regarded the guns, then took the Colt from McKenna and threw it to one of the Senderistas, who caught it. "That one is ours. You may return Detective Hoffmann's revolver to him once you're off the boat."

This guy's got a lot of class, McKenna thought in spite of himself. "Thanks," he said. He opened his jacket and put the revolver in his empty holster. The Senderistas switched their rifles back to the manhole.

"Gus, come on up!" McKenna yelled into the bilge.

Gus appeared at the hole, squinting into the light. Then he stood up for the first time in two days and McKenna heard his back crack. Standing in the bilge, the engine-room deck was at his chest level. Gus tried to raise his arms, but it was too tight. So he submerged into the bilge and came up again, arms first. Placing his elbows on the deck, with his legs still in the bilge, he tried to pull himself up, but didn't have the strength.

McKenna bent down and grabbed Gus's shoulder, but Gus shrugged his hand off, saying, "Don't. I can get up by myself."

So McKenna stood back and watched as Gus pulled himself out and shakily pushed to his feet, still squinting, filthy, soaking wet, and dripping water on the deck. As his eyes adjusted, he looked at the people around him, then stared at Felipe. "I'm ready to get off this boat, if that's all right with you, Commissioner," he said over his shoulder, still staring at Felipe. Then he turned around and smiled. "I guess we're losing this one, aren't we?" he asked.

"Yeah, we're losing," McKenna said, putting his arm around Hoffmann's shoulder, getting wet and dirty in the process.

*   *   *

Once onboard the launch, Hoffmann changed into a large pair of coveralls McKenna had thought to bring. Then he lay down on the floor inside the cabin as the launch headed back to the Wall Street pier. Hoffmann was snoring in under a minute.

McKenna and Camilia went out on the rear deck, ignoring the light drizzle as they contemplated the Manhattan skyline, both keeping their thoughts to themselves.

McKenna regarded the afternoon as a success. He had saved the taxpayers $100 million, was going to secure the release of another 200 hostages, and felt he stood a good chance of getting Felipe out of the harbor without any further deaths among the passengers.

Then he worked over in his mind the things Felipe had told him he planned to do if he won his war in Peru. McKenna didn't know what life would be like there in that event, but he was certain of one thing: Felipe meant to stop the drug traffic in Peru, and that would be a vast improvement over the efforts of the present government there.

Then he forced himself to think about the thing that endangered all the plans he had made for getting Felipe. If he couldn't find Elena and prevent her from accomplishing her mission, then Felipe would win.

He looked to Camilia and caught her staring at him. She smiled, self-consciously, surprising McKenna. ''You like him, don't you?''

McKenna looked back to the cabin. ''Not Gus,'' Camilia said. ''Of course you like him. I meant Felipe.''

Like him? McKenna asked himself, thinking over the question. Can you like a man who orders the death of innocent people? Admire his daring, his intelligence, his courage, and his single-minded dedication to his cause, maybe. But never like. ''Let's just say I respect him, much in the same way you would respect the cunning and courage of a tiger,'' he said.

''He just doesn't seem like a bad man. He's so . . . well, so . . .''

''Charming and gallant?''

''Yes, that's it. I know he's a murderer, but you wouldn't expect a man like him to do the things he's done.''

''I hear Ted Bundy was charming and gallant, but he was still a serial killer who murdered innocent young girls for kicks,'' McKenna volunteered.

Camilia considered that, but only for a moment. ''I know that what he does is still wrong, but he's not like Bundy,'' she retorted. "He doesn't do it for kicks, and I get the feeling he regrets every death he's caused."

Now where does she get that feeling from? McKenna wondered. She's been right in every instance since I met her, but I think she's wrong this time. McKenna believed that for Felipe, killing had become a matter of routine.

"There's good and bad in all of us, but I think the bad outweighs the good in Felipe's case," he said, uncomfortable that he seemed to be lecturing her.

Then it was Camilia's turn. "Do you think F.D.R. was a bad man?" she asked.

"No, he wasn't," McKenna answered, knowing where Camilia was about to lead him. "But you're going to tell me he ordered the deaths of lots of people, right?"

"Yes. He didn't pull the trigger himself, and maybe he couldn't have shot anybody. But he did authorize military actions that caused the deaths of many people, and some of those people were innocent. That's what war is, and Felipe's at war."

"But he's not at war with us, no matter what justification he uses," McKenna said after giving Camilia's viewpoint some thought. "We're not in Peru killing innocent people and he shouldn't be here. His excuse is expediency, which is the same kind of thinking Hitler used when he invaded Holland and Belgium to get to France. It's wrong, and that's why we can't let him win. Otherwise, we're going to be dealing with people like Felipe for a long time."

Johnny Pao was waiting for them at the pier when they docked, along with a detail of cops holding back twenty reporters. The ambulance McKenna had ordered for Hoffmann was also there.

The reporters shouted a hundred questions about the negotiations, but McKenna had no comment for them and answered only one question. They wanted to know who Camilia was and he told them. "She's my secretary, Camilia Wright. She's the best one in the police department, and, incidentally, the person responsible for any good ideas I might've had in the past week."

Camilia stopped for a second to adjust her dress and scarf in the glare of the flashbulbs, then pulled McKenna past the reporters to the ambulance.

Hoffmann simply ignored the reporters and followed Mc-Kenna and Wright until he realized the ambulance was for him. "Can't I just go home?" he asked McKenna.

"Tomorrow, Gus. Please just spend tonight in the hospital and I'll have somebody drive you home tomorrow."

"What time?"

"Is eleven o'clock okay?"

"Fine," Hoffmann said. "But I don't want to talk to any reporters."

"Whatever you say, Gus. I'll have somebody outside your room to make sure they don't bother you."

Somewhat mollified, Hoffmann got in the back of the ambulance, then remembered something. He got out and caught McKenna and Camilia as they were getting into the car.

"Yeah, Gus," McKenna said. "What did you forget?"

"I just have to ask you something," Hoffmann said, looking worried while he motioned McKenna to come closer. McKenna did and Hoffmann whispered in his ear. "You're not gonna let that guy beat us, are you?"

McKenna had to smile. "Not without a fight, Gus."

That's all Hoffmann wanted to hear. "Thanks," he said before turning and hobbling back to his ambulance.

Pao drove McKenna and Camilia to the rear entrance of city hall, but there was no escaping the reporters. The crew that worked city hall were the sharpest of the old hands, and they knew McKenna would be trying the old back-door trick. They were a determined bunch, but Pao was determined too. He got McKenna and Camilia in, pushing and shoving and ruffling some feathers of the Fourth Estate in the process.

The mayor, Brunette, and Heresford were in the mayor's office, watching CNN on TV while waiting for them. McKenna's city hall entrance had been broadcast live. He and Camilia arrived in the mayor's office just in time to watch Pao shove his way back into the car. Then, along with the rest of the nation, they watched a correspondent try to question Pao, and saw Mr. Personality respond by rolling up his window on the reporter's mike.

"Can't you do something with that guy?" the mayor yelled.

"No, Your Honor, I can't," McKenna responded simply.

They watched as Pao picked up a newspaper and started

reading before the cameras switched to a long-distance shot of the ferries.

"God, I wish I could get away with that kind of shit," the mayor said softly before sitting behind his desk. "I hope you've got something we can give the papers," he said, looking at McKenna. "Those guys are starved for a story."

"Nothing more than that the negotiations are continuing on course. The good news is that I don't think he's gonna be shooting any more people."

"What's the bad news?" Brunette asked.

"For one thing, one hundred and fifty million, with seventy-five of it by tomorrow."

"Can you do that, Mr. Heresford?" the mayor asked.

"Seventy-five million? We can manage that, but some members of Congress are going to have to be briefed," Heresford said. "What else?"

"Elena's going to release a deadly biological reagent somewhere in New York if Felipe doesn't arrive safe and sound at his destination."

McKenna expected the news to be greeted by resignation and gloom, but was pleasantly surprised by Brunette's reaction. "Don't worry about that," he said. "We'll get her."

"Wait a minute," the mayor interjected. "What kind of biological reagent?"

"Germ warfare," Heresford stated. "Probably something she'll introduce into the water supply, although I can't imagine where they got it from."

"From Cranston," McKenna said.

"I don't see how," Heresford said. "Brookhaven Labs never had anything to do with any germ-warfare programs."

"Could it be a bluff?" the mayor asked.

"I don't think so," McKenna replied. "*Sendero* doesn't bluff. If Felipe says they got it, then they do."

"Or they think they do," Heresford said, leaving some interesting possibilities for McKenna to think about. Could Cranston be scamming Felipe? he wondered.

But Brunette wasn't wasting time on it. "Whether they've got it or not, we'll take precautions," he said, still unfazed by the threat. "She'd probably go for the Central Park Reservoir, but I'll make sure she can't get near it."

"What about all of our reservoirs upstate?" the mayor asked, obviously nervous about the way Brunette was treating the problem.

"If we don't find her by the time Felipe's ready to leave, I'll send a couple of hundred men up there to guard them, too. She won't get near them."

"A couple of hundred?" the mayor exclaimed. "Do you know how much that would cost?"

"Don't worry about it, Your Honor. He's paying for it," Brunette said, pointing to Heresford.

"Let's worry about that if and when the time comes," Heresford said. "What else?"

McKenna told him, and thought he'd enjoy telling Heresford he was going to be taking a trip. But, in the end, he didn't get a chance to enjoy it. Heresford spoiled it with his blasé reaction to the news. "How long do you think we'll be gone for, if we manage to make it back at all?" was all he asked McKenna.

"I don't know," McKenna answered, hoping his disappointment wasn't showing through his voice. "Think you'll be able to squeeze it into your schedule?"

"Yes, I'll squeeze it in. Let's have the details."

Just when you think you really don't like a guy, why do they always have to surprise you? McKenna wondered while Camilia read them the transcript of the negotiations. Mr. Ashton Heresford is certainly a pompous ass who's enormously impressed with himself, but he might not be that bad a guy after all.

Then McKenna focused on Brunette. His friend seemed to be paying close attention to the discussion, but was adding nothing. Since Brunette obviously wasn't going to speak his mind, McKenna figured he would. "It's time for a decision. We have a plan that, once implemented, will be almost impossible to stop. When and if Colonel Savraada succeeds in bringing the Peruvian military onboard, they will attempt to destroy Felipe in Peru, no matter what happens here as a result of their action."

He was immediately treated to a glare from the mayor and suffered through a patronizing expression from Heresford. But McKenna was also good at making faces, and he tried a few. None of them worked on the mayor, but Heresford felt the need to say something. McKenna watched as Heresford searched for the right turn of words to put the neophyte local official in his place without damaging the working relationship.

Heresford thought he had found it. "I remind you that the

end result of your negotiations with *Sendero* should be to get them out of here with a minimum of damage. As you know, I wouldn't have selected you for this task, but I'm happy to say that you're performing it in an exemplary fashion. I've heard the elements of your plan, but you're still a police officer, and unless you plan on arresting those people for the crimes they've committed here, your task is basically concluded, successfully I might add, once they leave your jurisdiction.''

"And then what?'' McKenna asked.

"Then it becomes a priority diplomatic matter between our government and the government of Peru.''

"Suppose they become the government of Peru?''

"Correct me if I'm wrong, but from the things you've told me here, I was under the impression that wouldn't be such a bad idea.''

Heresford's condescending tone and demeanor was really getting to McKenna now, so he decided it was time to put him under the spotlight. "Then I'm correcting you. You're wrong. That is, unless you have a plan for dealing with them.''

"You're not operating in a vacuum here, Commissioner McKenna. This situation has been the subject of intense scrutiny by the National Security Agency, and they're not amateurs. I assure you that a comprehensive plan will be formulated to deal with Felipe and it will be implemented at an opportune time.''

"Care to give me a hint about this plan, or are these just vague rumblings you're giving me?'' McKenna asked, gratified to see that Heresford was struggling to control his anger and barely succeeding.

When Heresford didn't immediately answer, McKenna decided to pour some oil on the fire he had lighted. "You don't have a plan, do you?'' McKenna asked scathingly, knowing the answer.

"I'm not the person who makes the plans,'' Heresford replied in a condescending tone. "I review them and refer them to the President for his consideration.''

"Okay, have you reviewed a plan yet?''

Heresford apparently wasn't used to being questioned by local officials, but he had to answer. "No.''

"Then you and the rest of your think tank don't really have a plan, right?''

"Not yet.''

"Well, we do," McKenna stated. "We just need to get a few things straightened out."

Heresford had regained his composure and thought he had the upper hand. He gave the mayor a smile like they were sharing a secret before he answered. "By 'we,' you mean yourself, Commissioner Brunette, and Colonel Savraada, right?" he asked.

"That's the 'we' I'm talking about."

"As I understand it, your plan involves some high risks. It will endanger the lives of a large number of hostages and there is a substantial risk that *Sendero* will blow up the Williamsburg Bridge, not to mention the threat posed by Elena if you don't find her in time."

Now it was McKenna controlling his rage as Heresford waited for a rebuttal.

He's talking to me like he's explaining to a child why boys stand and girls sit when they pee, McKenna thought. What's important is that Felipe's plan must fail, but all Heresford's done is articulate the obvious risks. "Those are chances worth taking. We need a little time to minimize the risks, but we have to have a decision now," McKenna replied.

The mayor groaned, but McKenna kept his eyes on Heresford while bracing himself for the mayor's objection.

Heresford also waited a moment, but whatever objections the mayor might have had he kept to himself. He was still in a mood to listen.

Heresford looked a little disappointed that class was still in session, but he resumed his attack. "What you mean is, you need time so that you *might* find the location of the person with the detonator for the explosives on the Williamsburg Bridge, so that you *might* find Elena, and you also need to give Colonel Savraada some time so that he *might* win the cooperation of the military in Peru."

"Yes."

"And a fourth variable is that you must locate Felipe's parachutes, if he even has any, and you must do this without his knowledge."

"Yes," McKenna answered, starting to wonder if he really had a plan at all.

"And if all this happens, there will still be a substantial risk of failure, right?"

"I don't know if I'd use the word *substantial*," McKenna said, defensively. "We should know more about the risks involved by tomorrow. But tell me, what does the President think of all this?''

"I haven't discussed it with him yet."

McKenna smiled. It was time to drop the bomb. ''Well, I have,'' he said, enjoying Heresford's discomfort at that piece of news before he continued. ''He didn't say it was a good plan, but he didn't say it was stupid, either.''

That stopped Heresford and gave him something to think about, but the mayor thought it was time to put his foot down. ''He's not the one who has to know about the substantial risks in this city,'' he said. ''I am.''

McKenna knew when to shut up, and he did. Brunette knew when to talk, and he did.

''Speaking of substantial risks, Your Honor, there's a substantial risk you'll lose the next election if you cave in and let those people out of here without trying something to foil their plans, especially if a viable plan came to light and you did nothing with it. People would be writing books about it, second-guessing your decision.''

Brunette had said the E-word, the word that always got the mayor's attention and made him stop and think about the next election. He did for a moment, then said, ''If the Williamsburg Bridge goes down or Elena poisons thousands of people, I'll be sure to lose the next election.''

Brunette smiled at the mayor. ''Not necessarily. I'll agree with you about Elena, but not about the bridge. If we get her and the bridge goes, you'll still be a man of action in the national spotlight who lost a good fight. You know that Teddy Roosevelt lost an election for mayor, but he made a great president.''

McKenna watched as the E-word followed by the N-word and the P-word in the same conversation got His Honor in the right frame of mind. National spotlight, the thing every local politician craved, was usually something enjoyed by only the president, and rarely by a municipal mayor who would like to be president.

Then Brunette put the icing on the cake. ''You know, it's a risk like everything else in life, but if we do get them, you don't have to worry about the next election. You'd be a shoo-in. I don't think you'd even have to campaign, which means you'd be able to use that sizable war chest you've built up for something more worthwhile.''

The mayor liked it. He took a while to think while he looked around his office.

McKenna stole a look at Brunette and caught a wink, which meant they both knew exactly what the mayor was thinking. It was something like: This place is nice, but it sure isn't the Oval Office. But the mayor still wasn't convinced. "So you absolutely need an answer this minute on whether you should proceed with your plan?" he asked McKenna.

"Yes. If we can do our end here, we stand a chance of success."

"Your end?" the mayor asked, confused. "What do you mean by that?"

"I mean that the rest depends on Colonel Savraada. Once he gets his generals moving, it can't be stopped. We're asking you to think it over, recognize the risks, have some faith in us, and take a gamble."

"And where the hell is Colonel Savraada?" the mayor wanted to know.

Chapter 46

Whenever possible, General Ramon Hidalgo avoided staying in Lima. The city of his birth was no longer to his liking. As his driver negotiated the Nissan Sentra through the late afternoon traffic and the throngs of street peddlers, Hidalgo cursed the changes the two million newcomers had wrought.

When he was a boy, growing up in the same house his family had owned for 300 years, things were different. Although the weather had always been terrible, with the thick coastal fog blanketing the city and depositing layers of grime on the streets and buildings, in his youth everything had been painted once a year and the town had managed to maintain a cheery, almost provincial atmosphere.

But no longer. The newcomers from the mountains had brought crime and filth with them, living in crowded shantytowns that sprang up almost overnight and completely over-burdened the municipal services. The stately old government buildings Hidalgo loved were all in dire need of paint, the beaches were polluted, many parts of the city smelled like a sewer, and water and electric services were sporadic, at best.

But, despite the changes, he could still have lived comfort-ably in his own house in the middle of town if the newcomers hadn't also brought *Sendero* with them when they came. What had started as another provincial Indian revolt had dragged on for fifteen years, even spreading to Lima so that Hidalgo no longer dared to stay in his own house when he was in town and was forced to travel around the city in a common Nissan. He hadn't even seen his Mercedes in years, and visited his family only occasionally. Because of *Sendero*, he had been forced to move his wife and children to the safety of Spain, and even there they were living under assumed names.

Hidalgo thought the situation was intolerable, almost, but never thought of retiring and leaving, as many people in sim-ilar circumstances had already done. Because of tradition, that option was never really open to him. He wasn't just another rich man. His ancestors came to Peru with Pizarro in 1537, and if generations of conquistadors could stick it out, he wouldn't be the one to leave. His forefathers had fought the Indians for centuries, always winning and enjoying the spoils of war in the process, and *Sendero* wasn't going to beat him.

Still, sensible precautions had to be taken. Only rarely did he leave his secure and profitable base in the Huallaga Valley where he was safe from both *Sendero* and President Fujimori, the two banes of his existence. Since he had set up a small profit-sharing plan, the troops of the Sinsi Battalion were in-tensely loyal to him, and they were a force to be reckoned with, even for the president. His officers were from the best families and his men were dedicated, well equipped, and highly trained, one of the few effective fighting forces the army had in the war against *Sendero*. Although some sensible accommodations with the guerrillas had been made, the Sinsi Battalion kept *Sendero* from totally dominating the Huallaga Valley, the source of most of the nation's hard currency.

To further ensure his position, Hidalgo, unlike some other less sensible commanders, made sure that a good portion of the dollars that came into his possession found its way into the hands of men in high places in Lima. So, although he knew that Fujimori would like to remove him, the president didn't dare. It would just be too much trouble.

The Nissan slowed down. Having been Hidalgo's body-guard for ten years, the driver knew where he was going and stopped the car in an alley next to a stately mansion on the Prado in the fashionable neighborhood of San Isidro. Hidalgo left him on guard and he entered the mansion by the side door.

The madam was waiting for him just inside the entrance, in the foyer adjoining the sitting room. Although no longer a girl, Nadia possessed an ageless beauty that she knew how to ac-cent, wearing a demure tan business suit, her hair up in an aristocratic fashion, and her face adorned with what looked like a minimum of makeup. She looked untouchable, but Hi-dalgo knew better. He had known her for thirty years, since she was a young girl starting in the business. Although he doubted that she still made professional use of her talents, just seeing her always made him smile as he remembered the splendid times she had given him over the years. They knew each other well.

"So good to see you again, General," she said, offering him her hand and cheek.

Hidalgo took her hand and, pecking at her cheek, caught a whiff of her perfume. He didn't recognize the scent, but liked it. Like everything else about Nadia, it was subtle and aristo-cratic, but still exciting. Then he held her at arm's length and looked her over. "The years have been kind to you, Nadia," he said, admiringly.

Nadia responded by looking him over. "To both of us," she responded with a sincere smile.

Hidalgo smiled back, politely. "But no one would pay to spend time with me, and you could still be a rich woman," he observed.

"I already am," Nadia said, laughing but obviously appre-ciating Hidalgo's appraisal. "But I don't hear such compli-ments that often anymore. Are you ready to get to business, or would you care for a drink first?"

"Business. Maybe we'll have a drink together later."

"Do you already have a preference or would you like to see something new?"

"Remember the young lady I was with the last time?"

"It was a girl from the country, wasn't it?"

"Yes, very pretty, tall, but a little dark."

"That's Linda."

"That's right," Hidalgo said. "Linda. Is she available?"

"Of course. As a matter of fact, she was hoping you would select her. She has always preferred strong, tall men."

Hidalgo knew it was hype, but still appreciated it. "Then she must be upstairs waiting for me," he said, testing the madam's veracity.

She passed. "Of course she is, waiting in Room Four. Would you like me to take you up?"

"That won't be necessary. I know where it is."

"Then I'll see you when you come down. Enjoy yourself."

Hidalgo followed Nadia through the elaborately decorated sitting room, then climbed the stairs to Room Four, which lately had become his favorite room.

Linda was waiting for him, standing in the middle of the room, dressed in a scanty studded-leather costume that managed to cover her areas of interest, but still left nothing to the imagination. She was holding a short leather whip and looked like she could have been an Inca princess, the kind he saw depicted in the paintings and murals done by wistful national artists, but never saw among their descendants in the high Andes.

"You're late," she barked at him as she snapped the whip. "Get undressed."

"I'm not ready to start yet," he said calmly while looking around the room.

"Oh, I'm sorry, sir," Linda said softly and sweetly. "I thought you were."

The decor was medieval dungeon, but immaculately clean. The only furnishing was a long, wide wooden bench and a wooden table with large metal rings at each corner. The walls were lined with leather and metal tools and appliances, the purpose of which Hidalgo had no idea. He took one off the wall, a device that looked like a small pair of leather-covered tongs. "What is this used for?" he asked Linda.

"You're not ready for that yet, sir."

Believing the professional, Hidalgo replaced the device in its holder on the wall and locked the door.

Hidalgo realized that he had always been a sadist and had always enjoyed inflicting physical pain on others. He even got some sexual satisfaction from watching his men conduct forceful interrogations on *Sendero* prisoners. He accepted this trait as a part of his total being, something like his height and weight, and thought it was one of the things that made him a successful military commander. It was only recently that he had discovered he was also a masochist, and although it surprised him, he accepted that trait as well. The only thing about it that puzzled him was his preference for the type of woman he needed to indulge his aberration.

Hidalgo had always considered himself something of a ladies' man, and during his life had consorted with and enjoyed the company of the women of Peruvian and European high society, women with aristocratic good looks like Nadia's. They were nothing like the girl in front of him. Although he had to admit she was beautiful in her own way, he would never have considered her his type. He wondered if it was because he was changing, getting old, or if, subconsciously, he felt a need to be humiliated, as a sort of self-inflicted penance, by a member of the class he had spent a lifetime fighting and abusing.

In the end he decided the reasons for his preference in women for this type of activity weren't important, as long as the pleasure was forthcoming.

"You know what I require?" he asked.

"Yes, sir," Linda answered, softly and respectfully.

"Then I'm ready."

He watched as her facial expression changed from a look of respect and admiration to a sneer of pure hate. "Then get your clothes off, you filthy piece of trash," she growled, deftly snapping her whip so that the tip cracked close to his testicles.

The general hurried to comply.

Half an hour later Hidalgo was in the throes of ecstasy, naked and stretched facedown on the table with each wrist tied to a metal ring while Linda snapped her whip at his bare buttocks. She was an expert, missing most of the time while she degraded him and berated him with obscenities in Spanish and Quechua, and when she did connect with a flick of her wrist she inflicted a stinging blow, hard enough to cause pain but light enough to leave no wounds that wouldn't heal in a day or two.

Hidalgo knew that it wasn't the pain that excited him and gave him pleasure, but the anticipation of pain. He craved and feared the sound of the cracking whip.

But then she stopped, before he was ready. He knew this was part of the procedure, that she would bend down and bite his ear while she whispered promises and threats. He closed his eyes, expecting to hear her voice growling close to his ear, but the voice came from farther back in the room, near the door, and it wasn't Linda.

"Really, General, I don't see how that can be fun," Savraada said softly.

Hidalgo recognized the voice at once. He tried turning his body to look his new tormentor in the face, but couldn't. He did manage to turn his legs and buttocks, but his wrists were securely fastened to the metal rings on the table.

"You may leave us now, Miss," Savraada said softly in Quechua, and Hidalgo heard the door close as Linda left. Then Savraada accommodated Hidalgo by walking around the table so that he was in front of him and within view. Hidalgo glared at him while Savraada looked over the general's predicament. "I'm sorry, General, I seem to have caught you at a bad time," Savraada said without a trace of a smile. "I'm going to give you a moment to relax before I untie you."

Hidalgo felt himself relaxing very quickly. "How did you know I was here?" he asked as he waited. "Nadia?"

"No, General. Not Nadia. We've known for some time of your preference for this establishment and knew you were in town. It was just a matter of waiting for you to arrive," Savraada said as he untied the leather thongs securing Hidalgo's wrists to the metal rings.

The general sat up and rubbed his wrists, totally unconcerned with his nakedness, having spent many years in the barracks. "Is Nadia under arrest?" he asked.

"For the moment."

Hidalgo stood up, facing Savraada and towering over him. "Now why don't you tell me what you want before I throw you out of here, you little shit," he said menacingly.

Savraada was not perturbed. "Sit down and listen, General, or I'll have you tied to that table again," he said calmly.

Hidalgo raised his hands while Savraada stared at him impassively, then lowered them and sat down. "All right. I'm listening."

Savraada reached into his breast pocket and handed Hidalgo an envelope. "It contains a first-class ticket for Madrid on the Iberia flight leaving at eleven tomorrow evening. You will be on it. The envelope also contains a new passport good for thirty days. Your old passport has been invalidated and you won't be coming back."

Hidalgo was enraged at the matter-of-fact approach Savraada used in deciding his future, and considered ripping up the envelope and throwing it in the little man's face. But he decided to wait and hear more. "Then you think I'm retiring?" he asked.

"No. You're not retiring. You're just leaving."

The arrogance of it made Hidalgo laugh. "Or?" he asked, amused.

"Or you will be arrested."

"Over what? This little indiscretion? You expect me to give up my pension over this?"

"No, General. This just happens to be the place I found you and won't be mentioned in the charges against you. If you stay, you will be arrested and go on trial for your life for the crimes of murder, extortion, malfeasance, and bribe receiving."

"For my life? Peru doesn't have a death penalty," Hidalgo retorted, sneering.

Savraada smiled for the first time. "Ironic hearing that from you, General. I am prepared to document thirty-one instances in which you have had people executed in the name of the state. And although we don't *officially* have a death penalty now, I am assured by the president that we will have one by the time you go to trial. Your case will warrant it and public pressure will demand it."

Hidalgo remained unfazed. "I remind you, Colonel, that I have been previously investigated and cleared of any wrongdoing," he said.

"Some of your excesses have been investigated by military tribunals and, for reasons we both know, you were never officially charged. You will be this time. I also think you should know that I have agents in every company in the Sinsi Battalion and they have documented your activities in the Huallaga Valley."

That stunned Hidalgo. He had assumed that everyone who was paid was in, but suddenly understood that he had underestimated Savraada and his Dinconte agents. He took a moment to wonder who they were, but couldn't come up with a single suspect for certain. Until that moment he would have sworn that all his men were loyal to him. But he was a general, and knew that accusations easily made are hard to prove against a man of his means and stature. "Then your agents will have documented that the Sinsi Battalion has been successful in thwarting *Sendero*'s efforts at every turn," he said defiantly.

"Really?" Savraada asked quizzically with raised eyebrows. "Do you know a man named Alfredo Stesso?"

"No."

"Strange. You should. He was the commander of the *Sendero* Chou En Lai Company in the Huallaga Valley. You met with him at the Taverna Gallo in Tia Maria last April 21st. Your meeting was videotaped. You may be interested to know he is currently with Felipe on a ferryboat in New York City."

"Then he must be the Senderista I met there to negotiate an exchange of prisoners. It's done all the time," Hidalgo said, managing to contort his sneer into a smile.

Savraada disregarded the general's explanation with a wave of his hand. "How about a man named Esteban Merced? Do you know him?"

That one got the general. "Why don't you refresh my memory, Colonel?" he said, no longer sounding so confident.

"You met him at a jungle airstrip near Tarapoto last March 22nd. You thought he was a Colombian drug smuggler, but he is actually one of my men. Under duress, he gave you sixty thousand U.S. dollars so that you would let him fly out with a ton and a half of coca leaves. Those bills were previously marked and recorded, and some of them have turned up in some very interesting pockets here in Lima. In addition, you were also kind enough to give the members of the Second Company of the Sinsi Battalion a little ten-thousand-dollar bonus. Some of the bills you gave them will be presented as evidence at your trial, if you elect to stay."

"We'll see about that," Hidalgo said. His confidence was shaken but his courage was up. "You must think I am completely without influence to make such absurd accusations."

The effort was lost on Savraada. "On the contrary, General. I am completely aware of the influence you wield, and for that reason the minister of justice will be sitting next to you on the plane. He has wisely decided to accept my offer to leave while he can."

That piece of information hit Hidalgo hard and deflated his bravado. "Carreras is leaving?" he said weakly, more to himself than to Savraada.

"Yes. It's a long flight and I'm sure you two will have a lot to talk about. You can discuss the amazing coincidence that you have rented safe-deposit box Number R236 at the Puerta del Sol branch of the Banco de España in Madrid while he has Box Number R237. I understand they are very large boxes, which leads me to conclude that neither of you will be in danger of starvation, even without your pensions.''

Hidalgo was beaten and knew it. But he was confused about certain aspects in this new course of events. ''Why now, just when we were winning the war? This country needs men like me to beat *Sendero*,'' he asked.

''Wrong, General. It is because of men like you that we might wind up losing the war. Because of *Sendero*'s activities in New York, the world will be ready to listen to what they have to say about men like you and your methods. We aspire to be a civilized nation and can no longer have people like you around and in charge.''

''Then why are you letting me go?''

''I never intended to, but events have forced this decision. The next few days will be the most crucial time in our recent history, and we cannot afford to add political instability to our list of woes. The world will be looking hard at the actions of our army, and it would be better if you weren't here to answer any questions that will bring further discredit to the nation. Besides, your political payoffs will enable the president to exercise a certain amount of leverage among some previously recalcitrant high government officials.''

Now Savraada was in Hidalgo's realm, talking about political blackmail, which was one of the things the general understood well. His respect for Fujimori and Savraada climbed a notch. ''One last thing, Colonel. Since you seem to have me and you want me out of here so badly, why tomorrow night's flight? Why not tonight?''

''Because tonight you are going back to your base. You have one more service to perform for your country before you leave. You are going to gather your staff officers and announce that the battalion is going to be making a military sweep through Pucallpa and that they are going to engage *Sendero* there. You will then promote Major de Soto to colonel and place him in charge of the operation.''

''Major de Soto? Is he one of your men?''

''No, but I wish he were. From the information available to me, he appears to be an honest and capable officer. Unfortunately, he is loyal to you, but once you're gone that won't be a problem.''

Hidalgo agreed with Savraada's assessment of de Soto but didn't say so. De Soto was courageous and capable, and his honesty had always bothered the general. After some deliberation, Hidalgo had managed to take it in stride, happy to keep de Soto's share for himself.

But the general didn't understand the objective of the military exercise. "Why Pucallpa?" he asked. "*Sendero*'s there, but they won't be by the time we get there. We've swept through that area before and they always seem to know when we're coming. They just set a few ambushes and fade away."

"They'll know this time, too. But Pucallpa's just the first stop your battalion will be making. Then they're going into battle."

The idea of battle aroused Hidalgo's interest. He'd always thought the trouble with the war with *Sendero* was that there was never enough real combat, just patrols, skirmishes, and ambushes. "Where?" he asked.

Savraada regarded him coldly for a minute before answering. "Get dressed, General."

Chapter 47

Because of the *Sendero* action in New York, security was already tight at Tegucigalpa Airport and Cruzco knew it was going to get tighter. The afternoon papers had reported that the Honduran president had ordered the army to augment the police and the airport's security forces on duty there. What they hadn't reported in so many words was that the president's order was inspired by the intense pressure of the American government and the American airline carriers that served the capital city.

Still, in a country where the army was distrusted and feared because of a long history of brutal military takeovers, it was a move that surprised Cruzco and everyone else. It had taken the civilian government many years to get the army out of the capital in the first place, finally managing to dispatch most of the forces to remote bases along the Nicaraguan border where they no longer posed a threat to their own citizens.

But they were coming back. Cruzco's intelligence information was that a battalion had left by truck at eight that morning from their camp near the border, giving him two hours before they arrived. Cruzco had no choice but to advance the timing of the mission by a day. He knew the army would make use of their manpower to blockade the entrance to the airport and search all vehicles before allowing them to proceed to the terminals, a procedure that would invalidate the plan.

Cruzco was tense, but not worried. Felipe had thought of everything and his backup plan was a good one, although Cruzco was mildly surprised and somewhat annoyed that it had to be implemented. He had not expected to be joining Felipe in Peru until November, sometime after *Sendero* was in power there. But once he read about the capture of the *Sendero* hijack team in New York, he knew exactly what had to be done.

Finding the suitable personnel among the unemployed Sandinistas in Nicaragua had not been a problem for Cruzco, and he had served in combat there with five of the six he had selected for the mission. They all knew the plan and the risks, having been among those who trained Felipe's men in Nicaragua for the New York hijacking. They were ruthless professionals motivated by greed, a sentiment that Cruzco understood well and had always preferred over dedication to some abstract cause. Those who survived knew they were going to make half a million dollars apiece for three days' work. Those who didn't were going to leave some very wealthy widows who would soon adjust to their loss.

At 7:00 P.M. the taxi pulled in front of the terminal used by United Airlines and American Airlines. Cruzco and Miguel, both dressed in American business suits, got out and waited on the sidewalk while the taxi driver unloaded their two bags from the trunk under the watchful eyes of two policemen standing at the terminal entrance. Cruzco and Miguel each took an American Airlines ticket folder and American passports from their breast pockets.

"How much?" Cruzco asked the taxi driver in English.

"*Viente lempiras, señor*," the driver answered.

While the two policemen looked on, Cruzco turned to Miguel. "How much did he say it was?" Cruzco asked in unaccented English, looking confused.

"You got me, partner," Miguel replied, looking equally

confused. "Just show him your money. He looks honest enough."

Cruzco took a wad of Honduran money from his pocket and spread the bills in front of the taxi driver, who promptly selected a fifty-lempira bill for the twenty-lempira fare. "*Eso es*," he said, putting the bill in his pocket, which caused the two policemen to smile.

"Thank you very much and have a nice day," Cruzco said as he and Miguel picked up the suitcases. As the happy taxi driver took off, one of the smiling policemen opened the door for the two dupes and waved them into the terminal.

While Miguel waited near the door, Cruzco checked the television monitor displaying the departing flights. American Airlines Flight 902 for Miami was on time, due to depart in ten minutes from Gate Two. Cruzco was satisfied and right on time. Looking around, he saw three pairs of uniformed policemen stationed in the terminal, with one man in each team armed with an FLN Belgian automatic rifle.

Since there were only a few other passengers in the terminal, it was immediately apparent to Cruzco that security had doubled since he had checked it that morning. Aside from the two cops at the terminal door, one pair was stationed at the ticket counter, one pair was at the metal detector leading to the United Airlines gates at one end of the terminal, and one pair was on duty at the metal detector leading to the American Airlines gates at the other end of the terminal.

Cruzco figured he was going to take some casualties because of the increased security, but he still wasn't worried. He had allowed for casualties, and the Honduran cops didn't impress him. They were a slovenly lot. Most of their uniforms were dirty and unpressed and more than half of them needed a shave. Cruzco knew they were low paid, loosely disciplined, and poorly trained. He didn't expect much in the way of heroics from the Honduran police once the shooting started and the confusion began.

Leaving Miguel at his post near the terminal entrance, Cruzco walked to the end of the terminal and put down his suitcase near the metal detector leading to the American Airlines gates. The two airline employees manning the metal detector regarded him quizzically, but the cops gave him no more than a passing glance. Reaching down, he took a copy of the *Washington Post* from his suitcase and began to read. As he looked over the edge of the paper, he saw that the police were talking to each other and still paying him no mind. There were no other cops visible on the other side of the metal detector in the long corridor leading to the gates. Then he looked through the front glass of the terminal and saw another taxi pull up. Simon and Antonio got out, also dressed as American businessmen. They paid the driver, picked up their suitcases, and walked to the terminal door.

For a moment, Cruzco thought things were going to go even better than he and Felipe had planned. Then one of the two policemen outside placed himself in front of the door, blocking Cruzco's two men as a delivery van pulled up outside the terminal doors.

Cruzco folded up his newspaper, picked up his suitcase, and placed it on the metal detector conveyor belt as Miguel and the two Honduran cops watched him. He opened up the suitcase as if replacing his newspaper.

It was the signal Miguel was waiting for. He took a pistol from his suitcase and fired four shots through the front glass, hitting both cops outside as the side door of the delivery van opened. Two of Cruzco's men inside the van opened up on the front of the terminal with an M-60 machine gun positioned at the side door of the van, shattering every pane of glass in the United end and hitting both cops stationed there. Miguel turned and fired at the two cops at the ticket counter. Though hit, one of them managed to return fire with his FLN, cutting Miguel to pieces as Simon and Antonio stepped through the broken front glass, firing back. The cop was hit again, but managed to direct a burst at Antonio, hitting him in the legs. Antonio hit the ground screaming just before the cop collapsed.

Cruzco kept his attention on the cops at the metal detector in front of him. They were in a state of confusion for a moment. Ignoring Cruzco, one of them raised his FLN to fire at the attackers, but his companion decided to retreat, running down the corridor leading to the gates.

Cruzco took his pistol from his open suitcase and shot the policeman before he could get off a round. Then he turned his pistol on the two airline employees, but didn't fire. They had wisely raised their hands in the air as high as they could and posed no threat to Cruzco. Leaning his pistol on the metal detector for support, he fired four rounds down the corridor, hitting the fleeing cop in the back.

Ten seconds had elapsed from Miguel's first shot till the

time Cruzco jumped over the body of the cop in the corridor.
Just as he burst into the gate area, the sounds of gunfire in the
terminal behind him ceased. He stopped for a moment, searching for targets and ready to fire, but there were none. All of
the passengers for the Miami flight had already boarded. As
Cruzco ran past the gate check-in counter he saw two American Airlines clerks on the floor behind the counter, but there
were no cops in sight. He got to the plane door just as a
terrified flight attendant was trying to close it. She took one
look at Cruzco and raised her hands in the air.

Cruzco stepped past her into the plane and faced the passengers, most of whom were bent over in their seats. He had
been set to make an announcement, but found it unnecessary.
The plane was full, but no one was moving.

Cruzco waited and listened. The terminal area was quiet.
Then he heard someone running toward him from the gate
area. He pointed his pistol down the loading corridor, ready
to shoot any pursuers, but it was Simon who appeared. He
gave Cruzco a thumbs-up sign, then brushed past him on his
way to the cockpit.

Less then one minute after the shooting started, Felipe had
his plane.

Chapter 48 McKenna and Pao cleared the first Ken-
nedy Airport checkpoint just after dark. Pao waited at the second checkpoint for Tavlin and Gaspar in the car behind them
to clear it also.

As far as McKenna was concerned, everything was going
great. The surveillance teams following Seymor Cranston had
reported that he had just gotten off the Long Island Expressway and should be home in five minutes, if he didn't make
any stops. Then Brunette called. "Better get a move on,
buddy," he advised. "Looks like they got their plane."

"Where?"

"Tegucigalpa, Honduras. It's still on the runway."

"A Boeing 727?" McKenna asked.

"You guessed it. Took it about an hour ago. Looks like they caused some damage down there, but we don't know much more than that right now."

"Did they bring parachutes with them?" McKenna asked, bracing himself for the answer.

"Don't know yet," Brunette answered. "Shields has got a line into the State Department, but right now it looks like nobody knows more than CNN. I'll call you when I hear more."

"Change of plans?" Pao asked as soon as McKenna hung up.

"Yep. We're gonna watch some TV, amigo."

Five minutes later the four of them were gathered around a TV in Lieutenant Ward's office in the Port Authority police station. CNN was running live footage of the drama at Tegucigalpa Airport. American Airlines Flight 902 was parked on the end of the runway, its path blocked by Honduran army trucks. While they watched, a CNN reporter came on-screen to announce that another one of the wounded policemen had died, updating the hijacking death toll to six cops, two civilian airline employees, and two hijackers. CNN then played the interview of Tonia Salazar, one of the United Airlines reservation clerks who had survived the attack.

McKenna paid close attention as the pretty young girl in her blood-splattered uniform related the horror she had witnessed. She said she had been returning to her work station from the ladies' room when the shooting started and had immediately dropped to the floor. But she kept her eyes open and what she saw in those few moments would be indelibly etched in her brain for the rest of her life. After the shooting stopped, one of the wounded hijackers was right in front of her, shot in the legs. Another one of the hijackers stood over him, then noticed her watching. She said he pointed his rifle at her and she thought her life was over, but instead he just said, "Close your eyes, señorita. You don't want to see this." She did, and then she heard some more gunshots. When she opened her eyes again a minute later, the wounded hijacker was dead, shot many times in the chest.

"How many hijackers were there?" the reporter asked.

Salazar stopped to think for a moment, counting on her fingers. "Counting the two who were killed, I saw six," she said. "But there may have been more."

The reporter thanked Salazar, then the camera closed on him. He said that as far as was known, there had been only one message from the hijackers. The pilot called the control tower and said they would blow up the plane if the army shot the tires out. The reporter said American Airlines was ready to release the passenger list, but were awaiting Honduran government approval before doing so.

As the scene switched back to the airplane on the runway, the reporter speculated that the hijacking was connected to the ongoing Shining Path activities in New York Harbor, but said that Honduran government officials had refused to comment on that possibility.

McKenna was lost in thought and couldn't take his eyes off the plane on the screen. After a minute he realized he was the only one still watching. Everyone else was watching him.

"What are you worrying about?" Tavlin asked. "We were expecting something like this, weren't we?"

McKenna kept his eyes on the TV while he answered. "I was just thinking. Unless the Honduran government screws this up with some drastic action, I'm gonna be on that plane soon." Then he took his phone from his pocket and called Brunette back. "Anything new?" he asked.

"Yeah. Shields just got off the line with the State Department and for once we know more than CNN can tell us. They've got one hundred and twenty passengers onboard, including eighty-two Honduran nationals. The hijackers called the tower and said they're willing to let the Hondurans go if they can take off."

"That's exactly what we want to happen," McKenna said.

"You think I don't know that?" Brunette retorted, sounding a little annoyed. Brunette didn't say anything for a few moments while McKenna pictured his friend bringing himself under control. "Sorry," Brunette finally said. "I gotta watch myself. Lately, I'm snapping at everyone around here."

"You're entitled," McKenna replied. "These folks are putting us under a lot of pressure."

"It's not the pressure that's getting me. It's just that those killings down there were so unnecessary. We would've given Felipe any plane he wanted."

"That's not his style."

"I realize that. Good news is that we're stretching his resources. According to the Hondurans, none of the hijackers looked like his usual troops. They were Spanish, but they weren't Indians."

"Then we made him use his Sandinista friends," McKenna guessed. "Nicaragua is right next door to Honduras. Those people shouldn't care about what happens to *Sendero* in Peru, so they have to be in it for the money."

"That's the problem," Brunette said. "If they were just some more crazy Senderistas, the Hondurans would let them go. But now they think they can talk and threaten them into giving up."

What good would that do us in New York? McKenna wondered. He came to the conclusion it would do nothing but complicate his negotiations with Felipe. "Then we better get some heavyweights talking to the Hondurans," he said. "We want that plane here in one piece."

"That's what I figured and Shields tells me it's being done. But look at the bright side. They haven't their parachutes onboard yet, so you're on the right track."

That *is* a bright side, McKenna thought. "Unless we're a bunch of dopes, I'll be calling you later with some good news," he told Brunette.

McKenna checked with the surveillance team by radio before Gaspar tackled the lock on Cranston's shed. They told him that Cranston was sitting by himself in a bar near his house, watching the hijack coverage on CNN. He was on his third drink and they figured he wasn't going anywhere for a while.

"Let's see what he's got," McKenna said to Gaspar.

With Tavlin holding the light, Gaspar gave the large and expensive lock on Cranston's shed no more than a passing glance. "This should only take a minute," he commented as he knelt down and spread his kit of lock picks on the ground.

Ten seconds after Gaspar had inserted two picks in the cylinder, he said, "Pull the lock down." McKenna did. The lock snapped open and McKenna pulled it out of the hasp and opened the door.

McKenna was ready to go in, but Gaspar held him back and made him feel foolish in the process. "Don't you think we should take some pictures first?" Gaspar asked.

Of course we should, McKenna realized. We want to make sure Cranston finds everything exactly the way he left it this afternoon. He stepped back and Gaspar snapped six Polaroid pictures of the interior of the shed. Then McKenna entered and found the light switch on the wall and also found that Cranston was a very neat kind of guy.

The interior of the shed was immaculate and freshly painted and McKenna was surprised to see that it was even carpeted. Cranston's tractor was parked in the middle of the room, with his tools and lawn attachments for the tractor hung on hooks along the wall. From the entrance he could see four large drums in a row along the back wall, each marked with a HAZ-ARDOUS MATERIALS sign, but there were no parachutes in sight. McKenna carefully wiped his feet on the grass before entering, then went straight to the rear of the shed. He knocked on each drum, and from the sound could tell that two of them were empty and two were full of a liquid.

Pao wiped his feet and came in. He took a quick look around and laughed. ''Looks like a bust,'' was his cheery observation, which caused McKenna to stifle an instant impulse to place his hands around Pao's neck and squeeze for all he was worth. But he didn't, because he knew the parachutes had to be there. Then Gaspar came in and looked around. Like McKenna and Pao, he saw nothing until he picked up a plastic container from a shelf near the door.

''What is it?'' McKenna asked.

Gaspar squeezed the container and was rewarded with a blast of white powder. ''Talcum powder,'' he commented as he wiped the powder from his face.

It was good news to McKenna. He went to the door and pulled up the rug. Underneath, the floor was covered in talcum powder, with his and Pao's footprints clearly outlined in the powder.

''Looks like Cranston wants to know if he has visitors while he's away,'' Tavlin observed from the door.

''That's why they have to be in here,'' McKenna said, looking up. But there was nothing to be seen but a plywood ceiling, eight feet from the floor. It looked like each plywood sheet had been nailed to the supporting cross beams it was lying on. McKenna walked around, looking for an opening or a trap door. There was none. Then Gaspar found a ten-foot ladder behind the steel drums and McKenna's hopes soared. Gaspar took the ladder and pressed the top against four of the plywood ceiling sheets, but they were nailed tight. The fifth one wasn't, and using the ladder Gaspar pushed it up and rested the top of the ladder against the ceiling cross beam. He held the ladder steady while McKenna climbed up and pushed the plywood sheet out of the way. Then Tavlin passed up a flashlight and McKenna shined it around the attic of the shed for a few moments.

"Well, what's up there?" Pao demanded.

"You're right, Johnny. It's a bust," McKenna yelled down.

"Thought so," Pao commented smugly.

It was exactly what McKenna was waiting for. He reached into the attic and threw down a parachute, hitting Pao in the chest and saying, "Nothing up here but seventy-five of those old things."

"What? You've never been wrong?" Pao said, sounding contrite and subdued for the first time in McKenna's experience. Pao picked up the chute and examined it as McKenna climbed down. Pao was the old Pao again by the time McKenna reached the floor.

"What you have discovered," Pao said authoritatively as he held up the chute, "is a standard U.S. Army military surplus parachute which, when opened and properly deployed, should dispense sixty square yards of nylon above the head of the person who would dare to jump from a plane in flight."

"Thanks for that information," Tavlin said.

"But I have more, of course, Inspector," Pao answered.

"Please further enlighten us, Johnny," McKenna asked respectfully.

"If you insist," Pao said, pointing to a small canvas pack attached to the front of the chute. "This is a reserve chute attached on a front harness which, as you can see, has been packed and sealed under federal supervision. The daredevil jumping from a plane would deploy this chute in the event of any malfunction with his primary chute."

"Thank you, Johnny. You've been a big help," McKenna said as he took his phone from his pocket and dialed.

"Who you calling?" Pao asked.

"A General Sneadman. He tells me he has quite a few guys hanging around who, like yourself, profess to know a lot about parachutes. If they know as much as he says they do, we might be able to play a little joke on Felipe and his boys."

Chapter 49 July 31, GRAMERCY PARK HOTEL—
McKenna had hoped to sleep late after a long night at the
airport, but it wasn't to be. It seemed to him that he had just
conked out when he was awakened by the sound of the TV in
his room. Reluctantly he opened his eyes, searching for the
source of irritation. It was Brunette, very much at home, seated
at the table eating breakfast while watching CNN. "Gonna
sleep all day?" Brunette asked.

"No, but I could've used a few more hours," McKenna
answered as he swung his legs over the side of the bed. "What
time is it?"

"Late. A little after nine. But I thought you'd want to see
this," Brunette said, pointing to the TV.

So McKenna sat in his underwear and watched the TV as
Flight 902 took off from Tegucigalpa Airport. "Is that live?"
he asked.

"Live from Honduras."

"What did it cost to get them out of there?"

"I don't know what the State Department promised the
Hondurans for their cooperation, but the locals still wound up
striking a pretty good bargain with Felipe's men. They released
everyone on the flight but twenty American men."

"So they're headed for New York now?" McKenna asked.

"They didn't say, but we can assume so. But they're gonna
have to refuel somewhere."

"Find out how many hijackers are onboard?"

"The passengers they released said there's five hijackers left
and you were right about them. They're Sandinistas."

"How can you be so sure?" McKenna asked.

Brunette took a folder from the chair next to him, opened
it, and took a photo off the top and handed it to McKenna.

"Because their leader is this guy," he said.

McKenna studied the photo of Cruzco in a Soviet military uniform, taken when he was younger and without his beard. "He's a Russian?" McKenna asked.

"Yep. Nikolai Kevensky. Supposed to be one of their best agents. They infiltrated him into the Sandinista movement in 1979 and he wound up being a big shot in the Ministry of Defense in Nicaragua. Calls himself Cruzco now. After the Sandinistas lost the election there he was demoted, but he still has a pretty good job. Sort of a minister without portfolio. Here's a recent picture of him in his Sandinista getup," Brunette said, handing McKenna another picture.

McKenna looked at that one, a picture of Cruzco in a green Nicaraguan uniform. "So the Russians *are* involved in this, somehow," McKenna observed.

"Not anymore. The world's changed and they're changing with it, whether they like it or not. They wanted to get out of the revolution business, so they promoted him to general a couple of months ago and recalled him to Moscow for his retirement party. He never showed up."

"Didn't that worry them?"

"They were a little worried then, but now they're frantic."

McKenna could imagine that they were. "We know why he didn't show," he said. "He was too busy training Felipe's men in Honduras for bigger stakes."

"That's what it looks like," Brunette said, handing McKenna the folder. "Here's the deal on our Felipe, but he's not a Russian like Gleason thought. He's a Georgian. His real name is Alexi Demorschnadze."

"Stalin was a Georgian," McKenna said. "But we sure called him a Russian, didn't we?"

"Yeah."

"So all it should mean to us is that Felipe used to be a Russian until the Soviet Union fell apart," McKenna observed, opening the folder. On top was a picture of a younger Felipe in a Soviet military uniform. He could see that even then Felipe had an arrogant air about him as he stared into the camera. "What story are the Russians giving about his status?" McKenna asked.

"Like I said, as far as they're concerned he's not a Russian so he has no status. They retired him as a colonel in April and suggested he seek a commission in the Georgian army. He didn't even bother to reply to their message."

"Seems to me they don't treat their help too good. Didn't they put him in Peru?"

"Sure did, just the way we figured. They infiltrated him into Peru in 1983 after they figured he was burned in New York. Turns out he was perfect for the job. He had lots of training in guerrilla warfare and they gave him high marks for revolutionary fervor. He also had a real knack for languages, which helped him move up fast in *Sendero*. The Russians say he speaks French and some Italian, in addition to Russian and Georgian."

"Along with his Spanish and English," McKenna observed. "If anyone on their side is still keeping track, you can tell them to add Quechua to their list."

"They aren't. The Russians just want this whole thing to go away. Felipe isn't doing them any good."

McKenna took a minute to thumb through the thick folder. He closed it when he realized that what he had in his hands was Felipe's KGB personnel folder, translated into English. "I guess the President extorted this from Yeltsin, didn't he?" he asked.

Brunette smiled, like he was about to share a joke. "Had a job doing it. Boris told him he checked with his intelligence people and nobody on their side knew anything about Felipe. Now, the President knows Boris is having some problems with those folks since most of them are KGB hard-liners and not exactly in his corner. So he believed Boris and gave him some ammunition. Told him to check with Leonid Kantorovich and Werner Bachmann."

Leonid Kantorovich and Werner Bachmann? The names meant something to McKenna, but it took him a moment to remember exactly who they were. Then it came to him: the two KGB agents Shields had developed from Gleason's exploits. But the moment's hesitation was too much and he was sure Brunette had noticed his blank look. "Kantorovich is at the Russian embassy in Berlin and Bachmann's lost someplace in the Motherland, right?" McKenna asked, trying to sound like the bright guy in possession of all the facts.

"Of course," Brunette said, giving McKenna an amused smile. "So Boris sent someone to talk hard to both of them and they confirmed everything the President told him. Then he called his intelligence people onto the carpet."

"And they said, 'Oh, you meant *that* Felipe, Your Worship,' " McKenna speculated. " 'Why didn't you say so? We seem to remember something about *that* Felipe.' "

"Must've went something like that, once their memories were throttled. Apparently they thought he was doing a fine job in Peru until the world changed. The speculation in Washington is that when the USSR fell apart they lost track of their Cruzco and Felipe types, and after a while they just forgot about them in the confusion."

"Doesn't it sort of make you wonder how many more of these recently unemployed characters they left running around the Third World?" McKenna asked.

"I don't think they even know, but that's not our concern right now. Let's just worry about Felipe. We've got a lot of information on him now."

"Including, I hope, the names on the forged birth certificates the KGB provided him with."

"Yeah, there's five of them, all real tongue twisters. The Intelligence Division is working on them in New York and Shields is running them down nationwide. I was thinking you might want to give the names to Bob Hurley just to keep our functionaries honest."

"I think Hurley is all we need. He'll do it and save the taxpayers a bundle in the process."

"Whatever," Brunette said with a wave of his hand. "I don't care who we pay or who gets the credit, as long as we find Felipe's real estate holdings."

"Didn't the Russians give you the locations of the safe houses he set up for them?"

"Yeah. Besides the two we know about, there were another three. Sheeran checked them out. None of them are being used."

But with the names, maybe we still have a chance of finding the Williamsburg Bridge detonator, McKenna thought, though he still found it incredible that the Russians had given up so much information. "Do you know the deal the President cut with Yeltsin that makes us so smart right now?" he asked.

"Sure. It's simple. As long as Boris is in power, neither Felipe or Cruzco were ever Russian agents. That means we don't enlighten the press, the Peruvians, or the Nicaraguans. We don't embarrass Yeltsin in any way, whether we win or lose with *Sendero*."

Not a bad deal for Boris, McKenna thought. It never happened. McKenna tried to put himself in the beleaguered Russian president's head and came to another conclusion. "So the way it stands, whether we win or lose, Boris still wins. We gave him a weapon to whip his KGB in line so they have to stop giving him headaches.''

"I'm sure that went through his mind," Brunette said without interest. "His motivation isn't our concern, as long as the information is good.''

It occurred to McKenna that his friend, the guy who used to be a rabid and very vocal anticommunist hard-liner, only had room in his periscope sight for one target at a time, and Felipe was the one sitting in his crosshairs. "Anything about Cranston in here?" McKenna asked, hefting the folder.

"It's in there. According to them, it was just a case of industrial espionage. Felipe had told him that he represented a company called Eurotech Pharmaceuticals. Whether Seymor believed him or not at the time is a matter for conjecture, but he sold Felipe every Brookhaven Lab project he could get his hands on for three years.''

"But they never did anything in the way of biological warfare, right?''

"Right.''

"So Felipe must be blackmailing him to play ball right now, and maybe as a form of revenge Cranston sold him a bill of goods and called it a great case of germs.''

Brunette didn't think Cranston's motivation was important. "Who cares why he's doing it?" he said. "He's still a slimeball and we're gonna square away with him once this is over. We'll get them all.''

McKenna was satisfied with the answer. To him, it gave a hint that life was going to go on for Brunette once the crisis was over. But McKenna wanted to be alone for a while. "I'm gonna need some time to go over Felipe's history. You got my schedule for the day?" he asked, hoping Brunette got the hint.

He did. Standing up, he answered, "Far as I can see, you're free until lunch with Heresford at one o'clock at city hall. He's in Washington right now, but he'll be back.''

"I hope he's getting the State Department to twist some arms to keep Felipe happy.''

"I wouldn't worry too much about his end," Brunette said as he headed for the door. "He's a pretty effective guy. I'll see you before you meet Felipe.''

Brunette exited, leaving McKenna feeling guilty for a reason he couldn't articulate. He showered and got dressed, then ordered breakfast from room service. While he ate, he went over

Felipe's folder, not only to learn his background, but also to get a better understanding of what made him tick. In spite of himself, as he read his respect for Felipe increased. He had to admit that Felipe was simply the best at what he did, and it hadn't been easy for him. Being a product of the Cold War and having been raised in a totalitarian state, Felipe had spent a diligent lifetime working, studying, and taking risks, always achieving some degree of success in his assignments, but receiving few rewards along the way.

Since they were roughly the same age, McKenna found himself comparing his life's accomplishments to Felipe's, but finally concluded it couldn't be done. It was like comparing apples and oranges. Both had worked hard to become who they were, but life had treated them differently. Felipe was desperate and making one last grab for the brass ring while his world was collapsing around him.

McKenna thought about Felipe and *Sendero* for another hour, but the prospect of the killing to come depressed him. He decided to call Angelita. He missed her terribly and called her whenever he wasn't too busy, which meant he hadn't been calling enough lately.

Angelita answered on the first ring. "I knew it was you," she said, sounding chipper. "How you doing?"

"All right, considering."

"Feeling a little down, are we?"

McKenna couldn't figure out how she did it, but she always managed to gauge his mood. He could never pretend with her. "A little."

"When are you gonna finish with those people?"

"Soon, but there's a problem. They're discharging you today, aren't they?"

There was silence on the line and McKenna could almost feel Angelita probing his mind. He didn't want to worry her and was almost sorry he had mentioned it, but he wanted her with him. After all, there was a problem.

"You're gonna be doing something dangerous," she said in a way that told him there was no use denying it.

"Yeah, I'm gonna be going to Peru with Felipe."

"I knew it had to be something like that. On that plane that was hijacked last night?"

"Yeah. If everything works out, I'll be on it."

"When?"

"I can't say, exactly. Felipe's doing all the scheduling up

here.'' McKenna waited for a protest or a demand for an explanation, but there was none. "Joe will rent a car and we'll be there by four," was all she said.

"Take your time," McKenna suggested. "I'm gonna be busy at four."

"Don't worry about me. Just do what you have to and I'll be there when you get back to the hotel."

Angelita sounded upbeat, but McKenna knew the signs and could tell from her voice she was crying and trying to hide it. "Don't worry about it, baby. We're gonna win," he assured her, putting all the confidence he could muster into his voice.

"I'm trying not to worry, but I know you, Brian. You always think you're gonna win, but sometimes you lose."

After thinking about it for a moment, he knew she was right. He hadn't always emerged a winner in the police department, but he was grateful she didn't go into case histories. "It'll be good to see you," was all he could think to say, trying to change the subject.

She let him believe he got away with it. "Keep a clear head, hotshot. I'll see you later," she said. He heard her stifle a sob before she hung up.

Angelita had given him some unpleasant things to think about, but he couldn't afford to dwell on them. So he got back to business and called Bob Hurley.

Chapter 50

Julio Montalvo and the other ten *Sendero* prisoners stood on the rear deck of the police launch tied up at the Wall Street pier, looking tired but happy. They hadn't slept for days, but they weren't handcuffed and obviously knew their situation had improved somewhat.

Their lack of sleep was McKenna's idea. He figured that all eleven would be subjected to intense scrutiny by Felipe. To try to keep him from guessing that Julio had talked and given up the information that led to Seymor Cranston, McKenna had the other ten subjected to a full day and night of interrogation, with Picciarelli and his team hitting them with a steady barrage of questions, all of which McKenna already knew the answers to, thanks to Julio. Up until the last minute, each of them had been offered every type of deal that Picciarelli's fertile imagination could produce, but not one of the other ten had cracked.

Feeling that one informant in the bunch might be enough and two would be too many, McKenna was just as happy with that result. But he feared that the time would come when he would need Julio as more than just an informant, but wasn't sure if the young Senderista would rise to the occasion.

It wasn't that McKenna doubted his bravery. After all, Julio had agreed to his return to Felipe and ultimately, Peru, even though he was placing himself in extreme danger if Felipe got even a hint that one of the returning prisoners had talked. What bothered McKenna was his suspicion that Julio was still a dedicated Senderista, although now richer than his comrades to the tune of $200,000, safely on deposit in his name. McKenna had thrown in the extra $100,000 with the understanding that Julio would help out in any way he could, should an opportunity present itself. But McKenna suspected that Julio had talked, not because of any disenchantment with the *Sendero* cause or any threats McKenna had made, but because he hated Felipe more than he feared him. In Peru, Julio had been one of those favored to share Ingrid Troutmann's bed, and he took her murder as a personal affront. His motive was revenge.

Standing on the pier looking down at the launch, McKenna marveled at the dedication displayed by the Senderistas. They were all young, looking about as menacing as a bunch of kids on a high school field trip to the harbor, but he knew they were all killers, trained and ready to cause mayhem and die for their cause. Since they had been taken prisoner in Brighton Beach three days before, they had been kept separated and uninformed of Felipe's exploits in the harbor. Yet, their individual morales had remained high and they wouldn't be shaken by the usual methods. They all had faith that Felipe would free them, so none of them had exhibited any degree of surprise when they had been reunited and put in the paddy wagon for the trip to Wall Street. Without being told, they had felt certain they were going back. It wasn't until they were placed on the police launch that McKenna saw the first questioning looks. According to Julio, Felipe's hijacking team hadn't been let in on the plan to take the ferries. They knew only as much as they needed to know to do their part of the mission, and no more. McKenna had filed another Felipe leadership trait in the back of his mind for future reference.

Partly in return for the respect Felipe had shown him on the ferry, McKenna had ordered the surprised Harbor cops to remove the handcuffs from the prisoners as soon as they were brought onto the boat. Another reason for the order was that he wanted to see how the Senderistas reacted to their freedom, and he was interested by the result. He saw Jesus Arroyo take charge: Arroyo was the one with the bandaged hand whom Julio had identified as their squad leader. Arroyo said a few words to his men in Quechua, and they all sat down on the rear deck, talking quietly among themselves, but certainly giving the Harbor cops no problems. As McKenna suspected, even in times of uncertainty they were a disciplined bunch. He noticed that they ignored the Harbor cops, but seemed interested in him.

Then Arroyo approached McKenna. "Would you mind telling us where we're going?" he asked in a thick Spanish accent while looking up into McKenna's eyes.

"Not at all. As part of a deal I worked out with Felipe, you're joining him on the ferry."

"The ferry?" he asked, confused.

McKenna was happy with the question, which meant that Julio hadn't been lying. "Yes, your comrades have taken over two of our ferries and Felipe is demanding your return as part of his deal," McKenna explained.

The young Senderista took it in without showing any degree of surprise, but displayed a look that McKenna couldn't diagnose for a moment. Then he got it. It was pride. Arroyo was proud of his leader.

"Could you tell us why we're waiting here?" Arroyo asked.

For a moment, McKenna didn't reply. There was the sound of many sirens, coming closer. He turned around and watched as three police cars and an Emergency Service truck leading an armored truck broke into view from the canyons of the Financial District. The caravan stopped at the pier and McKenna turned back to the Senderista. "That's what we're waiting for," he said.

"Money?" the young man asked.

"Lots of it."

Without another word, the young man turned and rejoined his companions sitting on the deck. They watched intently as the four duffel bags were unloaded from the armored truck and placed in the cabin of the police launch. The launch cast off as the first reporters, alerted by the sirens, arrived on the pier looking for a story.

It was a nice day to be on the water, but McKenna wasn't enjoying it. During the trip to the ferry McKenna kept to himself inside the cabin, going over in his mind the points to be discussed with Felipe. Not that there was much to be discussed, he thought. His mission for the day basically amounted to telling Felipe that what he demanded was being done. For that reason he hadn't brought Camilia Wright to record the details of the embarrassing session, and Heresford had agreed with his position. His reasoning was that the fewer people around to document the capitulation of the United States government to the demands of an itinerant bunch of Third World terrorists, the better it would be in case the time ever came around when the details had to be denied.

Half an hour later, they were once again tying up at the rear deck of the *Samuel I. Newhouse*. This time the Senderistas on the rear deck, although armed, kept their weapons pointed away from the launch. Felipe was there to welcome the returned prisoners. He was casually dressed in dungarees and a blue naval work shirt, which led McKenna to believe that relaxation had been his order of the day to his men.

McKenna stood on the deck of the launch as the Harbor cops brought the duffel bags out of the cabin, but Felipe didn't appear interested in the money. He gave McKenna a wave, then helped each prisoner board the ferry, hugging every one after a short conversation in Quechua.

It appeared to McKenna that the prisoners regarded Felipe with a mixture of adoration and a healthy dose of fear. He filed that away, too, concluding that however Felipe had engendered that attitude in his troops, it worked very well for him.

Once his men had been led inside, Felipe turned back to McKenna, smiling, and again offered his hand to help McKenna onboard. This time McKenna accepted. He stood next to Felipe, figuring that Felipe would want to stay to supervise the unloading of the money, but he was wrong. "Ready to chat?" he asked McKenna, and when McKenna nodded he led him back to the table in the main cabin.

Once again, Felipe was the perfect and very confident host. He was alone and unarmed, pouring the coffee as if he were standing in his suburban living room among friends. "Should we begin?"

"Yes. I'm sure you know that an airliner has been hijacked in Honduras. We thought it was coming here, but it has landed in Miami instead."

"So I've heard," Felipe said.

"Since it landed we've received no further word from the hijackers and there is some speculation that these people are not connected to you," McKenna said, hoping to convince Felipe that he knew nothing of *Sendero*'s plans.

Felipe eyed McKenna for a moment, then stated, "It's my plane."

"I thought so," McKenna said, and was mildly surprised when Felipe decided to elaborate.

"I was a little surprised at it myself," he said. "That action wasn't scheduled to take place until today."

"Then permit me to say I'm gratified to learn that everything isn't going exactly your way."

Felipe smiled. "Permission granted," he said. "Please don't bother concerning yourself with my minor problems. Flight 902 will be coming here at the conclusion of our business. I hope you will ensure its safe arrival without me giving you the usual threats."

"It'll be here when you want it, but as I told you before, those additional deaths in Honduras were unnecessary. We would have given you a plane."

"So you said, and I considered your offer. But I prefer to depend on my own resources, and you must understand that once plans are made they are difficult to change from here. However, I do regret those deaths," Felipe said, sincerely. "Let's get to the next order of business."

McKenna took a thick envelope from his pocket and pushed it across the table to Felipe. As he expected, Felipe ignored the envelope and remained focused on him.

"It contains a signed statement from President Fujimori agreeing to two of your original demands, modified by the stipulations we agreed upon. The document is a fax copy, but he will have the original delivered to any address you specify."

"That won't be necessary," Felipe said. "I believe Fujimori can be trusted. Have you read it?"

"Yes. You'll find that it also contains some suggestions Fujimori has to end your war."

"Enlighten me as to the contents, if you would."

"Fujimori agrees to provide an honest explanation on the fates of the missing persons on the list you provided me. These cases will be investigated thoroughly and he will update the press from time to time as cases are resolved. As a show of good faith, he has already investigated thirty-seven cases and concluded that they were all illegally executed by members of something called the Sinsi Battalion. As a result, he has removed their commanding officer."

"I'm impressed," Felipe said. "You wouldn't know, but General Ramon Hidalgo is something of a powerhouse in Peruvian politics. What about the amnesty provisions?"

"He has agreed to them. Amnesty for members of both sides, commencing thirty days from now, for all actions taken previously. To implement your demands, he also agrees to safe passage for members of the UN Human Rights Commission and Amnesty International through territories controlled by government forces and full access to government records for any members of those organizations to investigate illegal government acts alleged by *Sendero*."

"I'm satisfied with that," Felipe said. "What else?"

"President Fujimori suggests that a date be set for himself and the persons in charge of your movement to formally sign the agreement binding both sides to the provisions you specified. He states he would attend this conference with an open mind and that possibly some further agreements might come out of it that would end the war."

"I'm glad to hear that. I will pass it on to my superiors for contemplation," Felipe said blandly.

That's a lie, McKenna thought. You don't have any superiors in *Sendero*, and you expect to be in charge by the date any conference could be arranged. But he kept those thoughts to himself and said, "That's something you're going to have to work out between both sides after you're out of here."

"I'm sure an attempt will be made," Felipe said. "I assume this envelope also contains Fujimori's acquiescence to our demands concerning the prisoners held by the government."

"Agreement, not acquiescence. Through the offices of our State Department, Chile has agreed to accept the three hundred and twenty-one prisoners held by the government, with the provision that they be lodged in camps under the supervision of the UN. Chile will also accept any dependents of the prisoners, as long as they are also interned in the camps. The government of Peru will pay for the transportation costs as long as *Sendero* pays for the maintenance of the prisoners *and* the camps.''

''I presume those thrifty Chileans have a figure in mind?'' Felipe stated while smiling at McKenna.

McKenna smiled back. ''I thought it was a little expensive until I remembered that the figure bandied about to keep one prisoner in jail in the United States is fifty thousand dollars a year.''

''We're not sending them here, we're sending them to Chile, where things are a little cheaper,'' Felipe said, sounding a little testy. ''How much do they propose to hold us up for?''

''Thirty thousand dollars a year for each guest,'' McKenna said, enjoying Felipe's reaction to the figure. ''I've already done the math for you to save some time. Assuming each prisoner brings two dependents, that's about twenty-nine million dollars a year.''

McKenna enjoyed Felipe's apparent discomfort, but then he remembered something that ruined his fun. Felipe didn't intend to have to pay for those prisoners for more than a couple of months, because by then he would be in charge and would, presumably, bring them back to Peru. What a showman, McKenna thought as he watched Felipe's facial contortions and consternation. Wanting to put an end to the spectacle, McKenna suggested, ''You know, it's not like you can't afford it now.''

Felipe took the hint. ''Then it's agreed,'' he said, seemingly reluctant. ''They will go to Chile. Which, incidentally, brings us to the money. I'm assuming those duffel bags contain seventy-five million dollars in the denominations I specified.''

''I didn't count it, but that's what I'm told. The currency counting machine is also there so you can check it yourself,'' McKenna said, trying to sound testy about it.

He got the reaction he hoped for. ''Maybe we've talked just about enough for today,'' Felipe said calmly.

Good, McKenna thought. He thinks I'm on the ropes without a punch left to throw. ''I'm sorry,'' he said. ''I want to get this over with. Let's just go on.''

Felipe liked it. ''I understand,'' he said. ''These are trying times, but it's almost over.''

''What's next?'' McKenna asked, noticing that Felipe was smiling and looking concerned. So now I know what this guy looks like when he's gloating, McKenna thought.

"What's next is that I release the two hundred passengers I promised you. You have the boats ready to take them?"

"Of course, but that's not what I'm talking about," McKenna said, laying it on. "I mean what's next to get you out of here?"

"I see. I thought you might have guessed that part. What's next is that you, Ashton Heresford, and Cristobal Cervantes present yourselves here tomorrow at four o'clock, along—"

"I get it," McKenna interrupted. "Along with another seventy-five million dollars or you'll shoot two hundred hostages, right?"

"Not put very diplomatically, for a diplomat," Felipe said, openly enjoying himself.

McKenna decided he had laid it on thick enough. Felipe thought he was just about to succeed, so McKenna managed a small, contrite laugh. "Sorry, but I'm looking forward to ending my diplomatic career," he said, getting up. "There's too much pressure in this job and I don't get to park anywhere I want like the rest of my fellow diplomats."

"It is almost over," Felipe said without a hint of malice, but McKenna managed to look worried. "I'll be seeing you tomorrow?" Felipe asked smugly.

"Tomorrow at four."

Chapter 51 Wanting to avoid the reporters waiting
at the Wall Street pier, McKenna told the sergeant in charge of the Harbor launch to drop him at the Bay Ridge pier in Brooklyn. He called Pao and alerted him to the change in plans. Pao would pick him up and said he was bringing Inspector Tavlin with him.

Tavlin could only mean good news, McKenna thought. He must have some information on Felipe.

McKenna's hopes were justified a minute later when Bob

Hurley called. "Found out what your boy's been buying and renting," he said.

McKenna closed his eyes and asked the question. "Anything close to the Verrazano or the Williamsburg bridges?"

"Two of them are, both studio apartments. One is at 1263 Grand Street, right on the FDR Drive. Another one is 328 66th Street in Bay Ridge."

McKenna knew both areas and kept his eyes closed as he tried to visualize the buildings at those locations. After a moment, he got them both. He knew that a complex of high-rise middle-income apartment buildings was at Grand Street and the FDR Drive. The one in Bay Ridge was even easier: 328 66th Street was one of two apartment buildings right across the street from the 68th Precinct station house. They were luxury high-rises and the tallest buildings in Bay Ridge. "You get the apartment numbers?" he asked.

"Got both of them. The Manhattan one is 14B, facing the bridge. The Bay Ridge one is Apartment 17A. I'm trying to find out which way it faces right now."

"Where are you?"

"In the renting office of the Bay Ridge one."

"Can you meet me in the Six-Eight station house in half an hour?"

"Sure," Hurley answered. "I should know all about this building by then."

"Wonderful. See you then," McKenna said and hung up. He then went out on deck, took a seat on a box of life preservers, and enjoyed the rest of the trip.

The launch docked ten minutes before Pao and Tavlin arrived. There were a couple of reporters on the pier, so McKenna waited inside the cabin until Pao pulled up. Pao sized up the situation, opened the rear door, and McKenna made the dash and they were gone with a minimum of problems from the press.

"The Six-Eight Precinct, Johnny," McKenna ordered from the backseat.

Tavlin turned around to look at McKenna. "What's there?" he asked.

"Bob Hurley. He's got the locations."

"So do we," Tavlin said defensively. "Felipe's got one at 473 Grand Street, overlooking the Williamsburg Bridge, and a couple of houses in Staten Island."

"How about one in Bay Ridge?" McKenna asked.

"Nothing yet," Tavlin answered, eyeing McKenna suspiciously. "Why? Hurley got one there?"

"328 66th Street, Apartment 17A."

"Did he have the one on Grand Street?" Tavlin asked.

"Yeah, he had that one, too."

As he expected, the frown crossing Tavlin's face told McKenna the inspector wasn't happy that Hurley had aced Tavlin's detectives. "How did Hurley do it?" Tavlin finally asked. "I've had twenty men on overtime since last night working on this."

"I don't know, but he's good, and as far as he's concerned, he's working for a lot more than overtime."

"How much is it costing?"

"Nothing tangible. Just a public expression of gratitude to the Holmes Detective Bureau for their help in this case when it's all over," McKenna answered.

"Hurley's even smarter than I thought. You can't buy that kind of advertising," Tavlin observed as Pao pulled up outside the front door of the station house.

Hurley was waiting for them inside. The 68th Precinct captain was out, but Hurley knew him and made the captain's office his own. He had the coffeepot going and had thought to bring in some bagels and cream cheese. But Tavlin was in no mood for the amenities. "You sure about the place across the street?" he asked Hurley as he poured himself a cup of coffee.

"You've got my personal guarantee," Hurley answered from his perch on the CO's desk. "Why? Didn't all your sleuths get that one?"

"I'm sure they would have, eventually," Tavlin answered defensively.

But Hurley wasn't going to let him off the hook. "Would that be civil-service *eventually* or private-industry *eventually*?" he asked.

"What's the difference?" Tavlin asked suspiciously.

"Probably a week at overtime rates," Hurley answered, really enjoying himself. "How many men you got working on it?"

"Twenty," Tavlin answered, falling into the trap.

"So they checked the city real estate records for property transfers and came up with the Staten Island houses and the co-op on Grand Street, right?"

"That's what they tell me."

"How long that take them?" Hurley asked, smiling.

"They started as soon as we got Felipe's names at about five this morning. They've been working all day at the municipal building, going through the records."

Hurley laughed at that and Tavlin's discomfort increased. "And that took them all day?" Hurley asked.

"That's right. How long did it take you?"

"I didn't even bother doing it. My secretary had them in under an hour, sitting at her computer. You ever hear of Ferrari?"

"The car?"

"No, the computer investigating service. They have all real estate transfers in a database. Once you buy into their service, you go on-line and check all real estate transfers by county. You can make the inquiries using either the date of purchase, the name of the buyer, or his Social Security number. Once I had the names the KGB provided for Felipe, the Social Security numbers and all the rest was easy."

"What do you pay this secretary, if you don't mind telling me?" Tavlin asked.

"Don't mind at all. Tracy gets thirty grand a year, three weeks' vacation, six paid holidays, and I throw in a Honda lease every two years. Why? What do your twenty detectives on overtime make?"

"You know how much they make." Tavlin wanted to change the subject, but was still in the mood to learn. "How come my men didn't come up with the place across the street?" he asked.

"Beats me. Maybe because Felipe didn't buy it. He rented it in October under his Ilya Cherenkov name. Didn't your men check his credit reports?"

"I know they found out he's got cards under three of his names, but nobody rents an apartment on a credit card."

"No, but when you go to rent a nice apartment, you usually have to sign a release authorizing the management company to do a credit check on you, don't you?"

"Sometimes, I guess," Tavlin said.

"Not sometimes. Always," Hurley insisted. "The people across the street use a firm called Hansen Equities to check out their prospective tenants, and their inquiry showed up on the Ilya Cherenkov credit report, if you know what to look for. Now, Hansen Equities happens to be owned by Kenny Hansen, a retired detective and a pal of mine. So I gave him a call and he gave me the location. Only problem is he didn't know which way the apartment faced. I had to come here and get that myself.''

"It faces the bridge?'' McKenna asked.

"Great view, I understand.''

"You find out who's in there?''

"A woman in her sixties and a guy in his twenties, passing themselves off as Mrs. Cherenkov and her son.''

Suddenly McKenna was worried that Hurley had gone up and knocked on the door. "How did you find that out?'' he asked.

"Easy. I figured they'd be spending most of their time watching the ferries and the bridge, which means they wouldn't be cooking. They'd be ordering in food, and they're not poor. They'd be ordering from some of the better restaurants. So I just talked to Fat Albert.''

"I see,'' McKenna commented, relieved. "Good thinking.''

"Wait a minute,'' Tavlin protested. "I don't see. Who is Fat Albert?''

Hurley was going to answer, but then he looked at McKenna to do the honors.

"Fat Albert is Detective First Grade Al Muscumeci. He's three hundred and fifty pounds and has been working Bay Ridge for twenty years. Knows every restaurant owner in the precinct.'' He looked to Pao for confirmation.

"That's right,'' Pao said. "I hear they ask Fat Albert when he's going on vacation so they can close up and go on vacation themselves. Doesn't pay to open up when Fat Albert's not around.''

"I get it,'' Tavlin said. "So Fat Albert calls his pals to see if they have any take-out customer named Cherenkov living at 328 66th Street, Apartment 17A.''

"That's right,'' Hurley said. "Came up with two of them where they're steady customers. Ricardo's and Lorelei's. Then me and Fat Albert went over and talked to their delivery boys and we got the descriptions and the rundown.''

"Sounds simple,'' Tavlin commented.

"It wasn't,'' Hurley rebutted. "Cost me sixty dollars for a Fat Albert dinner and fifty dollars apiece to the delivery boys to keep their mouths shut.''

"Good advertising's never cheap,'' Tavlin remarked without sympathy.

"Thanks,'' Hurley said. "I'm sure you folks have things to

talk about, so I'm gonna get out of here.''

"You don't have to go," McKenna said.

"Yes, I do," Hurley replied on his way out. "Time is money." Then a thought hit him and he stopped at the door. "You know about the car Felipe rented last week on his Ilya Cherenkov Visa card, don't you?"

Tavlin wanted to lie and say he did, but couldn't. "No. Tell us about it."

"A gray Oldsmobile from Avis. Rented four days ago, so the bill's not posted yet. I don't remember the plate, so you'll have to give Avis a call."

McKenna looked at Tavlin and knew the inspector wanted to ask Hurley how he did it, but his pride prevented him. Then Hurley was gone.

"Well, that was certainly informative," Tavlin commented, more to himself than to McKenna.

"Sorry to put you through that, Inspector," McKenna said, not looking too sorry. "Hurley was never exactly a humble guy, but we have to let him have his fun. Let's get out of here. I gotta get back to city hall and report."

"Then go and leave me here," Tavlin said. "I'm gonna get some men here and set up a surveillance across the street."

"I'd like to stay on that one," Pao said. "That has to be Elena in there."

He's right. It has to be her, McKenna thought. We know *Sendero*'s personnel setup and they only have one woman left here. She's doing her older-woman act again. "In that case, you'd better come with me," McKenna said to Pao. "We don't want her getting away again."

Pao opened his mouth to say something, but not a sound came out as his face turned red. "I'll wait for you in the car," he said, heading for the door.

"Hey, Johnny, I was just kidding," McKenna yelled after him, but Pao was gone, slamming the door behind him.

"Little high-strung, isn't he?" Tavlin observed.

"Yeah, he's a barrel of laughs."

"Just give him a minute to calm down. Got any suggestions on what you want done here?" Tavlin asked.

"Nothing you don't already know. Get a wire on the apartment, but since she's probably using a cellular phone that'll be a waste of time. The thing to remember is that you have to keep her away from the reservoirs and be in position to get her after Felipe leaves."

"Then it's simple," Tavlin concluded. "Just a loose surveillance, try and see where she goes, and have men in position to arrest her when the time comes."

McKenna thought it over and couldn't find a flaw in Tavlin's reasoning. "Basically, I think that's it," he said, then decided he needed a cup of coffee after all.

Chapter 52

McKenna immediately knew something was up as he left the station house and got into the car. Pao was all smiles, something McKenna rarely saw. "Why the strange face?" he asked as Pao backed out of the spot.

"Gonna show you something," was Pao's only reply. He put the car in drive and started slowly up 65th Street. Then he stopped and adjusted his rearview mirror. "See her?" he asked.

Oh no! McKenna thought. He turned around in his seat and looked through the rear window. There was a gray-haired old woman with a cane near the corner behind them, wearing a frumpy print dress, laced-up black shoes, and watching their car. It can't be, McKenna thought. Then Pao horrified McKenna by putting the car in reverse. As soon as he did, Elena dropped her cane and ran, disappearing from their view into the private park separating the two large apartment buildings.

McKenna's mind raced furiously for the five seconds it took Pao to drive in reverse down the block at thirty miles an hour.

Pao's put us in a no-win situation, but maybe it isn't his fault, McKenna thought. Maybe it's Elena's fault, making Pao's actions unavoidable under the circumstances. She's exhibiting classic symptoms of Willie Sutton syndrome, that arrogant peculiarity of the brilliant criminal mind. When the famous bank robber was being sought all over the city, he took an apartment across the street from the station house where the Bank Robbery Squad worked and watched the detectives who were searching for him enter and leave all day long.

Wearing a disguise, he even ate in the same restaurants they did and by the time he was finally captured he knew all their names and all their habits.

Elena had been watching us from her perch on the seventeenth floor, McKenna guessed. Watched us leave the Bay Ridge pier and drive to the station house. Then she came down to get a better look at us and show that, when we were looking all over the city for her, we couldn't see her when she was standing in front of us.

Unfortunately, Pao could and now we're in this mess. If we catch Elena, Felipe will wonder how we found her and might guess that, if we knew where she was, then we know where his other places are.

McKenna's thoughts were interrupted abruptly when Pao slammed on the brakes at the spot they had last seen Elena. "There she is," Pao said, and there she was. They caught a glimpse of her running just before she rounded the corner of 328 66th Street and disappeared from view again. "She's headed for her nest," Pao said as he opened his door.

McKenna was surprised she would do that and wanted a little more time to mull over the implications of the situation, but Pao didn't give him any. "Wait a minute, Johnny," McKenna said, but he was talking to himself. Pao was out and gone, running after Elena.

Thinking time was over for McKenna. He got out of the car and chased Pao, catching him just as he got to the glass-enclosed lobby of Elena's building. The outer door was open, but the inner door was locked. They could see that nobody was in the inner lobby, but both elevators were in motion.

There were an intercom and 200 apartment buzzer buttons next to the locked lobby door, and Pao started pressing them while McKenna looked at the elevator floor-indicator lights above the elevator doors. One elevator stopped at the tenth floor and the other stopped at the eighteenth.

"Who is it?" a voice demanded over the intercom.

"Police. Buzz the door open, please," Pao shouted into the speaker.

"What apartment do you want?" the suspicious tenant asked.

"Any apartment. We're chasing a kid who just stole a woman's purse and he ran in here."

The door buzzed and they were in. "I'll take the stairs," Pao volunteered, entering the stairwell next to the elevators.

McKenna was glad to hear that. The police procedural rule was never to leave your partner when chasing a suspect in a building, but the rule was routinely disregarded by experienced detectives looking to make optimal use of manpower to box in a suspect and ensure a trip to Central Booking. Their procedure called for one detective to take the elevator while the other took the stairs. "Good idea, Johnny," McKenna replied. "I'll meet you on eighteen," he replied, pressing the elevator call button. The prospect of climbing eighteen flights of stairs didn't thrill him, but he thought it the perfect mission for Pao.

Both elevators descended to the lobby in answer to his call. He hoped he wouldn't be seeing Elena, but just in case he took out his gun and pressed the button for eighteen. The elevator went up faster than he would have liked, straight to the eighteenth floor. He took a deep breath as the door opened, then stuck his head out and looked up and down the hall. Nobody was there. Then he crossed the hallway to the stairwell and smiled as he heard Pao climbing up far below him. McKenna walked up to the nineteenth-floor hallway and called Brunette.

"Where are you? Heresford and the mayor are pulling their hair out," Brunette said.

"Bay Ridge. We just chased Elena into Felipe's building."

Brunette understood the implications at once. "Was that wise?" he asked.

"No, but you had to be here to understand. I think she's in the apartment now."

"I can't believe she'd lead you back there. Maybe she's not as sharp as Savraada thinks."

That gave McKenna something to think about. "Or maybe she's sharper than I think," he said.

"What do you want me to do?"

"Get Emergency Service here and a bunch of detectives. Tell them to make a lot of noise. We're going to do an apartment-by-apartment search, starting with the first floor. I wanna make it look like we stumbled on her and don't know which apartment she's in."

"I'll get right on it. Leave Tavlin in charge and get here as soon as you can," Brunette said before hanging up.

McKenna walked back down to the eighteenth floor to wait for Pao. His elevator was still there and he held the door open.

*　　*　　*

By the time he reached the eighth floor Pao was tired, out of breath, and making a lot of noise as he climbed the steel steps. Thinking it a waste of time, he had still checked each hallway on the way up for the first six floors, but he passed on seven and eight. That was his mistake because Elena had gotten off the elevator on the tenth floor and walked down two flights. She was waiting for Pao in the eighth-floor hallway.

As soon as she heard him pass in the stairwell, she opened the door and lined up the sights of her silenced .25 Beretta automatic on Pao's back as he climbed the stairs. Pao hadn't heard her open the stairwell door, but he clearly heard her say, ''Don't move, Detective Pao.''

Figuring Pao should have arrived by now, McKenna was getting worried about him. He went to the stairwell and listened, but heard nothing. Then he was really worried. He heard the other elevator move and watched the floor-indicator lights. The elevator stopped on eight and then descended to Level G.

''G''? McKenna thought. Then it came to him. ''G'' stood for garage. That's why she ran into this building. She did some tricky stuff to throw us off when she pressed the elevator buttons, but she's got Felipe's car down there.

McKenna stepped into the elevator he'd been holding, unsure whether to push the button for the garage or the lobby. He decided on the lobby. The twenty seconds it took for the elevator to descend seemed like an hour to him, and as soon as the elevator doors opened he ran out.

Once outside the building McKenna stopped. Which side was the garage on? He didn't remember passing it when they were chasing Elena, so it must be on the right side of the building. Then he heard a bell ringing and knew he was right. He ran around the building as fast as he could and arrived at the ramp leading to the garage. The warning bell was still ringing and a red light on the side of the building next to the door was flashing. Then the light stopped flashing and the bell was silent, replaced by the sound of the electric garage-door motor.

McKenna braced himself, standing in the middle of the ramp at the top with his pistol raised and aimed at the garage door. As it rose he saw a gray Oldsmobile with rental plates and Elena behind the wheel. She was a redhead again, having removed her gray wig. She was talking on a cellular phone and didn't see him at first. When she did, her eyes went wide and she put down the phone.

"Turn the car off, Elena!" McKenna yelled, never thinking she would. He was ready to get off a few shots and jump out of the way before she ran him down.

Instead she stuck her head out the window and yelled, "Okay, Brian. Don't get excited."

"I'm already excited," McKenna yelled back. "Turn the car off and throw the keys out the window."

Elena did, then stuck her head out the window again. "Okay, what's next?" she yelled.

"Put both your hands on top of your head."

She did that, too, and McKenna walked down to her car, keeping his pistol pointed at her chest the whole time. When he got to her door he was surprised to see that she was smiling up at him, still wearing the horrible print dress and theatrical makeup smeared over her face. "I'm glad you got rid of that awful hat," she said pleasantly.

McKenna kept his pistol pointed at her head and she looked at him like he was being silly. "I'm not too crazy about that dress, either," he replied. "Are you armed?"

He was still being silly. "Of course," she said. "There's a .25 Beretta on the seat next to me and a 9-mm Glock on the floor under my feet. Do you want me to get them for you?"

"No, please don't bother. I'll get them." McKenna opened her door. "Keep your hands on your head and come on out."

She did, swinging her legs out of the car and standing up while keeping her hands on her head and staring into McKenna's eyes the whole time, looking like she was having a great time.

Still keeping his pistol pointed at her head, McKenna reached under his jacket and removed his handcuffs from the pouch on his belt. He snapped one end on Elena's left hand while she kept her hands on her head. Holding on to the other end of the handcuffs, he ordered, "Now be a good girl and put your hands behind your back."

She did and he snapped the other end of the handcuffs on her right hand and put his pistol in his holster.

She turned around, still amused. "Aren't you going to search me?" she asked impishly.

"*Sí, señorita.* It's all part of the service," he replied. He turned her back around and quickly frisked her. It took only a moment and he didn't find anything he didn't expect, but thought she had just enough firm flesh in all the right places. Then he heard sirens from the direction of the station house and knew that Brunette had executed his request.

Elena ignored the noise. "You call that a search?" she complained when he was done and stood up. "I was hoping for something a little more exciting."

"That's all you get right now, Elena. Once you get into the station house one of the policewomen will give you a good going over."

"You know, you missed a few things."

"Do you mean the empty garter holster high on your left leg?"

"That's one."

"And the handcuff key taped under your right breast?"

"Ooo," she said. "Very good. That's two."

"How about the small thin knife taped to the inside of your left arm under your dress?"

"Three. Excellent job. You got everything. You should get a prize for that," she said, mocking him with her smile.

"Glad to hear that. Now please lie on the ground."

"Really?" Elena asked, her smile disappearing for the first time.

"Really. I'll help you." McKenna held Elena's arms and she let him lower her gently to the ground. Then he looked in the car and found the .25 Beretta automatic with the silencer attached, just like she said. "Nice gun," McKenna observed. "But you won't get much stopping power from a twenty-five after the bullet goes through the silencer."

"I know," Elena said from the ground. "I just needed something small. This is such a dangerous city, you know. Perverts everywhere."

McKenna smiled at the thought of an unsuspecting pervert meeting up with this particular girl. Then he reached down and found the 9-mm Glock on the floorboard, near the gas pedal. He took it out and held it in front of Elena's face. "Is this my partner's gun?" he asked.

"You mean that nice Detective Pao?" Her smile had returned.

The thought flashed through his mind that only a girl like Elena could ever consider a guy like Johnny Pao nice, but he didn't dwell on it. "Yes, is this nice Detective Pao's gun?"

"Yes."

"How did you get it?"

"He gave it to me."

"Is he still alive?" McKenna asked, dreading the answer.

"Of course. I wouldn't hurt him unless I had to."

"And where is he?"

Elena laughed again. "He's waiting for you on the stairs inside. I think he'll be very happy to see you."

McKenna heard footsteps behind him and was relieved to see Tavlin and two uniformed cops running down the ramp.

"What floor?" he whispered to Elena.

She winked and whispered back to him, "Eight."

"Thank you," McKenna said, putting Pao's gun in his waistband, then patting her on the head. Tavlin had arrived and caught both actions. He didn't say anything, but looked mystified, first down at Elena, then back to McKenna. "Where's Pao?" he asked.

"He's inside," McKenna answered nonchalantly as he picked up the key ring from the ground, removed the car key, and gave it to Tavlin. "I'll go get him. Could you take her and the car to the station house?"

"Whatever you say."

McKenna told him about the knife and the handcuff key, then started for the front door at a trot, leaving the suspicious inspector behind.

McKenna got off the elevator at the eighth floor and walked into the stairwell. He expected to find Pao in some distress, but Elena had exceeded his expectations. Pao was in a real state of discomfort, facedown on the stairs wearing his handcuffs behind his back. Elena had further immobilized him by passing the handcuff chain through one of the steel supports for the stairway rail. He looked at McKenna and wanted badly to say something, but couldn't. She had stuffed his handkerchief into his mouth and kept it there by wrapping his tie around his face. The total effect was that Johnny Pao looked very unhappy. His face was red with rage, and veins that McKenna didn't even know people possessed bulged from his neck, jaw, and forehead. To make matters worse, there were two boys standing over him, about eight years old, giggling and enjoying Pao's plight.

"Stand at the bottom of the stairs, boys," McKenna said.

"Who are you?" one of them asked.

McKenna took out his very elaborate shield and showed it to them. "I'm a policeman," he said.

"Oh!" they both said, and walked down to the landing.

"Are you a detective?" one of them asked as McKenna started untying the knots in Pao's tie.

"No. I'm only a commissioner."

"Too bad," the kid commented.

"It's not that bad," McKenna assured him. "Maybe if I do good they'll promote me to detective."

"What's the matter with him?" the other kid asked, pointing to Pao.

"He didn't listen to his mommy and daddy when he was growing up," McKenna explained as he worked on the knots. "He's always saying mean things to people and sometimes we have to tie him up like this till he's better."

"Oh!" they both said.

McKenna got the tie undone, then put his hand on the handkerchief. "Put your hands over your ears, boys. I don't think he's fixed yet."

They did and McKenna pulled the handkerchief from Pao's mouth.

"I'm gonna stomp you two little shits into the ground," Pao yelled with his first breath.

McKenna turned back to the boys. "See what I mean?" he asked.

"Yeah, he *is* nasty," one of them answered. "Why don't you put it back in his mouth?"

"Should I?"

"Yeah," they both answered enthusiastically.

"You two better get out of here!" Pao yelled.

"You know, maybe you should go home," McKenna suggested to them. "I have to let him go now. He has to go back to work, and I think he's gonna be bad again. I think he's gonna tell some lies to a lot of people."

The boys thought it was time to leave and took McKenna's suggestion. They ran down the stairs, leaving Pao glaring up at McKenna. "Did you get her?" Pao asked.

"Yeah, I got her," McKenna answered as he took out his cuff key and inserted it in the handcuff lock.

"Is she dead?"

"Nope."

"Shit!" Pao said softly.

McKenna unsnapped one of the handcuffs and Pao stood up and stretched, then rubbed his wrists after McKenna removed the other one. "I need a big favor and I'll be your slave for life," Pao said solemnly.

McKenna stood back, smiling, and handed Pao his handcuffs. Then he reached into his waistband and gave Pao back his pistol. "By 'a big favor' do you mean not one word about this to anyone, ever?" he asked.

"And I'll be your slave for life. I'll do anything you want, go anywhere you want, say anything you want."

"I don't know, Johnny. You haven't been that nice to me lately," McKenna said, thinking it over.

"I'm really sorry about that. I'll be real nice from now on."

McKenna shook his head. "I don't know if I can believe that," he said.

"Okay. How's this? If you ever have any kids, my kids will be your kids' slaves. Same deal, for the rest of their lives."

"But wouldn't it be better if we could charge Elena with illegally imprisoning you and stealing your gun?"

"Are you kidding?" Pao shouted, incredulous and horrified at the thought. "I'd never live it down. I'd have to walk out this building, drive straight to the Pension Section, and retire."

"Well, we certainly don't want that, do we?"

"No, we don't." Then Pao's eyes narrowed as he shrewdly played his trump card. "You know, I did save your life," he said softly.

Chapter 53

When McKenna and Pao entered, Elena was sitting in the 68th Precinct detective squad office, handcuffed to a chair and wearing a prison jumpsuit while Fat Albert sat and sweated at the desk in front of her, typing away on her booking report. She smiled and waved when she saw the two. "Detective Pao. How are you feeling?" she asked.

McKenna could feel the heat rising from Pao, but Pao kept himself under control. "Fine, thank you," he answered politely as they walked past her into the detective commander's office.

Tavlin had made it his own. He was seated with his feet on

the desk, talking on the phone. "He just came in. I'll call you back," he said, then hung up and focused on McKenna, but was having trouble doing so. He couldn't keep his eyes off Pao's crumpled tie. McKenna knew that twenty-five years of life in the detective bureau was raging inside the inspector, and the focus of that rage was Pao's new look. It just wasn't done.

Pao was sharp enough to recognize the signs of impending trouble for him. He had also been around for a while and could remember far back to the time when it was okay for a detective to be lying drunk in the gutter, as long as he was properly dressed. As Tavlin stared at him, he quickly realized that his appearance constituted a felony violation of the dress code. "I'll go get another tie," he said meekly. Tavlin simply nodded, but didn't say a word until Pao left.

"Gonna tell me what happened to him?" Tavlin asked McKenna.

"Let's just say he's having a bad day," McKenna answered as he pulled up a chair.

"I think we all are. Ray's happy you got her, but thinks your timing's off. Meanwhile, he's sitting with the mayor and Heresford, getting his balls broken while waiting for your arrival."

McKenna could imagine the unpleasant atmosphere at city hall. He was supposed to be there, reporting on his negotiations with Felipe. Complicating his absence was the fact that the press knew he had been on the ferries, yet here he was arresting Elena in Bay Ridge and nobody in city hall had any reasons why. The whole thing could be played as a police success, but first they would have to get their heads together and come up with the proper scenario to give the press. He knew they would have to be told something soon. There was already a bunch of reporters gathered outside the station house, and their mood was such that they constituted a hostile mob.

"Elena have anything to say?" McKenna asked.

"Yeah. She said she'll only talk to you, in private."

Well, that's something at least, McKenna thought. "She have anything else on her?" he asked.

Tavlin took his feet off the desk and stared at McKenna. "No. She doesn't have what we're supposed to get from her at the right time."

McKenna had worked for Tavlin before and understood the inspector's attitude. Tavlin was a realist and was willing to play the game, pretending that McKenna in his new role was smarter than everyone else. The inspector was an understanding man, but he was used to success and was not noted for his tolerance of stupid mistakes that jeopardized any case he supervised.

McKenna realized that this one had put them in role reversal. Tavlin knew that McKenna would be gone and back in Florida as soon as the case was over, leaving himself to be critiqued when it was analyzed over and over again, as famous cases always were. Tavlin had been a boss too long and just couldn't help himself. He was sitting there as the inspector of police regarding the detective who had just screwed up.

McKenna knew he had to change that attitude fast if he were to operate and survive in the civil-service system. He had to get Felipe's poison to nullify his threat, and at the same time still make it look like they found Elena by accident. "Then bring her in here," he ordered. "I'll get what we need from her and keep everybody happy."

It was exactly what Tavlin wanted to hear. "Okay, Commissioner," he said, smiling at McKenna as he got up and left.

McKenna positioned himself in Tavlin's seat and called his hotel while he waited. Angelita was there. "How was the trip?" he asked her.

"Okay, but I'm here by myself now. Have any idea when you're getting here?"

"No, but it'll be late. Something came up."

"I know. It's on the news," Angelita said, not happy with that. "You better be careful with that girl."

"I will, but that's only the first part. Then I have to go to city hall and report."

"So what are we talking about? Ten o'clock?"

"More or less. I'll get there as soon as I can. I'm really missing you."

"That's what I want to hear. Get back to work, then get here."

"I will. Love you, babe."

"Love you, too," Angelita said as Tavlin brought in Elena. She was staring down at him, still smiling.

Bad case of timing, McKenna thought. "'Bye," he said into the phone, wanting to hang up.

But Angelita wasn't ready. "Wait a minute," she insisted. "Tell me, is she as pretty as they say?"

Now McKenna really wanted to get off the phone, but the

question had to be answered and he was going to be the loser no matter what he said. He decided to go with job performance and fix the home front later. "She looks okay," he said.

Elena guessed that she was the subject of the conversation and lost her smile. "Just okay?" she asked.

Which gave McKenna another problem. Angelita had heard Elena's voice. "Is she there?" Angelita asked.

Great time to lie, McKenna thought, but decided against it. "She was just brought in," he answered.

"Like I said, be careful with that bitch. 'Bye," Angelita said, then hung up, leaving McKenna amazed at how Elena had gone from girl to bitch in thirty seconds.

Elena was more gracious, slightly. "Having some trouble with that skinny little Spanish girl?" she asked as McKenna replaced the receiver.

Defend or retreat? McKenna asked himself. Retreat. "No, no trouble," he lied, pointing to the chair opposite the desk.

Tavlin looked to McKenna and pointed at the handcuff on Elena's left wrist. McKenna shook his head, so Tavlin removed the handcuffs before he left, closing the door behind him. Elena moved the chair so that it was next to the desk, then sat down, crossed her legs, and put her elbows on the desk, waiting for McKenna to begin.

McKenna couldn't help but notice something that Elena already knew. Even in prison coveralls, she was a beautiful and very sexy woman. The theatrical makeup was gone, leaving her face clean and fresh. If he didn't know better, he would have assumed red was her natural color, perfectly complementing her green eyes. He thought she could have been on the cover of *Cosmo* instead of sitting in a police station in a lot of trouble. But it was time to deal with the realities. "What are you going to tell me?" he asked.

"What do you want to know?"

"Something personal first, okay?"

Elena liked that. "Sure."

"Why did you send the basket of fruit to Angelita in the hospital? Was that a warning to me that Felipe knew where she was?"

Elena looked at him like he had just asked a stupid question. "I told you I was going to do something nice for you, didn't I?"

"Was he planning something at North Shore Hospital for her?"

"Who knows with Felipe? I knew he was still mad at you and he knew where she was. That's enough."

"Did he know you did it?"

Another stupid question. "Of course not."

"Then why?"

Elena treated him to a big smile and he thought she was going to laugh in his face, but she didn't. She wiped the smile off her face. "I have my reasons," was all she would say on the subject.

McKenna saw he was going nowhere and got down to business. "Felipe mentioned something about a biological reagent in sort of a threatening way, and I think you have it."

Once again, McKenna got the impression he had said something funny. Her smile returned and she answered coyly, "Maybe we'll talk about that later, after I see how smart you are."

Smarter than you know, McKenna thought, but I have to remember to keep her thinking I'm still dumb and in the dark. However, there are a few things to clear up that have nothing to do with resolving this case. "Why didn't you kill Johnny Pao?" he asked.

She answered his question with a question. "Do you like him?"

"Yes, I like him. I don't know why, but I do."

"Then that's why. I like him, too."

"What do you like about him?"

"For one thing, he saved me some trouble and killed that pig Emilio. I was going to have to do that myself, sooner or later."

"That's why you like him? Because he killed somebody on your side you didn't like?"

The irony in McKenna's question was lost on Elena. "I understand it was a great shot, wasn't it?" she asked, innocently.

"Yes, it was a great shot. Anything else you like about Pao?"

"Yes. He was sharp enough to recognize me. It *was* him that recognized me, wasn't it?"

"Yeah, it was him," McKenna said, relieved at the question.

"And not you?"

"No, not me. It's because of him you're here. Knowing that, do you still like him?"

Elena ignored the question. "I thought it was him," she said, then smiled at McKenna. "You know, I've been next to you before."

That gave McKenna something to consider. Does she know about the Gramercy Park Hotel? "When?" he asked.

"Do you remember one day last week? You took a little walk around Little Italy, then met Gene Shields in a restaurant?"

McKenna struggled to keep the shock out of his face. "Forlini's, wasn't it?"

"Yes, that's it. Very good food, but a little expensive. You know, you surprised me when you ordered steak in an Italian restaurant."

"I remember. For your information, the steak was pretty good. What did you have?"

"The veal scallopini. Excellent."

"So you were following me?"

"Yes. I must admit I was surprised to see you leave police headquarters by yourself. That wasn't too smart."

"I can see that now. What were you supposed to do? Kill me?"

"Yes."

"Why didn't you?"

"Because I enjoyed watching you. You were so friendly and everybody liked you."

"They always say they like you when they meet you face-to-face," McKenna observed. "Believe it or not, not everybody really likes me."

"No, I know not everybody likes you," Elena said, laughing. "But *they* did. They said nice things about you to each other after they saw you. Still, I should tell you that I still thought about killing you after you left Forlini's, but Pao was there in that very ostentatious car."

That's twice Pao saved my life and I was right about that car, McKenna thought. "I don't use that one anymore," he said in his own defense.

"We know that now. Some of our men followed it to Harlem before they found out you weren't in it."

Getting rid of that car was another lucky decision, McKenna realized. "Does Felipe know you could have had me?" he asked.

"No. I told him you were too heavily protected."

"Why?"

Elena just shrugged her shoulders, then said, "You should be more careful."

"I will. Just so you don't think I'm an absolute boob, I'm going to tell you something. We didn't have any idea of your existence then."

"Oh? You hadn't spoken to Colonel Savraada yet?"

It was McKenna's turn to shrug his shoulders and change the subject. "Why didn't you run me down today? You might have done it and gotten away."

"And take a chance on killing you?"

McKenna liked the way she made it sound like a bad idea. "You could have done it," he stated simply.

"Maybe, but I was talking to Felipe on the phone when I saw you. I had told him about the mess I was in and he told me to get away if I could without hurting you. If I couldn't, he told me to surrender."

Felipe's concern for his welfare was a stunning revelation for McKenna, and he didn't care if Elena saw it. But it only took him a moment to make sense out of it. McKenna knew Felipe was on a rigid timetable and had made a lot of plans for his departure, plans not easily changed. By his own choice, McKenna was the only person he had negotiated with. So, even if it meant sacrificing Elena, McKenna had to live to bring the negotiations to a successful conclusion on time. "I guess I should thank him the next time I see him," McKenna said. "It makes me laugh to think he values me more than you."

"He values me," Elena stated. "You have me in some trouble here, but he won't leave me here for long."

Probably right, McKenna thought. Felipe still has a strong hand. "What's he going to do, demand your return before he leaves or he'll shoot some more hostages?" McKenna asked.

"I can see you don't know him," Elena said in a way that made McKenna believe that idea had never even occurred to her. "I was never listed in his demands, and he already made a deal with you. Felipe always abides absolutely by any deal he makes."

Once again, something like that coming from someone who knew Felipe well increased McKenna's respect for the man. "So what makes you think you won't be here long?" he asked.

"It's simple. I'm going to jail now, but Felipe is a man of action and, like I said, he values me. When he is ready, he will do something spectacular someplace in the world and you will release me," she stated with absolute confidence.

McKenna believed her. Holding Elena meant Felipe would pull another terrorist stunt to secure her release, if he were alive and able to do so. "Does he love you?" McKenna asked.

"It's enough that he values me."

McKenna blurted out his next question without thinking. "Do you love him?"

He thought she was going to answer, then thought she wouldn't. But she did. "No, it's not him I love," she said softly, looking him straight in the eye.

McKenna realized he was pointing himself down a road he didn't want to travel, so he consciously banished his next obvious question from his mind. It was time to change the subject. "Do you have an apartment across the street?" he asked.

She responded to his question by laughing at him.

"Getting a little hot in here, isn't it, Brian?" she asked.

"No, it's fine in here," McKenna said, but realized he was sweating. "Was that a stupid question?"

"Which?" She was smiling at him innocently.

"Do you have an apartment across the street?"

"Oh, that question. You have my keys, don't you?"

"Yes."

"And you used them to get into the lobby to get Pao, didn't you?"

"Yes."

"Then it was a stupid question."

McKenna realized that he might be overplaying his dumb act for a very smart girl, which put him on dangerous ground. It was time to smarten up a bit. "Then you don't deny it?" he said.

Elena wasn't denying anything. She just looked at him without answering.

"Which apartment?" he asked.

Still no answer, but she was still smiling.

McKenna took her keys from his pocket. "You know, I'm going to find out if I have to try these keys in every lock on every apartment in that building."

The smile disappeared. Something he said had disturbed her. She thought for a moment, then said, "Don't do it yourself."

"Why? Is the apartment booby-trapped?"

"Just don't do it yourself."

"Elena, we're going to find that apartment and I'm not

sending anybody else to get blown up. I'll be careful, but it's gonna be done and I'll do it myself.''

''Don't.''

''Elena, think about it for a minute. Getting extra people killed in this doesn't make much sense when it's almost over.''

The time it took Elena to think it over convinced McKenna she didn't suspect he already knew which apartment it was. ''Is it that there's someone else in there?'' he asked.

Elena made her decision. ''Yes. His name is Arturo. He's very young and very dedicated.''

''Then he shouldn't die for nothing, and neither should any more of my people. Right?''

''He might not see it that way,'' Elena said.

''Could you call him?''

''You would trust me to do that?''

''Yes, as long as I listen in on the call.''

''Then I think that maybe we can make a deal.''

''I hate saying this to a girl like you, but *shoot*.''

Suddenly, Elena was all business. ''Arturo is an orphan,'' she said. ''He looks older, but he is only sixteen. He thinks he's tough, but I don't want him going to jail with the kind of criminals you have here.''

''What?'' McKenna asked. ''Your kind are better?''

''You should come visit my country sometime. True, we are at war, but we don't tolerate the kind of excesses you do. The government doesn't, and we especially don't.''

McKenna was interested in how this world-class criminal would solve America's crime problem. ''What would you do with our criminals?'' he asked. ''Shoot them?''

''Only at first,'' she stated as if it should be obvious to him. ''After a while the rest would catch on and mend their ways.''

McKenna concluded that Elena was very much a cause-and-effect type of girl and he could have debated her all day long on her ideas, but time was a problem and he wanted to stay on track. ''Let's stick to Arturo,'' he said. ''How about, after some gentle questioning, I bring him back with me the next time I see Felipe?''

''That would be very noble of you,'' she said, smiling appreciatively.

''Which apartment?''

''I'm not done. There's something else.''

''What?'' McKenna said, a little exasperated.

''I assume I'll be on television when they take me out of

here, and I can't go looking like this.''

"What can I do about that?"

"There's a makeup bag in the glove compartment of my car, but they wouldn't bring it to me."

"Done," McKenna said.

But Elena wasn't. "I also have some clothes in the apartment. I want you to pick out a nice dress, something you like. That's what I'll wear when I leave here."

Another classic case of Camilia Wright syndrome, McKenna thought. "You might not like what I pick out," he commented.

"I'll like whatever you pick out, but don't forget to match the shoes to the dress. And bring me some nice underwear."

"Okay. Is what I'm looking for in the apartment?"

"The poison?"

"Yeah, the biological reagent. What were you supposed to do with it, release it into the water supply?"

Elena smiled. "Yes, but that makes no difference. You know, I never would have done that."

"You'd disobey orders?"

"Of course," Elena said. "If the time came when I was supposed to use it, that would mean that Felipe was dead. I wouldn't kill thousands of people on the orders of a dead man."

I'm learning something new about this girl, McKenna thought. "Glad to hear that, but I'd feel much better if we had it. Mind telling me where you got it from?"

"Maybe someday," Elena said, acting like it was a matter of little concern to her. "It's in a Thermos in the refrigerator. Don't open it and don't drop it."

"Which apartment?"

"Seventeen A. I'm ready to make the call now."

McKenna shifted a pad and pencil to her from the desk. "Write the number down," he said.

She did. It was a 917 area code, which meant it was a cellular phone. "You have to dial, let it ring twice, then hang up and dial again," she said.

"Okay, but remember, only Spanish. No Quechua. I'm going to put it on the speakerphone."

"Are you sure your Spanish is good enough?" she asked teasingly.

"I'll manage." McKenna dialed the number, heard the two rings, hung up, and dialed again. Then he gave the receiver to

Elena and pressed the speaker button. Somebody picked up, but said nothing.

"Arturo?" Elena said.

"Sí, señorita."

"Commissioner McKenna will be coming up there very shortly. Do you understand?" Elena said in Spanish.

"Sí, señorita. I understand. Should I jump?" Arturo answered, also in Spanish.

"No, you must live. You are to disable the device at the door and surrender to Commissioner McKenna. He will return you to our comrades. Do you understand?"

"Sí, señorita. What about you? Have you been captured?"

"Yes."

"Will you also be returned?"

"Yes, but not yet."

It was a moment before Arturo spoke again. Then he asked, "Will I see you again, *señorita?"*

Elena looked to McKenna and he nodded. He was embarrassed and unprepared when she put her hand on his for a moment and said, "Thank you." Then she amazed him when she blushed before she put both hands on the receiver.

"Yes, Arturo. I will see you soon."

"Will Felipe be angry with us?" Arturo asked, almost unconcerned.

"No, Felipe will understand."

"Then I await Commissioner McKenna."

"See you soon, Arturo," Elena said, then McKenna hung up and looked at her quizzically.

"Like I said, he is very dedicated," Elena said.

"He would have jumped out the window if you told him to?"

"Of course."

"I think what he's dedicated to is you."

Elena smiled. "Brian, are you thinking bad things about me?"

"I don't know. Maybe."

The smile vanished. She replaced the receiver and said, "Well, don't. He is just a sweet boy and I already love a man."

McKenna was more than happy to let Elena have the final word on that subject.

Chapter 54

Pao was being so nice that he made McKenna uncomfortable. Everything was just "Yes, sir" or "No, sir" from the big detective, but McKenna didn't give up. "You know, you look like a color-blind altar boy in that costume. Looks ridiculous," he told Pao in the elevator.

Pao looked himself over. He had borrowed a uniformed cop's plain black tie, and it contrasted horribly with his white shirt and brown suit. The two Emergency Service cops just glanced at each other and braced themselves for the explosion from the famous Johnny Pao, but it never came. "Yes, sir. It does look ridiculous. It's a new look for me," was Pao's polite reply.

After they all got off the elevator, Pao wanted to use the keys and go in, but McKenna decided not to take a chance on opening the door. So, using Elena's procedure, he called Arturo from the hallway outside Apartment 17A. Once again, Arturo picked up the phone but didn't say anything.

"Arturo? This is McKenna. Do you speak English?"

"A little, Commissioner," Arturo replied.

"Good. We are in the hallway outside. Open the door and come on out with your hands on your head."

"Okay, I'm coming out." Arturo must have been waiting at the door. It opened immediately and he was there with the phone in his hand and his hands on top of his head.

Looking him over, it was easy for McKenna to see why Elena liked the kid. He was obviously scared. He was wearing shorts and his legs were shaking as Pao took the phone and handcuffed him. But that didn't stop the kid from smiling. It was a wide, friendly smile that said: You can trust me.

McKenna didn't. He kept his pistol trained on the kid as Pao searched him, knowing that the young man standing before him must have spilled a lot of blood in Peru to be considered eligible by Felipe for their mission.

As it turned out, Arturo was nothing to worry about. He had accepted his fate and was happy to be going home. Pao kept him in the hallway while McKenna and the Emergency Service cops entered the apartment.

The first thing they checked was the door and McKenna saw that Elena was right. There were three locks on it and Arturo had been prepared to extend a blast of welcome to any unexpected visitors. Four C-4 plastic explosive charges were still stuck on the door frame, but Arturo had followed Elena's instructions before they arrived. McKenna saw the indentations in the explosive charges where the blasting caps had been before Arturo removed them. The two cops removed the C-4 from the door while McKenna went right for the refrigerator in the kitchen. It was empty except for three bottles of Budweiser beer and a silver Thermos. Not wanting even to touch the Thermos, he closed the door and looked around.

The small kitchen was clean and bare, but McKenna smiled when he saw the two menus taped to the wall: Ricardo's and Lorelei's. The cabinets and drawers contained nothing more than two dishes, two glasses, and two sets of silverware. Finding nothing else of interest, he rejoined Pao in the main room.

It was a bright and airy studio apartment, clean and unfurnished. Rolled up against the wall were two sleeping bags on top of four suitcases. Four blasting caps with long lead wires and detonator switches attached were lying on top of the sleeping bags, along with a .45 Colt automatic.

McKenna ignored those for the moment and concentrated on the communications gear. Routine radio messages on the citywide detective band were coming from a base radio set on the floor next to the window. A second radio next to it was receiving messages on the 68th Precinct frequency. McKenna turned off both radios, took a pair of binoculars from the windowsill, and looked out the window.

The view was expansive. He could clearly see the ferries in the harbor and every part of the Verrazano-Narrows Bridge, as well as the Bay Ridge pier on 69th Street. But he couldn't see the 68th Precinct station house from the window and concluded that Elena had watched them leave the ferries, then had gone to the roof to see what they were doing at the station house before she put on her disguise and went down to show how clever she was.

He knew he was right when he went into the bathroom and saw the theatrical makeup kit in the sink. He saw that Elena had been in a hurry when she applied her disguise and hadn't bothered to replace the caps on the tubes of foundation.

McKenna went back into the main room and removed the pistol, blasting caps, and sleeping bags from the tops of the suitcases. He was just about to open it when one of the Emergency Service cops suggested, "We should have them X-rayed before you open them, Commissioner."

McKenna disregarded the advice, knowing that if Elena wanted him dead, she would have just let him open the door.

Three of the suitcases belonged to Elena. She had lots of nice clothes and had taken care in packing them, with everything neatly folded and her underwear and stockings rolled and secured with rubber bands. As he had suspected, Elena didn't own a bra. He thought about selecting an outfit for her as she had requested, then decided against it, thinking it better to keep further personal contact with her to a minimum. So he just searched the suitcases for weapons or anything else she might use to help her out of her predicament, but found nothing.

Arturo's lone suitcase was even less interesting than the others, yielding only three sets of casual outfits and the books and writings of Chairman Gonzalo. McKenna leafed through one of the well-worn books and found that Arturo, in his studies of revolutionary nonsense, had underlined and highlighted some passages of his leader's thoughts.

McKenna closed the suitcase, went into the bathroom, and closed the door. Then he called Tavlin.

"Find anything?" the inspector asked.

"Yeah, it's in the refrigerator. I'm just going to leave it there until you can find out what to do with it."

"Fine. I'll send some men up to guard the place until then. Anything else?"

"Nothing we didn't suspect. They've been monitoring our communications from here."

"What now?"

"Don't bother booking Elena. Just keep her at the Six-Eight. I'm sending her clothes over with the Emergency Service cops. Let her pick out anything she wants to wear."

Whatever Tavlin thought about McKenna's unusual order he kept to himself. "What about the other one?" he asked.

"He's going back, so don't bother booking him either. Just give him the interrogation show all night."

"You're not coming back here?"

"Nope. It's city hall for me. I have to go take my medicine and give them some ideas they won't like."

McKenna called Angelita as soon as they got back in the car.

"Glad you called. I was just wondering about you," she said.

"Wondering what?"

"Did she give you anything?"

"Some information," McKenna replied innocently, but knew it was time to change the subject. "Looking forward to seeing you again, babe. I really miss you."

McKenna's attempt had no effect on Angelita. "What did you think of her?" she asked.

"I think she's a stone-cold killer."

"That's it?"

"Yeah."

"But she's a beautiful stone-cold killer, right?"

McKenna had been with Angelita long enough to recognize the Spanish-woman jealousy signs, a very dangerous side effect for the man so blessed to have one. He went into calculated retreat. "Some of the guys think she's pretty, but I don't see anything special in her."

"Why not?" Angelita asked, suspiciously.

"Because I've got something much better. I've got you."

It worked, for the moment. "Then get here," she said.

McKenna hung up after love and kisses and thought how really good it would be to see Angelita again. But though he tried to prevent it, Elena kept popping into his mind. Pao was surprised when McKenna felt the need to call Angelita again and tell her how much he missed her. He kept his eyes straight ahead and didn't appear to be listening as he drove through the press crew in front of city hall and waited for McKenna to finish his call. But he had been listening. "Want some advice, sir?" he asked after McKenna hung up.

"Okay, Johnny. I guess I could use some."

"You're getting in trouble and overplaying your hand," Pao said.

It gave McKenna some more to think about.

Chapter 55

AUGUST 1, GRAMERCY PARK HOTEL—
It had been a great night after a long and hard session at city hall. McKenna awoke to the sounds and smells of breakfast, feeling mentally refreshed but physically tired, in a pleasant sort of way. Angelita was standing next to the table, smiling innocently and watching him. Although she was still showing a few bumps and bruises, she was also wearing one of his favorite catch-me-if-you-can nighties, so he did, again, while breakfast got cold. It didn't matter. After the fun and frolic they sat down and ate it anyway, talking furiously the whole time about everything but Felipe, Elena, or anything to do with *Sendero*, the things that were foremost in both of their minds.

After they showered together and dressed, McKenna turned on the TV and opened the curtains. Sunlight filled the room as McKenna's mood brightened further. "Looks like a great day to be in New York."

Angelita was sitting on the bed, watching Elena's face on the TV. "Then it's got to be a bad day to be leaving," she said.

McKenna sensed her mood change; he'd known it would have had to come sooner or later. After all, it was the big day, quite possibly the last day of his life. That afternoon he was leaving on the *Felipe Limited*. He had hoped to get another hour or two of sunshine out of Angelita with both of them having fun while pretending nothing special was going on, but saw that wasn't happening. The new Miss Crankyface was watching the TV with interest, so he knew she would be asking some questions and he would have to tell her some things she didn't want to hear. That was never a pleasant experience with Angelita.

On the TV the commentator was reporting on Elena's arrest.

467

A picture of her again filled the screen while he gave a short and speculative account of her life and activities within *Sendero*. He ended the report with the information that Elena had not yet been officially charged with any crime, but he listed a number of possibilities that should ensure a lifetime in the slammer for her.

Angelita turned down the volume and turned to McKenna. "Well, what is she being charged with?" she asked.

"Not much."

Angelita regarded him coldly. "What exactly do you call 'not much'?"

McKenna concentrated hard and managed to put a look of reasonable confidence on his face. "She's not being charged with anything," he said.

"And why's that?"

"Because it would be a waste of time and some things might have come out at her arraignment that we don't want Felipe to know."

"Whose idea is that?"

"Mine, I guess."

"What did she have to give you to get that kind of consideration, might I ask?" she said, standing up with her fists clenched.

"She gave us what we needed, but it's not part of any deal. She doesn't even know I'm sending her back."

"What's this *sending her back* stuff? You're *taking* her back, aren't you?"

Oh-oh, McKenna thought. I see where this is going, and I don't want to get there this way. "Yeah, technically I guess you could say I'm taking her back," he said, as if it just occurred to him for the first time.

"And you're going to be sitting on a ferry with her, and then you're going to be sitting on a plane with her. And I guess she'll be pretty grateful, right?"

"I don't think she'll be unhappy to be freed, but I won't be sitting next to her. Don't make a big thing out of this, Angelita."

"Then give me some good reasons why you're doing it."

"Okay. I will, if you sit down and calm down."

She glared at him for a moment, then sat back down on the bed. McKenna could see she wasn't calming down, but he had no choice except to take his chances and continue. "First of all, if we charge her and keep her, *Sendero* is gonna pull another stunt somewhere to get her back. We don't need that.

Besides, keeping her in jail when we've already been forced to give so many of them back would have to sway her jury. They might find her not guilty.''

"Not if I were on that jury," Angelita commented.

Don't I know that, McKenna thought. "There's more things to consider," he said. "I want Felipe real happy and relaxed on that flight and I'm counting on Elena to do that for me."

"Why? Is he one of the men who care about her?" she asked sarcastically.

McKenna didn't like the "one of the men" part of the question, but felt it better to leave it alone. "Of course," he replied. "From what I've seen, he's real good with his people."

She scoffed at that, but didn't attack his reasoning. Instead, she used a different attack. "What did everybody else think of this grand gesture of yours?" she asked.

"The mayor couldn't care less. He's already got his good press out of the capture, but Heresford thought it was a good idea. He knows that in a trial some embarrassing things might come out about the way this was handled."

"And Ray?" Angelita asked.

"Ray wasn't crazy about the idea. But you don't know him anymore. He'd kill each one of them himself and he doesn't want any of them leaving alive."

"Neither do I," Angelita said, surprising McKenna.

"But he came around and saw the reasons it has to be done."

"I don't believe that," she retorted.

"Maybe there's other reasons he knows that you don't," McKenna snapped back.

McKenna thought he had made a mistake, but he had said it and the damage was done. He didn't want her thinking and worrying while he was gone, so maybe it was for the best, he thought. He waited for her to ask, What other reasons? and was ready to answer that he was sending Elena to her death, if everything worked out as planned.

But she didn't. Instead she lay back on the bed and closed her eyes. "More bullshit," she said under her breath after a few seconds.

"What are you doing now?" McKenna asked.

"I'm tired. I'm taking a nap."

"Want me to join you?" McKenna asked, hopefully.

"No."

Now isn't this just a swell development? McKenna thought as he watched her, feeling helpless and not knowing what else to do. Then Angelita stifled a sob, so he sat on the bed next to her and stroked her hair.

It worked, as always. She took his hand and put it to her face, her eyes filling with tears as she stared into his. "Sorry, it's not your fault," she said.

"It's not your fault either."

"Yes, it is. I got us into this mess and I might be getting you killed in the process."

"It's not your fault. I'm just doing something that has to be done. You should know by now that I'd probably wind up doing exactly what I'm doing, even if you didn't want me to. You just gave me a little boost in the right direction and made it easier for me."

Angelita continued staring into McKenna's eyes and said nothing for a few moments, causing him to wonder if his statement had been news to her. Finally she smiled. "Then it is your fault after all, isn't it?" she asked.

"Sure, just like always."

"Then you're in a lot of trouble, hotshot," she said, still smiling.

"And how do I get out of this trouble?"

"Simple," she said as she pulled him onto the bed next to her and held him close. "You're gonna have to clean this mess up you've gotten yourself into, come home in one piece, and give us another baby."

Simple? McKenna thought as he held her face and kissed her tenderly.

Chapter 56 McKenna heard the good news on the radio as Pao drove him to the Wall Street pier. Flight 902 had taken off from Miami and was on its way north. It meant the end was near and he just wanted it to be over, one way or the other.

The mayor and Brunette were waiting on the dock, present for the big send-off. Heresford and Cervantes were already on the launch, posing for the photographers like they didn't notice the press gang was there on the pier. Heresford was dressed casually, wearing a yellow sports shirt and khaki slacks, looking like he was off to watch his friends race their yachts at Newport. Cervantes was a small, slightly built man, dressed stiffly and formally in a pin-striped blue suit and looking like everybody else was standing on his lawn and trampling his grass.

During the trip from the hotel Pao had maintained his Detective Slave routine, but it changed just before McKenna left the car. He held out his hand and said, "Good luck, Brian."

McKenna took it. "You gonna pick me up from the airport when I get back?" he asked.

"If I got nothing better to do," Pao said. "See you later."

"I hope."

"Get to work."

Good to have him back, McKenna thought as he got out of the car. He saw that the mayor looked to be in a good mood, but Brunette was wearing the same frown left over from the night before. He was obviously unhappy and McKenna guessed there would be no statements to the press coming from him. Nothing that could be printed, at least.

That was good, and right according to plan, McKenna thought. For the benefit of the reporters, and figuring that Felipe was watching everything live on TV, he decided to keep it businesslike. He nodded to the mayor, then shook Brunette's hand. "Money onboard?" he asked.

"Yeah. Had it loaded before we got here with the press following."

"Any changes?"

"You heard the plane's on the way?"

"Yeah. To JFK, I hope."

"No communication from them, but it's JFK. You might like to know that Felipe's not perfect. Cranston pulled a scam on him."

I sure would like to know that at this point, McKenna thought. "The stuff in the Thermos?" he asked.

"Just Chlordane. Bug juice exterminators used to use it for termites. It'd kill you if you drank it outright, but I'm told that dumping it into a reservoir would dilute it so much that it would have no effect on anyone."

"How can you be sure it was Cranston? Fingerprints?"

"Yeah. He was fingerprinted for his Top Secret clearance

and his prints are on the cover of the Thermos.''

"So maybe he's not such a bad guy after all," McKenna offered. "At least not as bad as we thought he was."

"He's still a scumbag, just like we figured. He didn't have access to the stuff Felipe wanted, so he scammed him, figuring it wouldn't be used anyway."

"I like it. Gives me some ammunition to use on Felipe if I need to bring him down a peg. Wish me luck."

Brunette did, hugging McKenna while the cameras clicked. "Good luck, buddy," he whispered. "We'll hold up our end, but try and get back here."

"I'm sure gonna try," McKenna answered as soon as Brunette released him. There wasn't much else to be said, so McKenna got onboard the launch, introduced himself to the Peruvian ambassador, and thanked him for coming.

"Wouldn't have missed it," Cervantes said. "Life has been a little dull lately and it's nice to get a chance to go home."

The ambassador's cavalier attitude surprised McKenna. "You know there's an element of danger in this, don't you?" he asked.

"Yes, but life's a crapshoot, isn't it?"

McKenna liked this guy. "It sure is, Mr. Ambassador," he said, then signaled to the Harbor Unit sergeant to cast off.

All things considered, it was a pleasant trip to Bay Ridge. McKenna sat on the rear deck, watching Manhattan recede, and thought about his promise to Angelita. Could he keep it? If he couldn't, what would happen to her? He tried to imagine her married to someone else, but the other guy's face kept changing into his own. Then the Harbor Unit sergeant called his name and McKenna went to the bow of the boat.

As the launch tied up at the Bay Ridge pier next to the empty lifeboats, Tavlin and Fat Albert arrived with Arturo and Elena in the backseat of their car. McKenna was glad to see that neither of them were handcuffed, a fact that caused some confusion in the press corps standing behind the barricades. They started shouting questions as soon as Elena got out of the car. McKenna saw that she looked surprised to be there, but she quickly adjusted to her new circumstances as he watched her.

The reporters' voices mixed and drifted to McKenna as an unintelligible jumble, but the way Elena looked gave McKenna a few questions to ask himself. She was wearing the dress and shoes he would have picked out for her, a tight white-and-red-flowered print and the red high-heeled shoes. With her red hair put up in a bun, she looked like a sweet and innocent girl stepping out on her first big date, ready to be bad. She gave a wave and a few poses to the reporters while Fat Albert opened the trunk and removed the suitcases. Then, Tavlin and Fat Albert picked up two suitcases apiece. Elena and Arturo followed them to the launch, with the cameras clicking and film running.

I hope Angelita isn't watching this spectacle on TV, was all McKenna could think as he helped Arturo and Elena come onboard. He took the suitcases from Tavlin and Fat Albert, then the two men turned and walked back to their car without saying a word to him.

Arturo took a seat on the bow of the boat, leaving Elena and McKenna alone on the rear deck. "Doesn't look like you're very popular anymore," Elena observed.

"Yeah, my ratings are down."

"Is it because you're releasing me?"

No, that's not it, McKenna thought. They know that, if everything works out, you're being released to your death, and maybe you'll be taking me along for the whole trip. It's that Tavlin and Fat Albert don't trust their acting abilities enough to mimic a cheery send-off.

McKenna didn't look at her and didn't answer. Instead, he watched the Harbor cops cast off. With the Brooklyn shore fading behind them, she respected his silence for a few minutes. But she still had something to say. "You know, in a few minutes we won't be alone anymore."

"That's all right," McKenna answered, still not looking at her.

"Isn't there anything you'd like to tell me?"

"Nothing you shouldn't already know. We're enemies and that can't change."

"Everything changes," she stated.

"And I'm a happily married man. That should make some difference."

"Like I said, everything changes. Is it okay if I thank you for releasing me?"

"Don't bother. I had my reasons. You're not really free until Felipe agrees to something for me."

"Is that what you're telling yourself?"

He looked at her for the first time. She stared back into his eyes, wearing a confident and amused smile.

He had to smile himself. "Yeah, that's what I'm telling myself," he said. "Let's just leave it at that."

She wouldn't. "You could stay with us," she suggested. "It would be an exciting life."

He laughed at the idea and Elena's smile lost some luster. "Elena, you've already given me enough excitement for one lifetime," he told her.

"There's always room for more excitement," she offered. "Maybe?"

It was a question McKenna didn't want to answer. No was easier than maybe, but no wasn't working on this girl. The launch slowed, giving him his excuse for not replying. He turned around and saw that they were approaching the *Samuel I. Newhouse*. Felipe and four of his men were standing on the rear deck. "Excuse me, Elena, but I'm gonna be busy for a while," he said. "Could you make it easy for me and put on a happy face for Felipe?"

"You mean, like I'm really glad to see him?"

"Really glad. We're all going to be spending some quality time together and in my situation I don't need an angry Felipe on my back."

"Okay," she said. "I'll be good." Then she turned and waved to Felipe. He looked surprised, but waved back.

Once again, McKenna caught a line thrown by one of Felipe's men. Heresford and Cervantes came on deck and Heresford caught the other and pulled the launch into the ferry. Cervantes was the first one off, and Felipe offered him his hand as soon as he was on the rear deck of the ferry. "So nice of you to come, Mr. Cervantes," Felipe said to his new hostage.

Cervantes fell right in stride. "So good of you to invite me," he said. "I've wanted to meet you for a long time. We might have a lot to talk about."

"I'm sure," Felipe said as Heresford came onboard. "Mr. Heresford, a pleasure to meet you," Felipe said, extending his hand.

Heresford hesitated for a moment, looking back at the Brooklyn shore. The newsmen were still standing on the pier, watching. But he shook Felipe's hand anyway and said, "Likewise, but I hope you understand we don't have much to talk about at all."

Felipe smiled. "I understand, Mr. Heresford. We'll keep it very proper."

McKenna was up next, leaving Elena and Arturo standing on the deck of the launch. "Good to see you again, McKenna," Felipe said as he shook McKenna's hand. "I see you've brought me something nice."

"Yes. Seventy-five million dollars."

"And two comrades, no?"

"Maybe two," McKenna said. "You can have Arturo back, but Elena might not be staying. We have to talk first. I need something from you right now."

Felipe raised his eyebrows, obviously amused. "Are you suggesting another deal?" he asked.

"Yes. I want a promise from you that *Sendero* will never again commit terrorist acts against Americans anywhere in the world."

"Just a promise from me?"

"That'll do."

"But I might not always be in a position of authority," Felipe said.

"Let's assume you will be," McKenna countered.

Felipe laughed and said, "An assumption I like. But I'm sure it has occurred to you that, on the surface, your position appears ridiculous."

"Only on the surface. I think I've come to know something about you and the way you do business, Felipe. I think that if we don't arrive at a settlement right now, you'll watch that boat take Elena back to jail."

While Felipe was thinking that over and staring down at Elena, McKenna added, "I just had her brought along to save us some time, in case the proposition suits you."

Arturo was nervously staring at his shoes while Elena leaned against the rail of the launch, gazing unconcerned at the Brooklyn shore while her fate was debated.

"Would you consider a modification to your proposition?" Felipe asked.

"Try me."

"If we don't arrive safely at our destination or, in the event of open warfare between our two countries, our agreement in this matter will be null and void."

"Fair enough."

"Then it's a deal," Felipe said. "You know, I was just thinking that it's a dangerous thing for a man when his enemies know him so well. Please instruct your men that, after the money is handed over, they will ferry the two hundred passengers I'm releasing to the Brooklyn shore."

McKenna did. Felipe then turned, walked to the cabin door, and said, "Would you follow me inside, gentlemen?"

McKenna, Heresford, and Cervantes followed Felipe into the main cabin, leaving the Senderista guards on the rear ferry deck and Elena and Arturo on the launch. McKenna was surprised when Felipe walked right through the *Samuel I. Newhouse* and jumped to the *Andrew J. Barberi*. Everyone followed him into the main cabin, where three armed Senderistas were waiting for him. Felipe stopped in the center of the cabin and said, "I assume you gentlemen aren't armed or carrying any types of transmitting devices. However, I must insist that you submit to a search."

Felipe didn't wait for a reply. He nodded to his men, and McKenna, Heresford, and Cervantes were patted down, each in turn. Nothing was found, and when the searches were completed Felipe pointed to the row of benches along the wall. "Please make yourselves comfortable over there, gentlemen," he said.

When the three were seated, one of the Senderistas gave McKenna a portable radio.

"It's set to your frequency," Felipe said. "Kindly inform your people that our plane will be arriving at Kennedy Airport and that it is to be refueled on Runway Four Right. The tower will receive further instructions from my men aboard the aircraft."

McKenna relayed the message and his instructions were acknowledged. He gave the radio back to the Senderista and asked, "Now what?"

"Just wait here," Felipe said. "I have a number of things to do, so I'll leave you here with my men."

"And then?" McKenna asked.

"And then we'll be getting underway, of course."

Chapter 57
It was near dusk when both ferries raised their anchors. The *Andrew J. Barberi* crossed under the Verrazano-Narrows Bridge at full speed, leaving the *Samuel I. Newhouse* adrift in its wake. After ten minutes the *Barberi* turned to port and the ferry followed the Brooklyn coast, a half mile offshore from the crowded beaches of Coney Island. By eight o'clock it was in the Rockaway Channel between the Brooklyn shore and Rockaway. Two drawbridges were opened to let the ferry through and twenty minutes later the *Barberi* again turned hard to port, still running at full speed, headed for the Queens shore at Kennedy Airport.

In the main cabin, McKenna, Heresford, and Cervantes braced themselves. The Senderistas guarding them took the hint and, still keeping their M-16s pointed at their three hostages, held on to supporting stanchions in the cabin. They all heard the sound of the hull scraping the bottom, a second before the ferry beached and came to a complete and violent stop. Then came some shouting and screaming from the decks above, but no one in the main cabin was injured.

A minute later, Felipe and Elena were the first ones to appear on the stairs, descending from the salon deck. "You'll be the last ones out," Felipe yelled to McKenna, then headed for the rear deck, followed by Elena and his men shepherding fifty hostages, all male passengers. All of these passengers had been put to work by the Senderistas, carrying the duffel bags of money, boxes of ammo, packs, Stinger missiles, and recoilless rifles. McKenna saw that the Senderistas planned to arrive home prepared and well armed. He watched as the passengers stopped on the rear deck to pass down their loads before they jumped into the water at the prodding of their guards.

When the Senderistas and all the passengers who were going

had disembarked from the rear deck, the guards left inside indicated that it was time for McKenna, Heresford, and Cervantes to leave. They did, but McKenna paused for a moment on the rear deck to survey the scene before him.

The airport was in darkness, though he could see the black outline of the control tower and the terminals in the distance. Closer were the flashing wing lights of an airplane on the ground, sitting on Runway Four Right about 100 yards in front of him on the other side of the bulrushes. There was lots of movement in the bulrushes as the Senderistas and hostages pushed their way through. Straining his eyes, McKenna could make out the outline of Cranston's storage shed next to the plane.

"Get going," one of their guards behind them ordered, and McKenna jumped from the deck three feet down into Jamaica Bay. It was high tide and the water only came up to his knees, but the bottom was soft mud and it was uncomfortable sloshing through the ten yards to shore. He heard Heresford and Cervantes splash into the water after him, followed by their three guards. When McKenna reached the shore, he turned around and waited. Heresford and Cervantes were right behind him, with two of their guards bringing up the rear, their rifles pointed forward. The third Senderista remained behind in the water. McKenna figured his job was to discourage the curiosity of the lucky passengers left behind on the upper decks.

"Keep going and don't turn around," one of the Senderistas ordered.

McKenna, Heresford, and Cervantes followed the order, plunging into the sedges and following what had become a well-worn path in the last five minutes. Taking more time than he thought it would, McKenna was the first to emerge from the bulrushes, close to Cranston's shed. The door was open and Senderistas were unloading the parachutes and carrying them to the plane.

"Keep going," the guard behind them ordered again, and they started marching to the plane. When they got close they saw the hostages from the ferry sitting on the ground in a group next to their loads, ringed by a cordon of Senderistas. Other Senderistas had set up a defensive perimeter around the plane.

McKenna's group passed through the perimeter and stopped at the edge of the group of hostages. At their guard's order, they sat down on the runway.

McKenna looked around, searching for Felipe and Elena. In

the darkness, he didn't see them until the rear ramp door of the Boeing 727 lowered. They were standing at the rear of the plane. There were some interior lights on in the plane and some light splashed onto the runway so that McKenna saw Cruzco emerge. He hugged Felipe and the two men talked for a moment before Cruzco went back up the stairs into the plane. Then two cabin attendants came down the ramp and stood at the bottom, soon followed by the passengers who had just spent two days on the plane with Cruzco and his Nicaraguans. McKenna couldn't be sure, but he thought he heard the cabin attendants say, "Welcome to New York and thank you for flying American," to the departing passengers as they filed down the ramp before being herded by Senderistas to the far side of the runway.

The unloading took five minutes. Then the ferry passengers were told to pick up their bundles and they were lined up at the rear door before they entered the plane, single file. That took another five minutes. Once they were all in, their guards escorted McKenna's group to the ramp. Felipe was waiting for them, smiling, but Elena seemed to take no special interest in them.

"Please board the plane, gentlemen," Felipe said. "I have a few more things to do, but you'll be sitting with me. My men inside will show you to your seats."

"First Class, I hope," Heresford said.

"Of course, Mr. Heresford. I always fly First Class."

On his way up the ramp, McKenna saw that the slipstream lock was still in place on the fuselage next to the ramp door, but he knew it wouldn't be for long. At the top of the ramp stood a Senderista holding a small oxyacetylene torch kit.

Seymor Cranston sat on the bed in his mother's room at the Port Jefferson Nursing Home, watching TV with the volume turned down. A CNN camera with a long-range night-vision lens was focused on the plane on Runway Four Right. Everything on the screen was in shades of green. The passengers who had boarded the plane in Honduras were walking in a group away from the plane and toward the camera. "See, Mom. That's where I used to work," Cranston said softly as he stroked his mother's hair.

As always, he got no response, and hadn't for many years. He looked down at her anyway, searching her face for some sign of recognition, but her eyes stared straight ahead. He put his face in front of hers and saw no change in focus in her pupils. Since her last stroke, he was never sure if she could see him or if she even knew she was alive.

Cranston returned his attention to the TV while he held his mother's hand. Flight 902 taxied down the runway and took off with the camera following its path. He turned off the TV when the plane was just a speck in the night sky.

"I have to go now, Mom," he said, then bent over his mother and kissed her on the forehead. "Don't tell anyone, but I may not see you again for a long time. We fooled them all and we're very rich," he whispered in her ear. He left the room, turning out the lights and closing the door behind him.

Leaving the nursing home by the rear door, Cranston stopped for a minute to look at the stars in the night sky, then walked toward his van at the end of the parking lot. His wife and kids were waiting in the van, all packed and headed for a new life.

What Cranston didn't know was that he was headed for Johnny Pao. He knew the big detective walking toward him from somewhere, but couldn't place him until Pao was in front of him and blocking his path. Then it came to him. He had seen Pao on television. Pao said, "Trick-or-treat, genius."

Cranston turned, hoping there was a place to run. Men in suits were getting out of cars all over the parking lot and the exit was blocked by another unmarked car.

"Come on, Seymor," Pao said, putting his arm around Cranston's shoulder. "I want you to meet a friend of mine."

"Who?" Cranston asked, his throat dry and his voice weak.

"Ray Brunette. I know he looks forward to making your acquaintance."

Chapter 58 After a long and busy day, Pao emerged just before midnight from the subway tunnel on the Manhattan side of the Williamsburg Bridge. He felt foolish, dressed head to toe in black with his face and hands smeared with light-absorbing camouflage makeup, wearing a front-mounted black knapsack and carrying a slung M-14 rifle with an enormous scope on top. He wouldn't have minded his mission if it wasn't for the costume they were making him wear.

It had started already and he knew it wasn't going to stop, ever. That big-mouth Joe Sofia was the first one to say it when he and Sheeran met Pao at the headquarters range. Pao had been busy sighting in his scope, already dressed in his costume, and it had been a simple Sofia statement, the way these things always started. Just a chuckle accompanied by a "How ya doin', Ninja?" and Pao was stuck with it. His new and unwelcome moniker was officially pasted to him when they had dropped him off at the deserted Delancey Street subway station, the first Manhattan stop of the J train. Sheeran had reported on his radio, "We're putting the Ninja out," and that was it. Once an inspector of police calls you something, that's your name.

Pao was fuming as he walked along the tracks, headed for the Manhattan-side bridge tower set in the riverbed 20 yards from shore and 100 yards from the subway-tunnel entrance. In spite of his appearance, Pao had always considered himself more Irish than Chinese. He hated Chinese food, loved spending an occasional free night dumping suds in Higgin's Shamrock Pub, and marched in every St. Patrick's Day parade. But now, through no fault of his own, he was the Ninja.

Pao stopped thirty yards from the bridge tower and checked his bearings by looking south to 1263 Grand Street, a twenty-three-story apartment building one block south of the bridge. From where he stood, Pao was level with the sixth floor of the building and not yet visible to the occupants of apartment 14B, which faced the river. Deviating from the plan, Pao left the tracks, crossed the Manhattan-bound inner roadway, and stood on the outer roadway, surveying with morbid fascination the solitary truck 300 yards ahead at the center of the bridge. There was a line of cars behind the truck, but they were all vacant, the occupants having fled on foot back to Brooklyn after Felipe had revealed his surprise.

Before Pao had accepted the mission, Brunette had made him aware of the risks. He had one shot, and if he missed, his target would press the "Fire" button on his M129A radio remote detonator, exploding the ton of C-4 in the truck and dropping the center span of the Williamsburg Bridge and errant marksman Johnny Pao into the East River, 137 feet below. Even if he survived the blast, which was improbable, and even if he managed to cling to the bridge tower, he would be ripped to shreds by the bridge cables after they snapped. One shot.

Nothing to it, Pao thought as he crossed the roadway back to the subway tracks occupying the middle lanes of the bridge. But the time for walking was over. Pao got on his stomach next to a three-foot steel wall that separated the eastbound tracks from the westbound tracks. He crawled uphill toward Brooklyn on the northern side of the wall, shielded from the view of anyone watching from 1263 Grand Street. Ten long minutes later he was twenty yards past the Manhattan-side bridge tower. Raising his head, he looked over the wall toward 1263 Grand Street. His view of the building was blocked by the bridge tower, which was good, and meant that whoever was watching the bridge from there couldn't see him.

Whistling as he stood up, Pao jumped over the wall and walked across the tracks and the Brooklyn-bound roadway to the Manhattan-side bridge tower. He peered around the tower and saw that he was at the tenth-floor level of 1263 Grand Street. Then he went up, climbing hand-over-hand up the interlocking steel girders, always staying on the river side of the bridge tower. What had looked like a difficult climb seemed easy once he realized it had been done many times before by that artistic and agile bunch inhabiting the low-income housing projects of the Lower East Side. The tower was covered in graffiti, with street names and gang affiliations spray-painted in letters ten feet high.

Fifty feet up, Pao was opposite the fourteenth-floor level of

1263 Grand. While holding on to the girder with one hand, he reached into his knapsack, removed two snap-on web straps, and attached himself to the girder. One strap he wrapped around the girder at his knees, and pulled it snug until his knees were pressed against the steel. The other he wrapped around the girder and snapped onto a waist harness he was wearing. He adjusted the web strap until it permitted him to lean back two feet from the girder. Then he took a large pair of night-vision binoculars from his knapsack, peered around the edge of the girder, and focused on the fourteenth floor, third window from the end.

There were no lights on in apartment 14B, but that made no difference to Pao. The man standing at the window looking at the bridge filled Pao's enlarged field of view in shades of green. There was a set of binoculars hanging around the man's neck, but he hadn't seen anything suspicious and wasn't using them.

Pao took the portable radio from his knapsack and keyed it. "Pao to Inspector Sheeran," he transmitted.

"Go ahead, Ninja," Sheeran replied, causing Pao to grimace before he answered.

"I have a target, Inspector. Are you ready?"

"Ready when you are. Good luck."

Don't need no luck for this one, Pao thought as he put the radio back in his knapsack and unslung his rifle. Simple shot, he told himself, precise known range of 229 yards, no wind, match-loaded 7.62-mm rounds, and with my own rifle instead of one of those fancy *Star Wars* gadgets those lobolas from the Firearms Unit wanted me to use.

With his M-14, the same type of weapon he had carried and used extensively in Vietnam, he thought the whole mission was a piece of cake.

Pao took the covers off his night-vision starlight scope and switched it on before tying the barrel of his rifle to the girder for additional support. Leaning back in his harness, he placed the stock in his shoulder and sighted around the edge of the girder through the scope. It took him ten seconds to reacquire his target standing in the window of apartment 14B. The man was looking in Pao's direction, but couldn't see him. His upper torso and head filled Pao's green field of view, with the crosshairs centered on the heart.

*   *   *

Filotico Malvado, lately of Huancayo, Peru, and recently one of the occupants of apartment 14B, was in a very sour mood as he stared out the window at the truck on the bridge. Everything was going good for everyone else but him and Angel. The rest were all on their way home, while he and Angel were stuck in New York in the most boring of assignments, watching a truck on an empty bridge, twenty-four hours a day. No action and no glory.

Making matters worse was Angel's snoring. It was loud and disgusting, sounding like the man had a ball of phlegm stuck in his throat. It always started five minutes after Angel climbed into his sleeping bag and always lasted until ten seconds before he woke up. Because of it, Filotico hated Angel. It was a consuming hatred that kept him focused and vigilant during his entire twelve-hour watch. He was always conscious of it, but felt his hatred subsiding. That meant his watch was almost over and he would get the chance to kick Angel awake.

Filotico checked his watch and saw that he was right. Midnight, end of tour. He took the detonator from his pocket, placed it on the windowsill, and was removing his binoculars when a small movement on the bridge tower caught his eye. He stared hard at it, but saw nothing, so he brought the binoculars to his eyes and surveyed the tower. Then he saw it: two cables tied around one of the girders. Were they always there? he wondered. Looking through the binoculars, he strained his eyes and saw a tube of metal that shouldn't be there, tied to the girder right above the other two cables. Could that be a man up there, tied to the bridge? he wondered.

It was Filotico's last thought. He saw the muzzle flash, but didn't hear or feel the bullet that crashed through his window, through his heart, and through the front steel door of the studio apartment. He was dead before he hit the floor.

But Filotico was the only one who hadn't heard the bullet. Angel heard it and also heard Filotico's fall. He was a combat veteran and knew exactly what it was, but the apartment was in darkness. He sat up, prepared to react to the changed circumstances, but he wasn't given the time because, in the recently darkened hallway outside apartment 14B, Sheeran, Sofia, and the two Emergency Service cops had also heard the sound. All considered themselves lucky. After Pao's bullet passed through the door of apartment 14B, it zipped between the two rows of cops waiting outside, each of whom was holding on to the universal police door key, a utilitarian invention that consisted of a 220-pound fire hydrant with two long steel handles welded on each side. Each cop held a pistol in his free hand and all wore night-vision goggles.

''Now!'' Sheeran yelled, and they swung the key into the door. On the second swing, the locks gave and the door swung open. By that time, Angel was crawling to Filotico's body to search for the detonator. As he reached his comrade, he was hit in the legs, buttocks, and back by fifteen 9-mm parabellum rounds.

Angel died four seconds after Filotico. The Williamsburg Bridge wouldn't last forever, but it still had a few years left.

Chapter 59 AUGUST 2, 3:00 A.M., AMAZON JUNGLE—*Comandante* Segundo Torres lay under one of the landing-light towers at the edge of Iquitos International Airport, binoculars to his eyes as he surveyed the scene in front of him. What he saw gave him cause for satisfaction. Against the backdrop of the lit-up runways and terminals, it was easy to spot the government defenses. Many of the army outposts in the thin security line facing him were unmanned, and he could clearly see the soldiers in those that were defended. It was obvious to Torres that the government soldiers were unaware of *Sendero*'s presence. They were smoking and joking and the sound of music drifted back to the Senderistas.

Torres watched as his scouts crawled forward in the darkness, marking a path through the minefield. They got far enough to cut the barbed wire directly in front of the government lines. Their actions went undetected, another good sign in a day full of good signs after the horrible month of marching through the jungle. So many men in the battalion had come down with yellow fever or malaria that, for a while, Torres thought he wouldn't arrive in Iquitos with enough effective fighting men to take the airport and then hold it for the day or two necessary.

But in the last three days, things had gotten better. Although he was down to 280 men of the 400 who had started the journey, the health of his remaining soldiers had stabilized. By that time it seemed to Torres that those men who hadn't already succumbed to sickness wouldn't. The strongest of the strong, he called them. He dispatched a platoon north to clear the drop zone, just in case, and then his attack force picked up the pace. They had arrived at the outskirts of Iquitos just ahead of schedule with morale high and his men hungering for glory.

The news that afternoon was even better. He had heard that the Sinsi Battalion had left its base in the Huallaga Valley and begun a sweep through Pucallpa, 300 miles away. It seemed the government was in disarray. Major political and military personnel changes had been reported in the last day, and the new and apparently inexperienced commanding officer of the Sinsi Battalion suspected that Felipe was returning via Pucallpa, not knowing that the runway at the airport there was too short for a Boeing 727 to land there. Better yet, *Sendero* spies had reported no increase in security by government forces at the Iquitos Airport.

So with major enemy forces far away and inferior enemy forces in front of him, Torres waited impatiently for the signal to attack. His company commanders knew exactly what to do. It was a simple plan, with the battalion advancing across the runway in line. One company would stop to secure the control tower, one would secure the terminals, and the remaining three would push through to the end of the airport, clearing out the government defensive perimeter on that side and then feigning pursuit before manning the perimeter. To create a distraction and spread confusion among the government troops, two of the four fuel tanks would be blown by satchel charges of dynamite.

As he went over the plan in his mind, Torres couldn't see how it could fail. The only thing that troubled him was his lack of a company in reserve. Because of the toll exacted by disease during the journey, all his companies were understrength, so he didn't have sufficient personnel for a reserve in case of the unlikely event of a counterattack by government forces.

Still, Torres was getting nervous after half an hour of waiting, but then the signal came at 4:00 A.M. Torres's radioman crawled to him and reported, "Comrade *Comandante, Com-*

andante Felipe reports he is a half hour from Peruvian airspace.''

''Sancho, signal the company commanders to attack,'' Torres ordered his radioman, then raised his binoculars and focused on the targets in front of him.

The response to his order came a moment later. Four outposts on the defensive perimeter were hit with rifle grenades, and the response of the surviving government troops exceeded Torres's expectations. They left their defensive positions, most of them without returning fire, while Torres's men filed through the minefield on the paths marked by the scouts. Torres didn't think he had sustained a single casualty by the time his men were regrouping at the government defensive line.

Then came the first sign of opposition. Some of the fleeing government troops stopped at the edge of the runway and began firing on their former positions. The Senderistas responded with a heavy volume of automatic weapon fire. Many of the government troops were killed, and the rest left their weapons and ran down the lighted runways.

Following *Sendero* battle policy, Torres's troops fired over the heads of the unarmed fleeing troops to hurry them on their way, acting on the theory that the terrorized and disorganized army troops would inspire panic in any of their comrades in position they encountered along the way.

As the Senderistas left the government position and advanced down the runway in good order, Torres and Sancho hurried forward to catch up with them. They had reached the edge of the runway and were fifty yards behind their advancing troops when the runway lights went out, followed by the lights in the control tower and the terminals.

Torres considered it an ominous sign, briefly. He could understand the control tower and the terminal lights. Government forces should extinguish them to mask any emergency defensive positions they might have set up there. But he couldn't understand the runway lights. The government forces were depriving themselves of an advantage, with his attacking forces clearly illuminated on the runway. But nothing detrimental came of it. He could make out the shapes of his troops in front of him, still firing and proceeding forward in good order, so he concluded that the extinguishing of the runway lights was the action of a panicked and inexperienced government commander.

Torres's conclusion was buttressed a moment later when his

troops blew the designated fuel tanks with their satchel charges. In the glare of the flames he could see more government troops fleeing their positions unarmed, running for the far end of the runway. As he watched, two companies of his men detached from the main body proceeding down the runway and began their advance on the control tower and the terminals, forming themselves and advancing in line.

It was there that some government troops found stomach for the fight. They fired from the terminal and some Senderistas were hit. The rest dropped to the ground and returned fire. Machine-gun fire raked the terminal as the Senderistas crawled forward. Then Torres's troops fired some rifle grenades into the terminal, but the sporadic return fire from the army troops inside continued.

The noise of battle was terrific, so Torres didn't hear his radioman until Sancho grabbed his arm and shouted in his ear, "*Comandante*, Felipe wants to know how the attack is progressing."

"Tell him surprise has been achieved, but we are encountering some resistance. It will take us another fifteen minutes to secure the airport."

"Another fifteen minutes. Yes, Comrade," Sancho acknowledged, then began talking into his headset as Torres ran in a crouch for the terminal.

Suddenly a green flare was fired from the control tower. Torres figured it was the signal for the government troops to surrender or withdraw, but changed his mind when things started going badly. The first sign was the sound of heavy firing coming from the far end of the runway. His troops must be encountering some resistance, Torres thought, but he attributed it to a final stand by government troops at their own perimeter. He turned and yelled back to Sancho, "Find out what's going on down there!"

Sancho raised his hand in acknowledgment, and Torres continued toward his men attacking the terminals. Then he saw discipline disintegrate in his ranks. There was still sporadic fire coming from the terminals, but some of his men were getting up and fleeing toward him. None of them made it. They were all cut down and Torres didn't understand how it happened. He knew the return fire from the terminals couldn't account for those casualties, and was further puzzled when some of his men left on line started firing at the sky.

Helicopters? Torres thought. It was impossible. He heard

nothing above him, and if they were there they were shooting in the dark. Yet, as he watched, his troops were being slaughtered by fire from far above.

Sancho arrived running and added to his confusion. "*Comandante*, First Company and Second Company report they are under attack at the airport perimeter. They say they are being attacked by soldiers from the Sinsi Battalion."

"The Sinsi Battalion? Impossible," was all Torres could think to say. Then Torres was hit hard on the top of his left shoulder and went down, still conscious but not knowing what went wrong. "Inform Felipe!" he yelled, but got no response. He assumed Sancho had dropped to the ground to avoid enemy fire and crawled to him, still shouting the order, but found that Sancho was dead, his blood and brains spilling onto the grass at the edge of the runway.

In the darkness, Torres searched for the handset and found it in Sancho's hand. He tried to transmit, but the radio had been shattered. Behind him on the runway, he saw the impossible happening. Helicopters were landing. He could clearly hear them and recognized their distinctive outline. Huey troopships from the Sinsi Battalion, he knew.

Torres took his .45 Colt from his holster and fired at the dim shapes of the soldiers emerging from the helicopters. The soldiers returned fire, and although Sancho's body was hit again, Torres wasn't. He fired his eight rounds and was reloading when the advancing soldiers found their target.

"Treachery!" was the last word on Torres's lips.

Chapter 60 Five hours into the flight Elena came from the lavatory and sat across the aisle from McKenna in the First Class section. She had changed into the Elena of Savraada's picture of her, wearing camouflage fatigues and a floppy jungle hat. McKenna avoided eye contact with her, but in the brief glimpse he allowed himself he had to admit she made something of a fashion statement, even in those clothes.

McKenna knew she was staring at him while he made the effort to look everywhere but at her. It happened each time Felipe left the First Class section, and he was sure that Cruzco and Julio had noticed. He knew that Cervantes had, because every time he looked at the little man, Cervantes responded with a wink. He felt McKenna staring at him, so he turned in his seat and did it again.

Unusual conduct, under the circumstances, McKenna thought. It seems the old guy is positively enjoying his little adventure.

Since they took off from their refueling stop at Miami, Cervantes had talked to Felipe about almost everything under the sun during most of the flight, their discussions ranging from world politics to Peruvian wine. McKenna noticed that the only thing they hadn't talked about was the politics of Peru, which gave him the impression that the subject didn't really interest either of them. The only time McKenna had joined in the conversation was when the topic turned to the French, and he found they all shared the same opinion on those folks.

Heresford was another matter, and McKenna regretted sitting next to him. Heresford didn't discuss anything with anybody but McKenna. It seemed he treated the whole thing as just another business trip and, when he wasn't sleeping, his only comments had been complaints, so many that McKenna found it irritating. He had complained about the in-flight meal, about the lack of ice for the drinks, and about the unhygienic smell coming from the passengers in Coach, those fifty poor people who had been Felipe's hostages for five days on the ferries. The only time McKenna had smiled was when Heresford had complained about the lack of a movie.

Aside from the fact that he was forced to wear his seat belt during the entire flight and there was always somebody standing close by ready to shoot him, McKenna had found nothing to complain about. He liked the food and had even eaten Heresford's. He didn't drink, so the lack of ice didn't bother him. All in all, he concluded that Felipe was still being the gracious host and the cabin attendants were doing a remarkable job under the circumstances. His only discomforts were his wet shoes and Elena when she was staring at him, as she was then.

He was relieved to hear Felipe announce over the PA, "Gentlemen, I am pleased to announce we have just entered Peruvian airspace, so we should be landing in about half an hour."

Just like on a charter flight, the people in Coach amazed McKenna and greeted the announcement with clapping. McKenna remembered that he was one of the snotty people in First Class, so of course he didn't clap, but the noise was another in the long list of annoyances for Heresford. He had that patrician look on his face as he stirred from his sleep. "What did he say?" he asked McKenna.

"Half an hour to go."

"About time," Heresford commented, then closed his eyes and appeared to go back to sleep.

"Nice talking to you," McKenna said under his breath.

But Elena had heard him. She reached across the aisle, tugged at his sleeve, and asked, "Want somebody to talk to?"

Cervantes was sitting in front of Elena, and McKenna saw him smile. Don't do it, McKenna thought, but Cervantes did it anyway, again, twisting his head slightly and giving McKenna that knowing wink he had come to hate.

I've trapped myself with my own big mouth, McKenna thought, but I can't risk being impolite, because one thing I don't need right now is an Elena very mad at me.

He looked to her and was relieved to see she was smiling at him. "Okay, let's talk," he said. "Where are we going?"

"You mean us?"

"I mean all of us."

Elena shrugged her shoulders. "Hell, eventually, I'd guess. Let's talk about something else."

"Like what?"

"Like where we'll meet again."

"We won't. I don't plan on coming here again."

Elena was still smiling. "That's all right. I don't plan on staying here after we win."

"No? If you win, wouldn't you be a big shot?"

Elena stopped to think for a moment. "I guess so, but I don't think I'd like that," she said. "I'm not into power."

"Then why are you doing it? For the people?"

"That's what I tell myself, but I think I do it for the fun."

McKenna thought, The fun? "Yeah, I've been having a great time since you folks got to town," he said.

"Brian, don't lie to yourself," she said. "If you think about it, you have been having fun. You like the excitement."

"The excitement? Yeah, that's fine. What about the fear?"

"The fear is just part of the excitement. Think about it."

The thought disturbed him and he didn't want to think about

it. It was just as well that Felipe came out of the cockpit and saved him further deliberations.

Elena sat back and smiled at Felipe, but he didn't seem to notice. He whispered something to Cruzco and Cruzco replaced him in the cockpit.

McKenna thought Felipe looked worried and took that as a good sign, sort of. He noticed that the plane was descending as Felipe resumed his role at the front of the plane, ready to continue his social chatter.

So was Cervantes. "You know, Felipe, I can see that you must be from a good family and I'm sure I would recognize your last name if you told me, but I don't hear Lima in your accent. What is it? Arequipa?"

Felipe wasn't getting into that one. "No, not Arequipa," he answered, then switched the topic to diplomacy. "How long have you represented our country abroad, Mr. Cervantes?"

"Forty-three years."

"And in the United States?"

"Thirty years."

"So, through many changes of government in Peru, we have always kept the same ambassador to the United States?"

"Of course. It has nothing to do with the prevailing political viewpoint at home. The national interests don't change, so it's really just a job which is best done by somebody who knows his way around. It amazes me the way the Americans change ambassadors after every election." He turned to nod at Heresford. "I'm sorry, Mr. Heresford, but some say that's not very smart."

"I agree," Heresford said.

"Interesting," Felipe commented. "Mr. Heresford, just between us, would you say that Mr. Cervantes has been an effective ambassador?"

"I'd say so, although he's given us our problems. Are you considering keeping him on in the unlikely event that you win your war?"

"Yes, but what makes you think it's an unlikely event?" Felipe asked, an amused smile tugging at the corners of his mouth.

"You'll be a little richer and you'll be able to keep the air force on the ground with your Stingers, but the government still has one hundred and twenty thousand soldiers to your five thousand."

"With the money you've loaned us, we're going to change

the numbers. Do you know how much a private in the Peruvian army makes right now?''

"Almost nothing, I'd imagine," Heresford replied.

"Very close. He makes thirty-eight dollars a month, if the government bothers to pay him at all. We will pay him two hundred dollars a month, about what an honest government captain makes, if there is such an animal.'' Felipe stopped to let the implications sink in, and it didn't take long.

"So you expect the government soldiers to defect to you en masse,'' Heresford observed.

"Exactly, and they would all be welcome, as long as they brought their weapons with them.''

Heresford didn't look convinced. Felipe let it drop and turned again to Cervantes. "Mr. Cervantes, if we *were* to win in Peru, would you still be willing to remain in Washington and represent the country?'' he asked.

Cervantes thought it over for a moment before replying. "No offense, but I don't think so. It's not your politics, it's just that Washington is beginning to tire me after so many years there, especially since the young people took over in the United States. It's socially awkward, at times.''

"Well then, how about New York?'' Felipe offered.

"The UN? That would be different and much less demanding.''

Both Cervantes and Felipe were content to leave it there, but McKenna was sure Cervantes would have slipped Felipe a résumé if he had one handy.

McKenna tuned out the conversations and kept to his own thoughts, wondering how Savraada was doing on the ground. If everything went well, Felipe would soon lose his social graces and there would be some unpleasantness forthcoming. It was going to be a bad time for everybody on Flight 902.

It began when Cruzco came out of the cockpit and whispered something to Felipe. Then Felipe turned his attention on McKenna. "It seems nobody is talking to us in Iquitos, McKenna. I don't suppose you would know anything about that, would you?'' he asked harshly.

What happened to the polite tone of voice? McKenna wondered. "Where?'' he asked, trying to look as geographically uninformed as possible.

Felipe stared hard at McKenna for a moment before turning to Julio. "Watch them,'' he ordered. "And I mean *watch* them.'' Then he turned and followed Cruzco into the cockpit as the plane continued its descent.

Julio took Felipe's instructions to heart. He called another Senderista from Coach and the two of them stood at the front of the First Class section, their pistols in their hands, glaring at the passengers. McKenna tried to catch Julio's eye, but the Senderista paid no mind. McKenna gave up and decided to stress his stupidity. "Where's Iquitos?" he asked Heresford.

Apparently, Heresford decided he was just as stupid as McKenna. "Damned if I know. It must be someplace in Peru," he whispered back.

But Cervantes had heard him. He turned in his seat and said, "It's a miserable city in the Amazon jungle. A phenomenon really. More than a quarter of a million people, but there are no roads going to it."

"Oh!" McKenna said. Then Elena caught his eye. She had produced another .25 automatic from somewhere, and she was holding it on her lap. She was still staring at him, but there was something in her eyes, a glint. She raised her eyebrows and smiled in a way that said to McKenna, Is something exciting happening here?

This girl's happy with the change in plans, McKenna thought, but he kept his face impassive and stupid, hoping he was fooling her. Then he heard the landing gear go down and his heart sank as the plane banked right. He looked out Heresford's window and saw nothing for a minute. Then they passed over Iquitos Airport. It was brilliantly lit up, but the lights weren't necessary. By the light of the burning fuel tanks McKenna saw that there were trucks parked all over the runway preventing their landing, but he saw no sign of any helicopters.

McKenna heard the landing gear being raised and felt the plane start to climb. It continued banking until McKenna figured they were headed north, back the way they came. Then Felipe came out of the cockpit, and McKenna saw that he was not easily affected by adversity. He was his old smiling self again. "Commissioner McKenna, did you happen to get a look at our airport?" he asked.

"I saw it."

"Were you as surprised as I was?"

"Yeah. Looks like somebody got wind of your plans and doesn't want you back."

"But you are surprised."

"Yeah, I'm surprised."

"Mr. Heresford?" he asked.

"I'm surprised too. What's next?"

"I wonder," Felipe said, staring from McKenna to Heresford. Then he seemed to reach a decision. "In any event, I sense your friend Colonel Savraada's hand in this, but it's only a small setback."

"Where are we going next?" McKenna asked.

Felipe ignored the question. "As is customary in airlines, the passengers in First Class will be the first to deplane. You gentlemen will be leaving well ahead of the passengers in Coach."

"Meaning?" Cervantes asked.

"Meaning you will be leaving this plane by parachute with me and my men."

"That can't be done," Heresford said. "There are safeguards built into commercial airliners to prevent people from parachuting from them."

"You will find that it can be done and you will do it," Felipe said.

Heresford accepted the information stoically, but Cervantes wasn't at all happy with it. "Wait a minute," he said. "I was led to believe that we would be released once you arrived in Peru. We are in Peru right now, aren't we?"

Felipe smiled at him. "I'm surprised at you, Mr. Cervantes. You should have read the fine print. Our agreement stipulates you would be released once we arrived *safely* in Peru, and I don't feel very safe right now. I'm a little worried about our air force shooting at us on our way down, so they will be informed at the last minute that you are with us. Besides, your company on the ground would do much to alleviate my concerns."

"I've never jumped from a plane before," Cervantes protested.

"Then you'll have one more thing to tell your grandchildren about," Felipe countered. He grabbed a PA microphone from the wall next to him and announced, "Gentlemen, there has been a change of plans. You are going to Lima, but we will not be going with you. The plane will be depressurized shortly, so do not be alarmed. All passengers are to place their hands in the pouches in front of them, then bend forward and rest their heads on the seat in front of them with their eyes closed. There will be no talking. Anyone who deviates from these instructions will be shot. These instructions also apply to the cabin attendants.''

Felipe hung up the microphone and McKenna heard movement in the Coach section behind him as the passengers complied.

''For the moment, those instructions also apply to you three gentlemen,'' Felipe said.

McKenna, Heresford, and Cervantes obeyed, but before McKenna closed his eyes he saw Elena get up and head for the rear of the plane.

There was a rustle of activity and a lot of shouting in Quechua behind him. Not long after that, the plane was filled with the noise of rushing air and the sounds of the engine. He knew they had succeeded in getting the rear ramp door open in flight. He could breathe easily, so he also knew they were below 10,000 feet. Still, for somewhere over the Amazon jungle, it was cold. Then the plane went into a steep, banking left turn and started descending. He heard people walking back and forth in the aisle next to him, then nothing for a while. But it was getting warmer. McKenna knew they were flying in circles and that it wouldn't be long.

''Felipe's ready for you now,'' a voice said from the front of the plane. ''Get up.''

McKenna looked up and saw it was Julio, pointing his .45 at the three First Class passengers. He also saw that it was to be a full combat jump. Julio had bandoleers of linked machine gun ammunition across his chest, grenades and pouches of M-16 ammo hanging from his belt, and a parachute strapped to his back with a smaller reserve chute strapped to his front. He cradled his M-16 across the crook of his arms as he pointed the .45 pistol at them. There was another Senderista standing next to him in the same getup.

Julio, this might be a good time to earn your money, McKenna thought, but he kept it to himself. But Julio must have read McKenna's mind, for he gave McKenna an almost imperceptible shrug. McKenna got the full translation of the small movement, and agreed. Any action at this point would be suicide. McKenna, Heresford, and Cervantes unbuckled their seat belts and got up.

''There are three parachutes on the seats in front of you,'' Julio said. ''Put them on.''

McKenna and Heresford did, but Cervantes had some trouble. McKenna helped him, then pointed to the D ring on the front of the harness. "When you leave the plane, count to three, then pull that ring," he told Cervantes.

"Hurry it up. Felipe's waiting," Julio insisted, so the three First Class passengers headed for the rear of the plane, followed by the two Senderistas.

There were three seats on each side of the aisle running to the lavatories and the wide galley located just before the open ramp door at the rear of the plane. The plane was only half full, and all the hostages were crowded into the front part of the Coach section. None looked up as they passed.

Felipe and Elena were waiting at the rear door, with the rest of the well-armed Senderistas behind them formed in a line down the aisle. All were wearing parachutes and all were heavily armed. It was the first time McKenna had seen them together and he estimated there were fifty of them. Julio yelled a command in Quechua and the Senderistas stepped out of the aisle to let them pass.

The four Stinger missiles were tied into a bundle stacked at the rear of the plane and five recoilless rifles were tied into another bundle. A parachute was tied to the top of each bundle, with a twenty-foot static line from each chute tied to the ramp railing. Behind Felipe and Elena on the other side of the galley were the duffel bags filled with cash and boxes of ammo. Julio and his comrade left the three hostages with Felipe and Elena and returned to the rear of the line.

Through the open rear door McKenna saw that dawn was breaking. "Some last-minute instructions?" he asked Felipe.

"Yes. You should know that we are circling at four thousand feet. Three seconds after you leave the plane, you are to pull your D ring. When your parachute opens, you will see below you a patch of ground my men have cleared. You are to head for that, because you'll be in trouble if you land in the trees. To go right, you pull down on the right strings of your parachute. To go left, you pull down on your left strings. Understood?"

The three of them nodded, then Elena left Felipe's side and pushed past Cervantes, Heresford, and McKenna so that she was standing behind them, across the galley from Felipe. Then McKenna heard Felipe ask, "Cruzco, how's it look?" He turned and saw that Felipe was talking into a portable radio.

"We're circling the drop zone," Cruzco answered and McKenna realized Cruzco was still in the cockpit.

"Any company?" Felipe asked.

"Negative. Radar scope is clean."

"We're on our way. See you on the ground," Felipe said. He put the radio back on his belt, then yelled to Elena, "Watch them!" before signaling the first Senderista in line to the door.

So Felipe's the jumpmaster. This is very bad, McKenna thought as he stood in the galley behind Cervantes and Heresford. Then he felt the barrel of Elena's gun in his back. "Are you sure you've got nothing to tell me?" she asked.

"Yeah, but I'll wait till we're on the ground."

"Looking forward to it," she said.

McKenna saw that Alfredo Stesso was the first. Together he and Felipe pushed the bundle of Stingers down the ramp and out of the plane. They stepped back and watched as the static line attached to the parachute tied to the top of the bundle went taut and the chute opened. Then they repeated the process with the bundle of recoilless rifles. Again, the chute opened and the recoilless rifles began their slow descent to the ground. Then Stesso walked down the steps of the ramp, holding on to the rail to keep his balance in the steeply banking plane. He turned and waited for the signal from Felipe.

"Go!" Felipe yelled.

Stesso jumped and Felipe watched his parachute open. The next one in line was a big man, so Felipe gave him one of the duffel bags of money to carry down. The man jumped and that was how it went, with Felipe giving many of them something to bring down. The smaller men got boxes of ammunition while the bigger ones got money. McKenna could see their parachutes opening and billowing behind the plane as the Senderistas slowly descended toward the ground. Before McKenna had finished saying his prayers, Julio was at the door. He was the last in line and Felipe gave him a box of ammo before he jumped without giving McKenna a glance.

Well, there goes a bad investment, McKenna thought. He was paid to do something to help if he got the chance, but the opportunity never presented itself. Maybe if he knew he was jumping to his death he would have created an opportunity.

Then it was Cervantes's turn. Felipe motioned the little man to the ramp with a wave of his pistol. The old diplomat held on to the railing, but froze at the last big step on the ramp, the four-thousand-foot one. He remained frozen until Felipe fired a shot over his head. Cervantes turned to say something, then fell off the ramp. McKenna saw his chute open, but knew that probably didn't mean much.

Then it was Heresford's turn. He walked two steps down the ramp and turned. "Hey, Felipe!" he yelled.

McKenna's heart froze when he saw that Heresford wanted to say something. Was he going to make a deal and tell Felipe that many of the stitches holding the parachute panels together had been cut, along with all the strings on the reserve chutes? Would he tell him that the chutes were designed to fail after one or two thousand feet of descent and that we were all probably jumping to our deaths?

But Heresford surprised him. He yelled to Felipe, "See you on the ground, scumbag!"

Heresford's stock soared in McKenna's estimation. What an exit line! Compared to Heresford, G. Gordon Liddy was a blabbermouth squealer.

But then Felipe replied. "Heresford!" he yelled.

Heresford stopped and turned. Felipe said, "I want to make sure you wait for me on the ground." Then he quickly raised his pistol and fired, hitting Heresford in the left knee before swinging his pistol back to McKenna.

McKenna watched as Heresford fell forward on the ramp stairs without uttering a sound, but managed to hold on to the railing. McKenna thought he was unconscious until he raised his head to glare at Felipe.

"Want another, Mr. Heresford?" Felipe yelled down.

Heresford didn't. He pushed himself off the stairs and was gone.

McKenna was watching and waiting to see if Heresford's chute opened when Felipe said, "Your turn, McKenna."

"You gonna shoot me, too?"

"I don't know yet. I don't want to be chasing you around down there, either."

Then McKenna heard Elena's voice behind him. "Don't shoot him, Felipe. Please." McKenna turned to look at her. She was no longer smiling and her gun was centered on his chest.

"He's going to, you know," McKenna said to her.

"No he won't. Not after I asked him not to. Now turn around and get going."

McKenna knew he was in no position to argue, but when he turned he saw that Felipe was glaring at him with hatred in his eyes.

I know what that look means, McKenna thought, thinking

of Angelita. That's jealousy. I'd better hurry, because this man is certainly going to shoot me.

McKenna was right. As he hurried down the stairs, his mind was on Felipe, not on the ground 4,000 feet below and the wind threatening to suck him out of the plane before he reached the bottom of the ramp. Then Felipe fired.

McKenna didn't want to scream but, unlike Heresford, he did as the bullet entered his right thigh. As he went down, holding on to the railing, he heard another shot behind him. Instinctively his body stiffened, braced to accept another round, but the bullet wasn't for him.

How could Felipe miss me at this range? McKenna wondered. When he looked up, Elena was standing over him, holding on to the railing with one hand and her pistol with the other. The wind blew her hat off and her hair was blowing all around her face. But she was smiling again as she asked him, "Are you going or staying?"

"Where's Felipe?"

"He's staying," she said and pointed up the ramp.

McKenna tried pulling himself to his feet. At first he thought he wasn't going to be able to do it, but keeping all his weight on his left leg, he managed through the pain. But the pain eased and he felt stronger when he saw the shape Felipe was in, lying facedown at the top of the ramp with his gun in his hand and a bullet in his head. Felipe's face was frozen in shock and his dead eyes were staring down the ramp at McKenna.

Things were happening too fast for McKenna. "You killed him?" he asked her.

"Well, you heard me ask him nice, didn't you?" she said.

Yeah, I heard you ask him not to shoot me, but you killed him over that? McKenna thought as he stared at Felipe.

"Going or staying? But you better make up your mind quick," Elena said impatiently. "Cruzco should be coming soon."

McKenna's mind was racing. Should I tell her about the parachutes? he wondered. She's crazy, but she just saved my life. But if I tell her, she just might think she made a mistake and kill me.

Then Cruzco helped him decide. He appeared at the top of the ramp and looked from Felipe's body to Elena standing on the ramp holding her gun on McKenna. He bent over Felipe, and that was when Elena raised her pistol and fired twice. Her first shot caught him in the chest and, as he fell, the second one took off the top of his head. Cruzco fell on top of Felipe's body, with a matching look of surprise on his face.

"Now look what you made me do," Elena said, sounding annoyed at him. "I really liked Cruzco."

And you really like me, too, McKenna thought as he stared at Cruzco's body. "I'm staying, Elena, and you should too."

"Why? So I can spend the rest of my life in jail?"

"Maybe I'll be able to work something out."

"Why take a chance?" she asked. "Except for maybe Alfredo, I'm in charge now."

Rank sure moves fast in their army, McKenna thought. "Elena, I'm staying," was all he said.

Elena took the news in stride. She was the picture of calm contentment. "I'll see you later. But don't I at least get a kiss for saving your life?"

Before McKenna could answer, she grabbed him and kissed him hard, both of them holding on to the rail with one hand. Then Elena pushed off. "Remember, there's more where that came from." She turned and jumped.

McKenna stayed on the ramp long enough to see her parachute open, then started climbing the ramp stairs, feeling physically weak and not too good about himself. When he got to the top he saw that the hostages were still hunched in the same position. He tried to remove his parachute, but didn't have the strength. "Hey," he yelled. "Somebody help me."

Nobody moved, so he tried again. "Hey, it's over. They're all gone. Somebody help me."

First one head raised, and then another. A man turned in his seat and looked at McKenna. "Who are you?"

"Commissioner McKenna of the New York City Police Department. It's over, but I'm shot. Help me out of this parachute and get me to the cockpit."

Four men got up and ran back, stumbling over each other to get to McKenna, but they stopped at the door when they saw Cruzco's and Felipe's bodies. After all, the hostages were still New Yorkers. "You got any ID?" one of them asked.

With some difficulty, McKenna took his shield from his pocket and showed it to them.

It was all they needed. The four of them removed his parachute, then half-carried and half-dragged him to the cockpit. As they passed the rest of the passengers, McKenna saw they were in a party mood, laughing and shaking hands. But he knew there was nothing to party about, yet.

The pilot and the copilot had the same questions for him, but they were in more of a hurry than the passengers.

"I'm showing a lot of radar blips coming our way from Iquitos and we might not have enough fuel to make it to Lima," the pilot said as he brought the plane to level flight.

"Don't worry about it," McKenna said. "Those blips are Peruvian army transports and helicopters. We can go to Pucallpa."

"Can't do that. Runway's too short. The book says this plane needs forty-eight hundred feet to land and theirs is only three thousand."

"It isn't now. The army should've been working on it all night. They've been extending the runway with corrugated steel sheets."

"That's good to know," the pilot said, hitting a switch on his control panel. "I'm going to raise the rear door and get some altitude to see what the fuel looks like. Maybe we'll be able to make Lima."

But a red light started flashing on the instrument panel. "The rear door's not closing tight," the copilot said.

"Then it's gotta be Pucallpa," the pilot said. "We won't be able to pressurize."

"So?" McKenna asked.

"So I'd need twenty-five thousand feet of altitude to get over the Andes and get to Lima. We'd run out of oxygen and freeze to death in here."

"I just thought of something," the copilot said. "Just because they built us enough runway to land doesn't mean we'll have enough to take off again. This plane might be stuck in Pucallpa."

"Who cares?" McKenna asked.

Nobody did, really.

It was an hour-long trip flying at 4,000 feet, with McKenna strapped into his seat in First Class, slipping in and out of consciousness and losing a lot of blood. As they approached Pucallpa, the pilot issued his crash instructions. McKenna managed to stay awake for that and listened carefully. Everyone had their seat belts on tight with their heads close to their knees as the pilot made his approach.

As soon as the wheels touched the runway, the pilot hit the brakes and flaps hard so that McKenna's head was forced into the back of the seat in front of him. But they had slowed by the time the bumpy part of the ride began when the plane left the concrete runway and started down the new corrugated steel extension. He said a small prayer and, when the plane finally stopped, he clapped like everyone else.

The last sight McKenna had of that day was of the soldiers and flashing ambulances approaching on the runway before he fell into unconsciousness.

Epilogue AUGUST 3, LIMA, PERU—Even before he opened his eyes, McKenna knew he was in a big city somewhere. The sounds of traffic outside were loud and the drivers were impatient honkers. He was dimly aware that he had been moved and had been on another plane, a much smaller one, but he didn't know when that was or how long the flight had lasted. He wasn't in pain, but he felt a little groggy.

When he did open his eyes, the first thing he saw was Brunette. "How you doing, buddy?" his friend asked.

"You tell me."

"Forty-five-caliber bullet wound to the right leg, tibia bone chipped. Some people would call that a broken leg, but not us. Then there were the usual complications. Loss of blood, shock, et cetera. Serious stuff for a sissy, but nothing to guys like you."

"Guys like me?"

"Yeah, guys like you. You know, heroes. That must've been a serious gun battle up there."

"Yeah, it was for two of them, but I wasn't in it."

"You weren't in it?"

"No."

"Then who killed Felipe and Cruzco?"

"Elena."

"Elena?" Brunette asked, astonished. "Why? Did they forget her birthday or something?"

McKenna didn't want to answer, so he tried changing the subject. "Where am I?"

It had never worked with Brunette before, and it still didn't. "Lima," he answered perfunctorily. "Why did she kill them?"

"Let's just say she had a thing for me, and Felipe shot me and made her mad."

That astonished Brunette even more. "A thing for you?" he asked. "Why?"

"Who knows, but it presents me with a big problem."

"What? No medal?"

"No. Angelita."

Brunette understood immediately. He knew the dangers involved when Angelita's man had been chased around by another woman, especially a Spanish woman like Elena who killed to save her man's life. Her first emotion certainly wouldn't be gratitude to Elena, and she would be sure to have some disturbing questions for McKenna. But Brunette had been around a long time and had the answer to most problems of that sort. "So, correct me if I'm wrong," he proposed. "Felipe and Cruzco had a falling-out on the plane and they killed each other, right?"

"That would be wonderful," McKenna said. With the most important issue resolved, McKenna turned his attention to the things he needed to know. "They all dead?" he asked.

"A lot of them are. But Savraada's got twenty-three prisoners. Most of them are wounded and quite a few of them are in real bad shape."

Hope rose and the next question leaped from McKenna's lips before he even thought about it. "Elena?"

"Sorry, buddy. She's dead," Brunette answered softly.

"How?"

"I don't have all the details. You'll have to ask Colonel Savraada."

"Where is he?"

"He's in the room next door talking to Heresford."

It was McKenna's turn to be astonished. "Heresford? He's alive?"

"Sure. You think it's easy killing politicians nobody likes? He's not in great shape, but he's gonna make it."

"How?"

"There's a few things about that prick we didn't know. First of all, he was a paratrooper."

"I should've figured that from his personality."

"And second of all, he's a sky diver. Now, he knew his chute wouldn't last long with his weight, so he did a free fall and guided himself away from Felipe's men and into the jungle. He says he pulled at about a thousand feet, and his chute held for a while. By the time he started losing panels, he was right at the treetops. That's where the soldiers found him, hanging in the trees. Cut up, shot, with a broken leg and a broken arm, but still alive. Savraada says they had a hell of a time getting up there to cut him out, but he was conscious and in charge the whole time."

"I'll be damned," McKenna said. "You know, never tell him I said this, but he's really quite a guy. I'd vote for him for anything he wanted."

"Me too, but he'd spit in both our eyes."

"That might be one of the great things about him," McKenna observed. "But our chutes got a lot of them, right?"

"Not as many as we expected," another voice said. McKenna looked to the door and saw Savraada standing there, his arm bandaged and in a sling.

"Come in, please, Colonel, and fill this lad in," Brunette said.

"Yeah, come on in and tell us what happened to you," McKenna added.

Savraada came in, but he was not the kind of guy to describe his own injuries. He ignored McKenna's question and got right down to business. "In many cases, General Sneadman's parachute riggers erred on the side of caution. We know that the parachutes had to hold up for some time or Felipe would have aborted the jump and gone someplace else. But as far as we can figure, twenty-one of them made it to the ground intact and ready to fight."

"Their chutes didn't fail?" McKenna asked.

"Not all of them. From the inquiries I made, I see what went wrong. When the general's men tested their work, they made their calculations using the weight of an American soldier carrying a sixty-pound combat load. That's two hundred and forty pounds, and on the tests they did with those weights the chutes failed four out of five times after two thousand feet."

"I see," McKenna said. "The Senderistas were smaller than us, and much lighter than that. Except for the ones coming down carrying something heavy, that is."

"Yes, something heavy like bags of money," Savraada continued. "My men and the Sinsi Battalion soldiers found bags of money scattered all over the jungle."

"Did they find it all?"

"I think they did, but there is a little embarrassment in this for me. One bag is missing."

"How much?"

Brunette answered. "From what we can figure, there's under five million missing. If the Sinsi Battalion took it, they're real dopes. They took the bag with the tens and twenties."

"But it *is* five million dollars," Savraada stated.

"And you know what Heresford said about it? 'A measly five million? They've earned it, so let them keep it.' "

"And what do you say?" McKenna asked Brunette.

"I'm not sure. Maybe I agree with him. After all, they did win two battles yesterday."

McKenna was having a hard time with Brunette's attitude, especially when he would personally arrest a decorated detective who took five dollars. But then again, McKenna reasoned, the Sinsi Battalion doesn't work for him. "Tell me about the battles, Colonel," he said.

"The airport battle was an overwhelming victory. We achieved complete surprise. Two hundred and twenty *Sendero* soldiers were killed or wounded and eleven were captured. I'm happy to say that the Sinsi Battalion accepted their surrenders, and those prisoners are still alive, which is a real change for that battalion. A few escaped into the jungle, but we didn't have time to chase them down."

"And on your side?"

"Twenty-three casualties. As we expected, and we're going to have to live with it, most of our casualties were sustained in the opening moments of the attack on the airport."

McKenna could see that Savraada was having a hard time with his casualty list, so he decided to help him out. "Yes, Colonel. Effectively, we sacrificed those soldiers to bait the trap and achieve victory and we will have to live with that," McKenna said. "Now tell me about the jungle."

"That didn't work out as well as we planned, either. We didn't expect so many of them to survive the jump and had also hoped to catch the survivors together near their landing zone. But we had to wait out of the radar range of the airliner, so by the time we got there they were already organized and in the jungle, looking for the money. We also forgot to take into account that they had twenty men on the ground who had cut down the trees to prepare the landing zone.''

"Heavy casualties?''

"I think so. They shot down a Huey with small-arms fire before it even landed. Lost nine men right there. Then, because of the jungle, the helicopters couldn't land, so the battalion had to do a combat jump around *Sendero*'s drop zone.''

"You jump, too?'' McKenna asked.

"Yes, I jumped,'' Savraada answered, like there was nothing to it. "We lost a lot of men coming down. Then the fight in the jungle was hard, with heavy losses on both sides until your man organized the surrender.''

"My man?'' McKenna asked.

"Yes. Julio Montalvo. Stesso's chute failed and the rest of their commanders were killed in the battle. After Elena's death, he was in command. He surrendered with his men and Mr. Cervantes was saved.''

"You mean Cervantes is alive?''

"Of course. Came out of it without a scratch. He is very light, so his parachute held, and he landed directly in their drop zone. He seems quite pleased about the whole thing. Says he's got some good stories for his grandchildren. Anyway, it was still a victory, but barely. We suffered forty-two casualties and they lost forty-five. We took twenty-three prisoners, but most of them are injured.''

McKenna tried to listen, but couldn't concentrate on the numbers. Aside from all the good news, there was still a question he had to ask. "So Elena died in battle?''

"Not exactly. She suffered injuries to her face and hands from a grenade. Disfiguring injuries. She was found dead with a bullet in her brain. I had all the bodies taken to Pucallpa, but when I saw hers I became suspicious and had her brought here for autopsy. The bullet was a twenty-five-caliber round, and none of the Sinsi soldiers had twenty-fives.''

But Elena had a twenty-five, McKenna thought. It figures. She was much too vain and wouldn't want to live if her face wasn't perfect. She killed herself after she survived the jump. Down in battle. That would excite her, and I didn't kill her when I didn't tell her about the parachutes. "How about little Arturo?'' he asked.

"We found his body next to Elena's. Looks like he was killed by the same grenade blast that wounded her.''

So faithful little Arturo's gone with the rest of them, Mc-

Kenna thought. He lay back on his pillow and closed his eyes to think it over. They had won and the enemy was all accounted for. He figured Savraada's news should have made him feel better, but somehow it didn't. When he opened his eyes again, Brunette and Savraada were both looking at him with puzzled expressions on their faces.

Savraada cleared his throat and his face and went on as if there had been no interruption. "There might be some good to come out of all this bloodshed. Fujimori is serious about peace and *Sendero* has won some sympathy and credibility around the world. I've talked to him and he intends to honor all the provisions of your agreement with Felipe."

"Except for the money, right?" McKenna asked.

"Except for the money. As far as he's concerned, he just found some money in the jungle and returned it to the people who lost it."

McKenna turned to Brunette and asked, "How about you, amigo? Seen enough bloodshed?"

Brunette laughed. "I guess I seemed a little bloodthirsty for a while, huh?"

"You *were* bloodthirsty. A stark raving lunatic."

"Well, I'm not anymore. I went to Pucallpa to meet with the colonel and saw more bodies than I ever wanted to see. It's over for me and I'll be ecstatic if I never see another one."

"I'm glad to hear that."

"What about you? What are you going to do?" Brunette asked.

"Depends on when I get out of here."

"Probably in a couple of days. As soon as the wound heals enough, they'll put a cast on your leg to immobilize you. Then you and Angelita will be on your way home."

"Me and Angelita?"

"Oh, didn't I mention that?" Brunette asked, really enjoying himself. "She's on her way down here to take you home to Florida."

Back to Florida? McKenna thought while Brunette watched him with interest, waiting for McKenna to comment.

But McKenna didn't, so Brunette said, "So I naturally got to wondering. Are you going back to be a bum in Florida, or are you going to come back to work?"

It was the same question McKenna was asking himself, and he had a lot to think about before he could answer. The end had come too suddenly, but it was definitely over. He had kept all his promises and looked forward to seeing Mrs. Crandall and Gus Hoffmann again to give them the news. They had won, but at what cost? He remembered Savraada's comment that nobody wins in a civil war, and in beating his ruthless but brave adversaries, he had left many more grieving, innocent widows and orphans. He wasn't satisfied with the decisions his role had forced him to make in the affair, and he certainly wasn't content. But he knew himself well enough to believe that he would learn to live with the results, eventually.

Concerning him most were the promises he had made to Angelita. He loved her dearly and desperately wanted to make her happy, which shouldn't have been hard. After all, he was sure she loved him as much as he loved her and they wanted the same things out of life: children and a nice place to raise them. They had lost one child to *Sendero*, but they would make a second. It was the place that was the problem. Although he had promised her they would return to the peace and comfort of Florida, McKenna had rediscovered himself in the Bright Lights, that vibrant place where he knew he belonged, the place where he could make a difference.

He recalled Elena's observation: "You like the excitement." And maybe fear *was* part of what he liked.

As these thoughts were flashing through McKenna's mind, his eyes were fixed on Brunette, who was smiling down at him, obviously enjoying the effect his question was having on his friend.

What to say to Ray, the man who can see through me and knows me like a brother? McKenna wondered. I'm too tired to think straight, but Ray deserves an answer and only one comes to mind. "Buddy, I'll have to get back to you another time on that one."

"I understand," Brunette replied, looking like he did understand. "We're gonna leave you now and let you get some rest before Angelita arrives."

"Great, thanks," McKenna said as Brunette and Savraada headed for the door. He was fading, falling before they closed it behind them. Asleep.

WATCH FOR *HYDE*,
DAN MAHONEY'S EXPLOSIVE NEW THRILLER
Featuring Detective Brian McKenna:

He had an hour to himself before he had to go, so Hector decided to devote himself to his latest obsession: Detective Brian McKenna. Three days before, he had visited the New York Public Library's main branch on Fifth Avenue, a building the size of a soccer field that was totally devoted to research. He had been amazed to find that, over the years, there had been one hundred and thirty-one separate articles in *The New York Times* in which McKenna had been mentioned. He had made copies of all of them and brought them home to Oldwick for study.

What he had learned delighted him. This Brian McKenna would be a worthy adversary. After studying the articles, he had surmised that McKenna was hard-working, intuitive, honest, intelligent, courageous, popular, politically connected, and, most important, lucky.

Hector hadn't counted on a McKenna type when he had first undertaken his mission in New York, and had initially been disappointed when his opponent had discovered his work after only one day on the case. But, since then, he had developed a new way of looking at his mission, and his disappointment had been replaced by pure personal pleasure. He felt certain that he was going to hand the detective the first major setback in his long and successful career. It had become a game played for the highest stakes Hector could imagine—his life and freedom. As far as he was concerned, a game played against an inferior opponent was simply boring—no fun and not worth playing. But this one was developing nicely and was bound to be loaded with new moves on the detective's part.

Hector relished the thought of placing McKenna in check for all the world to see, but realized that won games were sometimes lost by underestimating opponents and failing to perceive and anticipate surprise moves. That wasn't going to happen to him in this game, Hector resolved. Daring play was called for, but strategic retreat had to be kept ready as an option. However, the retreat must be dignified to keep the opponent off-balance and unsure of himself, so Hector prepared a package and left it on the bed, just in case.

After finishing his studying for the evening, Hector dressed in a fresh shirt and tie, and a clean suit. Then he checked his appearance in the mirror. He decided that his beard needed combing and did that without removing it. Satisfied with his appearance, he went downstairs to inform Mrs. Sweeney of his plans for the evening.

As he had hoped, she had already turned in for the evening, but he wrote her a note anyway, telling her that he was going to Bethlehem to take in a movie. It was his usual story to her, and she believed that he must be quite an expert on the Spanish-language movies playing in Bethlehem. She didn't know that he hadn't seen one of them, but used the Spanish-movie routine so that she would never think to question him about the films.

He left the note on the kitchen table where she would be sure to see it if she came down during the night. Then he left the house, locked the door, and went to the garage.

Inside the garage were three cars. He ignored the Mercedes and the Cherokee and started up the Buick station wagon. The Buick belonged to Carmen, but was registered to Mrs. Sweeney at her Philadelphia address and had been provided for her use to do the shopping and visit her family when she was off—which was most of the time when he and Carmen weren't staying at the house.

After fifteen minutes of driving on the tortuous winding back roads, he was at the East-West interstate highway, I-78. West led to Bethlehem and east led to New York. After another hour of driving at fifty-three miles an hour, he paid the toll at the Lincoln Tunnel. He saw by the large clock above the toll booth that it was exactly eleven P.M. He was right on schedule.

By 11:05 he was in the city, heading crosstown on East 30th Street. At Lexington Avenue he made a right and drove south nine blocks. There the avenue ended at Gramercy Park. He found a parking spot on Gramercy Park South. He made some final preparations, checked his beard in the rearview mirror, put on his gloves, wrapped his scarf around his face, and left the car, slowly walking east. He passed a few people on the street, but none gave the well-dressed, bearded man a second glance.

Hector stopped in front of an old brick synagogue, down the block from where his car was parked. It was Saturday night and the lights were on in the synagogue, but that didn't bother him. In fact, he had counted on it. The building stood alone, with an alley on each side leading to the rear. He stood and waited for ten minutes until there was no one on the street for a block in either direction. Then he entered the alley and walked to the rear of the synagogue, unseen by anyone.

There was a bamboo shed abutting the back wall. Hector had visited the location before and had done some research before he had learned the reason for the shed's existence. It was a Succoth hut, built to accommodate the synagogue's caretaker when he and his family observed the rituals associated with the Jewish holiday celebrating the harvest. The hut was used only a couple of days a year for the purpose for which it was intended, but Hector could see by the light spilling from the synagogue windows that someone else had decided to call the hut home, at least for that evening. A man was lying on the floor of the hut, wrapped in a sleeping bag. The squatter was sleeping, breathing loud and rhythmically. Next to him was a black plastic trash bag containing his possessions.

Hector smiled. Once again, his information had proven correct: sleeping at his feet was the thin, weak man he wanted. He took a small penlight from his pocket, turned it on, and held it in his mouth, taking care that the beam didn't shine directly into his quarry's eyes. Then he removed a steak knife from his pocket, got on his knees, and bent over the sleeping man. He moved his head so that the penlight was shining directly on the side of the man's neck and he stared at the spot until he saw what he was looking for—the almost imperceptible pulse movement that indicated the presence of the carotid artery. He held his knife over the spot and was bearing down to make the small, fatal incision when a dog barked somewhere on Gramercy Park South and the man's eyes opened.

Hector still could have accomplished his purpose exactly as he had intended, but he waited a second too long, surprised by the terror in his victim's eyes as he struggled to remove his arms from the sleeping bag. Then Hector put his right hand on his victim's ear and pushed his head hard against the floor of the Succoth hut while he placed the blade of the knife on his victim's neck.

But the man knew what was coming, and although he was weak and dying, he was determined that his death not occur just then. As Hector began his incision, the man twisted his head against the pressure being exerted on his ear and overcame it. His neck turned, and although Hector could see that he had made a cut, it wasn't in the exact right place. There was blood, but it wasn't coming in squirts as it should have if he had succeeded in severing the artery.

Then the man did the one thing Hector hadn't planned for. He opened his mouth and screamed.

Hector sliced again, but the man was wildly thrashing inside his sleeping bag and pushing himself along the floor of the hut as Hector pressed his right hand into his ear, struggling to hold him still. The slice was ineffective, producing a long cut on the neck, but inches behind the artery. The scream continued and then the man managed to free one of his arms from the sleeping bag. It came out of the top of the sleeping bag and he waved it frantically in front of Hector's face, screaming all the while.

Hector knew it was time to leave. He dropped the knife, let the penlight fall from his mouth, and pushed himself to his feet. Then he walked toward the street with long, purposeful strides. The screaming continued. As soon as he reached Gramercy Park South, he casually looked around. There was no one on the street, but inside the fenced park was a woman holding a leashed Golden Retriever. She was staring at him and, after a moment's hesitation, she yelled to him, "Where's it coming from?"

Hector turned and made a show of listening, gratified to hear that the screams were echoing through the backyards of the buildings on Gramercy Park South. It was impossible to tell just which backyard the sound was coming from, but Hector turned and faced the woman again. "I think it's coming from the next block. I'm going to call the police," he yelled to her.

"Please hurry," she yelled back.

Hector did hurry, walking directly to his car. He took his gloves off and pulled his keys from his pocket, but his hands were shaking so much that it seemed to take forever to insert the key in the door lock of the Buick. When he finally got behind the wheel, he took some time to regain his strength and calm down before he started the car. The woman was still standing in the park when he drove by, and the screams were audible through the car's closed windows. . . .

**Don't Miss _HYDE_—
Coming in January in Hardcover
From St. Martin's Press!**

Harry Bosch's life is on the edge. His earthquake-damaged home has been condemned. His girlfriend has left him. He's drinking too much. And after attacking his commanding officer, he's even had to turn in his L.A.P.D. detective's badge. Now, suspended indefinitely pending a psychiatric evaluation, he's spending his time investigating an unsolved crime from 1961: the brutal slaying of a prostitute who happened to be his own mother.

Edgar Award-winning author Michael Connelly has created a dark, fast-paced suspense thriller that cuts to the core of Harry Bosch's character. Once you start it, there's no turning back.

MICHAEL CONNELLY
THE LAST COYOTE

THE LAST COYOTE
Michael Connelly
_____ 95845-5 $6.99 U.S./$7.99 CAN.

The Dollmaker was a serial killer who stalked Los Angeles and left a grisly calling card on the faces of his female victims. With a single faultless shot, Detective Harry Bosch thought he had ended the city's nightmare.

Now, the dead man's widow is suing Harry and the LAPD for killing the wrong man—an accusation that rings terrifyingly true when a new victim is discovered with the Dollmaker's macabre signature.

Now, for the second time, Harry must hunt down a death-dealer who is very much alive, before he strikes again. It's a blood-tracked quest that will take Harry from the hard edges of the L.A. night to the last place he ever wanted to go—the darkness of his own heart.

THE CONCRETE BLONDE

"Exceptional...A stylish blend of grit and elegance."
—Nelson DeMille

THERE'S A SECRET WAR ON THE STREETS OF THE CITY. ONLY A NEW YORK COP CAN WIN IT.

His claim to fame is finding the guns on the bad guys, and Detective Second Grade Brian McKenna has just spotted the beard carrying a piece. What he doesn't know is that he's about to shoot his way into a war with a highly disciplined, well-armed enemy so treacherous, not even the NYPD knows they exist.

Exiled from the bright lights of Manhattan for breaking one too many rules, pressured by his girlfriend to quit the job, this is McKenna's last chance to win back his reputation and make the coveted rank of Detective First Grade. But if his moves aren't swift and right, a new breed of criminal—who has found a leader in an exotically beautiful and ruthless woman—will own his city....

DAN MAHONEY

DETECTIVE FIRST GRADE

"First-rate...explosive...a winner."
—William Caunitz